The Still Brimming Twilit River

CollectiveInk

First published by Liberalis Books, 2025
Liberalis Books is an imprint of Collective Ink Ltd.,
Unit 11, Shepperton House, 89 Shepperton Road, London, N1 3DF
office@collectiveinkbooks.com
www.collectiveinkbooks.com
www.liberalisbooks.com

For distributor details and how to order please visit the 'Ordering' section on our website.

Text copyright: Nicholas Hagger 2024

ISBN: 978 1 78535 851 7
978 1 78535 852 4 (ebook)
Library of Congress Control Number: 2024909473

A CIP catalogue record for this book is available from the British Library.

Design: Lapiz Digital Services

Printed and bound by CPI Group (UK) Ltd, Croydon, CR0 4YY, UK

We operate a distinctive and ethical publishing philosophy in all areas of our business, from our global network of authors to production and worldwide distribution.

The Still Brimming Twilit River

Nicholas Hagger

LIBERALIS
BOOKS

London, UK
Washington, DC, USA

Also by Nicholas Hagger

The World Government
The Secret American Dream
A New Philosophy of Literature
A View of Epping Forest
My Double Life 1: This Dark Wood
My Double Life 2: A Rainbow over the Hills
Selected Stories: Follies and Vices of the Modern Elizabethan Age
Selected Poems: Quest for the One
The Dream of Europa
The First Dazzling Chill of Winter
Life Cycle and Other New Poems 2006–2016
The Secret American Destiny
Peace for our Time
World State
World Constitution
King Charles the Wise
Visions of England
Fools' Paradise
Selected Letters
The Coronation of King Charles
Collected Prefaces
Fools' Gold
The Fall of the West
The Promised Land
The Golden Phoenix
The Algorithm of Creation
The Tree of Tradition
The Building of the Great Pyramid
A Baroque Vision
The Essentials of Universalism
The Oak Tree and the Branch

"I'll tell you a story
About Jack-a-Nory;
And now my story's begun;
I'll tell you another
Of Jack and his brother,
And now my story is done."

> Nursery rhyme first recorded in *The Top Book of All for Little Masters and Misses*, c.1760, sometimes quoted by Nicholas Hagger's mother during the war when he was very young.

The front cover shows the River Stour in the Vale of Dedham at twilight near Le Talbooth, a 16th-century ex-toll-house Constable painted, now a restaurant.

Acknowledgment

I am grateful to Ingrid Kirk, my excellent PA, for assembling these short stories.

CONTENTS

Contents

Contents

Contents

PREFACE

The Unity of the Universe Reconciling Contradictions:
Flawed People Within Universal Harmony

This is volume 7 of my *Collected Stories*. My *Collected Stories* (volumes 1–5) spanned 40 years in five decades (1966–2006) and contained 1,001 short stories. Volume 6, *The First Dazzling Chill of Winter*, contained 201 short stories (2009–2016) set in early old age. Now volume 7, *The Still Brimming Twilit River*, contains a further 220 short stories (2016–2024), bringing my total number of stories written over 58 years to 1,422.

Philip Rawley in old age
These short stories are all set in Philip Rawley's old age. Philip Rawley is now in his late 70s and early 80s, and we follow him through the perils of old age, before, during and after the pandemic which leaves him with a heart condition. Death is never far away but throughout he maintains his zest and appetite for life and his sense that he is in harmony with the universe, and remains active despite health setbacks. The society he is living in has changed, as has the world, but he is determined to keep going.

Reconciliation of contradictions
The titles of the short stories often involve a pair of opposites, in accordance with the algebraic formula, $+A + -A = 0$, which I discovered in Japan in 1965 and made the basis for my Theory of Everything in *The Algorithm of Creation* (2023): $0 = +A + -A = 0$. The algebraic formula expresses the wisdom of the East and can be found in Taoism's *yin* + *yang* = the *Tao*, Great Nothing, the One. All opposites – day and night, life and death, time and eternity, the finite and the infinite – are reconciled in an underlying unity. The same applies to the many contradictions thrown up by these, and all my, short stories.

Universalism's sense of the unity of the universe and all disciplines

The reconciling One and underlying unity of the universe can be found in all my works: my literary works (my poems, verse plays and other literary genres I have written in as well as my short stories); my mystic works; my philosophical works; my historical works; my religious works (which see all religions as approaching the same One Reality); my works of international politics and statecraft; and my writings on world culture. My *Collected Prefaces* contains 55 of my Prefaces – with this book I have now written 64 works – and behind all my Prefaces and works is my Universalist approach to life, that all contradictions, opposites, conflicts and disciplines are reconciled within the underlying unity of the universe.

Blending the two aspects of the fundamental theme of world literature: quest for the One and follies and vices

Universalism blends the metaphysical and secular strands of living and engaging with society and the universe, and balances the two aspects of the fundamental theme of world literature I identified in *A New Philosophy of Literature*: a quest for Reality (the One), and condemnation of social follies and vices in relation to an implied virtue. The Metaphysical poets quested for the One, and the Light is mentioned in many of their works and in the works of the Romantics. The Roman satirists (including Horace) and the English Augustan poets expose follies and vices. Universalism blends Romanticism and Classicism in an enduring unity, the One, and in these, and all my, short stories can be found the Oneness behind all the social situations and also instances of follies and vices that would satisfy Horace, Pope and Swift.

Metaphysical wit: yoking heterogeneous, dissimilar ideas together

The Metaphysical poets' approach is important, as their wit was seized on by Dr Johnson in his 'Life of Cowley' as "a combination of dissimilar images" in which "the most heterogeneous ideas are yoked by violence together". Universalism reconciles all opposites, and many of the titles of my short stories yoke together heterogeneous, very dissimilar ideas and present them within an underlying unity.

The ubiquity of Death

The quest for Reality involves confronting Death, and Death is never far away in these short stories. Awareness of Death is a consequence of knowing the One, and Death lurks behind social situations, and as Philip Rawley ages becomes more ubiquitous.

Miniature short stories a new literary genre: verbal paintings

These short stories create a new literary genre: the miniature short story. They say a lot in a very short space. They are vivid, and being miniature stories they can focus on telling details which convey truth found during questing, and can dwell on follies and vices. They reveal character through key moments, epiphanies that are revelations. They are often verbal paintings. Just as a portrait in the National Portrait Gallery shows its subject in a particular situation which throws light on the character and feelings of the subject, so these short stories paint a picture that reveals character and inner feelings which are either laudable questings or condemnatory follies and vices.

Revealing the Age

These short stories also reveal the Age, a sense that the West is in decline and faces an uncertain future, even (as the last short story suggests) a new Dark Age.

Flawed people seen from universal values

These short stories show dozens of flawed people in terms of universal values. Philip Rawley's meditating consciousness is aware of the hidden harmony behind all conflicts and contradictions in situations, and his contact with the One enables him to see the behaviour he describes in terms of the universal virtue within this harmony.

Those living through their egos are more likely to be conflicting than those who have undergone a centre-shift away from the rational, social ego to their universal self or soul which is in contact with the One. As a narrator Philip Rawley is able to view difficult events from a quiet serenity that recognises the universal values of goodness, openness, honesty, sincerity, love, compassion, kindness, patience, tolerance and peace – all of which are known to those who instinctively live within the universal harmony, the hidden Oneness, of the universe.

10 February 2024

PART ONE

The Still Brimming Twilit River

The Still Brimming Twilit River

For my birthday Pippa drove me as a surprise to Dedham in the Stour Valley. We checked in at Maison Talbooth, a spa hotel that overlooks the Vale of Dedham. All the twelve rooms are named after poets. We were in Shakespeare. Other rooms were Browning, Masefield, Tennyson, Wordsworth, Brooke and Shelley, and so on. There was a volume of Shakespeare's poems by my bed and on the wall, framed, was 'Shall I compare thee to a summer's day?'

We lunched on smoked-salmon sandwiches overlooking the Vale and had body and facial treatments in a spa room on two massage gurneys. We were then served pots of tea in the small garden outside our room. There were bluebells and violets on the bank that sloped down to a brick wall by where we sat. A column of ants lugged pale green balls along the brick wall to their nest. I watched, deeply relaxed.

In the evening we were driven to the hotel's sister restaurant Le Talbooth, a sixteenth-century beamed ex-toll-house on a bend of the Stour which Constable had painted. We sat in a window and sipped champagne and soaked in the eighteenth-century countryside.

After dinner we sat outside by the still, brimming twilit river. I gazed at the tranquil green surface and the curve of the bend and reflected that my current was still brimming while a hundred gnats danced in the floodlit dark beneath the humped bridge behind me.

Next morning we had breakfast and then coffee overlooking the sunny Vale. Then we drove back and had lunch at another hotel, where the family were waiting. They all came back for tea and I took the grandchildren down to feed our carp. There were phone messages from my brothers and cousin on what had been a close, family weekend. But I could not get out of my mind the still brimming twilit river and beyond the curve of the bend the dark beneath the humped bridge behind where I sat.

A Cliff Path and Dark Winter Evenings

There was a knock on the front door as we finished supper and Claire stood on the front steps.

"I'm just walking and I saw the car and I knocked to see if you're here."

"Come in," I said warmly.

She took her shoes off and I noticed how much weight she had lost.

"Hello-o," Pippa said, welcoming and in surprise.

Claire sat between us and talked about her regime of long walks along cliff paths, including the cliff path near our front door, and about the people who looked in to see her. It was all positive.

"Have you seen Charlie?" I asked.

"Yes, he's moved."

"Good," I said, "and he's got the same mobile number?"

"Yes, but his mobile's not working. He can't move his SIM card until he's got a new phone."

"Ah," I said. "I've rung him twice. I've got an envelope to give to him."

"I can take it," she said. "I can take it to him on my way home now."

She talked with Pippa about her Pendeen relatives. "Do they have a St-Just accent?" she asked. "I could listen to it all day. We knew someone who lived in St Just, he was in Harry's family. He was a fisherman. Stewart Granger stayed with him. There's a picture of him smoking a pipe near fishing nets. Stewart Granger paid for him to have new nets. He took the new nets out for the first time. The coastguard was watching and turned away, and in a trice the boat was gone. Dragged down beneath the waves by the nets. His body was washed ashore several weeks later, very decomposed."

"How awful," I said. "How kind of Stewart Granger to give him nets and how disastrous."

"Yes, exactly," she said.

She spoke of doing something on 24 April, which was "the second anniversary of Harry's death."

"That's the anniversary of my father's death," Pippa said, reaching for a family tree I had just written out for her on a sheet of A3 paper. "He died when he was forty-seven."

"It's young," I said. "A policeman."

"It is," Claire said. "Were you with him when he died?"

"Yes," said Pippa. "I was seventeen. He'd driven me to college interviews and got me into college. I'd just had a driving lesson and the car broke down. I came back and asked my mother where my father was. She said, 'He's mowing in the garden.' I went out into the back garden and he was lying on the grass having a heart attack. We called the ambulance and the ambulancemen revived him. But he went straight into another heart attack and died."

"Dreadful," Claire said as I nodded.

They looked at the family tree.

"I want to get it all down while my aunt's still alive," Pippa said. "She's ninety. She might not be here much longer. I drove her to a small restaurant next to a cottage where she once lived, in Geevor. Being so near the cottage triggered a memory. When she was three, she ate some dog-biscuits and was told off, shouted at. She ran out to Geevor Mine nearby where her father was working to tell him she'd been told off and shouted at. She was missing for a while and her mother was very worried. Having lunch next door brought the memory back.

"Bill and Daphne and I went to graveyards earlier this week to find the graves of some of the older relatives," Pippa continued. "We found them all. Bill had to scrape grass away on one of them. But we wrote down the dates of birth and dates of death." Then suddenly she said: "We had a budgerigar in my father's time."

"I remember it," I said. "It was still there when I first visited your mother's home."

Claire said, "Last time I saw you I was getting some birds. Do you remember? I had four or five. They took up all my time and they scattered seed on the floor. Someone I knew at work said, 'If ever you decide not to have them I'll have them for you.' She has a lot of animals, including a snake as well as cats and dogs. It got to it I couldn't do it any more. I rang her on Christmas Eve, and said, 'You know what you said about taking my birds?' 'Yes,' she said. I said, 'I'll be with you in half an hour.'"

We laughed.

"Well," she said, "I must be off. I'll take Charlie his envelope."

As she left she asked about the conversion of the toilet block round the corner from us. "The house has gone up, hasn't it?" she said.

"Yes," I said, "but not very high and not overlooking us. They're driving cars up the cliff path to the house and reversing them back, delivering materials. The weight could cause a landslide. Shall we go and have a look?"

And so we wandered round the corner to the narrow coastal path that traversed the eroded cliff. The cliff had once been ten yards on the sea side of the path all the way along up to the field, but a section had fallen away a few winters previously and the safety wire fence was almost alongside the path in one place.

"Look," I said. "There's a concrete wall at the bottom of the cliff on the beach but it stops halfway across and the waves pound in to the cliff beneath the path. See the stone the other side of the fence? It's got a hole in it where there was once a railing. And the sea wall just there, on the top of the cliff, ends abruptly, it sheared off with the cliff."

We walked further up the cliff path. To my astonishment a wall of stones was being built on either side of the cliff path to make a garden through which the path would run. Stones had been piled along the top of the unstable cliff to make a wall.

"The cliff will collapse," Claire said.

"*We* can see that, but those doing it can't," I said.

"I'm surprised the Council haven't said something."

"Perhaps it's not being done through the Council," Pippa said. "The top of the cliff has always been waste ground. The owner before Richard Dawkins may have retained it. Perhaps they bought it from him. There used to be a seat here."

"Yes, where Harold Wilson sat when he was no longer Prime Minister and had dementia. Mary Wilson brought him to sit and enjoy the view."

"Yes," said Pippa. "She had a relative near here. She sometimes brought him to sit here."

"You see those holes in the wall of that house? Those were for the pilchard barrels. As early as the 1780s pilchard fishermen levered the lids onto their barrels by using those holes."

"I never knew that," Claire said.

We wandered up beyond the wall and stood and looked at the rebuilt toilet. The new windows still had squares of paper on them, it was still a building site. There was a joiner's sign by the cliff path. In the first plans, immediately vetoed by the Council, the model who had bought the toilet block had a bath and a floor-to-ceiling window pane just above the sloping path. She was now loading weight on the edge of an eroding cliff. I shook my head.

It was all wrong. The wild, rugged beauty of the cliff was being turned into a suburban front garden with walls. It would be dissected by the cliff path and public right-of-way.

"Anyway," I said to Claire. "It's a good time of the year now, June. You've got light evenings ahead and warm weather and you'll be able to walk and get out."

"Yes," she said. "All those dark, lonely winter evenings...."

And I saw how lonely she had been and how her walks put her in touch with people and drove her to knock on doors like ours and why she was so eager to take the envelope she was clutching up to Charlie. She was looking forward to the light summer evenings so she could take cliff paths high above the eroding sea and not think about the dark winter evenings when she seemed to be miles away from humankind.

Cricket and Champagne

We arrived at the Oval early and ate scampi and chips behind the pavilion. Then we walked round towards the Vauxhall end, entered the OCS block and found row 7. We sat in seats 96 and 97. They were quite close together and my arm was touching Paul's as I produced a contract that had arrived by post and witnessed his signature while the toss took place. Essex won and chose to field, and the Surrey opening batsmen came out. One was Wilson. Runs were hard to get although it was a Twenty20 and Wilson ground his way to 17 while Surrey lost four wickets.

The two seats on my right were empty. Now two young girls entered our row. People further along stood up to let them past. They sat down in the two empty seats next to me. One of the girls crossed her legs, which were covered with black stockings, and produced a large glass container of champagne and two fluted glasses. She poured a glass and gave it to her companion and then poured one for herself. They raised their glasses to each other and sat sipping champagne as the cricket progressed and Surrey lost more wickets. Each time the girl next to me turned to her companion her pony-tail flicked and caught me on the side of my face. There was warm sunshine, and they poured themselves a second glass of champagne.

Surrey reached 117 for 9 at the end of their innings. We got up and stretched our legs and edged past the two girls to walk outside the seated area. We returned and the girls stood and smiled to let us by.

Essex scored quite quickly. Wilson was fielding near us. Several in the crowd called out, "Wilson, Wilson, give us a wave." Wilson, wearing a cap, turned and gave a brief wave. Next time he fielded the ball the crowd round us cheered and several sang, "Wilson, Wilson, he's on fire." Wilson turned and smiled and shook his head. The interaction between Wilson and the crowd continued until Essex reached 89 with only 2 wickets down.

Now there was a light shower. The players went in and Paul and I stood up to shelter outside the seated area. The two girls stood and smiled as we edged past. We watched a penalty shoot-out on a large screen – Poland beat Switzerland in the European knock-out competition – and then we returned. The two girls put down umbrellas and stood up for us and smiled. I said, "Thank you."

Now the sun was out and they filled their glasses from the last of the champagne. At least three times I was flicked on my cheek by my neighbour's pony-tail as she turned to talk to her friend. They finished their champagne and put the flutes away in a bag, wrapped in tissues.

The sun was out and it was warm on my neck. Hair flicked my cheek. I turned and saw the two girls fling their arms round each other and embrace. They had finished their champagne and were locked in each other's arms.

Then it dawned on me that there had been a Gay Pride parade earlier that day. I realised they had been to the Gay Pride event and had then come to the Oval to celebrate, what, the anniversary of the beginning of their relationship? The anniversary of their same-sex marriage?

They were polite girls who smiled when they were asked to stand, but after three glasses of champagne they were completely uninhibited and openly remained locked in each other's arms and an extended kiss. They only had eyes for each other as Essex made the winning hit and reached 121 with a boundary.

A Doctor and his Godmother

I entered the Hall and took a glass of orange juice and saw a tall white-haired man in his mid-eighties standing with his wife in a corner. Other visitors to Speech Day stood and sipped from glasses in a dozen groups. I threaded my way through.

"Dr James Pippin?" I asked.

"I just said, 'I wonder if that's Philip Rawley?'" he said.

"You've just flown in from Portugal," I said.

"Yes, and I've had a meeting with Simon and looked at the plans."

I shook hands with his Portuguese wife. Pippa was now by my side and talked with her.

"Good. The last time I saw you properly was in 1952. We were both in *Julius Caesar*. You were Cassius and I remember you saying, 'Forever and forever farewell, Brutus.'"

He nodded and smiled.

"I was in the crowd," I said. "I was a pleb, and a messenger. We had to duff up Cinna the poet, 'for his bad verses'. Do you remember?"

"I do remember."

"It was George Hokham's production. When he died I was rung up and was asked if I could attend his funeral as there weren't many Old Boys. I was to travel to Cornwall that day, so I diverted across the Severn Bridge to Wales. In the car park at Brecon I saw an old man standing with a boyish look and I said, 'I'm going to speak to him, he was my Head.' I sat with him. After the coffin was removed Pippa pressed a button on a kind of bust in the church foyer saying 'Press', and we heard his voice, 'This is the Reverend George Hokham.' All about how he came to be a priest in Brecon." I shook my head.

"I left in 1953," James Pippin said, struggling to get his words out of his creased face. "I had to tell the Head. You know, I wanted to be a doctor and the science wasn't very good at school. The founder of this school, Milly Watkins, was my godmother and she said, 'You must leave and go to Walthamstow Tech.' I told the Head and he laughed, he thought it a ridiculous idea. But I did it and became a doctor."

"And you've remained in touch with Milly's school ever since," I said.

He nodded. "I was a Governor, and a shareholder. While Milly was alive I'd come and chat about the problems. As I was saying, I've seen the plans and I think what you're doing is very good. I approve. I'm going to tell the solicitor I support you."

"Good," I said. That was what I and Simon were waiting to hear.

The Headmistress, Gale, who was leaving the school at the end of term, approached. She was tall. I told her how sorry I was to hear of the death of her husband.

"These things happen," she said. "We're moving through to the marquee now." She said to Dr Pippin, "I hear you and Philip have been quoting Shakespeare."

I wondered who had overheard our conversation and told her.

Dr Pippin said, "I feel like David before Goliath."

I said, "No, you're Goliath. You were a big boy in long trousers, I was your junior by five years."

He smiled and said, "I have to leave for a short while."

I saw him pick his way unsteadily towards the loo.

The Speech Day began with scenes from Shakespeare. There was a large picture of the Droeshout First Folio portrait on the stage. Simon sat beneath it and I noticed a symmetry between their eyebrows. James Pippin and I sat in the front row, separated by an aisle.

The prizes were given out by a former head girl who had trained as a nurse at the London Hospital. The organisation was under-rehearsed. Prizes were not in the right order and there was a hunt while girls waited. Certificates were given out to the wrong recipient now and again, and had to be brought back and swapped. This was the school we had found, which the Headmistress, Gale, had cheerfully coped with. It would be very different next year.

After the prize-giving was over Dr James Pippin unsteadily stepped up onto the stage and talked to the guest of honour. I joined him and the three of us talked about the London Hospital. Then I withdrew and patted his arm in goodbye and left him talking. As I reached the marquee's exit and turned round he was standing on the edge of the low stage by himself. The speaker had vacated the platform.

He had flown in from Portugal to assess the state of his godmother's school, and he had seen it as it was and, having looked at the plans and what it would become, he realised it had to change. It could not remain in his godmother's bumbling time.

A Burnt Croissant and a Wrong-Way-Round Cap

For Pippa's birthday I booked a spa near Frinton. We drove along Frinton front – all houses, no hotels or shops – and turned and drove back and parked in the only empty space for cars. It was by a stone path that led across the crowded Leas towards the sea. We peered down and saw a line of beach huts with the sea beyond, and immediately below us was a zig-zag path that people were descending or ascending. And then it came back to me. This was the 'zig-zag path' we took when, a boy, I stayed in Frinton in 1954, sixty-two years ago. My family trailed up and down this zig-zag path.

Pippa had been looking online to see if she could find a place by the sea on the Essex coast, and I said to her, "You wouldn't want to have a place here. You wouldn't like trailing up and down the zig-zag path to get to the sea, and if you drove your car out of a space to go to the shops you couldn't get back in. And the shops are a long way away, inland, too far to walk."

She said, "I agree, for all those reasons."

We drove four miles and found the sign to the Lifehouse Spa. We drove half a mile up the drive to the car park and carried our bags to reception. We checked in and were walked along a maze of very modern corridors to room 49. I flashed my card on the door panel and inserted it in the slot for electricity inside so the lights came on.

We had a modern room with a door that opened onto a half-mown lawn, beyond which, behind trees, was a lake with lilies. Ducks waddled tamely on the grass.

We unpacked and walked to the bar for diet cokes and a shared club sandwich. Then it was time for our full-body massage in a couple's room. I undressed in dim light and lay on a gurney with my chin on a towelled breathing-hole, and to relaxing music for the next hour a deep-touch massage ironed out my knots and invigorated the knobbles on my spine. At the end I was deeply relaxed and we were shown to a block of 'quiet rooms'. On a raised platform were several walled-off low double beds with curtains and relaxing music. Two of the curtains were drawn. We stepped up into our 'quiet room' at the end and pulled the curtains, and I lay in a stupor for three-quarters of an hour in the dark, paralysed into inactivity, and, almost asleep, breathed to the relaxing music.

Dinner was at 6.45. Outside the restaurant many barely-dressed youngish men and women sat in groups in the sun under the blue sky without any regard to possible future skin cancer. Inside, the dress was so casual that my long-sleeved shirt and grey trousers seemed excessively formal. Pippa had scallops and I had smoked salmon for starters, and we then had lobsters. There were 'nut-crackers' to break the shell round the claws, and a thin 'scooper' to scoop out the lobster meat. It had an indent in its handle so two prongs could spear lobster meat. I had a glass of red Merlot. Then I had a slice of vegan dark chocolate with raspberry tart, and we sat outside and sipped iced amarettos in the dusk among the post-Brexit Essex English whose informality and sloppy lolling I studied with fascination.

The next morning was sunny. Before breakfast I stepped out onto the lawn and walked twenty yards to the lake. A moorhen was standing on one of the lily leaves. It picked its way from leaf to leaf without sinking into the water. I watched entranced.

Breakfast was in the restaurant. All the men were in T-shirts and shorts and shuffled in slip-ons or wore sandals. I was easily the oldest there, by at least two decades. One young man in a track suit wore a cap the wrong way round, with the peak down his neck. From our corner near the self-service area (which was a bit bangy and slammy) as I sipped my orange and ate my bowl of cereals, fruit and Greek yoghurt I again studied the English, more than half of whom had voted to leave the EU without realising the danger, and, to me, the new Brexit English were epitomised by the young man with his cap the wrong way round. Then I thought I was being unfair.

I went up for toast and he was before me in the queue. He took a croissant – a French and therefore European delicacy – and put it in the slowly-rolling two-tier toaster.

I tapped him on his track-suited arm and pointed to a large sign to the right of the toaster: "Please don't put croissants in the toaster as they will burn."

"Oh," he said, "I didn't see the sign."

Immediately there were clouds of smoke and a black croissant like a large cinder was deposited in the bottom of the toaster. I handed him the plastic tongs that stood in the bread basket.

I sat at my table with my lightly-toasted brown bread and made 'soldiers' of toast, butter and honey to have with my coffee, and reflected on the new England which had been created by voters who had not grasped the subtler issues. It was a casual and informal, leisured and materialistic England. It had turned its back on the EU, it had burnt the EU croissant without seeing the danger sign. It had put the country into a new precarious predicament out of ignorance, and it wore its new distinctive identity with pride, like a wrong-way-round cap. Now I knew I had not been unfair.

A Rape and a Dying Mother's Love

We arrived early at the Cornish Methodist chapel that Saturday morning. I was in a lightweight suit, white shirt and tie and Pippa wore a fascinator. She said, "Bride," to an usher and we entered through the bride's door and encountered the "financé" as one of the family had called him, the groom, Charlie, in the minimally-decorated left aisle, a young primary-school teacher in his early twenties with an open face and hooked nose.

He said, "I was nervous an hour ago but talking to family and friends has put me at ease. The new flat's ready for a move-in between Winchester and Southampton, and we are leaving for Egypt for our honeymoon on Monday."

We sat in mahogany pews. Above the surrounding first-floor mahogany balcony was the organ and a large screen. The church soon filled up. The bride's mother's second husband, Victor, sat in the pew in front of us on his own. He had a bulging stomach and a thick neck. He was joined by the bride's grandmother's two sisters-in-law. The bride's mother, Martha, took her seat wearing a blue hat that hid her eyes beside her third husband, a small and balding man. The two sisters' brother Bill and his wife Daphne sat alongside them. The Minister, a white-haired elderly man in a clerical collar addressed us informally. He made jokes and asked us to rehearse a collective response he would ask us to make, "With God's help, we will."

The musicians from the groom's chapel softly played Pachelbel's Canon, and there was a procession from the back down the bride's aisle. First came the four bridesmaids, the last of whom was Sonia, an overweight young lady with red-orange hair who had just dropped out of media studies in Leeds. Ginnie followed, escorted by her father Albert, Martha's first husband. The bride was in a white dress with a veil.

They stood at the front beside the groom and best man, and after the welcome and a hymn ('Love Divine') the marriage took place. A tiny baby the size of a doll wauled in the pew behind us. Its father, husband of one of the bridesmaids, was baby-faced and 'shhed' it.

The words of the marriage were modern. The groom was asked if he would support the bride, and he replied, "With God's help I will."

The Minister ad-libbed, "You'll need his help," and everyone laughed.

Between the vows there was banter, and everyone laughed each time the Minister joked, seemingly unaware that the vows were being devalued by the light-heartedness.

There was another hymn ('Be thou my vision'). Now the mood was evangelical. A singer with a guitar and a backing group led the singing at a microphone, and there was clapping to the beat. There were two readings, one by the bride's half-brother Lionel, and an address by the groom's godfather who was also a Methodist Minister in a clerical collar, and there were two more jazzed-up hymns, sung by a jigging congregation ('This is Amazing Grace' and 'Joyful').

The register was signed and there were prayers, and after one more strummed hymn ('To God be the Glory') the bride and groom exited up the right-hand aisle on the groom's side of the chapel to loud applause.

Outside it was misty and there was a faint drizzle. Photos were taken under the chapel's columned porch whose roof proclaimed '1828'. I had a few words with Martha.

"You're teaching secondary science?" I said.

"Yes. Chemistry. I'm looking forward to it."

"And you're a preacher?"

"Yes, but I'm not allowed to do it at school."

Pippa and I walked up to the chapel hall nearby for coffee and (for those who wanted them) cream-and-jam scones, and I saw the baby-faced father of the two children on hands and knees. Daphne, who sat with us for coffee, said, "He changed the baby's nappy while the baby was still doing it and it's gone all over the carpet."

Ellen sat with us. She had been an auxiliary nurse for thirty years and was now seventy-one. She had retired and was living in an ex-almshouse in Barnstable. She asked if we could give her a lift to the lunch.

As we drove to the Britannia she talked about Victor's weight, and Sonia's. "I blame it on Victor's mother," she said. "She was controlling, Sheila. She fed them chips for breakfast. Both Victor and Sonia told me, 'We don't want chips for breakfast, it's not going to reduce our weight.' She did it deliberately to have control over them. Then she found a new man on the internet and disappeared to Falmouth four years ago and they haven't traced her. She told lies. Victor's adopted. He wanted to find his real mother but Sheila told him, 'She's not interested, she doesn't want to know.' But he did trace her. He found he had a brother in Ireland and got her address through him. He was looking for her under the wrong name – she had remarried – and *she* was looking for *him* under his original name, which isn't his now. So they couldn't find each other. She was living in Oxford. He met her once and they made their peace. Then she died. He took Sonia up for the funeral. It's a sad story."

We were early in the Britannia car park, and she asked if she could get out of the car. She walked and sat on a seat and smoked a cigarette. Then Victor arrived and walked to the same seat and he too sat and smoked a cigarette. I could see them talking as I sat in the front seat of the car with Pippa. Albert arrived and then Martha, so we got out of the car and joined Ellen. By now Victor had gone. She whispered to me, "He told me all about finding his real mother. I'll tell you later."

We queued at the entrance to the small marquee to write a message in a guest book and scoop chocolate drops from a jar into a bag which announced the wedding of Charlie and Ginnie. There were nine round tables with white tablecloths and blue sashes round white chairs. Our table was laid for five: we were with Ellen, Daphne and Bill. I was next to Ellen.

During my starter – brie and bacon – Ellen told me what Victor had said. "His father beat his mother up, and she left. She went back to collect her things, and he came in and found her there. He raped her, and Victor was the product of that incident. She went to her mother's. She had three children and when the fourth one, Victor, was born, her mother said, 'I'll look after the three, but you've got to get rid of the latest.' Because she had been raped. She had no choice. She was a woman and she had to make sure the three were provided for. So Victor was sent for adoption after a few weeks. In later life she looked for him as Christopher Gibbs, the name of her first husband. But his name had changed following his adoption from Gibbs to Hathaway. He looked for his mother as Christina Hathaway. But her first husband had died, and she had remarried and her second husband had died, and she remarried and her third husband had died. Her name was completely different. When he finally found her he wrote to her four times before meeting her. They had just the one meeting. Then she died in her early seventies, I don't know why. He took Sonia to the funeral and her family welcomed them with open arms, and Sonia stayed with them for a few days before returning home. He welled up while telling me. First when he described the rape, and then when he described how she left him to be adopted. It's a terrible story."

After the main course and pudding – I had chicken and chocolate torte – there were speeches. Albert spoke. His current wife was near him on top table. He now had a senior job administrating within the

DHSS and prosecuting fraudsters. He had a four-bedroomed house in countryside outside Birmingham.

In his speech he was gracious towards Martha, and said she had been a good mother. He seemed to be addressing much of his speech to me. He kept looking at me as he spoke. Charlie, the groom, spoke next and thanked Albert for his financial support. Albert had paid for the hire of the marquee and the lunch and the other costs of the wedding, and had given Ginnie a car. She had a new job doing youth work out of a chapel, and would be a lay preacher like her mother Martha.

After lunch we sat in the bar for coffee with Daphne. Bill went back home to rest, having had a heart operation which required ribs to be broken and reset. Ellen joined us. She told me, "I suffer from macular degeneration. I've had thirteen injections in my right eye and four in my left eye, fortnightly and alternating recently. They don't think they can save my right eye, so now they're trying to save my left eye. Until recently I've made the next appointment while having an injection, but now they've changed the system. They have to write to me, and six weeks may go by before I'm given my next appointment. They're delaying appointments to take pressure off the NHS."

The disco began at 6. Green laser lines filled the marquee, and to flashing lights the young danced or swayed or in some cases jumped up and down. There was a hokey-cokey. The elderly sat at tables sipping drinks, the music too loud to talk. I spotted Victor standing alone in the garden near the far entrance to the marquee. He had changed into a black T-shirt. I rose and joined him.

"I was at your wedding," I said, "with Pippa. I remember you talking about Arsenal. You still support Arsenal?"

"Yes," he said. "That was twenty years ago. Sonia was a baby. Yes, I work shifts, a lot of nights. I'm a manager in a warehouse, getting newspapers out. I worked from 11pm till 9am this morning, so I haven't slept for nearly twenty-four hours. I'll have some time off during the day and I may be able to get to see them play."

"Newspapers," I said. I told him about Richard and Kevin, who arranged the delivery of my daily papers.

"I oversee that," he said. "The vans come out of London and stop at Exeter, Plymouth, here and then Falmouth. Your shop meets the van at Bugle and I make sure four pallets are unloaded. I oversee your papers."

I said, "Say 'Hello' to Richard and Kevin for me next time you're speaking to them. I've helped Pippa compile a family tree, and Ellen was telling me about how you found your real mother. It's a very moving story, and well done for finding her. It will have been very important to her to have found you. At the end of one's life one wants everything to be put right. Can you tell me your mother's name? I'll add her to the family tree."

"Snow," he said without hesitation. "Christina Snow. I was looking for Christina Hathaway, my name, and she was looking for Christopher Gibbs, the name I had before I was adopted as Victor Hathaway. Sonia's the spitting image of her, and so is Lionel. Sonia and I share the same genes, we're both overweight. I shall walk home when I leave here, walk off some of my weight. And Sonia's doing well, she's lost ten pounds, but she gets disheartened that she hasn't lost more. She's in a chain of sandwich bars and is looking to be a manager of several places like me on good money."

"Good," I said. "And Lionel's doing well. He's reading Theology, he may be a lay preacher?"

"Yes, he may."

"Your real mother would be very interested in it all," I said.

"Yes, she would. I was lied to when I was growing up, and I found her late, but at least I found her. The trouble was, she was dying."

I could not bring myself to ask how she died, as much as I wanted to know.

I returned to the noisy marquee and sat on my chair as deafening music and green laser lines blasted through me. I saw Victor go and order himself another drink at the bar. He was the product of a rape and therefore unwanted by his grandmother, but his mother had wanted him and the high point in his life had been locating her despite the lies of the woman who had adopted him. His mother was then dying but she had been searching for him, and at the end of her life it was not the rape that had preoccupied her but its product, the vulnerable baby and older man who had so desperately missed his dying mother's love.

18

A Cut Wire and a Whippersnapper Bully

An Openreach engineer thundered on the door, a portly fellow with untidy combed-forward hair in a green-yellow high-visibility short-sleeved safety vest. His van was behind him near the harbour.

"You've got a line down?"

"Yes," I said, "line number 2. It stopped working when an engineer went up the telegraph pole at the back."

"I'd better come in and find where it enters the property."

I showed him how the cable came through a wall behind the sitting-room television. I helped him lift the heavy television to one side so he could crouch at the wall behind it. He took the front off the socket and tested the wires on a computer that sat in the palm of his hand and looked like an old-fashioned bulky mobile. He shook his head.

So I took him into the garden and showed him the telegraph pole in our hedge and the line coming off it to a gable window. He climbed the telegraph pole using the foot rests each side and opened the box at the top. I returned inside.

He came back to the socket behind the television and said, looking at his bulky computer, "Its range is longer than that. It may be the cabinet. I'll go and have a look."

Through the window I saw him walk to his van and drive off.

Half an hour later he was back.

"I found it," he said, as he knelt behind the television and tested the wires and nodded. "A cut wire. The previous engineer. The engineers don't care. They're only thinking about their job, any wires in the way get cut. That's how it works. It's the bullying culture in the company."

"Bullying?" I said. "In what way?"

"Time," he said. "Everything's costed for time. I've already taken too long on this job, I'll be criticised and told off. What's galling is that it's the manager's son. He's never got his hands dirty and he wouldn't know what to do if he came on this job. Nothing's simple, everything's complicated in every job we do. He allocates the number of minutes I can spend on finding the fault and when the time's up I get bullied. He says, 'You're incompetent.' But actually *he*'s incompetent for not being able to assess the time correctly. When a line's not working, it takes as long as it takes to put it right. You can't just do it in five minutes. They're actually using time to get rid of you. They constantly suggest that if you're slow you won't be with them much longer. I've known men who've been told to go because they took too long. The bullying means you have to get your job done, and you don't care what wires you cut to get it done.

"There isn't enough work down here. You'd think they'd be putting in fibre to up the broadband speed. The Japanese put fibre in during the 1970s, that's how far behind *we* are. They say they're doing it and they don't. They say they've split the company to keep the MPs quiet, but they're moving things around, appearing to be two companies with the same staff, and some redundancies, and the MPs are deceived.

"I hate this job," he said. "I've been doing it for sixteen years. I came down from Southend because it's expensive up there. I've been with my partner for most of that time down here. I've got a ten-year-old son, he's about to start his new school. I like it down here except for this job. I'll work for another four years and get my pension secured, I'll have done twenty years. Then I'll leave and do something I really want to do. Until then I'll be bullied every day, 'You've been too slow, you're incompetent, you oughtn't to be in this job.' From a whippersnapper who's never done this work."

He had finished screwing the front of the socket back and reinstating the plug.

"There you are," he said. "I can get out of your way now. I've enjoyed meeting you, hope you have good weather, but it's going to be stormy, I've heard." He shook my hand. "I'm well over. I've just got to email in with my time and hear where they're sending me next."

I watched as he keyed an email onto his mobile.

"There," he said. "I'll go and sit in my van and hear where I'm going next, and I'll be too slow there as well. I'll have to drive really fast to make up the time. It's what I'm always doing, making up the time."

I thanked him and waved him off, and watched him through the window sitting in his van. He was Essex like me, and I thought how lucky I was that I did not hate my daily life.

A Walled Garden on the Cliff

Further up the coastal path from us in Cornwall was a boarded-up toilet block. Up in Essex I heard it had been sold at auction for £116,000, and that the new owner was an ex-finalist for Miss UK whose boyfriend would convert it. I then heard that the plans for the Council included a downstairs bathroom with a floor-to-ceiling picturesque window and a bath that would be visible from the cliff path. The plans were turned down. Then I heard they had submitted new plans that had been approved.

I received an email from our neighbour Maisie, telling me about the situation. She said the new owners were difficult. They were making a garden alongside the coastal path on both sides and were blocking her double gates with a hot tub. She had remonstrated with them. There had been an altercation. She sent pictures showing several vans blocking her main entrance, all parked by workmen who were doing the conversion of the toilet block, and an early view of the garden work either side of the coastal path.

I could see flower-beds and potted plants. The new owners were trying to build a suburban garden on the wild Cornish cliff.

Maisie said the new house was going to be on *Amazing Spaces* on TV in October.

I said, "It's not an amazing space, it's a horrible space. It's out of keeping with a rugged Cornish cliff."

We were down in June for a few days. Claire knocked on the door one evening and we all walked up to see what the garden was now like.

I was shocked. They were building a wall of stone boulders on either side of the coastal path. Part of the cliff had already sheared away and there were protective railings alongside the tarmac on the path so great had the erosion been.

I said to Claire, "Harry would say this wall's going to end up on the beach. It's a health-and-safety hazard. Anyone sitting on the shingle at the foot of the cliff may be buried in an avalanche."

We came down again in August. Claire appeared within a couple of hours of our arrival, and we walked up again to look at the garden.

It was all finished. Between the coastal path and Maisie's house wall was what could have been a Japanese stone garden, with shingle and rocks. Elsewhere it might have been quite aesthetic but it was totally out of keeping with a wild Cornish cliff. On both sides of the coastal path were posts with nautical ropes suspended between them. At the top of the coastal path on the sea side, opposite the new glassy property that had once been the toilet block, was a garden with potted plants. Access was by a gate with buttons to key in a code. But all you had to do was swing your leg over one of the ropes suspended between posts and you would be in.

Then an architect looked by. I took him to view the house.

He said, "It's on the market for £600,000. I can't understand how planning permission was given for such a garden on the cliff. The buyer is to be responsible for this. Our firm's surveyed the cliff in the past for another client. There's no rock underneath. Water will pour down from the field and sooner or later, now the weight of the stone wall's been added, it will go. All this lot will end up on the beach below."

Just before the end of our visit I went for a walk around the harbour and saw Richard Dawkins' Range Rover parked outside his office. I climbed the external iron staircase and found him sitting by the open door. He said, "I'm off to Colchester on Wednesday."

Then he took me out and showed me the restaurant he was building alongside the car park. He was retaining the old Cornish stone walls, had two shop units downstairs and a restaurant that would seat a hundred upstairs. He said he would supply the space and lease it out to a tenant, who would install tables and chairs. He said, "I sold the harbour and so haven't needed to borrow a penny. Selling the harbour means I can have projects like this now."

We stood outside in the sun. I noticed how white-grey his hair had become. I thought he had put on a bit of weight. I asked him about the coastal path and the toilet block.

He said, "I'm irritated by the new owner. I sold it to Peter White for £15,000. I had to sell as I needed the money. It went to auction. I only heard about the auction two days before the day of the auction. I emailed the auctioneer and said, 'There's no access, you need to say

"Buyer beware".' The auctioneers don't seem to have mentioned it. It fetched £116,000. Now the owner's visited this office and said he has access, but he hasn't. The key case is Stokes v. Cambridge, 1961."

Stokes v. Cambridge determined that if a parcel of land allows access that can result in the development of a neighbouring property, the owner of the parcel of land is entitled to one-third of the value of the development. "There was a field and a coastal path, and it was found that the buyer did *not* have access. I was hoping to get something out of the access. But it's the new harbour owner's problem now. Anyway, they may not be able to sell, £600,000 is a lot to ask for not very much, when there's no access."

The boyfriend of the ex-finalist in Miss UK was a developer who had weighted the unstable cliff with a stone wall and wanted to be away before the cliff collapsed. His idea of good taste was to build a gated suburban garden with flower-beds on the cliff, and somehow his taste had not been challenged by the Council's planning department. It would serve him right if he was unable to sell because of the lack of access – and because no one wanted the responsibility of preventing the cliff from collapsing under the weight of the stone wall he had installed without professional consultation.

Rock Pipits and iPads

The grandchildren arrived at our Cornish house with their mother after lunch. Al, aged seven, and Minnie, aged five, soon asked if they could go down to the beach beneath our window. The children put on beach shoes. I put on my sand trousers and trainers and, holding a shrimp net and two spades, we clambered down the steps past the tunnel to the stony beach. We walked past the breakwater until we could see the caves. Before us was a deserted beach.

"Grandpa, can we explore?" Al asked.

"Yes," I said.

They ran off. Now the shingle turned to sand. They stopped at the first cave and peeped inside, and then ran on to the second cave. Rock pipits flitted higher up the cliffs.

"Look," I said. "Two rock pipits."

They looked.

"Can we go on the rocks?"

Rocks meant more to them in their world than rock pipits.

"Yes, but be careful. The boulders may be slippery."

They scrambled from boulder to boulder, each double the children's size. Al came to rest before a colony of black-backed gulls that sat on distant boulders and had not moved.

"We must stop now," I called. "The tide's coming in. We don't want to be cut off."

So they returned and I supervised shrimping. There were not many rock pools and there were no shrimps in the curling waves or on the mixture of sand and stones in the clear water close to the shore.

"We'll walk back now," I said.

They took off their beach shoes and walked through the water, occasionally stopping to throw a stone.

Back among people, I supervised the putting-on of their beach shoes and led them to the steps. We walked through the echoing tunnel and up to the iron bridge.

I said, "We're going to cross, hold my hand."

"That's not the way home," said Minnie.

"No, we're having a surprise."

Beyond the bridge, up the slope, was a Kelly whip van selling ice-cream. There was a picture of all the ices on the outside.

"What would you like?" I asked when it was our turn to talk through the side window of the van.

Without hesitation they pointed to a double whip with a chocolate flake, the most expensive ice-cream of the dozen on offer: £3.50 each. I had a choc ice on a stick. We took our ice-creams to a nearby bench and sat looking across the harbour at our house, which was the most seaward. The struts of the bench were spaced out.

"Ow," Al exclaimed, still licking his ice-cream. "I've been stung."

It wasn't a mosquito, wasp or bee. I investigated. A stinging-nettle had poked an edge of a leaf between the struts, and Al had somehow brushed his free elbow against it.

I coaxed him into finishing his ice-cream. Then Minnie dropped a chunk of hers on the dusty ground below us. Immediately an enormous herring-gull appeared and gobbled most of it up near my toes.

We returned across the iron bridge to the house, holding the net and two spades.

The next day the children's father, Simon, came down by train. Al's wobbly tooth came out and Simon asked me for an envelope so it could be placed under Al's pillow for the tooth fairy.

"There's a tooth fairy in each room," Al said confidently.

That night Simon and I walked to the end of the pier, talking, and then round the harbour as I caught up with his news. There was a brilliant full moon and the sea had a causeway of moonlight.

The next morning Al came and said, "The tooth fairy left me £3."

Simon looked mystified. "Three pounds?" he asked.

"Yes. A £1 coin, and a £2 coin on the floor."

From Simon's reaction I wondered if the £2 had dropped out of his pocket.

"You're a lucky boy," I said.

"Yes, I am."

"I think I've got a wobbly tooth," I said, pretending to attempt to pull out a tooth.

"No you haven't. Your teeth are all second teeth, I've got four more first teeth."

The next day we all visited Maud. We ate in the Kota Kai restaurant. We were joined by Sue, her daughter-in-law, and her daughter Josie. Then we walked to an ice-cream parlour and all had cornet ice-creams. After that several of us walked to the pier. The wind buffeted my head and filled my lungs, and oxygenated my brain.

We returned to Maud's house, and her son Richard appeared. I asked after his health, standing in the small kitchen holding a mug of coffee while Maud was engrossed in conversation with Pippa.

He told me, "It's good. I had a lump on my neck and went to a doctor but he said it was nothing."

Maud, aged ninety, was looking at a family tree Pippa had shown her, and she interrupted the conversation and called across the room, "A lump, you say?"

Richard reassured her it was nothing, but her hearing was acute. She had Richard's voice on a special frequency and could hear him above the nearby chatter.

Later Simon took the children to the Harbourside Inn and watched the first half of Arsenal v. Leicester, which was on a BT channel and not available at home. I joined him for the second half. I sat on a tall stool near the door and watched the screen. The children sat with earphones and iPads at a low table in the window, immersed in their world, oblivious to the 0–0 draw that held the adults' attention.

The following day we had Sunday lunch in a restaurant up the road. The grandchildren were very well behaved over their roasts. Minnie described two of her school friends. Aged five, she said: "They're pretend 'twins'." She did double-inverted commas with the second and third fingers of each hand. "They're not really twins." She said it in a very adult way.

Later that day Simon took the children down to the beach in the other direction, to the rocks near Gull Island. They walked back across the sand between the sea and the mouth of the harbour at low tide.

Later still, sitting in her chair, Pippa locked her hands and said, acting it out with her fingers (folding her two hands together and steepling her two second fingers), "Here's the church, and here's the steeple. Look inside and see the people. Here's the parson saying his prayers." She had turned her hands inside out so the upright fingers were the people and she wiggled her thumb for the parson.

I continued, "'Dearly beloved brethren, do not eat food out of pigs' bins.' That's what I was taught," I said.

"It doesn't rhyme," Minnie said. "'Brethren' and 'bin' don't rhyme. It should be like 'log' and 'hog'."

I was astounded at the sharpness of this five-year-old. I did not explain that the pronunciation in some dialects could turn 'brethren' into 'brethrin'.

"Grandpa," Minnie asked, "do you know everything?"

"Yes," I said straight-faced, "I know everything."

"What's the Japanese for 'Please can I have an ice-cream?'"

I said, "*Minfadlek, isu creamu gozaimasu.*"

On reflection, '*minfadlek*' is Arabic and '*gozaimasu*', though Japanese, may not be appropriate here. I should have said, '*Watashi wa aisukurīmu o motsu koto ga dekimasu shite kudasai.*' My reply was a bit made up.

"I said 'Japanese' because it is the hardest language," Minnie, aged five, announced.

"I lived in Japan many years ago," I said.

"Grandpa knows everything."

"With Daddy," I said. "Between us, Daddy and Grandpa know everything."

I remained straight-faced.

When they left to drive home the grandchildren checked their car knapsacks in the sitting-room.

"iPad," Al said. "Earphones. Kindle."

They had returned to their world. I had led them down into my world on the beach, of caves and boulders and observing rock pipits, but they had returned me to their world of tooth fairies, rhymes (which were also in my world) and technological gadgets.

I waved them off and knew they would soon be lost in their iPads. But while they stayed with us they had learned about rock pipits.

A Drone and a Child

I looked up from my work in the Cornish August evening. By the sea wall a tall man in a black T-shirt was holding a square drone. Its lights came on, two red and two green, and its four blades were spinning round. I went out and watched over his shoulder as he released it.

The drone flew out to sea and soared to a height and hovered.

"How high?" I asked.

He looked at a hand-held screen. "Two hundred and fifty metres," he said.

I thought, 'Seven hundred and fifty feet. Not long ago a plane was in difficulty when landing because a drone was in its path at six hundred feet.'

I looked up. The drone was like a star, quite still, two green lights and two red lights within a tiny ball. It was directly over my house.

"How much does it cost?" I asked the fellow.

"All that I've got here, eight hundred and fifty pounds a year ago," the fellow said.

An Indian approached, wearing yellow shorts.

"Is that your child in a car up there?" he asked. "He's bawling his eyes out."

"Oh, yes," the drone operator muttered.

The drone came down very slowly. "You've got to be careful, you don't want it to fall out of the sky," he said.

The drone flew out towards the sea and then came in and landed gently in the hand he held out, green lights and red lights still on, blades still spinning. He quickly dismantled it over a black square bag. He removed each blade in turn and packed it away, and then placed the square drone and his small screen in the black bag. He zipped the bag up.

"Got to go," he said, and clutching his bag he ran up Quay Road towards his car where his son was crying.

I returned indoors pondering the drone's potential uses. It could take photographs and spy by transmitting pictures onto the hand-held screen. Could it fly close to a window and spy inside? Probably. More sinisterly, could a terrorist arm it with an explosive and fly it to blow someone up? Yes, because Amazon were exploring delivering orders by drone. And I lurched into a future where privacy had given way to commercial convenience and death could come out of the sky at a terrorist's whim.

Because of his drone the fellow had neglected his son. I had found my encounter with the drone exciting but its potential, though thrilling at one level, could not fail to disturb for its uses would be at the cost of human freedoms and feelings we had taken for granted for hundreds of years.

Wasting Muscles and White Dust

We had a wasps' nest where a gutter joined sloping roof tiles, and I rang Derek. He came around 11 and got out of his van leaning on a stick, white-haired and early seventies. He shook my hand and I pointed to where half a dozen wasps buzzed round that part of the roof.

He squinted and said, "It's under that tile by the gutter."

He returned with a canister and a long thin white pipe, which he assembled. He rapidly plunged a plunger up and down several times.

"How have you been keeping?" I asked.

"Not well," he said. "I've got muscle wasting disease. Muscle atrophy. All my muscles, everywhere. It's made me unsteady on my legs. My knees gave way in the kitchen three months ago, I fell backwards on my ankles and ripped all my upper-leg muscles. The pain was unbearable. I cried out and Myra came running and tried to get me up. I said, 'Don't touch me, let me just lie here.'"

He plunged violently and puffed through his long white pipe. White dust gathered round the lifted tile. Wasps with white on their wings and bodies crawled and buzzed round. One or two crawled in under the tile through the white dust.

"They take it in," he said. "It'll be all clear in half an hour, an hour. I say 'twenty-four hours', but half an hour's enough."

"Thank you," I said. "Have you been to a doctor about your muscles? Have you asked if there are tablets that can slow it down and firm your muscles up?"

"No," he said. "I've had an MRI scan. That's what found it. They don't seem to be able to do anything. I'm waiting for a letter. My legs are weak. I can't lift my legs. Look."

He raised his right foot three inches off the forecourt.

"That's all I can do. My muscles are all getting weaker. But you're right, I need to fight it. I've given up all the pest control I used to do, I just do wasps' nests. I can just about puff the white dust. But I only do that for my friends, like you."

I said, "I shall be going to Manila in November."

"Congratulations," he said, shaking my hand. "You'll love it there. It's all safe. Take the labels off your luggage before you leave the airport so they don't think you're new. And remember, don't pay WST, white skin tax. The price of a taxi goes up if it's for a white man. Myra always got me taxis. I hid round the corner or else I have had to pay WST. Your biggest problem will be all the young ladies who'll be after you."

I laughed. But then I realised he was reporting on what he had found before he met Myra. He was seventy-two, and she was thirty-two.

"See you next year," I said, "when we have another wasps' nest."

"Right," he said.

He got into his car and waved to me, and as he drove off and a wasp covered in white dust flew past I wondered if I would see him again. He had wasting muscles, muscle atrophy, and puffing white dust was the last work he could do. He was on his last legs. He would soon be dust.

As he turned his car and headed for the open double gates I had a strong feeling I would not see him again.

A Salon and Just Looking

I had my hair washed and sat in the chair and had it cut. Only Lyn the stylist and I were in the salon. The glass door to the High Street was wide open and through the large window I could see a little old lady with a stick walk slowly in.

"Just looking round," she said in a very upper-class voice.

She had a velvety coat and a hat over a bun and a very creased face. She looked ninety. She walked slowly round the salon, pausing to look at the bottles of spray, and then she stopped and examined herself in the mirror. She turned and walked slowly back towards the door.

"You'll look very beautiful when she's finished," she said to me.

"Did you hear that?" Lyn asked, sniggering. "She says you'll look very beautiful when I've finished."

I smiled.

The old lady lingered by the pile of magazines. Then she was back out in the High Street.

"She's often done that," Lyn smiled. "I've no idea what she's called."

"She's got a kind of dementia," I said.

"Yes."

"If this were a bookshop, 'Just looking' would be an acceptable thing to say. But not in a salon."

"No, it's not right here."

"She might be eyeing up what to steal. But she wasn't. She's lonely and wants some human contact and she's going into all the shops and not speaking and just looking round, in her demented state."

"That's right," said Lyn.

She had finished gathering lengths of my wet white hair in her fingers and snipping, and now started blow-drying.

But I was still haunted by the little old lady who wanted to look round and studied herself in the mirror and had an eye for beauty even though she seemed to be in a dream of the now and may have been cut off from the past and future by her dementia.

A Car-Park Attendant and Interference

When I reached my College, and noticed the blackening 18th-century stone under the clock with gold numbers and hands, I turned right and, soon after, sharp left and edged through the narrow gate that was just wide enough to take my car. I thought of how I had climbed over the gate's predecessor as an undergraduate. I drove to the end of a hedge and saw a parking space immediately in front of me that would suit me fine.

A bald man in a blue sweater approached. "Over there, on the lawn between the trees, sir," he said, directing me to the end of the orchard.

"I'd rather park in *that* space," I said. "I've got to leave at ten-thirty tonight, it'll be hard to get out over there."

"Oh, all right," he said.

"And hello from last year," I said. "You parked me last year."

"I thought I recognised you. How have you been?"

"Well," I said. "Have you had a good year?"

"Busy," he said. "There's so much building happening. I just come occasionally, I live outside Oxford, I am in and help when there are events. Each time I come I see something new."

"Has the college coped with Brexit?"

"I don't think they're too happy about it," he said. "One in five of the staff could have to leave the country. But speaking for myself, I voted Leave. It was Obama who swayed me. He came over and said we'd be in the back of the queue. I thought, 'Who are you to tell us what to do?' So I voted Leave. We British have never been told what to do, certainly since the Victorian time. So I voted Leave. How about yourself?"

Obama had warned that the UK would be at the "back of the queue" in any trade deal with the US if the UK chose to leave the EU. But I let that pass.

"I don't want us to be impoverished," I said. "Of our £510 billion in exports, we exported £224 billion to the EU. And there are over 15,000 nuclear weapons, some not too well guarded, and terrorists might steal one. Such issues need sorting out. Countries have to co-operate at the present time and sort the terrorists out on the continent. It's complex."

"I understand," he said. "I don't want us to be impoverished and I don't want nuclear weapons to get into the hands of terrorists. I voted Leave because I didn't want Obama telling us what to do."

"But actually, his advice may have been right," I said, "even if it came across as interfering."

"I didn't want the American President interfering," he said. Then another car came, requiring his parking advice. "Nice to see you again, sir," he said.

And as he walked to speak to the driver through the window I thought I didn't want *him* to tell me where to park, *he* had been interfering but he had not seen that. He saw his job as a nice little part-time earner, and did not think about the consequences to others of his ill-judged decisions.

A Chaplain, a Funeral and God

The Gaudy (reunion, literally 'a rejoicing') took place on a showery day in October. I had tea with the Provost, and chatted to him in the foyer before he addressed us. He told me his next book would be on Wordsworth.

I went through to the seated area and sat halfway back. The Provost sat at the table in front in an open-necked shirt whereas we were all in jackets and ties, and talked informally. He said he had raised £80 million in pledges of the £100 million for college improvements and the last part was the hardest. "If you come into a windfall, please think of the College and" (he looked at us Older Boys) "please remember the college in your wills."

Afterwards I wandered by the lake and gazed at the stone seat beyond the arch, near the fallen tree and before the weeping willow, where I chose my future fifty-eight years previously. Then I changed into my dinner-jacket. Because I was driving back that evening I had not been allocated accommodation so I changed in the disabled toilet, which was spacious and had one low hook that could be reached by someone sitting in a wheelchair.

I attended choral evensong in the chapel, surrounded by the Victorian Neronian-style decorative paintings.

At 6.45 I walked to the drinks reception. I was early and found myself in step with 'the Reverend Donald Baxter' (as his name badge announced).

"Have you been a vicar?" I asked.

"Yes, I've been a vicar of a parish and more recently I was chaplain at a school."

"And do you still take services part time?"

"Yes, I get roped in. This last week I've had four weddings and a funeral. The funeral was very trying, it was the daughter of my neighbour and she was only twenty-six."

"It must have been awful for you," I said.

"It was."

"Did you interpret what had happened for the congregation?"

"I was bewildered and baffled. I didn't know what to say, and I said as much. You know Archbishop Rowan Williams was in a similar situation and he said, 'I just don't understand why.'"

We entered the reception. I declined champagne and took an orange juice.

"What do you feel about the world?" he asked.

"I see the universe as a unity, a oneness," I said. "A Light which can be found in the Metaphysical poets can break through from the beyond into one's soul. There is a cosmic plan and we are all within it. And fruit and people fall within the plan."

"That's very good," he said. "I should have said that at the funeral. But it's all right to say you don't know."

"Like the Bishop of Durham," I said, "who said he was not sure that he believed in God at all."

"Yes," he said. "And do you see all humankind as being open to this Light?"

"Yes," I said. "It's like the sun seen on top of a mountain. There are many paths up from different sides, but there is just one sun."

"Very interesting," he said. "I'm appalled at what's happening in Syria. I think the world is now in a very dark place."

And at that moment I saw my old Law tutor. He was eighty-three but looked younger. I turned to greet him and gave him my news. He was very attentive and radiated interest. Then I spotted the Provost in the foyer outside the hall. He had a sore throat and was saving his voice for his after-dinner speech by not shouting in the hubbub.

I slid my way past standing groups of old and young men to the quiet of the foyer, and spoke to the Provost.

I never got back to the Reverend Donald Baxter. I saw him further down our long table during dinner, later, grey-haired with a round white collar. I did not know if his lack of metaphysical vision had caused his bewilderment at the death of his twenty-six-year-old neighbour's daughter and his bafflement at funerals for the very young.

Barley Risotto

I clambered over the long bench in the dining-hall and sat as I used to sit nearly sixty years ago. I was the nearest to top table in my year. Beside me was an empty seat for the previous year, and a large, old-looking man puffed to my side and with great difficulty raised a leg and got it over the long bench and, half standing and half sitting, gripping the table and the pre-laid cutlery, swung his other leg over without tearing my dinner-jacket. "That was challenging," he said. He turned to me and said, "Did you play football for the college?"

"Yes," I said. "I was inside left."

"I was outside right," he said. "I played in that position because I didn't have to do as much as in some of the other positions. I was mostly in the Seconds. You were in the First Eleven. I had a few games in the First Eleven. I recognised your face. Jim Last."

"Good to see you again after nearly sixty years."

We shook hands and I noticed he had a very thick and prominent hearing-aid in the ear nearest mine, his right ear.

"I can't hear a thing on your side," he said, turning so his left ear could hear me.

I commiserated. "We're all getting old and falling apart in different ways," I said.

He was very unsteady and it was hard to imagine him on the football field. I was glad I had gone to the gym once a week for the last sixteen years.

He studied the menu, a folded stand-up booklet.

"Have you seen the starter?" he asked. "Barley risotto. That's an oxymoron. Can you tell me why and where the oxymoron is?"

"An oxymoron is when contradictory terms are alongside each other," I said.

"Risotto is rice," he said. "Barley and rice are contradictions. You can't have barley risotto."

"Perhaps there should be a hyphen," I suggested.

He laughed.

"Who else was in the team?" he asked.

"Brian Basildon was the First-Eleven Captain," I said. "He played centre half. Do you remember Mike Holloway?"

"Oh yes," he said. "I was thinking of him this morning."

"He died young," I said, "when he was about thirty."

"I didn't know."

"Do you remember Doughy Ross?"

"Doughy who?"

"Ross."

"I don't think so," he said. "Oh, it's coming back to me, yes."

"He's dead too," I said. "He died about the same time as Mike. Over forty years ago. That time was like a field of barley or rice, and now it's just stalks."

He was silent. I saw the faces of the team who were now fallen like reaped barley or rice.

"Do you remember Hugh Cobham?" he asked.

"Yes," I said. "Thinnish, tousle-haired, set-back eyes and a bit ungainly. He was centre forward."

"That's right. I saw him last week. He's a baronet now. He was the son of a baronet and he's inherited the title. He doesn't come to reunions."

There was now a hubbub and he had difficulty in hearing me. Our barley risotto, which looked like a heap of rice, with (allegedly) barley in it, and pumpkin sauce, had been placed in front of us. I thought of the paddies in Japan, the rice fields and peasants picking the rice, standing up to their knees in water....

I studied Jim Last. He was like barley, he had grown and his fleeting memories were like reaped grains of barley that were now barely visible. My memories had been picked and had been turned into stories, my visible risotto. Sitting beside each other, although we had been in the same team we were contradictory, an oxymoron: barley risotto. He had asked me what the oxymoron was. The real answer was: us.

Three Negotiations and Pleased Faces

We entered a large room used for weddings where many of the 800 guests stood in groups in evening dress. I took champagne from a tray and was greeted by a middle-aged couple. The wife asked, "Hello, do you remember us? Do you know who we are?"

"Yes," I said, and Pippa nodded with a look to me that suggested she had no idea who we were talking to. We made neutral conversation about Brexit. "My husband is passionate about it," she said. "He's a Brexiteer."

I spotted David Kipling and pulled away.

"Here's a young Turk who looks older than a schoolboy," I said. He had just come back from his home in Turkey at a time when the papers were running stories of migrants posing as schoolchildren to enter the UK.

He grinned and told me he had just had an eye operation in Turkey as his diabetes had affected his sight.

Then I saw George Osborne entering with Edith Small. She saw me and immediately introduced me to George Osborne. For a man who had been unceremoniously sacked he did not look disappointed. He was as tall as I was, the Chancellor of many budgets, and we stood side by side in dinner-jackets and chatted effortlessly, watched by several hundred of the guests.

I said to him, "I have something to ask you. Last night on television a negotiator for the EU was saying that there would be *two* negotiations: the divorce, which will take two years; and the negotiation for a European deal, which will take five to six years. And they won't run concurrently. So is it true that we will lose 44 per cent of our exports for about four years while we wait for the negotiations for a European deal to happen?"

He said, "It will be a difficult time. And there are three negotiations: the divorce; the transition, however long that will take; and then the EU negotiation. So it will be longer."

I said, "As the truth of the situation sinks in there will be a change in the national mood. Your time is coming."

He smiled and nodded, and Edith Small was saying, "I have to move him on."

I said, "The way you ran the economy was very helpful."

"Thank you for saying that."

George Osborne moved away, at ease, self-assured, with poise.

Hilda Strawson was behind, looking strained, and I bent and greeted her and said very quietly, "I was very sorry to hear your news."

Her business had gone into administration.

"I'm relieved," she said quietly.

I said, "I do hope everything will be all right."

"Yes it will," she said. She told me she owned the buildings and would have the rents but Gordon had given up his directorship as he had to declare his interests as an MP on the House of Commons Register, and so he would get nothing. "He only has his salary, so long as he keeps his seat. He's over there in the corner."

I said, "I'll go and talk to him." Leaving Pippa, I walked over and intruded on the group of four. Gordon was laughing as though he did not have a care in the world. "Can I congratulate you on being elected Head of a Committee," I said. "I read it in today's paper. Science and Technology."

"Thank you," he beamed as I shook him by the hand.

"Will you be an inquisitor and interrogate people who come to the table?"

"Yes, I'll be an inquisitor," he smiled.

I stepped across the group and said in his ear, "I was very sorry to hear about the business."

He said, "It's been difficult for some while."

"It's a social trend," I said. "The internet. Thirty years ago there was a demand for printing, but now people can print off the internet."

"I agree."

"Something's happened to our society. It's like the advent of the railway in the nineteenth century, which disrupted things."

"Yes, I agree." Then he mentioned his wife. "Unfortunately Ava hasn't got a job," he said and looked at me half-appealingly. At that moment there was an announcement that we should proceed to our tables, which were further back in the same large room.

I found Pippa at our table, table 17. I was seated next to an elderly couple who, I knew, had lived abroad. I did not know the others, but as I walked round and shook hands I discovered one of them was the owner of a garage up the road that Jim Dawson had done jobs for, collecting a car at a dock and driving it back for a small fee. His wife was glamorous and buxom but said little.

The tables were named after past Chancellors – we were Reginald Maudling – and there was a quiz of 20 questions, the answer to every question being a different Chancellor's name. There was an introduction and then Gordon said Grace and we were served duck pâté with crostini chutney and a dressed salad. The elderly couple on my left talked about their time in Iran, Qatar and Kuwait.

Then suddenly George Osborne was saying, "Hi there." The men stood and he shook hands. He came to me. I said, "We've already spoken."

"I know."

I could tell he wanted to continue the conversation and I wondered if he had sought our table out as I shared his views.

"What will happen?" I asked. "Will Article 50 be triggered or will it never be invoked?"

"There's a ten-per-cent chance it won't and a ninety-per-cent chance it will," he said. "It's very difficult, the majority of MPs are against invoking it, but they're all Brexiteers now and may vote it through. It's difficult."

I said, "Over the next two years things will get worse. You don't have to do very much and there will be disillusion. People will see they have been misled, your time will come. Do you secretly believe you will be leader?"

From the look in his eye I could tell that he did.

I said, "People will turn to you when they see they were let down."

He nodded.

"And thank you for tackling the deficit," I said.

He raised a thumb and jerked it forward with intensity. "And thank you for not charging £76,000," I said mischievously, his going rate for speeches in America according to what I had read in a newspaper, and he laughed and he moved away.

I liked him. I could have talked to him for hours.

We were served braised lamb shank and I heard about Kuwait and Qatar. Then Edith Small was welcoming George Osborne from a hand-held microphone at the edge of the room. "We entered

Parliament about the same time and I can tell you, he was the brains behind the Coalition. The Coalition would not have happened without his vision and organisation." There was loud applause. She said with a flourish, "George Osborne."

George Osborne strode through the tables to join her, full of self-possession, a self-pleased smile on his face. He took the microphone and free-wheeled effortlessly like a patrician, steering clear of Remain versus Leave, and Brexit. He spoke of past Chancellors who got things wrong: Neville Chamberlain and Winston Churchill. "His father Randolph Churchill was also Chancellor. He was a very bad one. He never gave a budget and threatened his resignation, which was immediately accepted, and he contracted syphilis – the very things I have been trying to avoid." There was a gale of laughter from the eight hundred. Then he made a plea. "Please like the rest of the world, otherwise they won't like us." He finished to loud applause.

Edith Small announced that he had come to us straight from Heathrow, having been in America, and that he was jet-lagged and would now be leaving. He stood to applause and slowly made his way to the door, stopping to be photographed from time to time.

We were served summer berry pavlova with fruit coulis and refilled our glasses with red wine. We stood for the loyal toast and raised our glasses and said, "The Queen."

During coffee there was an auction. It was conducted by an auctioneer, and Edith Small held up the items being auctioned. An inexpert drawing of Margaret Thatcher, signed by Theresa May, fetched £9,500. There were loud and slightly drunk men who were competing to announce that they were *nouveaux riches* to all present.

For some of the items – prints, a film poster and some chef's knives ("these are not Michael Gove's," the auctioneer announced to laughter) – Hilda Strawson bid in the region of £200 or £300, money I knew she could ill afford. But she was announcing to the world that everything was normal and she had no problems, even though her face permanently wore a strained frown.

I sat back and finished my red wine and nibbled on a chocolate mint. And I pondered on the Strawsons, whose business had gone under partly because of the advent of the internet and changed social conditions and partly because mother and son had neglected their printing for politics, which did not pay as much as the business had when it was thriving. Despite Ava's involvement I was sure the business had died of neglect.

I thought of the public world of British politics. George Osborne and the Strawsons had had disappointments, but you could not tell from the way they conducted themselves. Everything was excellent, that was the impression they gave. Gordon had just been elected to chair a committee, and this was proclaimed to applause. It was a boasting world and boastfulness was expected and warmed to, even though the boasters were privately worried. But the truth peeped through like a hole in the heel of a sock: there would be three negotiations. I realised I had just taken part in three negotiations: in Gordon's divorce from his business, in Hilda Strawson's transition and in George Osborne's hope regarding the negotiation with the EU that there was a ten-per-cent chance that Article 50 of the Lisbon Treaty would not be invoked.

I looked at Gordon and Hilda. They were standing and laughing and chattering vivaciously as if they had not a care in the world. They both had a front, like George Osborne's self-pleased expression as he strode to speak. The three of them had problems and all three put on pleased faces to maintain their standing among people whose respect, for varying reasons, they badly wanted.

A Pinged Cable and a Dark Hole

The CCTV engineer was little more than a boy with a quiff of curled hair and an earring and a sleepy look. He had not been able to complete the installation of the new cameras the previous day. "It's a mixture of old and new equipment," he said, raising his voice at the end of the sentence as if asking a question. In the cupboard under the stairs he removed part of the floor to create a hole and lay face down and shone his torch under the floorboards and worked on a cable amid a run of cables from the telephone, internet, cameras and goodness knows what else.

Some time later he came in to me and said, "I've lost the cable. It suddenly went 'ping' and it's disappeared and I can't find it. It leads up to the joystick that controls the cameras in your office."

He had a bit of black plastic bag wound round his thumb.

"Have you cut yourself?" I asked.

"Yes, it happens all the time."

"Would you like some Savlon?"

"Yes, please. Have you got a plaster as well?"

So while he removed the black plastic bag I found my tube of Savlon and squeezed some on his thumb and found a plaster and took the wrapping off the sticky part and left him to position it and seal it. It was like coping with a fourteen-year-old.

The next day he returned to look for the cable. I told him about the trap door in the kitchen pantry floor and he lifted it and climbed down the steps with some reluctance and at my instigation groped for the light switch under the floorboards. I gave him a cobweb broom, for there were large cobwebs.

With great unwillingness he set off to crawl underground to the place where the cable went 'ping'. I shone a torch through the hole in the floor under the stairs and he called, "I can't get there, there's something in the way."

At that moment his boss arrived, Ron. He was slim and had a pony-tail. Many years ago he had had a motor-cycle accident and the scars still showed on his face. He knelt in the cupboard under the stairs and called down the hole, "Alan." I heard a muffled conversation. Then Ron called, "If you take much longer you'll go to sleep."

Ron came through to the sitting-room to look at the quality of the pictures the CCTV cameras showed on the six-split screen of our television. Pippa had the television on and the pictures had gone blue. The cars were blue in the road outside, and the road itself was blue.

"You're a hard taskmaster," I said.

"He shouldn't have let go of the cable," Ron said. "He should have held on to it. When I was younger I had to go down holes and find cables, and now I'm the boss I think someone else can do that side of the work."

"In Victorian times you'd have had him go up chimneys," I said, and Pippa laughed.

Ron had to go. He had to be in Greenwich in an hour's time.

Alan emerged up the steps into the pantry, his clothes covered in dust. He went outside and dusted himself off. Then he returned.

"You've got a headband for your torch," I said. "Why don't you put it on your head, and try looking down the hole again with both hands free?"

"Yes, I'll do that," he said.

But first he went up to the joystick and sent a message down the cable.

Almost immediately he found the end of the cable. It was under the hole. He had been looking at it all the time but had not realised that that was the cable that had pinged.

By the time Ron returned Alan had completed his work, filled out the form I had to sign and was packing his car.

"Are you taking the old equipment?" I asked.

"I haven't got room," he said.

"Well, there are two boxes in the gardener's area," I said. "We want them gone. Can you repack your boot to take them?"

And I went to the gardener's door and saw the two boxes Alan had neatly packed away in a corner so no one would see them, and carried them to the car. I stood while he reluctantly put them in the boot.

Ron returned and they conferred. Ron came and had a word. I waved them off.

As Alan drove off I felt sorry for him. He was a young boy and his boss was a hard taskmaster and sent him down holes and he bloodied his fingers regularly because of the nature of the work. It was a solitary life except when his boss came and told him to hurry up. Miraculously, the cameras now worked. I could control them so they turned. But one slip of his fingers and a cable could ping away into a dark hole and condemn him to crawl under floorboards to find the end he should have held onto and not let slip. He was a put-upon latter-day slave who lived permanently on the edge of a dark hole.

Portraits and Harps (Or: A Napkin and a Bath)

That year the family gathering was above the National Portrait Gallery. We entered from St Martin's Place and took an escalator up past the 18th-century portraits to the Portrait Restaurant and, early, sat at the table laid for nine and ordered sparkling water. Pippa was by the window as she was to have a knee operation in two days' time and she did not want to catch any colds. We absorbed the view over London rooftops – spires, The Shard, Big Ben – and we were joined by Rex and his wife Winnie and almost immediately by Rupert. I was shocked by how thin and gaunt and grey he looked.

"How are you?" I asked, shaking his hand across the table.

"I'm ill," Rupert said. "I'm breathless and wobbly on my legs. I'm exhausted. I can't walk more than a hundred yards. To get here I left Charing Cross station, crossed Trafalgar Square and stopped at St Martin-in-the-Fields and sat in a pew to recover. I've had tests, I don't get the results until the middle of the month. But they've already found fluid in my lungs. I may not be alive much longer. You may be attending my funeral later this year."

I said, "I'm sorry to hear this, stay within what you can do. Don't be exhausting yourself."

He said, "I've done well. When I became a diabetic at fourteen I was told I might not live beyond sixty. I've had an extra fifteen years on top of that."

We were joined by Raymond and Florence, and Jack and his wife Alison. Jack sat at the end of the table. The other tables had filled up and now we almost had to shout to make ourselves heard across our table.

Rupert held up a page from the Old Boys' magazine. It was about the death of Raymond Cutler. "Do you know the story about him?" Rupert asked everybody. "Our father was invited to sing at the opening of the Debden Methodist church in Mannock Drive in the late 1950s and asked Raymond Cutler to accompany him on the piano. They arrived with their music and sat, and the evening went by and they weren't called. Dad came home and said, 'I took my harp to the party and nobody asked me to play.'"

There was laughter.

Gracie Fields' song was a wartime hit in 1944 and it would still have been in circulation in the late 1950s. I wondered if David in the *Psalms* had said something about not being able to play his harp that had passed down into the song.

"The church has recently closed."

The lunch progressed. After my pumpkin soup Florence called out, "I want to change places with Winnie so I can talk to you down at the far end, including Pippa."

When she arrived she had said to me, "I've got flu but it's the fourth day and I'm not infectious."

She did not have much of a voice, and she thought a cold was not infectious after two days unless there was a streaming nose. Regardless of her professional interpretation of when infectiousness stops, I was not keen for her to sit near Pippa.

Pippa had said, "I'm not doing any kissing, I mustn't catch any germs before my operation."

Now Winnie said, "I don't want to change places, I don't want your germs." She said to Pippa, "Flu's infectious for five days."

Pippa said, "You can come if you don't breathe."

Jack said to Florence, "Stay where you are."

I did not know that Florence had encountered Winnie in the museum, among the portraits, before coming up to the restaurant, and that Winnie had said to her, "You look thin, you've lost weight," annoying her by seeming to suggest that she had been previously overweight or that she was now fundamentally ill. Winnie had also imitated Florence's cough.

When Florence's husband Raymond went to the Gents at the end of the first course I moved to his seat and sat next to Jack. I thought if I sat opposite Florence she would drop her request to change places with Winnie as she could talk to me. When Raymond returned he sat in my seat. We swapped wineglasses – we had been served white and red wine – and plates of pheasant, which a waiter had just brought. My pheasant was less rare than Raymond's.

All the in-laws were now together. Raymond said to Pippa, "We are the out-laws." There were smiles down the far end of the table.

I talked with Jack about the international situation (the Middle East and Brexit) and we progressed to our pudding (in my case chocolate, vanilla and lemon ice-cream) and coffee.

Florence was still agitating to change places, and again Jack said, "Just stay where you are."

Now Florence put her white napkin over her head in a public sulk. She sat still like a parrot with a cloth over its head, and the napkin had turned into a 'sulk-kin'. Rupert then took the napkin off her head and put it on his own head, to lighten the atmosphere.

When we were all standing after the end of the lunch Rupert said to Pippa, "I hope the operation goes well."

Pippa said, "All I can do is go along with it."

Rupert said, "No, sometimes you don't go along with it. I had a client. He had an allotment and he often gave me flowers he'd grown. He was ill, and I prepared his new will. There was a lot of money and he left most of it to the Forestry Commission. His new wife had been his neighbour, and he had married her so she could inherit his pension. He also left her £100,000. One son had £50,000 and the other son had nothing as my client considered him a wastrel. He discussed it with me and explained it all to everybody, and everyone seemed in agreement and happy. Then he said to me, 'Now I have disposed of my assets, as I'm ill and have no quality of life I might as well commit suicide.' He was serious, and he said, 'I'll walk into the sea at Rye and drown myself.' I said, 'That's a terrible idea. Your body may not be found for seven years, and the will won't take effect until they've found your body. If you really have no quality of life you should do it in your bath.'

"He discussed it with me and I saw his point, it made sense. He was ill, he had no quality of life and he'd had enough. I thought that in his position this was a sensible thing to do. I told him, 'You must have alcohol and tablets on the side of the bath. Otherwise it might seem you've been drowned and that might trigger a murder inquiry and affect the will as it was changed so recently.' So he announced to his family, 'I'll do it in the bath. Leave me alone for the night and look in the next morning.' They all reluctantly accepted what he said, they were upset but understood about the lack of his quality of life. He carried it out and was found dead in his bath the next morning."

Pippa was not sure why he had told the story. He was not saying that she should not go along with her operation, and she had a sense, female intuition, that he was toying with doing something similar if his test results were bad and he concluded he had no quality of life.

We said goodbye to each other and left in the lift. (I did not know that Florence and Winnie then went to the Ladies, and that Winnie hogged the one hand-drier, making Florence wait.)

Outside in the car Pippa told me what Rupert had said and murmured in an undertone so our driver could not hear, "You need to monitor it, to make sure he doesn't do the same."

I nodded and said I would. I said, "If he wants to commit suicide, all he has to do is to withhold his insulin, just not inject himself."

On the way home the harp haunted me: "For I took me harp to a party/But nobody asked me to play."

Rupert had taken his life to our family gathering, his exhaustion, and had strummed a few chords at the beginning of the gathering. But, trapped in their own lives and preoccupations, nobody had asked him to play any more. At the end, in frustration, he had strummed some more through his story about his client's suicide. But then I thought we all had harps. Florence had wanted to strum her harp to Pippa, but to keep Pippa germ-free for her operation nobody had asked Florence to play. And I had just finished my latest book and had not volunteered this, and that too was a harp I had not played.

I thought of Rupert saying, "You may be attending my funeral later this year," and I thought we were all approaching the end of our lives. We all had funerals ahead of us. We were all angels-in-waiting with harps we would all soon be playing. But right now we were all besieged with our own preoccupations and problems and did not ask the others to play the harps of their concerns, which under different circumstances the others might want to 'harp on about'.

A Baby in the Bookshop

The publishers held a party in their London bookshop on a cold night in January. I was early, and to pass some time until 7pm I loitered in the alley-way and looked in the nearby windows of antiquarian booksellers and a shop that sold knick-knacks and rows of small busts of historical figures.

I was among the first to arrive. I saw my two new books on a shelf facing the bookshop door. I was given a glass of red wine and as there were only two other guests decided to go down to the basement and look at the books on the shelves. There were several by Colin Wilson, and I recalled attending a book-signing by him in this very bookshop in 1978.

I turned back from the shelves and found myself talking to a balding, stout man in a blazer and open-necked shirt. (I was in a blazer and sweater.) He told me he lived in Wiltshire and was an illustrator: "I provided black and silver photographs for the *Tao Te Ching*." This book had recently been reissued.

There were now half a dozen guests downstairs, and I noticed a plate of olives and nuts and brownies, which had not been touched. As he talked about his life in Wiltshire the plastic bottom on the stem of his wineglass fell onto the carpet. He was unaware, and I said: "Be careful with your wineglass, don't put it down, otherwise it will tilt and deposit red wine on the carpet."

He looked, and realised that his stem had no bottom. He said, "It's surreal," and bent and picked the plastic base off the carpet and tried to fit it onto his glass. He gave up and said, "Shall we go upstairs and see who's there – and I'll ask for another glass."

I was about to suggest going upstairs as the fall of the plastic bottom had somehow dislodged his mask and I had ceased to be interested in what he was saying.

Upstairs had filled up. I was approached by a lady with a guest list on sheets of A4. She peeled off a label bearing my name and stuck it on my lapel. She had all the guests on her sheets and I worked out that those present had no labels above their names on her list and that those not present still had labels above their names. I established which of my contacts in sales and marketing were present.

The illustrator went off in search of wine, and a young lady approached me, dressed in black. She was enormously buxom. She said, "Are you an author?"

Looking over her great chest into her eyes I said, "Yes. Are you?"

"Yes." Then I looked down and noticed she had a baby inside her bra within her dress. The bulge before her was her baby. I could see its closed eyes and screwn-up face. I said, "Well done for being here with..." and glanced down.

She smiled and said, "Thank you."

"What's your book on?"

"Parenting."

Did it urge women to put their new-born babies inside their bras, so there was skin-to-skin contact?

"Have you got a book just out?" she asked.

"Two," I said. "In fact, they're on the shelves round the corner, facing the door."

"Oh," she said, "I want to find them, what are their titles?"

The lady with the guest list then butted in. "The publicity lady you're looking for is behind the bar table," she said (exactly where Colin Wilson had sat in 1978), "and next to her is the Head of Sales talking to the lady in charge of foreign rights."

"Thank you," I said, and to the lady with the baby, "I'm sorry, I've got to go over there."

I elbowed my way in their direction. Soon I was talking to the publishers' staff who had been promoting my books.

I did not see the lady with the baby again. She seemed to have left when I came to leave. I wondered if she was on her own, a sole parent, and why she had brought her baby inside her bra. Had I not been interrupted I would have asked her how she came to write her book on parenting and I would have got her to talk about her relationship with her baby.

I had heard no words of explanation. I had just seen a visual statement of how to approach parenting. She was living by example, and so far as I was aware she had come with her buxom baby and left without a word about why she was making such an eye-catching statement. She had brought her baby to the bookshop – and how.

A Furred-Up Heart and Wobbly Stress

Rupert rang me. He asked after Pippa's knee. I said she was doing well but had had an infection on the glued gash and was on Flucloxacillin.

"You've had your test results," I said.

"Yes. They show I have serious heart problems. I'm wobbly and anaemic, and I've grown worse. I had an echocardiogram. They squirted jelly on me and moved the probe round my heart and turned up the sound of the ultrasound machine and I heard what sounded like my heart struggling." He imitated the squelching-groaning sound he heard. "It was the stress of the heart through the furred-up valves. And I've fluid in my lungs, and being a diabetic I have other weaknesses, including my kidneys. I can't walk more than a hundred yards, my valves aren't opening properly. In March last year Henry took me to Berlin with his family and I walked round Berlin, and I walked a mile across the Common here three times a week. I can't do it now. I'm exhausted. I'm sleeping three times during the day –"

"That's sensible," I said, "if your body needs it. Churchill used to nap."

"No, it isn't sensible," he said crossly. "It's evidence that I have no quality of life, sleeping during the day. Anyway, I am being sent to a heart consultant in early March. My appointment's for March the eighth."

"Will he recommend a cure?" I asked.

"He has options. He may propose a stent. But my diabetic body won't stand up to it. I'm sure that's what I'll be told on March the eighth. There's no cure and I have no quality of life. I wanted you to know the situation so you can understand as I feel I might not be around by March the eighth. I might not live much longer."

"Oh dear, Rupert," I said. "We shared a room together in the old days and talked, and I would have urged you then to live on and do the stent."

"I have to go," he said hastily.

And with a quick goodbye he rang off.

I pondered his call. I did not like the sound of his 'I have no quality of life'. That afternoon I had to be at one end of our new computers while a troubleshooter remotely repaired our Microsoft Office and found our portable hard-drive back-up and transferred some missing files of Pippa's from her old computer to her new one. I could not ring Rupert back until 5.30.

Rupert answered warmly, "Yes."

I said, "Rupert, I've been thinking, I'd like to come down to see you and talk as we used to when we shared a room and reminisce. I could manage Tuesday. I'd come about 12 and go about 2.30 before the rush hour. I'd take you out to lunch. Is there a restaurant within a hundred yards of where you live?"

"Two hundred and fifty yards."

"OK, well I could pick you up and drive you there and look for parking nearby, so you aren't exhausted. If necessary we could go to a pub so I can park in their car park. And we'll talk about our childhood."

"I'd like that but I can't do it on Tuesday. I'm stressed, it will increase my stress –"

"The idea's to de-stress you, not distress you."

He said, "I've got a heart that's stressed because of its furred-up valves. Can I get back to you and let you know when I can make it?"

Then he said: "I had a friend whose will I drew up. He lived opposite me and gave me flowers from his allotment. He was ill and decided his quality of life had gone. He wanted to drown himself in the Rye, and I said, 'No, you won't be found for seven years, it will invalidate the will.'"

I interrupted him. "I heard that story at the Portrait Restaurant. But you still have quality of life. If you do a stent you'll have some quality of life back."

He said heatedly, almost violently, "That makes me irritated and stressed. I may be breathless and wobbly but I'm capable of thinking things out for myself."

I was taken aback. Then I grasped that he might already have taken the decision to die and did not want his lack of quality of life to be contradicted. That was why my visit would be stressful, for I would urge him to believe that he could still have quality of life with a stent and enjoy his grandchildren. Any wobbling I urged would be stressful.

He said, "I'm writing the story of my life so my family can read it at my funeral."

I said quietly, "I hope that won't be for ten or fifteen years yet."

He said, "I hope it will be sooner than that."

I said, "Let me know which Tuesday will suit you. I'll come and collect you and drive you to a restaurant where we can talk about the old days, reminisce on the war, the people in the High Road and what it was like in church. If necessary I'll bring sandwiches and we'll have lunch in your home."

He said, "I'll ring you when I know when. Goodbye." His tone made it feel very final.

I gently said, "Goodbye."

I rang off and sat and reflected. Had Rupert already planned to die? He'd been waiting for his test results, and he'd heard that he had a furred-up heart. Had he convinced himself that realistically his diabetic condition would not permit him to have a stent?

But that was *his* judgement, not the heart specialist's. It would be better to hear what the heart specialist had to say. It would be preferable to take the risk of having a stent fitted as he would have a chance of surviving the operation and of improving his quality of life than to choose to die before seeing the cardiologist as he had no quality of life.

I felt he was not thinking clearly. His lack of quality of life was causing him stress, and his wobbliness had furred up his feelings and clogged his capacity to feel. He was dwelling on his funeral. All he had to do was to miss his daily insulin injections, and he would slip into a coma from which he would not emerge. For him not to act would be a fatal act. Was he putting on an act of going to a cardiologist when active inaction could end his life before he got to see him?

But then I remembered he had booked a four-day coach tour to National-Trust houses in May. He was looking forward to this holiday, and planning his funeral was surely a routine piece of forward planning? That is what I wanted to believe.

Even so, I sat and sombrely stared at the shadows of the late afternoon, and I thought I glimpsed Death, hooded, watching my response and biding his time.

Screams and a Tool-Box
(Or: A Carer and a Painful Knee)

"Percy is such a nice person," Pippa said of her driver when she returned from her consultation with the Professor who had operated on her knee. "His parents live near him in the gated community at Ripley Park, and his mother has dementia and screams out. Every morning he goes round and carries her into the shower as she can't go in herself and he's the only one who can lift her. Sometimes he takes her to the Day Care Centre for dementia patients in Broadstrood Road. There's a bus that picks everyone up but she's so far away from the road beyond the gates and the bus takes so long that he drives her to the Centre for 8.30. At the end of the day the bus leaves at 3, but he collects her at 3.30 and drives her home so she's got the maximum time there.

"She's been in and out of homes but she's with other dementia sufferers and they all scream. He was so unhappy about the last one that he'd go up and take her away from the others and find two chairs in a bay window just to get her away from all the screaming and sometimes take her out for the day, so she was only with the screaming for the night and breakfast. She's at home now and he's looking for another home. But it's £1,300 a week, and he said, 'I can't afford £1,300 a week.'

"Today he dropped me off in London, and drove back to take his father to a supermarket. His father's going the same way as his mother. He took a tool-box to bed. The next morning he woke up and wondered why it was there and decided he had planned to demolish the bedside cabinet, so he took it to pieces. His father really ought to be in a home himself and Percy is looking after him as well as his mother.

"Then there's his daughter and the wedding. She's getting married in Crete and she's choosing a wedding dress. So he's driving her and looking at the wedding dresses and helping her to choose. His mother's not going to get to the wedding in Crete.

"He's supposed to be a driver, but actually he's a family carer who's fitting in occasional drives, such as taking me. And he'll have to take me now and again as Professor Corner said my knee was really bad, behind the kneecap was all ground down, and he's surprised the pain isn't worse. It is painful, it hurts all the time, but it's tolerable and it may ease after six months. I'm not to overdo the walking. I can swim – he wants me to swim – but I can only do local drives. I can't do long drives. I don't know how our next drive to Cornwall will work as I won't be able to drive down. I'll have to think about it."

A Spouting and a Booed Bishop

I arrived in the front quad at seven that Shrove Tuesday dressed in a suit, white shirt and blue tie. I slipped through a side gate to the back of the school in the dark, and because the Old Boys were still in chapel and I was slightly early I walked to the list outside the dining-hall and looked for names I recognised. I did not see many. Then I returned in light rain and encountered the Head's wife.

She was holding an umbrella and she beckoned me to join her beneath it. I carried it for her as we walked to the new glassy Sixth Form Centre.

She said, "You're number 3 in seniority on the list, there are only two ahead of you."

Being number 3 gave me some status so I did not feel ancient or jest that she would soon be greeting me in a wheelchair.

The brightly-lit rooms were furnished with tables and chairs in light wood. She led me into the modern-looking sixth-form recreation-and-refreshment area.

I bought a glass of Merlot and stood while Old Boys drifted in from chapel. I hardly knew any. I recalled how the Under-12s sat on benches near where I was standing, and how I waited to bat in matches on the field outside. One by one some of my distant contemporaries gathered. I talked about the Forest with Leach and the war with Dee, who told me his experiences of being bombed up the road. He told me, "Tom Soubry is staying with me."

I knew he was the new President of the Old Boys, and that he had been a Bishop. I saw Tom standing apart, grey hair sleeked back and horn-rimmed spectacles, looking very lordly in a smart suit and Old Boys' tie.

Then Nutty Bray came and squinted up at me. I was shocked at how much he had let himself go. He was very unshaven and his dry grey hair hung forwards, uncombed. It needed brushing, he looked unkempt. I noticed the others avoided him.

We were called upon to follow prefects back to the dining-hall and take our glasses with us. It had stopped raining, and it was a pleasant walk past the chapel in the dark. I found table 4 and waited beside a tilted chair while contemporaries whose names I barely knew arrived in dribs and drabs. Dee stood beside me and Nutty Bray opposite me. Leach was the other side of the tilted chair.

Then I saw Derek Minstrel. He had flushed cheeks, a white shirt and Old Boys' tie. He was with Garfield Mayers, the retired surgeon from Devon.

Derek saw me and I pointed to the tilted chair. He said, "Garfield's staying with me. I had to meet him and then go home and change, and I thought we'd never get here."

I shook hands with Garfield Mayers who sat next to Nutty Bray on the opposite side of the table.

Later, grace was said: *"Benedictus, benedicat, per Jesum Christum, Dominum nostrum. Amen."*

We sat down to a curried starter of king prawns, a buttermilk chapatti-style pancake, chutney and coriander shoots that was served as we poured wine and water.

In the growing hubbub Derek Minstrel told me his throat still hurt from his bout of cancer and he could not sing properly. He said his wife had been told she had Alzheimer's after tests: "Even I couldn't answer some of the questions. She was asked the President of the US and the British Prime Minister. She knows it's Trump and Theresa May but she couldn't think of their names. It's very early Alzheimer's if she's got it at all. She's resigned and accepts what she's been told, but I don't think she's got it. Do you remember when I first saw her in Rome? Do you remember the nuns guarding the school party in the Vatican with their arms folded?"

I nodded, and recalled the nuns in brown ankle-length robes with traditional crisp veils and was sad that my youthful memory of her should end in Alzheimer's.

Our plates were removed and were replaced with fillet beef Wellington, a herb pancake, wild mushrooms and baby roots. Garfield Mayers leaned across and asked above the hubbub, "In one word, is Brexit good or bad?"

I said, "It's a bad thing. It's reckless. We're walking away from 44 per cent of our exports, £224 billion out of £510 billion, and we don't know to what. It's a risk to the NHS. Then Scotland might become independent and the UK might break up. And we need to stick together because of Russia. We might be in 1938 with a Third World War looming if Putin invades Estonia, which will make two theatres of war, the Baltic and the Middle East, by definition a Third World War."

Garfield Mayers had been listening. He nodded and said, "I'm very worried by it all."

Dee was listening and he said, "But we've got our sovereignty. Nothing else matters." And I saw how voters had voted for partial perceptions.

It was now pudding time. We were served chocolate mint pavé, chocolate soil and mint sorbet. It looked like a thin oak tree on a hill with soil around it.

Garfield Mayers said, "It's all very serious, what's the solution?"

I said, "A democratic World State. The UN, which has failed to stop 162 wars, should be turned into a World Parliament with elected representatives. It may not happen in our grandchildren's lifetime but it may happen in their grandchildren's lifetime."

Dee said, "It's against human nature. Human nature promotes national interests. I can't see it happening for 100 years."

I did not say that the constructivist view of international relations sees international relations as being socially constructed and transformed by human practice, not given by nature. And that it is therefore possible to construct a World State even though human nature has promoted national interests that lead to war.

Coffee was served and the speeches began with applause and cheering for the kitchen staff, who lined up on the sloping railed walkway to the kitchen which served as a platform. Then the Head introduced Tom Soubry from where the kitchen staff had stood.

Tom spoke like the Bishop he had been, without notes. He said, "Until last year, when I retired, I was Bishop of Leicester, where Richard the Third was found under a car park and reburied. And now it's rumoured that he has been joined by Claudio Ranieri, that's wrong."

There was laughter. Ranieri had won the Premiership for Leicester and had just been sacked as they had slid towards relegation.

He said, "I was Chairman of the Bishops in the Lords. And I'm pleased to see they will do their duty in the next day or two."

He meant that the Lords would defeat the Government on the issue of EU citizens remaining in the UK. Suddenly there were jeers and catcalls, and distinct boos. I turned round expecting to see smiling faces booing humorously, but I saw young men in white-shirted suits and ties with hate on their faces genuinely showing intolerance and outrage.

Tom Soubry was taken aback. "That sort of booing doesn't happen in church," he said. And everyone laughed.

But we had heard the new tone of intolerance and disrespect that Brexit had introduced, and I was shocked.

With admirable composure he said that as the new President he had toured the school and found it very good. "It stands for values, tolerance, fairness and truth-telling," he said, and everyone applauded, including the Brexiteers, who had not detected a veiled criticism of their booing.

Then he said he had been a speaker on a cruise with Dee and Sir Robert Field, and they had seen whales. He said, "There was a sperm-whale with her child, and I understand she said, 'When you're spouting you're a target.' And on that note I'm sitting down."

There was laughter as he took his place at his table.

After that the Head spoke about how different the school was from 100, 200 and 300 years ago. There were sketches of the school in these previous years. Good things were said about the school, and these were corroborated by the Head Boy. Then we all sang the school song – Derek Minstrel's contribution blended in this year whereas it had dominated the hall in previous years – and we sat and chatted.

Harry Denton, the part-time maths teacher and Old Boy with long hair curled round his cheeks like an aged angel, came and spoke to Garfield Mayers, who told me across the table: "I operated on his hands."

Dee said, "He was in the Royal Navy at Plymouth and Garfield was based in Devon."

"My daughter taught in one of your establishments," Harry said to me.

"Of course," I said.

It was time to depart, and I said goodbye to several on my table. I spoke to Daniel Rivers, who said, "Lance is in Switzerland. He's got a house there."

"He's still advising Qatar's ruling family even though the Prime Minister's died?" I asked.

"Oh yes, he just moved down a generation."

I found myself standing alongside Tom Soubry as I drifted towards the door. I introduced myself and said, "I was ahead of you, we overlapped by two years."

He nodded.

I asked, "Did you walk away from being a Lord when you retired?"

"Yes," he said, "Bishops are only Lords until they retire."

"But you have contacts in the Lords," I said, "and they are right to be dutifully holding the Government to account as it's being reckless, unrealistic and over-optimistic about our trade prospects if we walk away from half our exports."

"Yes," he said.

"Don't worry about the booing," I said.

"Oh, I won't –"

"But it's disturbing," I said, "that free speech is being shouted down when it's perfectly legitimate to criticise a reckless approach to the country's future."

"I agree."

"And it's in a school like this one, this new intolerance, not even this excellent school can escape this new tone."

"No."

"Major and Heseltine have suffered it."

He said, "And Blair and Mandelson. Boris Johnson has a lot to answer for."

"He does," I said.

I chatted on with Tom Soubry, and then realised that Pippa would have arrived in front quad to give me a lift home.

I walked back past the chapel shaking my head. He had spouted, and yes, he had introduced the Lords' political role, but he could not have expected the blustering vituperation of his audience. The country was polarised, and the half that had won the referendum hooted down every attempt to point to the dangers of withdrawal from Europe as bitterness, re-fighting the referendum, being pessimistic and wanting to benefit from Europe. The time had become nasty. The issue had been divisive and the Bishop had never been booed in church. Time was when booing was a kind of joke, not an intense and almost violent disapproval.

The *bonhomie* and gentlemanly debating of issues in my youth had given way to revolutionary jeering, and I had a sense of foreboding about the future of the UK as I turned the corner in the dark and saw Pippa's car in front quad. The venom at the collegiate dinner had shocked me, and I felt the country had changed, and things could never be as they were when I was a young man.

A Cage round her Head

Pippa said, "Do you remember the Maudlins? They've been on our table for the Forest supper. Sue has blonde hair and it's always with a flick at the bottom, always with a flick. I saw her a couple of months ago, and she looked dreadful. She'd had a fall and she had a cage round her knee, internally, and she'd had a hip done. She was trembling, and I thought she hadn't long to live.

"I saw her again today, and she was transformed. She looked really good. I asked, 'How are you?' and she said, 'I've got Parkinson's.'

She must have known something was wrong because of her shaking, but when it was diagnosed she was put on medication, and the medication's working. It doesn't always work – it doesn't work for Carol's husband, who's shaking now – but isn't it strange? She's worse, yet because of the medication she looks better."

I nodded and recalled her sitting over the quiz at our table a couple of years back. She had had a cage round her knee and now she had a different kind of cage round her head that masked her deterioration.

A Signal from Market Place

I had lost a tooth after biting on a biscuit, and as Pippa drove me eastwards to a birthday surprise I reflected that I was falling apart. I had a tender spot on my left shin which I suspected was thrombophlebitic and made walking painful.

Pippa took a scenic route through Suffolk towards Sudbury and forked off along Bridge End Road with fields on either side and no houses. Then suddenly we were in Lavenham, and parking in the car park of The Swan, a 14th-century hotel. I carried our bags in through the rear entrance and we were led to the Assington Room, a beamy suite of a bedroom and sitting-room on the ground floor. Soon we were munching smoked-salmon sandwiches and sipping green tea in the hotel's sitting area.

Lavenham is a medieval town with more than 300 surviving timber-framed white buildings. It became rich from the wool trade of the 14th century. We sauntered – in my case, limped – in sunshine up High Street to Market Place, which is surrounded by timber-framed buildings, and we looked in at the Guildhall. It did not seem eighteen years ago that Pippa booked us in at the pargeted Priory for my 60th birthday and that we ate in The Great House, which was before me now, where in dribs and drabs my children joined us in a surprise family dinner.

We sauntered back down Lady Street to Water Street, and I turned left and wandered to De Vere House, which I had contemplated buying nearly twenty years previously. It was a 14th-century Hall that had been extended after the Battle of Bosworth and had been owned by Edward de Vere, the 17th Earl of Oxford. (In those days I had wondered if Edward de Vere was Shakespeare, but did not think so now.) I stood before the ancient wooden front door and saw the carved star and boar from the de Vere coat of arms on the wooden lintel.

We returned to The Swan and sat under the ancient beams while I recovered my breath. Then I went to our room and changed into my dressing-gown and climbed the stairs to the Weaver's House Spa, where Pippa had booked me in as part of my birthday surprise.

I filled in a form sipping a red smoothie and was taken up to a candlelit room, Cashmere, by a Suffolk girl, who studied my form and suggested the treatments I should have. She left the room while I clambered onto the water-bed and lay face down with my nostrils and mouth through a circular hole in a special pillow, and she returned and to soothing music rubbed the treatment oils I was having into my skin: Drift-Away oil for peace and relaxation (sesame, avocado and lavender); Breath of Life for energy, strength and brain-boosting (tea-tree, eucalyptus and lavender); Aaahhh! for aching feet and limbs (dandelion, peppermint, lavender, clary and black pepper); and Be Gone as a cleanser for calming, anti-stress and soothing (olive, liquorice and aubergine). I also had Repose for sleep (frankincense, hops and jojoba); Toning Essence; and Giving it the Brush Off for detoxing my skin and removing my dead skin cells.

At the end of the hour I was deeply relaxed. I was given an ice sorbet and later led to the Quiet Room. There I lay on a couch for half an hour, drowsed by soft music, and sipped herb tea (olive and camomile) and nibbled at a macaroon. Then I quietly left and returned to our room. Pippa had now taken my place in Cashmere.

I lay on the bed and dozed. I was old and had become the Shadow I had known since my youth, my shadow cast by the sun which I saw as a future self that had wisdom and lived in harmony with the universe, beyond ego and nationhood. I was my Shadow, but I still looked forward. I had more to do although I walked with difficulty and my teeth were falling out. I was still very much alive.

Pippa returned and we went for dinner at 7 in a beamy, high-ceilinged dining-hall with coats of arms at one end. We had glasses of sparkling wine and as we waited for our starter, goat's cheese, Pippa checked her phone. There was a message from my sister saying she had rung all the numbers to wish me a happy birthday but had been unable to locate me, could I ring her. Pippa tried to text her but there was no signal. A waiter said, "We are in a hollow down here. It's best to walk up to Market Place, there's a signal there."

We ate our duck and pudding of different kinds of chocolate, and then sauntered – in my case, limped – up High Street to Market Place. It had once been a centre of commerce packed with people, animals, stalls and goods but was now a quiet backwater. The sun was setting and there was distant reddish cloud in a green sky. We sat on a bench facing the Guildhall and watched house-martins fly round the eaves of timber-framed buildings. There was a notice on a wall about the dancing in Market Place the previous Saturday to commemorate the American pilots of 487 Squadron, who had visited Lavenham many times during the war from Mildenhall and Lakenheath. The past was present, along with The Great House where I had celebrated my 60th birthday.

The twilight deepened to dusk and still the birds flitted and dived and swooped round Market Place. Three well-dressed elderly men approached, one tottering in an exaggeratedly decrepit way. He saw us and stopped being anciently old. One of the men broke away and headed across the square behind us. The other two approached us, and the 'decrepit' man said, "Good evening, it's a lovely evening, isn't it?" The man behind us called to us, "Don't believe a word he says," and they all laughed. "You've got a good seat there," the 'decrepit' man said, "with a good view of the Guildhall." He was well spoken and pleasant, and we smiled and wished him good night.

It was getting dark now but I sat on, in harmony with the universe in this remote and historic part of East Anglia, at one with all I could see, the fading clear sky over the medieval rooftops, in solitude and out of my time among 600-year-old buildings. I was contemplating all round me and motionless as Pippa texted my sister that we were staying at The Swan, Lavenham, and had walked to Market Place for a signal, sending a signal that I was well and still leading a full life despite my advancing years.

I sat very still, taking in all I could see and removed from all bustle and movement, as her signal went out from her interactive, market-place phone from where we sat in stillness and tranquillity in Market Place.

A Leap and Bees

We checked in at the once ducal Hunting Lodge in Sherwood Forest. The original building had been visited by so many monarchs since the 1100s, but had been pulled down between 1862 and 1865 and been rebuilt as a stone, turreted Victorian Gothic building. We had to wait for our room to be ready so we sat in the bar before a stone fireplace under a stone balcony on three sides, and took in a large tapestry, carvings of jousting knights, cloths of woven lions and unicorns and faded photos of the turreted Victorian Lodge. After a long wait we munched sandwiches made of white bread as thick as doorsteps, and drank milky coffee. Then we climbed a staircase to our room, no.6 off the stone balcony, and I changed into DJ.

The wedding guests had been encouraged to walk to the church through woods. We drove, parked nearly outside and joined a line of waiting members of the ducal family and friends, the men all in DJ.

The church had been completed in 1865, like the Lodge. It had recently become disused, and someone said that volunteers had cut the long grass and picked the wild flowers. Edward's uncle, Lord Mark, was holding a box of posies. I greeted his father, the Duke, and his stepmother and we chatted.

He said to me, "Some of my ancestors are in these graves."

Knowing his grandfather had sold the estate in 1943, I said, "How many are after 1940?"

He mused and said, "There's one who died in 1934."

Then Edward himself emerged from the church, bearded, and saw me and smiled. He came across and shook my hand. He had a sprig of pansy ironed onto his lapel, and he had two bees on his dress shirt, as I commented. Smiling, he showed me a bee on one of his cuffs.

He had told me in an email that he was assembling hives in their Welsh smallholding, and the invitation had suggested wedding presents might include a donation towards beehives. Keeping bees was his dream of peaceful living, and I had sent him a cheque to put towards some bees.

He was making a leap into the unknown by marrying a lady eighteen years younger than him, who would one day be the next Duchess.

Edward said to me, "There's been a hitch. No one has been asked to play the piano for the hymns. I'm hoping someone will sight-read. I have to go inside and sort it out." And he disappeared within the church porch.

The head usher, a portly American with a double chin, announced that we could now take our seats. We entered the tiny stone church. There were wild flowers in glass carafes on the floor by each pew. Above the altar on a curved ceiling there were circles, in one of which I could see the sun and stars, and in another a lightning flash on water. The circles suggested the universe and also contained apostles, and lines led up to an alpha and omega and to a connecting point where they were reconciled in unity.

Pippa and I sat on the right of the aisle among the groom's family and friends. A black lady with a very small black girl came and sat next to me. Her husband came and joined her. I did not know he was one of twins who were Edward's half-brothers, and that the little girl was his niece.

The head usher alerted us that the bride was about to appear. We turned and saw the bride float in with her father. She was in white, her face unveiled. She looked in charge and nodded to particular guests as she came down the aisle. Her long train was clutched by six young bridesmaids and page-boys, some of whom were black. She joined Edward at the front.

The vicar, a lady, welcomed us and announced the first hymn, Blake's 'Jerusalem'. There was a silence.

The stand-in organist was sitting at the church piano, not the organ, and hunting for the music in a book so that he could sight-read.

"Coming up," he shouted, but the delay went on. One minute slid by, and a second minute. Edward stood impassively and stared in front of him, above the fray. Then at last the stand-in organist found the music and strummed the hymn. The piano was out of tune.

There was then a reading from *Ecclesiasticus* 1, 1–10, by a young boy, and then the marriage took place. Edward and Sophie exchanged rings, and there was applause.

There was another hymn, and an Italian lady with an enormous black hat read a poem by Rumi from the pulpit. After prayers Edward's son, William, stepped up into the pulpit to read 'Sonnet 116: Edward de Vere'. It was Shakespeare's Sonnet 116. Edward, being descended from Edward de Vere as well as the Earl of Southampton, had long campaigned for the author of Shakespeare's works to be recognised as Edward de Vere.

There was one more hymn and then the signing of the register and a blessing. And then we were outside.

Edward stood awkwardly with Sophie and the bridesmaids and page-boys. He was joined by his father, the Duke, and his stepmother, and later by his mother. I noticed Edward's father did not speak to him although standing near him, and there seemed to be a distance between them. There were spaces between each of them, there was no togetherness. I knew they did not often meet and the family appeared dysfunctional.

All the wedding guests now took their wild flowers in glass carafes and walked back through the woods to an old fountain that stood in a large grassed bowl where a blessing was to be given by an "artist and lightworker". Pippa was not good with her walking, and I was not walking too well, so we drove back to the Lodge. We walked through the restaurant and out onto a terrace that looked down on a box garden and a red carpet at the top of a long flight of steps.

From the top of the steps I saw Edward and Sophie standing hand in hand in the grassed bowl near the fountain, being blessed. The Duke and his Duchess had also driven back. They had begun to descend the steps but changed their mind. They joined me.

"It's too risky," the Duchess said. "I broke my ankle in a fall a couple of months ago, the steps are too steep. I'm not doing that."

At the drinks table on the terrace glasses of a cocktail were being handed out. The Duchess asked what was in the glasses.

"Prosecco base, blood orange and cassis (a syrupy blackcurrant flavouring)," a waiter said.

The Duchess said, "I just want champagne," and she took a Prosecco base in a glass and tipped it into another glass and did the same again from a third glass so she had a glass of clear Prosecco.

I spoke to the Duke. "Do you recall visiting this Lodge when you were a little boy?"

He looked at me. "I was born in 1939," he said.

"So was I," I said. "I can remember things before 1943. Were you brought here before 1943, when your family still owned this Lodge?"

"No, my branch of the family were not close to the owner of the Lodge."

"Will you drive to see Edward in Wales?"

"I can't drive that far now. I'll go by train. In fact, it's two trains, you have to change. He'll meet me at Aberystwyth."

"And you still go to work at the accountant's office?"

"Yes, I'm a partner, I still do two days a week. But I prefer bridge."

"You're not in the Lords now?"

"No, that ended in 1999. I wasn't one of the 92."

"Did you make many speeches in the Lords?"

"I made my maiden speech. The same day that Yehudi Menuhin made his. He went on and had to be pulled down."

I said, "Blair cleared out the hereditaries to make spaces he could fill with preferment, so he could bribe MPs to do what he wanted them to do, bribe them with peerages. And the stock of the Lords went down."

"Yes," he said.

Then the Duke's half-sister came up. She said she had heard about me. She worked with child refugees from Calais, and we talked refugees. She said she lived in London.

The Duke had moved away. I asked her, "Do you meet Edward's father there, your brother?"

"No, we never meet."

And I thought again how dysfunctional the family was.

Then I saw Sophie standing near my elbow. I turned and kissed her.

"We meet at last," she said. "I've heard so much about you from Edward."

And I talked to Sophie about how Edward had come and worked with me and helped me, until the head usher announced that we should go through and take our seats. Pippa joined me, having sat and rested on her stick.

In the restaurant the eight tables for ten had white tablecloths. We were on table 2 in the far corner. I was between the Polish wife of Edward's uncle and the Italian wife in the large black hat who had read a poem by Rumi. She told me she had six-month-old twin boys she had left with her in-laws. Her bearded husband, a herbalist and lecturer on chiropractic, was seated next to Pippa.

The Italian lady told me she was a restorative architect who had learned her skills in Renaissance Florence. She loved restoring Renaissance buildings. At present she was restoring the church where Newton was baptised in Lincolnshire. She said, "I have called my two boys Francis and Isaac, after Bacon and Newton, philosophy and science." But, she said, she preferred designing modern buildings.

I called across to her husband, "Two thousand years ago I would have said to you, you married a Roman."

"No," she said, "I'm an Etruscan from Tarquinia."

"Pre-Roman," I said, remembering an afternoon visiting the inside of several Tarquinian tombs.

She nodded.

Dinner was vegetarian, perhaps vegan. We had shredded mushrooms on toast, then a red pepper stuffed with rice and vegetarian bolognaise, and then a fatless sponge of nuts and fruit, with Prosecco, white and red wine, and at the end port. I did not think the meal contained any animal fats.

Edward's bespectacled lean-faced uncle, the Duke's half-brother, told me he was in "international development" and that he lived in Oxford. His Polish wife said he worked in charities, mainly in 'Save the Children'. He said he was a socialist and lamented the British educational system and all grammar schools. His wife was teaching in an Oxford primary school.

To the Italian architect I said, "You're Sophie's friend, you've worked with her."

"Yes, and I shall continue to work with her."

"What's she like?"

"She's a very kind person. She would give you her last pound. She's like Edward, she's soul. I'm rational and logical, and mathematical, but she is like Edward. They are both living in the soul."

I nodded. I said so Edward's uncle could hear, "Edward is spiritual. His key word is sovereignty. Sovereignty of the monarch, sovereignty of the nation and sovereignty of the soul." Lord Mark nodded.

At last it was time for speeches. The father of the bride spoke first. He did not look unlike the Duke. The microphone did not seem to be working so it was switched off. Most of his speech was too quiet to reach our table. He praised his daughter's projects and unwrapped a parcel in brown paper containing an enormous scrapbook on whose plain pages he thought the guests could leave messages for Sophie and Edward. He toasted Sophie and Edward.

Then Edward spoke, and at least I could hear him. He praised words Sophie had used in the conversation when they met: "epic", "ethical" and "magical". Perhaps with a nod to the Italian lady sitting next to me he said that these words in Italian would be "*epico, ethico and magico*". He spoke of his magical relationship with Sophie as being a relationship of soul mates, and spoke of "the sovereignty of the soul". Lord Mark, his uncle, bent forward and knowingly caught my eye. Edward called for a toast to marriage, and then another one to "A pledge of better times", which I knew was on the ducal shield, a translation of the Latin *auspicium melioris aevi*.

There was applause and then the best man spoke. Nobody could hear a word he said, but I gathered he recited Edward's career from a website he had found.

Lord Mark bent forward and said that Edward had a gift of loyalty: "Anyone who has helped him is imported into the family."

I agreed. I said he also had a rebellious streak. "He relabelled Shakespeare Edward de Vere on the Order of Service, and he defied the Government when the hereditary peers were abolished by leaping onto the Woolsack in the House of Lords. He was protesting against the loss of his birthright. He discussed with me what he was going to do, and he was heavily influenced by the teaming-up of the Earl of Southampton, his ancestor, and the Earl of Essex for a protest against Elizabeth I, recently described as a *coup d'état*, in 1601. Southampton was imprisoned for two years but Essex was beheaded. Edward described the protest as a beautiful act and by his leap he was attempting a similar protest that would also live for 400 years."

"I see," Lord Mark said.

I saw Edward's mother on a nearby table and crossed and introduced myself. I said to her that his first marriage had been difficult – I had seen at close quarters, there were days when his wife was too drunk to take his son to school – but hoped all would be straightforward now. I said, "He told me he wanted to leap onto the throne. I stopped him. I said that could be interpreted as treason, as violating the Queen's space. He would be laying himself open to misinterpretation. He really wanted to protest against the extinguishing of his hereditary right to sit in the Lords, and he leapt onto the Woolsack – and then told the journalists outside that he worked for me." I said, "Thank you, Edward," and got myself down to Cornwall. And there I opened *The Telegraph* and saw a picture of him sitting on my settee in my Great Hall holding court to the journalists."

She laughed but looked embarrassed.

I said, "He was thinking of his ancestor the Earl of Southampton, following his example in 1601."

She shook her head and said, "I heard about it on the news. I spoke to his first wife. She said, 'You're bourgeois.'" She pulled a face.

I saw William, Edward's son, standing taking photos. He was taller than me. I moved towards him and said, "I remember you in short trousers, and now I'm looking up to you." And I repeated to him, "Your father's leap onto the Woolsack was inspired by your ancestor the Earl of Southampton, Shakespeare's patron, and was a protest against the abolition of all but 92 hereditary peers' right to attend the Lords." I said, "It was intended as a beautiful act that would be remembered in 400 years' time. And when he inherits the Dukedom from his father, and you become his heir, an Earl, he needs to go to

Black Rod and say the situation has moved on now he's the Duke and that the lifetime ban on his attending the Palace of Westminster should be lifted."

He listened and said, "I've often wondered what happened. I never heard that perspective put so eloquently and beautifully by you. Thank you for telling me. It's something I've wanted to know."

It was 12.30am and the band were playing softly in the background. Pippa was tired and had signalled she wanted to go upstairs to bed. So I headed out with her.

She said, "You should write in the big scrapbook." So I went back and wrote a message from us both.

As I passed through the bar to rejoin Pippa I saw Edward standing by himself. He had ordered a couple of glasses of red wine and was waiting by the bar counter.

"Have you enjoyed this evening?" he asked.

"Yes. I've talked to most of your family: to your father –"

"Yes, he said he really enjoyed talking to you."

"And his half-sister who's been helping refugees and his half-brother, your uncle Mark, who works with 'Save the Children' and was on my table; and to your stepmother, and your mother, and to William. I told William that your leap onto the woolsack was inspired by the Earl of Southampton and he said it gave him a new perspective on the end of all the hereditaries except for 92. So you can discuss it with him."

"Good," Edward said, "thank you."

"Will you be around at breakfast?" I asked.

"What time do you have to leave?"

"We ought to be getting off about 10."

"No, we're going to Langham Hall for the night. We won't be back by 10. And we're going to Ireland on Tuesday."

"Very nice," I said. "And then, bees."

"Yes."

"Keeping them and studying their social habits like Virgil."

"Yes."

"Can you bring it into your teaching of Latin?"

"Not really. I have 13 pupils I teach Latin to over the internet. An agency finds them and takes a small cut. There are 13 syllabuses, and I can't do Latin poetry with them yet."

I nodded.

The bees were his dream. He lived up a mountain in Wales with a view of the sea, and he would have his own honey from the bees on the hillside.

The barman placed his two glasses of red wine near his elbow, so I shook his hand and embraced him and thanked him for inviting me. I rejoined Pippa, who was sitting on her own at a table in the bar, waiting to go upstairs.

Edward had made a leap into marriage, a leap into the unknown after the failure of his last marriage. His dream – Sophie's dream – was to have bees on the hillside of their smallholding in Wales. He had been held back by another leap, his protest at having his right to attend the House of Lords removed along with all hereditary peers except for 92. Enemies such as Black Rod had stung him like bees.

He had had a troubled life with his first wife but now he had a second chance, and from the serenity of old age I hoped that this new leap would bring him peace with Sophie and harmony with the universe among the bees on his remote mountainside above the sparkling sea.

Truth like a Champagne Flute
(Or: Fudge and Gooey Cake)

I entered the village hall in shirtsleeves because of the heat and was greeted by our MP Edith Small. I kissed her cheek and she greeted Pippa and asked, concerned, if a secretary had addressed her by a wrong first name at the door (the MP relating to one of her constituents at the level of names). I told her I had left her a card showing an aerial view of a river among the flowers and bouquets on the floor, and I said she had more of her course to run.

We had all been invited to celebrate her twenty years as our MP, and we crossed to the bar and took glasses of champagne and then headed for the garden, where eighty people stood talking in shirtsleeves. I noted that only one wore a tie.

Immediately in front of me was John Brakely. He was Secretary of State for Northern Ireland, and I shook his hand and asked if the deal with the DUP, to shore up the minority Conservative Government, was happening.

Black-haired with steel-rimmed spectacles, he said, "Yes, it will happen."

I asked if there would be a price, how many billions would be going to Northern Ireland and had the Treasury objected?

He said, "No." But I was not sure if I believed him.

"And Sinn Fein won't bring its seven members to London to cancel out most of the DUP's ten votes?"

"No, they won't want to swear an oath to the Queen, so they won't attend."

"And will the talks with the EU lead to a soft Brexit now the Government's in a minority?"

He said, "'Soft Brexit', 'hard Brexit', I don't know what they are. They're just words."

I knew the Government was split between the two – the Chancellor favoured a soft Brexit (staying in the single market and customs union) whereas the Prime Minister favoured a hard Brexit (leaving the single market and customs union), and I realised he had been told to say that to prevent a split in the Party outlook. He was fudging, he was a fudger. I had been fed fudge.

Before I could reply Edith Small appeared and said, "I need to take John away, I'd like him to meet someone over there." And she took his hand and led him through a throng of people.

I spotted a couple I knew and went over and shook hands. I spoke to the owner of a gardening business and to the wife of a dentist, who told me about her life of travelling to children and grandchildren in Paris and Dubai. I spoke to another MP, Gordon Strawson, who asked me questions about the Middle East, particularly Syria.

Eventually Edith Small called for silence: "Order, order." She called for her son, "Martin, Martin." She called several times. He was nowhere to be found, but then made an appearance to applause, a dark-haired, thinnish young man.

Edith Small said, "I planned this gathering in February. I thought I'd have all my friends, and you are my friends. It's Martin's birthday, and he's just taken his last GCSE. So here's a cake."

A helper carried forward a large square cake with gooey white icing and three lit candles.

"When I told him I would be announcing his birthday he said, 'I hope they won't sing Happy Birthday.' So let's sing it."

She smiled wickedly, and, slightly embarrassed, all sang 'Happy Birthday' and Martin, looking embarrassed, blew out the candles.

There were piled plates, burgers, cheese and pasta under a small self-service awning, and guests now queued to eat. I was not eating. Pippa had helped herself to some pasta and sat at a garden table. She asked me to find her a glass of orange, and on my way to the bar, still holding a champagne flute, I found myself standing next to Edith Small.

I said, "I watched the meeting of the new Parliament and thought I might see you dragged unwillingly to the Speaker's chair."

"Not this time," she said. "*He*'s still there. He's unpopular with the Conservatives but he's still got the job."

"In the near future?" I asked.

"I hope so. I'd like to be Speaker."

Then Martin came up. He said to his mother, "Dad shouted at me over the phone. Will you ring him?"

Edith said to me, "He's lunching with his father tomorrow at the Waterside as it's Father's Day."

Martin looked at me and curled a lip and rolled his eyes.

I said to him, "You will be calm and relaxed, it will all go well."

Edith nodded.

Martin said, "I'd rather be with mum. She doesn't shout at me."

I went on to fetch Pippa's orange, and when she'd drunk it she said she was ready to leave.

I took a last look at Edith Small's friends, who were still drinking champagne in the garden of the village hall. I saw John Brakely talking to a group of men, no doubt fudging the Government's position. And I saw a helper carrying Martin's birthday cake around, offering slices of gooey icing to everyone.

There were two standards of truth in the garden, a blurring fudging regarding the EU talks and a gooey cake which had masked the real and raw situation, dressing up the 'telling it as it was' which I associated with Martin (who had talked of being shouted at openly in front of me). I had not accepted the fudge and I had not eaten any cake but I was at home where the truth was.

I reflected that truth is best unembellished, neither blurred nor masked. Truth is plain and simple like the champagne in the flute I was still holding, which proclaimed a gathering to celebrate and did not conceal any underlying splits.

A Resuscitation and a Ghost
(Or: A Farmer and a Pig)

Arthur, who had been crippled for many years and was in a wheelchair, had been taken ill with prostate cancer. He was in pain and had been admitted to a nursing home and after two months had died, aged 91. His funeral was at Guildford Crematorium at 10.30.

Pippa and I stayed overnight at The Jolly Farmer, Bramley, once a Saxon village. The front of the pub dated back to the 1550s, and we had a bedroom and sitting-room on the first floor with wattle and daub by the bed's headboard. The open window looked out to the sign of a ruddy-faced farmer riding jollily on a pig and beyond it to a twelfth-century church.

We ate in the restaurant at the back, which looked as if it had been a beamy barn. It dated to the early 19th century. On the walls between the beams hung agricultural tools including mattocks, and early electrical devices. There were stuffed pheasants on the upper beams beneath the slopes of the roof, extensive twigs and many hanging bottles. I had haddock and chips followed by scoops of vanilla and white-chocolate ice-cream and coconut-and-pineapple sorbet, washed down with Chilean Merlot.

We then went upstairs to our sitting-room and, poleaxed by the Surrey air, dozed in front of a Panorama programme about farmers, food and Brexit.

Next morning after breakfast in the beamy restaurant I changed into the suit I had brought in a suit-carrier, white shirt and black tie and we drove three miles to the crematorium. We arrived at 10 and sat in the waiting-room and greeted my two nephews. One of them, Jeremy, told me his wife had stayed behind to look after his son, who had had a fever for the last four weekends, picked up at the nursery he attended. He showed me a text he had received from his mother, who was following Arthur's coffin in a hearse: "Limo late, hearse blocked in, stuck in traffic, Dad in a strop."

We saw the hearse arrive and went outside and stood while Doreen and her two daughters Alison and Eliza entered the glassy front doors. We followed and sat in the third row from the front on the right, behind Jack and Alison and Doreen's family.

I noted the family wore coloured ties. Half the guests wore black ties like me.

We stood as four pallbearers bore the coffin on their shoulders, sloping down slightly as the front two men were shorter than the back two, and placed it on the raised bier.

There was a hymn and there were readings by Arthur's granddaughter and his two grandsons. Jeremy read a parable on immortality about a ship disappearing from sight over the horizon of an ocean but being welcomed by other eyes watching her approaching. There was a tribute from his two daughters who spoke of how Arthur had always loved cars and mowers, how as a builder and designer he had believed that every job should be done well, and they spoke of his sense of humour. His dying words were, "I can't thank you enough for all you've done for me."

The coffin remained on the bier at the end as the furnaces were not working. We trooped through a door at the front and stood on a covered walkway outside among laid flowers and watched light rain. Arthur was discreetly loaded into the hearse and driven to a crematorium whose furnaces *were* working.

I spoke to Jack. He said, "He was terminally ill and was supposed to die two months ago. We were all called and spent the night there, everyone gathered and a surgeon resuscitated him by pumping him full of drugs. He was still terminally ill. I said to the surgeon, 'Didn't you read in the paperwork, "Do not resuscitate"?' He said, 'We believe we are there to save our patients medically.' So his terminal illness and his suffering were protracted two months, and the misery of the family as well. The family were put through daily visits when we all sat round his bed."

The lady vicar had said that during these last weeks he had doubted God but had re-found his faith and had consented to have holy unction applied to his forehead shortly before he died.

The guests were invited to drive to the Withies Inn, Compton, which was about two miles away. It was a 16th-century beamy inn, and glasses of elderflower wine were waiting for us at the bar. I spoke to Doreen, who, aged 90, said (social proprieties uppermost in her mind), "Thank you for coming."

I talked to my nephews. I told Jeremy that besides having "missionary and sceptical" genes the family had "early and late" genes – some were always punctual, like me, and some always late. He said his wife was always late. I sat with Walter and his wife and talked about Greenwich. They lived near Christ Church C of E Primary School, which had 120 pupils. I wondered if it was in the premises of the old Riverway School, where I had once taught, whose registers (perhaps including my own) were now in the National Archives.

I talked again with Jack. "It was a difficult death," I said.

"Yes," he said. "It would have been better for everyone if he'd died when he was supposed to two months ago and if that surgeon hadn't prolonged his agony."

"I'm not sure he would have seen it that way."

"No, he wanted to cling to life. He fought to survive, he didn't want to die. He was terminally ill but he could not accept that."

I turned and by my elbow stood – Arthur. I froze. He had his bald head, slightly-hooked nose and crumpled ears. What was he doing there when he was dead? Was it his ghost, come back to argue against what Jack had been saying? I asked Jack quietly, "Who's that?"

"It's his cousin," Jack said.

I had seen a family resemblance. It was in the family's genes.

Coffee was served. I wandered away and sat down with my coffee. Arthur had been crippled and when told he was terminally ill he had not accepted his impending death. He had not been resigned to it and although the family had requested that a DNR ('Do not resuscitate') notice should be raised, he had clung to life and had had an additional two months of tortured living with pain relief for what would otherwise have been acute pain and had finally, to everyone's relief, died. He had become a ghost, and how could I be sure that Arthur was not in the inn with us, standing invisibly alongside his cousin and listening to the irritated pontifications of his younger relatives, and countering them with humour, like a farmer riding a pig?

The Infirm and the Sea

On the way to Pippa's birthday surprise I drove to a convalescent home on the south coast. Pippa had said she would like to visit it some time as it was one of the few homes left where you could recuperate after an operation for a week or two by the sea, and she wanted to get a feel for it in case any of our family ever needed it.

I turned off the coast road and drove past lawns in sunshine and parked behind the large imposing Victorian building and rang the bell. We were expected, and a youngish lady in a white uniform wearing a badge saying 'Care assistant' opened the door and led us into a corridor. "I'll give you a tour of the ground floor," she said. From all the front windows we could see the sea across the distant road, grey and calm beneath the sunshine.

"There are twenty rooms," she said, "and three guest rooms where relatives can stay overnight. It's a convalescent home, not a nursing home, so the inmates are expected to get themselves up and come down in the lift to breakfast. That's part of their convalescence. They can walk outside, but no staff accompany them to the sea, they are expected to do that on their own. Inside we are halfway between hospital and home. There are medical facilities – doctors, nurses and drugs – but also four sitting-rooms where they can sit and watch TV."

We sauntered past several medical rooms and in one of the sitting-rooms I saw a picture of the founder over the fireplace, Sir Henry Harben of the Worshipful Company of Carpenters, who had opened the convalescent home in 1897. Then we were by the entrance to the dining-room. There were round tables laid for lunch with pink tablecloths.

"They can sit together or on their own, wherever they like," the care assistant said. "Guests can stay to lunch, for £10 each."

Suddenly there was a loud gonging from a large free-hanging wooden-framed gong: "Gong-gong-gong-gong-gong."

"It's lunch-time," the care assistant said.

And from the far end of the corridor came a slow procession of the sick and infirm. They were led by an old lady hunched over a Zimmer frame who moved very slowly. Behind her was an elderly woman on a crutch, walking in slow motion, and an elderly man hobbled on two crutches. There was an old lady with a bandage over one eye. An elderly gentleman was bent over a walking-stick. More gathered in groups behind them and stood and then sauntered towards their lunch.

We pressed back against the wall to let them pass and I was reminded of Pieter Bruegel's painting, *The Blind Leading the Blind*, where the infirm follow a blind man who seems to be falling into a ditch. They were a shuffling, decrepit lot. Looking the place over for anyone in our family who might need a week or two to convalesce after an operation, I was struck by how unsteady they all were, and how slow they would all be in taking their seats at the lunch tables.

We were escorted on, past a medical room with a padded massage couch, to a large sitting-room where communion was celebrated every Sunday. Then we were led back past the dining-room, where the inmates were sitting in groups round half a dozen tables, to the Administrator, a woman in her early forties in a white uniform.

We talked about the length people stayed. "Mostly it's a week or two weeks," she said. "But it depends on what operation they've had and how long it takes to get them on their feet. Recently someone who had an ankle operation was here for six weeks. She couldn't put pressure on her feet for the first two weeks, but she could walk normally by the time she left."

We thanked the Administrator for our tour and talked about the notice needed before a new arrival. "Three weeks is generally enough." Then we returned to the front door and descended steps to my car, and drove back through the grounds to the sea. We stopped and got out and gazed at the calm water lapping the beach between breakwaters.

I had stayed several times further along the coastal road when I was young and able-bodied, and I thought of how the elderly and infirm had gathered in the convalescent home to overcome their operations near the same sea. I had a sense of the transience of our lives. The sea was permanent and in some strange way eternal, and we humans who aged with time became unsteady in our limbs. I had seen beyond the rules and regulations of the social institution, and had looked deep into the underlying decaying process of the physical human condition, from which Pippa and I were not immune.

Normans and Peacocks

We parked outside Bailiffscourt Hotel and checked in. Our room was not yet ready so we left our luggage with a concierge and had tea in a 12th-century-looking room that had been re-created in the late 1920s.

In 1927 Lord Moyne had bought 750 acres by the sea, which included a Georgian farmhouse and a Norman chapel. The chapel had been built in the 12th century, demolished and rebuilt in the 13th century. It had been given to the Abbey of Seez in Normandy, and the Abbess sent a monk to act as bailiff and watch over its interests. Lord Moyne, Minister of Agriculture from 1925 until 1929, had demolished the Georgian farmhouse and, using many 12th- and 13th-century stones in its walls, reassembled them into windows and doorways in their original form to create a 'new' medieval building.

We ate sandwiches and drank tea alone in the 12th-century-style monk's cell with pointed windows where the Norman monk would have lived. Through a window I could see a peacock on a nearby first-floor roof.

After tea we collected our luggage and walked to the Court House, where I had booked the Elmere Room on the ground floor. A bottle of French Belle Combe pinkish rosé was on a table with a card saying 'Many Happy Returns' – of Pippa's birthday, but also, perhaps, to this hotel.

Pippa left for the Spa, where I had booked her in for a massage, and an hour later I followed, walking between knee-high lines of lavender, changed in a shower room with lockers and sat in the foyer in my dressing-gown and complimentary white slip-on towelling slippers. Pippa came out and sat with me after her treatment, and then I was taken in by a local girl and lay face down on a water-bed and had a 'drift away' massage in candlelight to soothing music as my skin soaked in a number of different oils.

I returned to our room, my skin saturated, and soon afterwards we sauntered to reception and took our seats in the dining-room. There we were served duck, and a dark-chocolate ice-cream with white-chocolate sorbets, and glasses of red wine.

Out of the old windows I could see a grass tennis-court and two peacocks were pecking seed. They had been fed there and would soon be roosting in the tree near the hotel's entrance.

We walked back to our room in the dusk and slept early. The next morning we breakfasted in the same dining-room on muesli, fruit, yoghurt, nuts, scrambled egg, bacon and mushrooms, toast, honey and coffee. I settled our bill and the Administrator gave me a key to the Norman chapel, which was down a path from the Court House.

It too had been restored. I unlocked the door and entered beneath the arched lintel where the Norman bailiff had come to pray. The chapel was tiny and devoid of furniture. It felt very empty. I stood before where the altar would have been and looked at the pointed Norman windows and the arched niche to the right of the altar, and thought of the Norman bailiff praying that he would receive enough from the locals to keep the estate solvent and send surplus funds back to the Abbess in Seez. I also thought of the decorative peacocks that were encouraged to grace the place.

As I walked back I thought that the tradition behind the estate and its outer buildings and the rule of the Norman bailiff blended with the more modern restoration and keeping of peacocks to convey an image of a tranquil, timeless past and of the secrets of centuries that was in fact a re-creation of the late 1920s, not unlike the antiquarian image of the estate's antiquities I would re-create in these few carefully-wrought strokes of my pen.

A Collector and an Honorary Grosvenor

I was given an introduction to a private GP in Devonshire Street, off Harley Street, by Jack, who had worked for the Duke of Westminster. The Duke's staff had annual MOTs at this GP's practice, and as I shook hands with Dr Erdmann, who had smooth black hair sleeked back and wore black horn-rims and a dark suit, he said to his PA, 'We're going to treat Mr Rawley as an honorary Grosvenor.' That meant I would receive discounted treatment at the Grosvenors' special rate.

Dr Erdmann sat at his desk and asked me questions. I had had a blood test and completed a lengthy form in the waiting area, which he scanned through. Then he examined me from head to toe for two hours. He was meticulous, nothing escaped his attention. He said, "I can't find a pulse for your feet. There's no pulse in the ankles. You might have poorly-functioning arteries in your feet. You will need an ultrasound to look at your arteries."

He scribbled out a referral to a consultant and during the examination made four other referrals on the inner workings of different parts of my body. As he continued his examination he dictated his observations onto a hand-held Dictaphone, which at the end he handed to his PA to type up.

Dr Erdmann was a collector of modern paintings and sculptures, and entering his practice was like entering an art gallery. Paintings of shapes and scribbles and doodles graced every room. He said, "This is the last time you'll see this place, from next week we're in Harley Street, in new premises." When I visited him there I was seated in a waiting-room to the left of the entrance, and an enormous painting showed two black smudges shaped like cancerous lungs, and in one corner fingers held a magnifying glass.

As previously, he greeted me very warmly as if I were an old friend – an honorary Grosvenor – and I swiftly developed a close affinity with Dr Erdmann, who ran a vast practice that linked with dozens of specialists and consultants and spanned five or six properties in Devonshire Street, Devonshire Place and Harley Street. He told me he had bought some of his paintings during visits to California. His PA told me that all the paintings in the new place were new, the staff had not seen them before.

He was like a spider sitting in the centre of a vast web. He was an aesthete and a collector who, judging from his properties and his paintings, was rich enough to retire from medical work if he chose. He gave the impression of continuing to work out of love for his patients rather than the money his private practice brought in, and of caring deeply for his patients. His medical work was his life, and I had no doubt that besides being a collector of paintings he was a collector of people, who (so long as they could afford his fees) swiftly became his friends.

Not-Breathings and a Mask

That spring and early summer I spent three months having an 'MOT test' on my health. I was generally healthy but I had had varicose veins treated by foam sclerotherapy and I had a cold right foot and walked unsteadily. I often dozed during the day and sometimes dribbled and drooled as my control over my saliva weakened.

I went to my GP in Devonshire Street, Dr Erdmann, who examined me for a couple of hours and put me through blood tests of many conditions. I had my arteries examined by ultrasound, I had a CT colonography on my prostate and I had a scan of my brain. My heart was tested (and ratcheted up to 130 beats a minute to check it could cope) and I had a colonoscopy.

All this established that I was clear of cancer and had no hidden disease that would suddenly burst upon me. And just as I was congratulating myself on being a Ulysses, cleared to "sail beyond the sunset and the baths/Of all the western stars" in search of fresh adventures, I was sent to a sleep specialist who said I should be tested for apnoea as I nodded off during the day.

I saw Dr Maghreb in a 4th-floor room in Devonshire Place. He seemed to be an Arab – there were many Arabs in the waiting-room downstairs – and was extremely courteous. He had an assistant of enormous girth who gave me a monitor that looked like a phone, which I was instructed to strap on my front before my sleep that night. There was a nasal mask with two prongs to check my breathing, and the next day the equipment was collected by a courier who biked it to a laboratory.

I visited Dr Maghreb to hear the result. He said, "The test worked. The chip has given us a lot of information. You stopped breathing 118 times in 404 minutes, the longest for 70.9 seconds. You did not breathe several times for more than a minute during your sleep. The body self-regulates and makes you breathe to keep you alive, but such long spells of not breathing mean you are low in oxygen. The reading is 93 per cent, it should be above 96 per cent. Lack of oxygen is bad for your heart and your brain. You should use a machine until the end of your life. I have one here for you to take away. It is a CPAP machine. There is a central piece of equipment with this black lead, this plug goes in that hole, there is a tube here and you have a full mask from the top of your nose to your chin. It will change you, improve your consciousness during the day. You will not fall asleep any more. It is strapped on like this."

He put me into the mask. I tried it out.

I took it home and wore it for a month. But air leaked out of the sides, as the results on the machine showed, and the reading showed I was having 'events' (not-breathings) at the rate of over 5 per hour, over 30 in a six-hour sleep. Dr Maghreb decided I should have a nasal mask with two prongs that just covered my nose.

I tried this and my 'events' were cut to under 2 per hour, sometimes 1.7. So I stayed with the nasal mask and left my mouth free.

For six weeks I felt more tired than usual as I woke several times in the night, conscious of the mask and the hiss of air from the tube. But little by little I got used to it, and I discovered I became more thorough during the day. My work was meticulous, I paid greater attention to detail. My brain grew sharper, my powers of observation more acute.

And so here I am, sleeping in an undignified mask while a hiss of air prevents me from not-breathing for ever, yet with my faculties undimmed and a Ulyssean appetite for life and new experience that belies my years. I remain interested in everything with a clear-sighted intellect and soul, while my body slows and I walk more unsteadily than I used to do and defiantly mask over my not-breathing that could result at any time in my immediate death.

Cog-Wheels and Houses

The ride-on mower only drove in high gear. The gear stick was jammed and would not return to neutral. For a week the gardener was still able to start the mower, but then it would not start at all as the teeth of the starter cog-wheel did not enmesh and engage with the teeth of the larger cog-wheel. I called Mart, the servicer.

He came about 10.30 with his van and a new cog-system, for which he had quoted £389, VAT inclusive. He was a healthy-looking man who had lived in the open air and had a head of well-groomed hair. I would have said he was in his early fifties.

The gardener had parked the red mower on a patch of grass at the front of our house, and Mart lifted the bonnet and took the front to bits. He spread the parts out on the grass. He said to me, "I think it doesn't need the new part, I think I can solve the problem and keep the old part."

I left him sitting on the grass among his tools, his head close to the engine as he peered at the toothed wheels. Later, looking out of a window I saw a shower of sparks spraying the grass as he ground the teeth of the starter cog-wheel.

I went out about 12. He said, "It starts seven times out of ten. But that's not good enough. It's not up to my standards. I'm not going to be beaten, so I'm working on. It's got to start ten times out of ten." So I left him sitting on the grass in the sunshine, his head close to the engine.

At 2.30 he looked as if he was clearing up, so I went out.

"I've made the old part work so I don't need to fit the one I brought. I've started the mower ten times and it started each time," he said. "And I've started it another ten times and it started each time. You see this smaller cog-wheel, I've ground each of the teeth. You see they're silver at the edges. They'll engage now." He started the engine first time to show me. "And I've put a pin in the gear stick so it won't come out again."

I thanked him and stood with him as, still sitting on the grass, he replaced the parts, tightened them with a spanner and replaced the red bonnet. Then he stood up.

"I'm glad you were able to come today," I said. "I know you're busy."

"Very busy at present," he said. "It's the harvesters. The farmers are getting their harvests in and with the bad weather around they're pushing the harvesters and they break down. They ring and it's urgent as they might lose their harvest. So I have to go to where they are. We operate in several counties, Essex, Suffolk, Kent, Sussex, and I have to keep the machines operating. I start work at 6.30am and finish at 9pm, and I'm on the go all day. I live in Saffron Walden, and I have to get back home. I'm off to Bishop's Stortford now. I like Bishop's Stortford, I've got two houses there. The first one I bought in 1968 and the second one's in the same road. I let them out, there are always tenants. I've only had a few weeks' void since 1968. The first one I bought when I was 21, the second when I was 28."

With a shock I realised he had bought his first house 49 years previously. If he was 21 in 1968 he must now be 70, although he only looked 50.

"You've made good investments," I said.

"Oh, yes," he said, "they've been brilliant investments. An agent collects the rents, I don't go there. But I bought them when I was young and carried on working and paid the overheads out of my salary and now I am reaping the benefits. Now I'm off to Bishop's Stortford. I like Bishop's Stortford."

Soon afterwards he was driving his van out of the gates. I reflected that he travelled round all the farmers who were desperate to save their harvests while he had already harvested his properties and was living more comfortably than they were as a result of his youthful eye to the future. Through his inherent wisdom he had an earner whose cog-wheels always enmeshed and never broke down.

An Epileptic in Corfu

We arrived at our Cornish house during daylight and it was soon clear there had been a power cut or a power surge. I found two switches had tripped on different fuse boards in different parts of the house, and restored lights. But there was no internet, the Sky box was dead and so was a television in the same room. So I rang Ron.

He came the next morning, a large man with spectacles and a bulging paunch. He drove from Newquay and got to work immediately. He installed a second-hand Sky box he had brought with him and held in his hand, and a new power supply unit he fetched from his van, and got us back on the internet. He improved the aerial to the television but pronounced it blown. He said, "It'll be the condenser. I can take it back to Newquay and repair it and bring it back and you're looking at at least £110. You can get a new television from Asda for £110, so it's better to buy a new one. I'm going to the dump, shall I take this old one?"

I had offered him coffee ("Milk and two sugars," he said with alacrity before I had finished asking) and as he drank it standing up, with Pippa sitting on the sofa and me standing, he talked in an over-calibrated way.

"My phone hasn't been working over in Newquay because of the mast," he informed us. "It cost me thousands' worth of business, so I rang them and said, 'Put it right.' 'No, we don't know what's wrong.' 'Well let me do it.' 'No, we can't let you near it.' 'Well, install a new mast, then.' I've done work for companies like them before. In the 1990s I did work at the RAF base at St Mawgan." (RAF St Mawgan is generally referred to as an 'RAF station'.) "They've got seven floors underground, it has to be a top-secret NATO base, and they allowed me down five but they wouldn't let me go down to the bottom two. If there's a nuclear war that's where NATO will operate from. The internet comes across the Atlantic to the UK and the base is on the western tip of England, so there'll be a direct link with Washington."

"Like the phone in the War Rooms' loo that Churchill used to use to speak to the American President," I suggested.

"Yes. The internet goes straight up to London and then comes back down to Cornwall, but for the seven underground floors at St Mawgan there will be a direct secure link with Washington."

Pippa said, "My parents were both at St Mawgan during the war."

Ron said, "I was in the Canary Islands when the Americans contacted me. They were so keen to get me they laid on a plane and offered to fly me back. They didn't book me on a plane, they sent a plane specially from St Mawgan to the Canary Islands to pick me up. When the Americans left they left behind all their equipment, even their keys. They walked out and said, 'Take what you want, we'll get it all new where we're going.' I don't have that kind of holiday any more. My second wife took me for forty thousand in six weeks, she was evil. Now my partner's died I'm single and I just go to Greece, to Corfu.

"I love it there. Last time I was there I arrived at the airport and the customs fellows said, 'Oh, you're back.' I shook hands all round and the customs fellows said, 'We'll take you to your hotel.' I said, 'No, pub.' I spent all night there, and next morning I realised I hadn't got my luggage. I'd left it in the airport. I was driven there, it was still there, where I'd left it on the floor. No one had touched it. I said to the customs fellows, 'You didn't blow it up.' 'No, we know you.' I checked in at the hotel. They said, 'Oh, we were expecting you yesterday.' Then I went back to the pub. 'You're banned, you drank four bottles of Bacardi and we've got none left. Oh, wait a moment.' She returned with a couple of bottles of Bacardi. 'Got them from down the road.' I speak Greek while I'm there. It comes back to me when I arrive, I forget it when I'm over here.

"I enjoy myself because I know I may not have long. It's my epilepsy. I was diagnosed after a seizure in 2000, caused by my second wife. I was really stressed over the forty thousand. I felt a pain in my head above my right ear and before I could say anything, within three seconds I was gone. It happens to me every twelve to eighteen months now. I don't say anything about it because they ban you from driving for a year. They don't ban you for a heart attack, when you can lose consciousness, but they do for epilepsy. The second time I rang and said, 'I lost consciousness yesterday.' The hospital said, 'You're banned from driving for a year.' I said, 'But you haven't examined me.' 'We know your condition.' I can't do with being banned from driving, I came to you this morning across Cornwall. So now I say nothing. I just get on with it and enjoy myself. But I don't drink as much as I used to, and I stopped the smoking and I'm looking at my stomach. So I go to Corfu. They're friendly there, they look after me. I'm on my own, single, here, but over there they all care about me. I love it in Corfu.

"Now I need to relieve you of some money. That'll be ninety please."

We had made him coffee and listened to him and he had charged us only £90 for his return journey across Cornwall, his call-out charge, a working Sky box, a power supply unit, repair to a TV aerial and his assessment of the condition of the television. He could have charged us much more. As I watched him carry our defunct television to his van I thought that he regarded us as like the people of Corfu: we cared for him, and so he did us for little more than at cost. But then I realised he would repair our television and sell it on to a future customer, like our replacement Sky box.

A Painter and a Cripple

I walked up the path to the bottom of the garden to see how the semi-retired Cornish painter, Mervyn Rocks, was getting on painting the door to an outhouse.

"I renewed a plank," he said, balding in white overalls, "you can't see which one it is."

"That one," I said, "the others have bobbles on them."

He nodded. "I've got to leave soon to collect my car," he said. "I'm in the van today. My car's being serviced. All my family's number-plates reflect their ages at different times. Mine is M22 ROX, because I married at the age of 22. My wife's is C18 ROX, because she's Christine and she married me when she was 18. And my son's car, a BMW, is C40 ROX, because he's 40. He's Christopher. When I pop my clogs mine will go to my other son, Martin, who will begin with an 'M', and Christopher's BMW will go to my wife as they are both 'C', and he'll get a new one. So it will all work out.

"Talking of clogs we had to attend a funeral on Friday. My father-in-law died. He was 88. He seemed very healthy but he complained of pain in his stomach. He went into a nursing home on the Saturday and we went to see him on the Monday and were told, 'We're getting him washed so he's ready for you.' He was dead, and we hadn't been told. He had a malignant ulcer which burst and blood came up out of his mouth. His funeral was at Carclaze and six of us had a meal round a table to remember him. We've been cleaning up his bungalow. His partner died 20 years ago, and he had another partner. He was a soldier. My mother had dementia. She put butter in the oven. She had to have someone living with her.

"Your neighbour, Jim the undertaker, buried my father-in-law. I saw him just now. He came in a wedding car. His weekly tenants next door had a wedding and he drove up in a large black Rolls-Royce with two white ribbons tied from the mirrors to the front of the bonnet. The bonnet ornament on a Rolls-Royce is called 'The Spirit of Ecstasy' and sometimes 'Emily', 'Silver Lady' or 'Flying Lady'. I said to him, 'Your tenants have got too many cars. I couldn't turn the other day, there were so many, and I had to reverse back to the top of the road.' I said to him, 'Your wife wouldn't like to do that, would she?' I said, 'That car on the corner of the green is the worst, he's always down looking at the sea.'

"The driver was sitting in the car and Jim said, 'He shouldn't even be here, I'll tell him.' So he went and had words with him, told him it was a private road for residents only. The man shouted back out of the window. Jim said, 'There's a notice at the top of the road, you should go to Specsavers if you don't know you're not supposed to be here. You're causing parking problems.' The man shouted at him. There was a loud argument, just five minutes ago. The man said, 'I'm on crutches, I'm a cripple, I can't walk,' with a lot of expletives.

"Jim said to me afterwards, 'I feel sorry for him but he has no right to be there, he's making it worse for everyone else.' I'm glad Jim told him because he's always in the way for me. Jim's a good bloke, he's known me through his undertaking, he buried my father-in-law, he's sorted out the parking for me. Now it's time I went and collected my car."

As I walked back down the garden path I reflected on the skill with which our painter had manipulated our undertaker-neighbour into getting rid of a cripple who had caused him parking problems. He was a tradesman, but he acted more strongly than would have befitted a resident. We live in a regulated society and he had insisted on parkers following the rules, but had his self-interest made him heartless and uncaring towards a disabled man who lacked the ability to walk?

Fate Smiles at the *Fête*
(Or: Trusting the Universe)

"Al had a dream last week," said Simon, "that he was at the school *fête* and won 20 bottles at the bottle tombola. He's only eight but he talked about his dream as if it was his fate. I wonder what will happen at the fête this afternoon."

I attended the *fête* on a warm, sunny day. Several hundred people wandered between many stalls on the sloping field. There was a huge bouncy castle and near the bottom of the slope Al was kicking a football at Teddy Sheringham, a former England footballer who was doing a stint in goal.

Then I saw Al go to the bottle tombola. Thirty or forty bottles with raffle numbers on them stood along a table, and Al was the only customer. I sidled up without his seeing me and observed from a distance as he bought five tickets for £1. If the ticket ended with an '0' as his first ticket 490 did, he won a bottle. He bought another five tickets for another £1. Two of them ended in a '0'. He showed no emotion as he chose his bottle each time, it was his allotted fate.

Weirdly, after buying 10 lots of five tickets for £10 (given him by his mother) he amassed 15 bottles.

His mother saw the row of bottles from where she was sitting and hurried over to help. Al had no more money left, and seeing the situation she gave him another £3. By the end he had 20 bottles in rows. I came forward and tucked bottles of wine and soft drinks under my arms and helped his mother carry his trophies to a table where her mother was sitting with Pippa.

"Did you win all those?" Pippa asked with magnified astonishment.

"Yes," he said calmly and matter-of-factly, aged eight. "I dreamed that I would win 20 and I did."

"And if you dream something," I said, "it happens."

"Yes," he said. "I dream it and it happens. It's nice."

I smiled at the trust his eight-year-old mind had placed in the universe, but as he ran off to see what else was exciting at the *fête*, I thought, 'Maybe he's right, maybe the bountiful universe has things in store for all of us as on a table at a fête and all we need to do is trust the universe and assume Fate will smile and push some of its bounty in our direction.'

A Ruby and the Universe
(Or: "Find it, Anubis")

For three years I had kept a rough-hewn ruby Pippa gave me on our Ruby Wedding Anniversary in my shirt's breast pocket. I wore it over my heart as a lucky charm. It was misshapen and had a ridge on one side and I would have recognised it anywhere.

I went to Cornwall and shortly after my return became aware that it was not in my breast pocket. I thought it might be on top of my desk, where I turned out my pockets last thing at night before going to bed, but it wasn't there. Nor was it on the floor. Once I had found it under a box on wheels near my desk. It wasn't there. I began to wonder if I had left it in Cornwall, or if it had fallen out when I had bent to pick something up.

"Find it, Anubis," I said aloud one morning in the direction of my Egyptian antiquities, which were in my wooden shelves. "Find my ruby, Anubis."

Soon afterwards I was aware I had strained my back. It was as if I had dislodged a vertebra. That afternoon I went to the gym to walk off my discomfort. After thirteen minutes walking and ten minutes cycling I went to the stepper machine (an elliptical or cross trainer) to do my next exercise. My movement was constricted, and as I prepared to mount a stepper I tripped on one of the star-shaped 'arms' of its base and felt myself falling between two steppers. I had stubbed a toe and I banged a hand as I (successfully) tried to save myself by clutching one of its middle bars. I jarred my back, which immediately appeared to improve. Somehow my half-fall seemed to have improved my back. In the short term, for it later transpired I had twisted my pelvis and my back was a lot worse.

When I returned home I drove down the stony drive to the stony turning area, parked and lifted my gym holdall out of my BMW's boot. I took a few steps and then untypically stopped and put my holdall on the loose stones, something I had never done before, and, feeling my back, surveyed the great stony parking area (perhaps 60 yards x 30 yards) and the stones up the drive to the gate. I thought there might be a couple of hundred thousand small stones between me and the grassed banks and distant flower-beds.

Suddenly a reddish stone caught my eye. It had been half-buried as a car had driven over it. I bent and with my fingernails prised it out and picked it up. It was my lost ruby. Without a doubt, the misshapen contours and distinctive ridge immediately established it as mine.

I was astonished. What was it doing there? It was the last place I would have thought of looking. And how could I have found it amid a sea of small stones?

Then I realised. I always kept pen and paper in my breast pocket, including a shopping list, and perhaps when I had gone out to do my weekly shop on a Saturday I had pulled my shopping list and biro from my breast pocket to write down something I had just remembered I would need, and had inadvertently pulled the ruby with it and dropped it where I had briefly stood to scribble.

The fact remained, I had said aloud that morning, "Find it, Anubis," and it had been found. My bad back had caused me to come out and drive the car to the gym, and the apparent improvement to my back after my half-fall had led me to put down my holdall on the stones – and find my ruby. How much of this was a coincidence and how much was Providentially planned to get me to stand where my ruby had lain for several days?

I did not know. But as I picked up my holdall and resumed my walk to the front door it seemed as if I lived alongside a parking area lined with rubies, and I thought that the angels had given me a bad back and then apparently cured it so I could be reunited with the ruby I had for so long worn close to my heart. And for the rest of that day I was very quiet for it seemed that I was living in an interactive universe which heard my requests and reconnected me with what I had lost.

A Black-Out and Wooden Chairs

One morning our domestic help, Carol, said almost tearfully, "I don't want to leave but I think I'm going to have to. My husband's getting worse. On Saturday we went out to a restaurant and we ordered and just after the food arrived and he had had a few mouthfuls he passed out, his head went down to his food, and he wet himself. Then he came to and was repeatedly sick. I had to use a container on the table for him to vomit into. An off-duty policeman was dining nearby. He came over to help. It's the fifth time that's happened and each time's in a restaurant. He can't go out to a meal any more. He knows his Parkinson's getting worse. When he goes to the toilet he misses and I have to clear up after him. He said the other day, 'I want to pack it in.' He used to go cycling and to the gym and watch documentaries but he can't follow programmes any more, he has a short attention span. I'm looking after him all the time, he can't be left, and it's got to the point I need help.

"Jenny" (her daughter) "has found a flat in a sheltered block near her that would do us fine. It's only two bedrooms with a view over the car park – not over the river, like some of the others – but it's the last one, and there's a communal sitting-room downstairs and it's between Marks & Spencer and the doctor's. I could leave him sitting with others to keep an eye on him while I go out to the shops, and it's near Jenny, so she could look in every day. It would be too far to come here unless I come one day a week to do the ironing, but he would have someone looking after him all the time.

"We've sold our house, except that we haven't. Our buyer said he had one house to sell but now it turns out he has to sell two houses to fund his purchase. We got rid of all our furniture last week, before we were told this. The British Heart Foundation, a charity, took it away. We had to pay them, £470 it cost us. We had a piano and they said, 'You've got to pay to get it downstairs and then we'll think about whether we'll take it.' Someone across the road said she'd have it, so we let her take it away. They've taken all our sofas. We're sitting on wooden chairs, expecting to move.

"We'll have money in the bank after selling our five-bedroom house and buying the two-bedroom flat, money to live off. But now the new place is saying the price will go up if we haven't exchanged contracts by the end of the month, and our estate agent's gone on holiday and no one else can talk to our lawyer. It's the last flat and others want it. I don't know how long they'll wait. I feel it's not going to happen. My daughter's had a heavy massage chair delivered so we can sit in comfort. Donald is saying, 'Aren't we moving on Friday?' He doesn't understand, and Jenny and I haven't told him the real situation as we don't want to worry him.

"I don't want to go, Mr Rawley," she said tearfully. "I like working here. I like doing the hoovering and the bed changes and doing the ironing – and speaking to Mrs. Rawley. I don't want to leave but I'm going to have to, so we can all cope with Donald's Parkinson's as it gets worse."

Noisy Voters and an Orange Moon

At Paddington I lugged my bags to the first-class waiting-room, showed my ticket and found an unoccupied armchair. I made myself a cappuccino and sat and kept an eye on the television news and the constantly-updated train-journey screen. I munched oat cornflour biscuits from a packet and read some newspapers from my bag.

Eventually the 19.03 was shown as 'preparing', no platform listed yet. I left with my bags and saw a Great Western Railway train immediately in front of me.

"Is this the Plymouth train?" I asked a male cleaner.

"Yes, the 19.03."

I walked up to the front of my train and climbed into the first-class carriage, L, and found seat 36, a window-seat with a table by itself. I unpacked my bag of newspapers and work and my glasses, put my three bags on the train rack and, relishing my own company and quiet, finished reading the newspapers until with a sudden jolt the train jerkily pulled away from the platform. I looked forward to solitary concentration in this quiet carriage.

Across the aisle before me were two tables laid for dinner with white tablecloths. An elderly man in a tie said loudly and self-importantly to a waitress with short dyed-red hair, "So I have you again, twice in a week." A young lady squeezed in front of him to the window-seat and he sat on the outside by the aisle, his back to me. Then a father with a teenage son arrived and sat in the opposite seats. From their introductions and subsequent conversation, which I could barely hear, I gathered the elderly man was an MP in the South-West, and politics figured spasmodically during their meal. I watched from the solitude of my seat while working on my table.

At Plymouth it was all-change. I had to proceed on a local train going to Penzance, which was across the platform: only two carriages. I lugged my bags to the middle of the train so I was within reach of the only two doors, which were near each other and closed. All the passengers on the train I had left who were travelling on lined the platform, two or three deep. It was 10.30pm and the train for Penzance was due to depart at 10.42pm.

The push-buttons by the two doors lit up after that time. The door into the rear carriage would not open, so everyone converged on the only other entrance, the door to the front carriage. Everyone pushed. I managed to use my holdall as a barrier. It was barged aside – I was barged aside – by a young man with a short pony-tail who powered through. I fought my way in and inside the train saw rows of two seats on either side of an aisle rapidly being taken. I found an empty pair of seats and heaved my luggage up on to the luggage rack and squeezed in by the window. There was no leg-room and I had to sit with my knees turned sideways against the back of the seat before me.

There were too many passengers for the seats, and soon the carriage was full. I had a young man nursing a shoulder-bag next to me, causing me to jam my knees against the back of the seat ahead of me. Many had to stand at each end. But what shocked me was the noise. Everyone was shouting. There was a terrific hubbub. I could see four men further down opening large cans of lager at their table. A blonde woman standing in the aisle was yelling to her husband, who was standing at the end of the carriage, as she supervised two young children who were in seats. Two young men in front of me were taking selfies. One held the camera above his head and I realised I would be in the selfie and turned and looked out of the window so my face would be obscured.

The train started and trundled through the dark. The lights inside the carriage were dim. No one was reading any sort of a book or newspaper, all were in shouting conversation with their neighbours, and what shocked me most was that this was natural to them, this was how they lived. My world of a first-class quiet carriage and written or computer work at a table was another world from theirs.

Then I realised that these were the new British voters. I peered over the seats in front of me and behind me and looked at them. The men were all in sweatshirts, no one was in a suit or tie. They had all been to Plymouth for the day with family or friends and were going home. Very few were looking at phones. No one considered that their words could be heard by others, that their voices were intruding on silence. There was no silence on which to intrude; as everyone was shouting, they had to shout even louder to be heard. These were the voters who had voted for Brexit, who wanted the English to be apart from other nationalities, who wanted borders and visas, a Little England in which they could all be together with each other.

As I studied their faces as they talked to each other, unaware, I realised that this was a different race from the one I knew when I commuted to London in the late 1950s, when everyone was quiet and smart and read *The Times*. Somehow, my race had changed. I had followed a solitary way to be close to my inner thinking, and was an outsider, isolated, in their chattering and shouting and loud laughter. ("The loud laugh that spoke the vacant mind," I thought, recalling Goldsmith's words from the late 1760s.)

When I reached my station at 11.46pm and had lugged my luggage through the gate, Pippa was waiting for me in her black car. We drove to our harbour and she sat on a wooden bench outside our front door and looked for shooting stars while I unloaded the car. It was the time of the Perseid meteor shower when, after 11pm, there were many shooting stars.

When I had finished unloading I walked to the sea wall a few yards away, and a full orange moon took my breath away. There were two triangles of shimmering orange light on the calm sea, one on the horizon tapering to an apex halfway towards me and another (its mirror image) whose apex was near it and spread outwards towards me so its base covered the sea beneath the wall.

I stood and soaked in the orange light on the dark sea under the orange moon, and I was glad to be me, in my solitary's consciousness, and not one of the noisy, yelling, shouting voters who I had sat among for an hour, who had determined the new direction our country was taking.

A Hammer and a Flat

We collected Maud from her home in Porthleven. I helped her into the car – at 91 she found it an effort to climb up into the BMW X5 – and we drove to the Housel Bay Hotel, which overlooked the Lizard. We sat in the window, and I looked across dozens of blue agapanthuses to the Lizard Lighthouse and the rock at the end of the promontory that stuck up like a huge dorsal fin. We ordered fish and chips, and Pippa had sea bream.

"I was with Daphne yesterday," Pippa said to her aunt of her cousin. "Edna's buying a house near Duporth. She and her husband have been renting, and it's only recently they've worked out they'd be better off having a mortgage. Daphne told me about Sonia. She was at university for a year in Leeds doing Media Studies and 'doing well', *she* said, and then she dropped out and worked in a chain of shops, and she told her father Victor (Daphne said to me) she was going to be a manager. Well, she dropped out of that. She's been living with her mother, Martha (Daphne said to me), and Martha has been doing more and more at her school in Bodmin, and taking after-school clubs, and she's been doing things at the church, and she's not been home very much. And Ian, her husband (Daphne said to me), has been drinking. He's nearly an alcoholic.

"Well Sonia, his stepdaughter (Daphne said to me), is very clever and manipulative. She has told the Cornwall County Council that she wants to attack Ian with a hammer because he's drunk so much. She's not going to attack anyone with a hammer, but that's what she's told the Council to get an assessment. She's got herself assessed for mental health problems, and she's announced to the assessors she's a lesbian and can't control her urge to attack Ian with a hammer.

"She's been given a flat in Newquay, in a block of flats for people who've been assessed. Newquay was where a flat was available, it could have been in Penzance. Once you've been assessed you don't have to be assessed again, you have the flat for life. So she's got a flat and she won't have to work. Martha and Victor have moved her out of Martha's house and into the new flat as she's a potential danger to her stepfather. She's more or less said to the authorities, 'Give me a flat or I'll attack my stepfather with a hammer.'

"Ginnie hasn't visited her mother since the wedding. She's been to her husband's parents twice, but she doesn't want Charlie mixed up with drinking and mental health issues. She's supposed to be going to Martha's this weekend – now that Sonia has gone. Martha, with all she's doing in the school and the church, has had to go backwards and forwards to Newquay to visit Sonia. Victor's been visiting and has been helping with furniture. He's had a chequered past but he's coming up good now.

"Daphne told me all this but she's not well. She's been dizzy and has been told it might be labyrinthitis. And Bill was put on antibiotics and they renewed his prescription for the same antibiotic eight times. He's now been told that was a mistake, the body becomes immune with too much of the same antibiotic, he's had the wrong treatment. They're not well, and are watching what's happening to their children, Edna and Martha, and though Sonia is Victor's and not theirs they've been very worried by it all. Nothing's gone smoothly for them."

When we returned to our house by the sea, the Red Arrows were performing in the sky towards the horizon, trailing red smoke for the Fowey Regatta. They looped the loop and made a heart of red smoke above the distant headland, and a Red Arrow roared down trailing red smoke and thrust an arrow through the heart. And I thought that with her convincing tale that had hoodwinked the Council and won her security for life Sonia had thrust a painful arrow deep within her family's aching heart.

A Christening and a Crutch

Claire came and sat on the seat outside our Cornish house with Pippa. She looked very slim with a lacy top, and her hair was very wild-looking round the sides of her face. She looked young for someone in her mid-sixties.

"It's Harry's birthday next week," she said to me. "We had an event for him last night and we raised £1,100 for the football club he was associated with. There was a football match, and we won 3–2 and his son scored the first goal. There was a speech and the man at the microphone said, 'And Harry's ex- is here. No, his wife, his widow. Sorry about that, Claire.' And then he called me and my card partner 'Claire and Harry'. I said, 'No, Claire and Graham.' He hadn't a clue."

I smiled and shook my head. Then I made the two of them coffee and went indoors to cope with phone calls while they looked at the sea and talked.

"Claire is doing all right," Pippa said after she went. "She's looking after children two days a week. She's always had a child-minding job. She's dropped collecting money, that was too much for her. She's allowed to work sixteen hours a week without paying tax, and she's applied to Asda for part-time work. Not on the tills, I'm not sure what exactly. She's waiting to hear. She's financially comfortable with what Harry left her and her other income.

"She's seeing two men. One was a friend of Harry's, and he's not a boyfriend, just a companion. They go for walks together. And the other, Pat, calls her his girlfriend but she doesn't call him her boyfriend. She's closer to him. She's got herself christened and confirmed all on one day at her chapel, St John's. She didn't tell her family she was doing it. Pat said he'd like to attend but she said 'No'. He insisted, so he did attend."

"She talks to Harry late at night," I said, "and that suggests he's in an after-life, and so by being christened and confirmed she's getting ready to join him in the after-life. Not long ago she was talking of killing herself to join him."

"Yes," Pippa said, "that's right. She took Pat to the event yesterday. She told her children, and they supported her. But she was worried about it; she said, 'I was thinking, "What will people say? What will they think?"' I said, 'It doesn't matter what they think. It's your life, not theirs, and you can do what you like with it. What they say is irrelevant.'"

I nodded, admiring her strong advice. "It's very easy to be in a relationship and say someone who isn't shouldn't be doing something," I said.

"Yes," Pippa said. "She should ignore what people say. In fact several came up to her at last night's event and said, 'I'm glad you've found someone.' She told me, 'I discussed it with Harry and he said, "After I'm gone you should find somebody else." I said "All right" but I never thought I would. And even now I haven't, but we'll see what happens. But it's the company. We go on excursions, shopping to Plymouth for the day, that sort of thing, and it's not being alone. We'll see what happens.'

"He's on a crutch," Pippa added. "He's waiting for a knee operation. He needs an operation on both knees, but they'll only do one. So he attended last night's event on a crutch."

And I thought Claire was using Pat as a crutch while she finally came to terms with Harry's death, which she had still not got over.

A Swim and a Rescue Operation

Ross, the ex-Zimbabwean soldier, came. He had taken 300 pages of letters I wanted put on computer to a special machine which turned them into a Word document that could be moved around on screen, for £65, saving us hours of work. His scans were on a CD and he uploaded the file onto my computer.

Then he sat back in my PA's special support chair (careful not to re-arrange the movable arms) and said, with expressive eyes, thin-faced with a thin moustache, "I must tell you, I go swimming. I've swum for years. I do three kilometres and I begin to get tired then and I know it's time to stop. I hate doing it in a pool, that's so boring. So I go to Southend. Normally swimming there's so interesting. The tide's often in, and there's the pier to look at, and pedalos and water-skiing, and I do one kilometre each way and keep one kilometre in the tank in case I get into difficulties. I wear a green fluorescent cap so I can be seen, and often a wetsuit.

"Five weeks ago before I went away I went to Southend for a swim. I put my 'kit' – my towel and wallet and watch and phone – on the beach as usual, wrapped up in my towel. There was a couple there who often wave to me and I wave back to them, and that's the level of it. The tide was out and I had to walk into the water. It seemed I'd waded half a mile and the water wasn't above my waist. So I tried to swim in this really shallow water. I did one kilometre one way, on my back as I was scraping the shingle and I made sure it was my rump that scraped, and one kilometre the other way. I stood up in about six inches of water and I was really fed up as I walked back through the shallow sea as I hadn't had my usual exercise. So impulsively I walked to Shoeburyness and walked rather than swam the exercise I should have had.

"As I walked back to my beach," he said, very animated with wide eyes, "I could see something had happened. There were crowds lining the front and coastguard helicopters in the air and so many police cars with blue lights and police in uniform. And I thought 'Oh, my God,' and I put my hand over my face in embarrassment. I just wanted to find my 'kit' and go. But most of it had gone, so I had to go and speak to a policeman. He said the couple who waved to me had reported me missing and there was a huge search-and-rescue in progress. They thought I'd left my kit and waded out and drowned."

He laughed infectiously.

"My kit was held by six different people and I had to give my name and address six times. I thought I was going to get done for wasting police time, the operation involving the coastguard helicopters must have cost thousands. But the English police were so nice, no one shouted at me. On the Continent they've shouted at me when I've been swimming, especially the French police. In Greece there are huge tall-masted, flat-bottomed ships for about sixty tourists, and their navigators hate swimmers as they are a danger to their ships. In the Greek islands I was swimming near rocks and one of those ships came near and deliberately headed for the rocks immediately in front of me and its water nearly pushed me onto the rocks, which is what the ship's navigator was trying to do. Of course I immediately swam into the wash so I wouldn't be thrown onto the rocks. And I thought, 'You idiot, you could have killed sixty tourists, not to mention me.' I could have needed rescuing then. Swimmers are not popular with ships. It's like cyclists and cars."

He chuckled.

I had smiled and chuckled as he spoke with animated facial expressions that effortlessly held my attention.

It was time for him to leave. "I'm going to Earl's Colne now," he said, "near Colchester. There's a Zimbabwean community there, including someone I haven't seen for years. They said, 'You can come on two conditions: that you don't bring anything with you (such as a bottle) and you come again often." He laughed.

I took him down to the front door and waved him off as he got into his car and drove out of our gates. He had been a soldier in the Zimbabwean bush and he was used to being self-contained. He swam to keep himself fit. He was energetic and motivated, with an infectious laugh. For him, life was good but he made it good out of his own efforts. Southend was a long way to drive to, but he put himself through the drive, he made the effort as part of his control over his body.

He was like a backwoodsman, he was in command of his body within the open-air life he had once known in Rhodesia and now perpetuated. He deported himself with quiet purpose, he was self-organised with the bearing of a soldier, and I admired him for routinely swimming two or more kilometres in the sea.

Magic in the Osteopath's

A couple of months back in the gym I had tripped over the footrest of a cross trainer and fallen through the gap towards the next cross trainer. With my left hand I clutched a middle bar and with my right missed the middle bar and saved myself from a complete fall by holding on to the base beneath the middle bars. I twisted as I fell, and bruised myself in one or two places but thought I had escaped a worse injury.

But after that I had slight pain in my lower back on my left side. And again in the gym, while walking on the treadmill something aggravated and I now had a pain in my lower back on my right side.

So I rang the osteopath's number and found myself speaking to his son, Martin, who I had known since he was about nine. He said, "My dad's in France, renovating his property there, but I can see you."

I parked up the road and walked past shops to his shop-window, and arrived for 4.30. Martin was a hefty young man in his mid-thirties, with a cropped head. He looked very overweight. He led me to the treatment room. I undressed to my pants and lay face down with my mouth through a hole on the treatment table while he examined me and oiled my lower back and rubbed it with a circular movement of his right hand for twenty minutes.

I said I remembered his father buying the French property twenty years back, and that it reflected his quarter-French ancestry.

He said, "It's several hundred years old. And very dilapidated. He goes over there for two weeks twice a year, and during the last twenty years he hasn't made much progress. I told him he should sell it and buy a property in better condition. He's gone with his Ghanaian wife. He met her over here fifteen years ago."

He told me he lived in Eastbourne with his wife, that he had worked with his father for twelve years and that he had paid off his mortgage, had no credit cards and owned his own car.

He made me turn over and held my left arm and placed it across my chest and folded the other one over it and drew my knees together and when I was in a parcel, with his hands between my crossed arms he thrust heftily down on my right side and as I involuntarily gasped with pain said, "It's in, first time." He did the same to my left side. Then he put a hand on my head and another at the base of my back and somehow sat me up so my legs were over the side of the couch. "That's how paramedics and firemen do it," he said.

I dressed and paid him £38 and asked when he was next available in case I needed him. He said, "I'm here tomorrow. I shall return to Eastbourne mid-morning and see my patients down there and then go to Derby as I'm taking part in a card tournament and if I win I will play for England in Las Vegas, all expenses paid. You should put ice-cubes on both sides of your back for the rest of the evening to prevent any inflammation."

Back home I put the rectangular blue thermoses with frozen water we took to Cornwall in our cool-bags into the freezer, and when the water inside had frozen, put two inside the back of my pants so they were in contact with my skin. From time to time I returned to the freezer and put the two I had been wearing back in and replaced them with two more frozen ones.

I slept well, but next morning I still had pain on my right side so I rang Martin and left a message. He rang back: "Can you come at 10.40?"

I arrived at 10.30 and he was sitting alone at his desk in his shop-window, waiting for me. Again I undressed in the treatment room. I had difficulty in crossing my legs to take off my shoes, and said so.

He said, "That means you've got a twisted pelvis."

I indicated a knobble in my back on my right side where the pain was.

He felt it and said, "I think you've got a twisted pelvis, which I missed yesterday. The pain is in the pelvis joint. Lie on your back. If I'm right, one leg will be longer than the other."

I lay on my back on the treatment table. He held my ankles.

"Yes," he said, "one leg's longer than the other. Turn over on your front."

He again massaged oil into my lower back with a circular movement of his right hand.

I said, "In the old days, your dad would have me on my left side and hold an arm and rock me with a finger at the base of my spine, to push anything back in place."

He said, "I do things slightly differently. We were both taught by the same man. My dad was taught at the beginning of this authority's career and I was taught by him at the end of his career, and he changed his ideas during his career. So I'm now teaching my dad the new way of doing it."

We talked about the necessity of keeping up to date in all fields.

"When I've finished treating you I shall drive to Eastbourne," he said. "I've got no patients till 3, which is why I can be here now. I've got patients from 3 to 7. Then I shall leave with my friend and drive back up to Derby. The tournament is for a fantasy card game, Magic: The Gathering. I was introduced to it when I was thirteen. It had just been created in 1993 by Richard Garfield. Each game represents a battle between wizards. I played the game until I was eighteen and then gave all my old cards to my brother. I returned to the game by Fate a year ago. My wife's best friend had tickets for a trade festival at the Eastbourne Conference Centre and couldn't go, so she gave the tickets to my wife, who took me. As we walked round I saw a table with Magic: The Gathering and I said, 'I used to play that.' My wife said, 'You should take it up again.' I said, 'It'll cost a lot of money.' She quietly bought me a £5 ticket to enter a tournament. There were 3,000 playing nine 'rounds' and scoring points, and I won, by 0.2 of a point. Luck was with me throughout the game, Fate. I've had the same cards since and the same players, but Luck wasn't with me anything like how she was that game. The teenagers were shocked that I won as I was older than them. I told them I had the old cards but my brother got rid of them. They're worth a fortune now, thousands. Twenty million play the game now. I sold other bits and pieces I still had to a Magic shop for several thousand pounds. I've spent £6,000 on buying new cards and equipment.

"Anyway, in Derby this weekend there will be 4,000 in a large room playing at lots of tables with aisles, nine rounds, and I'm looking to win. Then I'll go to the US to play for England, and my wife will come with me. I'm used to being the best because before I found Magic: The Gathering again I played video games and was world champion at *Warframe*. I am the best in the world. But I don't acknowledge my game name so I've given the £20,000 I've won to a children's charity. People laugh when I say I'm the world's best video games player. But Magic: The Gathering is different.

"Now," he said, "I'll put your pelvis back. It's twisted. Turn on your back. Your pelvises should be like this." He showed me his two hands with his thumbs standing up. "But yours are like this." He moved one thumb further upwards. "That's the knobble. I'm going to magic it so the knobble is back down, where it should be. First I need to pull your legs so both legs are the same length. Hold on."

He pulled hard at my right ankle. My leg felt it was coming out of its socket. I slid along the treatment table.

"Good. Now put your knees up. Press your knees against my hands."

I pressed my knees inwards and he pushed them sharply back outwards and there was a sharp stab in my groin.

"It's back. Turn on your front. Yes, both sides of your back are flat. There's no knobble now. Get dressed."

He left the room to write up my notes. Now I could cross my legs. I left the treatment room and went to where he was sitting at the desk and paid him.

"As if by magic, I'm cured," I said.

He said, "The man I treated before you this morning has been to my dad for many years but he said, 'I like the way you do things, I'll come to you from now on.'"

I nodded.

As I walked back to my car I reflected that I had tripped and fallen in the gym and without realising it had twisted my right pelvis in saving myself. He had been in charge and was confident of his diagnoses. He had tugged at my ankles and pushed hard against my closing knees to untwist my pelvis. He had shown a knowledge of how the bones in my lower back operated, and how to untwist them.

But at heart he was still a child, playing video games and fantasy cards to do with magic. All magicians have techniques and he had had a technique while he performed his magic at the gathering of his patients as if they peopled his fantasy card game.

A Forest Glade and Princess Anne

I still had pain on my left side after the weekend, especially when I got in or out of my car, so I rang and left a message. Martin, my new osteopath, rang me back and said he was free at 10.30.

I found the room behind the shop-window empty. Anyone could have walked in and helped themselves to the money in the desk drawer. I sat down and waited while he finished with his patient. I saw a new oil-painting of Princess Anne propped on a radiator behind his desk.

Martin came out of the treatment room in a smart blue uniform. A middle-aged lady followed, looking in her bag for payment. Martin said, "You can go through."

I went to the treatment room and stripped to my pants. When he came in I showed him a small knobble on my left side. He said, "It's a locked pelvis muscle, it just needs pushing in."

He spread a role of paper towel over the couch and I lay face down with my mouth over the hole while he rubbed oil with circular movements of his right hand in the middle of my pelvis.

"How did you get on in Derby?" I asked.

"All right," he said. "Each game is a battle between wizards. On Saturday we had the standard, three games, and I won all three. But then we had the draft. The cards are machine-shuffled and you have three booster packs and have to build a forty-card deck. I had three cards that were good value but were useless in playing an opponent. Basically I had a rubbish hand. And I lost. I was disappointed. But my friend Ryan won all eight of his games – standard, draft and modern – and he's joined the National team, he's going to Las Vegas. I'm pleased for him. I told him mid-week, 'You've got to believe in yourself.' I talked him into winning. There are several in the National team. There were about 2,500 who were playing but only 390 qualified to compete for the National team, I was one of them. We sat in a hall with an enormous digger in the middle. It must have still been a building site, it all looked very new. We were in rows like a clock face, like the hands on a clock.

"My favourite card has always been of a forest glade, because it reminds me of when my dad took me to see the sunrise through the trees in Epping Forest. We took a rug to lie down and watch it because of the dew. The artist who painted the pictures on the cards is very famous, John Avon, and he was there, walking about, and after I'd won my three standard games I stood up and talked to him when he came by. I told him about that card and what it meant to me, and he told he hadn't been painting for a while as he had been depressed. I showed him an acupuncture point he could press to get himself out of his depression. When he heard I'm an osteopath he asked me questions about his back and I was able to treat him while we spoke. He said, 'Wait here a minute, don't go yet,' and he came back with a last poster of the card I'd been telling him about, and he signed it 'Best wishes from your friend, John Avon'. I was so pleased. It's going on my wall.

"When I got back my dad gave me an oil-painting he had commissioned of Princess Anne. When I qualified as an osteopath I got my certificate from her. It's to go in my practice in Eastbourne, on a wall. He said I should put up my qualifications and that oil-painting. I'm not so sure, it's a form of boasting. I don't know where I'll put the painting, I'd rather have the poster of the forest glade on my wall in Eastbourne. I'll have to think where Princess Anne is to go."

Then he said, "Now we'll do the manipulation. Turn on your right side."

He held my right arm and folded it over and took my left arm and wrapped me into a parcel and thrust his two hands hard down on the left side of my pelvis and said, as I recovered from being winded, "That's it, I heard the click, it's in."

I got off the couch with ease and knew I would be able to get in and out of my car now. As I paid him, standing near Princess Anne behind his desk while the next patient went through to the treatment room, he showed me a picture of Ryan on his phone. It was too tiny for me to see properly; I just saw a young man with hair. He showed me the messages he had sent him. He said, "I haven't got a picture of the forest glade. The poster is in my car."

I shook his hand and said I did not expect to have to visit him for a while. He stood up and headed for the treatment room. I lingered and looked at Princess Anne and thought about the forest glade. He was holding the fort for his father, and he vividly remembered watching the sunrise through trees when he was very young, and now he had an endorsement of his position in the form of a painting of the royal lady who had given him a certificate proving his qualification. He had taken a different path from his father into Magic cards but deep in his mind he was still lying on a rug in a forest glade with him, waiting for the sun to rise. His two pictures on his Eastbourne wall were different expressions of his father's love.

Rage and Tattoos

I arrived early and sat in the front row of the pillared hall just seats from a mobile platform on which stood a desk and three chairs, and a lectern. The screen behind it asked, "Who wrote Shakespeare?" and from time to time turned into seven images of Shakespeare. Three hundred crowded in and filled the seats behind me, and at 6.45 Sir Jeremy Boxham led a procession, wearing a pink suit and pink striped shirt and spectacles, and placed his papers on the desk above where I sat. He spotted me and nodded.

Behind him was Alex, the grandson of a famous 1920s novelist, and after a greeting at the lectern from a representative of the hall the moderator spoke from where she sat. All three at the desk wore wireless microphones.

The moderator was a youngish lady with long blonde hair in a pony-tail and an uncertain manner. She said that Alex and Jeremy Boxham were friends and had often talked Shakespeare, but had not debated publicly against each other before. She was the wife of a Conservative MP and had written a novel set in the 17th century, and she had bearing. Jeremy Boxham sat grimly staring at his papers while she summarised his career and glanced nervously in his direction several times. Then she invited Alex to speak for 15 minutes.

He stood to cheers in a suit, white shirt and tie with curly hair round his egg-shaped head, and he spoke rapidly and irritably. He said that 'Shakespeare' was a pseudonym, and quoted a dozen writers soon after Shakespeare's time whose phrases ("disguised", "masking through" and such like) allegedly declared that Shakespeare's works were not written by Shakespeare but by an aristocrat.

Jeremy Boxham then had 15 minutes. He said that Alex's family were contrary and loved an aristocrat. He read a list of all the Earls who were candidates to have written Shakespeare's works, including the 1st Earl of Essex, the 2nd Earl of Essex, the 3rd Earl of Southampton, the 3rd Earl of Pembroke, the 4th Earl of Pembroke and the 5th Earl of Rutland. The numbers carried on going up by one until he came to the 17th Earl of Oxford. He said that Shakespeare's identity had not been doubted for 240 years, that his tomb described him as a great writer with wit, with the wisdom of Socrates and the art of Virgil. He said that Jonson and many other writers including Meres talked of Shakespeare as a writer, that the handwriting of the 1612 signature corresponded to three pages of a play not performed in his day, *Sir Thomas More*, the 'a' being confused with a 'u'. He said the manuscripts of 600 plays had been destroyed as foul copies once the plays were performed, but this manuscript had survived because the play was not performed. He said that Shakespeare's collaborations with Fletcher had been confirmed stylistically by computer analysis. Shakespeare had given three rings to three actors under his will: Heminges, Condell and Burbage. He said that Jonson never went to Italy yet wrote *Volpone*, and that Webster never went to Italy yet wrote *The Duchess of Malfi*, and that Shakespeare never went to Italy but got information about Venice and other places in the plays from George Bryan, Thomas Pope and William Kempe, actors he played with who had visited Italy. And Shakespeare heard about Elsinore, where Hamlet was partly set, from Kempe, who had been there.

Alex was then allowed to rebut Jeremy Boxham. He said Boxham had got so much wrong it would take longer than 15 minutes. He said Shakespeare's wit was not referred to on the tomb and angrily recited a list of authors who had doubted the authorship during the first 240 years after Shakespeare's death. He said the 'five-Act' format was earlier than Boxham had said. He said that the three pages from *Sir Thomas More* were not in Shakespeare's hand. He worked himself into a frenzy and in an explosion of rage he said, "Fifteen minutes was too short a time for me to open my presentation. I had more to say that I could not say." He said he had discovered that Shakespeare was buried in Westminster Abbey – not Stratford – but would say no more on this occasion as there would be a special announcement in the near future. He said there was no evidence that the Stratfordian 'Shakespeare' had any education.

Boxham, rebutting Alex, said that Shakespeare's father, John Shakespeare, was a town councillor, and that town councillors were allowed to send their children to the Stratford grammar school, and that although the roll of entrants was lost Shakespeare must have attended the grammar school as the son of a town councillor. There he would have encountered the Latin poets he needed for his works. He did not go to university like the other dramatists of his time, and this was noted several times.

There were questions from the floor through a hand-held microphone: about Shakespeare's education, about academia's hostility towards those who raised the authorship question, and about the collaborations. And then I heard a familiar voice and turned and saw the famous actor Sir Richard Florid standing, looking like a homeless man with tattooed arms, asking about the Sonnets.

Boxham replied deferentially, saying he had asked a good question, and spoke of Shakespeare's 'bisexual imagination'. He pointed out that Shakespeare had said, "My name is Will," a self-identification.

There was an explosion of rage from Alex, who said, "That's stupid, it's bonkers. It's all wrong, no one's going to write that their name is a shortened name. Today if a writer wrote, 'My name is Chris' or 'Rob' or 'Sam' we'd think him bonkers." There was laughter.

Boxham said, "Jonson wrote, 'I, Ben Jonson.' He didn't call himself 'Benjamin'."

The questions revived points already made and resulted in repetitions. It was said from the floor that there were interpolations in Shakespeare's will, and that "Hamnet" was not "Hamlet". Boxham said, "Hamnet and Hamlet are variant spellings."

Eventually there was a summing-up. Boxham stressed, "Everyone has a distinctive linguistic register and this can be measured on a database now the entire *corpus* of a writer is online. The Warwickshire words are clear: keech, dowl, dey."

Alex said angrily, "I don't accept those words. Shakespeare's vocabulary was 31,000 words, of which 21 were allegedly Warwickshire and it's been demonstrated that those 21 words were widely used and weren't just Warwickshire words." He listed well-known readers who had doubted Shakespeare's identity from Freud to Ted Hughes.

The moderator held a vote. "Hands up who thinks Shakespeare wrote Shakespeare." I put my left arm up. She asked for another show of hands to the contrary. Impressionistically she then said, "It's a tie."

It was a tactful ending to her moderating, and everyone laughed.

I stood up. Alex crossed the platform and embraced his good friend Boxham. I then stepped forward to the desk and said to Boxham, who bent, "I reckon you won. See you in nine days' time. We'll look back on it then."

"Yes," he said, "in nine days' time."

As I headed for the door I saw Sir Richard Florid sitting and talking to his neighbour. There were empty chairs in front of him and I entered that row and crossed towards him. He saw me coming and beamed and we shook hands. "You're looking well," he said. Then he turned back to his neighbour to finish his conversation.

I studied his tattoos. He was wearing no sleeves in an actorish, hippy outfit that again made me think of a homeless man. The tattoos were like two interwoven strands of vine leaves that crossed and recrossed at regular twisted intervals like DNA. The tattoos went from his wrists right up the insides of his arms.

What if he was cast to play a Roman Emperor? His tattoos would have to be covered up with make-up. I saw Derek Jacobi sitting on the far side of the hall. He had played the Roman Emperor Claudius as a stammerer on TV. He was wearing a jacket, but I was sure he had no tattoos.

As I headed for the door I thought of the learned points made by both sides which had driven Alex to passionate rage, and I thought of Sir Richard Florid's tattoos. The theatrical debate on the authorship and its muscular scholarship that would live long in our memories had resembled in-your-face indelible tattoos up the inside of an actor's arms.

Knocked-Over Glasses and a Ringing Phone (Or: Sixty Years and a Fool)

I went back to Oxford for a gaudy at the end of September. I made my way to the new building which had a large glassy foyer and a tiered wooden lecture room. Tea was laid out in a large bar area with a view over the sports field. More than a hundred of us Old Boys stood around wearing jackets and ties, chatting and waiting for something to happen. Then the Provost Jeremy Boxham came in, in a bluish suit, open-necked heavily-striped green-and-white shirt, spectacles and grey parted hair in a slight wave.

He saw me and came and said, "Thank you for coming to hear me in London."

For a few minutes we talked Shakespeare. He said, "I was unable to convince many there."

I said, "Some of them are obsessive about who Shakespeare was, you were never going to convince some of them. But Alex was not evidential, it was all speculative."

He nodded.

I said his point about the 1612 signature and the 'a's in *Sir Thomas More* was a good one. I said Alex was not sure of his case as he would not talk about his candidate, Edward de Vere; only about Shakespeare of Stratford. I said, "He claims to have found de Vere's tomb in Westminster Abbey, but that's going to be speculative as well, there will be no clear evidence."

He nodded.

I said, "I saw your review of Plath's early letters this morning. She said Hughes is 'half-French, half-Irish'. I had not heard that before."

"Nor had I."

"I was looking in your book to see if I had missed that, but I didn't."

Eventually he stopped talking literature to me and circulated among the hundred waiting Old Boys, and then herded us into the auditorium. He stood at the lectern on the stage below our tiered seats, among screens that rose automatically from the floor, and said, "This is where I say as if we were in a London tube, 'Mind the doors.'" He pressed a button on his lectern and the many double wooden doors at the back closed automatically. There was a round of applause.

He said the new building had cost £12m (a gift from an Old Boy, the Emir of Qantoosh), and that the panes of glass were so large that only two companies made them throughout the whole of Europe. "And we chose the one that went bankrupt halfway through." There was laughter. He said the building would have a Royal opening in three weeks' time. He talked about the College's need for money, to recruit the best fellows – two had been recruited from Germany and the Netherlands, but both were anxious about accepting because of the situation after Brexit and he was worried that Oxford would not maintain its place as the world's number-one university – and to support the students. "Their debts have risen, they have to pay for maintenance now as there are no longer maintenance grants. And there is a mental-health issue as they are anxious." He said that 40 per cent of Oxford students and his College's students were from independent education, and 60 per cent from the public sector. Speaking without notes he came across well and there was strong applause when he finished.

There was time to kill and I walked in the grounds and saw again where I sat nearly fifty-nine years previously on the morning I gave up the Law. And then I changed into my dinner-jacket in the disabled loo – as I was not staying the night I had not been allocated a room – and then sat in my car and read until it was time for chapel with choral evensong.

I sat in the front row and across the central aisle; facing me I saw Jocelyn Twyford pointing at me and beaming and laughing, saying 'Hello'. He had sleeked-back hair and a ruddy face as if he had a heart problem and very expressive looks that projected his emotions like a highly-skilled actor who was aware he was playing the fool. Jeremy Boxham read a lesson clad in a long gown and Jocelyn Twyford was disconcertingly in my line of vision.

Drinks were in an old building the other side of the field. There were only six from my year there, including Jocelyn Twyford and me, and I did not know any of them well. I took a glass of champagne from a tray and stood in the crowded room and talked to a retired judge who was now a cross-bencher in the Lords and spoke on the state of English Law after Brexit. Then I saw Jocelyn Twyford approach. He helped himself to a glass of champagne from the drinks table just behind the Lord and turned to speak to us and – crash! Another glass of champagne fell and smashed and champagne ran onto the Lord's trousers. The glass had been caught by the back of Jocelyn Twyford's jacket.

"Sorry," Jocelyn Twyford laughed as the Lord grabbed a napkin and dabbed at the front of his trousers. Jocelyn Twyford laughed like the fool I thought he must be, and even the cross-bencher Lord, though cross, joined in the laughter before disappearing to the washroom.

Then I saw my old Law tutor, whose clutches I had escaped fifty-nine years previously, and I crossed and greeted him and told him that a document I had had to write had drawn on his Roman-Law classes all those years ago.

After half an hour we were called to go to the dining-hall. It was dimly lit and, nearest to top table, the six in my year swung elderly legs with difficulty over the benches to sit at the long table. I sat with a log fire leaping at my back and suddenly realised I was sitting in the very place where I took the week-long entrance exam sixty years previously the coming December. The tables were candlelit and the light dingy, and it all came back. I was sitting with a warm fire at my back in a shadow, and had difficulty in reading the examination paper and my own work, especially when after 3.30 the outside December light began to fade. The afternoon exams did not finish until 5.

I announced to the rest of my year that I was sitting in the identical place where I took the entrance exam sixty years previously. They were impressed. I was opposite Jocelyn Twyford. Weirdly, there was a triangle between Jocelyn Twyford, Jeremy Boxham on top table, and me. I was also opposite Bertrand Warner.

Bertrand Warner, now eighty-four and eager to collect my view on Brexit, was older than the rest of us, having joined our year while already working in the Foreign Office.

We had sole paupiette with scallop mousse, and progressed to juniper-crusted venison loin with black pudding and wild mushroom pithivier. I was served first white, then red wine, and sipped to taste each but then drank sparkling water as I would have to drive home later. At one point Jocelyn Twyford leaned across the table and said of his neighbour (who was a year below us), "We've been talking glebeland."

He said later, "I'm on the diocese. I live in a rural community near here. The Council wants to sell glebeland for building land but I know the local sensitivities and mark them in the margin of the official document. I'm a kind of community consultant. What's your see?"

I said we were under the Bishop of Chelmsford.

"Stephen Cottrell. He's a seriously good egg. I know him."

And now he came across as a shrewd adviser.

But then he said, "I'm going to check my phone. I'm sorry to be crass, but my wife is visiting her mother in a local hospital. She's just had an operation, and I need to go when she rings." He checked his phone. "Nothing, that's all right."

We were served apple-and-blackberry brioche pudding, and then cheese and biscuits, coffee and *petit fours*. Suddenly there was a crash and a tide of white wine approached my pudding bowl. Jocelyn Twyford had knocked over his wine glass. My pudding bowl acted as a dam and it did not pour onto my trousers as it had on the Lord's.

Jocelyn Twyford said to a Polish waiter, "I'm sorry, I've foolishly knocked my glass over. Can you bring a cloth to place over the wet tablecloth? And bring me some more wine?"

The others in our year were beside themselves with suppressed mirth. I had been coping with not having the wine spill onto my dinner-jacket, and had not joined the general merriment until I had checked that some wine that had reached my napkin on my knees had not reached my trousers. The Polish waiter brought two paper serviettes bearing the College crest.

At around 10.15pm Jeremy Boxham stood to speak, still wearing his long gown. He told us, "This is your hall." He said it was about to be redecorated for six months as the paint was flaking off and bits were falling onto the floor. The Victorian panelling we had all known as undergraduates would not be returned, it would still be Georgian in style but would have panels to improve the acoustics near the bottom, and underfloor heating.

"Tomorrow the new students will be starting with us. You have all been through that and remember how you felt, and you may want to donate to the College to help them get through the same experience." Then he said what excellent progress the College was making, and how it had come fourth in the University's Norrington table. "Standards are high, but thanks to the grounds and drama, the students take it in their stride and don't get anxious."

Suddenly there was a loud ringing sound. Jocelyn Twyford clutched his pocket and produced his ringing phone. He tried to turn it off and failed. He stood up and with difficulty extracted his legs and swung now one, now the other over the bench. He headed for the door fighting his phone. He successfully stopped it.

Jeremy Boxham stopped speaking. All eyes in the hall were on Jocelyn Twyford. We tried to suppress our mirth.

Jocelyn Twyford turned round and caught my eye. He was the centre of attention throughout the entire hall. He pulled a triumphant face. He was a perfect fool.

Then the phone began ringing again. This time no amount of fighting with it could silence the ringing. Grimacing, Jocelyn Twyford turned and headed for the door, pushed it outwards and disappeared into the night. Even after the door closed I could still hear a distant ringing.

Jocelyn Twyford wisely did not come back. He had evidently received the call to visit his mother-in-law.

The six of us were shaking with laughter and trying to keep a straight face as Jeremy Boxham continued. If any of us had been asked in advance who would be the most likely of all those in the hall to perform foolish acts – to knock over and break a glass of champagne and knock over a glass of white wine and then interrupt the main speech with a ringing phone not once but twice – we would all have said without hesitation: Jocelyn Twyford. It simply could not have been anyone else.

I had been reconstructing – acting out – a memory from nearly sixty years ago, sitting where I sat the entrance exam, and the past crowding back into my mind had been invaded by the carelessness of a fool. Or was his clumsiness due to a medical condition, perhaps a slight stroke, of which we were all unaware and ignorant? And perhaps *I* was the fool for not having seen this?

Hand-Made Bricks and a Wall

"Do you remember Mandy?" Pippa said when she was sitting down after her monthly group had left. "I told you about her husband, how he had many things wrong with him. He had a broken hip and went into hospital and fell out of bed and broke his arm and ended up worse than he went in. She developed shingles and other things wrong with her and as she said over tea, it affected her mind. She told us a story that took about twenty minutes and left us all appalled. But I'm telling you in less than twenty minutes. Anyway, with all that going on she was rushed off her feet, and someone they'd known for years, who'd done odd jobs for them, who they both trusted more than anyone else, Sean, helped them. He visited her husband and sat with him and he looked after her, drove her to the hospital because she doesn't drive, fetched and carried. And with so much illness happening, because they trusted him more than anyone else they gave him a power of attorney. They have no children and were afraid they'd get too ill to cope with their house.

"They live in Benders' Hill, and there was a problem with a wall at the back. It was falling down. He offered to fix it for them, and he did. It was quite a big job. He bought the bricks. More of that in a minute. Then the wall at the front had problems. It was a smaller wall, and he asked if he could do that too. She said to us, 'I was so beleaguered with all the medical problems I didn't want to think about it, so I said "Yes".' He went away and did his calculations and came back and said, 'It will need hand-made bricks. I can do it for £6,750, but if it's for cash, just £6,000.'

"She was shocked at the amount but her mind was on her husband, and she went along with it. They went to Santander, and she asked to withdraw £6,000. The cashier said (with him listening), 'Are you sure you want to do this? It's a lot of money.' But she said, 'Yes, yes I want to do it.' So she received £6,000 in £20 notes all paper-banded in small piles. She gave them to him.

"Three weeks went by. She didn't hear from him so she rang. He said, 'I'm working on it. I've bought the bricks and I've made arrangements for a skip.' Another three weeks went by, and she became suspicious. She doesn't use her computer, but with one finger she found the builders' merchants that had supplied the bricks. She rang them. A man said, 'They're not hand-made bricks, and the total came to £500. I've got the receipt here.' So she had paid him £6,000 and the bricks were £500.

"She didn't want to worry her sick husband so she discussed the situation with people she knew. They all said, 'Call the police.' So she did. A female police officer came and spent an hour with her. Mandy told her she had given him £17,000 for the back wall. She said that wall had been badly built, it had sand instead of cement in places and parts were already falling down. The police officer said, 'He's a conman. He's been grooming you.' This was a shock. She said to her, 'But we trust him. We've given him a power of attorney.' (He hasn't got a power of attorney now.) The police officer said, 'You have proof, the builders' merchant's receipt. This could result in a custodial sentence.' Mandy didn't want him to go to prison on her account after all he'd done for them.

"She knew Sean so well that she knew his family, especially his mother-in-law, and she asked her to come round. She told her what had happened and mentioned the £17,000 as well. At first his mother-in-law defended him and pointed out he had two small children. The mother-in-law said, 'I don't know where the money's gone, they live from hand to mouth, it's not getting to my daughter or the children.' Mandy asked the mother-in-law to make sure Sean came to see her.

"Sean came round, abject, sorry. She said of his over-charging, 'I've been advised by the police that you could go to prison but I'm thinking of your two young children. You must never do this again to anyone. And I want my £6,000 back.'

"He went away and returned with £2,500 and excuses. She said, 'I want it all.' He reluctantly returned with another £500 and more excuses. She said, 'I want it all.' He returned with another £2,000 making £5,000 in all. The paper-banding round the notes was identical to what she had received from the Santander cashier, they were the exact notes she had given him. She said, 'I want the remaining £1,000.' Then he got nasty, and said his honour was being impugned.

"He had spent it, but he returned, having borrowed it from the in-laws. He was surly and slammed down the last £1,000. He said angrily, 'You've cast aspersions on my good name. You've questioned my integrity. I've worked for well-known people.' He mentioned a couple of names. Then he said, 'I've worked for Mrs. Rawley.'

"Mandy said, 'Oh, I know her. What work have you done for her?'

"He backtracked, and eventually said, 'No, I didn't do the work, I just quoted.' But he didn't," Pippa said.

I said, "It's interesting that Mrs. Rawley is held up as an icon to work for."

She nodded.

"Mandy then found out that one of her friends had got him to quote for her ninety-year-old mother. So she put a stop to that quotation.

"Mandy told us at the end, 'When you're elderly, you have to watch out for being conned even by those you most trust.' Dr Pannier said he felt sick."

So here was someone she and her husband had trusted so much that they had given him a power of attorney over their assets and their house in case anything happened to them and they were both too ill to cope. He conned them by telling them the bricks had to be hand-made bricks and upped the price by about six times – having done the same to get £17,000 out of her. And as he built the wall – and that one, too, had begun to fall down in places – a barrier went up between them.

The trusting relationship between them which had been enshrined in a power of attorney now had a wall across it. He had walled himself out from their trust.

The loving, hands-on care he had put into sitting with her husband and driving her were like hand-made bricks, and when Mandy had found out from the builders' merchants what was going on, it was as if he built a wall between him and the object of his affectionate attention for so many years. I shook my head in disbelief and wondered at the self-interested darkness within the human heart and the evil kink in human nature that had put it there.

A Bid and a Junction

I walked to the evening reception alongside the Forest and arrived at shut electric gates at 7.40pm. A man in a navy body warmer emerged from the bushes. I wondered if he was a plain-clothes police officer or a privately-hired security guard. He asked if I was going to Manor Court and keyed in a code which opened the gates. In the entrance hall I took a glass of champagne and nodded to people talking in a circle. I saw Edith Small in a back room all on her own. I turned left into a narrow corridor and encountered burly black-haired Gordon Strawson coming the other way.

"Hello," he said, stopping.

We talked in the corridor.

"What's the atmosphere like in Parliament?" I asked.

Sexual harassment was the running issue, and there were daily complaints against different MPs for inappropriate behaviour going back several years, a trend that had spread from Hollywood to the Palace of Westminster. The experienced Secretary of State for Defence had resigned and been replaced by the Chief Whip, who had no ministerial experience.

"It's 'Oh, not another one.'"

I nodded and went through into the large sitting-room, where 150 people stood talking loudly, holding champagne. I knew nobody. Gone were the days when it was like a parents' evening and I used to accost the Planning Officer with news of the latest planning application. I hovered by the central table and helped myself to nuts. I would have liked to sit down but there were only half a dozen chairs at one end and they were taken by elderly guests and everyone else had to stand.

Then I saw Gordon Strawson talking to a dark-haired lady near the door, and returned past groups of people to him.

The lady greeted me as though she knew me: "Are you still at the house? Did you walk tonight?"

I could not place her, so I said, "Yes, yes, I did walk."

"With your wife?"

"No, she can't come. She had a cataract operation yesterday and she's convalescing."

We were served cocktail sausages on sticks.

To Gordon I said, "We were in mid-conversation."

"Yes, sorry."

I said, "Last time I saw you, you were Chairman of the Committee for Science and Technology."

"Yes, I lost the Chairmanship –"

"Because of the unnecessary election."

"That's right. The election was bad for me. The Chairmanship had to go to the Liberal Democrats. My career has gone into nosedive."

"You'll come out of it. Give my best wishes to Ava." (Ava was his wife.)

"I will. She's got a job now. She's working in a school for retarded and autistic children, helping the leavers to find work in the community. I want to talk further with you on this –"

At that moment the cocky Sam Smith, who had stood for MP unsuccessfully, barged in. He shook hands all round with a past Chairman of the Association's self-importance, took Gordon to one side to discuss arrangements and then led him off to the other side of the room.

There were more *canapés*. Holding my champagne in one hand I took a pastry being offered and put it in my mouth with my free hand. I felt a searing pain on my tongue. The pastry had just come from the oven and was burning. I munched in agony and could not speak.

Then Bill Temple from the nursery across the road from me joined us and I realised I had been talking to his wife Sally. Unable to speak, I shook his hand.

At that moment the guest of honour, the Secretary of State for Transport and former Lord Chancellor, a Brexiteer, came in, holding a glass of champagne. He had carefully trimmed hair round his bald head and was sprucely turned out, with a buttonhole stitched in white.

Edith Small was behind him. She pointed at me in greeting, said, "I want to speak to you," and then absconded into the standing guests.

The Secretary of State for Transport saw me and perhaps because I am tall – he was 6 foot 5 – he shook my hand.

I said we had met at Hilda Strawson's. "How's the atmosphere in Parliament?" I asked after he had shaken hands with Bill and Sally.

"Not too bad." He began to speak about sexual harassment.

I interrupted him: "Fallon was good, he stood up to the Russians."

"Yes, he did."

"And the EU. Are you confident, is it going well?"

"Yes, we're confident." He did not say that it was going well.

"Davis and the PM aren't depressed and in gloom?"

"No, we're all confident."

"After the resignation of Fallon I thought there might be a little reshuffle and Boris Johnson might be moved to look after the Party and you might be made Foreign Secretary."

He stared at me. I had surprised him.

"Stranger things have happened, you never know."

I sensed he already knew that he might become Foreign Secretary. I said, "I have a project on global Britain involving reforming the UN. If you're Foreign Secretary I shall ask Edith Small to arrange for me to come and see you, and I'll visit you if I may and explain it to you."

"Yes, do come and see me if I become Foreign Secretary. I'll look forward to that."

Bill and Sally had listened in silence.

The Secretary of State for Transport said, "I've only just arrived, I'd better circulate." And he moved away.

I chatted on and then headed across the room between talking groups to speak to Edith Small. She was being briefed about the coming auction. I looked at the items on display, envelopes with tickets for events, pictures of two past Ministers with handwritten messages beneath, two books on Brexit. Then Edith saw me and came to be kissed.

"You got my email?" I asked.

"Yes, I did," she said in her Scottish accent.

"I'm serious about approaching the UN with an initiative for global Britain, with some official backing."

"Unfortunately my contact at the UN has just been withdrawn by the Foreign Office. He's back over here."

Then Sam Smith approached. As Chairman of the Association he had points to discuss regarding the auction. Edith talked on to me, but he was at her elbow and trying to interrupt.

I said to her, "I'll be in touch with you next month."

She said, "I'll speak to you later. I want to speak to you." And she turned aside to go to the display table.

The Association's current Chairman, an Asian councillor, called for silence, and Edith shouted, "Order, order," her Deputy Speaker's call. The councillor then made quite a long speech thanking individuals, and handed over to Edith Small.

Edith said, "I have nearly got a bad throat. Of course, I am strictly neutral and impartial when I am Deputy Speaker" – there was laughter – "but I was Deputy Speaker last night, and the Labour Party gave me such a hard time I've nearly lost my voice. Anyway…." She introduced the Secretary of State for Transport. "We've known each other for many years," she said.

The Secretary of State for Transport spoke fluently and quietly for 20 minutes. He paid tribute to Gordon Strawson, his former PPS, and to Sam Smith, his special policy adviser for the last two years. I was shocked. I had not realised he was a special policy adviser.

Much of what he said was about Brexit and how well things were going, and how it was in the interests of the EU countries to reach a deal, and what nonsense it was to say there would be no flights to Europe if there was no deal. He ended by saying, "There is a cloud on the horizon. The Labour Party is like nothing we've experienced before. They're Communists. They had a leg-up at the last election because the young don't know what it was like when we had State ownership, when we had British Leyland and British Rail and all the strikes. They must be stopped at all costs by argument. We've got three and a half years to make the arguments."

Edith Small thanked the Secretary of State for Transport and said, "We're going to start the auction shortly. We want every glass filled. We want you to be full of champagne so you will be generous with your wallets."

The auction then began. Edith Small read out details of a lot being auctioned, and Gordon Strawson did the actual auctioning. Four tickets for a week at a hotel on a famous golf course near Chester were bought, after bidding, by an ostentatious, loud, tall man in a dark suit with black hair who was holding a champagne glass and sipped repeatedly, called Mike Bentley, a developer who lived in Kent and had bought a local golf course in Edith Small's constituency. He seemed to want to brag about the money he had, and he was linked to a flamboyant dyed-blonde woman standing apart from him near the speakers. He won the four tickets for £800 and she pushed through the bidders behind her to kiss him in thanks.

There were then two tickets for a concert featuring the pop group The Script at the O2 in February. Again there was competition and the tickets went for £600 – again to Mike. And again the flamboyant lady turned and pushed through the bidders to give him a kiss for winning.

Then the two pictures of Ministers were sold. One was of Nigel Lawson with, in his own hand, a text in Latin, which Edith Small translated to laughter as: "The job of Chancellor requires a lot of hard work and a lot of bloody lucko." Again Mike won the two pictures, for £300. This time the woman cheered raucously.

There were two massive Jeroboams of red wine (each holding the equivalent of six bottles), which, after competition, Mike also won for £600, and this time the lady's push-through and kiss seemed very attention-seeking.

Finally came the *pièces de résistance*: two books on Brexit. Edith announced, "One is by Tim Shipman, *All Out War*." She did not read out the subtitle: *The full story of how Brexit sank Britain's political class.* "I've read every page, what happened during the referendum campaign, and it's true. It's signed by the three main Brexiteers: David Davis, Liam Fox and our guest of honour. Then there's a book by Liam Fox, *Rising Tides*. It's signed. It's about threats to global stability."

Gordon Strawson said, "What shall we start with? £50?"

The bidding went up to £600. Mike seemed to have won the two books. Suddenly he lurched and half-fell backwards. Someone behind saved him from falling, but he spilled his champagne on the fawn carpet.

There was a lull in the bidding. A waitress came in with a salt cellar and shook salt onto the fawn carpet. Someone had a word with our host, the owner of the carpet, who nodded phlegmatically and turned his attention back to the bidding. It seemed that Mike was drunk and had nearly fallen over.

The bidding continued. Mike shouted, "Twelve hundred pounds."

Edith and Gordon had not heard because of the background chatter.

"Twelve hundred pounds," Mike shouted, perhaps trying to cover up or compensate for his spillage, which had held up the proceedings and inconvenienced everyone. There was applause and Sam Smith stepped forward and whispered to Edith and Gordon to explain the situation, as a policy adviser should.

"That's magnificent," Gordon said. "Any advance on twelve hundred pounds?"

Mike shouted: "Two thousand five hundred pounds."

Everyone in the room was stunned. There was renewed applause. The atmosphere was one of astonishment. The spillage of wine was now completely forgotten. The two books could be bought from Amazon for £6.98, and he had overpaid by nearly £2,500.

Mike was drunk, he had stumbled backwards. He was a fool, he had made judgements about his money while under the influence of alcohol. But he was also a donor. He had made a donation in the form of buying every item being auctioned, funding the entire auction takings, and collectively the 150 people in the room admired that.

All right, I thought, he's decided to make a donation to the party in the form of winning all the bids at an auction, but he's doing it in a show-off, self-important, boastful manner that is actually quite objectionable. It was 'In your face' and 'Look at me' and 'I've got more than any of you', and Essex; and I did not want to be among such people. I thought, 'What am I doing here, condoning this vaunting of wealth?'

"I want you to sign it with a message," Mike called out to the Secretary of State for Transport. "To M2, junction 5."

Mike was publicly asking the Secretary of State for Transport to endorse by implication his plan to develop a local golf course, and perhaps another development in Kent near the M2 junction 5, in return for his donation. It was blurted humorously but it smacked of appalling corruption. He seemed to be attempting to buy a policy from the Secretary of State for Transport, he seemed to be bribing the Minister.

The Secretary of State for Transport said in a rebuffing tone, "I'll write my own message," and he opened the copy of *All Out War* and wrote in the front. Mike pushed his way through to the front of the bidders and stood beside the Secretary of State for Transport to receive his signed book.

There was more applause and that was the end of the auction.

"We're going to have the raffle now," Edith Small said, "but first you should refill your glasses."

I had bought a raffle ticket for £5 and had written my name on the ticket, which had been put in the draw. But my back was aching from all the standing. It was nearly 10 o'clock, the party was supposed to end at 9.30pm. I had not sat down, because there was nowhere to sit, for getting on for three hours. It was announced that the Secretary of State for Transport was leaving. As he walked past me he nodded to me. I let a minute pass and then quietly slipped away.

I walked down the dark drive. The electric gates were closed. I peered at the lit keypad the security guard had keyed an entry code into, but there was no indication of how to get the gates open. The gates were very high to climb. They had steel spikes, and I was in a suit I did not want to tear.

Then behind me a car's headlights approached. I saw the Secretary of State for Transport in the front passenger's seat tapping on his mobile phone, perhaps entering the code to open the gates. The gates swung slowly open. I waved in acknowledgment to him and strode out in front of his car.

The half-drunken atmosphere of the auction had gone and had been replaced by sober coping with gates in the dark for both the Minister and me. As I walked home I reflected on the ostentatious display of wealth we had all witnessed. It was vulgar. It was Mike saying to 150 people, 'Look at how much wealth I've got, I can buy influence and get junctions built if I want.' It was an obscene display, like something from the early Roman principate. He had shown off his money, thrust it into our faces. He had no taste, he was a *nouveau riche* trying to impress, he wanted to be in with the Secretary of State for Transport. But now the moment had passed. Out in the cold dark the boasting seemed folly, and the Secretary of State for Transport had switched off and gone, perhaps as nauseated as I was. The bids were supposed to be for party funding but had turned into a request for a junction, and the ignorant bidder did not see what a *faux pas* he had made and in what bad taste his 'joke' had been.

Then I realised he had come with an agenda and an objective: to persuade the Conservative councillors to give him planning permission for his controversial development of the local golf course, which would include giving some land back to the local community. He had come with the calculated intention of winning every lot in the auction to come across as a party donor to the councillors who would be voting on his planning application, most of whom were present, and to obtain what he wanted as a reciprocation. His intake of alcohol, which resulted in the slopping of his champagne on the carpet, was not the cause of his high bid, and his *faux pas* was not a *faux pas* but his statement of his long-term objective which had culminated in the events I had witnessed, and judging from the Minister's writing of his own message, the success of his attempt to develop near the M2, junction 5, where he lived, perhaps a development near his home, was by no means guaranteed.

The Superintendent and the Friends

I changed for the Forest Supper on Thursday evening and stood before Pippa at 6.45, the time she wanted to leave.

"There's a tiny problem," she said. "It's not happening. There's been a mess-up. There's no catering staff, the meal can't happen. The catering staff have been inadvertently booked for tomorrow. I had missed a phone call from Holly and rang back. They're ringing people and telling them not to go. They'll be in the foyer turning people away."

It was appalling organisation by a voluntary group. Dressed up with nowhere to go, we went to Miller & Carter and had steak with peppercorn sauce and then *crème brûlée*.

The next day the Forest Supper was on again. Everyone had paid in advance and the food had been ordered, the event had to happen.

We arrived in the foyer at 7. I wore a blazer, a tie and a sweater, for it was late November and cold. Jillian Appleby, bespectacled, ticked us off on her list. I sympathised with her for having to do it all over again. "What happened yesterday?" I asked.

"The catering staff didn't arrive. We looked back at emails and saw the date was wrong. I don't want to point a finger, these things happen."

I knew her husband Patrick was terminally ill with cancer. She said he had not been able to do his voluntary work in the Forest, clearing and pruning, until last week. We collected glasses of orange in a large ante-room and then entered the large assembly hall. There were ten circular tables with laid places. There were only five places on our table and there were large spaces between each place.

Pippa said, "Jillian told me there were 59 yesterday, and there are 65 today. It's still only half the usual amount. The elderly generation is dying off and not being replaced by the younger generation. That's why the two organisations, the Friends and the Centenary Trust, amalgamated. Together they can't get half the people that one could provide a couple of years ago for an event like this."

Pippa went off to speak to Holly, who was sitting at a table with her Indian husband. I saw Lady Myrtle sitting at the frontmost table, and went over and stooped. She had silver hair and a lined face and she looked very ill. She was nearly bent double, and very tiny.

"How are you?" I asked.

"Not well," she said. "But we won't dwell on that. The world's turned into a horrible place. I don't like what I see."

Taken aback I said, "As we get older we become increasingly alienated from the world out there. The world of our childhood is a different country, a lost kingdom."

"Yes," she said. "I'm ninety-four, you know. I wonder what I'm doing still here. I've had one illness after another, all since Lee died. I've got cancer right now. I live alone, a domestic help comes in from time to time. Yes, I've got stairs but I've got a stairlift. Stanley's very good, he comes to see me every day. He lives so near, only ten minutes away. I can't go out. I've only come here tonight because he's brought me. I've walked in with a stick, but that's all I can do."

Stanley approached, tall in a dark suit, white shirt and tie. "I'm part-time at the school," he said. "I still do the 'A'-level class, UK Government and Politics. I work hard on it to keep ahead of them. My mother helps. I'll soon be retired. I'm on committees."

"And the church," Lady Myrtle said.

"Oh yes, I'm a steward at the church."

"Do you have to read notices at the front of the church?"

"Yes."

He talked on about what he was doing. The Superintendent of the Forest was sitting a couple of places away. He was in his late forties with rimless glasses. I excused myself and crossed and shook his hand. He stood and we chatted at the front of the hall.

"Are you based at The Warren?" I asked. I knew he had been appointed by The City of London nearly ten years previously and ran the organisation of the Forest in a professional way.

"Yes," he said.

We talked about the future of the running of the Forest. He said he would like to visit me to continue the chat. Then I realised that Jillian Appleby was at the microphone on the platform ready to start, and I returned to our table as did Pippa. Theresa Moston sat between us, large and overweight.

A middle-aged man in a suit I did not know sat 'next' to me a long way away. He had blond hair and spectacles. His companion was listed on the guest list as 'guest' followed by his surname.

I asked if he had tried to attend yesterday.

"Yes, they told us in the foyer it was off. We went over the road for something to eat."

We had to fetch our first course from a long table at the side of the hall. We sat and ate chicken with honey-mustard sauce and mashed potatoes. There were two quizzes on our table: 30 clues to radio or TV programmes (with the numbers of letters in each word), which had been compiled by Patrick Appleby's brother. Another quiz was entitled 'Leaves, Trees and Places'. On photocopied pages there were colour photos of a leaf and its tree in a local place. The quiz had been devised by the verderer Patrick Appleby and the Deputy Lord Lieutenant, verderer Gabriel Fellows. We had to state the tree and identify the local place.

By now we had been served our puddings – Pippa and I had panna cotta, lemon tart and cream – and I had collected mint tea for Pippa and green tea for me. The answers to the leaves quiz were announced. Patrick Appleby and the Deputy Lord Lieutenant alternated. Patrick Appleby spoke in a thin voice and stood unsteadily, as he battled his cancer. The two hardest to identify were a wild service tree and a spindle.

Our table won the leaves quiz with 33 correct answers out of 40. Our prize, a large box of chocolates, was brought to our table.

The Superintendent then left. He headed for the door and passed our table. He stopped and gave me his card. "I'll come and visit you," he said.

After the raffle all stood up. I saw the bearded Deputy Lord Lieutenant approaching me, and I extended my hand. We had spoken a couple of years back, as he recalled. He said, "I've got a beard like George the Fifth looking exhausted."

I smiled, "I can't see the exhausted, but yes, it's a George-the-Fifth beard." I asked, "Will you be Lord Lieutenant in due course?"

"No, there isn't time. The Lord Lieutenant will be a lady from Writtle."

I said, "When my cousin died the Lord Lieutenant of Sussex attended his funeral and his sword took up an entire pew. Do you find that with your sword?"

"Yes, but these days you have to hand it over in the porch and it's looked after. At one national event 20 Lord Lieutenants had to leave their swords in the porch and they were in a pile, not looked after, and they all got mixed up. At the end each Lord Lieutenant was trying to identify his sword. No one teaches you how to use a sword. In the end I went to Colchester barracks and had sword tuition. It was very helpful."

We talked about the future of the Forest. He said, "My idea is that The Warren should be handed over to Jillian Appleby's organisations. It makes sense."

I could not see The City of London doing this.

As we came away I said to Pippa, "There's a proposal to take The Warren away from The City of London and give it to the lot we've been with."

"It won't happen," Pippa said. "Jillian's not happy with the support she's been getting. Everything's left to her and her husband, no one does anything. She can't even count on the Friends to get the date right. It will stay with The City of London."

I could not but agree. The organisation of the Friends had been amateurish and shambolic. Jillian and her husband had sent out the invitations, compiled both quizzes, manned the microphone and presumably booked the caterers without help. She had been nursing her husband through his final illness while all this was going on, and attention to detail had understandably suffered. But to take the organisation of the Forest away from the professionally-run City of London and give it to this group of ageing volunteers, whose President was Lady Myrtle and who were all in varying degrees ill, would be chaotic. The Superintendent and the Deputy Lord Lieutenant stood for both views of the Forest organisation and I was sure the *status quo* would be perpetuated.

A Seaside Dream and Institutions

I sat in my window overlooking a grey sea. A message from Alan Frost had taken me back. His father, Rowan, and Pippa and I had shared car journeys to Simon's school, and I had often driven Simon and him. I had found him monosyllabic in those days:

"What have you been doing, Alan?"

"Er."

I rang him and found him fluent.

"Hello Phil, I'm driving," he said, "hands free. It must be thirty years since I last spoke to you. That was when my parents left for Lyme Regis."

I said, "We saw a lot of your parents up to that point. They were very kind to us. They had us to Sunday lunch and your father organised a short game of cricket in the garden. I believe I bowled to you." He laughed. "We've always stayed in touch. We send Christmas cards."

"That's why I've contacted you," he said. "I should have been in touch a year ago. Sadly my father died last year. I found your card a couple of days ago and realised you and Pippa didn't know."

"Oh, I *am* sorry," I said. "He gave up at the Bank of England and went to Lyme and ran a bed-and-breakfast –"

"They sold that home and bought nearby. He had a long history of depression, as you know. He was on lithium, and that led to mental problems. He had TIAs, six we knew about, and many more small strokes. We wondered if the lithium brought on mental deterioration. He was in a mental hospital in the end, and died of cumulated strokes. The house is still there. It's still got his two thousand books but my mother has moved into a nursing home in Lyme. She's got dementia, she doesn't recognise Charles." (Charles was Alan's younger brother.) "He's been a thorn in my flesh for years, and he still is. He turns up and asks for money. I believe he's living in the Hastings area. I'm living near London, and I drive down and see my mother and check the post in the house.

"I've been married to a Polish woman for ten years. We've got two boys. They live in Poland, and speak Polish, Swedish and

English, as she does. They're not far from Berlin. I'm in computers – I'm researching in Hull University right now, a lovely campus – and work allows me to spend a week every month in Poland, so I go back every month. When I'm over here I keep an eye on my mother. We took her out of the nursing home for her eightieth birthday last year, but otherwise she doesn't leave the nursing home. The Council pay her fees every month. I have a power of attorney and reached an agreement with them that the house will be sold on her death and they will recoup what they've spent."

"Good for you," I said.

I thanked Alan for reacting to our Christmas card with this news and after a few more reminiscences rang off. I sat in the window and pondered, a grey wintry sea beneath me.

Rowan had hated the Bank of England and claimed it made him depressed. He had not wanted to go to Lyme, and he complained that Maria had made him go. She had been a teacher and was half Rowan's height and spoke with a demotic accent, but her intentions were commendable. She was looking for a project that would give him a purpose and take him out of his depression and would not be too stressful, and bed-and-breakfast by the sea would mean he would relax for part of each day by the sea. But he was still depressed and whether or not because of the lithium he had TIAs, mini-strokes, and it all went wrong. Between them, they had come to a sad end, her dream of stress-free living by the seaside had ended in their both being institutionalised, and I had a great respect for Alan who was in regular touch with his mother in Lyme Regis despite living between London and Poland.

Anno Domini

I visited Dr Erdmann to hear the results of my blood tests. There was modern art in the waiting-room, a picture of two bulging blob-like round eyes and a bulging stomach and blobby legs, and I realised it was a mirror in which I could find my humanity and proneness to disease.

In his room on the first floor Dr Erdmann presided over human frailty and illness like a god. He reviewed my tests on his screen and urged me to pull my chair round to the side of his long desk so I could see. Then we chatted. I told him I was organising my papers so everything would be tidy when I departed.

In a dark suit, white shirt and tie, with black hair and spectacles, he said, "Don't be introspective, you're not about to die."

I explained that there was a tradition in my family that we all left our affairs in tidy order so the younger relatives had nothing to do.

He retracted and said, "That's admirable." He added, "Individualised scanning saved you from having cancer in two years' time: the polyps. I've known an actress for forty years, she is very famous now, and I found she had early lung cancer. The radiological report said it was all right but I was suspicious. She is now completely cured of cancer. It was the same with you. I was suspicious of the radiological report about the polyps and now you're completely cured."

I was fortunate to be in the hands of a master doctor who could detect any condition by following his instincts. He wanted his patients to be positive and outward-looking, as he was, and he had covered his walls with works of modern art that suggested bodily disease that could be diagnosed and got under control.

We talked about my tendency to nod off between 5 and 6 o'clock, and he said, "That's *Anno Domini*, I'm afraid. There's nothing you can do about it, it's just *Anno Domini*."

To him, old age was a fact of life which had to be accepted with good grace and not dwelt on. And one should keep on doing what had to be done, regardless.

He was like the Greek god Asclepius who could be visited in his temple in the ancient Greek time. His walls had pictures of mortality, distorted beyond immediate recognition by modern art into subtle backgrounds, like drapes in an ancient temple, but nevertheless still there. He sat in his temple like an Oracle and I consulted him and was told enigmatically, "It's *Anno Domini*," and I came away with a new acceptance of my mortality and a still-brimming appetite for life in my remaining years.

A Retirement and a Stranger

With his Christmas card my former bank manager (and later Bursar until he retired) sent me a letter about his wife. He wrote: "She was diagnosed earlier this year with Alzheimer's disease. It wasn't a complete shock to me as I had already noticed the signs the previous year. These prompted a memory test with our GP and then a consultant. Sadly the past few months have seen a slow deterioration, despite the medication, and the intelligent, lively and fun-loving Coleen has effectively been replaced by a stranger possessing none of those qualities. She now has very limited short-term memory and has already lost much of her past. What a cruel disease. So far she has resisted any professional help towards her care and, for the moment, I'm able to cope with her needs. I suspect, however, that in the next year or so I may find it necessary to enlist some help, and my preference would be a live-in carer – the house can easily accommodate such a person – and only resort to a care home when absolutely necessary. It has been five years since I retired and, obviously, this is not the retirement I had hoped for. Bad things can't always happen to other people."

I felt sad. I closed my eyes and saw the warm, vivacious, alert and friendly person who was the old Coleen. Kim had worked hard in the bank and then for me, and his retirement had not turned out as he had hoped. At least it was better than the retirement of his predecessor in the bank who, the week after he retired, went to the Canary Islands and went swimming and drowned. One worked hard, and when those nearest got ill, one had to be strong to sustain them. Life in old age was a feat of endurance as much as enjoyment.

I thought, we grow old and confront our mortality and co-exist with it like a pensioner co-existing with a silent and dependent relative. And as we care for the mortality of others we recognise and become ever-more-deeply involved in our own mortality. One had to be strong, fearless and bold while supporting those who depended on our continuing stability. Life often presents the elderly with ongoing caring that was not of their choosing and which could not have been foreseen.

A Fallen Snowman and a Ghost

There was a heavy fall of snow. I walked round our long garden and wondered at the beauty of the branches and the twigs, which were all decorated with two inches of lacy snow. I looked back at the house, which was magical with a long white roof against a white sky. That night it froze and the next day the side roads were treacherous. I had a dental appointment the following morning and parked in the road where I used to live, outside the house where I survived the war. The pavements were slippery and I walked down the centre of the road. There was no traffic, it was quite safe.

When I returned something remarkable had happened. On the corner of the road where I used to live and Priory Road there were two large balls of snow that I had not seen when I passed the spot earlier. One was waist-high, the other was a head. Then I realised it was a snowman whose head was in the icy gutter. It was as if a snowman had gone out walking and had fallen where Priory Road began.

Suddenly I lurched back to my boyhood, to a foggy day one weekend. The fog was thick, visibility was about 10 yards. Grandpa was visiting us, a man of 71 with snowy white hair. He went out to buy a newspaper and had not returned by lunchtime. My mother asked me, aged five, to go out and look for him. I walked towards the High Road and on the corner of Priory Road I found him lying half face downwards, half on his side. He had fallen over and he had cuts on his head and the side of one hand. I could see the scarlet blood. I helped him get up and led him back home. My mother fetched a bowl of warm water and wiped his cuts with wet cotton wool, and bathed his wounds.

The snowman had fallen exactly where my grandfather had fallen during the war. Behind the fallen snowman was an unexpected ghost. I walked on down the centre of the road, icy snow covering the pavements on either side, and was aware of my layered life. In this road where I used to live, where I saw our windows fall out from dropped German bombs, I walked in the present but memories sat up in the gutter and called me. And it seemed that the snowman was holding a gravestone to remind me of my long-dead Grandpa.

A Rod and Seasons

Gully, our gardener, was slow and vague but had a good grasp of the mowing, seeding and planting that needed to be fitted into the seasons. He had a painful back and had been unsteady on his feet for some months. He was diagnosed as having what he described as "dead foot". He was now falling over every day. He had an MRI scan. He saw a consultant, who said he should have an operation. He had a broken piece of disc that needed to be plated together, he needed a small rod in his lower spine and he needed the removal of a spur that was digging into a nerve. All this would improve his "dead foot".

On the way home he stopped at a pub to have a drink and think about what he had been told. He did not want to have an operation on his back. He entered the saloon bar and tripped over his own feet and fell headlong.

"I shouldn't serve you," the barman said, suggesting he was drunk.

Gully protested, "I haven't had anything to drink, I've got 'dead foot'."

Gully had the operation. It lasted five hours. He awoke in agony. He had shooting pains up his back. The surgeon visited him and said his back would settle in a few days. Gully was in hospital for five days instead of two because of the pain, then he was sent home, where his shooting pains returned.

"I thought I'd be back at work in a couple of weeks," he told me over the phone, "but it's going to be at least two months."

He had used up all his sickness and holiday entitlement, so I made arrangements for him to begin SSP (Statutory Sick Pay).

I had to ring him about a certificate. His wife answered and said casually, "I've had the same operation. I was off work eighteen months."

I did not think Gully would be away that long, but I wondered how much he had known about his likely length of absence before he had the operation. It occurred to me that he might always have known that he would be away a long time and that he had pretended to be surprised that it was not only two weeks.

I immediately thought this was unlikely. Gully worked for us in the mornings and went to other clients in the afternoons. He wanted to be back earning a full week's wage, not sitting at home on SSP, which in his case was £83 a week. He wanted to get back. He was just not very good at planning his life, he had drifted into the operation without asking practical questions. Perhaps he did not want to hear how long he would be away. But he *had* tackled what was wrong with him, and after a period of convalescence he would be able to work again, assuming he made a full recovery and the shooting pains went.

Gully was a law unto himself. He lived amid the rhythm of the seasons, and his back would heal in the rhythm of the seasons. Everything had a time and a place and a season, and in the fullness of time he would be back to full strength. In his own way Gully was in harmony with Nature and therefore with the universe.

A Deer and Hospitals

The ironing lady lived the other side of Ongar. When she lived in Woodford she had many clients our way. She was forever collecting sheets and shirts to iron and returning them three days later. She whittled her clients in our area down to a few after her move, which took place after her father died, but when Carol left she took us on. She came on a Monday evening to collect the sheets and returned them, ironed, on a Thursday evening. She was in her early sixties with shortish blonde hair and had bright eyes.

That week she came to the door at 9.30pm on a Tuesday. It was cold outside but as always she stood and chatted to Pippa and me.

"Sorry I couldn't come yesterday," she said. "It's exposed our way. We're in the middle of fields, just four houses at the end of the road in the fields. There was a tree down and we couldn't get out. There's a hedge on each side of the road and one day nine years ago a deer ran out when I'd just set off. I saw the deer's bright eyes and instinctively swerved. I avoided it but crashed into a telegraph pole. Two neighbours had no phone but one neighbour successfully got the pole moved. It was erected a few yards further down the road away from a gate he used. It cost £3,000 to install a new one. That neighbour said I was his hero. I'm small, I could have broken my nose. Airbags don't inflate from the sides. You wouldn't think one deer could cause so much trouble, would you?

"I've just come from Whipps," she said. "My mother's in hospital. She's ninety-two, she's got dementia. I found out she was seriously ill when I found her naked on the floor of her bathroom. She'd had a towel round her after a bath and she'd fallen over.

"My father was in the same hospital all those years ago. He was asleep downstairs the night he died. He got up to draw the curtains and had a heart attack. He died in the ambulance on the way to Whipps, and later I drove past the house on my way home and saw the curtains undrawn. I sensed something had happened. I got back home and heard he'd died when I got through my door. I had to turn round and drive all the way back to the hospital.

"I'm having a small operation at the same hospital the same day I next see you, so I hope I'll be all right. Do you know, I had eight letters from the hospital all saying the same thing, the date of my operation. I do hope I'm only having one operation, not eight." She laughed. "You're going to Cornwall, I gather. When we were children my father used to drive us there. I had to wave to every AA man."

"Yes," I said, "I remember the AA men. They stood in uniform by the road and saluted the AA badge on all the cars that had them."

"That's right," she said. "I had to wave to all the AA men. That's what I remember about going to Cornwall."

She took our laundry bag and put it in her car. As she drove off into the dark I reflected that she collected and delivered. She came to the door like a deer with bright eyes, and I did not have to swerve to avoid her. She had the raw good sense of a countrywoman, and she was always worth listening to. And hospitals featured strongly in her conversations. Her memories were dominated by her encounter with a deer and by her several encounters with hospitals.

A Sale and Providence

Carol was having a dreadful time with her husband, Donald. She was selling their house so they could move to a flat near their daughter and have money in the bank for their old age. He had been in Whipps Cross Hospital and had been discharged, despite being incontinent. At home he was wetting his bed, the floor and the carpet. His carers were shocked at the soiling, and got him readmitted to Whipps, into Peace Ward. It was noisy, it was filled with dementia patients. The first time she visited him a black nurse shouted, "Number 10's wet his bed." It was said very publicly, everyone in the ward turned and stared in her direction. She squirmed in embarrassment and humiliation. The nurse made Donald stand and then pushed him back into a chair. Carol was appalled at her treatment of him. She wanted to complain but thought better of it in case her husband was systematically bullied after she left.

"I rang Carol," Penny said. "She's moved to her new flat, and her husband's still in hospital with dementia and incontinence and she doesn't want him back. Her daughter's found a nursing home nearby. She'll have to pay £850 a week, the Council will pay £150. There's some money from the sale of the five-bedroom house, but they sold it quickly and at a rock-bottom price to make the move happen and the two-bedroom flat was expensive. The money will be used up in three or four years, and what happens then? She'll have to sell the flat and move in with her daughter and use the proceeds of the flat to fund her husband's care at the nursing home. It's all a nightmare. There isn't enough parking at the building that includes her flat. She can't drive or she loses her space in the car park and then she's out in the town, where there's no parking. There's just a multi-storey car park. Her daughter has to collect her to visit her husband. Anyway, she doesn't like driving through Harlow, she gets confused by the roundabouts. She's really stressed. She can't sleep because everything's going round and round in her mind. She's been prescribed antidepressants but she won't take them as she doesn't want to become dependent on them. Her husband's moving into the nursing home next week, and she's got no help. It's down to her and her daughter to afford it all, except for a token payment by the Council."

I sat and pondered. She had had a five-bedroom house and had down-sized to live with her husband in greater comfort, and his dementia had suddenly got worse and turned into incontinence. She had moved from her family home at just the wrong moment, and was now living apart from her husband and would be visiting him in his nursing home. Or perhaps she had moved at just the right moment, to release funds from her house to pay for the nursing home.

I sat and pondered the ways of Providence and the more I thought the more I detected the hand of Providence in the events. Carol had somehow muddled along and taken the right decisions needed to pay for her husband. And then I grasped that she needed to have no property of her own so the State would step in and do some paying. She had bungled her way halfway to this point. Yes, it was possible to see the guiding hand of Providence in those apparently hopeless events.

Good Manners and a Bull

That November I drove down to Hampshire to visit an old friend. The drive was through countryside. I knew I had to stop at a particular garage on the way that had a shop where coffee was hand-served at a high counter and where there were toilets. The garage came up without warning. I was in the fast lane and although I slowed to try and move to the inside lane I was hooted and had to continue. So I decided to keep going to The Hen and Egg, where I had stopped once before. It had a toilet and served coffee. I pulled across the road and parked outside and went to the door. A notice said, 'We are open at 10am for coffee and breakfast.' It was 9am and the pub was on winter opening hours. So I walked to my car. I had been thwarted again.

I had been brought up to have good manners. I had been told in my youth that I should always relieve myself before being received in a house. It was non-U to arrive and immediately ask to use the loo.

Near the bottom of his long lane there were fields on either side. There was a pull-in off the road before a farm gate. No one was about. I thought, 'From the cavemen to the 19th century men relieved themselves in such spots, it's only in the 20th and 21st centuries that we expect comfortable toilets.' So I got out and relieved myself.

A black cow without horns ambled over and put its head over the hedge and carefully watched what I was doing. With a shock I realised it was a bull. It began snorting and looked as if it was about to charge through the hedge, which was not very thick. Quickly I got back into my car and reversed and carried on up the narrow lane.

Social decorum dictated that I should find a garage or a pub with a toilet and empty my bladder there. When that proved impossible I had to find an appropriate place in the countryside. How could I have failed to see the bull until I was relieving myself?

Having been brought up to be attentive to good manners I had no doubt that I had done the right thing. But I could have been charged by the bull and killed. As Shakespeare might have written, 'Exit Philip, pursued by a bull.'

In the light of this possibility, had I carried observing good arrival manners too far?

Drama Queens and Pink Pheasant

We arrived at the National Portrait Gallery before 12 and went up by escalator, which took us to the Stuarts and Tudors on the second floor. Pippa spotted a full-length portrait of Queen Anne by Michael Dahl, painted in 1702 when she was 37. We sat before it. Queen Anne looked morose. She had had seventeen or eighteen pregnancies, all of which ended before birth and she was pointing a finger towards a nearby crown. She had only been on the throne for three years, and I wondered if she found being a Queen weighed on her.

"Look at the velvet and the ermine, and the lace. The paintwork is exquisite," Pippa said.

Her pose looked a bit theatrical. She was projecting moroseness and blaming the crown. She looked a drama queen.

We took the lift up to the third floor and reported in at the Portrait Restaurant, where a waiter was standing behind a computer inside the door.

"There are nine of us in all," I said. "Seven still to come."

"Oh," the waiter said, looking at his computer, "they are already here."

He arranged for a lady to lead us to the far end of the restaurant. Rupert was sitting at the end of a long table before the end wall. Florence and Alison were sitting with their backs against the wall next to Raymond, and Jack was sitting next to Rupert opposite them. They all stood and there were hugs of greetings and air kisses across the table, and I took Jack's seat and sat with my back to the other diners next to Rupert, facing a portrait on the wall of Aldous Huxley wearing round spectacles above a caption 'Brave New World'.

Rupert had been talking about his bypass. I asked, "How are you doing?"

He struggled to reply. He spoke slowly and seemed to forget what he was saying. "My wound is still weeping," he said, "and my eyes are not good. I had both cataracts done a year ago and one of them has to have laser treatment. I…."

Jack and Florence were listening to him and he was revelling in the attention, and I wondered if he too was a bit of a drama queen.

Rex and Winnie arrived and we all stood. Rex edged his way along the seat under the wall and sat under Huxley. Winnie sat opposite him, next to me, and Jack was now further down the table. She was in a polo-necked sweater and said how hot she was. She had pink cheeks.

We ordered. I ordered artichoke soup and pheasant. The foreign waiter tinkled a glass with a knife to gain our attention and asked, "Who wants their pheasant pink and who well-done?" I asked for my pheasant to be well-done.

After a while I said I needed to talk to Jack, and Winnie and I changed places. I talked to Jack at some length about a contact he had in wealth management and the prospects for the UK economy in the coming months.

Our pheasant arrived, by itself on the plates except for a small helping of salad. I ate and talked and realised that somehow I had been given pink pheasant. It was very pink, not slightly pink. The pink meat had more bacteria and was therefore more risky than well-done (which would be more dry). I cut away the pink flesh and pushed it to the side of my plate.

Now Florence called that she wanted to change places with Jack so she could talk to those at the far end of the table, where Raymond sat facing Pippa. So Florence changed places with Jack. Jack moved next to Rupert and I had Florence next to me. Raymond now sat next to Rupert, and Jack said to me, "That end's the Bypass Club," for Raymond had also had a bypass the previous year.

Florence wanted to talk about her family. She told me about her visit to Kosovo with Raymond to spend Christmas with Archie and his family. "I don't know how long he'll stay," she said. "He's done four years. I want him to come home but they'll do another three years I think, and look at the schooling and decide then. I want him to keep his skills up so he's not unable to find a job when he returns. Raymond says it's their decision and we should not interfere." She told me how she had looked after Raymond after his bypass and got him walking and doing things.

I suddenly remembered I had a camera and I asked a waitress to take a picture of us all. I said to Rupert, "Can you turn and look at the camera."

He turned the wrong way, towards the wall, and presented his back to the waitress. He tried to turn to see her, and was looking over his shoulder at the camera.

"The other way," I said.

He still did not get it.

"Sit in the empty place there," Jack said, indicating the end of the plush seating against the wall.

And so he did.

"You're in the way," Florence said to me. "I'm not going to be in the picture. I'll stand."

And before anyone could say anything she stood above me as the waitress took a picture. There was a flash.

"One more, please," I said to the waitress, and I sat back so Florence's face could be seen. Pippa was beyond her.

There was another flash and the waitress gave me back the camera. When I looked at the picture of Florence standing I saw Pippa's face beyond her unobscured. If Florence had remained seated she would have been clearly seen.

Florence had made a big issue of something trivial – all she had to do was sit slightly forward – and had invested the situation with melodramatic emotion, and I saw her as a drama queen seeking attention.

Menus were handed round so we could choose our puddings. We continued our meal. Most of us ordered "choc pot", which all pronounced "pot" as in 'hotpot' but Jack pronounced "pō" as in the French 'pot-pourri'. I said that a proofreader would say the menu should have put 'pot' in italics if it was meant to be French. There were smiles.

Then I reminisced how Rupert and I, aged 13 and 11, got up at 4am and caught the first tube at 5 on our own and queued outside the Oval without a ticket and watched the 5th Ashes' Test, England v. Australia, completely unaccompanied. And how when we were even younger, together with Rex, we were put on the tube, changed at Bank, got ourselves to Waterloo by 'the drain' and took a mainline train to stay with Rex. Rex reminisced how he was put in the care of the guard when he came to stay with us, and on reaching Waterloo had to find his way up to the tube on his own.

Rex said we went to see Kent v. the West Indies at Canterbury. I said the crowd went onto the pitch at the beginning and spontaneously formed a guard of honour, and Gomez, the West Indies' captain, led his team between the two rows of spectators and sang softly as he passed us, "Here comes the bride." He was bringing emotion into the routine procedure of leading the players out to play, he too was a bit of a drama queen.

Pippa and I left the restaurant just before 3.30pm. We said our goodbyes with hugs and air kisses and took a lift down to the second floor and then took the escalator down to the foyer to get out.

Our car was waiting for us. As we drove home I reflected that Florence and (to some extent) Rupert had shown signs of being drama queens like Queen Anne, and that the pink pheasant was bloodied and suggested the two bypasses.

I had listened to narratives Rupert and Florence had wanted to bring to my attention and had sympathised with Rupert's and Raymond's operations. I had spent three hours with drama queens and had heard about their pink-pheasant-like bloodied flesh.

A Mince Pie and Vacant Eyes

Jasmine came to the front door to return the ironing. It was misty and dark, and she had red cheeks and bleary eyes.

"I've had the flu since Christmas," she said. "My mother's back in the home, I think I got it from there. She's fine, she's ninety-two. They're all sitting in front of the television not watching, vacant. She sits and hums and dribbles. They had mince pies to eat. She took her false teeth out and put a whole mince pie in her mouth so it was up where her teeth should be and sat with her mouth full and her cheeks bulging like a hamster. I think she'll choke to death. She's had scans, there's nothing wrong with any part of her except her dementia. It's just her mind.

"I took a photo album to her. She didn't register. Then she said, 'That's a nice little girl.' I said, 'That's me.' A few pages on I said, 'That was your husband, do you remember him?' Nothing. Then six pages later she suddenly said, 'That's me.' Two pages later, nothing. She's ninety-two and no quality of life, just sitting humming before the television, vacant. If I were in charge of the home I'd take the lot of them to Switzerland and give them all an injection. I hope she chokes, it's the kindest thing when you get to that stage.

"I haven't been going to the clients because of my flu. I've come to you and to Simon, and that's it. One of my regulars rang very demanding, wanting to know when I was coming. She thinks she's more important than other clients. No, I'm just doing Simon and you. Simon texted me and said, 'There's loads, I've left it in the porch for you.' I texted, 'I've got flu.' He texted, 'Oh no.' He thought I wasn't coming but I'm here. See you on Thursday."

And she picked up the bulging laundry bag full of sheets, duvet covers and shirts and struggled to heave it into the back of her car. I buzzed the gate and her car headed up the drive to return to the countryside beyond Ongar.

A Broken Christian

I had a heart-rending Christmas card from Kathleen, who we used to know when we were living in South London.

She wrote: "I am sorry to tell you that Ronald passed away on 10 November, entirely peacefully surrounded by those he loved and who loved him best. A Requiem Mass was held at Newport Pagnell Parish Church on 4 December and he is buried in our village churchyard. Broken, but life must go on. K x."

I thought back to those days, and the day we all met for dinner at the house of a friend of Pippa's who had pinned butterflies and African carvings in her sitting-room. Ronald was an accountant, Kathleen was intense and small and spoke with a plum in her mouth. He was quiet with a thin beard and had little to say, but she made him the centre of her family. She would say "Ronald did this" and "Ronald did that", and it came across as unconditional Christian love. They were very church-based and attended the local church whose curate had been there that evening. They had two daughters the same age as our two sons. They had moved away from South London to Buckinghamshire, and had continued their church involvement.

They had lived Christian lives of blameless service and now Ronald's life had come to an end and Kathleen was "broken". I knew no details beyond the card. But it seemed they had not been rewarded for all the good they had sought to do with a long and happy old age.

The card had a picture of Mary and her child on the front. To Kathleen this signified that she was now a mother – and a widow – looking after her family.

A Cleaner and a Prefab

Katie came. She was blonde with her hair tied back and horn-rimmed spectacles. She was a thorough cleaner and had cleaned for us as part of a team three or four times. Now she was doing it by herself two days a week. On her second solo day she came into my room and began polishing the surfaces. I lifted piles of papers out of her way and replaced them when she had sprayed and polished. She talked while she cleaned.

"I like doing this house," she said. "I liked doing your gas stove yesterday. I think now the best job I ever had was on a fruit-and-veg stall. I loved that, talking to the customers when they came for fruit and veg. I did that for ten years. Now my husband's not well. He had gallstones removed before Christmas and he won't be back to work doing his driving instructing until the end of January. He's sixty-one, he's older than me. He's not earning much at present, but we still love each other. I worked really hard yesterday. I had to clean two flats in Docklands. Carly didn't have a permit so it had to be in the evening for parking reasons and I wasn't home until 9. I had no breakfast yesterday and hardly any lunch and just a little at 9. And my boy played up. You know he's autistic, he began to have a tantrum. If I see a bit of dirt on the carpet I get up and I get him to pick dirt up too. I'm looking forward to my lunch today. Then I'll clean my own house this afternoon.

"We live in a prefab. There's a lot of iron to hold it all together. Is that screen for your security cameras? I thought so. We've got a screen split into four, with four pictures. It's good, I've got it on my phone. Look."

She stopped and turned her phone sideways. I saw the word 'RING'. Then a picture of part of a house came up, and a view over a green with houses in the distance the other side.

"That's our house," she said. "I can look in on what the cameras are showing while I'm at work. And I've got 'front door'. If the doorbell rings it buzzes on my Fitbit and rings me on my phone. And I can say to a tradesman, 'Can you leave it round the back, please?' Technology's good today. I'm in constant contact with my home. Who'd have thought I could be a few years ago?

"Yes," she said, "I'm looking forward to catching up with *my* work. I shall polish and hoover my house this afternoon. I love cleaning, it's so satisfying. I want to do ten thousand steps a day on my Fitbit. Polishing counts as a step. If I do circular rubbing like this, that's ten steps.

"Right, that's the polishing done, I'll plug my hoover in now. It's my Henry I've brought, not Carly's. It's used in my house and yours and nowhere else. I don't believe in bringing germs from other people's flats in Docklands and houses. Everything has to be clean, then everything's all right."

She had had a hard life working in fruit and veg and doing her cleaning, but she knew what pleased her, and I could only admire the hard work she put in. She was a hard worker and she had made the best of her prefab and her sick husband, who was sixty-one, and their autistic son. She was a hard worker who had had a hard life and had a prefabricated template in her soul for everything to be clean.

A Surgeon and a Red-Stained Shirt
(Or: A White Shirt like a Pure Soul)

No sooner had I arrived at the Sesquicentennial (150th anniversary) Shrove Tuesday school supper and reunion and bought a glass of red wine in the old library (my sixth-form classroom), wearing a suit, white shirt and old-school tie, than one of the Rivers twins said, "Garfield Mayers is here, he's telling everyone he wants to sit next to you."

"Thanks for tipping me off," I said, and then I saw Derek Minstrel standing looking dazed and shook his hand.

"Garfield Mayers is staying with me," he said. "I couldn't get here any earlier, I had to meet him at the station and we drove straight here. This is my son."

I shook hands with a thickset young man in his early fifties, and said to him, "Many years ago I went to Italy with your father. I did the itinerary and got your father to the Vatican on a certain day. Your mother was visiting at the same time in a party of schoolgirls under nuns. I got your father to see your mother, and if they hadn't got together you wouldn't exist."

"Oh, right," he said, "right."

"And during that visit we saw Hitler," Derek said. "It was definitely Hitler. I was thinking of him only this morning."

"In the Youth Hostel in Sicily," I said.

"Yes," he said. "Hitler was definitely living in Sicily, it was him."

"Who's dead?" I asked.

"Clement what's-his-name. Oh, I've forgotten his name. Who's died?" he asked his son. "Oh yes, Clement Steward. His funeral was this afternoon, I couldn't go."

"He was our inside-right," I said.

"And Henry Cardew, just dropped dead a couple of months ago, at home, no illness."

"His Honour," I said, "a Brexiteer." He had said to me across the table three or four years back, "Don't start me on Europe. I'm pro-Europe but anti-EU."

We went through to the dining-hall and found table 6. The hall had been enlarged, out onto the lawn, and some Old Boys were sitting in the extension. The wooden panelling had been painted a pale grey, and all the central lights were on. It was too bright and had lost its atmospheric associations with the hall I remembered from my school-days.

We stood by table 6. It had a white tablecloth and white napkins by laid places.

Garfield Mayers joined us. He shook my hand and said, "I'm so impressed by all you've done. I want to tell you something about what I've done."

Derek Minstrel was standing next to me. "It's secret," he said. "You can't say."

"In confidence," Garfield Mayers added. He was clearly full of good news he wanted to share with me. We all sat down. There were six of us on the table: Derek Minstrel, Garfield Mayers and me, the two Rivers and Dee. There were two empty places facing each other at the end on my left. One of the two no-shows was Nutty Bray.

The Headmaster called for silence and said grace in Latin: "*Benedictus, benedicat, per Jesum Christum, Dominum nostrum.*" All chorused, "Amen."

From the other side of the table Dee said, "Robin Roach can't be here because his daughter's got an impacted wisdom tooth. I saw them last night. She's suicidal, and he's got to stay with her."

"Yes," said Derek. "Robin has a suicidal daughter."

I did not say that she was all right when Pippa taught her, but developed suicidal tendencies at senior school.

During our starter of smoked salmon and a large prawn on a pancake, Garfield Mayers asked me questions about what I had been doing. We were interrupted by the serving of the main course, beef fillet with mushroom dauphinoise and roast root vegetables. A *maître d'* in a smart suit stood in the centre of the hall and directed a team of waitresses to the tables. Each carried two plates. I tried to catch up with Derek Minstrel, who told me he was going to stay in Balmoral village in May. But Garfield Mayers had things to tell me.

"I was a surgeon until I was 75," he said, "and the last five years I've spent a lot of time making a garden for the hospital. I've dug the beds and planted flowers and put up seats for the patients and staff to enjoy, and we've got wildlife areas. Look," he said, showing me a picture on a small iPad, "that's a hedgehog pot – or home – in our wildlife area."

I said I had not seen a hedgehog recently as we had foxes, which are reputed to eat hedgehogs despite their spikes.

"Well," he said, "we've won a national garden competition. Five of us will be going to Torquay to accept our award. It's so exciting. I planted it, look."

He leaned across the table. On his iPad I saw a heath of clumpy grass, a few distant benches and small round flower-beds that looked out of place on the heathland as though cultivation had strayed into a wildlife habitat.

He thrust his iPad towards me like a surgeon probing with his scalpel.

"Hmm," I said admiringly, not sure of what I should say. He had overstated the importance of what he had been doing. It was no big deal, and its being secret was hyping up a very local project.

"And look, here's another, also secret –"

He leaned forward again and again thrust his iPad towards me and a large glass of red wine went flying. I saw a river of red wine advancing across the white table, a tidal wave rushing up a narrow estuary like the Bristol Bore. Instinctively I pushed my chair back and most of the wave poured onto the floor between my legs. Some fell on my napkin in my lap, then I noticed I had splashes of red wine on my shirt and a few blobs on my suit jacket and trousers. My tie was untouched.

"I'm *so* sorry," Garfield Mayers said loudly.

"A good thing you're not a surgeon now," Derek Minstrel said caustically.

"I'm really sorry. Salt's good for it."

I beckoned to the *maître d'* and pointed to the large pool of 'blood' that had soaked into our tablecloth, and to the splashes on my shirt.

"Salt's good for it," the *maître d'* said. He left and returned with a salt cellar. He sprinkled salt on my shirt and trousered legs and left the salt cellar with me.

I laid my napkin, which had small pools of 'blood' on it, over the lake of red on the tablecloth, to hide it, and took a clean napkin from the unused plate that had been laid to my left.

"All's well," I said, making light of the accident. "The shirt would have to go in the washing-machine anyway when I get home. I'll put it into the Stains 60 program. No problem."

When Garfield Mayers leaned forward, probing like a surgeon inside an operation, to show me his family near a Christmas tree, I was wary of what glasses might be near his elbow.

"That's my wife," he said, "and two daughters and two grandchildren. And me."

"A lovely family," I said admiringly but guardedly.

Daniel Rivers leaned across the table from the other side of Derek with *his* iPad. "That's my wife in the royal palace in Qatar," he said. "Sitting all alone in that vast room of grand curtains and carpets. They said, 'She looks lonely.'" He laughed. "I'll tell you a secret," he said, leaning across Derek.

I was wary of 'secrets', they could be accompanied by spillages. I kept an eye on all glasses between him and me.

"The ruler of Qatar is coming to live near you. I've bought him a 28-acre estate in High Beach. I'm getting it ready for him. I'd like to bring him to see you."

"Fine," I said. "I'll look forward to it. Come and have coffee, but best to ring first."

Derek said, "I had a bond with Henry Cardew. The two kitchen maids let down our tyres as a prank, so we went up to their room and ruffled everything up to leave it dishevelled. The Domestic Bursar complained to the Head, and the whole school was kept back on an *absit* until the culprits owned up. We owned up and were whacked. We each had six. It was only banter. The two maids were so embarrassed they left, embarrassed because their prank led to those consequences."

"I was a boarder," said Daniel Rivers, "and some of us went for a midnight swim with the maids in the swimming-pool. We were caught, and I was banned from the swimming team as a punishment. The Head said, 'Why's Rivers not in the swimming team?' He ordered my reinstatement. For him, the school came first."

We were served sticky-toffee pudding and ice-cream with toffee sauce. Then coffee was being served and I was aware of a microphone on a stand by my elbow. The current Head was standing behind it. We had suddenly become the front row. A hundred-and-fifty pairs of eyes were looking at me, it seemed. I folded my arms to conceal the red stains on my shirt and pulled my napkin up.

The Head introduced the Head Girl and then the President of the Old Boys, the ex-Bishop who had been barracked the previous year. He spoke of the challenges of the next fifteen years, of automation and artificial intelligence. He said, "Many of today's pupils will never drive a car, because cars will be self-driving. The whole pattern of training, work and retirement may be completely different in the coming digitalised society."

The Head took over and spoke of the school 150 years ago. He said there were 925 pupils in the school at present. I listened, shielding my shirt with crossed arms.

We stood to sing the school song. I buttoned up my jacket. Then Daniel Rivers said, "We haven't had a toast to the Queen." He raised his glass and tried to get me to toast the Queen with him.

Henry Davids, floridly bearded, approached. Daniel Rivers said, "He's a millionaire, he owns Stonards Hill."

Derek said, "He teaches maths."

Henry Davids fell on Garfield Mayers, clutching his shoulders, and said, "The surgeon, look, you've been operating." He pointed to the wine stains on the tablecloth and napkin. "That's what your operations looked like." He laughed aloud and then chuckled. "But you saved my life."

"It's true," Garfield Mayers said, "I operated on him many years ago."

Derek said, "Do you still teach maths?"

"Yes."

"And are you a millionaire?"

"Yes," Henry Davids said. "*You* live by 10 to the power of 9 whereas I live by 10 to the power of 12." He then threw his head back and laughed while we tried to fathom his meaning.

I left in a drizzle. Pippa picked me up in her car. As we drove home I reflected on how my shirt had begun the supper pure and white. The surgeon had wanted to tell me about his garden and winning first prize, and I had been stained by the egotistical declarations on our table. The purity of my soul had been stained like my white shirt. My blood had stained the tablecloth like red wine.

When I took my shirt and silk vest out of the washing-machine an hour-and-a-half later, the stains had gone. I looked at my clean shirt and silk vest and knew that my soul was pure again. I lived a solitary life out of choice and protected my soul. I had found the slow rhythm of living through my soul fecund and productive. I was not one to talk my evenings away or spend hours listening to others' memories and achievements for their own sake, to pass the time. I always had things to do. I lived with purpose.

I kept my soul pure and white and did not like to see it bloodied and stained with the red wine of probing conversation. Sitting at length with other people stained my pure soul red as if it had been attacked by a surgeon, and I was pleased to be tranquil and at peace again in the nourishing night.

A Locked Memory and a Reconfigured Bar

Kay picked us up at Malaga airport in the large Caravelle that now lived near the Spanish apartment. Our grandchildren Al and Minnie were grinning in the back. Simon loaded our luggage. Our grandson Bernard, Pippa and I clambered in and we drove to Malaga, parked in an underground car park and sauntered to the port.

There was a glorious blue sky and it was warm for early April. Al and Minnie scooted off on their three-wheel scooters, standing on the tread on their right legs and scooting with their left legs. They swooped along like skimming swallows in summer.

We stopped at a Gaucho steak and tapas restaurant and sat in bright light near the Mediterranean and were served swordfish and chips and red wine. The children had ribs.

Then we retraced our steps along the promenade to an ice-cream parlour. Simon and I left the others and, guided by a map on Simon's phone, walked towards a crag and after turning to the right and left several times in a maze of streets we came across the orange walls of the bullring and then the Hotel Miramar, a palatial white-marble building in railed-off gardens with a crest over its grand entrance. It had taken four years to build and was inaugurated in 1926 by King Alfonso XIII.

We wandered through the courtyard-like lobby and came out at the back. Beyond diners, wide marble steps led down to the gardens, and beyond railings was the sea. We plodded down the steps and it all came back to me. Nearly 59 years previously Ian and I had been to a bullfight at which Chicuelo II was slightly gored. The American writer Ernest Hemingway was sitting a row from the front and a Spaniard sitting next to us said, "If you want to meet Hemingway, he'll be in the bar at the Hotel Miramar in the evening."

We went on to the Hotel Miramar, which was nearby, and went out to the back. Danny Kaye was singing below the marble terrace, to the right as we stood with the sea at our backs. We returned up the marble steps, found a long bar and there, standing in the middle on a fawn-gold carpet among fifty drinkers, was Hemingway, white hair combed forward, white beard, still massive despite having just turned 60, holding a tumbler of what looked like gin and tonic. A couple of young writers were talking to him. We spotted the *Observer* reviewer Ken Tynan sitting in the window.

We loitered nearby and when there was an opportunity we spoke to Hemingway. Just turned 20, I told him I wanted to be a writer and that I had read the Nick Adams stories and the story about Krebs. I said I had been to the bullfight.

He gave me his full attention and nodded gravely.

I told Hemingway that one day I would write more stories than he had written, and he nodded attentively, tolerant of the boasts of youth.

He said, "There's a *mano a mano* ['hand-to-hand'] tomorrow. Ordonez and Dominguin. It will be the best bullfight of the year. You must see that. You should get tickets if you can, you won't regret it." He was very gentle.

Then a middle-aged man interrupted, "Oh Mr Hemingway, don't you feel the bulls of today aren't as big as they were some years ago?"

Hemingway put a hand in his pocket and slapped three 100 peseta notes in his hand and said aggressively, "Go and buy yourself a book on bullfighting," followed by a blunt expletive. The man returned the banknotes and withdrew abashed.

His few kind words to me left a permanent impression which remained with me throughout my life.

We slept on the beach at nearby Torremolinos, and the next morning we queued at the bull stadium and bought a couple of tickets.

Simon and I hunted for the bar. It had gone. The space had been converted into a restaurant with glass divisions, but I could still see the window Ken Tynan had sat in, and I could work out where the long bar counter used to be and the exact spot where Hemingway stood. I stood where I had stood that day and pondered that my boast that I would write more stories than Hemingway had turned out to be true.

The next day Ian and I sat in the second row from the front in the bull stadium, and Hemingway was also in the second row but further round, wearing a maroon shirt. The *mano a mano* was between the number-1 matador Antonio Ordonez and the number 2 and challenger, Luis Dominguin. The first three fights went without a hitch. Ordonez, strutting and darkly handsome, killed two bulls and Dominguin one. Then Dominguin fought a huge bull and made several passes. Just below us, ten yards from the side of the ring where we were sitting, he threw caution to the winds, knelt with his back to the bull, threw away his sword and cape and raised his hands in the air in a V for Victory gesture.

The bull kicked sand back with its hoofs, bent and charged. The crowd screamed. The bull's horns hit Dominguin in his right side and he was tossed and thrown. Then the bull was charging at his body and goring him.

Matadors ran on with capes to distract the bull. Ordonez was one of them. One got Dominguin to his feet. Blood oozed through his tunic. He waved the matadors away, picked up his sword, performed a series of perfect passes to "*Olés*" and then completed a perfect kill, plunging his sword over the bull's horns. The crowd roared. Then he walked stiffly towards us, slowly, his face twisted with pain, blood oozing through his tunic down his right side, and collapsed by the wooden inner ring just below us. He was stretchered off.

The crowd was on its feet and there was a deafening noise. We all stood on our seats. I saw Hemingway standing in his maroon shirt, waving his arms. The fight was the climax of his book about the rivalry between Ordonez and Dominguin that summer, *Death in the Afternoon*.

Hemingway shot himself nearly two years later in 1961, aged 61, after being diagnosed with alcoholism and hypertension, which had revealed itself in his reaction to the man who asked about the bulls. It later emerged that, having fought with the republicans in the Spanish Civil War and recorded his experiences in *For Whom the Bell Tolls*, he had been recruited by the KGB in 1940 and supplied Stalin with information, and that he shot himself in 1961 as he was apparently depressed and deeply ashamed of what he had done.

Simon and I reached the orange walls of the bull stadium. I saw the name Antonio Ordonez over a closed doorway, and nearby a sign: Plaza de Antonio Ordonez. Ordonez had had the bull stadium square named after him. We walked all round the stadium looking for an open door so I could work out where I had sat, but it was completely shut up. There was no way in.

I pondered my memory from nearly sixty years ago. It was out of reach. Hemingway was dead and the bull stadium was closed. My journey to supplement what I remembered had ended in failure. That day in 1959 was out of reach. Bits of it were tantalisingly close but the setting where Hemingway stood had been reconfigured and the stadium where Dominguin was gored had been locked.

I reflected that in life we seek what is lost but most of the time it remains out of reach and our seeking ends in disappointment. But I would rather have the bits I had retrieved than not have tried at all. In life we hang on to the bits of the past we are able to salvage from time's relentless advance.

Smiling Sun and Si Si

The gated estate of apartments was off the A7. The villas were angular behind white walls and railings with orangey tiles and in discreet colours – pale blue and olive green – against the blue sky. The small lawned gardens were separated by beautifully-kept hedges.

We parked in the road and entered the compound through a high, locked gate-door and walked past frondy banana trees and bushes with fluffy scarlet flowers.

Our front door – the one to the apartment Pippa and I shared – was next to Simon's. The marble interior was cool. There were sliding patio doors and shutter-blinds that raised at the push of a button. The taps had to be turned sideways and the plug for the kettle was round with two prongs.

Then I became aware that on the table were two A4-sized drawings, both saying "Welcome to Spain". One from Al showed a giant sun with a smile and on either side two figures labelled "Grandma" and (taller) "Grandpa", both smiling. The other from Minnie showed a sun with eyelashes and a neutral mouth (neither smiling nor sad) and teeth, and the seven members of the family who were then in Spain were in ascending order and labelled. Minnie was the shortest on the left and "Grandpa" was the tallest, on the right.

Pippa and I supped with the others. We walked round the hedge into the next garden and sat on the covered patio, where Simon grilled burgers and sausages. We had salad and red wine at a table. Sparrows chirped from the hedges in the evening sunshine.

"It's good here," Kay said. "We came over Christmas. On New Year's Eve we stayed up until 12 and it was warm, we could sit out here on the patio. On New Year's Day we went to Marbella and they played on the beach. We sat and watched them, it was warm. It's a lovely way of life. I prefer it to England. There are so many playgrounds for the children, the beaches are better, and it's warm all the year round."

"We let this when we're not here and the rents cover the mortgage and there are euros to spend when we're here," Simon said. "It's lovely while the children are this age. They can scoot in safety, there's a lifeguard, Pueblo, at the pool, it's safe. They can't do this in England. When they get older we'll probably sell our apartment and buy a house by the sea on the Costa del Sol. We'll see."

Simon played some music after supper, and Al and Minnie began dancing. Al did a Highland fling he had learned at school, with complicated steps. Minnie, seven, was indefatigable. She hopped from one foot to another, shooting out her arms, wagged a finger, pointed, fixing her audience with her eyes, improvising imaginatively. I could see she could be a dancer one day.

The music stopped and we sat and enjoyed the fading evening. A black bird I could not identify called "Si si" in the twilight.

I looked at the coloured houses against the darkening blue sky. There was a stillness, it was warm. I liked Mediterranean living with its villas, its sunshine, the nearness of the sea.

We walked up past a line of shrubs to the swimming-pool, which resembled a large figure 8. The lifeguard was surrounding it with protective rattan safety-fencing for the night. Everything was orderly, everything was good, Mediterranean living was safe.

You sat in the sun and ate and slept in a rhythm that slowed you down. As the black bird called "Si si" I too said "Si" to the Spanish way of life.

Orange Trees and a Tossing Catamaran

We parked the Caravelle at Isdale and caught a 79 bus to Marbella Centro. We walked to the Old Town and found the Plaza de los Naranjos, a square of orange trees. The first oranges of the year were out and hung like lanterns in the green leaves.

We sat and had drinks at one of the tables under the orange trees. A slim middle-aged waiter brought a tray of glasses and handed a hot chocolate to Bernard and, to Pippa, a "mint tea for your sister", and as he put two glasses of beer before Simon and Kay, "still water". Bernard, Minnie and Al played top trumps and the same waiter ostentatiously sidled up and studied Al's cards without his being aware and when Al turned round, nonchalantly pretended to study the orange trees.

We walked down to the front. As we sauntered we discussed Brexit. Simon said, "Those who voted for Brexit fall into three groups: the North, the blue-rinse brigade and the Great Unwashed. Most of them didn't know we are in a customs union or single market."

We sat at the front of the beach restaurant La Pesquera and I ordered Iberian pork steak and rosé. Minnie and Al played in a slide on the beach. Al shovelled sand into the exit of the slide and Minnie slid down and landed in his sand.

Through the thatched umbrellas on the beach I could see Gibraltar, a rock rising on the horizon. It looked detached from the mainland near it. As I looked a terrific wind got up and shook water from a puddle on the canvas roof of our restaurant left over from the previous night's rain. It showered Simon, who immediately stood up and said, "Let's go inside."

We were shown to a table at the back underneath a hanging bicycle with a suspended joint of cured ham, both on offer for a combined price of 99.99 euros. We went on to have cheesecake. I had Bernard's caramel ice-cream which he did not like.

We bought boat tickets to cross the bay from a man with a leather bag looped round his neck to hang on his right side. We walked to the end of the pier and caught the 3.30 catamaran. We sat on the front deck. The sea was rough and we tossed up and down as we progressed, and we were drenched by a flick of spray. Minnie and Al were sitting on the netting at the front with the waves visible beneath them, and they were thrown into the air each time the catamaran hit an oncoming wave. Pippa and I sat inside to escape the spray. Simon and Kay sat on. I was afraid Minnie would be swept overboard, hit by a wave and slid under the railings as she was not holding on.

Soon afterwards Simon and Kay came in with Minnie and Al, who were drenched and cold and nearly tearful. Minnie was cuddled by Kay, Al by Simon.

We rounded the mole and moored at Puerto Banus, a white town with orange roofs. It began to rain. We abandoned seeing any of the town and headed for taxis. Simon, Pippa, Minnie and Al took a taxi straight back so the two children could have a shower. Kay, Bernard and I took another taxi to the Caravelle at Isdale and then drove home.

The square of orange trees had been relaxing, but the tossing catamaran had filled me with foreboding and stimulated my sense of danger. I had lived through two opposites during the day, peaceful oranges and dashing spray, but now they were reconciled and in harmony, and I was calm, beyond all turmoil and turbulence, beyond all confusion, in a place where all contradictions co-existed in an indissoluble unity.

A Barbary Ape and a Full English

We left early on Sunday morning for Gibraltar. We drove alongside the Atlas Mountains and crossed the border – a young Englishman in uniform checked our passports by our car window – and then the runway. We passed the petrol station where the SAS gunned down three IRA suspects in 1988. We drove through narrow English-looking streets and parked near the cable-car.

I looked up at the scudding clouds round the top of the Rock. The cable-car swayed and knocked against the supporting structure halfway up and at the top.

We had coffee by windows that overlooked the Spanish coast: Algeciras and the sweep towards Cadiz one way, and up to Marbella, Malaga and the Atlas Mountains the other way, and Western Beach and the open sea.

Then we climbed steps and reached the viewing platform. I looked down at Rosia Bay, where Nelson's body was carried ashore in a rum barrel from HMS *Victory* after the battle of Trafalgar in 1805. I peered unsuccessfully for the cemetery where dead English seamen were buried after Trafalgar. I reflected how easy it would have been for the Spanish to invade the tiny British rock if it had not been ceded 'in perpetuity' by the Treaty of Utrecht in 1715. It was astounding the Rock had remained British for 314 years since 1704.

Then I was aware of an ape by my knee. It walked on all fours and leapt onto the railing and sat and looked and allowed itself to be photographed. It was one of the Barbary tailless apes that occupy the Rock. The legend is that British rule will end when the apes die out, and mindful of this superstition during the Second World War Churchill introduced more apes.

We went on to the Battery and saw several more apes clambering on its walls. Then we caught a cable-car down to the bottom.

We walked along Main Street until Pippa's legs gave out and we went into The Horseshoe and ordered 'full-English' breakfasts: eggs, bacon, baked beans, tomato, mushroom and hash browns. We all declined black pudding. The breakfasts came with coffee and rounds of toast, butter and 'bitter marmalade', so I ate these as well and then had an ice-cream. We sat as a family with pictures of horses all round us, and I could feel the bonding over our 'full English'.

Kay left to collect the car. We sauntered on to the San Pedro Battery and waited in the car park. Kay picked us up and we drove to Gibraltar's Morrisons. I looked in and was fascinated by the trolley storage. Shoppers could store their full shopping trolley for £1 and have coffee and then retrieve the £1.

But I was thinking of the primitive primates, the Barbary apes which had come from the Barbary coast of North Africa during the Berber assault on the Visigothic domains in South Spain in 711. The Moors had remained in al-Andalus, which became Andalusia, until 1462. I was thinking how the British had seized the Rock from Spain in 1704 and civilised the Gibraltarian inhabitants. I thought of the 'full English', a meal that stood for English culture in its struggle to colonise the backward peoples of the world. The Barbary apes so at ease with people had been civilised, and the 'full English' signified that the new lords had come to stay and had no intention of leaving.

Leaping Towards the Sun
(Or: Yachts and McLarens)

We lunched on baked potatoes, cheese, baked beans and ice cream and then Kay drove us to Puerto Banus. She put us all out and went off to park. We walked along the front between wide-open restaurants and bars and a long line of cars parked beside white two-storey powered yachts, all packed together so tightly that they were separated only by a tyre. One yacht was named *Far Too X-clv* [Exclusive]. Al and Minnie scooted ahead on their scooters. We passed a blue McClaren P1 (price £1m) and many Ferraris and Porsches, but did not see a Bugatti (price £2m).

Kay was waiting for us halfway along the front. We stopped at Portside Banus, one of the Linekers' bars. Simon and Kay had beers, I had green tea.

We passed on and came to the statue on a column greeting yachts with his arms in the air: La Victoria, or Victory. We strolled on to the cocktail bar Simon and Kay often went to, shaped like a ship, and came out on a wide road. A McClaren was revving up loudly at traffic-lights. It roared forwards and soon returned on the other side of the road, showing off the owner's wealth. I reflected that Puerto Banus was a place that catered for the super-rich who had to extend their wealth in leaps and bounds and wanted not the moon but the sun.

We wandered inland and came to a park with a playground. It had four bungee-jumping poles thirty feet high. Al and Minnie were strapped into harnesses and then they were jumping on the trampoline and leaping thirty feet into the air with looks of delight on their faces at each leap.

The rich had the waterfront but here in this small park there was a sheer joy of living that had nothing to do with how many millions you had, leaping up into the blue sky and towards the brilliant sun.

Ladies by the Pool

I sauntered up to the swimming-pool, a large figure 8 surrounded on four sides by set-back houses of many colours against the blue sky. Several ladies were lying on sun-loungers. I saw Kay lying on her front, head up, and Pippa sitting alongside her, talking to two ladies in bikinis. One lying on her back smiled at me.

I said, "Hello," and introduced myself.

She sat up and said, "I'm Isabel." She held out her hand which I shook. She looked half-Spanish: dark with short hair and a Spanish face.

"I've heard all about you," I said. Simon had tried to buy an apartment but it had fallen through. She had rung Simon to say that another apartment was going, which she had viewed, and he bought it immediately. I knew she was an orphan who did not know who her parents were.

The other lady in a bikini held out her hand, a pretty, slim woman: "I'm Felicity."

"I've heard about you," I said. There were three children playing near Al and Minnie. "Is that Jim, Isabel's son, upside down wearing green trunks?"

"Yes," said Felicity, "that's Jim upside down wearing green. The other two are mine: Frankie and Lisa."

I left the ladies to continue their chat by the pool and strolled back through exotic plants to the apartment to watch Arsenal's second half.

Simon said, "They didn't like their children's school so they moved to mid-Essex and the three children are now at another school. Felicity's divorcing."

Later Al and Minnie came and Minnie said, "Lisa couldn't find us. She cried for a quarter of an hour. We said we'd be in a garden and we were, and then we went somewhere else and she couldn't find us and cried." And I thought how sensitive she must be at this difficult time for her while her parents were divorcing.

That evening we went to the Cambano restaurant. Al and Minnie scooted there, Kay and Bernard walked with them. Simon drove Pippa and me and parked. We ate in a semi-enclosed space on the first floor. There was a lot of glass which gave good views, but there were gaps in the glass on the flat roof and rain would have come through. There were jets of flame to warm the outside area.

We ordered – I had fish and chips – and it took an hour to come and then came in dribs and drabs.

"That plate's been here five minutes and is getting cold," Simon told a young male waiter. "She's waiting for the other plate before she can start. There should be two waiters, not one."

"It's only me, one did not turn up," the Arab-looking waiter said apologetically. "They" (he indicated inside) "have said how it should be tonight."

At that point Isabel and Felicity walked by with their three children. They were waving. Sitting ten feet above them I turned and waved through the window and they all grinned and beamed. They were ladies by the pool and they waved to their fellow ladies by the pool and their family wherever they were.

A Tearful Sun and a Mohican Skull

Our flight home was delayed by about an hour. Simon brought Al and Minnie in at 10.30. They gave us 'goodbye' drawings on A4. Al's had a huge sun looking miserable with a tear falling from its right eye. On either side, labelled, were Grandma and (taller) Grandpa, looking miserable with down-turned mouths. The drawing said, "Goodbye Grandpa and Grandma". Minnie's had a picture of herself with a turned-down mouth, also saying "Goodbye Grandpa and Grandma".

Simon took us to have coffee by the pool and we had a good chat. Kay joined us. We returned and collected our luggage. We said goodbye to Minnie, who was feeling unwell and was staying with Kay in case she was carsick. Then Simon, Al, Pippa, Bernard and I left for Malaga airport. We took the AP7 toll-road which runs all the way to Barcelona and beyond and was fast. We drove alongside mountains all the way.

In the airport we queued at the bag drop. A family of six was ahead of us. The husband wore a green track-suit top above a T-shirt that showed a huge skull with Mohican red-tinted hair and blood dripping round its mouth. He had greying hair smartly cut. His wife had maroon-tinted hair. She was in decorated jeans. The children were all floridly and hippily dressed. As I watched, his wife sat on the floor and rummaged in an open suitcase and handed out sandwiches and drinks to the four children, who were all loud and undisciplined. She knelt on the floor rummaging in her case for some while.

Eventually it was our turn. An English woman in her twenties, smartly dressed, pushed in and spoke to the Spanish lady in uniform who was checking in our bags. She said in an estuary drawl, "I've been told to go to the wrong queue and my flight goes in half an hour. Will I still catch my flight if I queue?"

The Spanish lady did not properly understand and said, "You must wait like all the others."

"But you haven't answered my question. Will I catch my flight if I queue? If not, what do you suggest?"

She was hoping we would allow her to go in front of us, but she was bad-mannered and rude and we looked down. The Spanish lady repeated, "You must wait like everyone else." And with bad grace she slammed the counter with her passport and went to the back of the queue.

I said to Bernard, "There's the voice of an English voter: pushy, pushing-in, aggressive, not-her-fault. When you're Prime Minister you must prevent people like that from having the vote."

He laughed.

We all went through. Simon and Al said goodbye to us at Security.

"We're being led by Bernard," I said.

We snaked round four times and waved to Simon and Al. At the gate a man in uniform pointed us to a table.

Bernard said, "We go to this table and take a tray."

We took trays.

"Excuse me," a man said on the next table. "It's a crazy system, but the queue starts way over there. You have to go past several tables to get here."

"We were told to come here," I said.

"But others on those other tables have been queuing."

"We were told to come here," I repeated.

We progressed through Security. I said, "Bernard's our leader." Bernard headed towards an American sports bar for lunch. On the way we passed the Mohican family.

The wife with maroon hair was sitting on the floor with her suitcase open again. She was rummaging once again. Something was clearly missing. As I passed she gave up looking and slammed both hands down into the suitcase. Then she got up and stroppily strode off, leaving the family.

"She's got to go back to the other side of Security," I said, "to see if she dropped something when she was handing out food and drink."

"Yes," Bernard said.

Bernard led us into the American bar. The rest of the family followed and queued behind us. We were seated and when I turned they had gone.

We ordered grilled chicken and fries, carrot-and-celery dips and sparkling water.

The family were sitting nearby and were joined by the lady with maroon hair. She picked at the food they had ordered, and called the waiter, who arrived with sparkling water.

"Where's my coke?" the lady with maroon hair asked.

"Did you order one?" the waiter asked.

"They did."

But they didn't. The waiter checked and told her.

"I want my coke," she said, making a scene. "You must be stupid."

The waiter disappeared.

I thought of the pusher-in who wanted to push in front of us, and of the lady who lost something from her case and now called the waiter 'stupid', and I realised that *she* was the Mohican skull who challenged the way society was run. His T-shirt was reflecting her. I thought what a rude front English families presented in Europe these days.

We found gate C35 and when we queued for our delayed flight the Mohican family were immediately in front of us, talking loudly in a Northern accent and again munching sandwiches and drinking bottles handed out from the (again) open suitcase. And again I was ashamed to be English.

I saw the lady wore a badge on her jeans jacket's lapel. I tried to decipher the words. They said 'A parroty Parliament', and I grasped she was an anarchist. She with her loudness and stroppiness was an

English voter, and she was against Parliament and all forms of order as well as being a Mohican.

I shook my head. The world had changed and I had been left behind in the old democratic world of tearful suns. Quite simply I had outlived my time. And I realised that as a reflecter of the people of my time I would also have to reflect the anarchistic people who frequented this new world and paraded their Mohican skulls.

Swollen Legs and a Fractured Shoulder

"Jean's in a bad way," Pippa said, sitting in the suspended basket while I finished my lunch. "Medically. She's gluten intolerant and she's not eating much. She's had lymphoedema for many years. She has swollen legs and she wears compression garments over them, she always wears trousers. No one in this country knows how to treat it and she's been for treatment in Switzerland, which hasn't been very satisfactory. Now her husband's got it as well, he looks dreadful. But that's by the by.... Some years ago she also had cancer and that was treated. It may be the lymph nodes were damaged or removed as part of her cancer treatment, hence her lymphoedema and her swollen legs. She had a mastectomy at Princess Grace Hospital.

"She's found it increasingly difficult to walk. She went to Holly House for an X-ray, and that showed a lump on her knee. She went to Whipps, thinking that if there was going to be expensive treatment ahead she should be in the NHS system. They said there was nothing wrong with her knee and she hadn't got a lump.

"She's been on a cruise to the Caribbean and America, because George thought it would do her good. It was a dreadful cruise, she could hardly get out of bed, she couldn't go on any excursions and she was in pain the whole time, her lymphoedema was worse. She couldn't move one leg and had to lift it to get herself out of bed. She felt trapped on the ship. Anyway, five weeks ago she was putting on her compression stocking when she fractured her collar-bone. Her arm's been in a sling ever since. She's recently had a pulley to lift her leg up and lower it when she's getting out of bed, but she can't operate the pulley with her hands now she's in a sling.

"Three weeks ago she went to the Royal Orthopaedic Hospital in Stanmore for a private consultation on her knee. They did tests and she got the result yesterday. She's got a cancerous tumour on her knee, which Whipps didn't see. And the cancer's returned to her breast area. I think she's got bone cancer, which is why her collar-bone was so fragile and snapped under the strain of pulling on a compression garment. Next week there will be decisions and she may have an operation on her knee. But it will have to be done privately now as the NHS missed it, and it will cost.

"Every Friday I play bridge and there are four of us who play together: Jean, Edwina, Marie-Louise and I'm the least decrepit. Last Friday George came to help put the tables out. Jean was in a dreadful way, she sat with her leg up, her face was twisted with pain and she couldn't get up to go to the loo. We had to move her leg and she then had to be pushed to get up, and she stood for a long time before she could begin walking. She brought her daughter and she was a treasure. She complained of feeling cold and her daughter went to the car and brought back a cardigan. And she was looking after her all the time. So her lymphoedema's got worse, her bones are fragile and she's got cancer in her breast and her knee and perhaps elsewhere too.

"Lily Borage is the most decrepit of those who play on a Friday. She won't play with anyone as she thinks she's better than them. But last Friday she was telling the others before I arrived, 'I'm going to play with Pippa. I know her family.' She's taken to waiting for me, and she's attached herself to me. It's made us laugh. Edwina said to me, 'I knew your mother-in-law' – your mother – but I don't talk about it.'"

I had listened sympathetically and had winced and pulled faces as Jean's pain and discomfort grew worse. Jean was falling apart and it seemed that nothing could be done.

The next week her bone cancer was confirmed. She had cancer in six places, including her jaw and her knee, and she made daily visits to London by car for radiotherapy and chemotherapy. Then I heard she was in the Harley Street Clinic at the end of her course of treatment. George had talked of taking her to Poland for proton treatment as he reckoned there was only one person trained to do it in the UK, who was in Manchester, and no equipment – he did not know they do proton beam therapy on the NHS at UCL in London as well as in Manchester, and private hospitals provide it – but he was in too bad a way himself to take her to Poland.

Jean was now terminally ill, and all the plans to cure her condition had collapsed. She had struggled along, but what began as swollen legs and developed into a fractured shoulder as she tried to cope with them was now cancer in her head, her body and her knee, and she was now at death's door. A swelling, a fracture, and suddenly she was facing her end.

A Laundry Bag and an Enlarged Heart

Jasmine came to the door after dark to collect the ironing bag. She said, "I'll have to bring this back on Wednesday, not Thursday. I've got a medical appointment on Thursday, my hands are really cold. It was really cold this morning. I went out to the stable and came back. I had my appointment last Thursday and they looked at the X-ray and said I've got an enlarged heart. Hypertrophic cardiomyopathy. It's what killed George Michael. If you've got it a blow on the chest can be fatal. It's a genetic disease. It's a thickening of the heart muscle. It must have been all the coughing I did when I was a child." She nodded, her nose was slightly red from the cold. "I've got to take a tablet for it but I forgot to take it this morning as I went out to the stable. The tablet does things to you, it gives side-effects, it affects your waters and.... I had to have an ECG, and then another. I thought, 'I don't want this, my father had thickening of his heart muscle and died two months later.' So perhaps with my big heart I'm on my way out. Anyway, I'm going again on Thursday and I'll hear what they're going to do. I don't want to go because I'm going away for the weekend, I haven't got time to be ill.

"I'm going down to Dorset to see my uncle. He's eighty-seven. I'll stay in a hotel, he's in good health but it's not fair to stay with someone who's eighty-seven. I'm going down to see him because he won't be around much longer, he's the one who's well and I'm the one who's now got a heart problem, I could have a heart attack or stroke." She shook her head.

"It's because you're big-hearted to all you iron for," I said, and she laughed.

"But some of them want me to bring the ironing back the next day," she said. "I shall tell them, 'I've got a big heart, you mustn't kill me.'" She laughed and said, "See you on Wednesday," and lugged the enormous blue bag of ironing – bed-change sheets, shirts and nighties – off into the dark and put it into the car.

I fobbed the gates for her and the lights came on down the drive, and as the gates opened, with her cold fingers and red nose she drove off in her little car into an uncertain dark.

Mountbatten and a Magpie

For my birthday Pippa took me to Sopwell House near St Albans. It had a long yellow *façade* and was the home of the Mountbatten family, who leased it from 1900 to 1909. Lord Mountbatten, the last Viceroy of India, spent his boyhood there, and Prince Philip's mother was proposed to in the gardens. Henry VIII had married Anne Boleyn secretly in Sopwell nunnery nearby. Sopwell House was now a hotel and spa, good for meetings as it was just off the M25, and used by professional football teams who could have some anonymity among its 129 rooms.

We had a three-course lunch in a self-service restaurant with many choices and we were then shown to our room on the second floor. It had a narrow balcony with just enough width to sit with maple and ash trees leafing round us and a view towards distant trees that hid five lakes. Inside we had round-pin plugs with just a couple of square-pins to accommodate the electrical equipment we had brought.

After 3.30 we walked to the spa and were shown to separate treatment rooms for a 'hot stones' massage. I lay face down and felt searing surges of red-hot laval black stones dragged on my back and then along the back of each leg by a strapping girl to soothing, relaxing moonscape music. I was drowsy when I turned over and nearly drifted off as the burning of the stones pervaded my arms, my chest and the fronts of my legs.

We were near a door to the gardens and later we strolled out to the large pond (or small lake) where *koi* carp saw us and swam towards us, mouths open as if expecting to be fed. We walked in the grounds and looked at how the House had been extended at the back to create the spa and then returned to our room for green tea and iced French *macarons* which had been left on a slate saying 'Happy Birthday' in icing.

We went down to the restaurant for dinner and sat in a longish room with two other couples. One – Pippa spotted and found on her phone – was a well-known actor who had acted with Meghan Markle. We had glasses of champagne and toasted *canapés* with the chef's compliments – duck's liver – and then asparagus broth, and I had asparagus as a starter and then guinea fowl, followed by chocolate and orange mousse.

I slept fitfully and showered next morning. When I left the bathroom Pippa said "Shh" and pointed to the door to the balcony.

A magpie was sitting on the outside doorknob, tapping the window with its beak.

We went down for breakfast. There was a huge choice. I had fruits, cereals, Bircher muesli, a cooked breakfast, toast, honey and coffee.

We packed and settled the bill and I went out to our car with our luggage while Pippa went back inside to find a leaflet about the spa.

I thought of how the House would have been in Mountbatten's youth, when it was an Edwardian home with round-pin electricity, modern in its day, and how the public had now taken over and filled it with a diverse clientele that reflected the previous weekend's royal wedding between Prince Harry and Meghan. When I was born before the Second World War the UK had ruled a quarter of the world, and Mountbatten had come to India as the last Viceroy ('Deputy King') and had begun the post-war withdrawal from the British Empire. Mountbatten had stood for the equality of Indians and British, of dark-skinned and white, which Prince Charles would now stand for as the next Head of the Commonwealth.

Now we did not have to be imperial. We had declined as a world power but now, in my eightieth year, I could see that the world was better with satellites, the internet and satnavs, and black and white could share in a world harmony. And for a fleeting moment I thought that Mountbatten had come back as a black-and-white magpie to tap-tap-tap on my window to stress the need for this diversity today.

A Coffin Trunk and a Dressing-Room Honours Board

Simon took me to Lord's for champagne tea in the Long Room. We sat near a string triplet of violinists down the far end and ate sandwiches, scones and cakes and sipped champagne and tea.

Then a guide took us to the Lord's museum to see the Ashes, the urn that is supposed to contain a burnt bail following a satirical obituary in *The Sporting Times* after England lost for the first time to Australia at cricket in 1882.

The guide wanted to know what countries we all came from and he told the story of the Ashes very fluently and asked us questions. We then wandered round the exhibits and I was struck by a large trunk in a glass case. A placard described it as "Nasser Hussain's coffin trunk" which he had taken on tour to South Africa in 2000. It was large enough to hold his bats and pads and other cricketing gear, almost large enough to be his coffin. I had known him and had spoken to him during my previous visit to the Long Room, and I reflected sadly that now his cricketing career had finished and was buried in his coffin trunk.

We returned to the pavilion and climbed stairs and walked along corridors to the home dressing-room, which was also the England dressing-room. There was green padded seating all round the walls and a waist-high island of lockers in the middle. The hyperactive guide went round the room pointing at seats and reciting who had sat there during the last 50 years. In a *tour de force* of memory he recited getting on for 50 surnames of past cricketers, so we all knew who had sat where. He said that Flintoff was the untidiest, and that his bats and pads were strewn all over the floor. We went out onto the balcony and looked down at the deserted pitch and then returned to peer at the honours boards: centuries for batsmen, five/ten wickets for bowlers.

I saw Hussain's name as one of the centurions. This was his immortality. His career was in the "coffin trunk" in the museum, but here his century for England would live on a board for ever. All my boyhood cricketing heroes like Denis Compton had gone the same way: they had left behind a relic in the museum and been fêted on a dressing-room honours board.

A Great Star and a Green Band

Simon took me to Lord's by car to see the third day of the First Test between England and Pakistan, who were 166 ahead in their first innings. Paul and Bernard came too. We climbed the outside staircase to the Marylebone Suite for breakfast about 9.30, and had a green band tagged on our wrist and our tickets put in a holder round our necks. We ate bacon baps at our table, and were served coffee.

Then we all walked round the ground to catch the excitement of a full crowd arriving. I was greeted by an Old Boy in a blazer and an MCC tie, a member who would be sitting in the pavilion.

We found our seats, cunningly just under cover and sheltered from both rain and morning sun. Then we went back to the Suite for champagne, and Graham Gooch was standing by our table in an open-necked shirt and shirtsleeves. He was looking after us for the day.

I asked him about the state of the game.

He said, "England are up against it." They would have to score a lot of runs later today if they were not to lose.

I asked him why England was behind: "Is it accurate bowling by Pakistan or lack of resolve by England?"

He was reluctant to answer, so I said, "When you made 333 against India here at Lord's in 1990, and we saw it on television in Cornwall, you had resolve, you went on and on."

I had mentioned his greatest feat. He said, "You have to be patient. When I got out I went back to the pavilion and Micky Stewart, the tour manager, said, 'Why are you back here? You should have gone for the record.' He gave me a bollocking for getting out. I didn't know about the record. What was it, Hutton...."

"364," I said, "and Sobers got more, and Lara."

He nodded.

"The present England team could do with you coaching them again," I said. "You were doing well until the batsmen let you down in Australia by swiping and getting out."

He nodded again. We found our seats and sat and sipped champagne while Pakistan increased their lead to 179 before getting out. England batted and lost early wickets.

At lunch in the Marylebone Suite – duck's liver, then help-yourself to chicken, smoked salmon, prawns with a very full salad, followed by chocolate and orange tart with more champagne and red wine – we encountered Gooch.

"It's definitely a shock for England," he said. "They've come here, the seventh side in the world rankings, and are doing this to us in our backyard in English conditions. Something's definitely wrong."

England were 110–6 but rallied through a late stand. At tea I watched Gooch go from table to table, an ex-cricketer and England captain, perhaps earning a couple of thousand as appearance fee, giving his opinion on the game, talking to people who were pleased to meet him. I thought, 'I believe he lives alone, having been divorced in 1992. He can earn money here where he's remembered – here, where he scored 333 – and go and see the players. It's a good life for him.'

Later Simon returned to the Marylebone Suite and found the official on the door challenging Gooch's identity: "Where's your green band?"

Simon had his ticket round his neck and a green band on his wrist, and Gooch did not have these. He said to Simon, "Several of the officials don't recognise me now."

It was a new set of circumstances for the ex-cricketer to come to terms with in the present phase of his life: no longer being recognised. In his heyday in 1990 he had been a great star, the most recognisable man in the ground, scoring century after century, worshipped like a god by whole swathes of the England crowd. But now his achievements had slid into the past, and he was not always even able to get into the Suite so he could tour the tables and earn his latter-day match fee by reminiscing about his awesome feats.

A Hole in the Carpet and a Stately Garden

Gully was bending in the rose-beds when I got back. I went out and he straightened, wincing at the discomfort to his hip. He wore a hat against the sun and there were weeds in the green wheelbarrow.

"Have you heard of Guerdon Hall?" he asked.

"Yes," I said. "Dawn owned it. Her husband was a local landowner and was found drowned in mysterious circumstances in Hobbs Cross pond. It's not clear whether he passed out after wading in to cut weed or whether he drowned himself. She inherited the Hall and the stately garden. Her son Tom was an MP but he lost his seat. I've been there a couple of times. Elizabeth I was supposed to have stayed there but it was burnt down and rebuilt and what you see inside today is not what Elizabeth I saw. And the lawn's large enough to put up a very long and large marquee."

Gully nodded. "It's near the motorway. It's noisy. I've worked in the afternoon for Clara," he said. "Her daughter-in-law. She lives in the road behind the NatWest Bank, I forget what it's called. She moved into the Hall to look after her, and was with her when she died. Dawn's left it to Clara's husband. They've not got the money to keep it going. There are gardeners but they can't afford to pay them. I've been asked if I'll go and work there in the afternoons."

I was surprised.

"It's a huge garden," I said. It was only the previous day that he had told Pippa he was too tired to work in the afternoons following his convalescence after his operation on his back (during which we had paid his salary for three months).

"I need something in the afternoons," he said. "I've been £270 a week down since I came back. I had to miss an afternoon last week as my hip was hurting. That was 40 quid I lost. Because I was with her behind the NatWest she's taken me with her there. There are things that need doing to my house and I can't pay for them, I have to do everything myself. My son's room's wiring had to be done. My wife's in Australia seeing her sister, as you know, so I've had to do it on my own. I couldn't find where the wiring went so I cut a hole in his carpet and had the floorboards up and there's no wiring there. I couldn't solve it, I haven't been able to find the wiring, and now he's got a hole in the carpet, and my wife will find out when she comes back from Australia. I need to go to Guerdon Hall to get my finances back on track."

And I thought how a cedar split and lost a branch in a storm in our garden, and how it was wedged against a branch from an oak. Gully had wanted to climb the tree and dangle like a spider and cut the branch up for £120, but he could not even get on the mower seat, let alone climb a tree with a harness, and he was not insured, and we had asked Wayne across the road to bring his professional fully-insured dangler.

I knew that the size of Guerdon Hall's garden was beyond him. He could not keep up with the grass-cutting and the weeding in our garden working five mornings a week, and there was no chance he could keep up with the grass-cutting and weeding at Guerdon Hall, where a team of gardeners currently worked. As with our cedar, he was saying he could do something when he couldn't. It was a dream, that a fit Gully from thirty years ago with no spinal or hip problems could do masses of heavy work, but the reality was different. I doubted whether he would ever fulfil his dream of breaking free from living off his credit card and breaking out of financial hardship.

A New Wife and a Septic Tank

On the way home in the car Simon and I talked in undertones on the back seat so the driver would not hear.

"Stan's losing interest in what he's doing for us," Simon said. "He sometimes does half a day's work instead of two, so I've got him signing on in reception when he comes in and signing off, so I know how long he's been working. You remember he wanted to move to Canvey Island. He did, and he became a councillor there for a while, which is what he wanted to do, while coming back to work for us two days a week.

"His wife Jane died soon after the move. There was a funeral there. He put news of his wife's death on Facebook and a school friend of his wrote to him saying she was sorry he had lost his wife, and they're getting married. They will sell their houses and buy a bigger one on Canvey Island. He has a boat there. His life's there now. It's strange how life turns out, isn't it? He announced his wife's death and the announcement found her replacement, all on social media."

I mused. It came back to me that in the old days we had a septic tank installed before there was main drainage. It was like a yellow submarine, and the fire brigade came and lowered it into the hole we'd dug. Stan had helped us and as we stood near the hole I handed him an envelope containing his month's wages – he was paid in cash in those days – and while cement was being pumped round the septic tank he dropped his envelope and it disappeared under the cement. When I heard this I paid him again so he would not have to take the hit, and he was very grateful.

I reflected. I paid him, he dropped the envelope in the cement and I paid him again. And now his wife had died, he dropped news into Facebook, and he had a wife again. Somehow there was a pattern that was hard to fathom. He had always been someone who had lost and then found, and now he would be living with a new wife who he had found by reporting his loss.

A Lurch and a Wall

The dental surgery rang: "You've got a six-monthly appointment tomorrow but Dr Clerihew's retired, she's not seeing any more patients."

"Oh dear," I said, "what's happened?"

"She thinks she's got a virus. It's affected her balance. Anyway, she's retired. Can I put you in for Thursday at 9.45 with the senior partner, Will Lee? Dr Clerihew's coming in to clear her room, you may see her then."

She had been a good dentist. She had taken out two of my upper teeth after finding pus in my gum which could have gone to my brain. She had been very thorough and always X-rayed me and studied the X-rays for signs of abnormality.

I was slightly early on Thursday. Dr Clerihew was standing near the receptionist, looking very elegant despite her green scrubs and green mask. She had curly brown hair and was made up to give her cheeks a bit more colour, and she greeted me with her customary reserve. There was no one else in the waiting-room.

I pointed at her in recognition and said, "If you've got a moment when you are ready come and have a chat."

Standing at the counter, I was given a form to fill in asking me to tick Yes or No to two dozen medical conditions I might have had. Pressing on the counter I ticked No to the lot and sat down and began reading my newspaper.

Dr Clerihew was now sitting alongside the receptionist who was studying her screen. She stood up and came round the high counter. She lurched and nearly staggered into the wall as she advanced and sat down beside me. I immediately thought, 'She's got a brain tumour.'

"I *am* sorry to hear you're leaving," I said. "And I'm sorry you've not been well."

"It's probably just a virus," she said, not wanting to talk about it. "It's affected my balance."

"Would you come back if your balance came back?"

"Oh no. I made the decision to leave before my balance went. The virus was coincidental."

"When were you aware of first losing your balance?"

"Oh, in March."

"It's now mid-June. Have you had tests and scans?"

"Yes, but I'm awaiting the results." It did not sound true. Surely she was not still awaiting results after three months? I noticed the orangey blush she had painted on her pale cheeks.

"You look well," I said, "really well. Sometimes I see someone and think, 'God, he looks ill.' But with you it's the opposite."

"It's because I've been sleeping late and doing nothing," she said, "getting the hang of retirement."

"Will you be all right financially?" I asked. "Pension? Welfare State?"

"I'll manage," she said with reserve.

"You may need looking after."

"It's probably just a virus," she said. But we both knew it was more.

"I want to thank you for looking after my teeth so well. You've been an excellent dentist."

She smiled.

"I've got to go back to Buckhurst Hill now," she said.

"How will you travel?" I asked, wondering if I should give her a lift after my appointment.

"Oh, Uber."

She stood up and with difficulty walked back to the receptionist.

"I've lost my bag," she said.

I thought, 'That's a consequence of the brain tumour. It's affected her memory.'

"It's here," the receptionist said, handing it to her.

Then she was heading for the door.

"Goodbye," I said as she passed me.

"Goodbye."

I instinctively thought I would not be seeing her again.

I was called up to Mr Lee. He was a small Chinaman with stick-up hair, and I grasped that he was really Mr Li. He did a holding operation. He found I had no fillings, "You have excellent teeth, sir," and instead of using the scaling machine he hand-picked at the base of my teeth and when I mouth-washed and spat at the end a dozen bits of what looked like sliced-off gum filled the swirling bowl.

I said, "You will keep an eye on Dr Clerihew, won't you? She could be ill."

"Oh yes," said Mr Li, "we will."

"I've known her for thirty years," said his large assistant, "I'll keep an eye on her."

I paid the receptionist downstairs.

"It doesn't look too good about Dr Clerihew," I said while she coped with my card.

"No."

"You'll stay in touch with her?"

"Yes."

I left. I had witnessed Dr Clerihew's last day at work. That was how it was, you got in early and worked all hours with a full waiting-room and then you got giddy and stopped. For all I knew she was terminally ill, but she had presented her illness with lightness of touch during our social chit-chat as a virus, even though she had lurched into the wall. Ahead of us all was a wall, and we were all waiting to lurch into it. Her time had come, and our time would eventually come.

A Shower and a Threat

Gully buzzed the gate. He had lost his gate fob and key. I fobbed him in and walked down to the front door and waited. He parked his car, got out and came over. We talked about where his key might be: in the car boot, under his car's front seat, in another pair of trousers or on a floor in his house.

"Can I have next week off?" he asked. "I've got a lot to do." He pursed his lips. "It's my wife," he said. "I didn't do enough while she was away in Australia. I've got to do the bathroom. The shower leaked and I took it out, but I haven't fitted a new one. I bought a new one from a shop that was closing down. It was a good one, £997 reduced to £270. She said, 'You do realise that was a display model and it's probably not got an inside, and the shop's closed now, don't you?' They wouldn't do that to me, would they? They would...." He laughed ruefully.

"And there are tiles to fit all round the shower. The old ones haven't been fitted properly, there's mould behind them, so I've taken them off. And the bath's encrusted. I've got a new bath in the garage but it's green and she says, 'I'm not getting in a green bath.' But beggars can't be choosers. And the new light downstairs in the hall doesn't work as I've not fitted a wire to it. She found the hole I cut in the carpet looking for it....

"Her attitude to me's completely changed since she got back. I've put in new garage doors, but she's only thinking of the bathroom. She said, 'You should have finished the bathroom while I was away, you've not done enough. I'm going to leave you.' At first I thought she was bluffing, but now I'm not sure. It's as if she's threatening me. I haven't got the money to get someone in to do these jobs. I have to do them myself. I'm afraid she's going to leave me.

"She looks good.... She's been used to luxury at her sister's in Australia, and the pool they've got, and the sea. And I think she wants to go back without me, sell the house and take 50 per cent and go out with my son permanently, having dumped me." He smiled ruefully and disarmingly.

"Sure," I said. "You can have next week off. I can see what's happened. She's got used to the life of luxury with her sister, who's said, 'Come out and join us.' She's had an immaculate bathroom there and now she's got one without a shower or tiles and an encrusted bath, that could do with a good clean. You've got a son and son-in-law who can help you. Make it into a family event. Go to your daughter's this evening and ask her to get her husband to buy a new shower at Wickes or somewhere and come in and fit it over the weekend and also wire up the light. He's an electrician and gas fitter who also fits showers. Get him involved. And ask your son to buy some tiles and fit them over the weekend. He tiles places for a living, you've told me. Say to both that you're still recovering from your operation and need their help. Make it a family event, all hands to the pump, so your wife can see you're serious about putting the bathroom right. So over the weekend sort the structural problem out, the shower, the tiling, the bath and the light. Then spend the rest of the week cleaning up the house."

Gully nodded. "I'm tempted to tell her to clear off," he said.

"You mustn't do that. Go with what she's asking for. Australia will recede. She won't want to live the other side of the world from her children. Make a comfortable home for her in the next ten days."

He nodded. "Thank you," he said, "I'll go and see my daughter this evening."

He went off to begin his work. I watched him plod slowly along. His back or hip was still impeding the way he walked, he was only just coping, life was a struggle for him and mislaying his keys didn't help. He scraped along and somehow his wife had put up with living in a home that was chaotic. He started jobs around the house and did not finish them. He began work without thinking it through and so areas of his house were unfinished, tiles were off the bathroom wall, he had removed the shower and not replaced the bath, and now his wife had an escape route to Australia, but she needed to do up the house first to maximise the amount she would get if it were sold.

The next morning he came in late as usual as I was returning from collecting the papers. I had left the gates open for him.

"Did you find your keys?" I asked.

"No, it's a bit of a mystery. There are plenty of places I can still look, in the boot of the car, down the side of the sofa."

"Did you speak to your daughter?" I asked.

"No, I got back from my other job too late and we had to go shopping. And my wife went out to meet my daughter. She looked fantastic, she's 64 but she looks very good, she's always been a good dresser."

"Did she fix up for your son-in-law to help this weekend?"

"No, I couldn't ask her to do that."

"Did you speak to your son about helping you with the tiles?"

"No. I've got to do preparation first, plastering, I won't be ready to tile until I've done the plastering. And the shower can't be fitted until the tiles are in. And I have to sort out the financing of the tiles."

I had given him a week off to sort out his bathroom but I doubted he would be any further forward in a week's time. I could see how his wife felt about it all, having had many years of constant delays and nothing finished. If I had been her I would not have stood for his excuses. I had lost patience with him now. There was no more I could do. So I nodded and took the papers indoors and glanced at the headlines, and soon he was out of my thoughts.

A Mask and a Quiche

"I've been to see Jean," Pippa said, sitting down after parking her car. "It's all dreadful but she's doing well. George let me in. She's had the radiotherapy, five sessions. I don't know what happens normally, but they put her in a tight-fitting heavy mask from the top of her head to down below her shoulders – it has gauze in it – and fastened her down, I believe screwed her to the couch, so she couldn't move, so she was trapped in her mask. She was in the Harley Street Clinic for a week after that because she was so frail. Now she's having the chemotherapy. The first dose was up there, then it's every fortnight at home. There's a machine that stays at her home and people come and operate it. She had the latest dose yesterday. She was all right today but she won't be tomorrow and the next day. She can hardly move. Her leg is very swollen at the best of times because of the lymphoedema but now with the tumour on her knee it's enormous.

"What happens at the end she doesn't know, but there's a plan. I guess they'll assess the chemotherapy when it's finished and decide if they're going to operate. Under the circumstances she's bearing up well. George went across the road and came back with a bacon sarnie for himself and for me, and a quiche for her. She can't have the pastry, so she just had the quiche filling. She's just going with it and not thinking about the future. She'll see where she's got to when this round of treatment has ended."

I shook my head. She had worn a mask for the first part of her treatment and she was wearing a mask of quietly going with it, a mask of acceptance, of making light of her ordeal, and ahead was her hair falling out and a possible operation on her tumour and the prospect of trying to live on when she had cancer in six places, trying to appear normal, eating savoury quiche even though she couldn't eat the unsavoury pastry.

Outside a song thrush was singing in the large oak tree, four clear piping calls and then a trill. I thought of the beauty outside and the horror that was being endured in Jean's house, alleviated by a treat of quiche, and I shook my head. Life was full of beauty and terror, and the two were held in balance by the mind's harmonious reconciliation of all the opposites encountered each day. It was a truly wretched business which she bore with fortitude and aplomb.

A Tudor Hall and a Woman Priest

Pippa went back to the very historical Tudor house we used to own. It was associated with many Tudor and Jacobean events. The owners Patrick and Celia who had succeeded us had had two young children, and were selling fourteen years later, following rumours they had split. The property had been on the market for two-and-a-half years and this might be the last opportunity to visit for a while. She had seen a notice on a board and had applied to be one of the party from our area who were to meet down there. The last time we went I had been recognised and as the owners had threatened to sue us over a nearby footpath immediately after the sale I had had to beat a hasty retreat. Celia had become the local vicar and had used the house as a place of silent retreats rather than as a living museum where history had happened.

Pippa went with Amy. I said to her, "Ask Amy to find out what happened, why they're selling." She left about 8 and was back around 5.

"How did you get on?" I asked.

She sat down and said, "Fine. There were about forty-five there. We didn't know any of them. Patrick, the owner, made a short speech saying it's a home, we were welcome to take pictures but his son's shoes might be under a table. There were two guides and we were split into two groups. Amy and I had a man of about sixty. He gave a complete history of the Hall and its owners as we toured the rooms, which are pretty much the same, with some no-go areas now. He barely mentioned our predecessors, but there was a lot on us. 'Philip and Pippa' featured very strongly, all the research you did for the guidebook, which they are still selling. He said we transformed the place and opened it, and that all his knowledge was based on your research. We were shown in a very positive light. Our organiser was with us and remembered my name on her list and at lunchtime she asked me, 'Are you the Pippa Rawley he's been speaking about?' I had to confess. She told Patrick, and Patrick came over. He was very nice. He said, 'Hello, how nice to see you. You can come at any time. I'd be delighted to see you any time. How's Philip?'

"I said, 'You're selling, things change, children grow up....'

"He said, 'All Suffolk knows things have changed. Yes, the children have grown up. I've divorced Celia, she's living in Felixstowe with a woman priest.'"

I was staggered. "In a Lesbian relationship?"

"She said, 'I think so.' I went back and told Amy, 'I've found out what happened, we don't have to try now.' When I told her, her jaw dropped. She didn't say anything, there was nothing she could say. She was amazed."

I said, "This must have happened two-and-a-half years ago. There's a team that runs getting on for a dozen of the local churches in a Benefice. They must both be in the team."

"I would think so. Perhaps under the divorce settlement Patrick and Celia will get 50 per cent each of the house when it's sold." Then she said, "Afterwards we had a tour of the gardens with the three-day-a-week gardener. He's a conservationist, he likes wild flowers, so in many areas the wild flowers and weeds are waist-high and there are nettles everywhere. Under us, our gardener used to say, 'Ten acres and you won't find a single weed.' Not any longer. The grass is cut by a contractor and sometimes Patrick does it to save money, so he just conserves. The gardens are very overgrown, and my aster bed and the hostas and hollies I put in have completely disappeared. Round the moat's very overgrown and a wild hedge and small trees block views of the moat."

I shook my head and mused. Celia had been horrid to our guides and had sacked most of them – one because she pulled out of a tour and got herself covered to say goodbye to her dying father – and, a lawyer by training, she had threatened to take me to court. She had then astonished everyone by becoming the local vicar and preaching 'Love thy neighbour', having sacked most of her staff. And now this. I wondered what God thought of her setting aside her family for the woman priest. I did not think He had been sacked like our guides as she was still in the Benefice team, so presumably He had come to terms with the changing mores of England and had gone along with it and put aside the family-based morality on which the confessionals of Catholic priests had been founded. Now Christians could do what they wanted, and that was right, and what had been right and supported by the Church had changed.

She had progressed from being a member of a family that owned and ran the Tudor Hall to being, in her own right, a woman priest who was now co-owner of a Tudor Hall, and her husband had been cast aside. I could see that her choice of her sexual identity was behind the sale of the Hall I had lovingly renovated and restored.

A Car Park and Marathons

The school *fête* was in full swing as Simon and I walked round the field which I owned and remembered from my own schooldays covered in buttercups, looking at the stalls, dodgem cars, bouncing castle and a roundabout with a whitewashed policeman turning at the top. There were several hundred parents and children doing things at the tables and queuing at the attractions.

A parent stopped and chatted to Simon. He said to me, "I can see you're his father, you look alike."

We walked on and Simon said, "He's a comedian for a living, he does children's parties and is often dressed as a clown. He's a clown."

Al came and hugged my knees. He had already won eight bottles of wine in the tombola, all with a raffle ticket stuck on them.

We had reached the corner of the field. Simon said, "I'll show you the car park. No one's looking. Can you swing your legs over this low fence?"

We followed a path through bushes and came out to an open area of flattened hard core.

"Room for fifty cars," Simon said, "that won't have to be parked on the road at the front. They'll come in through the gates and there'll be a road round to the drop-off point where you're standing. Cars will continue out through the gates. There'll be a button-system to open the gates out of hours. It'll put our numbers up and pay for itself in three years. I was held up for six months because there were adders. Seven were caught and relocated at a cost of £10,000."

I pulled a face. We climbed back over the low fence and walked on round the field. We passed a recently retired England footballer who had just ended a stint as a manager in India. I had a word with him about the coming world cup in Russia. He said, "Things are going in the right direction, we've got a manager who believes in going forward. It's all down to the manager."

There was a free table under the shade of the big oak tree with four wooden chairs. I sat on one of them and Pippa came and joined me. Kay's mother sat opposite me.

She said, "Trump's just met the North-Korean leader in Singapore. You know I lived in Malaya as a little girl. I've been wondering, do you know why Singapore left the Malayan Federation in 1965?"

I thought and said, "President Li Kuan Yew was Chinese. I think there were tensions between the Chinese and the Malays. He looked at Taiwan and wanted Singapore to do well on its own as a Chinese state, like Taiwan." She nodded. "I was reading about the Malayan Federation only last night," I said. "I've been reading Maugham's short stories and several are set in the Malayan Federation. 'The Outstation' for example. There's a Resident, living in an outstation in the middle of nowhere, and an Englishman who's an upstart and calls him a snob comes to assist him, and they hate each other. It was how we ran the Empire, which was good. It brought the remote places on. Maugham describes the way of life. There's a club in a distant city, there's tiffin in the afternoon and they dress for dinner. And the upstart's refused to give his Malay boy three months' salary and gets killed with a *kris*, a Malayan knife." She nodded. "Maugham doesn't explain the Malay words, you'd enjoy the stories."

She nodded. "I was in an outstation. My father took us to a remote place and I went to school with Malays. There was an American complex nearby where we could go and swim...."

Then I spotted the Chairman of our accountants, Jim O'Shaughnessy, in a white sweatshirt buying a burger for his son. "Excuse me," I said, and I stood up and crossed and he shook my hand, holding a burger in his other hand and supervising his small munching son.

"You're Chairman now," I said. "In football terms, the manager."

He nodded. "And Senior Tax Partner. I'm sad to be because Mervyn died. I'd rather he was still alive."

"I last talked to him in that event at the Tower," I said.

"It was our 65th birthday," he said. "He'd come back from being ill with throat cancer."

I nodded. "I dreamt about him two nights ago," I said. "I had to visit my accountant who was in a shop at the top of Church Hill. I took my receipts in and Mervyn was standing behind the counter. I knew he was dead and nearly asked, 'What's it like being dead?' He said I had to bring four empty third-of-a-pint milk bottles like the ones we had at school when we were children. I knew I'd forgotten them and I walked back towards my house, which was also in Church Hill, to bring them – and woke up. So I dreamt about the last Chairman. The clients dream about the Chairman."

He laughed. "Mervyn died six years ago," he said dreamily.

I knew he ran marathons for charity, and had run seven marathons in seven continents in seven days, starting in Antarctica (–20°C), flying to Chile (South America), then Miami (North America), then Madrid (Europe), Marrakesh (Africa), Dubai (Asia) and finally Sydney (Australasia, 36°C). He was one of only nine people in the world to have done this. But he looked overweight and slightly out of condition, especially after finishing his burger.

I reminisced how in the old days he and I had tried to persuade our staff to join one of Mervyn's share schemes, and how reluctant the staff had been to believe that this would be to their advantage. I said, "I remember saying to them, 'I feel as if I'm saying "Free £5 notes are going here, come and take one,"' and you're all crossing over the road, suspicious of being given free money.'"

He nodded and laughed.

Simon came and joined us. "Your dad was just saying he'd like to take over from you," Jim said with a twinkle in his eye, and Simon laughed, knowing I would not say that.

"I showed him the school," I said to Simon, "and now he's a parent."

"Lovely school," Jim said.

The *fête* ended with a raffle at 3. The Head stood with the Deputy Head and called out numbers and handed over two lions, which were larger than the children who won them. They handed out many other prizes.

In due course I left to carry the bottles Al had won up to Simon's house. I passed a small crowd.

The Deputy Head, a blonde with a full face, was gamely sitting on a chair under an oilskin that looked like a cycling cape and was dodging a wet sponge thrown at her by children and adults who had paid for each throw. She screwed up her face as one caught her chin.

I walked through the gate from the field where I had spent much of my childhood. I reflected on the hard-core car park that would keep it all going and the isolation of the lives of some of the hard-working parents and grandparents: the clown, the football manager, the resident's daughter and the marathon-running Chairman. Everyone there was running some sort of marathon in their busy lives, and Simon's marathon included laying the hard core for a new car park that would allow more children to enjoy the beauty of the field and its ancient trees.

A Scraped Knee and Tattered Hands

Paul led the way into the Queen Victoria, a beamy pub, and at the bar ordered drinks. I carried my red wine to a table laid for six in the restaurant round the corner and sat alongside Pippa and opposite Paul and Elza, who wore lacey platform shoes. Paul raised his glass and said, "Happy Father's Day. Susan and Mike are coming but have been held up in traffic so we're starting."

We studied the menus and Elza said how much she had enjoyed cycling at the weekends: "I go to Theydon Garnon and sometimes as far as Greensted church and avoid the wide roads and stick to narrow lanes and the countryside. It's a complete change from sitting in front of my screen all day. I really like it."

"Only she fell off her bike," Paul said.

"Yes, I did. I grazed my knee."

"It was more than a graze. It was a scrape, skin off."

"Is it painful?" Pippa asked.

"Yes, still. I hit something uneven in a path I was cycling on. But it won't stop me cycling into the countryside. I love it."

We ordered roasts. Then Susan and Mike came. Susan said, "The traffic's at a standstill on the A127. We managed two miles in half an hour."

Pippa and I had sat down and shuffled sideways along a long leather seat beneath a table overhanging our knees, and I could not get up. I kissed Susan from a sedentary position and put my hand out to clasp Mike's hand across the table.

"No, his skin's erupted," Susan said, sitting next to me, opposite Mike. "He's had a relapse. We haven't slept, he was so uncomfortable last night. It's from within out."

His hands were bright pink and there were many splits in the skin. It looked as though his right hand had been in boiling water. There was a plaster round one finger.

"The doctors are hopeless," Susan said after the waitress had taken her order. "There's no appointment for three months, then they don't know what to prescribe and the tablets don't work, like the present ones he's taking. We've been sent to dermatological consultants by the GPs but I think we should be going to an immunologist at Southend Hospital. It's one of the best places for immunology. He was completely clear until he had a burst appendix – peritonitis – in Germany when we were at Hintlesham Hall for your 70th birthday. He was told he'd be dead in an hour unless he had the operation." (I remembered her in tears as she left for Germany.) "I think the peritonitis caused a weakness in his immune system and caused him to have pernicious anaemia, which cuts across the tablets for a skin condition that he's been prescribed. So the tattering and splits are coming from within because his immune system can't control it. He's got another appointment but it's in three months' time. And he's performing on his keyboard on stage next weekend. He can hardly hold a knife and fork, let alone perform. He can't wear gloves for playing. He's in agony, playing through pain."

"Perhaps you should go to Southend Hospital's A&E and say, 'Look, this is urgent, please admit him to see the immunology consultant tomorrow,'" I said, "and force an appointment without waiting three months, appeal to their sense of feeling they should help."

"They don't feel like that," said Susan. "They go on holiday without saying. You turn up and find you're seeing someone else. They don't seem to care. They've got their system of three-monthly waits and that can't be changed."

I said nothing and our food arrived.

"I've started a 'banned foods' list," Susan said, "based on research I've found online."

"No tap water," Mike said, pulling a face. "No all sorts of things. I've had allergy tests and they couldn't say I was allergic to any one thing. But I can't have blueberries, and I like them, I have them every day."

"So do I," I said sympathetically as I ate my roast.

"We've got to go to a funeral on Monday," Susan said. "In Bournemouth. Mike's uncle went round to his neighbour and said, 'I'm short of breath,' and dropped dead in front of him at 83."

I said I was sorry to Mike. Then I turned to talk to Paul and Elza to bring them into the conversation.

An old man sitting opposite an old lady got up at the next table and knocked into Mike as he left. "Sorry," he said. "I'm here for Father's Day but my sons are elsewhere. One's in Scotland and the other's in Litchfield. They can't come. I'm with the mother of one of my son's wives. We're celebrating Father's Day without them."

Everyone was coping with some difficulty, and everyone had a cross to bear. Elza was in pain from her scrapes, and Mike could hardly fork food into his mouth from his tattered hands. A Bournemouth family were mourning Mike's uncle, and the man at the next table was without his sons on Father's Day.

Life was a struggle, but it was still enjoyable. I tucked into my three flavours of ice-cream – honeycomb, vanilla and chocolate – and explained to the family as they had heard many times that I had been deprived of ice-cream by Hitler during the war and I was making up for it now.

There was laughter.

I said I could remember sitting in my high chair during the war and seeing a map of Europe on the wall, the troop fronts marked by my father with coloured pins, and that I could remember sitting in my pram outside the post office while my mother went in to buy stamps. "And anyone could have pushed the pram away," I said. "I might not be here now, I might be sitting over there. I might be the old man at the next table who can't see his sons."

And again everyone laughed.

Yes, life was enjoyable amid the family even though knees and hands were sore.

A Slipper and a Clout

Simon took Pippa and me to The Bald Faced Stag (as I think of it, it's now called Toby Carvery) for the grandchildren's early 'Grandpa's Day' lunch.

Al showed me his mouth and said, "Guess what's new."

I said, "You've got a brace," and he nodded.

Minnie showed me her broken finger, which looked as if it had healed now.

Bernard showed me his phone and I saw a picture of a red car.

"It's my new car, Grandpa," he said. "It's a Ford Fiesta. It's going to be parked outside Dad's. I've had six driving lessons already. I'll be able to drive it on my seventeenth birthday."

"Before then," Simon said, "I'll take you to a place in Romford. There's a village off the road with streets and speed limits and you'll be able to drive the car there."

Kay had joined us and we sat round the table. She said, "Al cried in Spain because he didn't want to come back."

"But then he remembered Daddy was here and that was all right," I said.

"I remembered I'd better want to come back," Al said with a wicked gleam in his eyes.

We queued at the carvery and returned to our table with laden plates, and the conversation turned to schools.

"Did any of you ever get the cane at school?" Al asked.

"Yes, I did," I said.

Al's eyes widened. "Why were you whacked?"

"I was captain of cricket and I was put in imposition school ('impot', detention) and the master wanted me at cricket nets and not in detention so he did a deal with another master that I could be free to go to nets if I was whacked."

Al took it in with wide eyes and nodded.

"Did you, Grandma?"

"I got the slipper," Pippa said.

"Why?" I asked.

"For semantic reasons," said Pippa, who was good at semantics and doing Sudoku. "We were told not to run so I skipped. To me skipping was not running. I thought it was unfair, I hadn't been running."

"It is interpreted as cheek," I said.

Pippa ignored my remark.

"When I got home I told my father. He was a policeman," she explained to Al, "and he was so cross with me for breaking school rules that he clouted me. To get slippered meant getting one from him. I thought that was unfair."

"It was tough at school in your days," Al said.

"It was a bit like *Tom Brown's Schooldays*," I said. "Schools were places of violence in those days. Sometimes it was like a battlefield, there would be bodies strewn all over the playground."

Al laughed. "I don't think so, Grandpa, you're making that up."

"But things were tougher in those days," I smiled. "Some would say a good job too as you youngsters have it too easy today. Do you agree?"

Al and Minnie vigorously shook their heads to general mirth.

Tests and Cappuccinos

I went for my six-monthly review with Dr Erdmann in Harley Street. I arrived at 9.45 having fasted, and sat in the waiting-room for my 10.30 appointment. I headed off for the loo and was stopped by the receptionist who was in a loose black *hijab*: "You have to do a urine sample, shall I give you the bottle now?"

At 10.30 I was taken up in the lift to the first floor by a secretary and shown into a large treatment room where an Australian nurse weighed me, tested my sight, measured my breaths (getting me to blow into a tube three times), took four phials of my blood and sat me stripped to the waist on a couch to have sticky pads placed over my body for an ECG test. Then I was taken through to Dr Erdmann, who was in a dark suit and tie.

For 90 minutes he tested me from head to foot, searching through the seborrhoeic warts on my back for possible carcinomas, hitting my knee bones with a tuning-fork and pressing my groin for hernias and squeezing my scrotum for cysts.

At the end he said, "You should have a shingles vaccine as you once had chickenpox and so have the virus."

I was led to another treatment room and sat on a bed and was vaccinated for shingles.

Then I went downstairs to the waiting-room and sat amid his modern art and poured myself water and took my tablets. Then I made myself a cappuccino and munched a packet of biscuits to break my fast.

I settled up with Dr Erdmann's secretary in the ante-room outside his room, and she made me an appointment for 9am the following Wednesday to review the results.

I was at the door at 8.30 and Polish workers politely and apologetically said they could not admit me. Then Dr Erdmann arrived in cycling clothes (a white T-shirt and track-suit bottoms).

I was shocked, I had only ever seen him in a dark suit and tie. He looked different. His sleeked-back black hair looked less dominant. He allowed me to enter and I sat amid his modern art and sipped a cappuccino. His secretary came in and gave me a 25-page medical report to look through.

Eventually I was told to go upstairs to the first floor. I climbed the stairs this time, and was admitted to Dr Erdmann's room. He was now immaculate in suit and tie and sleeked-back black hair, and sitting in front of a lumpy abstract plaster sculpture that seemed to be full of bulging breasts.

We went through the medical report. I noted some minor mistakes but it was all good and my cholesterol was optimal. However, I was short of Vitamin D, despite having taking 20,000 iu once a month for the last year, and I now had to take this amount weekly for 12 weeks and then fortnightly.

He told me that he wanted me to have a scan of my leg arteries in November, and a scan of my heart to look for warnings of possible coronaries. But otherwise I was healthy. He said my thinking was sound to give up my medical insurance and have a regular thorough MOT in its place.

He escorted me to his door and I settled up with his secretary in the ante-room while a second secretary amended my 25-page report and gave me a perfect copy. Then I took the lift downstairs.

I sat in the waiting-room and had a mid-morning cappuccino and biscuits and dipped into my 25-page medical report and reviewed my results.

The older one grows the more the premium for medical policies rises, and I would have been paying £15,000 a year, which I had cut to under £2,000 twice a year. I felt pleased for I had made a decision on monitoring my health that was actually saving £10,000 a year, and the results all showed that I was stable.

I looked at a painting on the wall that suggested two lungs with black cancerous smudges inside them, and sipping my cappuccino I was aware of being on the healthy side of a cost system that made elaborate provision for coping with unseen smudges of illness.

Lunching Ladies and Solitary Work

Once a week Pippa went swimming at a pool that specialised in sloping-ramp access for swimmers with hip problems or disabilities. "They're all more decrepit than I am," she told me.

She invited her co-swimmers back to our house. The idea was that they would all bring food and would have lunch in the garden. Gully was told a month in advance that the rose garden should be immaculate and the grass cut, and incredibly, it was. All the plants in the pots along the terrace looked delightful. There should have been nine but in the event only seven could come.

I kept out of the way but after the first arrived Pippa rang up and asked if I'd put the umbrella up. The first guest had firm views on how I should do it, but I did it quickly my way, holding the heavy umbrella downwards, putting the pin through the pole and then dropping the pole into the hold in the stand. That way my head did not get trapped in the umbrella while I fumbled for the hole against the gravitational weight of its folding down.

Six more ladies arrived in six separate cars around 12. I looked in on them again three-quarters of an hour later. I had had some lunch upstairs, and Pippa rang and invited me to have some strawberries. The island in the kitchen was stacked with platters of left-over viands, a quiche, salads, a trifle, strawberries and cream, all in separate containers and brought by separate ladies. They had just finished their first course outside and the plates were stacked near the sink. I put them in the dishwasher along with various containers and set it going.

Three of the ladies had come in from the garden and were helping themselves to trifle, and one said, "He's well-trained." I said that everything else would be one later load.

Pippa had asked me to take pictures of them, so I went out with my camera. They had pushed our garden tables together into a circle and were eating their pudding. It had been cloudy but now the sun came out and I took four pictures of the group from different angles, and then left them to finish their lunch.

The ladies later walked round our garden and looked at all the plants. They stayed until 4.30. They left in separate cars and I went down and tidied up, unpacked the dishwasher and loaded it with the remaining cutlery and crockery. Pippa said we were eating the food that was left, and she and I repackaged it and covered it and put it in the fridge. I noticed the containers said 'Waitrose', much of the food had come from Waitrose.

By all accounts they had had a good time and had got to know each other better. They had bonded into a unit and had thoroughly enjoyed themselves.

I thought, 'If you're a lady who has had a medical condition and needs to go to a pool with a ramp, it must be very nice to sit with seven others in a similar condition and compare notes while sharing good-quality food in a timeless setting, and get to know each other better while walking among trees and flowers.' It was how to live. I looked in on their togetherness from the isolation of my study as I carried forward my proofreading and (to me) important and urgent work.

A French Court and a Retreating World

I took Pippa to Hartwell House in the Vale of Aylesbury for her birthday surprise. We drove down the road towards the House and turned the corner, and spread out before us was a lake spanned by a stone bridge, green fields and a cornfield. The Jacobean front was this side of the lake with an equestrian statue of Frederick, Prince of Wales (George II's son who never became king). It faced an avenue of lime-trees.

We unloaded at the Jacobean entrance and a uniformed porter took our luggage into reception. We registered and, leaving our luggage as our room was not quite ready, we drove the car up to the car park and lunched on a shaded balcony in the Spa café in the warm July air, looking down on an old courtyard. We savoured the peace of the place, which had already slowed us down. I had haloumi cheese followed by a chocolate brownie and caramel ice-cream. I studied a map of the grounds in a booklet I had picked up.

We walked back to a courtyard behind a gate and an arch in the centre of an old building. On either side of a lawn stood a statue of Zeus and Juno (the Greek Hera). They were on plinths and looked old and pitted. Zeus had a beard.

We wandered on down past the House and the lime grove to the lake, which had been built by a rival of Capability Brown's, Richard Woods. We sat on a stone seat in front of the stone bridge, which had once been the central arch of the 18th-century Kew Bridge. Near us there were ducks and coots round tall yellow pond plants, and through the arch of the bridge beyond blanket weed were two swans. Behind us was a herd of Friesian cattle and in the middle of the field was a statue of William III on a column; a statue in the middle of pasture near where the high-speed train line was supposed to come in a few years' time.

It was all peaceful and ordered, the pastures had not changed since the 18th century. All round if I turned 360 degrees the past was present. Here in 1809 had come Louis XVIII in exile when Napoleon became Emperor, forced to leave France. He came with a Bourbon court of a hundred retainers (the number King Lear took with him) and set up a court in exile here until Napoleon went into exile and he was allowed back in 1814. Louis XVI had been guillotined and his son Louis XVII had died at the age of ten, and the throne had passed to his nephew Louis XVIII. Here to the French court came the future king Charles X and Gustavus IV, the exiled King of Sweden, both Bourbons.

It was a place of exile, and sitting on the seat I reflected that I too was in exile. I had "missed the march of this retreating world" (Owen's words in 'Strange Meeting') and was in exile from social media, mobile phones and the digital revolution – though I did have digital television and worked through my computer – and lived a life of observing Nature and human nature while all round me people were checking their smartphones.

We sauntered back. A receptionist said our luggage was now in our room, and we were given a tour of the classically-decorated ground floor, the large Great Hall, the bar, the morning-room, drawing-room, the stairs which had large carvings of Jacobean soldiers holding raised swords in a guard of honour all the way up on the banisters, and finally the library.

We took the lift up to our first-floor room – the wallpaper in the corridor was of 18th-century hunting scenes – and savoured the views from our windows from the front of the house down to the equestrian statue and the lime grove; and from the side of the house down to the lake and the Friesian cattle in a cornfield.

We sat for a while and then walked back to the Spa for our aromatherapy massage. My body soaked up the oil and 'body butter' the masseuse rubbed into my dry skin.

Afterwards we walked back to the library, which had shelves lined with old bound books, and some busts. There was nobody else in it, and we ordered tea. Pippa had Earl Grey, I had green tea. It came with home-made biscuits, and we sat exactly where there was a desk in the 1840s according to an old painting, the desk at which Louis XVIII signed a document that entitled him to return to France as King and resume the Bourbon monarchy there in 1814. A portrait of his full face and grey early-19th-century-style hair looked down on us from above the door. This was my world: of books and reading in depth, not the spoken word and tweeting in 140 characters.

We wandered back to the Great Hall and sat by the fireplace and admired the 1740 decoration and many portraits in oil on the walls, and from my booklet I realised that there was a stucco ceiling showing 'Genius rewriting History among the ruins of antiquity'. Genius held a blank artist's drawing-book and was about to draw the future, and nearby was a Minotaur. I gathered from the columned temple and broken columns Genius was in Knossos, imaging the future within the ruins of the past. And that too, I had done. I had not just escaped "this retreating world" into the past, I too had looked forward and foreseen the future. This was my kind of place: it had the spaciousness of Capability Brown's rival and echoes of monarchs and a royal court, and it looked forward towards the future.

We went back to our room and at 7 went down for dinner in the dining-room. We sat near a pillar with glasses of champagne and ate a three-course meal of scallops, guinea-fowl and (in my case) treacle pudding with almond ice-cream.

Afterwards we sat in the Great Hall with Baileys and I studied the stucco work again: Genius with eyes closed, seeing the future and the ruins of the past just as I had looked beyond nationalism and had detected a united world in the far-distant future. My attention was drawn to the fireplace. Between portraits of Charles II and Nell Gwyn was a 1740 image that I thought was Orpheus holding a torch, his lute, book and poetic mask nearby and birds he had tamed by his music, including a cockerel. He was about to enter the Underworld to look for Eurydice. There was a Greek 'key' design all round to emphasise the Greekness of the image.

Then I realised that all the carved images in the House were in classical dress: William III, Genius, Orpheus. It was an 18th-century Neoclassical environment.

We slept fitfully. Early next morning the cattle were lying down. Two flocks of Canadian geese were grazing. We went down and had breakfast in the dining-room, sitting near the open door, and later wandered outside to the terrace where there were a couple of sphinxes. I took a picture of Pippa beside a sphinx.

We vacated our room and settled our bill. Just before I walked to collect the car we wandered out to have one more look at the front down to the lake before we left. And I found two lines by Byron from 'The Age of Bronze' (1822): "Why wouldst thou leave calm Hartwell's green abode?/Apician table and Horatian ode?" 'Thou' was Louis XVIII. Byron, who knew Hartwell House, was saying: 'How could you leave the calm of Hartwell and go back to France? Hartwell is too beautiful to leave.' And the food was unbeatable: Marcus Gavius Apicius was a Roman gourmet who loved luxury and only ate the best food.

With a faint sigh I concurred. Byron was right; the peace and the associations of the past – Zeus, Genius, Orpheus – made it hard to return to the 'real' world out there of gadgets, mobile phones, laptops and 24-hour news.

I was quiescent. I had made my peace with the world. Yes, I was still an exile, but I co-existed with the world, I did not oppose it. I was happy for it to continue as it was. Others used the gadgets and lived materialistically, I was glad I had missed the march of a world retreating into machines, technology, artificial intelligence and robots, and Hartwell House had objectified what I felt about how one should live in the stucco work of its splendid 17th- and 18th-century rooms.

It was a retreat from the constant unrolling out there, it mirrored my soul and my soul mirrored it, and my soul and Hartwell House had a definite place for Zeus, Genius and Orpheus the poet in the trafficky road I now found myself back in, and the voice of the satnav lady. I had returned to my exile after a blissful twenty hours in traditional environmental reality.

A Mystery Play and Death

Pippa and I arrived in York about 1pm on a Sunday and unloaded the car opposite the Minster. We checked in at our hotel (Dean Court) while our car was driven away for garaging, and we were shown to our second-floor room, which had a view of the front of the Minster. People in medieval dress were walking to and fro. Some of the women looked like brides, some wore medieval caps. Some men had drums.

We had ham sandwiches in the downstairs sitting area looking out at the Minster and then set off. We walked along Low Petergate and stopped at Guy Fawkes' birthplace in 1570. It was a spacious house with a wooden staircase, now a pub and a restaurant, and he evidently came from a well-to-do family. I stood and touched woodwork that he would have touched without knowing that he would be hung, drawn and quartered on Tower Hill.

We walked on to King's Square. A young black-haired fire-eater with tattoos on his legs was juggling three fire sticks before a crowd several deep. He talked as he juggled, and now juggled five fire sticks. Then with a flourish and a build-up he swallowed a sword, putting it between his lungs and turning with his mouth open, bent double, so all could see the hilt.

Then he co-opted three men in the crowd to hold a bike with one wheel and a tall saddle. He clambered up and sat twelve feet from the ground and kept his balance by pedalling forwards and back and nodded his bowler hat off and caught it with one foot, and pedalling with the other foot, kicked it back up onto his head to loud applause.

Then he juggled three fire sticks, pedalling backwards and forwards. He put on a black hood, still juggling three fire sticks. He was now joking that he would be passing the hat round and that foreign tourists were expected to donate £20, and we left.

We walked on to the top of the Shambles, the old butchers' street mentioned in Doomsday Book and rebuilt c.1400. ('Shambles' meant 'slaughter-houses'.) We were going to attend 4pm evensong at the Minster, so we turned to go back and not far from the top end of Church Street encountered a stationary procession.

Behind a T-shaped cross saying 'Plague' at the top about forty men and women were dressed in white. Some were brides, one wore a mask with a pointed nose like a bird's beak, one wore a grimacing mask like a fierce animal. They were all completely still.

I grasped that this was a York mystery play, performed by locals. I went down to the front of the waiting procession, took a photograph of the waiting medieval people and tried to work out the meaning of what I was seeing. I knew the population of York had been halved by the Black Death in 1349.

A man in white with a pointed nose stood near me. He had been watching me. I looked at him, and had the feeling that he represented Death. Before I could move he took a step forward, reached out and touched my arm. His face was hidden beneath his mask.

Death had touched me. In my eightieth year I had been touched by Death. Chillingly I looked at him and involuntarily smiled. I hurried back past the medieval figures, some in old caps, to rejoin Pippa. I turned and a waggon was trundling from Swinegate into Church Street. The procession had been waiting for it, and suddenly all the white-clad, masked figures were on the move behind the waggon, and the air was full of shrill medieval music from pipes. Pippa and I walked back to the Minster. I was haunted by my encounter with Death.

In the entrance of the Minster we were greeted by a prelate in black. He asked if we were attending evensong and directed us in. I asked him what the procession of people in white had been.

"It's a mystery play," he said. "I don't know too much about it, it's not under the Minster but the guilds. The Cycle of 11 plays started last Sunday and continued on Wednesday and it's finished today. I think you saw the last one, the Mercers' play, *The Last Judgement.*"

We went into the Minster and queued near the Quire to wait to be admitted. Pippa sat on one of a row of nearby chairs.

As I stood in the line I began to understand what I had seen. The York Cycle of 48 mystery plays began with the Creation and ended with the Last Judgement. We had seen the last of 11 plays featured during the previous week and that day. All the souls in the procession were waiting for the waggon, as the medieval York-Cycle plays were performed in the streets on a waggon. They were the souls of the dead waiting to hear the consequences of their cruelty and kindness. They were all in white because they were dead, they had died of the plague, and some would learn they would be brides of Christ in Heaven, and others that they would be devils with animal faces in Hell. Somehow Death was among them, and Death had singled me out and touched my arm.

I had to face it. I was nearly 80, and Death would come for me one of these days. It seemed that Death had made himself known to me. I had been touched – notified that my time was coming – and the York Cycle of mystery plays wanted me to repent and turn to God in preparation for my impending death. Now the queue began to move and I was in a sombre mood as we jostled along up steps into the Quire and I was shown to a chair in the Presbytery at the same level as the high altar.

Every seat was taken, and all were waiting in anticipation of evensong. But I had been touched by Death, I felt different. It seemed I was like Dr Faustus, I had been touched by Mephistopheles, my soul was in the balance and I had been approached by Death, Hell loomed and I was weirdly witnessing in a metaphysical discussion in the atmosphere about the timing of my demise.

A Canon and Everlasting Life

As I sat in the front row of York Minster's Presbytery waiting for evensong to begin, holding the Cathedral notice-sheet and musing on Dr Faustus with more people coming up the three steps to take their seats, a tall man of the Church in a cassock, with a bald head, bent and said, "Do I recognise you from the school, are you Mr Rawley?"

I stood and recognised his face from my past and, trying to place it, said, shaking hands, "Hello, I didn't expect to see you here. Very clever of you to spot me among all these people."

He smiled and said, "I'm trying to remember your first name."

"I'm Philip, and this is Pippa."

"And is Simon still with you?"

"Yes," I said and then it came back to me. He was Christopher Collison. He had married Simon – conducted his marriage service – ten years previously.

"I didn't know you'd come here."

He smiled. "I have to go now. Speak to you afterwards."

I nodded and he left. I sat down and said to Pippa, "That was Christopher Collison. Fancy that, his name's on the notice-sheet. He's in bold at the top, 'In Residence: The Reverend Canon Dr Christopher Collison, Chancellor.' He's Chancellor, just beneath the Archbishop of York."

In some strange way I felt my handshake with him had counterbalanced and neutralised the touch of Death.

The Quire was soon full. Then there was distant singing and everyone fell silent and a procession entered the Quire from the Robing Room outside. After the first dignitaries came the choristers, all in cassocks and surplices, and at the end came Christopher Collison. He made his way up to a Quire-stall at the back.

There was a lot of singing from the young choir and periodically we all stood up and sat. At one point they sang the Magnificat. Christopher Collison sang three almost inaudible solos – he had no microphone – and was answered each time by the voluble choir. There were readings from *Exodus* and *Matthew 7*.

Then there was a sermon. The Pastor was escorted to the steps of the pulpit by a server with a mace. The sermon was based on *Matthew 7*, "Judge not that ye be not judged", which the Pastor said he did not understand because it contradicted other passages in the *Bible*, and he dwelt on dogs and swine, which were also in the passage in the reading from *Matthew 7*.

At the end of evensong the procession left and we all followed. Christopher Collison was standing in the nave near the Quire screen, and we chatted. He said, "I left the school for Gloucestershire and then came here."

I said, "With the Archbishop of Canterbury being questioned for his criticism of Amazon when the Church has investments in Amazon perhaps there will be a vacancy soon and we may see the Reverend Canon Dr Christopher Collison being elevated?"

"No," he said. "This will be my last job. I have two more years to do. We're just starting an important project in November and I want to see that through."

"Can you say what it is?"

"Oh yes, it's no secret that York voted Remain in the referendum and the rest of Yorkshire voted Leave, and the project is to bring the two sides together, to reconcile them."

"That is very important," I said. "It's the most important thing to do at the present time. We're in the European civilisation, all the twenty-eight EU nation-states share a background of Roman Catholicism and the Reformation" – he nodded – "and bringing both sides together is the most urgent healing task."

He nodded again and said, "I'm very busy the next two days getting the project off the ground, otherwise I'd invite you for a drink."

It was as though the Church were offering me its protection, as though the Canon was pointing me forward on the path to Paradise.

We smiled and shook hands and we walked to the door and left the Minster.

I stood outside in sunshine. There was a blue sky. My soul had been in the balance and Death had tipped it by touching me. But now it had been reclaimed by the Church. I had been approached and recognised, I was out of the clutches of Death and Hell. I had everlasting life. But I had to face the fact that at nearly 80 I might have made only a temporary escape.

A Crypt and Hot Coals

We went back to the Minster next morning and walked round looking at the stained glass. There were many marble dead bodies lying on tombs, death was everywhere. Between the 13th-century doors was a statue of St Peter, a bald man holding a key and a book.

We looked in at the chapter house, an octagonal building dating to the early 1290s. There was a ledge round the inside wall where all the canons could sit. The Dean was in charge of the Minster and led the canons, and I gathered that even in the 1290s all the canons were of equal status, including the Pastor and Chancellor. Only the Dean had real authority, and even the Archbishop of York could not attend the Minster unless he was invited.

We joined two other couples for a tour of the crypt at 11. Roy, our guide, was a volunteer working from retirement. He took us to the Quire and showed where the old church with its curved apse (which contained the altar) would have been, the first Norman church built by Thomas of Bayeux between 1070 and 1100. Then we went down steps to the undercroft beneath it and he showed us the lay-out of the original church, which had been built a couple of metres above Roman remains. He showed us where Archbishop Roger de Pont

L'Évêque had extended the church in 1154–1181 – "he built that wall," Roy said – and we had sat above his extension at evensong.

He took us to a passage behind a locked and barred gate, let us in and handed out red hard hats for health-and-safety reasons. Then we followed in single file down a narrow passage between blocks of magnesian limestone that had been removed from the Cathedral, some with intricate carvings, many with lines gouged out from hot-lead fillings so they could be stuck to adjoining blocks. We saw the inside ledge of the old church on which the sick and disabled were allowed to sit, hence the expression "the weakest go to the wall". We saw the inside of the wall of the present Minster, built from 1354 to 1420.

He took us to a similar locked and barred passage the other side of the crypt and we saw buttresses from the old outer wall of the old church. They had been exposed to the weather for over 200 years from 1100 to 1354, but though of magnesian limestone, a soft stone, they had not suffered from the polluted air of smoke from the Industrial Revolution. We saw an old apse, curved.

We then returned to the undercroft and lingered at a round stone column decorated with Norman dog-tooth and a 'K', the initial of the carver (perhaps indicating that wages could now be paid for a finished job). Roy showed us the tomb of St William, an Archbishop who was greeted by the people of York on a bridge, which collapsed under their weight. He miraculously saved everyone and became a Catholic saint. Roy said, "We can safely assume it was divine intervention, so he became a saint." Everyone laughed.

Then he took us to a gravestone taken from just outside the Minster. It was heavily decorated with figures.

"Look," he said, "these are people being dragged down by devils, and there's the Devil organising it, and devils are burning the people, you can see the coals and the flames carved in stone. This is the Church sending out a message to impressionable people who couldn't read or write, 'If you don't do as we tell you, you'll end up like this.' It's Church propaganda, getting its message across to keep its power. It's the same with stained glass, stories for impressionable people who couldn't read or write."

And I saw the Church as a PR-machine safeguarding its own power and bombarding the poor with propaganda. 'Do as we say or the hot coals await you.' And I thought of all the stonemasons who had devoted their lives to building the Minster and had not lived to see it finished, and of the builders of the Great Pyramid in Cairo who had not lived to see the end of their life's work, and now of the exploitation of the gullible through extreme images. And I was glad I did not live in the medieval time and did not want to have anything to do with the mystery plays that perpetuated the myth of Hell.

There was the Light, and those who experienced it lived within a new dimension, and those who missed it did not realise what they had missed. Religion could take you to a positive experience that transformed living, but there were no hot coals waiting for those who failed to admit the Light to their lives during their brief lifetime on this earth.

Vikings and a Skeleton

In York we walked on to the Jorvik Centre, paid and took a lift down to the Viking settlement. We were escorted to an electric 'train' of open carriages. We were taken into the darkness while a voice spoke on screen, and came out into reconstructed scenes of everyday Viking life.

We passed Viking houses (wooden and thatched), dark and lit by candles, and many people, mannequins that moved and even blinked their eyes. There was mud everywhere and we passed Vikings of all ages, men and women, a Viking making combs, a couple arguing whether they should eat meat or fish, a grandfather teaching his two grandchildren a game like chess called *hnefatafl*. Boats were being unloaded, fish sold, and a man was in a woven-wicker toilet and a woman with a crutch was attempting to cross a road. The people were all animated, they looked very real.

We came to a halt and got out of our 'carriage' and entered the museum. "It's the evidence for what you've just seen," said a helper. We walked round looking at cooking utensils, crockery, combs and seeds that had survived, and then I was looking at a skeleton in a glass showcase.

She was a woman of about 45 whose right leg had been almost detached from its hip-bone at birth. She walked with a limp, and was in pain, the label said. And I realised this was the woman who had been shown trying to cross the road. There was her real skeleton pointing to what must have been a really difficult life.

We walked back to the Roman bathhouse. I looked into it, but it was small, just low walls showing hot and cold bathrooms (*caldarium* and *frigidarium*). We went on to Betty's and queued to get in and I had a cream tea and Pippa had a Fat Rascal. Many people crowded together in the tearoom, and everything was as could be wished, but I could not help thinking of the woman whose right leg had been disconnected from its hip for the whole of her life, who limped and lived in pain, and who died and was on show in a glass box in the Jorvik Museum.

Death had again confronted me in the form of a skeleton. I had looked into the Viking Age for its artefacts and achievements and had found Death, who was waiting for me now.

A New Garden and a Dead Baby

"The man next door's manager of a Telecom company," said Penny. "Twenty-eight thousand spent on the garden, designer clothes, expensive holidays. It's been a happy lifestyle.

"He's been with his girlfriend one-and-a-half years, they're both in their late thirties. They had a miscarriage, she became pregnant again, and now they've lost their child. They've had to have an abortion. The baby was Down's syndrome. He said they couldn't look after it, they haven't the time to care for it. He's got a son of fifteen by his first marriage, and they can't leave him to look after the baby after they've gone.

"His ex-wife has just told him she needs £14,000 more for their son, and he's going to have to pay it. 'It's sheer jealousy,' he said. They had made the house tidy, they were doing the garden to be ready for the new baby, and she was quite advanced, you could see she was quite round at the front. It's sad, very sad, isn't it?

"What's right? Christians would say the baby has a soul, but Down's syndrome...." She shook her head. "Whichever choice they made was wrong. Having the baby would impact on their social life and the social life of all they know. And not having it would impact on the unborn baby. What a terrible choice to make."

We sat in silence and contemplated the awful choice her neighbour had had to make. Do souls have priority over circumstances, or do consequential circumstances have priority over souls?

An Angel among Belsen People

"Jean's not all right," Pippa said in reply to my enquiry. "She's in and out of hospital. She thinks she may get better but they've abandoned the latest chemo as her body couldn't take it, and there's no plan to continue it, so the hospital are effectively saying she's terminal. Last Saturday an ambulance was called, she was in such pain. Everywhere, as her cancer is everywhere. They've put her on morphine. Before that she had antibiotics, and she and George thought she wasn't eating because of the antibiotics. But probably her body can't cope with digesting, she's no appetite. She gets out of bed in their flat and sits in a chair. George is like you, 80 and hopeless, and goes into a shop with a list and can't find anything. You're better than he is, he's completely hopeless. He doesn't cook at all. She's got to be gluten-free and can't have milk and certain dairy products. I took her a slice of carrot cake last week, which she loves, and she had a crumb. She can't eat. I've given her a tray that will go in a microwave and I took her some bacon. She texted me yesterday. George has learned how to put it in the microwave and she could have bacon. I got her some coconut-based milk but she couldn't drink it. I've been finding things she's still allowed to eat. Her brother was there on Sunday and I hope he's talked some sense into her about eating. She's a Belsen person, very thin, almost unrecognisable. I visit her every week, and sometimes talk to George. He's hoping she'll get better but realistically the cancer's taken control and she won't eat and she's not going to get better."

I shook my head. "You're an angel," I said quietly. "Finding her food she might be able to have, which her husband can't find."

"I'm lunching with Pauline now," Pippa continued. "She's not all right either. She's got a son who's got cancer. He's terminally ill and won't recover and hasn't got long to live, and he's got three children. He's in his forties. Pauline's in a dreadful state. I must go, I should have left by now."

I watched her drive out, being a comfort to families affected by cancer. She was a caring person with deep feelings for the sufferings of those she knew well. She was an angel among Belsen people. I thought of the two cancer sufferers and shook my head – and then returned to my work.

A Fall and a Nursing Home

"Maurice Baxter's done what you did last Wednesday," Pippa said that Monday evening when I got back from the gym. "Had a fall. Yours was only five steps, his was more. He fell downstairs, he's over 80, and hit his head and gashed it from ear to ear across the top. Blood spurted onto the wall. He's disabled anyway. He's always had scoliosis, and he's always had something wrong with one arm. At bridge he has to move that arm with his other hand. There's something wrong with a foot, he wears a high shoe. He was in acute pain. And he started talking scribble. Joan said, 'He was accusing me of having done all sorts of things and was using a strange language.'

"She said, 'I got a pillow and put it under his head. I could see there was something badly wrong with his leg. Then I called for an ambulance and then I called our daughter. The paramedics came within five to ten minutes.' He's now in Princess Alexandra Hospital, Harlow. He's broken his leg in two or three places. But they also found he had a blood clot on his brain. That must have affected his speech. His speech is better now but he's going to be in hospital for some while. He'll never be able to go upstairs again. A stair lift wouldn't work as his leg would be sticking out in plaster."

I shook my head.

"Will they move to a bungalow?" I asked.

"I don't know."

I reflected. That's how it is. You go down stairs one day and lose your footing and fall and hit your head and have a blood clot and break your leg and suddenly you can't live at home any more. You have to go into a nursing home. At least he hadn't died. I thought of quiet Maurice Baxter I used to know at school. He was a year or two ahead of me and he often went to see Muriel Iris, our old teacher, who used to mention his news. Yes, that's how it is. You start one day quite normally, have a fall and end up in a nursing home – or, worse still, dead.

A Legless Man and a Child with a Moustache

I had seen Bob, a smiling American with prosthetic legs who looked youthful, in his late thirties, and a boy who he pushed in a wheelchair, who was no higher than his waist and had a moustache, round the ship and on excursions, and I had smiled at them. We had a day at sea, and I was on the topmost desk queuing for an ice-cream when he nudged my arm and said, "Hi." I turned and asked how his legs were bearing up – he said "Fine" – and how well he was doing, unsupported by a stick.

He said, "I've had thirty years of training."

"Thirty years? Were you in the army?"

"I was hit by a train. I was in a suit and tie, there were two rail tracks close together, there was nowhere else to go."

"In America?"

"Yes. It hit me. I didn't feel a thing. There was a Fire Department nearby and a fireman came and I said, 'I've got to get to work.' He said, 'You're not going to work today.' I know that if you're in an air crash you don't feel a thing."

"And George?" I asked of the adult-looking boy whose wheelchair he pushed.

"A double whammy." Did he mean that he had been hit by the same train?

"He's your son?"

"Yes."

"How old is he?"

"Twenty-one." So he could not have been hit by the same train if Bob had had thirty years of training.

"He's got a mature face, he's all there."

"He's the life and soul of the party."

"And he's your wife's son?"

"Yes."

"She's doing well, looking after you, and then him. Very well."

"Yes."

Then I was being served. I chose a chocolate ice-cream.

"Are you having an ice-cream?" I asked Bob.

"Why not?" He chose a chocolate ice-cream.

"You'd better get back to George before it melts," I said.

"Yes."

"See you soon."

"Sure." And he was gone, striding on his prosthetic legs.

I saw him several times after that, pushing George's wheelchair about the ship, and he smiled and waved, but we did not have a chance to speak to each other again. And I never knew what had caused the "double whammy" that resulted in a child with a retarded physical development and an adult brain.

All I knew was that Fate had delivered Bob a double whammy, that he had endured for thirty years and had kept going and was stoically uncomplaining, and that in a compelling way he had triumphed over his predicament, he had risen above what life had done to him. And I could only admire what he had made of himself.

A Monk and a Right Hand

The ship berthed in Kotor on my eightieth birthday. I could hardly move my right hand, it was swollen and I was not sure whether I had had an insect bite or a touch of arthritis or gout.

We found our coach and climbed 1,400 feet above the Bay of Kotor, winding through twenty-five curves. From the top of the mountains we looked down on our tiny ship. We stopped at Njegusi and went on to Cetinje, the royal capital of Montenegro. We walked past King Nikola's house and the house of St Peter of Cetinje, and to pass the hour we had been given in what was a small town, walked past the tiny church to the Serbian Orthodox Monastery. I had heard that it contained the right hand of John the Baptist, the hand that baptised Christ in the River Jordan, and I asked a gardener where it was.

At that moment a friend approached and greeted him with kisses. The gardener spoke to him and the friend said to me, "You have to ask the monk." He took Pippa and me inside the monastery to a little room, and spoke to an Orthodox monk, who pointed and said airily in English, "In the church."

We walked down the corridor to the church. A baptism was in progress, and an English-speaking guide, a smartly dressed man, was saying, "Only the main monk can open the coffin of St Peter of Cetinje." I returned to the monk and asked, "Is the hand in the coffin of St Peter of Cetinje?"

"Yes."

"Can we see it?"

He asked, "Where are you from?"

"England."

"Are you Catholic?"

"No. Anglican, but I'm very interested."

"I'll open it for you."

He got a key from the 'bookshop', which sold icons, and led us to the coffin which stood on the floor, nearly waist-high, near a window. It looked like a decorated chest. He opened it and lifted the wooden lid. The 18th-century St Peter (who had died around the age of 82, in 1830) lay back, his head covered – his flesh had not decayed since his death in 1830, and near his brown hand were two glass containers with decorations round them. One held a wooden fragment of Christ's cross, and the other two bent forefingers of a right hand. Two fingers were stubs and a thumb was missing.

"John the Baptist's right hand," the monk said.

I bent down to get a closer look. It was brown and almost furry, a bit like a claw. Local Montenegrins were suddenly behind me – word had spread that the monk had opened the coffin, a rare event – and had crowded round me, touching the glass and praying with eyes closed. It was a special event. I let my imagination wander. That hand had dipped into the River Jordan and had baptised the adult (30-year-old) Jesus shortly before he was tempted by the Devil in the wilderness, and had witnessed its own beheading shortly before John the Baptist's severed head was placed on a dish to be served at a dinner table.

The monk closed the lid and locked the coffin. He held a bag with half a dozen 10-euro notes in it. I put 20 euros in and thanked him. He said, "There is an icon." This was in a museum elsewhere, decorated by St Luke.

I asked him about the provenance of the hand. "How do you know it's the hand of John the Baptist?"

"I don't know," the monk said.

The English-speaking guide overheard me and said, "It was brought by the Knights of Malta and was taken to Russia. It was sent to Montenegro by the Tsarina at the beginning of the Revolution to keep it safe. Ever since the Revolution it has been here."

We left the monastery and resumed our coach journey to the other side of the mountain and looked down on the Budva Riviera and the open Atlantic coastline. I was thoughtful. How could we be sure it was the hand of John the Baptist? It must have been cut off as a relic when he was beheaded. Where had it been taken and where was it kept until the Knights of Malta took possession of it?

I thought again of the two forefingers that baptised Christ. The baptism was an event of huge significance in history, and the fingers and hand were so claw-like. And now it was a relic of the Orthodox Church in a glass container in a monastery. I had received a blessing on my eightieth birthday. I had been allowed into the presence of this relic, part of the body of John the Baptist. I had spoken to a gardener, and his friend had taken me to the monk, who seemed to be an Anglophile. The coffin was opened rarely, but he had opened it for me.

The hand was a call to a spiritual life, just as it had called Christ to a spiritual life while it baptised and cleansed him. I had already had spiritual experiences and this image, which Providence had revealed to me, was like a seal, it confirmed the experiences I had had. I gave thanks to the unity of the universe for sending me this message that I had responded to, a call to the spiritual life. But on a practical note, it was a right hand, and my right hand had lost its pain and discomfort. And on a practical note it was my right hand that did my writing. Providence had sent me a message that my writing hand would soon be free from the swelling that had made it hard to move.

A Tiller and a North Wind

There was light rain as I walked past Thorney Island, a stretch of still water and low tree-clad beaches where the Special Boat Unit had prepared for D-Day, and into the marina within the enormously far-flung Chichester Harbour. I was wearing a mac and carrying a shoulder bag, and looked down at the row of boats on pontoon B. It was 8am on a Monday morning, and no one was about. I walked to the nearest shelter and sat in a rattan chair.

At 8.15 I walked back to pontoon B and James drove in. We shook hands. He said, "I'm really sorry, there was an accident and the road was closed."

We walked down the sloping gangway, he punched three numbers into a keyboard and displayed a card, and we boarded his crabber, a 22-foot boat with a cabin down steps from the back.

The rain stopped but it was still overcast as I helped untie the cladding round the mainsail. James put on waterproofs and reversed out using the motor. He chugged out of the marina and followed a channel, and he pointed out Thorney Island, where there was still a secret military base and airfield behind trees. Our course led into the Emsworth Channel down the east side of Hayley Island amid cries of oyster-catchers. An oyster-catcher flew over our boat, flapping fast, black head and white, intent on its destination.

I was doing the steering and keeping to the right of a succession of posts with beacons on top. I watched a screen which showed our ship in the middle of a light-blue channel, and steered away as we neared the dark-blue shallows. I sat at the helm, and when we needed to swing to the right I pulled the tiller to the left, and when we needed to swing to the left I pulled the tiller to the right. Below the screen was a depth reading in feet. It must never go below six feet. "If it gets to five feet we run aground," James said. "But we've got a retractable keel which gets us afloat again."

We came out into the open sea, which was calm, and James hauled up the triangular mainsail, which was maroon with a crab in the top corner. I steered into the wind and tacked slightly when the sail flapped in the wind until it was taut. I thought of Virgil's helmsman Palinurus who fell asleep at the tiller and slumped overboard and drowned. The funeral games of *The Aeneid*, book 6, were held in his honour.

Light rain was falling again, for June it was cold. James handed me a hat, a scarf and gloves. I sat in the light rain, and my waterproof jacket and maroon trousers got steadily wet.

"Look," James said when we were a mile out, pointing across the calm waves. "The Isle of Wight, Bembridge on the left." I saw a low island in the mist. "And that's Portsmouth over there you can see in the distance." It was too far to be seen clearly. "Three forts were built by the Navy in the nineteenth century to defend it. The nearest fort was built down into the seabed, there was no rock. It was an architectural feat for its day. The farthest two forts are on either side in the distance." I could make them out towards the horizon. "And in there, at the top – northernmost point – of Langston Harbour was Porchester, the second-largest Roman town after Londinium."

He loved the history of these ancient waterways that had been central to the Roman occupation of Britain and to Britannia's rule of the waves in the time of Nelson and Trafalgar.

It came on to rain more heavily, and it was 12. James said, "I think we'll go back into a cove over there, anchor and have some lunch."

We headed back towards the land, tacking into the wind several times (which meant I hauled the tiller I was sitting holding to one side as far as it would go and the mainsail swung over my head, and as the boat inclined to one side James tugged one of the thin ropes to adjust the sail and return the boat to an upright position). Zigzagging we made use of the wind, we rounded the last buoy and anchored about twenty yards from land in a deserted cove.

We climbed down steps into the cabin, cold and damp, and James put the kettle on, and a heater that blew warm air round my right leg. He produced ham and goat's-cheese sandwiches and summer pudding, which we had with coffee. We talked about the world the UK faced after Brexit, and he saw the UK as losing its influence and facing a dismal future.

We went up on deck. James said, "Look, the wind has changed. It's coming from the north. See the arrow on top of the mast, it's pointing to where the wind is coming from. We've got to go into the wind. The channel is too narrow to tack far, we're going to have to motor-sail."

We got going again. We sailed out of the cove along the coast to the Channel round Hayley Island. It was a long way, and we had to cross open water. We zigzagged with regular tacks. James said, "Normally when I come out, we only have to tack a couple of times. Because we're heading into a north wind we've already tacked about thirty times."

Eventually we entered the Emsworth Channel. As it grew narrower he turned on the motor and hauled down the mainsail. I had to steer into the wind as the mainsail came down.

Back on dry land I felt alive. I had sat in rain and steered with the tiller while James coped with the mainsail, at one with the elements, in harmony with the conflicting universe and its squalls and north wind. I had steered through opposing forces, and I was aware that behind the weather that created difficulties was One principle which directed and moved everything to accord with its will. I had left the social world of the marina and had gone out into the universe and I felt the better for confronting its conflicting forces and experiencing its underlying, reconciling unity.

Lugworms and Snakes

We had breakfast by a window overlooking the sea. It was overcast. The estuary tide had receded a long way during the night but was now coming in. Four men were digging about a hundred yards away on the wet sand. It looked as if they were looking for lugworms for bait.

Then there was a squall. Rain lashed the windows and snakes streaked down, each head a raindrop falling down the large window and leaving a trail. And I was taken back to when I was eighteen and travelling back from London on the tube and snakes slithered down the window as the tube emerged from the underground tunnel to overground before Stratford and then Leytonstone.

I looked at the four diggers. They were unfazed by the rain and were digging furiously as the incoming tide approached. They were shovelling and tipping mounds of sand and then stopping and bending to see what they had revealed. They were looking for lugworms for bait and I was looking for snakes, and we were at one under the harmony of the overcast sky and the estuary at low tide with an incoming sea.

Death at My Door

That Saturday I was sitting in my window in Cornwall with the sash up, working at my desk with the late-afternoon sea beneath me beyond the wall, and I heard a voice call "Philip". I looked out and twenty feet below it was Maisie, with immaculate blonde hair, red nails, holding a cigarette. She called up, "Did you hear the loud music last night?"

"No," I called back.

"We did, we could hear it two miles away."

"The harbour acoustics didn't carry it to us," I shouted down.

Then I realised her tenants were sitting on the balcony, listening. So I said, "Come to the front door," and shut the window.

Wearing shorts and sandals I went to the front door and sat on the seat inside the porch. She approached and stood below the steps.

"How are you?" she asked. "We heard it, it was from the Rashleigh at the end of the harbour. But here you don't hear what's going on down below in the drinking area beside the dock? Perhaps we heard it because it carried up the hill."

She chattered away. Then her husband appeared, bald. He came and shook my hand.

"How are you?" he said.

"Fine, thanks. How are you?"

"Oh, now I'm seventy-five I'm doing three hundred funerals a year instead of five hundred. But we're still busy."

He was a funeral director.

I said, "I've just turned eighty."

"You're looking very well on it," he said. "Whatever you're doing keep doing it." And suddenly in his eyes I saw tape-measures. He looked at me as if he wanted to measure me for my coffin, so I could be one of his three hundred funerals this year.

"I'm very active," I said. "We've been in Russia. I'm still able to travel."

My message was clear: I'm not ready for a coffin yet.

And as I watched him I realised he was Death disguised as a funeral director. Death had come to my door to measure me for my coffin, and I was having none of it.

"Well, nice to see you again," I said, and got up and went in and closed the door.

I had shut Death out. He was standing outside but he could not get in.

But the next day Susan rang and said, "Mike is not very well. He's in hospital. He went to hospital on Friday. The cancer has got into his liver and he's got hepatitis." And I thought, 'Death is abroad, I hope Mike is all right.'

A Rapid Death and a Stoical Wife

That Sunday Susan rang when I was still in Cornwall to say Mike was not very well and had been in hospital since the previous Friday.

She said: "He hasn't slept most of the time for a week and hasn't eaten much. He was worse on Friday night. He was taken to hospital by ambulance as he couldn't sit up. He was put in an 'acute medical ward'. He had a scan last Tuesday and tests for hepatitis. At first they thought he had side-effects from blood-pressure tablets. The scan showed he's got bladder cancer that's spread to his liver. He's on a drip. His kidneys aren't working properly and they are trying to dehydrate him to get rid of his fluid. His abdomen's enormous from retained fluid. His colon's affected and he's also got a hernia in his right groin. He has a colostomy bag, and cried when he heard he had to have it. He's got an appointment with a surgeon on Thursday, and the hospital are keeping him until then. They are planning to cure the other problems so he can have an operation for bladder cancer and the remainder of his prostate.

"I didn't tell you on Thursday as I knew you were leaving for Cornwall and wanted you to have a good night's sleep. He's been getting up every hour and I've only slept in snatches of half an hour."

I said how sorry I was to hear all this. I said, "You must take this opportunity of his being in hospital to have seven or eight hours' uninterrupted sleep."

I asked if he had made a will.

She said, "No."

I urged her to get him to dictate something while he could.

She said, "I'll ring a friend of ours who's a solicitor."

The following Tuesday Susan rang me again from the hospital, around noon. She said, "Bad news on Mike. He's still in hospital, he has a week to live. It may be tomorrow or the next day. I've slept in his hospital room the last two nights. He knows. He was asked, 'Where do you want to die, at home or in hospital?' First of all he said, 'Home.' But that would mean getting an ambulance and he's comfortable where he is. So he said, 'Here.'

"I managed to speak with a doctor in the corridor for five minutes. It's his liver and kidneys not working. It's a shock that it's so sudden."

She broke down for a short while, and when she resumed tears were not far away. Then somebody came to his room and she hurriedly said she had to go, and would keep me informed.

I had sent Mike a card showing a spiral staircase of ascent back to health, each step being a keyboard key. Sadly the card now had to be interpreted in reverse: the keyboard steps descended into oblivion.

I later sent Susan an email saying there had been reports from people who have died and come back to life that they floated down a tunnel towards Light, and then heard a voice saying, "Not yet," after which they turned back.

The following day, Wednesday, Susan rang. She said, "It may be later today. Mike is sleeping." His mother and son by his first marriage, Susan's stepson, would be with him that afternoon. She said, "His will got done last night. The solicitor we know came, heard his requests, and returned with the will for his signature."

I was relieved.

Susan said, "There may be a small humanist funeral followed at a later date by a memorial service fans can attend." She meant his keyboard fans.

The next morning I woke suddenly at 6.40 with a slight nosebleed that left blood above my upper lip, as if I had to be aware of something.

Susan rang from the hospital at 8.15.

"How are you?" I asked.

She said calmly, "It happened at a quarter to seven."

"Oh, I *am* sorry. But it's a merciful release."

She said, "He fought to the end, which began about 2.45 this morning. In the end they gave him a large dose, and for the last half-hour he wasn't aware. I'm still talking to him. I've read in medical bulletins that organs die slowly and he can still hear me for a while."

I said, "His spirit may be attached to his body by an umbilical cord, and may break away after the funeral and go to where all spirits go next."

She said, "I've been here in the hospital since Sunday. His mother's coming up, and I've more calls to make, and very little battery." We were cut off by her low battery, and she rang again. "His liver packed up and so did his kidneys. They tried to reverse it but they couldn't. I just want to get home and have a shower. I'll ring tomorrow at greater length. I'm making short calls on my phone now. Will you tell everyone your end?"

Susan rang the next day. She had had eight or nine hours' sleep and made 70 phone calls the previous day. She said, "While in hospital Mike went from 3 months to 3–4 weeks, and then suddenly to 1–2 days and 'get your financial affairs sorted out tonight'."

She talked of Mike's harrowing death. The hospital would not give him morphine "as it might kill him" – but he only had a few hours to live anyway by then. She said she should have had a sponge, but was wiping his lips with cotton buds. "He was terrified." She said the hospital was not good at pain management. "This was not supposed to happen. It was bladder cancer and prostate, then hepatitis, then the kidneys not functioning." She said, "When I woke this morning he wasn't there. I thought he'd gone to make coffee."

After she rang off I sat and pondered. She had had a lot to endure, and I wished I could have been of some help, but I clearly could not live in his hospital room as Susan had. Mike had undergone a rapid decline and death, with one organ after another shutting down, and I was full of admiration at Susan's stoical support at his deathbed. She had seen things during his last hours that could haunt her in future nights, and I hoped she would never fall ill and come face to face with what she had seen during his rapid death.

A Toiling Mower and a Dancing Wasp

We had mid-August Sunday lunch at the Carlyon Bay Hotel. We sat in the window. The sun was dazzling, and I screwed up my eyes to stop myself from sneezing. I moved the butter dish into the shade and all through our starter (chicken liver parfait, sourdough and chutney) and main course (salmon) a gardener in a high-vis yellow jacket pushed a petrol-driven hand-mower across first one, then the other of the two oval lawns. The lawns already looked cut, and he was trimming, turning very good into excellent. From time to time he stopped and picked up a small lump of grass, and every so often he emptied his mower's bag. Meanwhile a wasp danced up and down the long sash-window against the sky, and then flew to the window the other side of long curtains, where an old man picked up his newspaper, rolled it into a club, and whacked it several times on the wide internal window-sill and killed it.

After our pudding – Pippa had strawberries, I had chocolate torte and vanilla ice-cream – we walked to the lounge for coffee. It was hot in the window and there was a wasp dancing up the pane, so we sat at a table near the bar. No sooner had we tucked our feet under the glass-topped round table than a waiter set down a tray with two cups and coffee. From the window-table beneath the wasp an elderly man with grey hair combed forward to just above his spectacles remonstrated and waved his arms. The waiter realised his mistake and picked up the tray with an apology and carried it to the couple in the window. On his way back I said, "I was impressed that you anticipated our arrival, please don't leave us too long." And the four elderly people at the next table smiled and laughed.

Our coffee (and mints) came soon afterwards. We talked about Susan and what she would do after the funeral, how she must not be bounced into a new life, how she needed time on her own in peace and quiet to work out what she should do. I thought of Mike lying in a Hadleigh mortuary alone. Susan had had a dream in which she went through Mike's last hours and at the end she heard a voice saying, "It's not your turn." At over eighty it would be my turn soon.

Not long afterwards I got up to settle our lunch bill at the bar. The mower was still toiling outside – he had progressed to mowing the circular lawn round the round flower-bed – and the wasp was still dancing up the sky on the long sash-window, and I wondered how many of the guests sitting over coffee at round tables and being served by the waiters were anything other than natural toiling mowers, watching wasps while they waited comfortably for their death.

A White Face and Pasties

We went to visit Aunt Maud. She came to the front door with a stick as we parked the car around 12.30, and although I knew she was housebound – indeed roombound – I was stunned at her white drawn face and lined skin. As I climbed her steps and kissed her I thought she was very frail and had not long to live. She had her death in her face.

I followed her into her bedroom, which used to be a sitting-room – there was a discarded sofa in the garden awaiting collection – and sat in a chair by the window in the small room. Pippa sat opposite me. Aunt Maud sat in a chair by a frame bed, and propped her stick against the mattress. I asked her about her time in hospital.

She said she was glad to be back, and she had had to have the downstairs bed or she would still be in hospital.

"It's a four-foot bed, I'd like it to have been a bit smaller. I'm all right now," she said. "But I had a bad night in there, my worst night. I had a nebuliser, I couldn't breathe. And there was a male nurse there. He was good. He sat with me for three hours while I was in difficulties, and next morning he looked in and sat with me. He was caring. It was noisy in hospital," she said to Pippa. "There was a woman in her fifties in our ward. When her husband visited her she was quiet and well-behaved, but when he left she was shouting out 'Help me, help me'. Even at night, 'Help me, help me.' A voice further down the ward said, 'I wish someone would.'" She laughed and Pippa and I laughed.

She had more colour now, she had perked up. She was no longer deathly white as she reminisced about her time in hospital.

Pippa produced the three pasties she had bought at the pasty shop on the way down. We ate them with their bottoms in paper serviettes, Cornish-style. Maud asked, "Did you get any seed-bread while you were getting them?"

"No," Pippa said. "They'd sold out, they only have small loaves. They do two bakings a day. The first lot sold out, and the second lot were proving, the dough was still rising."

The talk turned to her grandson. "He gave blood," Maud said, back to her old self now, "and recently they tested his blood and wouldn't take it. It's got too many red or white corpuscles. In his childhood he had intolerance of wheat, and he may have gone back to it."

"Coeliac disease," Pippa said.

"Yes, coeliac disease."

"Brought on by contact with gluten, proteins in cereal grains. Intolerance of wheat. The pastry in pasties will be affected, he won't be able to have pasties like these. He'll have to shop for gluten-free."

"Yes," Maud said.

Maud said there were mint-ice-cream cornets in the freezer. Pippa got three and we all ate our ice-creams. Maud chatted and was more animated now.

Looking at her I could not help feeling that I might not see her alive again. We had had pasties together as if we were picnicking near the sea, echoing a past normality and making the best of her inability to come out with us, but I could not forget the white face I had seen in the doorway, which the pasties and talk of hospital and her grandson covered up.

Rain and Ten Thousand Steps

I drove to Lord's with Simon, Paul and Bernard, to watch the third day of the second Ashes Test. The tickets were part of a hospitality package, a birthday present to me from Simon, and he had also organised a car to take us. We arrived as the gates opened and walked round the ground to the Nursery Pavilion. We were shown to a table and were served breakfast: orange, granola and yoghurt, and a sausage-and-bacon bap. Two former players – Mark Butcher, the ex-England cricketer, and the Australian Merv Hughes, who had a handlebar moustache, spoke to us, saying England were on top, that their score had been good considering the difficult conditions. We left and at Simon's prompting walked round the ground, past nets where players practised and past stands to the pavilion that overlooked the pitch. A small crowd stood behind barriers to watch players arrive, and we saw Ben Stokes sign autographs and pose for photos the other side of the barriers.

We watched the morning session from Grand Stand C. The bowlers were on top and the Australians only scored 50 for the loss of three wickets. Steve Smith, who had modelled himself on Don Bradman, was in for an hour (during which he went through two pairs of gloves, which he changed every half-hour) and only scored 8. He left the ball and blocked, each time performing his idiosyncratic twirl of the bat and miming letting the ball pass him.

The crowd watched each ball, electrified. A bee buzzed over our heads, looking for flowers. In the middle batsmen played defensive shots with great concentration, someone was out, and the bee buzzed round our heads looking for flowers. Each tiny thing had its own priorities in the bowl of the stadium.

We returned to the Nursery Pavilion for lunch. Five young men, four in open-necked shirts, joined our round table with an older man who was also in an open-necked shirt and talked loudly about a medical operation he was expecting to have, and all the others listened and laughed when he laughed. He was their boss. From what they said I could tell they worked at Goldman Sachs and were on a day out from work, bonding their personal relations.

It came on to rain over lunch. We lingered over our tuna, steak and lemon-meringue tart. On a wall screen there was talk of a coming inspection, but the wicket was covered and Lord's looked a bleak sight amid umbrellas. We took our time and then at Simon's instigation we went for another walk round the ground. It was now 3.30, and we decided to go back for tea in the Nursery Pavilion as there was talk of an inspection at 4.15.

Paul said, looking at his Fitbit, "I've done around 8,000 paces today. I'm supposed to do 10,000. I went to the gym two days ago and did 10,000. If we walk round the ground once more I'll have achieved it."

The rain began again just before 4.15 and by 4.30 it was announced over a loudspeaker that there would be no more play that day. Simon called our driver. He was on his way back from Heathrow and would be some time. We walked round the ground once more. It was dry now, but it would take over an hour to prepare the wicket after covers were removed and the authorities were keen to guard the outfield from skids and slides so it was in good condition for the next day. We stood near the gate and watched as a succession of cricketers, now commentators, ambled past us: Warne, Atherton, Boycott, Botham, Holding, Hughes, David Lloyd and others. They were intercepted and asked to pose for photos by groups drinking in the adjoining open-air bars.

We left the ground and crossed the road to wait for our Mercedes. Boycott crossed after us and waited nearby for his car. He made a smiling comment as he passed me. Botham came out and stood across the road from us, waiting for his car. He was pestered by members of the crowd who were leaving and wanted to stand beside him and be photographed, which he did with some bad grace.

I thought of the cricket and the cricketers. The present players wanted to play and the past players wanted to commentate, but they had all been obstructed by the rain. But thanks to enterprising Simon we had feasted and walked off our cholesterol and burned our calories by taking 10,000 steps, which I was sure the ex-cricketers had not done, particularly Botham, who looked very overweight and had difficulty in walking. The rain had held up the proceedings and the old cricketers' commentaries, but every cloud has a silver lining and we had all taken 10,000 steps towards fitness we would otherwise not have taken.

A Humanist Funeral and a Self-Controlled Widow

We arrived at Southend Crem for Mike's funeral about 1.30pm. We waited in the car park. I wore a light-weight suit, a white shirt and black tie. Pippa, Simon and Paul went and sat on a seat, and as I was about to join them a car reversed nearby and I saw Susan waving through a window. Sibyl was also waving from a far seat. Mike's brother-in-law had driven them. We talked through their open window.

Then a lot of the mourning congregation started arriving, and I shook a lot of hands, including several well-known musicians' and Susan's stepson's. He was very tall. Sibyl's son Don arrived with his wife and four youngish daughters. I met Mike's mother, a small lady in her mid-eighties. Sibyl approached, and I noticed her creased face and thick lipstick. Susan was greeting the congregation at the door, completely natural and in charge.

Mike's coffin arrived, and we lined up behind it in pairs in the Crem's foyer. Susan led the way behind it, Sibyl and I followed. The Crematorium's chapel was packed, there were many people standing along the sides and at the back.

We peeled off and sat in our designated seats in the centre of the front row. There was a rose and an order of service on our seats. Mike's mother and two sisters sat further down. Simon and Paul were behind us with Florence and Raymond.

The celebrant had a beard. There was no mention of God. The contributions were memories of Mike and readings. There was a tribute from Susan, who ran through his life, and Susan's stepson read some family memories of him. An uncle and Mike's two sisters reminisced. A representative of the band's fan club spoke, and there were songs: 'Days' (by Ray Davies); 'If I Shall Go' and 'He is Gone'.

At the end, led by Mike's mother and sister, and then Susan's stepson, everyone went up and laid their rose on Mike's wild-hyacinth-woven coffin covered with flowers. I too went up and laid my rose and then headed back to the aisle.

The curtains closed and the coffin was removed to the cremation oven. Susan watched in full control of her emotions, perfectly composed.

Afterwards Susan was at the door greeting everyone on their way out. She was very much herself, stoically in control.

Outside there was a mêlée. I talked with Pippa, Simon and Paul, and with Florence and Raymond.

Then I found myself next to the lyric-writer and singer Ray Davies, and he said correctly that we had met in Ipswich. He said, "Susan was the best thing to have happened to Mike." I knew he had Parkinson's disease, but his memory was still good. He said he wished he was as old as me, 80. "I'm 75." He said, "Mike and I phoned each other every Sunday, the one who wasn't drunk did the phoning. He told me in disgust, 'I've got to have a blood test.' It was actually a very important blood test, and after that he changed."

We drove to The Lawn, Rochford, a spacious place for a wake: many large rooms on the ground floor inside, a terrace at the back and a triple fountain with water splashing down three bowls, a lot of grass and horses in stables. About 140 went inside for a cup of tea and for food in the Orangery, but it did not seem that many.

Then I took off my black tie and pocketed it, and sat on the terrace at the back. I talked to Don, who was sitting next to his mother Sibyl, a lieutenant colonel at Abbey Wood, near Bristol, where 10,000 worked on projects to upgrade British weapons. He said he was in a team of 60, representing the army, working under a civil servant. He said, "It's threat-driven. Intelligence says there is a threat, in my case a warrior tank is the best way to counter the threat, and I work on getting better air-conditioning and greater armour to survive roadside bombs. Russia is the main enemy, followed by China and North Korea."

He said wars are best fought in coalitions, the UK has not enough ships and aircraft following successive Tory cuts. He said he had a desk job and liked being a soldier, but would rather live in Devon at home with his four daughters.

Inside, Susan was talking to many of the 140 who had come to The Lawn. Periodically, between chats, she put her head round the door to check we were all right, to smile and say a few words and then go back inside. She handled the mourners very well, giving each her individual attention and listening to all they said. I thought again how stoical she had been.

When the time came we went inside and found her, still surrounded by a group of mourners, still composed and attentive. We said our goodbyes and I congratulated her on getting through it all so convincingly.

In the car I reflected that she was in control of her inner emotions throughout the day. She had displayed remarkable self-control. Mike had requested a humanist funeral, and he had had what he wanted. Susan was now a widow, but she did not give the impression of being in widow's weeds and in mourning, she had handled the sudden and rapid end of her husband's life with great aplomb. I did not know – no one knew – about the ordeal that was ahead of her.

An RSM and a Blocked Drain

That October the rainwater drain in our Cornish back garden backed up with foul-looking water and bits of toilet paper. Through an agency I managed to find a drain man who jetwashed.

He arrived about 2pm from Exeter and Plymouth, on £195 + VAT an hour, in a large van with two fire-engine-type hoses on large drums inside its back doors. He was a competent, energetic-looking fellow in his early sixties, and he knew what he was doing.

I showed him the round South-West-Water cover he'd parked over, and, working back to the problem, a rectangular manhole cover alongside our house and another inside our gate. He lifted both with two screwdrivers and showed me they were clear. I pointed to two more small covers near our back door, where foul water had backed up, and he got a long coil with a torch at the end and threaded it through and looked on a screen he'd erected outside the back gate and said, "There's a blockage, it looks like tree roots." He withdrew the torch and connected to the fire hydrant on our front lawn and with another hose blasted from the manhole by our gate. There was a short drainpipe beside a chest-high wall with shrubs above it and the drain beneath it blew up clouds of spray.

"That's where the blockage is," he said.

He made preparations by his van and talked to me as he worked. "I was with South-West Water until I was sixty. They got rid of me because I failed a medical to do with my chest. I'm sixty-three, still going strong."

"You're doing well," I said.

"I was in the Army for twenty-two years until 2000. I was in the Chelsea Barracks in the King's Road, RSM."

He had a regimental sergeant-major's efficiency, and I thought of the young recruits he had barked at and licked into shape.

"Just after I joined I was told, 'You're on ceremonial duty.' I was on the QE2."

"The Falklands," I said.

"Yes," he said, surprised that I'd worked that out.

"I was there some years ago. Were you in the strait where the *Sir Galahad* was bombed?"

"Near it. I had no training for it."

"Did you yomp with a thirty-pound back-pack?"

"Yes. The British troops were left without cover. We had to."

But I would have to pay £195 + VAT an hour for his drain clearance, so I stopped talking. He said I should not be outside because of possible spray, so I went indoors and watched through the window of the back door. He did a couple of blasts, and foul water backed up onto the outside path to the gate. He changed the head of his hose and increased the power, and suddenly the foul water disappeared in all the drains, including the one where there was trouble.

I opened the door.

"It's done," the RSM said.

"Excellent. And the roots?"

"They've gone."

"Did they split the pipe?"

"No."

I said, "It was Nature that caused the blockage, with some human help with bits of loo paper."

"Exactly. Can you flush all the toilets, sir?"

The RSM was speaking to me as if I was an officer in the Falklands.

I went inside and flushed four toilets. They cleared immediately. Whatever had prevented them from flushing by causing an obstruction and water to back up had gone. I returned to the back door.

He had hosed the concrete between the back door and the gate and now slooshed it with a bucket of pink disinfectant that had many bubbles as it spread round the drains. Then he hosed all the water, leaves, dirt and bits of loo roll down all the drains until there was nothing visible. He returned to the back door.

"That's it," he said, "fifty-nine minutes. I'll fill out my form. Can you come to the front and sign it there?"

I joined him at the front of the house and signed his form. He was very much in charge, still an RSM. Coping with the fire hydrant, the hose and the coil with a torch at the end all happened with military competence. He lay face down by the drains as if militarily trained. He said, "I've got four more places to go to today but I'll just get myself together." Our neighbour wanted to reverse out so he pulled his van forward.

Pippa returned from shopping and we had to take papers, cardboard boxes and household rubbish to the dump. We were away about half an hour. When we returned I saw the RSM sitting at the wheel of his van on the phone at the end of the harbour, next to the ice-cream shop. It was now 3.45 and it would be dark by 6. I wondered how many of his four destinations he would go to that day.

A Baited Trap and Two Mice

Twice I had found bait taken from the wooden mousetrap, so I bought a plastic one that looked more efficient. That morning I went up to the loft and looked at the plastic mousetrap. It was upside down and there was an enormous mouse which had taken my bait. I carried the trap downstairs and tipped the mouse onto a dustpan and carried it to our forest fence and slid it over into the undergrowth outside. I reset the trap with new bait. Before lunch I went back to the loft again. The mousetrap had disappeared. I found it upside down in a hole near a pipe and a smaller mouse was attached to it. I lifted the mousetrap out and took it downstairs and again slid the mouse over the fence. Two mice in a day, and I was trying to prevent a huge family of mice from colonising our loft.

As I was finishing the first course of my lunch, Bernard came. He had a reading week at university and had come home to see everybody. He came through to our kitchen and sat in our hanging basket in our window, facing Pippa, and he talked about his course and about his maternal grandfather's death. He had been summoned as his grandfather had been given half a day to live after a stroke a few days earlier, and he had flown to Newcastle and arrived to find him barely conscious. Bernard said, "He was breathing and rasping but his eyes were closed. I held his fingers and spoke to him, but I don't know whether he heard me and his fingers didn't respond. He died the next morning at 12.30." He said, "I went back to uni and discovered I had this week off so I tried to book a ticket for Wednesday. I checked on Tuesday and found my train went in three hours' time, I only just caught it." Bernard then told me how he would be spending a week in work experience with the City broker (again) when he got back in mid-December, and how he was looking forward to it.

The gate buzzer sounded. It was his mother in a blue car with a black hood. She had blonde hair carefully brushed and a hooked nose. "Sorry to hear about your dad," I said as she got out and came in. She looked sombre.

As I made tea and put in the sweetener she had, she talked to Pippa about the death. "It was unexpected," she said. "He'd been given five years to live when he was diagnosed with dementia and had to go into the home, and that was four years ago, and he seemed all right. The nurses didn't say he was that ill at first. I was up there for Saturday and I was coming away on Sunday and my cousin said, 'He's having a test tomorrow, can't you stay?' So I stayed. I had my car packed to come home for three days. I was set to drive back on Tuesday and said to a nurse when he was asleep, 'Well, I'm driving home now.'

She said, 'I'd wait if I were you. He may not be here tomorrow.' That's when I rang Bernard to come up immediately. He deteriorated very quickly. His food was going into his lungs, that was the problem."

She then said his house had been let to a young girl who had got behind with the rent, and that she and her cousin were going to give her notice and put the house up for sale in the New Year.

Soon afterwards Bernard and his mother left. He came to be hugged and I slipped him £20 as a grandfather should and wished him good luck during his exams next week and a good last few weeks of the term. They drove off, one in a red car, one in a blue car. And I returned to my lunch and finished my pudding: a bowl of fruit (banana slices, blueberries, raspberries and strawberries) covered with dollops of yoghurt. And I thought of the two of them. Both had scented bait: Bernard was looking forward to his work experience, where he had been before and where he could see himself landing a highly-paid job, and his mother was expecting an amount out of the sale of her father's house, which would make a difference to her life.

I thought of the two mice in my trap, and I hoped that as Bernard and his mother pursued their bait they would not find that life snapped over them as my trap had snapped over the two mice. I hoped they would take their bait away from Fate's mousetrap, like the earlier mouse, and not have the trap snap on them before they could enjoy their career and sale, the sort of things we all want from Providence but are often denied.

A Purple-Nailed Man and Clattering

I arrived early in Queen Square and found reception in the basement. Behind the desk sat a woman with a bun and a man's dark glasses. I showed my appointment for my MRI (magnetic resonance imaging) and she spoke in a loud low man's voice. She stood up and gave me a clipboard with a questionnaire to fill in, and I saw that below her red jumper she was wearing a black skirt and had long purple nails. But she was definitely a man.

I completed the form, sitting by a Christmas tree, and read a newspaper past my appointment time, 1pm, and studied the three others who were waiting. A woman with a swollen face came out. She had artificial roses in a band round her head. The man in a skirt with purple nails worked on a keyboard, clattering the keys. I stood and returned the clipboard. He wrote an amount. "That's how much it will be," he said. "And if you need a dye it will be this on top."

As it was 10 minutes after my appointment time I asked how long before I had my scan.

"Oh, when they're ready," he said brusquely as he typed at breakneck speed, clattering and unwilling to be interrupted. He did not seem to be interested in the patients, only in what he was keying in.

Then he was joined by a real woman who opened a swing-door, walked round the chest-high reception desk, edged behind the man and sat on an empty chair.

I stood again and asked her if I'd been forgotten.

"I'll check," she said, and she got up and walked round the chest-high reception desk and went through another swing-door. She came back and said, "Two minutes." I thanked her.

I had my scan. A middle-aged woman went through my questions in a small changing-room to establish I had no metal inside me, and told me to remove all metal things – my watch, my belt, keys and coins, even my collar stiffeners if they were metal. I complied and was led through to a room with a huge machine. I lay back on a thin padded couch, had a rest placed under my legs and was slid into a tunnel. I just had time to say, "You're looking for my cerebellum."

I had earplugs and a Perspex head cap and for twenty minutes heard scrunching and clattering and rat-a-tat-tat noises of different pitches. Occasionally I heard a distant voice and said, lying still, "I'm fine."

Eventually I was slid out and sat up and swung my legs down.

"You found my cerebellum?" I asked.

"Yes," the fellow said, 'it's there."

I returned to the dressing-room and put on my watch and my belt, put my keys and coins in my pocket, and then returned to the reception desk to pay. No one was sitting waiting now. The man was still clattering on his keyboard.

"I didn't need dye," I said, finding my card.

The girl printed out my invoice and looked at it doubtfully.

"Is that the right amount?" she asked the man.

"No, I'll do it," he said loudly.

He printed out an invoice that had the correct amount, and returned to his clattering.

I paid by card and left them. The man was still clattering as I walked to the door, and he spoke loudly to the girl. Was he transgender or a transvestite or had he merely self-identified as a man who would wear women's clothes? I was not sure. But he clearly seemed good at his job, even if he did not put himself out for his patients, and he was clearly producing something quite lengthy with his clattering, perhaps a report.

I left the warmth of the reception area, climbed the steps and went out into the cold of Queen Square.

A Schoolboy and Death

The dentist hived off the cleaning of teeth to a hygienist, leaving herself more time to look for fillings – and creating two invoices. I went for my hygienist's appointment at 9am on a Tuesday. The receptionist said, "She'll be here soon. She's got boys at the school where the boy was killed by a motorist who drove onto the pavement. There's security, and it means she's slightly late in getting here after she's dropped them off."

The hygienist came and called me up at 9.05. She was about 40. I sat in the room Dr Clerihew used to occupy, and I said I hoped her children had not been affected by the incident.

"My younger boy's thirteen, he saw it," she said. "He said there were legs in different directions and he was bleeding in his head, a lot of blood. He's not been affected. He asked me to sit with him as he went to sleep that night, but the next day he said, 'They're offering counselling, I don't need counselling.' My other boy didn't see it. But what's strange is no one must talk about it. The names of the boys involved in the incident are all secret, no one must refer to them. The man meant to do it, he drove past and turned and drove back and mounted the pavement and ran into the five boys, killing one. He's known locally to throw his weight about, he has a record of abusive behaviour. Because the names of the boys are now secret, it looks as if he was known to them. I wonder if he was in a relationship with the boy's mother and it was broken off because he was abusive and he tried to attack the boy as revenge, to get at her, and got the wrong boy. It can't be random. Anyway, we'll see what happens in June, when the trial starts."

I listened with interest. "You're probably right," I said. "I wondered if he'd had a son at the school who was bullied, and was trying to take out the bully and got the wrong boy."

Then she realised the time and got on and scaled and cleaned my teeth.

As I walked away from the surgery I thought of the man in his car. What caused him to make a run past boys outside the school gates and turn and then deliberately mount the pavement? If they'd given him some lip while they were crossing a road they could have enraged him, but these boys were walking in a group and were well-behaved, and he had driven past and turned back. What would cause a man of 51 to drive his car at a group of schoolchildren and kill one aged eleven? His action defied belief.

Then I thought, he threw his weight about, he was abusive. Standards of behaviour have slid, the UK is in decay. Knife crime is up, the streets are no longer safe, social media has made people angry and he threw his weight around outside school. We are living in a time of decline, and this sort of behaviour can be expected to happen. And I looked with sadness at the decline in manners since I was a boy of eleven after the end of the war.

A Donkey and Precipices
(Or: A Cave-Dweller and a Monastery)

At last I was at Petra, the lost Nabataean city which disappeared in the 8th century AD and was rediscovered by Johann Ludwig Burckhardt, a Swiss explorer, in 1812.

At the gate to Petra, at 8am in early March, we took a horse-and-cart as it was a good five miles' walk to the 'basin' and back.

It was a flimsy cart. Pippa sat between the Arab who steered the horses – at a gallop under a warm sun in a blue sky – and me, and the terrain was sandy with frequent boulders and several times we were sharply jolted off our seat. It was a bone-shaking journey and tired walkers were amazed to see us careering along as if in a chariot race.

We went into the shaded cool of the Siq, a very narrow gorge approximately 182 metres high and 1.2 km long, at breakneck speed and as walkers jumped clear I released my grip on the rail at the side of the seat as my knuckles could be scraped on the sandstone rock.

At last we came to a skidding halt before the 40-metre-high Treasury – six columns on the lowest level, and two more on each side of a funeral urn above them – beside a couple of other horse-and-carts. I got out and stood and looked at the façade well-known from *Indiana Jones and the Last Crusade*. The funeral urn in the middle at the top was thought by the Bedouin to contain treasure, hence its name 'The Treasury'.

John William Burgon, an American poet who became Dean of Chichester Cathedral, described it in a poem that won Oxford's Newdigate Prize for poetry in 1845 (without having visited Petra) as "a rose-red city, half as old as Time". It was rose-red as it was before 10am, but it certainly was not half as old as time. It was in fact a 1st-century-AD tomb, probably carved for King Aretas III of the Nabataeans. I took some photos on my phone and got back in.

We careered on along the Street of Façades, past the Royal Tombs carved high up in the sandstone rocks, along the Colonnaded Street, past the Great Temple and the Qasr al-Bint to the stopping point in the basin beside a bridge with no water beneath it. We got out and sat on the stone wall of the bridge. Our group were walking and we had to join them for lunch at 11.15. Pippa's replacement hips had required us to avoid the long walk.

An enormously fat man, who had told me he had been ill eight years ago and had eight operations and was recovering from cancer, got out of another horse-and-cart, followed by another horse-and-cart bringing his wife. They went off to the restaurant. Pippa and I carried on sitting on the wall, and a Bedouin came and asked, "You want to go up to Monastery by donkey?"

I shook my head.

But he was persistent. "My son take you."

To deflect him I asked him where he lived.

"For many years in a cave in Petra. Now in a village, that village." He pointed, and I could see sand-coloured houses.

The sun was getting warm and the sandstone was turning yellow.

"What was it like in the cave? Cool in the summer, warm in the winter?"

"Exactly. Very cool and very warm."

"Could you see the stars at night from the entrance to the cave?"

"Yes, beautiful stars."

He had lived like a Neolithic in the New Stone Age, and here I was discussing what it was like being a Neolithic.

"Your group is walking, you have to do something. My son take you. Thirty dinars. It's your last chance, you'll never go again and you are here."

He had a point, but I shook my head. "Nine hundred steps, very slippery, the donkey may slip."

"No hooves so it can walk up steps better. My son will look after you. You will be safe."

We had been warned by the tour group against agreeing to offers from Bedouin. I would not be covered by any insurance. But I was nearly 80, and fit and confident in my abilities. And had not Jesus asked a disciple to untether a colt which had presumably not been broken in, and bring it to him, and had he not ridden it into Jerusalem on Palm Sunday? If Jesus could ride on an untamed colt, I could ride on a tamed donkey.

Pippa said, "Go if you'd like to. I'll talk to Richard." (The fat man.)

"All right," I said, getting up from the stone wall off the bridge. And immediately his son was beside me, a Bedouin in a headscarf, with a donkey. He put my left foot in a stirrup and helped me swing my right leg over the donkey's back and I was in the saddle, holding onto a steel grip at the front of the saddle.

And off we went, the caveman's late-teenage son cluck-clucking to hurry the donkey into a trot and keeping pace and holding my arm as we turned and headed towards the 200-metre-high mountain.

We climbed and climbed, first a slope, then uneven slippery steps with sand on them. Soon there was a precipice on my right side.

"Don't worry, the donkey knows where to walk. He's been doing this for five years. He's called Azeus." 'Azeus' reminded me of my protector Zeus. "When he goes up, you bend forward, when he goes down, you lean back and hold on to the handle." He indicated a leather thong fixed on the saddle. "I will be holding the rope."

The rope was in fact a silvery chain tied round the donkey's neck.

We climbed and turned and climbed again. We passed one or two walkers who had set off really early and several Bedouin stalls selling clothes and trinkets. Suddenly we stopped.

A wizened old lady in black got to her feet and greeted me: "Hello, I am Nain's aunt. Promise me you come here and buy something on your way down. Give me your little finger."

I complied and we interlocked little fingers.

"That means you will buy from me and not the woman up at the top. I trust you."

With apologies for being in a hurry I carried on climbing. Nain told me he had two brothers – "I am in the middle" – and three sisters, and his aunt was one of twelve children. He had never lived in the cave, nor had she, they were all in the village.

I recalled that in the 1980s, soon after 1985, when Petra was designated a world heritage site, Bedouin living in Petra had been expelled to a nearby village by UNESCO and the Jordanian government, but still felt they owned Petra.

We climbed and then stopped by another Bedouin stall.

"My sister," Nain said.

This was the woman his aunt had referred to.

"Buy from me. Will you buy a nice silk scarf now?"

I made my apologies, saying time was short, and passed on.

Suddenly Nain said, "We are three minutes from the top. Donkey stops here. You get off and walk."

A Bedouin lady had a glass of milkless tea for him, and he tethered the donkey by its silver chain to a tree. Reluctantly I dismounted – taking my foot out of the left stirrup and swinging my right leg over the donkey's head – and began climbing more steps with my bag, feeling exposed. I was nearly 80 and would one of the Bedouin attack me for my money? Eventually I came out above a plateau, descended uneven steps and stood before the Monastery, which looked similar to the Treasury – columns and capitals – and according to what I had read was either 1st-century-BC and perhaps built to be dedicated to the deified King Obodas I, or perhaps early 2nd-century-AD and built in the reign of King Rabbel II. It became a church and had crosses on the wall. Hence its name 'The Monastery'.

I wandered across the plateau past a flock of black goats and sheep to the brow of a hill, and then the brow of another hill, and when that revealed the brow of a third hill I gave up pursuing the view. On either side of the third brow I could see desert, and I knew I was looking into Saudi Arabia, down at Wadi Araba and the Great Rift Valley 4,000 feet below.

I retraced my steps and found Nain. He was reluctant to leave his conversation with the Bedouin girl who had given him tea. He unchained the donkey that was feeding behind the Bedouin stall and put my foot in the stirrup and I swung my right leg over its back, and making urgent clucking noises and getting the donkey to go fast he ran ahead of Azeus and we began our descent back down the steps.

We went fast. I managed to keep moving past Nain's sister but further down we were stopped by his aunt, who was in black. "You buy now, a nice scarf, like this one. One dinar." She held out a chequered blue and white scarf. "You will look like a Jordanian." She put the scarf on my head to shield me from the very warm sun.

I felt in my breast pocket and found a dinar and offered it to her.

"No, this one is fifteen dinars."

"I haven't got it." I opened my palms in a skint gesture.

"Here, drink this tea." A tiny warm glass of tea was thrust into my hands. "You promised me you would buy, we agreed with our little fingers. I trusted you."

"Keep the dinar for the tea," I said.

"No," she said. "The tea is hospitality, I cannot take any money from you without you buying something. Twelve dinars."

"I haven't got it," I said, meaning I had not got the exact amount in change.

Disgusted, she let me proceed. "But make sure you give Nain a good tip," she called as I continued my descent.

We went down very quickly, past many precipices with enormous ravines between high sandstone walls. The donkey was sure-footed and knew where to tread, and Nain held my arm whenever I was in danger of falling off.

"No one has ever fallen," he said. "It would be bad for our business. We care for all who make this journey."

Eventually I got to the bottom. "Your wife is in this restaurant," said his father, appearing suddenly. "Was it good?"

"Yes," I said, dismounting. I went to the restaurant wall, put my bag on it, and tried to find 10 dinars for a tip. All I had was 20. "Have you got change?" I asked Nain. "Can you give me 10 dinars?"

"No, I have no change."

He had kept me alive above precipices and I had seen the Monastery, so I let him have the 20-dinar note. He was surprised and pleased. "Thank you."

"I looked after your son," I told his father, the ex-cave-dweller, and to Nain said, "Tell your aunt I kept my promise to give you a good tip. Little-fingers promise was kept."

He nodded and was then off looking for another customer, number 4 of the day. He had told me I was number 3.

I walked under the awning in the garden of the restaurant. Pippa was sitting with Richard and his wife, and a minister. She looked at me and said, "You've caught the sun." Later she told me she had really meant I was puce from the exertion of being bumped about as the donkey descended the uneven steps. "Did you get to the top?"

"Yes," I said. "I didn't fall off. I reckoned if Jesus could ride on an untamed colt on Palm Sunday, I could ride a tamed donkey. But I'm a bit disappointed. No one was waving palm fronds when I came down."

All laughed, the minister a bit warily.

Then fat Richard leaned forward and said: "I gather you have a hobby, collecting Roman and Greek coins. I'm a coin dealer opposite the British Museum."

And I thought of Nain's aunt who wanted me to buy her wares, and realised it wasn't only Bedouin who touted for business.

A Fairy Shirt and a Cleaning Boss

Katie brought her sister Joanna as the cleaning company had decided to use their staff in pairs. They both had black company T-shirts with the name of the company and phone number, but Joanna had a picture of a pink fairy beside them.

"I never had one of them with a fairy on it," Katie said at the door as they prepared to leave. "I never got one. She did, but I didn't."

"It's a bit like a cricket cap. You get your cap for having played well."

Katie looked at me with disdain. "Thank you for saying that," she said, and we both laughed, and Joanna nodded enthusiastically.

"Carly forgot," Katie said of their boss. "It's like her driving. She's the worst driver. We sit in the back and she stops and says, 'I can't believe that, did you see what he did?' She's jerky, it's the accelerator, and then the brake, we're going backwards and forwards in the back. She stopped at a roundabout. There was a sign saying left or right. A car stopped to let her go. She just stopped and cars were just missing her. 'Did you see that? He shouldn't be allowed on the road.' He'd stopped for her but it was his fault. It's always someone else's fault when she's driving." Joanna was nodding along.

"If she wants lessons, you know who can volunteer," Pippa said, laughing.

Katie's husband was a driving instructor.

"No, no," Katie said defiantly. "She's beyond help."

"Thanks for today," I said, "see you on Monday."

"Yes, see you on Monday. Bye."

And they left to go to their next assignment. Both had Carly's company's phone number on their backs, one with a fairy, and I hoped their boss was better at organising their fairy work than she was at driving them.

A Fluffy Cloud and Swallow Harbingers

For several nights running after I put the light out to go to sleep and closed my eyes, in the dark I saw a small white cloud. It was puffy and fluffy and downy and was gently lowered so it was almost near enough to climb onto and lie on or sit on. I didn't know what it was. I half-wondered if I was looking at my soul.

That hot afternoon with storms forecast I went for my afternoon walk during lockdown (because of coronavirus) with a tub of fish food to feed the fish in the fish-pond and three parakeets that lived in the large foresty garden flew in front of me, screeching, saying, 'Hello and thank you for putting nuts in our bird feeder.' I fed the fish in the pond – the *koi* carp were hungry and fought with each other to gobble down the capsules and crowded out the goldfish – and then I walked across the lawn, avoiding the clover and buttercups and star-like lesser stitchwort, to the main field with forest trees on three sides. I put the tub on the ground by the gate and set off for the second field down the slope. There were no birds.

Suddenly I was being dive-bombed in a friendly way. Swallows swooped down, three, now four, and skimmed and swerved and climbed and dipped and came racing back alongside me. And I thought of how at least a year ago I went out onto my balcony and three or four swallows swooped round my head, playfully saying, 'Hello, we're back from Africa, good to see you again.' They accompanied me all the way to the bottom field. They vanished, but as I turned back they hurtled down from above trees across my path, skimmed and then returned. One flew at me and at the last minute soared up over my right shoulder and wheeled high in the sky. I waved my friends goodbye and returned to the top of the field to retrieve my tub, cross the lawn and go in.

The next day was cloudy and there had been rain. After I fed the fish at 4 o'clock I entered the main field with forest trees on three sides and held out my arms in an embracing gesture and beckoned with one arm. And from the trees beyond the fence to my left as I walked hurtled one, two, three, four swallows, dipping and swooping across my path to greet me, skimming and swerving to dart back near me and say, 'Hello again, we've come from Africa, we're still here.'

They accompanied me to the second field and rose into the sky and were lost in trees, but again as I walked back they returned, crossing my path, and two landed on the fence rail on my right and sat side by side showing their white bibs and allowed me to walk to within six paces of them. I lingered and studied their anatomies. They were definitely swallows – not (these days) rare swifts or house martins. I could tell by their long forked tails and their colouring.

I spoke to them. "I'm glad you're here again," I said. "You're welcome in my garden and these fields any time. Thank you for flying from Africa to roost here again." And they flew contentedly off.

That night again after I turned off the light to go to sleep in the dark I saw the white fluffy cloud, and I thought of Rubens' oval painting on the ceiling of the Banqueting House, showing James I ascending to Heaven on the back of an eagle. And I wondered if the angels were showing me a cloud my soul would be living on after it was escorted to Heaven not by an eagle but by these swallows, who were in fact harbingers of the next phase of my soul's life.

An Open Bonnet and Trickling Oil

Gully bought a VW he found for £700. His old car, a light-green Renault, had not been properly maintained for years, and a rear side window fell down inside the door requiring attention. The engine-warning light had been on and at the same time the repair got rid of it. He had decided it was costing him too much money to maintain, hence the purchase.

The Renault was standing outside his house with a notice stuck on a back window: 'For Sale, £500.'

"I was stitched up," Gully told me. "A couple of Indian men knocked on my door. They had a child with them, a small boy. One of them asked me to open the bonnet, so I did. He bent and had a good look inside. Then he said, 'Can you open the boot?' So I opened it and returned to the bonnet. He called, 'I can't see the spare wheel.' So I went to the back and showed his companion where it was stowed. I left the Indian looking under the bonnet alone, I wasn't observing him for getting on for a minute. I was distracted.

"The Indian under the bonnet said he wanted a drive. So I closed the bonnet and they all got in my car and we went for a drive round the local roads. When we got back outside my house the main Indian said he wanted to have another look under the bonnet. He said, 'Look, there's oil at the top.' I hadn't seen that before. Then he said, 'Look, it's trickling down the outside of the engine, the engine's gone.'

"I knew I couldn't put a new engine in to sell the car. I knew I had to sell it now to get something for it. All along I was clear in my mind that I'd accept £400. But the main Indian said £100. I was bounced into it. I said, 'Yes' – £100 was better than writing off the car as the engine was leaking oil – and I signed the paperwork. They drove the car off.

"After they'd gone I thought about it. I left the main Indian looking under the bonnet and went round to show the other one where the spare wheel was. He could have poured oil down the outside of the engine, *he* could have put it there. It had never happened before. Then I was sure that was what happened. They stitched me up. Their scam was to get me to open the bonnet, pour oil on the outside of the engine, go for a drive, then claim the car was worthless because it had got trickling oil. Why did they give me £100 if the engine had gone?"

Gully looked sheepish. He had been taken for a fool, and he felt foolish. I felt sorry for him and said as much: "I am sorry to hear this." He looked rueful. The £300 he had been deprived of mattered to him.

He wandered dejectedly off to continue working in his Lord's vineyard.

Red Kites High Above the Virus

Simon came for Pippa at 7.30 and drove her to Le Manoir aux Quat' Saisons near Oxford where she had a lockdown cookery class, the only pupil with two chefs, making dishes from Raymond Blanc's vegetable garden, including a soufflé. When the cooking was over and she had eaten what she had cooked she sat with Simon in the garden, and Raymond Blanc came and sat and had a long chat. He said it was tough out there after lockdown, and he was having to consider closing some of his outlets.

Paul picked me up and drove me to Le Manoir. We arrived at teatime – we walked between lavender beds to reception and all the staff wore masks and visors – and we sat in the garden with Pippa and Simon. Le Manoir went back to 1225 and had been rebuilt in the seventeenth century. It had only just reopened after lockdown. Red kites soared and circled overhead. We sipped Prosecco and were served tea with lemon-drizzle cake by a waiter.

We had all brought bags of presents, and Pippa opened her cards. I gave her a Victorian gold brooch with wings and seventeen tiny pearls, four of which were grouped together: our family and the two branches of her family.

Simon had brought a mauve balloon which waved 70 in large numbers in the gentle breeze in shade under a tree. Our grandchildren were in Spain, and rang and looked in on our setting and showed us theirs. We sat on for a while, our family of four at peace, celebrating a milestone, Pippa reaching 70, all basking in their belonging to a family unit with the coronavirus all round.

We checked in and went to our room, Crystal. The two boys were in Jade nearby. We unpacked and changed and got ready and met the boys in the bar. The four of us sat on a long window-seat, no one else was in the room. Then we were shown to our table. It was distanced from two smaller tables in a cosy room.

During the next two hours, to soft music, we had seven courses: *la tomate, le crabe, les légumes de notre jardin, le turbot, l'agneau à la pêche* and *le chocolat*. There were smaller courses slipped between them, some just a mouthful or two, and there were wines for each course, white wines from Germany, France, Austria and Portugal, and two ports. Pippa sat under her balloon, which let everyone know she had turned 70, increasingly smiling and laughing as the good food and wine had their effect.

Afterwards we sat outside in the garden, the only guests to do so. We were in comfortable chairs round a low table and there was a clear sky in the dusk, and then dark. Venus, the evening star, and the pole star could be clearly seen, and later a third star, the planet Jupiter. We were all in harmony, there was considerable mirth, a family enjoying togetherness and appreciating each other's company.

There was a gentleness beneath the conversation, a deep relaxation. We were all at ease with each other. There was a dreadful plague abroad, and everyone was apprehensive of catching it from a surface or another person, but our sitting-together confirmed a safe haven from the plague, and in our conversation and alertness we were like four circling red kites high above the virus. We felt the peace of our family beyond all viruses.

Isolations and Masks

I had not seen my London doctor for nine months. I had had an appointment in March but was rung by his PA, who said before lockdown, "Because of Covid-19 we're not seeing anybody, we're having video calls. It's better if you don't come for a bit."

Now in August, lockdown over, I had an appointment for a nine-o-clock blood test and then at 2pm with Dr Erdmann. I arrived on the Harley-Street doorstep holding my bag at the same time as a thinnish, neatly-dressed lady with black hair who later turned out to be the nurse in the basement I had to see.

She asked me to take off my shoes and she weighed me. She measured my height. She gave me an eye test (reading letters of the alphabet in descending size). She then studied her card and said, "I have to do the ECG now, take your shirt off and lie back on the couch." Then she said, "I need to think about what I'm doing. I've been at home for fourteen days and I'm out of practice."

"Quarantining?" I asked. "Have you returned from Spain?"

"No, I've had Covid, for a second time," she said casually as she placed electrodes on my body and legs. "I tested positive and had to isolate for fourteen days. I've had no symptoms. I had Covid in March, quite badly. I had a fever and a cough and lost my taste and smell, but this last time nothing."

"Perhaps the test was unreliable and gave a wrong answer?" I said. "If it didn't, your antibodies from March only lasted four months."

"No, the test is always right," she said.

When she finished my ECG test she took my blood. The needle on the inside of my left arm hurt and she took five bottles of dark red blood. She put cotton wool on my wound and as I held it strapped it down with a plaster. A dark bruise spread from beneath the plaster.

I was not allowed to sit in the waiting-room because of Covid distancing rules. It was raining as I left reception. I put up my small umbrella and took my bag and walked to La Brasseria in Marylebone High Street, where I had booked a table. I was shown to a small square table in a corner near the unused end of the bar, and got out my work: a proof I had to read. I ordered yoghurt and nuts and cappuccino, and began working. Every other table was occupied, and I could see a girl writing on a pad and a man bent over a laptop. The restaurant was used to being an office away from the office.

I ate my yoghurt and after an hour had another cappuccino, and after another hour another cappuccino and a slice of cheesecake. I concentrated on my proofreading, the door opposite me was wide open to let out any Covid germs, and light rain fell during the whole of my four-hour stint. Then the rain stopped, and I paid and walked back to Dr Erdmann's, put on a mask, completed a form and was shown to the upstairs waiting-room.

Dr Erdmann was a quarter of an hour late. He came to fetch me, dressed in scrubs as if about to conduct an operation: a surgical hat, mask and blue gloves. I could see his eyes behind the dark frame of his glasses between his hat and his mask.

He led me to his room and said, "I've had to swab everything down, including your chair." I could see a smear of disinfectant that was still drying on its seat. He said, "And I can't wear a tie and my shirtsleeves have to be rolled up. It's the only way, it's very depressing."

This was a new Dr Erdmann. For the three years I had been coming to him he was very much in charge and bustling.

"What do you think of it all?" I asked as I sat and unpacked my file from my bag.

"I think Covid's here to stay and it's not going to get any better and we've got to live with it," he said. "I think lockdown was a mistake. It's lost our economic stability. I can't see things getting any better. I'm very depressed about it all, the economy."

I said I agreed with him. "Sweden got it right, shield the elderly and vulnerable, let schools and businesses carry on, no lockdown, and they've had fewer deaths than the UK and only half the economic slump."

"I agree," he said. "I had Covid in March."

I was stunned. It was as though he had torn off his mask. I did not realise my appointment in March had been cancelled because he had Covid. His PA had masked the situation by presenting it as a new procedure to avoid face-to-face meetings on safety grounds.

"I had it quite badly. I didn't want to go to hospital and be on a ventilator. It was the same time Johnson had it, and at that time ventilators made things worse. I said to my partner, 'I'm going to stay and isolate here.' And I did."

"I'm sorry," I said. "I didn't know. Did you catch it from a patient?"

"Yes."

"Well done for keeping going," I said.

He nodded.

I realised that something had happened to him in the course of having Covid. He had lost his authority and was more uncertain than he had been during the last three years. He was more inclined to talk about himself and had twice admitted to being depressed, which the old Dr Erdmann would never have done.

Dr Erdmann asked me questions. We discussed my blood test and I said the nurse had been away for fourteen days.

"Oh, is she back? I didn't know."

"She says she tested positive a second time, so her antibodies didn't last from March until July."

He looked at me and said, "I think there was something wrong with her test."

But he was her boss and she had been asked to go home and isolate. It was a strange situation.

At his request I stripped to my underpants and he gave me a thorough examination, dictating into a hand-held Dictaphone as he examined me. I noticed he was still fluent but a couple of times he forgot the thread of what he was saying, which may have been due to Covid.

At the end he said, "I think you're extraordinary for your years, both mentally and physically. You're how I'd like to be when I reach your age."

I said, "Some people like to do Sudoku to keep mentally active. I proofread and tinker with words."

He said, "That's excellent."

Now he was back to his old self. Dr Erdmann had been shaken by Covid and the economy and his business were not as they had been before, and his life's work had been threatened along with his life. Everything was a struggle – he didn't know his nurse was back and the wiping down had got to him. But he had kept going just as my parents' generation had kept going during the war. All of us had to keep going with determination in the 'new normal' of post-Covid living – of masks and social distancing and wiping everything down with disinfectant.

It meant assuming that the virus was present on every door handle and surface, it was like living during the plague, the Black Death, and I reflected that he had let his guard down and revealed the vulnerable soul beneath the efficient mask of the head of a successful Harley-Street practice. We all lived isolated lives now, and hid our dismay behind masks.

PART TWO

A Death-Mask and the Bone People

A Death-Mask and the Bone People
(Or: Shouted Names and Sepsis)

On that May Bank Holiday I woke with a painful right arm. I couldn't lift my right hand without excruciating pain. I operated with one arm to dress, pulled first my vest, then my shirt, then my sweater over my limp right arm and then my left arm and ducked my head in three times without aggravating my right shoulder.

The next day, determined to see that mind triumphed over matter, I drove to the gym, holding the steering-wheel with my left hand and guiding it with my limp right hand, and managed to do all the exercises and weight-pulling two-handed, but with some difficulty. On the way home my car key slid out of my left pocket and fell down between the seat and the car's central island (the centre console), and I had to try and retrieve it left-handed, which was difficult.

For some days I had had a gash at the back of my right hand, and now my temperature began to rise. I managed to get a message to my GP. She sent me a message saying she could not see me because of Covid restrictions, but she was worried my rising temperature might have been caused by the gash and I should go urgently to A&E and have a blood test and an X-ray as I might have sepsis from my wound.

I knew that sepsis is sometimes fatal within 12 hours. Wanting to avoid the inevitable delay of going to an NHS A&E I made an emergency GP appointment at the local private hospital for 5pm.

The doctor was Indian. She appreciated the possible urgency and wrote out forms requesting two blood tests and two X-rays. She said she had ticked two X-ray boxes as she wanted me to have an X-ray and ultrasound. She said, "I'm used to working on computers, I'm not used to having to fill in paper forms."

Unfortunately the blood test and X-ray departments were now closed, so she gave me the forms and advised me to hand them to the receptionist at the Diagnostic Centre, which I did. The receptionist said they would phone me the next day, and I wrote my phone number on one of the forms.

The next day I heard nothing, so I rang the Diagnostic Centre. I was told they could not progress the requests as the form requesting

X-rays had two X-rays ticked when there should only be one, and there was no trace of the request for blood tests. It might have gone to Outpatients.

I rang Outpatients and they didn't have it. A receptionist there said it might be in "the back room", and she kindly said she would walk to the back room. She rang back to say it wasn't there, they couldn't locate the form and she would contact the doctor's secretary. The doctor's secretary rang me and said that she had no copy of the original request and would have to consult the doctor. She spoke with me later and said, "In view of the urgent situation as you may have sepsis, she says you should go to A&E immediately."

There was no escape from waiting several hours. Pippa immediately drove me to the recommended NHS A&E, and I arrived at 3.30pm. I registered at the entrance and received a laminated sheet with labels showing my name and medical details, which I had to carry with me. I was triaged. I explained I had lost the use of my right arm and there was a worry that I might have sepsis. I showed the wound on my hand. The Sri-Lankan triage nurse said aggressively, "That's a leap, there is no evidence that wound has caused sepsis. I'm sending you to the GP in the UTC."

He gave me directions on a piece of paper, and I walked to a nearby building and inside the revolving doors walked down a corridor and turned left past Marks & Spencer and found the Urgent Treatment Centre: about thirty sitting on spaced chairs, all in masks, under notices on the wall saying the wait could be four hours. I reported to reception and then found an empty chair.

In theory there was a queue. But a young girl came in with her arm in a sling and was seen immediately. There seemed to be only two doctors and each interview seemed to take at least twenty minutes. A new patient was called by name in a loud voice from a corridor or an inner room within reception. A lady in a wheelchair arrived and was seen immediately. A young man hopped in on one foot and sat on the floor with his back to the wall, and was seen almost immediately. He was out within five minutes on a pair of crutches.

Then a man in a Hallowe'en mask, dressed in black, came in. He had skull eyes and teeth and looked like a ghost. But as he sat, hooded, and looked at me, I realised he represented Death. He was not seen immediately, and I toyed with the idea that Death had turned up to claim me because of my sepsis.

Eventually I heard a distant cry down a corridor, "Philip Rawley." I gathered my bag and looked for where my name had been shouted from. I found a Sri-Lankan GP standing outside his room. He beckoned me in and asked me to explain my plight and then to strip to the waist. His phone rang, and he went to an inner room and shut the door. Later he came out and examined my arm and asked me to move it in different directions. Then he said: "I have to phone. Get dressed and return to the waiting area." He retreated to his inner room and shut the door.

I returned to a different chair in the waiting-room, not knowing what was next as it had not been explained, and I read a newspaper I had brought.

Then I heard a woman yell, "Philippa, Philippa."

I thought, 'That's a girl's name,' and stayed where I was.

Another patient called to me, "Are you Philip?"

"Yes," I said.

"You're being called."

So it *was* me. A rotund African lady led me through reception to an inner room and took three phials of my blood. She asked me for my sheet with labels, tore off the top part and put it on my wristband. She said, "Come with me, we are going back to A&E."

As we walked down the corridor I said, "Does my wristband mean I'm being admitted?"

"No," she said.

"Is it in case I escape while we're walking?"

She chuckled for a long while.

Back in the A&E waiting area I read another newspaper. Eventually a Chinese doctor called, "Philip Rawley." He told me his name was Chris and he was a doctor, and he led me through corridors to a room of cubicles with drawn curtains. I sat on a chair in one and took my top off (sliding it over my head and wincing) and he examined my right shoulder. I followed him to the nearby X-ray department and had my shoulder X-rayed front and back, stripped to the waist.

Back in my cubicle I sat and waited. Chris returned and said, "I have looked at your X-ray and your blood tests. You have a slight infection in your blood. I think you have fluid in your shoulder. A septic joint."

I said, "Can that turn into sepsis?"

"Yes. You may have sepsis. Either you have sepsis or you have bursitis, which is not a problem, or a frozen shoulder. I want to bring a consultant to see you."

I waited and a thick-set, more swarthy man came in, who I reckoned was also Sri-Lankan but might have been Pakistani. He examined my shoulder and asked me to move my hands in different directions. Then he said: "I agree with Chris. There's effluence there, fluid. You may have sepsis."

The two went out and conferred the other side of the curtain. Then Chris returned and said, "Dress, we are going back to the waiting area. I want you to see the bone people so they can take a biopsy from your shoulder and examine it."

'The bone people'. It sounded witch-doctorish.

And so I again sat in the waiting area. It was now 8.30pm, and people were getting hungry and thirsty. There was a refrigerated glass drinks dispenser. A large bald man of about forty in a sweatshirt and shorts was sitting near it. He was speaking loudly to people sitting near him. He asked a woman how long she had been waiting and what her medical problem was, and in breaching her privacy behaved inappropriately. He now sat himself in front of the drinks dispenser with his head immediately in front of the card-reader, which was fixed on one side. When a lady said, "Excuse me, I need to use my card," he bent his head so she had to insert her card just above his right ear. When she had finished her transaction he returned to his previous position obstructing the drinks dispenser.

Nine o'clock came and went. I stood up and crossed to the receptionist and said, "I'm waiting for 'the bone people'. They do know I'm here, don't they? Can you see if I'm on a list?"

She said, "Oh, the orthopaedists. They're operating in different parts of the hospital, they haven't arrived yet. It may be another hour before they're here." She looked at her computer screen. "Yes, your name is on their list."

I sat and looked at the waiting area. They were all waiting for a call. And thinking of how Death had joined us in the Urgent Treatment Centre I thought we might all be waiting for a call from Death, wearing a death-mask, to go forward to the next life.

Towards 10pm a Sri Lankan in blue operating scrubs called, "Philip Rawley." I joined him and he led me to a cubicle. A junior doctor appeared. She was his scribe, she had a pad of patient writing-paper and a pen and stood in the corner of the cubicle while the 'bone person' examined me. He said: "I am a consultant more senior than the last consultant you saw. I have studied your X-ray and blood test, and I do not think you have fluid in your shoulder but calcification. I'll tell you why while I examine you."

He asked me to strip to the waist and extend my arms, and he gave a running commentary to his scribe: "Right arm extended a hundred and twenty-five degrees." And so on. He ran through all the parts of the shoulder with a comment. He was very fluent and had an encyclopaedic knowledge of the shoulder that was very impressive. He said, "If you had fluid, you could not have done that movement." And: "That movement proves that you have calcification."

At the end he said: "I am referring you for an MRI. We will write to you. I will study the MRI and we will go on from there. I will prescribe an analgesic [a painkiller] and will not prescribe antibiotics as you have no infection."

"But the blood test said I have," I said.

"Yes, I don't think that came from your hand."

He was very definite and he inspired confidence.

I dressed and returned to the waiting area and rang Pippa to say I could now be collected. My analgesic was brought: Co-codamol. I sat and swallowed my first tablet beneath my mask. I did not want to risk drinking water in this Covid-present hospital, and anyway the bald man was still obstructing the card-reader, only moving his head out of the way after he had interrogated people who wanted to use their cards about their medical condition, a form of social bullying, so I washed my tablet down my throat with gulps of saliva. Then I moved to the door and sat so I could see Pippa arrive.

Somewhere back in the hospital hooded Death in his death-mask was getting to know his immediate victims, those with sepsis being easy pickings. But I had a way out as one of the bone people had said I did not have sepsis, and was going to study my MRI and restore my shoulder. After more than seven hours of waiting I had escaped. I was still wearing my wristband but I would soon be out in the night and driving away from shouted names and sepsis, back to some semblance of normality in this post-Covid time.

A Grey Top Hat and Dread

We parked outside the Carlyon Bay Hotel in Cornwall that Sunday. We put on masks to enter the hotel and its restaurant, and to reach our table. The doorman was in morning dress with a grey top hat as usual, and a black mask. He greeted me with recognition in his eyes as usual.

We ate at a socially-distanced table in the window with a view of the sea. The sun was in my eyes and a bright October glare off the bright gloss paint on the low window-sill made me squint as I read the menu until a black-masked waiter obligingly pulled across a blind.

Lunch was being served in style as usual despite the pandemic. Every table was taken. I had prawn-and-smoked-salmon *timbale*, then chicken and finally chocolate torte with raspberry sauce and clotted cream. Pippa had the same starter, then lamb and finally sticky toffee pudding. We had to have coffee at our table instead of in the lounge, and payment had to be by card in the restaurant and not at reception or in the lounge bar.

Everything seemed normal but it was different. The showcase of jewellery had gone, along with the armchair to sit in near the entrance. There was gel on a table. There were notices about keeping distance.

The doorman sidled towards me as we left and asked if we had enjoyed our lunch.

"You've stayed clear of Covid?" I asked.

"Yes. We've been busy. Eighty-nine in for lunch today. We like it that way, it's keeping all the jobs going. But for how long? What's going to happen as winter approaches?"

His eyes were between his black mask and his grey top hat. I saw dread in his troubled eyes. He seemed to dread losing his job more than getting Covid, his mask was a dress code. We were in an uncertain time, and no one knew if there would soon be another national lockdown as the R number – the rate at which infections spread – was rising in the north.

"We've just got to carry on as normal without taking unnecessary risks," I said. "We've got to keep the economy going. There's no sense in living for years in lockdown waiting for a vaccine that never arrives while the economy disintegrates and all the jobs go."

"I quite agree," he said. "That's exactly how I think. Thank you for coming, see you soon, I hope."

His eyes were appreciative and smiling. Then he was already back greeting another elderly couple who had just arrived.

He had been the doorman for a few decades, he had greeted me countless times, and the Hotel was his life. He was elaborately and immaculately dressed in a 19th-century style, and he masked his dread between his black facial mask and, pulled down over his brow, his perfectly worn grey silk top hat.

Michaelmas Daisies and Sycamore Leaves

We took old newspapers and a black bag to the Cornish dump. Under Covid you could only go on alternate days. If your car had an even number on its number-plate you could go on an even date, if an odd number on an odd date. Despite the halving of the number of cars there was still a queue in the hedged lane to get into the dump. There were only a dozen cars in front of us, but only one could go in at a time and there was a long wait before the next one could go in.

I sat and gazed at the hedgerow in the October sun. The blackberries on the brambles caught my eye. I could have wound down the window and picked a handful without getting out of the car. There was old man's beard entangled on some of the shrubs. There were nettles and gorse and there was a holly twenty feet high with clusters of bright red berries, a glory against the autumn sky.

There were mauve, tall Michaelmas daisies and I was taken back to my boyhood home where there were Michaelmas daisies along the fence by the rubbish dump where my father had his bonfires. I was back playing with a ball outside the back door and looking at the apple and pear trees, the gooseberry and red-currant bushes, and the roses and mint near the kitchen window.

Now we could join the last few cars on the right of the road, and as we waited a sycamore leaf spiralled down from an overhanging tree, and then another, and I was back at school in the last year of the war, listening to my teacher Mabel Reid, who was blind in one eye and wore an eye-shield, explaining that sycamore leaves bore their curved sycamore pods with seeds downwards like a spiralling parachute.

I had been queuing to lug and post newspapers through slits into a huge container and throw a black bag down into a skip, but before I had even done that I had been transported back to my childhood garden and to an early classroom. So does Nature feed us with images that by association take us back into our earliest memories.

A Colon and Perfect Design

On arrival at Princess Grace's Hospital wearing a mask I was asked to wash my hands under a tap near the door. I was taken to the accounts room, which resembled a small post office, and after a wait in a comfortable armchair outside I was taken to a small room and asked to undress, put on a gown and get into a bed on wheels. An Asian nurse in a mask came in and asked me if I had fasted and taken the "Moviprep" (Movicol preparation). She asked me if I had had about twenty conditions, which she knew by heart and rattled off separately. I said "No" to each. She fitted a cannula to my right hand. Then an Arab orderly in a mask came and explained what was to happen to me. I said I'd had it before, so I knew what to expect.

He wheeled my bed out across the corridor into a large room where there was a Chinese nurse, and after signing a consent form for her I was greeted by the surgeon. He was in scrubs and had a youngish face beneath his mask.

He asked if I wanted a sedative. I said I didn't need one last time. He nodded and attached the cannula to a tube to activate a drip-in local anaesthetic.

He asked me to lie on my left side with my knees up and while he questioned me how I had coped with lockdown he thrust a tiny camera on a thin flexible tube up inside me and its light shone into the dark tunnels I could see on screen as he began his colonoscopy.

I lay and looked as it travelled up near my heart. I said, "I can feel it just there, and pointed with my free left hand to just below my heart, and the surgeon said, "Yes, that's exactly where it is."

"No polyps found yet?"

"No, and no sign of any cancer."

I was looking at the folds we were passing through and was struck by the order and organisation of my inside. I said, "The organisation is wonderful, the design is amazing."

He said, "It is, simply amazing, and economical. Everything's necessary. You can't remove any part. It's all necessary to the whole, perfect for digestion. It can't be improved on. I see it every day, but I'm always filled with amazement at the intricacy, the perfection of what is there."

"Could it be an accident?" I asked as the camera passed more folds and turned into a new tunnel.

He said, "No," very finally, in a tone of 'no way'.

So there we were, on the threshold of agreeing that there was intelligent design in the universe, a deep philosophical point of view that finds evolution unsatisfactory, while I ignored the slight discomfort I was feeling inside and concentrated on following the progress of the camera's journey through my flesh on screen.

He finished soon afterwards. There were no pre-cancerous polyps and no cancer. "You're so clear you shouldn't come back for five years," he said.

"I'll be eighty-six then."

"Yes."

As I wiped myself free from gel and dressed I puzzled over how each human being had such perfect digestive organs that were so well designed they could not have happened through accidental evolution, and once again the mystery of a human being defied thought, there was no explanation as to how my organs had come to be as they are and to work so smoothly.

Sunday Best and Track Records

Pippa took me to see Aunt Maud in Porthleven. She was 93 and confined to one downstairs room which had a bed, a chair, a television and a window with a distant view of the sea. Her skin was sallow, her hair white and she looked very old.

Pippa opened the front door, which was not locked, and we greeted her. I fetched a chair from another room and sat, and Pippa sat in a comfortable chair in a corner and talked about how we had had lunch in Truro and walked by the sea to the pier, which was chained off as the sea was rolling in and fountaining up over the walls.

Maud soon got on to her family, and somehow her father's mother came up. "She was always erect," Maud said. "She wore black and she had no humour at all. Your mother was terrified of her."

"I remember when she came," Pippa said. "I had to be in my Sunday best, and my mother would wait for her, looking out of the window, not knowing what time she'd be driven in by my father. I was bored waiting and I was allowed to go up the road. In the playground there were some children jumping near a puddle and I thought I should do the same, and I fell and got mud on my legs, knickers and dress. When I got back she had arrived and my mother was horrified."

We all laughed.

"Do you remember riding on the rollercoaster with Pippa?" I asked.

"Oh yes, I do." Maud described how she sat in front of her, and Pippa's father was holding onto Pippa with one hand and her with the other hand. "I was always up for a challenge in those days," she said.

Richard came in from a day working in Marazion. He had a beard. I congratulated him for escaping from the oval-rugger-ball-shaped cancer he had had cut out from his stomach.

We sat eating slices of three different cakes and drinking tea, and I asked Richard, who had been a fisherman, how the French boats could come into British waters legally, as the negotiators in the talks with the EU seemed to be unaware of the situation.

"They have licences," Richard said. "They've bought them. When boats were decommissioned or sold the Government did nothing about the track records for quotas. Under the EU you might have a boat but you couldn't fish without a licence and track record. When I sold my boat, the one we went out in, my track record was sold to someone in the Channel Islands. If you had a large boat, a Spaniard came up to you and said, 'I'll give you £260,000 for your track record,' and many said 'Yes'."

The British Government were set to stop overseas fishing boats from fishing in British waters, apparently unaware that many of them had paid for licences and track records. It was a mess.

"I might go back to fishing. Anthony keeps asking me. I might go back when I retire."

"If so," I said, "I'll come out with you for a day as in the old days. We'll have a reunion, and a breakfast as soon as we've left Newlyn."

Richard nodded. Covid was raging and a 'weak-deal' Brexit was being confirmed the next day, but we were both forward-looking, and Aunt Maud was pleased that her son and I were looking ahead and being positive.

A Contract and a Mess

Gully the gardener came back from his week's leave. On his arrival I went to his door and asked if he could fill the bird feeders first. "A good week?" I asked.

"Yes. Oh," he said, "I've meant to tell you. I might be leaving. I may have sold our house and we may be leaving the area."

Thinking quickly, I asked, "For Norfolk? To be near your daughter?"

"Yes. My wife's afraid she's going blind as you know, because of her diabetes, and her consultant is seeing Covid-only patients. She wants to be near my daughter. She's found a house, she's very attached to it, wants me to get it at all costs. I don't like it. It's infuriating, I've seen several down there with large gardens, one that is fantastic, huge with an enormous garden, but my wife said, 'Not interested, too remote, don't want to live there.'

"She wants us to have a town house in Harleston, near Diss. It's only got a tiny garden. There's a brick wall on either side from other houses and a small garden to another wall at the end, and the house blocks the sun for much of the day and there's only a bit of sun at the end of the garden.

"The house she's found has six bedrooms. My two sons are living with us as you know. My eldest one doesn't contribute. He gives me £40 a week, and when I asked, 'Could it be £10 more?' he said, 'Can't do that.' He's living cost free. The other one works here as a gardener. They can come with us or else...."

"They'll rent?" I asked.

"I'm not buying them a house," Gully said. "I need capital. My sons aren't paying their way and we're short of money. I'm working and can't have time off and I'm not getting anywhere."

"Are you getting a good price for your house?"

"Yes, nine hundred and sixty thousand. The house with six rooms is a lot less. But it may not happen. The timings might not be right. We've got a buyer for our house, but he doesn't want to pay the increased stamp duty. He said, 'I can't do that.' Stamp duty goes up on the thirty-first of March, and it's now February the first so there's not long, and searches have to be done in lockdown. It may not go through in time."

"We'd be sorry to see you go," I said.

"Oh, and down in Norfolk things are difficult. My daughter has a bad relationship with her husband. He comes in and sits and watches football and doesn't speak to her. She's unhappy. You know I cashed in my pension so they could buy a house. It turned out he had debts, no one knows how much, so they've had to be paid off. The house is smaller than it could have been. He's an electrician and he's not working and he hasn't got enough money. She asks for money and he gives her £20 for a week. But £10 goes in petrol for the car to take the two children to school, and she has £10 for food for a week, and sometimes she goes without eating. She might leave him, and we need a large house down there so she and the three children can move in with us and my two sons. I haven't got a pension as it's all gone into their house.

"We'll all be down there and my daughter will be able to drive even when my wife goes blind, that's the idea. And I'll have some money in the bank. But it could all collapse, I may still be here.

"But we both want to leave our house, it's haunted. There are strange noises from the room on the top floor and no one's there. My sons aren't happy about it. My daughter won't come to our house now, last time she did the door was slammed behind her and she couldn't turn the handle to get out. Yes, we have to go, but I don't want to go to this house she's found. It's big but I wanted an Italian house we saw with a huge garden and a lawn I'd have to cut with a ride-on mower like yours, not this one she's fixed her heart on. I'm resigned to going."

I had listened sympathetically. I said, "The concept may be right, but this particular model may be wrong. See what happens, whether your buyer withdraws because of stamp duty. You're in the hands of fate. If you do leave, when do you think it might be?" I asked, thinking that six weeks of rush-up time were ahead, from towards the end of March to the end of April, when the two fields would need cutting twice a week.

Gully thought. "Six to eight weeks' time," he said, "I should think."

"So you'll exchange contracts in that time?"

Then he stunned me.

"I signed the contract for my house last week," he said. "But the owner of the house we are buying hasn't signed his contract, and there may be a delay as we wait for the seller and our buyer to sign their contracts. We're held up in a chain. They can't sign if they're in a chain. So I don't know when we're going. If it happens, six to eight weeks, I would think. But I might have to move out of my house with nowhere to go. It's a mess."

A Covid Jab and Cancer

I arrived at the Buckhurst Way Clinic for my second Pfizer jab well before 5pm on a damp day in March, wearing a black mask, parked and walked round to the back entrance. There was no queue and I was greeted inside the door and told to go and register at a desk. I showed my card and had it stamped and the batch number recorded, and was directed to a chair. Almost immediately a blonde nurse in blue came out of a room covered by a screen and asked me if I was next.

I said, "It seems so, no one else is coming forward."

"This way."

I was seated on a chair, and a West-Indian lady struggled to find me on a computer. I gave my surname and date of birth, and the blonde nurse helped her find me. I stood, took off my coat and sweater, then sat and the blonde nurse said, "Left arm?" and I nodded. She did the injection very quickly and very well. I scarcely felt it.

She said, "It'll be worse than the first one, but it will only last a few days. Take paracetamol if you're in pain or have a temperature."

I said, "Will Nurofen do?"

The pharmacist said, "Yes, it will do very well."

As I got dressed I asked, "How many have you done today?"

The nurse said, "I've no idea. When it gets to eight I have no idea how many I've done."

I thanked her and left for the waiting-room. I had to sit for 15 minutes. I had a sticky label saying '5.00', 5 o'clock, the time I could go. I sat and watched other elderly jabees shuffle in. Everyone seemed to have a stick. They were all clearly over 80.

Then a tall man came in and pointed a metallic stick at me and beamed behind his mask. I recognised him. I knew he was 85.

"Here's another 60-year-old," I said. Roland Marsh laughed and sat down. He was a local historian.

"How are you?" I asked. "Have you escaped Covid?"

"Yes," he said, "but have you heard of my cancer?"

"No. Are you all right?"

"Touch wood, yes, now. When did we last meet? This happened just over two years ago. I had terrific pain and many tests and no one could find anything. Then one day they found cancer, a nine-inch-long thin oval growth that was pressing into my bowel. That was what caused the pain. I'm OK now. But I've also had a new hip, and now I need a knee."

"So as soon as lockdown's over you'll have a knee?"

"That's what I'm hoping."

He chatted on about his illness. The others in the waiting-room did not give any indication that they were listening.

He had '4.58' on his sticky label.

"Look," I said, "it's gone five o'clock. My time's up. You're 4.58, your time's up as well."

"No," he said, "I'm staying here for a while."

"Half an hour?" I asked.

I could not hear his reply, which was muffled by his mask.

"Let's meet when lockdown's over," he said.

"Yes," I said. "I'll visit you or come and have coffee."

"I'd like that."

"Good luck with the knee."

And with that I stood and vacated my chair for a patient who was standing waiting for a seat.

I reflected as I returned to the fresh air and headed for my car that I had now had my second jab and would soon be 97% protected from falling ill with Covid and going to hospital, and that Roland Marsh had cancer and a replacement hip. The news was dominated by Covid jabs and also by the ignoring of cancers due to lockdown, and it was strange that the two subjects should have dominated our conversation when we were both writers. Then I thought how hard lockdown must have been for him, living alone. He had been very eager to talk and tell me his condition, and I wondered if he was sitting on in the room so he could latch on to someone else waiting who would listen about his failing body and disabled knee, which had provided him with a topic of conversation when for a few minutes he could escape the loneliness of his elderly failing life.

A Beanie and Tears

Gully was late into work for his last day. He had to sell the contents of his loft – he had often said, "I'm a hoarder" – to a reclamation site: a large heavy green bath, eight bikes and many wheels. His 8.30 start became 12. We had coffee and chocolate cake ready and we sat on the terrace at the garden table without masks in the warm March sunshine.

He sat in his beanie hat, looking like a medieval peasant sitting with a Lord, and talked about his move to Norfolk. He said he didn't want to go, he didn't like the house his wife had insisted on their having – and (he told me the previous day) he didn't like the fact that his wife had asked for half the profit on the sale to be put in her separate bank account. He was leaving behind his eldest son to feed his two grandchildren every evening, even though he was living separately from his partner. His youngest son had worked in the district and would be moving down to a new area. He just didn't want to retire. It was evident from the way he spoke that he had put his heart into our garden and fields for ten years to the month.

I said he had put his family first and realised the asset of his house, and had a bankable sum that would tide him over during his retirement. I knew that after his back operation he was ready to retire. He said, "Thank you for looking after me after my operation."

He said, "I showed Arnold the wildlife. You have mice living the other side of the shrubs, I saw six or eight in one morning last week, and there's a fox burrow in the corner with another entrance or exit under a pile of sticks. I showed him those and explained I leave them for the wildlife."

He spoke lovingly and protectively of the creatures, it was unthinkable this would be his last day.

Pippa said, "Look, there's a buzzard soaring about over the field."

She was right. Gully had often pointed out two buzzards circling. I said, "It's come to say goodbye to Gully."

Gully gave a sad smile.

Pippa gave him a box and he stood, embarrassed. It was two rose-bushes, one called "Happy retirement" and the other "New home". I said, "You'll have to plant them either side of the entrance in Norfolk and rename them Philip and Pippa." And he smiled.

I gave him a book and he opened the card that was with it.

I said, "It's been a good ten years. You must come back and see us."

Pippa said, "We'll miss you."

I said, "If we're in Norfolk we'll contact you and look in."

"You'd be welcome visitors," he said.

We left him to do his hours. He picked up twigs and put them in a wheelbarrow and I went down and he showed me the hole the mice made and the foxes' holes he was referring to. He gave me the keys to the sheds and to the tractor, and I left him to cut the lawn, one last cut on a golden day. Then he came to my door and handed me the key to his door and his fob.

Suddenly he was sobbing, his eyes wet and tears on his cheeks.

"I don't want to go," he wept. "I've loved it here. You've been really good to work for."

Drawn into his emotion I said, "If it doesn't work out and you stay up here I'm sure we can find you something."

"Oh thank you. I don't want to go. I like it up here."

I said, "But your wife may be going blind because of diabetes, and you need the asset to live off and it solves the problem. You'll be close to your daughter."

"But I like it here," he sobbed. "I don't want to go."

We went down the spiral staircase and waved to Pippa, who was on the phone. She pointed to the front door. I returned inside the house and stood with her outside the front door as he got into his car.

He started his car. He was in control of his emotions now under his beanie, but looked sad, and I felt sad. He waved and we waved. We had opened the double gates as he had surrendered his fob, and the last I saw of him was of a beanie and a wan, tearful smile as his car drove out of our front gates for ever.

Galling

I rang Florence on the Sunday after her birthday. "How are you?" I asked.

"You know I've got gallstones. I'm in pain and I've been waiting since October. Six months. It's incompetence. We're going on the twenty-ninth of March for a face-to-face, actually face to face. Six months. It's dreadful. We're steaming. The NHS, which I worked for, isn't seeing anybody, no face-to-faces. Covid only. If you hear someone's chained to a radiator in Bedford Hospital it will be me."

I said, "I'm really sorry to hear all this. I hope you received my birthday card."

"Yes, thank you. I'm at my wits' end. The system's incompetent, we're in no mood to let it last any longer. I'm taking Raymond with me on the twenty-ninth, I don't care about going on my own because of Covid. I want to know when an hour's procedure will take place. It was urgent in October – given high priority – six months have gone by. It's disgraceful. We're not standing for it."

"I'm really sorry," I said, "and I hope something can be sorted out. Is it worth considering going private?"

"We're very particular about their qualifications. Raymond will want to see how qualified the person is who's performing a procedure. We don't trust the qualifications in the private sector. But they've lied to us, 'Oh, you'll hear from us in two weeks' and it's six months. Covid's taken all their funding, there are thousands of operations that have been postponed. It's not right. I'm in constant pain with my gallstones and I was given priority for keyhole surgery on my gall-bladder, and six months have gone by. I'm forty-eight kilos, that's seven stone eight pounds, and I avoid fat and everything in the hospital's been diverted to Covid."

She went on for another ten minutes. I couldn't get a word in. She was in constant severe abdominal pain under her ribs on her right side. She had worked in the NHS all her life before she retired. I could understand how galling her painful predicament was.

A Club Man and a Tolling Bell

My grandson Al was playing his first game for the local cricket club Under-12s against a team from Orsett, near Basildon, and he asked if I would watch. I arrived at the ground at 9.30am.

There were a couple of hundred sitting around the sloping ground. I spotted Simon's wife Kay sitting by the boundary in front of the thatched pavilion, and my granddaughter Minnie was doing her homework, a word count, lying on the grass. I asked Kay to put up my collapsible chair, which I had carried in a long bag over my shoulder, and I sat in comfort.

The young cricketers were in clusters along the boundary, waiting to start, and some parents were sitting further along the ring of the ground. Al, looking very smart in his white longs, came up and said, "Hello, Grandpa. We're batting, I'm number 5." Then he turned and joined the team that was clustering round their coach for a team meeting.

I reflected on how I used to watch cricket on this ground with my father at the end of the war – and on one occasion received more than forty gnat bites – and how I played before a crowd sitting four deep all round the boundary on a hot day in 1956, and there was never a team meeting in those days. Things were said in the dressing-room as we changed, and that was that.

I said to Kay, "Who's the link between the club and the Essex cricket team? There's a man with an Essex badge on his shirt over there."

I indicated a portly man with silver hair who was standing stoutly in front of the thatched pavilion as if he was in charge.

Kay said, "He's the Chairman."

I stood up and walked towards him and called from a distance, "Are you the Chairman?"

The silver-haired thickset man chuckled, "On a good day I'll answer yes to that."

I smiled and said I might have had a letter from his daughter mentioning him or possibly it was the daughter of his predecessor?

He said, "I've got two sons but no daughters. So it wasn't me."

I explained I was Al's grandfather and had played on this ground sixty-five years ago, and said, "It is good that cricket is continuing after all these years."

My remark was merely a pleasantry, but inadvertently I triggered what had clearly become an obsession.

He told me at great length that they had had a lease until 2025 and it would then be surrendered to the Urban District Council which was no longer in existence. So he had gone to three solicitors, and there were three different opinions. All said he should avoid the Council as the field would be sold for housing and become a building site if the Council had it: "You'll be playing in a park." He was then offered an extension until 2047, and then, miraculously, there was a legal arrangement for the club to own the field for ever.

"That's excellent," I said.

Then a lady connected with the visiting team, wearing what looked like a black swimming-costume, tried to pass us to go into the thatched pavilion.

"The toilet's better in the new pavilion over there," the Chairman said.

He monologued to her about the facilities, and she lingered. He said, "Your club's doing very well to field eight teams. Stick at it."

After she left I got him on to his role in the club.

He said, "I looked after the Under-14s for twenty-five years. I recommended players to the Essex team. We had a tall lean boy in our team who was good at placing his shots, Alastair Cook, and also Bopara. They played every match on this ground while they were with me. They began in this sort of game we're having today. The club played Pakistan in 1964, you know."

I said, "Keep your eye on Al. He took five wickets in one six-ball over playing at Bancroft's. He may get in the Essex team one day."

He told me his name and gave me a small cricket-club booklet with all phone numbers, including his, of the management committee at the front. He said, "I'm here every match day and a lot of the other time as well. I oversee it all." It was his life, and he belonged.

Then someone came to talk to him, and I excused myself and went back to my chair.

The club's Under-12s batted. Wearing a helmet and going in at number 5 Al scored 25 out of 130. He hit the ball on both sides of the field before he missed a spinner and was bowled.

Shortly before 11am a bell tolled from a nearby church for five minutes, perhaps summoning the faithful to a service, but sounding funereal, reminding us all of the Covid plague and death. This coincided with the change of innings.

We then watched the club field. I noticed that many of the players seemed to be of Indian origin. They were all very good. Al bowled a couple of overs and the only run he conceded was a boundary four from a high full toss that slipped out of his hand.

At 12 noon the church bell tolled again, reminding us of the plague in our midst and death.

I was getting sunburnt, so I waved to Al (who waved back from cover point), packed my chair away and, saying goodbye to Kay and Minnie, walked back to the car.

I thought of the Chairman, and how he spent his whole time at the club. He was a club man, he had things to say about the organisation to everybody, he belonged, he defined himself in terms of the teams and the players, past stories and guaranteeing the club's future. He belonged within the management.

From time to time the bell tolled in the breeze, portending his demise, but he did not think of that. He gave his life meaning by belonging to a circle of locals who all held positions on the management committee, and he did not want to be reminded that one day he would have a funeral and that the end of all his organising would be announced by a tolling bell.

A Cushion and Swabs

The day before we went to the Oval Simon said he would give me a lateral flow test and register it with the NHS on his phone. There was heavy traffic as the M25 and M11 were both closed due to lorries being on fire. There was queuing, and having been out I drove to Simon's house to sit in the car outside and wait for him.

Kay drove in with Al, and I was invited to sit in the back garden where there was spacious white-cushioned seating under a roof.

Minnie appeared in a karate Gi and sat with me and told me about the cushion she was making at school, how she dyed the material and made a pattern and sewed it and did backstitches. "Can I show you?" she asked.

She ran off into the school next door through the side gate, and reappeared through the side gate holding a cushion, and with a girl of about her age in plaits. Kay was behind her and said, "This is Lizzie, she's in Minnie's class. Her parents work in the NHS and have been held up by the traffic. She's waiting for them."

I said, "Hello. I'm early because the traffic is bad. Sit over there, this is where people who have traffic problems sit."

She smiled and sat down.

Minnie sat beside me and showed me her cushion. I admired it. I felt it round the edges and examined the stitches, and commented on the buttons she had sewed onto it, and studied the pattern.

Then Kay said Minnie could take Lizzie to her room, and as they left Al returned and sat on the white-foamed seating. He told me about his cricket.

"I've been put up into the A team," he said. "I've been selected for three matches." He had scored 30 and had to retire, and he had batted with an Essex player who told him, "We need eighteen runs and there are five overs left, we can take our time." He was bowled next ball, slogging at a spinner and missing, and Al steered the school to victory, and was not out at the end.

Then Simon appeared through the side gate. He took me into the kitchen and gave me a thin swab and told me to scrape both tonsil areas for 10 seconds each, and then stick it up one nostril, using the loo mirror as a help.

The scraping of the tonsil areas made me gag, and tears came into my eyes as I swabbed the inside of my left nostril.

I returned to the kitchen, Simon put it in a solution and asked for my NHS number, which I dictated. He completed a form on the computer on the kitchen island, and registered me. Kay and he also used their mobile phones, and both Al and I were registered.

"Have you heard there's been a substitution?" Simon asked about the cricket the next day.

"No."

"Bernard can't go. He's still in Devon, isolating. Someone in his house has got Covid. Al is going in his place. Didn't he tell you?"

"No," I said. "But can he get off school?"

"I've arranged it. They've said Yes. That's why he's just had a swab."

So that's how going to sporting events was these days, I thought. Before the pandemic I focused on the comfort of cushions you sat on to watch, but now, during the pandemic, it was swabs that brought tears to your eyes. Life had become more basic, Bernard hadn't passed his swab test and could not go to the cricket, and the comfort of a cushion might help his isolation.

Covid and swabs were now a fact of life, living with Covid was the new normal, but Minnie was ahead of the new way of living and was making her own cushioned comfort and perpetuating how life used to be while we all stoically endured under this dreadful new plague.

Sweet Caroline and a Bleeding Spectator

We arrived at the Oval by car – Simon, Paul, Al and me – and had our Covid tests checked on Simon's phone. We took a lift up to the new hospitality area alongside the pavilion. We entered a large room with 30 or 40 laid tables, each of us received an event card and lanyard, and a wristband, and were shown to our table. We dumped our bags and took glasses of champagne out through swing-doors to the tiered white seats and found where we would be sitting. We strolled in the early morning sun and then went back in and had our lunch at 12 o'clock: lots of bite-sized nibbles to be eaten with fingers.

Sri Lanka batted first. A wicket fell before we could reach our seats. They were soon 12-3. There was a rally, da Silva scored 91 and by teatime they had set England 241 to win. We watched from our height, looking down on the cricketers who rushed about, seeing what was going on below as if we were in a low cloud.

We had tea at 4.30, and again we had plates of finger bites put before us. Graham Gooch and Alec Stewart appeared through a door from the pavilion. They stayed within ten yards of the door, and spoke to us through microphones and kept their distance to avoid catching Covid. When Gooch had given his view of the game and they had finished, they left by the same door to the pavilion without being in contact with anybody.

We sat outside in the warm evening sun and watched Roy score 60, and Morgan and Root see England home to an eight-wicket win. As the winning score approached, the crowd in our hospitality seating were happy – some had been drinking all day – and I heard strains from several rows back of 'Sweet Caroline', the rejoicing song, as victory approached: "Sweet Caroline/Good times never seemed so good." Then it sounded as if they were singing their own variation, "Sweet Caroline, I feel fine." The words they sang smiled as they expressed inebriated delight.

After the winning hit we stood up and returned to our table and collected our bags. We walked fast to the lift and stood, and managed to get down before the crush. The lift stopped at the ground floor and beneath us were steps down to the covered thoroughfare. A group of happy English supporters were holding out an English flag, a white flag with a red cross, and chanting, "Eng-er-land, Eng-er-land."

A policeman was bending over something nearby. It was an elderly man, a spectator. He had fallen down the steps and had blood on his head. He was lying bleeding and unconscious. In the middle of 'Sweet Caroline' and the chants of "Eng-er-land" round the English flag Death had intruded.

The elderly man was oblivious to his surroundings. He had come to watch the cricket in the hospitality area, and he had collapsed and fallen down the steps, and was unaware of England's win and of the chanting round the English flag.

That's what happened. You went to cricket, enjoyed the day, sang 'Sweet Caroline', and as you came away you collapsed and fell down steps and died.

A Portakabin and Creatures of Habit

It was a warm sunny August morning and there were splashes of light on the calm waves as I set off to look for the secretary to the new owner of the harbour, who had engaged a company to film all cars entering his private road and fine them. I started with the office where the previous owner, Robert, had worked, believing she might be there.

The door was open at the top of the steps and a notice said that mask-wearing was mandatory, so I put on my black mask and with no one around looked in on Robert's old room – and found Robert sitting there over a table covered with files.

He was pleased to see me and waved me into a chair. "I still haven't retired," he said, "look at all these files. I'm ready to retire. I'm seventy-eight, and we've just finished selling our properties near Colchester and I've been selling down here. We've sold the clay-dries. The restaurant next door, that's for my retirement. We'll just live on in our present house, I like it here."

I explained I was looking for the new owner's secretary.

"My PA did that job, Lynne, but she had her last pay cheque this month and she's in Bristol now. You need to see Connie. She reports every word you say back to him, so be careful. She's in a Portakabin in the car park just out there." He pointed towards his window. "Don't tell anyone, but I don't like the way he's gone about things. He's tough and ruthless. I believe in being fair. He wants to charge everyone for parking on his road."

I explained we owned the green mound in front of our house, and our parking spaces, and had a right in the deeds "to pass and repass" to get there.

He said, "You're right. If it comes to a court case I'll be a witness for you. But don't tell anyone I said that. Between you and me, he's leaving soon. He doesn't want the residents to know. He's caused some trouble with the residents. Is that a letter from him you've got there? I'd like to photocopy it."

I followed him out to a large photocopier with many buttons to press, near the door. He tried to turn it on and eventually succeeded, but the first sheet came out landscape rather than portrait and did not cover the new owner's letter. He gave up.

"My PA used to do this. I haven't touched it until recently. I miss her, I wish she was still here," he said. "I'm seventy-eight, but I'd have been bored stiff if I hadn't carried on working like this. I'll come and visit you while you're down, perhaps?"

"Excellent," I said.

I got away from Robert and went in search of the Portakabin. There wasn't a Portakabin in the main car park. Then I discovered a narrow lane that passed under his window. I could see a car park at the back thirty feet up, behind railings. I turned right and I was standing next to a small wooden Portakabin with three open glass doors. The rooms seemed to be full of boxes.

Inside the far open door I found three women sitting: two secretaries who were bending over computers, tucked away behind boxes, and a lady of around 35 with a precise face and hair tied back, who was sitting in the middle. There was no room to do anything but stand in the doorway between waist-high boxes. I put on my black mask.

"Is this the harbour headquarters?" I asked. "Are you the new owner's secretary? Connie?"

"Yes," she said.

"I'm Philip Rawley," I said, and I explained why I had come. "We got down last night and I found this letter on the doormat. I just wanted to introduce myself and say we've got the grassy mound near the harbour wall. You may not know that we own it and park on it, so we are not affected by the letter on parking."

"No," she said, "but you are for access. We've looked at all the deeds, you are affected by contributing to the upkeep of the road."

"That's not an issue. But parking is. I've a got a letter here that went to our neighbour, perhaps from one of you, saying Ringo, a private company, will film any car that enters the road. How will Ringo distinguish between cars with a legal right to park on their own ground and those that are parking on the road?"

"You give me your car number," she said.

"I can give you the car number we've come down in now," I said. "The family have several cars. Can I email those to you?"

She gave me a card. I gave her my email address. She wrote it all down on half a side of lined A4 paper.

"Thank you," I said. To the two silent secretaries I added, "Sorry to have disturbed your concentration, thank you for bearing with me." They both smiled. "You'll tell him about this conversation?" I asked Connie.

"Yes."

I left. I thought of Robert, who was bored and lonely in his retirement and was looking for excuses to talk and get involved in the new owner's regulation of the parking on the harbour. And I thought of Connie, the new owner's eyes and ears who was sitting among packing-boxes in a cramped Portakabin expressing the new owner's intention to fleece the residents and visitors of large sums of money. It was a job, probably well-paid, but the working conditions were awful. And in the winter, when the doors would be closed, the lack of space would be claustrophobic. The new owner was doing what he did, being an enterprise, making money by being tough and ruthless and then getting out, not caring about the working conditions of his staff.

Then I thought they were all prisoners of their work and walk of life in some way or another, creatures of habit who repeatedly did what they did. Robert couldn't stop his habitual way of passing his time and the three secretaries had all got used to their cramped working conditions in their Portakabin. And the new owner filled his time by running the harbour.

And I.... I was 82 and still writing my perceptions of life into stories, and was I not as much a creature of habit, fleeing boredom and loneliness by continuing what I always did, as they were?

Children of Light

I received a letter from a reader who described how her sister "suddenly transitioned from her earthly body at the beginning of the year" – "my soulmate, she and I were and are still intertwined" – and had come back to her in an epiphany that began with her saying, "I am a child of Light." And at the same time "a gigantic dragonfly" appeared outside her window and one of my books "fell off my bookshelf where it had been sitting for years". She picked it up and read "essence precedes existence" and "felt like I was reading the thoughts of one who understood us, my sister and I..., that I'd found a fellow child of Light". I replied that her sister may have come back to tell her that "we are all children of Light, and few know it".

I pondered on this "epiphany" down in Cornwall. The sun sparkled in the waves, and as I looked out of my window three ladies in swimming-costumes were standing between waist- and neck-deep, talking, and the exploding flashes of light in the incoming tide went between them and surrounded them, and I realised they were children of light. They were in the midst of white Fire, like angels. I could see the light from my first-floor window above the sea wall, perhaps 50 feet above them, but they could not see the sparkling, the jumping of lights between them. They were children of Light and did not know it.

A Pedantic Electrician and an Oven
(Or: Closed Eyes and a Western Way of Living)

The boiler servicer came to our Cornish house and serviced the boiler. I pointed out the electric shower wasn't working, and he looked at the fuse-board, which was in a cupboard beneath a shelf, behind rows of glasses. It did not appear to have any switches down. He said of the oven, "There are no lights at the top."

Pippa said, "The oven isn't working, I've booked someone to come on Wednesday."

"Something's happened that's affected the fuse-board, and the oven and the shower are off," he said. "I'm photographing it on my phone and I'm sending it to Ronald so he can visit you and get them going again."

Ronald rang the next day to say he would be with us at 4pm, and he was. He was a short fellow of about 60 with a parting on his right side and neat hair, holding his tool-bag. He was left-handed, I noticed his parting was in reverse, and he wore spectacles. With his lined face he could have been a pedantic lecturer who adhered strictly to spelling rules.

He opened the cupboard door and looked at the fuse-board and took out all the glasses stored in front of it, removed the shelf and tested input and output, and said, "In's working, out isn't." He began unscrewing screws with his screwdriver and took out two RCD (residual current device) fuses labelled 'oven' and 'shower' under a covering that did not show on the fuse-board, and matched their size with temporary fuses he had, which he installed so he could take the defunct ones into a shop and return with identical fuses.

I had made him a cup of coffee, and he took it and sipped it.

"I have to turn the electricity off," he said.

I went round the house and turned off the television Pippa had been watching and my computer upstairs.

He turned the electricity back on. I took him upstairs. The shower was running hot. "It's working now," I said.

We went downstairs. Pippa was by the oven. She said, "The lights are on at the top but it's not getting hot."

"The element must have gone," he said.

"Could that have caused the fuse-board problem?"

"It could have. Do you want me to look?"

"Yes, please," I said without hesitation. "You do everything."

"I'm an electrician, I do everything electric."

He pulled the oven out – it was sitting on a wooden cupboard with a wooden cupboard above it – and asked if I could loosen the cable which was caught up at the back, and find a dust-sheet for the floor, which I did. Then he asked me if I could help him lift the oven down onto the floor.

I held the back of the oven, and he gently lowered his end to the floor. Then he unscrewed the screws at the back to reveal wires. He pulled out two and tested them.

"This one's dead," he said. "It's the element."

He reached into the front of the oven and unscrewed and eventually came out with a double-circled element. He said, "These two rings are too close here, I reckon they touched and blew the fuse-board."

He went outside and rang a shop. He ordered an element to fit our model, and a "lamp" (a bulb) and a round white sparking battery.

Then he returned, turned the electricity on, and put the back on the oven. "We're going to put it back," he said. "I can put the new element in from the front."

So he and I held one side of the oven each and lifted it from the floor into the square hole in the wooden cupboard and pushed it in. I was amazed that at 82 I could lift a heavy oven and guide it in.

Then he drank his coffee.

"I cover all Cornwall," he said. "I've been with Luke for some years. We came from Poole. I was doing Dorset and Somerset and my wife wanted to move. I said, 'Where do you want to live?' She said, 'Cornwall.' So we came here. We didn't know where we wanted to settle, so we rented several places. We had two boys and we had to get used to the Cornish education system. They're thirty-three and thirty-one now, they had a wonderful upbringing, on the beach. I go round Cornwall. I was rung up this morning from Portsmouth and asked how far I go. I said, 'Many will only go half an hour but I do all Cornwall. I don't do Portsmouth, there'll be electricians in towns who'll cope with towns.' In Cornwall the people are scattered, so that's what I do. And I've kept up with the regs, the Regulations. I've just passed the eighteenth revision. The Regulations don't refer to light bulbs, they refer to 'lamps'. Efficiency and safety. This bulb I'm replacing, the Regulations call it a lamp. There's a fellow who looks after us who reads the Regulations every day, as we don't, and he said, 'A bulb is what you put in the ground. The Regulations say it's a lamp.'

"I have to implement all the formal rules in what I do, but sometimes I get there by luck. I had to key in the time on an oven, and I said to my client, 'Watch what I do', and I closed my eyes and punched in numbers, and it worked. I hadn't a clue what I'd done. Sometimes that's how I stick to the formal rules." He chuckled. "My job's fiddly," he said, "but you get used to it.

"Anyway, to get back to what I was saying, we moved and now I've bought and settled about ten minutes away and she loves it and we won't move again. Thanks for the coffee, I'll be back tomorrow morning with the element and lamp and plug, and next week with the two new fuses." And he collected his tools and put them in his bag and went.

I thought how hard his life must have been, travelling round Dorset repairing fuse-boards and ovens and showers, and bringing up two boys. He maintained appliances and kept everyone's Western way of life going, and put things right by strictly adhering to the formal rules and technical knowledge. He got built-in ovens out and put them on the floor. The oven on the floor was obedient when he was around. He was in charge of the machines that give us our Western way of living, and that was what kept him going through his busy working day.

An Undertaker and no Funerals
(Or: Getting Back to Normal)

I was eating in the restaurant by the pier in Cornwall, just finishing my two scoops of ice-cream (my pudding), when a voice said, "Hello." A man was standing above me, balding and small-bearded in a floral shirt, looking like Death. He held out his elbow to be bumped as a greeting, as if Death were greeting me and measuring me for my coffin, and I responded and realised it was the undertaker who owned the house next to us, but did not live there. "How are you, well?" he asked.

I said, "Yes, we're fine. Were you hiding round the corner?"

"Yes," he chuckled. "With Maisie and our daughter. Maisie's going to Spain tomorrow with the three grandchildren."

"To forty-eight Centigrade, leaving you in seventeen Centigrade?" I said.

He chuckled again. "Yes, but don't tell her that. I've got a few beers planned down at the pub."

"How's business been during Covid?" I asked. "Busier than usual?"

Pippa kicked me under the table.

But he was willing to talk. "No," he said, "lighter than usual. Hardly any deaths. It's lockdown and distancing. It's stopping people from catching things from each other. Fewer deaths from flus and other diseases as well. I was talking to someone who's in the same business and he said the same. He said, 'I've got two funerals, and then that's it. But it won't always be like this. It will all come back. We'll get back to normal.'"

"Sorry you've been having a lean time," I said, secretly glad.

Then Maisie appeared with their grown-up daughter. "Arright?" she asked, the Cornish greeting. "Are you well?"

"Yes," I said as the undertaker eyed me with a scrutinising look.

I was going to ask about the work that was about to start on the cliff under their windows, putting rods into the foundations to support their house, and I was going to ask about their dealings with the new owner of the harbour who wanted to bring a private company in to film all cars entering our road and fine them for parking illegally if they were more than 15 minutes, but they were clearly in a hurry as it was showery outside and they wanted to get out in the dry. They moved on out.

I thought of how Covid had terrorised everybody into distancing and how fewer had died, and how getting back to normal meant more dying so he was back in business. Death had his eye on me, but I wasn't going to be one of those who would help him get back to normal.

A Fused Circuit Board and Mended Gates

Ross came to fix a new circuit board for the electric gates. I had opened them manually (after unlocking a padlock on a chain) and pushed the gates open, and as he crouched by the box that contained the old fused circuit board, his pony-tail down to the small of his back, I saw a burnt slug.

"That's what caused the system to go bang," he said. "A slug." There were two holes at the bottom of the box for cables and I found some plastic bags and he stuffed them round the cables so no new slugs could climb into the box.

When he was nearly finished, and was standing after taking a phone call, I asked him about the funeral he had to leave to attend.

"It's my aunt," Ross said. "My dad's sister, ten years older than him. She was diagnosed as having cancer two years ago. She said, 'I'm eighty-seven. I'm not putting myself through all that.' She deliberately did nothing and now the family are meeting today. There will be tea after the three-o'clock service. Many would do the same thing at eighty-seven."

At 82 I nodded.

"I see my dad every weekend," he said. "He lives in Bishop's Stortford. We lost my mum in 2014. She was sixty-six. She had just celebrated her sixty-sixth birthday, and she said, 'I'm just going to lie down, I'm a bit tired.' Next morning my dad took her in a cup of tea. She was dead. She'd had a gastric ulcer. It burst. She probably died of blood-poisoning."

I looked concerned and sympathetic.

"So I'm going to the funeral now," he said. "I've got to go home and change."

I opened the gates for him as he drove out.

I thought of his two relatives' deaths. His mum didn't know she was going to die, her gastric ulcer burst in the night like a circuit board fusing. But his aunt knew. She preferred to let Nature take its course at 87. She was not a writer, and was not thinking of her next work, as I was. She lived with her cancer and consented to its spreading and choking her to death. She put her body's gates on manual and opened and closed them each day by hand. I was not sure that I would do that if I were faced with the same choice. I would want the gates in my body to be mended and work on my fob.

A Wasps' Nest and Vulcan

For a couple of months there were half a dozen dead wasps on the floor in the upper corridor each day. I could not see where they were coming from. Then some were dead on the floor of a windowless bathroom and they could only have come through the light fittings. I went to the front of the house and peered up at the roof tiles and gables and saw no sign of wasps. I went to the back of the house and again saw nothing. I told our gardener, Arnold. But he could see nothing.

The following day he tapped excitedly on my French window as I was hunched over a computer. He had found the nest. He took me down the spiral staircase and along the terrace to the middle of the house and pointed to a fascia board beneath the tiles. I now saw there was a round hole in it, and half a dozen wasps were dancing at its entrance. The nest was inside, between the ceilings and the tiles.

I rang the local pest control company, and about 11.30 a van pulled up. Ralph was a youngish man. I took him to the back and pointed to the hole and asked how he would reach it. He said, "Perhaps from one of the windows. But I need to make sure they're not honey-bees. We're not allowed to touch them." Hanging out of a window would be better than going up a ladder to the sloping roof above the ground floor and walking up it to reach the hole and the dancing wasps.

We went round to the front door and up the stairs. I showed him two possible windows, one each side of the hole. They opened outwards. He peered and confirmed they were wasps and not honey-bees. I had not found a single honey-bee on the corridor floor. He went off to get his equipment.

He returned looking like a bee-keeper, with a white hat, 'anorak', and masked muslin over his face, and white gloves. He held a canister containing Vulcan dusting powder. Upstairs he turned it upside down and shook it and then turned it the right way up and then upside down again. It had a long thin spike. He peered through an open window and put his spike through the gap between the hinges on the end of the window and the wall, and put a gloved finger on the spike's trigger and gave it three squirts.

He went to the room the other side and peered from the other window, and then returned and squirted again. Then he packed away his equipment, returned to his van and did the paperwork.

I told him we had mice chewing the cable of the clock in the annexe building and asked how they got in. He said mice always get in at ground level, and I should look for a hole at mouse level. (I later found a ground-level vent that had been chewed, and blocked it.)

I paid by card. He read the numbers out very quickly over the phone, it was speedily done. Then he was off to his next assignment.

As he drove through the double gates I thought that his whole working life was dealing with wasps and mice. He was not a lover of Nature but a killer of wasps and mice for nesting in places that were inconvenient to humans. Every creature had a rightful place and the rightful place for wasps and mice was not near humans, and so they had to be Vulcanised. He was like the Roman god Vulcan, god of fire, the Greek Hephaistos, and he enforced his godhood with his canister of dusting powder and kept the earth's Paradise free from noxious insects and rodents that spoiled the luxurious life of humans in this corner of the highly organised Western world.

A Fast Walker and a Sick Elm
(Or: Conflict and Placid Calm)

That day I went to the dentist to have a new crown fitted in place of an upper-right snapped tooth. The lady dentist, Dr Cherihew, said, "I'm quickly drilling out the base of the old tooth and the screw," but after ten seconds she gave up and muttered to her assistant, "That drill's not working." I had twenty minutes of drilling while she struggled to pull out the base of the snapped tooth and the screw. It did not hurt. Eventually she seemed to have done it.

The glamorous nurse kept calling me darling. "First of all there was no water, now there's loads of water from the drill. Are you all right, darling?" And, "Your mouthwash is there when you're ready, darling."

I could not reply with the drill whistling or I might have had a cut lip.

After I left the surgery I drove and parked and looked in at the bank. Four notices said, 'This counter is closed.' All four counters were closed. A receptionist standing by the door said of the cashier, "She's just come in, but it'll take more than ten minutes to get the system going."

I sat to maintain my place in the queue and watched a dozen more customers come in. Then a relief cashier, a middle-aged lady, appeared from a rear door and bent over me and said, "It's all changed because of Covid. We're not doing counter service. You have to get cash from the wall machines or do transfers on that machine over there."

I said I preferred counter service.

A couple of minutes later she relented, beckoned me to her counter and served me as usual. But it was a struggle as her machines were not working properly. Her computer froze, and I waited until it unfroze.

She was too busy to serve customers but she printed off instructions on how I could do my own banking from now on, and added helpful notes in handwriting as she explained the stages to me. She ordered me a PINsentry card-reader, which would give me a code: "It'll take a week to come." Then she criticised my paperwork: "You've written out the transactions you need to do, they could all go on one sheet of paper."

On the way back to my car I stopped at the health shop for brewer's yeast. When I came out a tall, elderly man in a dark-grey suit, pink shirt, red tie and black shoes walked fast past me. I half-recognised him but could not place him. Was he once a local Head, was he a solicitor? He went into Robert Dyas.

I crossed the road and sauntered towards where I had parked and he again walked past me, not carrying anything he had purchased. He was walking terrifically fast, I had never seen such a fast walker. Olympic walkers used to look as if they were nursing a baby as they half-ran, but he walked with his arms by his side and would have outwalked them. He was a really fast walker.

He took his jacket off and got into his Range Rover, did a U-turn and tore off down the road. I got into my car and followed him more sedately, for my car was pointing in the direction he was going.

Two roads away I encountered his Range Rover at a T-junction. He was stationary while cars whizzed past in both directions. Then he turned right, and so did I. He was holding me up, this fast walker. He was actually a slow driver, I had to check that I wouldn't go into the back of his Range Rover.

When I got home I received confirmation from Pippa and Arnold, the new gardener, that the elm she gave me for my birthday a few years previously might have Dutch elm disease. The sapling had been doing well but was now sick. Its leaves had turned yellow in late spring and then dark brown in August, when no other leaves had turned, and it was weeping a sticky, clear substance, oozing sap, down the side of its upper trunk. It was not a well tree. Elm leaves turning yellow and then brown in late spring and summer are a symptom of Dutch elm disease, and I had raised the possibility with Arnold. Arnold had now pointed his phone, set to his garden app, at it and had received confirmation on his screen: "Dutch elm disease". If the young tree had Dutch elm disease, then elm beetles had carried fungus into its veins and it was unable to breathe.

Pippa had sent a picture to the nursery where she had bought the sapling, and the reply came back that it probably had had too much water in January and February and would be all right next year.

I made myself coffee and took it upstairs and sat at my desk, and I thought: 'That's how life works, through a lot of little things that seem disconnected: a dentist struggling to wrench out a bit of tooth, a lady cashier struggling with her system and deflecting her work to her customer, a fast walker who was struggling with time, and an elm with fungus or water blocking its veins.'

Yet somehow at a deeper level, they were all connected. The humans were all struggling with material things or with time, and Nature was ever-changing and full of fungal disease or waterlogging. Life was a conflict, and as I went from situation to situation, and chore to chore, all was conflict which I somehow passed through with a placid calm that reconciled all opposites and contradictions.

A Carer and Acceptance of Death

When we had our historic house we always had a housekeeper and her husband, and Gino was one of the husbands. He came from Lord Swaffam, and at the interview his wife told me she had to get him away as his employer was disabled and Gino was dressing him, driving him to the House of Lords, wheeling his wheelchair, driving him back, cooking for him, ironing for the next day and getting him into bed for the night. He was dresser, carer, cook, housekeeper, caretaker, butler and chauffeur.

He came to us and was soon managing the events, which meant managing the public on coach tours and open days, presiding over the serving of teas prepared by his wife and over the grounds, which were immaculate. He always fed the swans and the geese at the right time, on the edge of the moat. I remember walking with him by a herbaceous border and he cried out "A weed" and he swooped and with his bare hand plucked out a weed the gardener had overlooked. He was butler, chauffeur, valet, handyman, gardener, caterer and events manager. He set high standards and cared about everything.

He and his wife left to return to Italy as there was a position in the village he was born in. Twenty years later I received a message he had died, and wrote to his wife.

She replied: "He was diagnosed with advanced prostate cancer three years ago. After two-and-a-half years of chemo there was no more they could do. Although the cancer was in his bones he actually suffered very little pain. About a month ago he took a real turn for the worse. Finally he couldn't walk, talk, eat or drink. It was so awful. He died peacefully here at home, holding [his son] Alan's hand. Even though we knew he couldn't go on, it was still a shock. We are never prepared or ready. We are all in pieces but trying to be strong as he would have told us to be. I can't believe he's gone. Even death is part of life and we have to accept it."

It was a heart-rending letter. In his working life with me he had been calm and quietly in charge with great composure, and I could imagine he would have been no trouble to anyone during his last months, he would have lain quietly and self-effacingly, not wanting to cause trouble, ever the butler and valet, quietly in charge and solving problems and carrying out the family's wishes.

And I thought of his wife's closing remark on death: "We have to accept it." She had been full of practical common sense and accepted that death is part of life, she accepted things as they were as she had done when she worked for me. I was sure now Gino had gone aloft and was somehow managing the new arrivals, making sure the grounds were immaculate and performing many duties behind the scenes in Heaven.

But most of all I thought of all the caring he had done and that in the last six months of his life he was cared-for by his family. It was a just return, a karmic boomerang, for a lifetime of caring.

A Moon Face and a Bent Screw

I had an arched moon phase longcase clock dating from c.1780 with a painted moon-phase dial: a full chubby moon with rosy cheeks, brown eyes and red lips. The dial had two peacocks on either side of the key spindles, and was on a turning disc at the top of the clock.

I had wound it for 20 years, and once, the framed-glass door over its clock face came off on its hinges as I opened it to wind the mechanism with a key, and it cut my wrist as it fell and the glass shattered. That was long in the past.

That day I saw the pendulums were hanging near the bottom of the long longcase door, and I opened the framed-glass door at the top to wind the clock, and as the glass door flew through the air I grabbed at it and knocked it onto my stuck-out foot which cushioned its fall and it clattered to the floor, glass unbroken.

I searched and found one tiny screw for the top hinge. It was bent, and I thought it might be a 1780s screw. I could not find the screw for the bottom hinge. It was too tiny to match from the screws at the bottom of my tool-box, so I went to the local jewellers.

I explained the situation to the elderly shop owner. He took the bent screw and retreated to the back of his office, searched and returned.

"I haven't got one here," he said. "But I'm going to the clock maker's on Wednesday and I can take it with me and match the size. How many screws would you like?"

"Four," I said without hesitation. "If two bend while I'm screwing them in, then I've got two in reserve."

"Good thinking," he said. And he put the screw in a plastic envelope and wrote "4 screws".

I began to leave, but turned back.

"Do you want my name?" I asked.

He said, "I shall never forget you."

He was the old-style shop owner I recall from my boyhood, who went by facial memory, and not by name. To him I was unforgettable. Something about me had lodged in his memory. Perhaps none of his other customers entered his shop and talked about a 1780s moon face with one bent hinge screw supporting its framed-glass door.

A Disabling Stroke and Buried Feelings

"Adrian's father's had a stroke," Penny said of her son-in-law's father. "He couldn't remember what had happened to him. His wife doesn't drive, they found him on the floor and Adrian took him to hospital.

He kept saying, 'Why am I in hospital?' The nurses told him, 'You've had a fall,' but it didn't seem to sink in.

"Yesterday he had a second stroke. Adrian, his mother and sister were all summoned to the hospital, which is very unusual over a weekend, especially all three together, and were given the news. It's caused vascular dementia, it will never get any better. He's staying in hospital. It was a thalamic stroke, he can walk – he's a bit wobbly – but he's slurring his speech and it's affected his memory, so he doesn't remember anything. He's still saying, 'Why am I in hospital?' He's told he's had a fall but he's forgotten that within a few minutes and he's asking again. He can't write. He can read, but can't remember what he's read for more than a few minutes.

"Rebecca" (her daughter) "has said, 'If I were living with him, I'd *make* him learn to write all over again. He needs an hour every morning, being pushed, and another hour later in the day. Now, fresh after the second stroke. Otherwise he won't be able to do it.' But his wife's not strong, she can't drive, and they sit and watch a lot of television and he's obese from overeating. Abuse of the body has consequences, and allowing yourself to become obese is no exception. He needs a completely new diet and way of eating. None of the family is strong enough to enforce it. I don't know what's going to happen.

"He's in hospital indefinitely, his wife can't visit him without being taken, their only son – Adrian – is a policeman, and though Adrian has been given compassionate leave to sort things out, he'll soon be back at work and can't drive her. And his sister is a teacher but doesn't like driving on a motorway. There's a fuel shortage as you know, and going to hospital and back uses a lot of fuel, and she makes excuses for not visiting him. Rebecca is on 15-hour shifts in her hospital and can't help. They've all been pampered.

"I had to knuckle down when I was young. My mother was never well, she had heart problems. She looked after my physically- and mentally-handicapped sister who was two years older than me. She carried her up and down the steep stairs to our third-floor rented accommodation each day. She collapsed and died when I was seven. I was there. My handicapped sister was taken into residential care and I took on looking after my father, who was very unwell. I did the shopping, the washing, the ironing and housework. He had a heart attack and died when I was fifteen. And after that I had to look after myself. I never had a normal life of being looked after as a normal child. But I got through. I wasn't pampered, I know what it's like to cope with illness, and they're older than I was. And there are complaints that Rebecca isn't doing enough, after driving home (having searched for fuel) after a 15-hour shift in her hospital, dog-tired."

There was a silence. I was more than 20 years older than she was, but I felt for her. I said, "It's very difficult. My father had several strokes, and I know what it's like to visit someone who's persistently ill in hospital. It's a worrying time for Adrian. It's a wretched time he's going to be going through." And to my surprise my eyes filled with tears.

She saw this and said, "I'm sorry, I didn't mean to awaken feelings in you."

"It's a wretched time," I said, "but under the circumstances he'll somehow cope, give him my best wishes."

"I will."

Later I thought that the two strokes had stirred up latent, suppressed feelings in both of us; in her case at being orphaned at fifteen, in my case at losing my father when he was 57. The end of a life fills us with emotions we control and suppress, that can emerge and wash over us at any time.

And I thought that seeing a loved one suffer strokes enhances our awareness of the significance of life, and gives memories we will never forget. And realistically, if they did teach Adrian's father to read all over again, as he was overweight and had neglected to control his weight by overeating, how could anyone be sure he would not have a third stroke before he had learned to write?

A Black Crow by the Drive-Thru
(Or: Waiting like Carrion)

The plague was reinforced by an infectious strain of the Delta variant that was sweeping through the country.

Penny was working at home that day. She had not felt well, she had a very high temperature, was achy and had a headache, and a lateral flow test result was positive for Covid. So she went to the Enfield drive-thru test site and got a PCR (polymerase chain reaction) test. She emailed me.

We had been sitting next to each other the previous day. I told Pippa and she drove me to the Assembly Hall test centre, which was deserted. We were shown to a couple of chairs and the receptionist put our details (names and NHS number, and Pippa's phone number) onto her phone and registered us for lateral flow tests. We were given swab-like nose-probes and told to put them up inside first one, then the other nostril and twiddle ten times. It tickled the lining of my nose and after my nose-probe was removed I sneezed three times.

We went outside and sat in our car for 10 minutes. The results came through onto Pippa's phone. I was positive, Pippa was negative.

I briefly thought back to when I could have caught Covid: I had been to London to see consultants, I had been to the bank and the post office and to two restaurants with my grandchildren. And Penny had spent a weekend with her family.

The Assembly Hall test centre had said that if one of us was positive we would have to go to Enfield, the nearest PCR site while the one in a car park across the road was closed for refurbishing. So we drove to Enfield's Valley Road. We drove past the test site and turned round and turned right at the cinema and right again and stumbled across the test site, which was parallel to the road but hidden by trees. At the gate we were turned away as we had to have appointments.

Pippa reversed and we parked facing the test site, in a wilderness of wire fencing and empty space and autumn leaves. Pippa went to her phone and found where to register. The questions went on and on, it seemed we were asked 50 questions on each of us. But eventually we finished our request for PCR tests and a message came through that we could be tested between 3.30 and 4. It was then 3.20.

We sat in the car park and waited for ten minutes. It was autumn and there were dead leaves all round us in the empty parking area. There was a lithe, sleek, agile black bird pecking among the leaves. It started on our left, progressed along the front of our car and ended on our right.

As I watched I was sure it was a black carrion crow. It wasn't a jackdaw as it was jet black, and it wasn't a rook. It was too sleek. It was too slim to be a raven.... I settled on a crow in my mind.

And then it dawned on me: this crow was a harbinger of death. It hung around near the entrance to the test site, spying on who was about to test positive so it could visit Death and usher in the latest Covid victim. It was on the look-out for potential carrion, it was the harbinger of Death and escorted the doomed into the presence of Death.

We were waved to the gate and were allowed to proceed with our hazard lights flashing. We had to wait while a Chinese lady talked to us through a panel window. We were swabbed down our throats – the nurse twiddled ten times while we said "Aaaah" until our breath ran out – and then up one nostril. Then we were free to go home.

I had a messy thick mucus that I blew out of my nose the next morning, but otherwise I was reasonably well. I had no headache or aches, and reckoned my booster was keeping me safe from Covid, supplying antibodies. I heard the next day that my PCR result was positive.

I sat and thought of the black crow. It had kept me company while I waited and now I had been introduced to Death. But I was not being taken this time. I could escape. I would have to isolate for ten days and then escape from Covid. I had got off lightly – unlike Penny, who was told her PCR was inconclusive, and, fuzzy-headed and coughing repeatedly, had to drive back to Enfield and go through the process all over again. I later heard that the black crow had kept her company while she waited for her test.

A Trolley and a Split Face

Richard rang Pippa about 95-year-old Aunt Maud. Pippa told me afterwards, "She's in permanent pain, and to reduce her pain she sleeps in her chair, and the only way she can get comfortable is to contort herself, twist the hip that hurts, and put her forehead on the trolley. Last night she fell asleep down in Cornwall with her head on the trolley, which seems to have moved, dropping her forward against the hearth. She seems to have hit her head on the tiled side of the fireplace and split her face open from one eye down to her lips. She woke up with blood everywhere, not knowing what had happened, and couldn't move. She had pain all over her. She had a buzzer round her neck and managed to press it. It went through to a monitoring place that rang Richard at 1am.

"Richard went round to her at 1.30am and called an ambulance – which didn't come until 5.30am. And then it was the wrong one as it didn't have morphine, it wasn't a team with pain relief, so they had to wait for an ambulance a grade higher, which came at 7am. She asked the ambulance men for a mirror, but the injury to her face was so horrific they wouldn't give her a mirror.

"They took her to Treliske Hospital. Ambulances were queuing. Her ambulance queued until 1pm, six hours. There was no urgency. The hospital had no beds, so she was parked in A&E and had to wait to be seen.

"I said to Richard, 'The NHS wasn't designed to cope with ninety-five-year-olds who need a new hip.' There's no prospect of a bed for a while, and her face is split open from one eye to her lips, so she can't eat, and she had trouble breathing. She's too old to have a hip operation, and so she'll be too old to have a face operation."

I thought back to my wartime childhood. There was no going to hospital for free before the NHS was set up in 1948, and if German planes bombed you and split your face open, you had to cope on your own to avoid paying. Somehow, with the pandemic and staff shortages caused by Brexit, we had gone back to the days of my childhood.

The next day Pippa heard from Richard. She told me: "Aunt Maud was finally admitted to an emergency ward. She had her face sewn up and is having tests for her long-standing irregular heart and her hip. But she can't have a general anaesthetic at ninety-five."

The next day Pippa had another call from Richard. She said, "Richard was working up scaffolding and he had a call from the hospital telling him Maud had been discharged: 'She's sitting in the room where patients are put to be collected.'

"Richard said, 'I'm up scaffolding at present.' He was told, 'You'll have to come. She's sitting waiting for you, she's been discharged.'

Richard said, 'Has she any home care?' He was told, 'We're short of staff. She can have half an hour a day at 1pm, that's all. She has to have liquid food only. You'll have to buy her liquid food.' Richard asked, 'How do I get that?' He was told, 'I don't know, that's down to you.'

"So Richard had to leave work and collect his mother. He put in a formal complaint at her being discharged without a care package or provision for her to have a diet of liquid food, and he's now working out how to get Maud up her steep steps and through her front door. She hasn't been able to walk up or down the steps for three years, and there's no ambulance or stretcher."

The next day Pippa had another call from Richard. His wife and daughter helped him get Maud up her steps in a wheelchair Pippa had bought for her, taking her up backwards with one pulling and two pushing and lifting from below, step by step.

"Now she's back in her front room again," Pippa said. "There's her bed, and her chair, the trolley and the hearth. She's got help at lunchtime, but she can only eat liquid food. Sue will make their porridge every morning and Richard will take Maud's round and empty the commode before he goes to work each day. She'll wait until the home help comes at 1pm. In the evening Richard is talking of going straight to her after work and sleeping there.

"In fact, Maud insisted she would be all right, and Richard just takes her breakfast and looks in on her in the evenings. And she is still twisted in permanent pain, and only able to relieve her discomfort by contorting herself and putting her forehead onto the trolley, which led to her fall and her nightmare queuing and waiting in A&E with her whole face split wide open."

A Solitary and Hardship

Arnold, our new gardener, talked about his coming holiday. "We're going to Gran Canaria," he said. "My wife wants to lie in the sun and I'll hire a bike and go up into the hills and explore. I'm looking forward to that. And after we return I shall go off on my own, drive to Little and Great Langdale in the Lake District."

"Where Wordsworth's Solitary lived," I said, "at Blea Tarn House between Little and Great Langdale."

"Yes, I know his house. I'll take my sleeping-bag and a tent and I'll sleep out at night and spend three days completely on my own. I'm a trained mountain rescuer and I've been taught to make wise decisions, and I won't take my phone. It's a fell walk of twelve or thirteen miles. I'll be alone in the environment and Nature up Scafell Pike. Except for when I go to Wainwright's Inn near Great Langdale when I'm down. I love it there, it's got a flagstone floor and open fires. It's in Chapel Stile, Ambleside."

"Wordsworth country," I said.

He said, "I was trained by a former SAS soldier. He's very well known. He was hit by two avalanches in Romania's Transylvanian Alps in 2003. He heard a crack, and a ridge 500 yards above him headed towards him. That was the first avalanche, which he survived by running. Then he heard another crack, and he was swept over a cliff down to trees and rocks. He crashed to a halt and tried to stand, and fell down another slope. He woke up in darkness, cut off from his supplies, suffering from over-exposure in a minus-15 temperature with what turned out to be a broken leg and a shattered pelvis, and he wrote a book about his struggle to survive. He crawled for three days through mountain gullies. He had a Leatherman multi-tool and a compass in his jacket pocket. I always take those with me when I go out surviving. He survived because of his mental strength, and he impressed that on me: being mentally strong.

"I used to help him. He had a survival school, and apart from me his staff were all from the Special Forces, and I used to go and work for him. The discipline was very strong, and anyone who was late was sent home straight away. It was ruthless military discipline, but it worked.

"Having been through that survival school I have to go out on lone forays and survive in difficult terrains. That's partly why I cycle. I'm often on my own – you know, I came 2nd out of 49 in the St Ives, Cambridgeshire road race – and only last night I went for a ten-mile run near where I'm living, in a 25-pound vest, a vest weighing 25 pounds. There was no path for some of the way and I was slipping and squelching with my weighted vest to make my endurance harder. I love pitting myself against hardship and surviving, as Ken trained me to do."

He was away for a couple of weeks, and his first day back I asked him how he got on.

"Not very well," he said. "I didn't enjoy Gran Canaria. My wife had a lovely time, just lying in the sun, but there was nothing for me to *do*, and the roads were poor for cycling. I wouldn't go back. The drive to the Lake District was longer than I expected. I spent Friday and Saturday nights in my tent in great rain between Little and Great Langdale, and visibility was down to 30 yards. I came away on Sunday afternoon, a day early, it was wet and visibility was poor. I survived all right, but it was too wet to do some of the things I had planned to do. It wasn't the kind of survival I was hoping for."

Arnold suffered from occasional bouts of asthma but he was incredibly physically strong, and mentally strong, despite having had Covid quite badly six months earlier and saying he was still not back to the energy and fitness he had had before.

My father used to say to me during the war when bombs were falling around us and we could hear the distant blasts, "It's mind over matter, mental strength." In a small way I had been trained to be mentally strong, too, and I could recognise the need to be alone and survive in *my* mental environment and Nature as I wrote my works. I had an instinctive respect for Arnold as I reckoned my mental struggle to survive amid words and bring my works into being reflected his mental struggle to survive among the hazards of Nature. I too forced myself into Herculean tasks of grappling with verbal avalanches and downpours, and survived to write again. Like Arnold I had rejected a life's comfort and of lying in the sun for a life of challenge, of doing, of pushing myself to my limits. My work came out of my solitude, and I looked to the Solitary's house between Little and Great Langdale as a symbol of solitude from which I wrote.

Arnold would continue to make regular forays into zones of discomfort which (like wearing a 25-pound vest) might seem masochistic to those who take the easiest route through life, and he would reinforce the strength he drew from his self-imposed ordeals. And I too would wear a 25-pound vest as I grappled with a new work and would derive further inner strength from my repeated ordeals. I wished I could talk to my long dead father about his "mind over matter", which he taught me under Hitler's bombs, but like Arnold separated from his teacher Ken, I was on my own now and was putting into practice the mental strength I learned from him as a little boy.

Covid and a Car

My PA Penny emailed me while working at her home that she had tested positive for Covid. I told Pippa, and Pippa and I immediately drove to Chingford Assembly Hall, registered on Pippa's phone and had supervised lateral-flow tests, cotton buds on long stick-like probes thrust down our throats and up our nostrils and twirled. We then went and sat in Pippa's car outside, and the results pinged through on her phone: she was negative, I was positive.

I knew Penny had gone to Enfield drive-thru for her PCR (polymerase chain reaction) test. Pippa drove on to Enfield and we found the Testing Centre. We were told at the gate that we had to register on our phone. We reversed across the entrance road to a parking area, and registered on Pippa's phone: answered about 50 questions each. I sat in the car and watched a sleek black carrion crow pecking among the late-autumn leaves on the ground until a message came through. We had been given a slot after 3.30, and at 3.40 were allowed to drive to where the tests were being administered. One after the other, we opened our mouths so a Chinese girl in blue gloves could plunge a stick down our throats until we gagged, and were then given the stick to twiddle it up each nostril ten times. Then we drove home.

The results came through on Pippa's phone the next day. She was negative, I was positive. Penny had been to Enfield before us, and she reported that she had been told her result was inconclusive. She had to go back to Enfield and be re-tested, and she received her positive test result the following day.

We seemed to have caught it at the same time. Did Penny catch Covid from her daughter Rebecca, who was in the NHS and in daily contact with Covid-infected patients and perhaps as an asymptomatic carrier gave it to her mother, who in turn carried it asymptomatically to me? Or did I catch it from one of the family and as an asymptomatic carrier give it to Penny?

Then I recalled a week back, the previous Friday. It was the day I was supposed to be interviewed for American television. Penny worked with me until 1pm. She went home and returned at 4pm for the 6.30 broadcast – which did not happen as we could not connect. The broadcast was postponed until the following Tuesday.

Then I recalled more. We were archiving, and I took a handful of papers to the annexe, where the boxes were kept. When I returned Penny said, "Your gates are open, and look, there's a lady in that car with the headlights on. She's level with the gates, and she's been watching us."

I said, "I'll go down and ask her what she wants."

I went downstairs and, outside, headed for the open double gates. The driver of the car came in, seemingly driving one-handed, wound the window down and said, about 40, quite smart and well-spoken, "Sorry, I took a wrong turning." But she didn't take a wrong turning, she had been parked in the entrance between our open double gates and had been watching us for a quarter of an hour. She seemed to be carrying a perfume bottle in her left hand, and to be driving one-handed. She turned and reversed awkwardly, and left. Did she squirt me from her perfume bottle?

Suddenly I was in Skripal territory. Had a hostile force found out I was broadcasting to America and tried to interrupt our efforts on our current work by spraying us with Covid?

The idea haunted me for the next ten days. I duly isolated until the following Monday week, and had Covid very mildly. But I thought from time to time that when we finally made our broadcast to America on the Tuesday, I finished with a slight snuffle and felt I might have a temperature. Two days later, for two days running, possibly days 5 and 6, I had a temperature of 37.5C instead of my usual 36.2, and my temperature was around 37.5 until the day before my isolation ended.

I thought of getting our CCTV engineer to look back at the CCTV footage and see if he could locate the woman's registration number so I could find out who she was. But realistically, I could have got Covid anywhere – in the bank, in the post office – and Penny's daughter and son-in-law, as an NHS doctor and police officer, were exposed to the virus every day, and it was impossible to pinpoint the moment we caught it. The car was a good idea that satisfied my enquiring mind with a specific moment when I could have been sprayed (in the open air) and could have carried my infection upstairs and infected Penny within minutes. But I had to accept that there was probably no neat solution, and either of us could have been infected, and infected the other, in at least a dozen ways, if our families had been asymptomatic carriers.

I was lucky to have had Covid mildly: no headache, cough, breathing difficulties, sickness or tiredness, just a persistent cold. I had had two vaccinations and a booster. I carried on working – with hindsight I did my broadcast to America while having Covid – and I got off lightly. Penny had it worse as she had had just two vaccinations and no booster. Her temperature was up to 39.5 for several days and she felt very unwell, achy, weak, tired and sick and had to spend long times in bed. We had both probably had the Delta variant, and having seen Indians on TV gasping for breath and queuing to buy rusty oxygen cylinders from what looked like a black-market rag-and-bone shop in Delhi so they could breathe properly, we could not complain. We did not realise that the much more infectious Omicron variant was about to land, and that it was more transmissible, could re-infect very easily and was not deterred by two vaccinations.

Another bout of the plague was ahead. I had survived a mild dose of one variant of the plague, but new variants were ahead and were unpredictable. We were now again facing a new wave of the pandemic, which for all we knew might be even more deadly. Like Milton, isolating from the plague in Chalfont St Giles, Buckinghamshire, I co-existed with the new variant of Covid and just got on with my work.

A Guard Dog and a Fox
(Or: Human Training and Animal Instinct)

On Christmas Day after dark Penny took her daughter's guard dog for a walk on a lead. She was wearing trousers. The dog, a Labrador Retriever, spotted a fox and bolted. Penny was pulled along the road by the tugging lead, and ran to try and keep up. She fell on the pavement and was dragged along, ripping her trousers and losing several layers of skin on both her knees. Eventually she let go of the lead and found she had a deep cut in her left hand.

The dog chased after the fox. Penny managed to get up and retrieve the dog and to struggle to her daughter's house. Her daughter, a Specialist Paediatric Registrar in the NHS, treated her hand and knees, put on surgical plasters and said the sooner the hand and knees could be left to heal in the air, the better.

Penny returned home. On Boxing Day she was supposed to go to her daughter's in-laws but she politely cancelled and stayed at home. She was too sore to walk far, and travelling in a car and sitting would be an ordeal. Her hands were sore and she was unable to type.

When I heard, I said how sorry I was to learn her news. I sat and reflected on the ambivalence of domesticated animals, especially dogs. Most of the time they obey human rules and bark when they hear a would-be threat or intruder outside at night, but beneath their humanised training was an instinct that could sweep all the training aside. The scent or the sound or (especially) the sight of a fox was enough to turn a well-behaved dog into an instinctively territorial and defensive animal that reacted immediately and bolted to see off a perceived threat to the friendly human it was guarding, so immediately that this dog mercilessly dragged the human it was guarding while trying to catch up with the threat – in Penny's case, a fox.

'Crystalline' and a Rancorous Shout
(Or: Adjectival and Harmony)

Bernard was seated next to me at the Boxing-Day lunch table. We had plates heaped with several meats and vegetables and dollops of bread sauce and horse-radish sauce, and sipped good red wine. He said to me, and to his father who was seated next to me at the end of the table, of his visit to his mother's family in the north from which he had just returned, "We played Trivial Pursuit last night. It was the men against the women. I was in charge of the men as I was back from university, and Chris wanted to be in charge." (Chris was his maternal grandfather).

"There was a question, 'Describe a transparent mineral.' I said, 'We're going to say "Crystalline".' 'No,' he said, 'it's "Crystal".' But I stood my ground and said, 'We're going to say "Crystalline".' He shouted at me: 'You're wrong. You're wrong. You're wrong.' He said it three times and banged the table and pointed at me."

"What did you do?" I asked, noting his father's eyes were gleaming with intense amusement.

"I kept my composure. I didn't argue with him. I said, 'We're going to say "Crystalline".' He shouted even more loudly another twice: 'You're wrong. You're wrong.' Then I didn't say anything and there was a silence. And Monica said, 'You need to listen to what Chris is saying.'" Monica was Bernard's maternal grandmother and Chris's wife.

"I didn't say anything, and she said, 'You're sulking.' The atmosphere was very strained. She didn't speak to me after that and *he* didn't speak to me this morning when we left. He didn't say goodbye."

There was a stunned silence round the table. Simon's eyes were gleaming with mirth.

Seeking to restore harmony, I said, "I expect he's ruled the roost for forty-five years, and now the younger generation are coming up with ideas that are challenging his set opinions and he can't handle it. You're not wrong, actually. The question began 'Describe'. A describing word is an adjective, grammatically the question was asking for a grammatical reply. And 'crystalline' is more obviously adjectival than 'crystal', which can be both an adjective (as in 'crystal ball') and a noun ('a crystal'). In a sense you were both right. He meant the adjectival use of 'crystal', but your 'crystalline', though not everyday speech, was more clearly adjectival. You weren't wrong."

I continued, "In a true democracy the voters can vote for whatever candidate they want. There are many opinions, and no one choice is right or wrong. He can have his opinion and you can have yours, but he can't say your opinion is wrong, because you've voted for a more obviously adjectival answer. He can say, 'I prefer "crystal"', not 'You're wrong.'

"So how's it been left?" I asked.

"I don't know," Bernard said. "He didn't speak to me this morning, which will make it awkward next time I go up north. If I go again...."

Simon said nothing but his eyes were full of 'I-told-you-so' mirth. He had had his own disagreement with Bernard's mother's family, which contributed to his separation and divorce, and his eyes expressed confirmation of what he had always known but had not expressed. He remained silent, and we carried on eating, and the conversation turned to relationships.

I said, "Life is full of apparent differences, opposite points of view, but they can all be reconciled. All opposites are fundamentally part of an underlying harmony, including pedantic ones. So I'd forget about it."

And what could be more pedantic than the difference between 'crystal' (adjectival) and 'crystalline' (more clearly adjectival) in a Trivial Pursuit that was, by its own nomenclature, 'trivial'. And with what rancour had Chris imbued his reaction to the word, and how long had it accumulated before it blew up, like a light-bulb going out?

Games and Harmony

After lunch my two sons and three grandchildren went up to the playroom on the second floor, and after a while I followed and sat and watched.

Al was playing table tennis with Bernard, up to 12 or a two-point margin above that if there was a tie at 12–12. Then Paul played Bernard, and after that I was called to play, despite being 82. I narrowly beat Bernard (with some diagonal back-handers that had the ball leaving the side of the table out of his reach). Then I played Paul, and lost as he hit the ball really fast. I then played Al and Minnie, who took it in turns to be my opponent, alternating after each point. I narrowly won.

I then watched Paul and Bernard play bar football. Then I was called in and Bernard and I played Al and Minnie. They were very good. They spun their players, who during their whirling round and round rammed the ball into the goal at great speed. I tried to block their shots, manning the two attacking rods, and Bernard blocked at our back and fired goals through my defending players and their attacking and defending players.

The match finished with us all breathless. Bernard and I had easily lost.

Al said teasingly, "I'm going to work in Bernard's room now."

"No you're not," Bernard said playfully, and affectionately caught him as he squealed.

There was a competitive spirit between the grandchildren, but underneath their love for each other was palpable, and they were delighted to be in each other's company and in their playroom. And I was accepted into the harmony because I had shared it with them.

They played in competition and yet were fundamentally at one, as was Simon when he joined us and played Paul at table tennis. We were a family at ease together, and all equal in terms of the games we played. Bernard's game of Trivial Pursuit between the boys and the girls was supposed to create a similar harmony, but raw self-asserting grievances had surfaced unexpectedly. This harmony was their norm.

A Fox by the Road

I put on my green mask and collected my trousers from the cleaner's that Saturday afternoon. The ticket pinned on the plastic bag over my hung trousers said 'Mr Rawed', as if I had been made raw by life. I checked that the seam between the legs of the trousers had been sewn together – it had – and I walked with the plastic bag containing my trousers over my arm back past the pharmacy and round the corner to Station Road, and, realising I still had my mask on, stopped to take it off.

"Mr Rawley?" said a voice, and I looked up and saw an Indian wearing a mask, who had been walking in the opposite direction on the pavement.

"Yes," I said.

"Perhaps you don't recognise me as I have a mask," the Indian said, taking off his mask. "I live in the road next to the school where you were living, and I saw you about the car park. And my son was a pupil at your other school then, around 1988."

"It must have been 1989," I said. "That was when it opened."

"Oh 1989. I remember you from those days."

"Oh yes," I said, "I remember now, we often spoke."

I was still not sure what his name was.

"Yes, we did," he said. "Are you still at the schools?"

"No," I said. "My son has taken over the day-to-day. He was good at computers, he computerised the schools."

"Yes," he said. "Very necessary. I am Dr Hunjan."

"Oh, I remember that name very well from around 1989," I said.

"Yes. In those days I would look out of where I was practising as a doctor and Lord Myrtle would walk by and I'd say, 'Hello, Lee.' And he'd say, 'Hello', and we'd talk. Those were good days. I'm 80 now. I'm still practising, but more part-time. I'm with Dr Danely. I live alone, and working keeps me in touch with people. I advise people on their joints." He looked at me as if I might be a future customer. "Are you keeping well?"

"Yes," I said. "I'm 82 now –"

"Oh, you're older than me. I look up to you –"

"I go to the gym once a week and I've kept going, I believe in moving the blood around the body. I walk for fifteen minutes and cycle and treadle and pull light weights. And on Sundays I do my exercises. They're based on the Canadian 5 BX – five best exercises – for the Royal Canadian Air Force. Fifty years ago they were in a Penguin book about them. In those days I began with twenty-eight toe touches but I've modified my exercises since then. I still end with 650 runs on the spot. And I run on the ceiling. You know, I lie on my back and raise my hips and cycle in the air as if I were running on the ceiling. It means the blood reverses and pours down into my head. It's very good for you."

"Yes," he said. "Not long ago I had swollen feet, and I lay on the floor and for an hour had my legs in the air, and all the fluid ran back

down in my body, and my ankles were all right. But my toes hurt...."
He told me a long story about his toes and ended by saying, "So I had
two broken toes and I ignored them, had no treatment. I want to write
down what you said: 'Canadian 5 what was it'?"

I found a pen and he hunted in his wallet for paper to write down
'Canadian 5 BX'. I said, "I've done these exercises for over 50 years.
The only other person I know of who did them longer was Prince
Philip. He was without a stick at 99 as a result. And Prince Charles
does them, Philip made his son do them."

"I want to find the book," he said. "Can I give you my phone
number? If you have any problems with your joints I can give you
advice on the phone. I like to stay in touch with people."

He wrote out his phone number and then his hidden mobile rang
loudly.

"You must take the call," I said, eager to get away. "Thanks,
goodbye."

I left him searching for his mobile in his pockets. He lived alone
and seemed lonely, he needed people to talk to and worked to give
advice on joints, and now he had given me his phone number in
case I needed advice on my joints, so he could talk to me. He was a
still-practising GP and I had given him details of a book on exercising
and had told him to move the blood around his body and keep going.
He had cunningly set me up as someone he could talk to in the future.

I walked on, carrying the plastic bag containing my trousers over
my arm, found my car and drove to the end of the road. Three people
were waiting to cross, waiting for me to pass, and strangely, waiting
on the other side of the road was a fox.

There was a fox by the road. I thought how Dr Hunjan had
cunningly manoeuvred me into being someone he could talk to, and
realised this was the second time I had encountered a fox by the road.

Greens and Parkinson's

I received an email from my sister Florence: "I had a talk with our
cousin Rex yesterday. Did you know a neurologist on 11 January
diagnosed Parkinson's?"

I didn't know. The next day I rang Rex. I said I was sorry to hear the news. I had rung to wish him well.

He said faintly, sounding a poor old thing, "Thank you. Yes, I've got Parkinson's. I've known for several months that something's wrong. I've got trembling hands, and I can't sleep."

"Are you still driving a car?"

"Yes," he said.

"It would be good if you could make it to the family gathering in March, so we can catch up. You'll get a very sympathetic reception."

"It's a long way," he said. "I'm still deciding whether we can make it. I've got a bad back as well from chopping wood. I don't do that any more, we've got someone who comes and does that."

"You're positive about it all," I said. "Arguably there's a reduction in life expectancy. You're 80, and you've got ten to fifteen years, that will get you to 95, well beyond the average life expectancy. Do you remember we used to talk as children of living to be a hundred?"

He laughed.

"I'm not unduly worried," he said. "I'm just looking forward to getting it confirmed by MRI on Monday."

"When we were children I told you, you should eat your greens and lettuce," I said. "Do you remember, we were taken to the coast, to the flat on the first floor above the shop, and we had a lunch of ham and salad. You didn't like the fat on your ham and you took it and some salad in your hand and threw it out of the window. You looked down and saw it had fallen on the hat of a lady who was walking down the street. She didn't realise she had your ham and salad on her hat."

We both laughed, bonded in our childhood naughtiness.

"That may be an apocryphal story," he said in embarrassed self-defence.

"I told you, if you didn't eat your greens and your lettuce you'd end up with Parkinson's," I said, "but you wouldn't listen."

He laughed. He was no longer a poor old thing, the old Rex had come back. We were back in our childhood. He reminded me how we travelled on our own on trains at a young age – "my mother put me on the train by the sea and I was met from the train at your station"

– and there was an ease between us which enabled us both to process his Parkinson's, put it in context and downgrade its importance amid mirth and a positive outlook.

Two Strokes and Being Positive

I rang my brother Rupert a week before Christmas, and had quite a chat. He said to me, "I don't think I shall live long."

I said, "But you've been doing very well, you'll be 80 in three months' time, you're on top of your diabetes."

"But," Rupert said, "I'm confused by numbers, I have been since my heart operation."

I said, "You walk two miles across the Common each day."

"I do," he said. "I've got to know a lady at church who has been in a wheelchair for five years after a bad stroke. She hasn't walked more than a few paces, and the other day she said to me, 'Can I walk with you across the Common?' And she did. She asked if she could hold my hand, otherwise she might fall. I was all set to catch her if she fell. She held onto my hand, and she was so pleased with herself. She was being positive. And now I do five-mile walks, after being told I wouldn't be able to walk a hundred yards after my heart operation."

"Because you were being positive," I said. "You led her forward by your example of walking across the Common."

"Yes," he said. "I'd like to visit you at home for three hours in March around the time of my eightieth birthday."

A month later his son rang after I had finished supper. Pippa handed the phone across to me, and Henry said, in a voice that was on the verge of breaking into a sob: "I'm afraid I've some bad news. Dad has had a stroke."

"Oh no," I said.

He spoke hesitantly, stifling a sob. "I rang him and he went strange during the phone call and didn't make sense. He wasn't completing his sentences. He's in a hospital in Maidstone. But the hospital tried to discharge him soon after he was admitted, to clear his bed. They regarded his physical mobility as good enough to discharge him. He can walk but he's…. He's confused. He doesn't know where he is. He's been diagnosed by observation, it hasn't been confirmed by MRI."

"How are his limbs?" I asked, processing what I was hearing. "Can he move them all?"

"He can walk all right," Henry said. "It's his mental confusion. He had difficulty in recognising me… and couldn't complete sentences. A nurse stupidly left a syringe and needle by his bed and disappeared, and he tried to inject himself with an inappropriate dose of insulin at the wrong time without being aware of his usual injection time. He'll need looking after. He won't be able to take his insulin on his own. He can't live on his own in this state of mind."

Henry sounded wretched and in tears.

It sounded as if Rupert had had a stroke in his left brain, which affects speech, rather than in his right brain, which paralyses left limbs.

I said, trying to be positive, "Our father, your grandfather, had four strokes in the 1960s, and he recovered from the early ones. I mention this in case it's genetic with your dad. He may recover."

Henry perked up. "That's very interesting," he said. "Very interesting." He now had the prospect that his father would recover, and his mood lifted.

I chatted to him a little longer, thanked him for ringing and said I'd stay in touch. "Please give him my love and my best wishes," I said.

Pippa had already got the gist.

"He can move all right but he's talking scribble," she said.

"Yes. Why him and not me?" I murmured.

I was thinking of Rex, and now Rupert. The younger older generation, those just or nearly 80, were cracking up. And weirdly I had gone on and on…. I thought of all the times I had been to the gym and taken vitamins, and had consciously looked after myself. Why not me? Because I had looked after myself? But I knew that my turn would come, and I had a similar ordeal ahead of me. I just needed to get my work finished and my papers in order before my turn came. That was what being positive meant to me. I was sombre for the rest of the evening.

Cussedness and Recovery

That Saturday I rang Rupert at his home just before lunch. "It's Philip," I said.

"Yes," Rupert's voice said clearly. "I'm not well, I can't concentrate, I lose the thread."

I said I was sorry to hear his news and had been following his progress in hospital.

"I could be dead now. I was near death. I was very frightened."

"But you didn't die," I said, "it's not as bad as we first thought, and you're getting better."

"Yes, I've stayed positive. Henry was on the phone to me, and I gave a stupid answer and he knew something was wrong and said I should check my mental health. He arranged for me to go to the hospital. I had a big argument with the staff. I've always had a problem with authority, people taking over and telling me what to do, what dose to have as my injection, and I have a streak of cussedness, I look after myself. When I went to Leningrad by ship in 1966 and had a turn on the ship on the way back and ended up in a hospital in Essex, a nurse told me, 'You must eat what I tell you to eat.' She wouldn't let me do my injection, without knowing anything about diabetes. She wanted to tell me how to manage it. And cussedly I insisted and looked after my injection myself. It was the same with this hospital. They tried to tell me how to do my injection, and it was wrong. Again I was cussed."

"'Cussed' suggests 'awkward, stubborn'," I said. "I prefer 'determined'."

"The Rawleys are very determined," he said. "Eventually they let me do it myself. I had excessive blood sugar yesterday, but today I'm all right. I'm back in balance because I'm doing it myself."

"Can you count all right so you can get your injection quantities right?" I asked.

"Yes," he said. "I've always been bad at reading and counting, at school. I was told, 'If you can't count properly you'll be caned.'" He laughed.

I said, "They ran school like a military institution, with strict wartime discipline."

"After I had my heart operation I couldn't read, I *could not read*, and I couldn't count."

"I remember your saying," I said.

"It was the same after my TIA."

"Yes, your stroke was downgraded to a TIA," I said. "But your counting's getting better now?"

"Yes."

"And can you feed yourself?"

"Yes, when I first filled a kettle, water spilled over the side, but I can do it now. Fifteen cups of tea a day." He laughed.

"And can you sequence going to bed, cleaning your teeth and then...?"

"Yes," he said. "I'm improving. Henry and Kathleen have looked after me. We've had some nice conversations. What happened to me has made them aware I may not be here much longer, and they're making the most of the time now."

"You're doing well," I said. "Damage caused by a TIA may not be permanent, you may get a lot better in the next couple of weeks. Keep going."

"The Rawleys *are* cussed," he said.

"Very determined," I said, "we all are."

"Yes. And the lady who was in a wheelchair after a stroke for five years rang me this morning."

"She'll be very interested in what happened to you, having had a stroke herself."

"Yes, she's got the next instalment of *Bleak House*, she's invited me to watch it with her. I did *Bleak House* for 'A' level. I took her onto the Common –"

"You told me," I said.

"Yes," he said, "and she's happy to take me for a walk on the Common this afternoon."

"Good," I said. "You're getting back to normal faster than we all thought you would a week ago. Will you be able to go to your 80th birthday party at Florence's? The 150th party, her 70th and your 80th?"

"I don't know," he said. "I'm going to see how I am."

"That's what Rex has said," I said. "See how you are nearer the time."

"Yes," he said.

"Keep going," I said. "I'm going to ring off now so as not to tire you."

I rang off and sat and pondered on Rupert. He had been near death, and his children realised this and were nice to him. And he'd been drawn closer to a stroke victim who was inviting him to watch *Bleak House*. He had nearly died, and he had been frightened. But he'd had the strength to fight his way back into the land of the living and resume his former life. He was determined and had a streak of family cussedness, but he was making a good recovery, and he'd be all right. There was an unspoken link between his cussed determination and his will to improve, his recovery.

O-oo Yes and a Good Death
(Or: Darkness and a Glimmer of Light)

Later that evening I thought of Rupert confronting death and being frightened. I thought of my own death, of facing death, and wondered how accepting I would bring myself to be when the time came. Then I thought of Mrs. Barton, who looked after my great aunt who lived near my grandmother when I was a boy. When I visited my great aunt and talked about what I was doing, white-haired Mrs. Barton would beam at me and say, "O-oo yes." Again and again, "O-oo yes." I don't think she said anything else.

But even she managed to die. So many terrified people had managed to die all right, with dignity at the end, and make a good impression. It would be like a light-bulb going out, for a few seconds I would be aware of the fading light as the bulb failed and then it would be darkness. And, who knows, I might be in a tunnel groping towards a different kind of Light as I moved on to my next stage –

perhaps after lingering to watch my own funeral, as happened to me when I saw myself after I was dead in an early-19th-century life during a regression I had had over 40 years previously. I had seen the two gravediggers in white shirts and braces digging my grave in preparation for me to be laid in it.

Yes, I thought, when my time comes I'll have the determination to die well, have a good death, and accept the darkness that follows – and look for the glimmer of Light I should move towards, from what my regression had taught me. I had died of cholera in that early-19th-century life, I could remember taking my last breath. There was nothing to death. It was so easy, dying. You took a breath and then did not take another one.

I told myself I did not fear death – and I believed myself for a few minutes.

Dandelion and Burdock

We took our granddaughter out to lunch as she was spending the night with us. We went to the Royal Forest Hotel. Eleven-year-old Minnie ordered a square fort of Yorkshire pudding filled with three sausages and gravy. I had scampi and chips and a diet coke, and Pippa had gammon with a poached egg on it, and a can of dandelion and burdock.

"We used to have it in Yorkshire when I was a little girl in the nineteen-fifties," she said, "and I haven't had it recently."

Minnie wanted to taste it, and Pippa found a spare spoon and poured her a spoonful. I also had a spoonful to taste. It tasted fruity and earthy, sweet and bitter at the same time.

Minnie was full of her news that she had passed all her interviews and decided to go to the same school as her brother Al. We had puddings. Minnie had a chocolate brownie, Pippa had sorbets and I had chocolate torte. Then we drove home.

I took Minnie out to feed the fish and then to look at our fallen tree. It had sheared off and fallen across our fence out into the forest. It needed cutting up into sections as a wildlife habitat.

It was still February, and there were no dandelions visible, and no burdock. Later Minnie swam in our pool and showed us her crawl, which she hoped would one day take her to swim in the Olympics. She was very good, and eager to please. She swam a length and did a very professional back-flip turn, somersaulting and propelling herself forward into her next length.

Pippa sat on a chair and gave her instructions. She said, "You need a swimming teacher to work on your strokes, hone and polish them to knock seconds off your time."

Minnie was all sweetness and eager to please like a yellow summer dandelion with a clock of downy seed-heads, and Pippa was sharp and curative like a burdock with prickly flowers and leaves like soothing dock.

An Opera Singer and a Blocked Evangelist

I went to my old school's Shrove Tuesday dinner. Pippa dropped me off and I walked through light rain past the few I could see through the open door in the chapel to the dining-hall. People were standing in the coffee-room off the far side, and I joined them and studied the list of attenders on the wall.

I was listed as the second oldest in terms of the year I started at the school. It was already clear that the event would be poorly attended as Covid restrictions had only recently been lifted. The Head's wife had emailed many, including me, asking if they could come. I had just heard that the Head was leaving and attended as this would be his last Shrove Tuesday.

My contemporaries were all absent. I hung around awkwardly, talking without a drink before dinner, and then made my way to table 6 in the dining-hall where I found myself between a sixth-former and an ex-sixth-former who was now at university, the grandson of my contemporary James Pink.

"How do you remember my grandpa?" asked the grandson, who had a central parting with wavy black hair on either side. His grandpa was sitting next to him at the end of our table, erect and self-contained at 83, and I thought he might be listening though he appeared to be studying the menu.

"He was a bit overweight in those days and got ribbed by the master taking us for jerks at break," I said. I added, "PE," seeing incomprehension in his eyes at the word 'jerks'. I recalled the master, a Pegasus footballer, saying, "You'll never be able to move in your old age unless you get rid of your stodge." But I was too tactful to say this.

"He used to be called 'Slogger Pink'," the grandson said. That was what he had expected me to reply.

I did not remember him playing cricket at all.

Dinner was served, first smoked salmon, prawns and pancakes, then round fillet of beef with pancakes of herbs, vegetables and mushrooms on pastry. It took me a long while to chew mouthfuls of the beef, and I had not got very far when the Head came by and loitered. I turned my chair and shook his hand and stood up.

Standing with him, I said I was sorry to hear he was leaving.

He said, "I think it's right that I should move on after fifteen years." He told me he was going to a school in Worcestershire (where I knew A.E. Houseman, the poet of "Loveliest of trees, the cherry now/Is hung with bloom along the bough", and Heseltine had been been). He asked me about my trip to Russia three years back – we had discussed it shortly before I left and lockdowns had prevented dinners on Shrove Tuesday since then – and how I thought Russia's invasion of Ukraine would end, and in the course of my reply I knew I had two more books to write. As I spoke the plates were cleared, including my half-unfinished beef.

We were then served vanilla pancakes with honeycomb swirl ice-cream, and the black-haired grandson told me he had been a music scholar, and that he would like to be an opera singer as grandpa hoped, but at the same time he would like to be a property investor as his father hoped as he had an older brother who was disabled.

"He has a mental age of one," he told me. "I want to be able to look after him for the rest of his life. I look into his eyes when I leave for university, and I can hardly bring myself to leave he is so upset. When

I come back the look in his eyes is one of immense joy. I can't describe it, but it's the most important thing to me – after singing opera."

"You can draw on that feeling in your singing," I said to him. "You should research the opportunities in opera singing in the UK and Europe, for example by meeting someone in the Royal Opera House in London, and looking into the opportunities in Italy. University is a good place to be as you can review what you want to do, listen to a voice inside you. I was to do Law but I knew I had to study English Literature and I changed, and I have never regretted it. You should listen to your inner voice, and it may be you get advice from outside too. Who knows what powers are around us, willing us on to do Heaven's work and planting ideas in our mind, encouraging us forward. You should be still and listen with an open mind to inspiration from a deep place, possibly from the beyond."

"That's very interesting," he said. "I'm a Christian, like grandpa. I'll go to the Royal Opera House and research Europe including Italy, and I'll listen to my voice, and I think I know what you'd advise."

"What would I advise?" I asked.

"Singing in operas," he said.

"Yes," I said. "If the right investment-property can be funded so your elder brother has enough to live on for the rest of his life."

"This has been very interesting," he said. And he turned back to his grandpa.

After dinner we had coffee, and there were speeches from the Head Girl and the Head on his fifteen years at the school, his move and his replacement.

The sixth-former next to me said the prefects had been asked to attend a dinner with the replacement to see if they liked him and to answer his questions, and he was very similar to the present Head. He might have the same approach to the school, there might be more of the same.

We all stood and sang the school song. Because the event was poorly attended it was sung thinly, and each of us sensed we were singing a solo. We could all hear our contributions. We were not taken over and stirred by a bank of sound.

Pippa would now be outside. I prepare to slide away.

But grandpa stopped me. With grey hair tidily cut, James Pink said, "Last time we spoke I said I would deliver *New Testaments* like this to one of your schools" – he held up a small maroon-coloured book with gold lettering and named a school – "and I tried but I was blocked."

"Were you?" I replied in a surprised voice.

"Yes, I was blocked. So I'm going to try again, and this time I'll say you approve."

The stodgy Slogger at school had become a missionary in his retirement, spreading the word of Jesus by giving out *New Testaments* to the heathen younger generation in local schools.

"But it's difficult," I said. "Schools have a tight curriculum these days, there isn't a lot of time for projects that hold things up."

But he was not having it.

"I'm going to try again," he said, as if inspired by the Lord.

I said I had to go and tried to head him off but he was still talking. I extricated myself and headed for the exit, went out into the light rain and walked to where Pippa would be waiting in her car.

I had heard the swansong of a Head who was leaving and had sung his operatic farewell to past pupils. I had advised Pink's grandson to listen to his soul on his ambition to become an opera singer, and I had been tackled by his grandpa, a blocked evangelist who was determined to inflict his philanthropic altruism on our curriculum. And underneath it all was a strange reconciliation as the school moved from an old Head to a new Head, an evangelist who might bring a new, hitherto blocked, evangelist's agenda.

Somewhere there was a symmetry that to me, then, in falling rain, suggested opposites – or contrasts – held in balance within an underlying harmony.

Barnstormers in a Churchyard

Our car pulled up outside St James's churchyard, which was the other side of a hedge. Raymond was greeting Jack in front of the church barn on the other side of the road, and seeing they were open-necked and tieless I immediately took off my tie and hid it under a cushion on

321

the back seat. I got out, holding a pot containing flowering plants, and greeted them while Pippa parked nearer to the hedge.

Jack was wearing an orange shirt. He was more lined than when I last saw him, from the cares of moving. His wife, also lined, stood beside him and greeted Pippa. He told me he had rung Rupert, who had had a second mini-stroke and was not coming to this combined family gathering for his eightieth and Florence's seventieth birthday.

"I rang him this morning," Jack said. "He was feeling guilty at not being here. He's all right, he's been to church. He's not as bad as he's let on. He's winding us up. He lives alone and I think he welcomes the attention."

"But once he'd said he'd stop his injections I had to tell Henry," I said. "If he'd done it last week and we were now at his funeral, I'd have thought: 'I knew and did nothing.'"

"I understand," Jack said, "but he has down times and up times, and I reckon you caught him in a down."

As the two ladies joined us, I said, "But let's get one thing straight. There are pre-war (pre-World-War-Two) babies like me, wartime babies like Rupert and Rex" (neither of whom would be coming) "and post-war babies like you and Florence. And being a pre-war baby I coaxed Rupert through the bombing."

Jack laughed out loud and said, "I love it."

Raymond was now standing inside the doorway of the barn. Clutching the pot containing planted flowers I approached him. I put the flowers on the floor and drew his attention to them. "They're for you and Florence," I said.

I went past the kitchen through to the inside of the painted brick barn. There were two long tables with a chequered tablecloth laid for lunch. A dozen people were standing talking near a table with plates. I shook hands with Archie from Kosovo, and then I saw Florence.

"Philip," she cried out as I hugged her, and standing back, "you look just the same as three years ago, you haven't changed, you've still got a thatch of hair. Emma isn't coming," she said, "she's got Covid, tested positive this morning."

Archie stepped forward and said, "She's on my tablet, say 'Hello'."

And I saw Emma, my god-daughter, lying in bed in spectacles, waving at me, and I said I was sorry to have heard the news that she couldn't be with us, and hoped she had Covid mildly.

Emma's husband Theo came up and shook my hand. "I had it two weeks ago and last week," he said. "I had a headache and found it clouds the head. She's got the same."

I hoped we would not catch Covid from his Covidy family: the children he had brought.

Sir Frank came and asked me how I was. He had been a civil servant who advised the Archbishop of Canterbury and had then become Parliamentary Commissioner for Standards. I said to him, resuming where we'd left off last time I saw him, "Johnson's compared Ukraine's break from Russia to the UK's Brexit, but Ukraine's applied to join the EU, not leave it, and the EU isn't a tyranny that's bombing civilians."

"I agree," he said, "the analogy was bad, inept."

"And you could have been asked to write Sue Gray's report if you were still doing what you were doing. What would you do about it, if the Met took it over and then a war broke out? Would you urge that it was made public quickly, or would you let everyone be slow as there's a war on?"

He smiled and said, "She's got little choice now the Met have got it. They will have to complete their investigations before it sees the light of day." Then his wife lurked and he recounted how they had driven down from the north in Fern's [his sister-in-law's] new Mercedes as she was trying it out, and they had had a comfortable ride.

Suddenly Raymond tinkled a glass for silence and welcomed us. He said it had been Jack's wife Alison's birthday last week, and we all sang "Happy Birthday" while she squirmed and blushed and looked bashful. We were asked to go to the tables and sit where we liked, and then come up to be served food.

Frank and I sat opposite each other, and I opened a bottle of sparkling water. We went up and I chose lasagne, broccoli and beans, and he had curry and rice. We returned to our table. Jack was sitting on one side of me and Alison on the other. Pippa sat next to Jack, opposite Archie. Florence came and sat between Archie and Frank, and then left to organise.

As we ate Frank asked me about my trip to Russia. And with the Ukraine war more than three weeks old, I narrated how I had addressed a roomful of people in Moscow two miles from the Kremlin, and how there had been military in the audience and how an Admiral and Vice-Admiral had come on stage at the end and raised my arms in a victory salute. I said, "I'm holding hands with a Russian Admiral and Vice-Admiral on the internet." He laughed.

I was giving a performance and I told him how I was asked to sign a book for Putin and met three of his advisers, and how I was supposed to make a return visit to meet him. I said, "Einstein should have sat with Hitler and said, 'Don't invade Poland after Czechoslovakia.' And I should really go back and say now, 'Don't invade Poland after Ukraine.'" He was attentive and asked me many questions. I gave a performance as I ate.

But then all the other members of the family were performing. Jack told me about his move to his high-rise flat overlooking the Thames. He showed me a picture on his phone. Archie was performing on what he had been doing in Kosovo. Frank was performing on his view of Parliament. He said at one point, "Johnson seems to have no judgement." Archie had already given a performance of Emma lying in bed waving live on his tablet. And Florence was performing as hostess on her 70th birthday. We were all performing in a barn. We were barnstormers, like the original barnstormers who gave theatrical performances in rural districts, often in barns.

After pudding (Swiss roll, cheesecake and cream) Raymond asked us to go outside to the churchyard for a photo. I found myself walking with Jack, who, being an organist, headed into the 11th- or 12th-century church of St James. It had a crenellated 15th-century tower. I went with him. I said, performing, "They're getting us used to where some of us are going to spend the next few hundred years," and Jack smiled.

Jack found the organ, which was free-standing, and rolled back the lid and identified the make. Performing, he raised his hand to play a few bars – but then his wife Alison was standing by the door and beckoning, saying, "They're waiting."

We walked between the waist-high leaning tombstones to where the group was standing. Archie was stooping over a camera on a tripod, making adjustments to the timer. Florence and the children were sitting on a garden bench. The adults were standing in a semicircle behind them. Jack and I joined at the back. Archie bossily said that everyone should turn their left shoulder towards the camera to squash everyone into the picture. I said to Theo, who had moved to stand next to me and was now my neighbour, performing, "I'm giving you my shoulder, not a cold shoulder," and everyone smiled.

"Smile," Archie called. "One-two-three...."

He ran, clutching his pockets, and joined the end of the semicircle just before the camera flashed.

He returned to the camera and looked. "One more."

Again he clicked and ran to the semicircle, performing. Again he returned to the camera and looked and said, "That's fine, that's all."

We broke up and I wandered among the graves and leaning slabs. Many over more than a thousand years had come to this church and performed, and some of them lay under the ground near where I stood, their performances done, at rest. The reclusive Rupert and Rex had opted out and elected not to attend, finding it hard to cope with the after-effects of a mini-stroke and Parkinson's disease, but the older members of the rest of the family had barnstormed in and played their part as I would shortly, when I called on all to raise their champagne glasses and toast Florence, and had just been seen within the context of their performances: tombstones and graves. Florence and Raymond would certainly be buried here as they were local church-goers.

One day we would all lie in a churchyard or a cemetery or be burned at a crematorium, and our bodies would turn to dust or ashes while our souls (our deeper core) might survive, and all the barnstorming would be but a memory, and appear as a passing moment, like dandelion fluff blown on a wind.

An In-Breath and Sandy Windows

"The windows are sandy," said Katie, our cleaner, as she dusted round my room in March. "It reminds me of my aunt. She died recently. I was there. I'd seen her a week before, she knew she was ill because she was told she'd have palliative care, and she knew that meant end-of-life. She said, 'I don't want to know what I've got, I know I'll be at my daughter's wedding in August.' We knew she had lung cancer, but we didn't tell her. And she won't be at her daughter's wedding in August.

"I was with her when she died. She was in her seventies, and she was in a kind of coma. Her colour changed, she went a kind of grey. She breathed in as if she was catching her breath, and that was it, she never breathed out. I knew she'd gone. An in-breath, and no out-breath.

"I attended her funeral last Thursday. It was the day that muddy, sandy rain came down and covered all the cars and windows on one side of her house with Saharan sand. I was behind her coffin in the sandy rain. Yes, your sandy windows remind me of my aunt."

She paused and shook her head. Then she picked up her hoover and began hoovering as though she had put her aunt out of her mind.

Chest Pain and Pericarditis
(Or: Fluid on the Heart Sac)

When I undressed for bed that Tuesday evening I was shocked to see I had red swollen ankles. I had a wretched night. Around midnight I had a pain at the bottom of my throat. As I lay on my back it was very central, and I found it hard to breathe. Eventually I got off to sleep for just an hour, woke and went to the loo. I walked about to try and get rid of what was on my chest. I slept for another hour and again woke and again got up and went to the loo and walked about. I slept for a third time and again got up after an hour and walked about, tried to walk if off by going to the loo.

Now I gave up trying to sleep. I crept downstairs and took an anti-acid-reflux tablet and a Nurofen between swigs of water.

I returned to my bed and lay in the dark. The pain was still there, but had eased slightly. I wondered if I was having a heart attack. I remembered that I was having a Covid booster jab at 9.30am. I decided to get up, and I went through to my office. I sat at my desk, tilting slightly forward, and the pain eased.

Just after 5.45am I did a Covid test. One line appeared by the C. I waited until 6.15am and decided I did not have Covid. I again wondered if I had had an acid reflux, if stomach acid had splashed up to my oesophagus. My temperature was 37.8C.

I went outside in the half-light and sat on my balcony in the cool air. I returned indoors and took my temperature again: 37.5C. In an hour's time my temperature dropped to 37.0C. I wondered if my pain-racked body could cope with more Covid antibodies from my coming jab.

I crept downstairs and had breakfast. My chest was hurting again. My at-rest pulse was 101 instead of 77 the previous day.

I forced myself to drive to Mayor's Pharmacy. I parked in a car park near Woodford Station. I reported to the pharmacy and was told to sit on one of the chairs on the pavement outside. I was called in and asked questions and given my jab.

I felt dreadful all morning. It hurt to lie down, so I sat bolt upright, tilting slightly forwards, and watched Prime Minister's Questions and then the Chancellor's Spring Statement, which I dozed through. I lunched with difficulty and took a Nurofen.

I kept going until the next Saturday, but I was not right. I was tired every day. That Saturday I found a large wasp crawling on the corridor carpet and, thinking it might be a queen, scooped it into a mug and took it outside, and as I tried to scoop a hole in the hard mud for it I lost my balance and fell on my hands and knees. The mug flew through the air and I had mud on my trousers and shoes.

I was shaken. I washed my shoes. No harm had been done, but my fall set me thinking. I went upstairs to my office and sat at my computer and put in symptoms: unsteady on feet, loss of balance. "Stroke" came up. I put in red swollen legs, which I had. "Embolism" and "clot" came up. Then I recalled how I could not lie down but had to sit upright. I put that in, and "pericarditis" came up: "pain in the chest at the bottom of the lungs", "painful to lie down", and significantly "3lb put on in a day". (I was 12st 9lb before the wretched night, and was 12st 13lb the next day.) Also came up: "water retention" (hence my hourly visits to the loo), "red-orange urine" (blood in my urine), "better sitting slightly forward", "swelling in ankles", "shortness of breath".

So I had pericarditis and perhaps also heart-valve disease, which had similar symptoms. I emailed my London GP, Dr Erdmann, the next day. He replied that I should go to A&E urgently as I might have deep-vein thrombosis and a pulmonary embolism: a blood clot in my lung.

Pippa drove me straight to Princess Alexandra Hospital, Harlow. I was there by 2pm. There were 170 patients, and it was three-and-a-half hours' waiting for triage and eight-hours' waiting to see a doctor. But when the receptionist read Dr Erdmann's email, which I showed her, I was seen immediately. I had an electrocardiogram (ECG) and was sent to the Same Day Emergency Centre.

I was there for seven hours. I had a blood test and my D-dimer was high. I was given medication and told to return two days later for a CT (computed tomography) scan. When I left the waiting area for the hospital's inner corridors, I was struck by the dreadful scenes: handicapped elderly people were parked in wheelchairs, and one side of the corridors was filled with emergency beds and patients who were gasping for breath and looked at death's door.

Two days later I returned to radiology there. I was injected with a dye before 10am. It dyed my blood so a blockage where blood could not flow might be seen. The dye was pumped into my cannula. I lay on a 'table' and was moved into a huge chamber. An automated voice told me, "Breathe in and hold your breath." And later, "Breathe." When it was over I sat outside the chamber for 15 minutes and then walked to Costa's and had cappuccino and millionaire's shortbread, and drank two bottles of sparkling water to begin getting rid of the dye.

I returned to the Same Day Emergency Centre and was called by a nurse. I had another blood test, and my blood pressure taken and another ECG. I returned to the waiting area and waited.

Eventually I was called by the doctor. She said, "There's no evidence of a blood clot, but something is going on because the D-dimer is high. You have fluid in the sac round your heart. You have pericarditis."

That was what I had diagnosed myself on my computer, I said.

She was amazed. "That's a really hard diagnosis to make. You are very clever."

She put me on Ibuprofen three times a day for pain relief, and Colchicine 500mg, one a day for three months and perhaps for a longer time. I waited for the results of yet another blood test, walked to the Harlow Pharmacy to collect my Colchicine and was picked up by Pippa at the nearby roundabout. I thought: 'I have pericarditis. Somehow I must co-exist with it. Behind all conflicts is harmony.'

A Fall and a Puzzle Ring

When I got back I found a message on my answerphone. I had an echo test booked in two days' time, and needed to report for a review before it.

At 10.15am the next day, back at Princess Alexandra Hospital, Harlow, I was given a blood test and had my pulse taken. The nurse said, "Your heart is high, no pains?" Then I had an ECG. Then I had to wait until 2pm to see a doctor. I went to Costa's and sat over a medium cappuccino.

I had my echo test. An Asian lady wiped my chest with gel and dabbed with her probe and examined my chest on her ultrasound screen. She said, "You still have fluid round your heart." She did not know if it was moderate.

I returned to the waiting area. I took my own pulse on my pulsometer. It was 121 at rest and should have been around 70.

At 3.40pm I was called in to sit with the Asian doctor and the consultant. The doctor said, "You have swollen lymph nodes and inflammation – and infection and fluid. We are referring you to cardiology to see if the fluid in the sac round your heart should be drained. It's moderate. You have leaking heart valves."

Eventually I returned to the receptionist who said, "The doctor has said you must be booked in for Monday, 11am." Pippa collected me at 5.40pm.

On the following Monday I was woken at 3.30am with chest pain, under my left arm and in my left side. I knew the irritated layers of my pericardium sac were rubbing against each other, and that I should get up and sit forward, which I did. By now the pain had spread to my left shoulder and nearly up to the left side of my neck. I told myself it was not a heart attack and not to call an ambulance. I walked through to my office. Online I read that cardiac tamponade, the condition of fluid on the heart, could make me faint. I dressed and crept downstairs and had early breakfast after only just over four hours' sleep.

I went back to the Hospital and told them about my pain. I was shown to a bed and told to lie down and wait for a cardiology doctor. I lay for four hours as cardiology was understaffed. I did some work I had brought with me.

At 3.15pm I was shown to the same consulting-room I was in the previous Friday and saw the same doctor and consultant. The doctor said of my echo test, "We will monitor your fluid, not drain it as that is too risky. Our strategy is to decrease the inflammation and therefore the fluid. You have had a virus." I had asked if I could go to Cornwall as planned. "You can go to Cornwall but you must come back in 16 days' time for a CRP (C-reactive protein) test and you must be seen sooner if you have fever, breathing defects and swollen ankles. There is no sign of lung cancer, just a viral infection that caused the pericarditis."

I went to Cornwall the next day. Pippa had bought a foldable wedge so I could sleep at a 45-degree angle (slightly forward) and escape pain from the fluid in my sac squashing my heart. The break seemed to be doing me good: I had my bedroom window open and the fresh sea air filled my room and my lungs as the sea crashed ashore thirty feet below.

Three days later, at midday, my heart problem crept up on me, first into my left shoulder. I lay on my bed and on the wedge, and the angle eased the pain round my heart. The pain round my heart lasted until I lay down in bed around 11pm.

That night I woke at 3.30am. There was faint light in the streetlamp outside shining through a gap in my curtains, and I did not put the bedroom light on. I got up to go to the loo, and, still half-asleep, began walking, unaware that my right toe was caught in the side of the counterpane, my bedspread that normally reached the floor. I could not go anywhere except fall. I felt myself falling in the half-light and put out my left elbow and fell on it with a crash, in what now seemed the dark. I did not hit my head on the wardrobe or the knobs on its adjoining drawers, or a nearby stool, but even so when, shaken, I got to my feet and put on the bedside light I had a bloody right knee and a very bloody right toe. I managed to stick a plaster on my toe and staunch the wound.

The fall shook up my left shoulder which was now clear of pain. I just had a sore knee and toe. I did not need my wedge now, and there was no pain in my heart now.

The next morning I was not fully well but battled on. I read the papers and then made adjustments to my wedge. I worked at my desk overlooking the sea in my bedroom-study, and about 4.30pm I made tea (a scone, jam, cream and chocolate Swiss roll). I took Pippa's through to her, and when I finished my tea in the sitting-room near her I went outside and sat on the bench with a view of the harbour and sea in warmish sun, although I felt cold.

I dozed. After about 20 minutes, I reckon, in my sleep I heard my deep source, my deep voice, say, "You've lost your ring."

I woke with a start and looked at the ring finger on my left hand. My puzzle ring (four rings slotting together into one ring) had gone. It was missing.

I looked around and below the bench but there was no trace of it. I went indoors and climbed upstairs and looked everywhere in my bedroom-study: in, round and under the bed, on the carpet, under the wardrobe, in case it had flown off during my fall. I looked at the wedge and behind the bed. I looked on the stairs and in the sitting-room, and in the kitchen, and returned outside. There was no sign of it. I reflected that I had been unwell for two or three days, and it could have been missing for two or three days, for all I could recall.

At 5.45pm I took my at-rest pulse: 111, which was high. I was labouring. I sat at my desk upstairs and looked out of my window across the sea and thought. My fall in the dark somehow encapsulated my fall from good health, and it seemed to have stripped me of my puzzle ring, whose four slotted-together rings symbolised many things: Pippa, me, Simon and Paul; my three children, including Susan, and me; my four main properties, two houses and two businesses; and my two computers, me and my Muse, my inspiration for my works.

My fall from good health was in danger of ending my immediate family and domestic life, my main assets and my working life. I needed to get to the bottom of what was really causing my heart to behave so erratically.

A Wind-Surfer and a Loud Laugher

Pippa drove me to the Nare Hotel in Cornwall, for Sunday lunch. We went down narrow lanes with high hedges and passed occasional pheasants. We checked in at reception and were shown to window-seats in a large lounge overlooking the sea, and ordered sparkling water.

The sea was choppy in wind that was shaking the clumps of flowers near our window, and I could see a large grey sail billowing like a kite or a parachute and then diving, and a wind-surfer came into view. He was a tiny figure on an otherwise deserted sea in the bay against the grey sky, and he was doing his best to travel in a straight line on his sailboard, tugging on the strings of the sail to catch the wind and move in his intended direction.

We ate our nibbles and our glasses were put on a tray and a waitress led us through into the dining-room. I was in a blue shirt and gold tie and blazer as Pippa had said it was formal. We ordered, and our starter arrived almost immediately. I had smoked salmon and Pippa asparagus and an egg. Outside the wind-surfer was still going backwards and forwards in a straight line, first to the right, then to the left. He disappeared from our view for a while and then reappeared. I saw a red kite hovering at my eye-level near our window. It was incredibly still in the wind, then flapped its wings and dived.

Pippa reminded me that her friend Holly came here with her Indian husband. She said there were good deals for sea-view rooms and they were met at Truro station by the hotel's driver and driven to the hotel and then returned to Truro station when it was time to go home. I recalled how sixty-one years previously Colin Wilson had driven me to Truro station after I had stayed with him, and how I sat on a cold, bleak platform in January, having just missed the train I was aiming to catch.

Our main course arrived: the hotel's speciality, beef, which was carved near our table by an Arab. Most of my helping of beef was raw, and I ate the vegetables and left the fatty very raw parts. At the next table but one an elderly couple were sitting with a younger couple. I was not sure which of the two the parents had brought into the world, but very quickly the young man, in an open-necked shirt, was saying things and pulling faces, and the young lady was filling the room with laughter. To her, everything was funny, perhaps because she was happy. The elderly couple sat in silence without saying anything, and after the tenth loud laugh I thought of Goldsmith's line in 'The Deserted Village', "The loud laugh that spoke the vacant mind".

The pudding trolley came. We had blueberry pavlova with raspberries and strawberries, and still the wind-surfer was fighting with the strings, trying to control the sail in the wind. The sail tugged and dived and then rose, threatening to lift him out of the water. And still there was regular loud laughter from the woman (who had blonde hair on either side of her face) even when they were being served.

I went to the loo on our way back to the lounge. There was a bust of what looked like a Greek god in the entrance. I thought it was Zeus but there was no label, it was just standing near the entrance to the urinals. I peered at Zeus. I asked the doormen outside, but they did not know who the bust was of.

We had coffee in the same window. The wind-surfer was still going backwards and forwards, struggling with the soaring and dipping sail, and I saw the laugher holding her partner's hand, walking outside. He was vaping, and clouds of white vaped smoke hung about them in the garden. She was in platform heels to bring her height up to his height. They reached the steps that led up to the door near our window and he puffed three times in rapid succession, and three enormous clouds of vaped smoke hung round them like a fog. Then they came in and sat at the table behind us, where the parents were already sitting in silence, but now there was no loud laughter, just sitting waiting to be served.

I thought of all-seeing Zeus in the Gents, and of the wind-surfer who was still relentlessly surfing backwards and forwards, trying to control the wind as I tried to harvest the inspiration that flowed from Zeus's world into my books. And I thought of the loud laugher and her partner, perhaps husband, who had paid for all four to have an expensive lunch and was perhaps staying overnight, and of the Epicurean laughter in the moment that is the opposite of a wind-surfer's dedicated direction backwards and forwards – the illusion of progress but in fact ending where he began but having filled his sail with blowing wind and skilfully tacked and veered, as in a poem or a complicated work of art.

I knew I was on the side of the stoical wind-surfer, who ploughed lonely furrows in the field of the incoming waves, sacrificing pleasure in the moment to achievement and a lasting legacy. But in our plague-filled Covidy time I did not begrudge their "Eat, drink and be merry for tomorrow we die" of Omar Khayyam and Epicurean enjoyment, and I hoped they would find happiness together (without distracting dedicated stoics with laughter about nothing very much).

Covid Inflammation and Double Heartbeats

During my last visit to the Hospital the doctor had said, "Good news, your fluid is getting better." I had taken Colchicine for three weeks, and it seemed to be working: "There is hardly any fluid now" was the verdict on my blood test.

However, just over a week later my at-rest pulse was 127, the next day it was 125, and the next day 124, all very high.

I had my six-monthly blood test at Dr Erdmann's in early May. I was also given an ECG. I saw Dr Erdmann in the afternoon. He still thought I had a blood clot and referred me for a CT (computed tomography) scan in a nearby building. No embolism was found, according to the technician when I asked. I then had a leg scan.

Dr Erdmann said, "I think what you've had was caused by your Covid in November. I am referring you to Dr Lennon as he's a Covid specialist, and I'm asking him if you should now go onto blood-thinners."

I saw Dr Lennon two days later, on a Friday. I had to sit outside his door until he opened it. He was a balding, youngish consultant in an open-necked white shirt and no jacket, with considerable charm. We had a general chat and discovered we had a mutual friend.

I asked him what was really causing my high at-rest pulse and my fluid.

Without hesitation he replied, "Covid. The majority throw it off after taking Colchicine, a minority find it comes back when the medication is stopped. You may be in the majority as you are well, but you may need to go on taking Colchicine. Your arrhythmia and tachycardia may be bad because of Covid."

He said I would have an ECG before I left, and that I would be fitted with a monitor for 24 hours and that I should post it back on Monday. He said I should have an MRI (magnetic resonance imaging) and an auto-immune investigation at the Royal Brompton Hospital.

I had the monitor fitted. It hung round my neck under my shirt for the rest of the day and that night, with three electrodes on wires attached to my chest.

I went to the Royal Brompton Hospital eleven days later. I had a blood test and then walked round to the new diagnostic centre behind it. I was taken for my MRI immediately as the previous patient had not turned up. I was put in a huge machine for more than 45 minutes. I lay back and amid the clankings a young man gave me instructions: "Stop breathing" and then "Breathe". He must have said those words a hundred times before my procedure was finished. I did not know that the clankings were investigating two problems at the same time: my auto-immune system and my heart muscle.

Three days later I returned to Dr Lennon. He was 40 minutes late in seeing me, but it was worth the wait. He said, "You still have inflammation in your pericardium, the sac round your heart, *and* on your heart muscle. You have five mills of fluid – 25 to 30 mills is concerning. You have Covid-19-induced perimyocarditis, the 'peri' means your pericardium or sac round your heart is inflamed, the 'myo' means your heart muscle is inflamed. Both your pericardium *and* your heart muscle are inflamed, and the heart muscle causes your heart to beat, so that must be taken seriously. You have been infected by the Covid-19 virus, you have the infection mildly. It will be another three weeks before the blood test you had will be back. You'll need to see me in six weeks' time, and then after three months. Your recovery will continue until the autumn. You haven't been to the gym since early March, and you should not go until September at the earliest."

I was all right during most of the next six weeks. However, in the morning of 22 June my at-rest pulse was 114, and two days later it was 120; both were high. I emailed Dr Lennon, who rang me two days before my appointment and said, "I'm afraid the new tachycardia is making you ill." He asked if I would go up to London and have a blood test and ECG, and have a monitor fitted, which I did.

I was back in time to attend a prize-giving inside a marquee. I had a chair by a side wall of the marquee. Some staff were sitting on chairs outside. There was a cool breeze, and I was relaxed. In my mind I had a low heart rate for the monitor I was wearing under my white shirt, tie and jacket.

The next day I handed my monitor over to Dr Lennon's reception by arrangement just after lunch. I asked the receptionist to forward the results to Dr Lennon in time for my appointment, and then sat in a waiting area and worked (helping myself to two cappuccinos and four biscuits), and then took a lift up to the first floor and sat outside Dr Lennon's door. That day the practice was understaffed and no one forwarded the results of the monitor.

When he saw me Dr Lennon said, "Your D-dimer is low and your auto-immune system is normal, your ECG is normal. There are two possible phenomena and diagnoses. Depending on the results you will either be on a blood-thinner or on a beta-blocker."

The next day Dr Lennon rang me before lunch. He said, "You have three readings. The first is not concerning. The second is that you have higher heartbeats during the day. The Holter monitor showed you reached 149. You averaged 102 (instead of 72 last time). The third reading is that you have had three episodes of arrhythmia. I am putting you on bisoprolol fumarate, a beta-blocker for heart conditions, for three to six months. Continue with the Colchicine until the next review in September."

And so I had got there at last. Covid had rampaged around my heart and left me with: fluid in the sac round my heart that caused me pain; an infected and inflamed heart muscle, arrhythmia; and high heartbeats.

Thinking back to my sitting in the marquee, wearing the monitor, it seemed I had had a heart rate of 149 while I watched and applauded at the prize-giving, double my heart's normal rate. My heart was pounding just to sit still, and if it had not been coped with I might have eventually died from an overactive and exhausted heart. I was very grateful to Dr Lennon for getting to the bottom of what had been plaguing me since I caught the modern plague.

Garage Doors and a Mobility Scooter

"I've had a phone call from Holly," Pippa said as she lay back, resting her arm. "It's not good. She drove her Volvo into her front garden and her foot slipped on the pedal and she drove it into the garage doors. Both collapsed onto her husband Raja's car, which he's had for twenty years. His car came off worse than hers, her Volvo is like a tank. His car is a write-off, and he'll have to get another one, a smaller one because he's eighty-three. There will have to be two new garage doors. And she wasn't really confident driving before, she's seventy-nine, but she's giving up driving now. She's going to have a mobility scooter to get to the shops at the end of her road. It's a seminal moment, like Miss Jacobs going into the railings on Roding Road at eighty-six and never driving again. It's shaken her up. She's mortified by all that's happened and has gone from coming here last week to not driving any more. She won't be able to come here on a mobility scooter, I'll have to go to her place to see her."

"I'm sorry," I said, and I thought of her last visit a week or so previously. "How's the patient?" I had asked pleasantly of Pippa, who had just come out of hospital having had a procedure on her arm. "Good," Holly had said, "the patient is doing well." Now she was a patient herself, recovering from the shock of demolishing two garage doors and her husband's car, and resolved never to drive her armoured car again. She was now immobile out of choice and only able to go out on a mobility scooter. So old age creeps up on us and suddenly takes us over.

An Adder and a Xylophone

The pool man came to replace the pump and found an adder outside the door. It hissed at him. I was called and, thinking that Orpheus would have played his flute and charmed the snake, walked to the field and beckoned Arnold, who was on the ride-on mower. He pulled up and said he'd get a bag. He set off at a brisk pace. By the time I had walked to the pool door Arnold was leaving with the snake in his bag. He was holding a grabber which had been very effective.

"It's not happy," he said. "It's been attacked and wounded on the back of its head. It's aggressive. The pool man said it's been living in the drain in front of the door. It came up with his backwash."

It must have hurt its head as it came up through the grating.

I looked. It was brown with black V markings, a black zigzag stripe on its back, definitely a male adder.

Arnold headed for the gate to the forest, where he was going to release the snake into the wild.

That afternoon I had to attend a prize-giving. The Head had tested positive for Covid the previous evening, and the Deputy was deputising. Pippa and I parked and were greeted by the Bursar, who led us from our car to a marquee in the tennis-court at the back. The children and the parents were drifting in. We sat on our labelled seats at the front and waited as the marquee filled up.

We were asked to stand for the platform party: Simon, the guest speaker (a County Councillor) and the Deputy Head. Simon spoke at the lectern. And then there was the first event: xylophones and glockenspiels.

Several girls sat at xylophones on the floor. The teacher, Mrs. Maybank, leapt up and held up the proceedings by repositioning each xylophone. Then they began playing.

The girls hit the tuned wooden bars with their wooden-headed mallets and played 'Pachelbel's Canon'. Not all girls knew what to do, and some blows on the wooden bars were missed.

Mrs. Maybank conducted with exaggeratedly closed eyes and exaggerated gestures. They reached the end and there was applause. The girls then had to stack the xylophones against the wall to clear the floor space. One xylophone was lurching from the top of the pile.

"It's going to fall," I whispered to Pippa. "Shall I get up and rearrange it?"

"No," she said.

I watched as the girls finished their stacking. Then there was a crash. The xylophone wrongly stacked had fallen and most of the tuned bars had scattered on the floor.

Mrs. Maybank hurried forward, looking flustered. She bent and swept all the bars into a pile with her right hand and re-stacked the pile of xylophones.

It was like an adder, it had hissed and not co-operated with humans and Mrs. Maybank had piled it out of the way against a wall. The xylophone looked very damaged, if not broken. It had a score down its neck.

The prize-giving continued with girls coming forward and lining up to sing 'Summer Time'. I thought of the adder which had come up from a drain and would not allow the pool man past it, and I thought of the xylophone that had not been spotted (except by me) and had collapsed and fallen to pieces and had to be moved, and Mrs. Maybank's striding presence to fiddle about with it and delay the proceedings and I saw her as a hissing adder that had been wounded by the collapse of the xylophone, and the parallel came back to haunt me when it was announced that she was leaving the school, and would be out in the forest on her own.

A Grasshopper and a Hostess

Arnold came up to my balcony with the hose to water the plants. I came out to talk to him, and saw a grasshopper on the stones.

"How did that get there?" I asked. "Look, it's a grasshopper. I haven't seen one for years."

Either it had been brought up by a bird and dropped, or it was on Arnold's boot as he climbed the winding staircase.

Arnold carefully scooped it up and took it down to the lawn beside the rose-bed and released it. I saw it jump as high as one of the roses and was back as a boy on the Stubbles, walking amidst screeching purple-and-green grasshoppers that occupied much of the grass on the Stubbles and occasionally jumped in front of me as I walked past the copse to the forest at the end. I was pleased we now had a grasshopper, the only one I had seen for perhaps 50 years.

That evening we went to Tom, Dick and Harry's for Bernard's 21st dinner. I parked and we walked for five minutes to get to the restaurant. It was heaving, there were about a hundred thirtyish women and men in shorts sitting at the roadside tables, eating and talking, and also inside. We found most of the family there at a long central table with two silver balloons shaped into a 2 and a 1, and Bernard sitting opposite Simon, his father. I sat opposite Angela, Bernard's mother, and Chris and Monica who had come down from the North for the occasion. There were three stag heads with antlers on the wall, two labelled Tom and Dick and one labelled &c.

Everyone was talking very loudly, some were standing talking to some who were sitting, and it was hard to hear what those on the other side of our table were saying. Then a blonde thirtyish woman in a summer frock was standing over Bernard and talking to him through a microphone she was holding.

"It's your birthday," she said, welcoming us as a hostess.

The background chatter was so loud it was hard to hear the words on her loudspeaker system. Bernard answered her questions and she moved to another table and engaged the ladies round it in welcoming conversation.

Our drinks were delivered and we ordered. I ordered croquettes and lobster by pointing to them on the menu as the waiter could not hear our voices.

And now, having been to every table, the hostess – she had started with ours – was at the door end with a sound system that began playing music and she started singing. The music stopped and she sang on, almost inaudibly, but she could just be heard above the excited chatter. Those on one or two tables sang along with her, but most carried on shouting to each other above the conversational din.

The place was rocking, everyone was animated and loving the moment. It was clearly the place to be. At eighty-three, I was from a different era but observed the animation with interest. And still she sang, seamlessly passing from song to song without a break like a grasshopper sawing in a summer glade – like the grasshoppers I heard as a boy just after the war when I ran on the Stubbles and looked for butterflies.

I had seen a grasshopper that morning, my childhood was back within reach, and the hostess was singing to us like one of my childhood grasshoppers which until that morning had been mere memories. The restaurant was heaving, the grasshopper was singing and I was content for Bernard who was celebrating his 21st among his family, and everything was right with the world.

A Wasp Man and Stings

We had two more wasps' nests, one outside the dining-room, near where we sat at a round table in the evening sun, and one above a Velux window in my study. Wasps in both areas could threaten us if we sat in the open air.

Wasps were dancing in two places round our house, brought out by the warm weather. I picked up the phone.

The wasp man came in a peaked cap and shorts. He put on his gear, and under a helmet and net, puffed powder into the brick and wood at the top of the dining-room corner, under tiles near where wasps danced. Then he climbed his ladder near his van at the front and edged along between a low wall and the sloping roof outside my study and puffed powder under lead flashing where wasps danced. His cull was over in five minutes.

"Don't go out at the back for at least two hours," he said. "They'll still be dancing around until then. When the powder goes in, the wasps send out a distress call and they all come back but won't go in as they know there's a problem. There may be twelve or fourteen queens. They'll stay for a while and then go. But they've nowhere to go, so they'll die.

"People say it's cruel, but there have to be culls, that's how I see it. Otherwise one animal or insect will dominate, and there won't be a balance. Did you hear them building their nests? Tap, tap, tap."

One of my sons and a grandson had both heard tapping a few weeks back, but we had not associated it with wasps' nests.

"That'll be sixty pounds. It's fifty for the first nest and ten for each subsequent nest. If it's a cheque I'll have to charge VAT."

As I went upstairs to find him £60 in notes I caught sight of bees in potted lavender, oblivious of what the wasps had been going through, and I was suddenly in a world where wasps and bees send out an alarm pheromone, small molecules that travel through the air and send other wasps into a defensive stinging frenzy. It was amazing that a pheromone, a mixture of slightly volatile chemical compounds, disperses quickly to alert other wasps or bees in the colony that danger is near. I was in a world where you only sting when you are threatened, and you transmit your being threatened to your community, which responded with pheromone-activated stings.

These creatures had intricate systems, and should be guarded rather than attacked. They were intricate creatures and I felt ashamed at having culled the two nests – for fear of being stung. Wasps and bees sent out a pheromone when threatened, and when threatened I had called in the wasp man, and had alerted him that there was a threat. They had a power of showing distress that humans did not have. I could not send out a distress call and bring fellow humans back from a mile or two away.

We were all intricate creatures, and we all reacted swiftly to feeling threatened, and I resolved that from now on I would be more tolerant of all creatures, which had every right to live regardless of their sting.

Fine Dining and an Uninterested Pair

For Pippa's 72nd birthday we were driven to the Berkeley Hotel in London's Knightsbridge. It was the hottest day of the year, with the temperature on the verge of 40 Centigrade, and from our air-cooled car we saw the smoke of the wildfire at Wennington on the skyline, three tree-like plumes of brown smoke on the horizon.

Pippa, Simon and I had a glass of champagne in the bar. At 6.45 we went through to the Marcus Restaurant (named after its head chef Marcus Wareing), and Paul joined us, having come on a slow tube that had been driven cautiously in case rails had buckled in the heat. We sat as a four, and re-bonded as a family.

Simon had made the booking, and at his insistence we opted for the seven-course menu. The courses came at regular intervals, and the contents of each course were described by a French waiter. Each course was fine dining and tiny, sometimes just three mouthfuls. We had another bottle of champagne and some red wine, and the conversation flowed and there were family reminiscences and mirth, and re-bonding.

Occasionally I looked to the table on my left. A young man sat with a white face and smarmed-down black hair. His face was so white I wondered if he had painted it, clown-like, and his hair was so smarmed-down I wondered if he had used Brylcreem. He had a slightly hooked nose and he looked like Dracula. Beside him was a possibly half-Chinese girl with heavily-made-up eyes and longish black hair. Once when I looked up at them he was trying to feed the girl with a long spoon, but she turned her head away. Next time I looked up they were sitting in silence with their eyes down, and next time they were studying their phones.

I asked Simon for his view.

"It's a new generation," he said. "The phone has replaced conversation. That's why we've banned phones at the table for Al and Minnie."

Then I saw a waitress stand before their table and recite a description of a new course.

'Dracula' looked down into his lap and made no eye contact with the waitress, and the girl similarly ignored her. The waitress turned and returned to her duties. The pair sat on, utterly detached from what had been placed in front of them, and from each other.

I wondered if they were on drugs. Perhaps the long spoon 'Dracula' had attempted to feed the girl with contained a drug? And now they were both in a drug dream in a restaurant costing £100–£200 a head depending on what menu was chosen? I wondered if they were staying at the Berkeley Hotel, or whether (like us) they were there for the restaurant and the fine dining. In either event if they were not both on recreational drugs it was baffling that they should be eating so expensively and yet be such an uninterested pair.

A Roman Sacrifice and Tapestry Rugs

We berthed at Waterford and showed our ship's identity card at the gangplank and walked to our coach. We were then driven through Waterford and out through green fields to the originally 12th-century

Kilkenny Castle, which had been owned by the Butler family for almost 600 years. We went through the withdrawal room and dining-room to the entrance hall and up the grand staircase to the tapestry room, which had thick 12th-century walls.

I froze for there were two large tapestries on the wall showing figures in the style of Rubens. The printed explanations on stands showed they were linked and told a story in Livy's *Ab Urbe Condita* (c.27–25BC) about the consul Publius Decius Mus, who, along with his fellow consul Manlius, had a dream that the invading Latins would be defeated if a Roman consul sacrificed himself in battle against the Latins in 340BC. First Decius Mus is shown holding a statue of Mars, who in turn holds a statue of Victory. In the other tapestry Decius Mus's body is lying in a couch, dead, with severed heads on spears and prisoners being dragged by Roman soldiers to look at Decius Mus's corpse.

We went on through to the library and the drawing-room and along the corridor past the nursery and through the bedrooms and down the Moorish staircase to the picture gallery, and there I saw three more tapestries in the same series, on the same theme. In one, Decius Mus has ordered his lectors to go to Manlius and inform him of his planned sacrifice of himself. In another Decius Mus stands before the high priest Marcus Valerius and with bowed head recites a prayer (*devotio*). In the last one, Decius Mus is shown being speared through his neck and falling backwards from his plunging horse, as another horseman raises a sword to finish him off. Decius looks to Heaven, bearing his pain at his death. The Romans, commanded by Manlius, rallied at his death and won the battle and the war.

I was stunned by all this and wanted to know more. We were driven back to our ship and as I got off our coach I asked our guide what was known about the dating of the five tapestries. She said, "You should speak to Fred." She looked. "He's there, at the entrance to the coach."

I went to the coach and said to the elderly, balding man on the coach steps, while the rest of our coach passengers queued at the gangway to the ship, "I believe you know about the dating of the tapestries of Decius Mus at Kilkenny Castle."

"Oh yes," he said. "They came from Paris and are dated about 1660. I've worked at Kilkenny Castle for forty years, and one day

Hugh Butler, my friend, said, 'Fred, will you go to Paris and bring back some rugs there?' I went and drove them home. There were ten tapestries, they were being used as rugs. I've been into it, they were designed by Rubens. Here's my card. Send me an email and I'll send you a book. There are ten in all, but five are in storage, there's no room to show them."

The gangway seemed to be about to be taken up, and I thanked him, excused myself and hurried up the gangway to the member of the crew who had been clicking on ship ID cards and was packing away, and got back on board in case the gangway was removed for repair work.

Over lunch I reflected on what I had seen and heard, on the nobility of Decius Mus who sacrificed himself to save Rome from invading forces, and on the manner in which Rubens-designed tapestries had been downgraded to be trodden on as rugs. Livy's story of Decius Mus's sacrifice had largely been forgotten, as had Rubens' designs, which had been relegated to be rugs to be walked over.

I reflected sadly that all art faced such a fate, and that one day my books might be torn apart to be used as paper-walks and my stories of noble sacrifice might be forgotten.

Dining Clergy and the True Cross

From our Waterford berth we were driven by coach up to the bridge across the River Suir (pronounced 'Sure') and back down to Reginald's Tower, named after Ragnall Mac Gilla Muire, the Irish-Viking (Hiberno-Norse) ruler of the city who was captured and held prisoner there by the Anglo-Normans led by Richard de Clare in 1170.

We got off the coach at the House of Waterford Crystal and crossed the road and went up steps to the entrance of the Medieval Museum, which incorporated several medieval buildings and part of the city wall within its basement. We were fallen upon by a bald curator who put us into an open platform-lift I operated by pressing and holding a button. It went down a floor and stopped and he was there (having run down stairs) to open the waist-high door and let us out.

He showed us a small tower and then took us into a dimly-lit stone-block building with arches that supported the roof and with slit windows.

"This will blow your mind," he said. "It was built in 1260 from ballast, look at those blocks in that arch. This was near the Bishop's Palace, and this was part of the Deanery. The Dean was number 2 to the Bishop, and it's where the clergy dined. It was their dining-room. Just imagine the tables on this uneven floor. Twenty to thirty clergy dining here. The slits guard against arrows, which are unlikely to find a way through, and they could look out and see what was happening out there. Just imagine, 1260 and it hasn't changed at all since then, and at that far end is the Mayor's wine cellar. James Rice was Mayor eleven times and he bequeathed his wine cellar. It's 1440. I get excited each time I come down."

As we returned I saw a notice calling it 'Choristers' Hall'. So, it was for the choirboys as well as the clergy, a general church officials' dining area.

We went up in the lift to the top floor and walked round a room about the 12th-century port city showing a model of what it looked like, and then went down a floor to the statues assembled to a theme: 'The Art of Devotion'. There were 15th-century cloth-of-gold church vestments and chasubles and I looked at the Great Parchment Book of Waterford which described cases of petty crime and the impact of the plague, and reflected the details of what medieval life was like.

On my way out my attention was caught by a fragment of the True Cross. It was in glass, a silver cross with a Russian-style double footrest, and the caption beneath said it was a piece of the True Cross brought home by the Pope after the capture of the Holy Land during the First Crusade, which began in 1096.

So was it really a fragment of the True Cross, or were we being told it was by an 11th-century Pope? And similarly, was the dining-hall for the Deanery's clergy or was it for choristers, as the labelling said? I was in among the imagination of curators and Popes, and how could I be sure that what they told me was objectively true rather than what they wanted it to be, and how their minds had come to believe it to be?

An Angel's Trumpeting and Framed Photos

Our ship moored in Kinsale Bay a mile and a quarter from the port. We clambered down to a Zodiac at the back of the ship and sat on the side, two of ten clad in waterproofs and life-jackets, and sped until we were beneath Charles Fort, a seventeenth-century star-shaped artillery fort built in the 1670s to guard Kinsale Harbour where the Spanish fleet had moored before the Catholics were defeated in a battle in 1601, and which retreating British anti-Treaty forces burned in 1921.

We landed and took off our life-jackets and waterproofs and were driven by coach through green Irish countryside, many green fields with cows, until we were let out in Cork (which means 'marsh' in Irish). Our guide Anne, an ex-teacher, then took us on a walking-tour of Cork, through the Viking and Anglo-Norman quarters and then the Huguenot quarter.

On the way we reached the Protestant St Fin Barre's Cathedral. It was named after the patron saint of Cork, the first Bishop of Cork, Fionnbarr (meaning 'fair-headed' in Irish). It was on the site of his monastery and a previous 1536 Protestant cathedral, which had been demolished in 1864, and the present stone-turreted Cathedral was rebuilt in 1870. It had a golden angel high up with two long trumpets. The guide explained that during cleaning by students in 1999 the trumpets disappeared and were eventually found in a field and returned. Their disappearance caused consternation as there was a legend that ill would become of Cork if the trumpets disappeared.

Inside we sat in pews in the nave and looked at the elaborate sanctuary ceiling and the stained glass while for a quarter of an hour the pastor gave us a talk about the Cathedral through a microphone that was not working, and no one heard a word of what he said. The angel's loudspeaker-like trumpet's message had fallen into incoherence.

We continued the walk through the English market and along Mutton Lane to St Patrick's Street and crossed St Patrick's Bridge to the Shelbourne Bar, an 1895 pub with yellow walls and green leather bench-seats and old pictures on the walls.

Pippa and I ordered cappuccinos and I sat on a stool facing the wall in a snug, glad of the rest and respite from walking at eighty-three, and became aware of the three old framed photos on the wall to my right and two ahead of me. They all looked like photos taken during the First World War, and I thought I recognised Patrick Pearse and John MacBride, two Irish patriots who were executed after the uprising in Easter 1916, when rebels captured the General Post Office and were suppressed by gunboats the English sent up the River Liffey in Dublin.

During my last visit to Ireland I had taken a taxi to the General Post Office, and the driver then said, "I'm taking you to Kilmainham Gaol to show you what the British did to our patriots." My taxi-driver was an IRA sympathiser. He knew someone at the prison entrance, and I was allowed to go in and see the wall against which James Connolly was shot in a wheelchair, having been injured during the uprising.

I asked the young man who brought our coffee, "Who are the photos of?"

"I have no idea."

So I asked one of the ship's team who were looking after us. She enquired and came back and said, "I've been told it's the family of the great-great-grandfather of the present owner."

I thought it strange that the barman I had asked did not know this, and wondered if they were indeed patriots, and if the woman in the framed photos was Maud Gonne, who had married MacBride and with whom Yeats had been in love. Was I being fobbed off with a family connection so the Shelbourne Bar could not be accused of having IRA connections?

I accepted that my imagination had seen the faces of 'patriots' in the old framed photographs, and put the pictures out of my mind.

We were taken across the road and we waited for our coach to collect us to return us to the Zodiacs. There was a delay and I noticed the Cork Baptist Church had an inscription in stone: "Christ died for the ungodly. *Romans*, V, VI–XI." (Chapter 5, verses 6–11.)

As I waited for the coach I thought of the Protestant angel with silenced trumpets meant to advertise the Protestant religion, and I thought of the patriots who died after the Easter 1916 uprising, sacrificed their lives for Ireland, and who may or may not be shown on the pub wall. And I thought of the martyrs' ungodly violence, and the Baptist rebuke, "Christ died for the ungodly". And everything blended, the history of troubled Ireland shone through. The Protestants' trumpets had been silenced by the Catholics, the British had set Charles Fort on fire as they withdrew, the Irish patriots were violent and ungodly, and now, under the EU, religious division was largely settled and there was co-existence, and a country that had been through an upheaval and independence was now a more harmonious place than it had ever been, with all its opposites in Protestantism and Catholicism now reconciled.

Shaw's Steps and Browsers

We got on the Zodiac in Bantry Bay in County Cork, and once ashore near Bantry House, where Richard White saw Wolfe Tone's ships that had come to unite Ireland and informed the British in 1796, we were driven to Glengarriff. By the sea-front stood Eccles Hotel, 1745, where George Bernard Shaw and other writers once stayed.

From there we took a cabined boat out into the bay in sunshine, past an uninhabited island occupied by a couple of dozen basking or swimming seals and black cormorants. We passed a white-tailed sea eagle's large-twigged nest high in a tree and three moving heads.

We put in at Garinish Island, which is alternatively known as Ilnacullin. It had been developed when it was bought from the London War Office in 1910 by the MP for a Scottish constituency, Annan Bryce, a regular visitor to Glengarriff for some years. His island is now famous for its Italian garden.

We took a path that led to the large walled garden, which was full of flowers of every colour. We walked down and sat on a seat. Pippa was still recovering from her operation, and I left her sitting on her seat and set off for the Italian garden without realising that its "casita" ("small house") was right in front of us across a large lawn. I took a path through woods and rare trees and reached the Casita from the side. It had one room with a marble floor and eight columns on each side.

Here, I had been told by our guide, George Bernard Shaw stayed with the Bryce family in 1923 while he was working on *St Joan*, soon after Eire broke away from the UK. In the guidebook there was a picture of Shaw standing between two pillar bases with sculptured heads of busts, now gone, his white beard prominent.

I walked down steps to a rectangular pool with a small bronze statue in its middle, and on either side were steps up, then a flat rectangle where (on the right) Shaw stood to be photographed, and then more steps and another two bases for statues, since gone. Beyond a stone balcony between two pillars and an arched roof were two distant small mountains. I wandered round getting back into the time of Shaw in 1923, the year Annan Bryce died, and imagined how Bryce built this garden between 1910 and 1923 when there was no telephone to communicate with workers and he may have had to send instructions from London by post. And I thought how Shaw and Bryce would have come to this remote corner of Ireland for privacy, to escape the attention of journalists based in London and Dublin.

"I'll see you in Heaven," Mrs. Bryce is reported to have said to Shaw, to which he is reputed to have replied, "Madam, we are already there."

I walked back by the lawn to where Pippa was sitting and sat with her as two robins hopped near our feet. Then we walked to the café near the quay and we had cappuccinos and carrot cake. It came on to rain, and as we clambered onto the boat to return to Glengarriff the rain became heavy. We got under cover inside the cabin and sat down, but many of our group got wet, and unwilling to sit on the seats in the open back of the boat, stood like strap-hangers in the old London tube as the boat chugged and got up speed to cross the open sea.

At Glengarriff we hurried along the front in rain and got into our coach. The Irish guide spoke to us as we drove back and then said on the outskirts of Bantry, "We're stopping here, there are two stores you can go in and look around, one over there and the other there. You've got half an hour. You can browse and see if there's anything you want. You can leave the coach now."

No one moved.

"Don't you want to go and see?" she asked.

Everyone shook their head. There was no shelter except in the stores, and all suspected the coach company would receive a cut from the stores for any purchase the passengers made.

"Oh," she said, "change of plan." And we returned to the Zodiacs to return to our ship.

Over lunch on the ship I thought of Shaw on the steps 99 years ago jovially comparing his face to the faces of the statues long gone. And I thought of the guide who had treated us as browsers who might make purchases. And had we not browsed events of 1923 to make purchases from the tour company and café – had not seeing the Italian garden become a browsing that had taken our money?

A Turtle and a Harbour-Master

I clambered into a Zodiac with seamen's grips (two hands touching elbows) and sat on the side. An elderly woman came and sat opposite me, then another sat next to me, and finally Turtle, the ship's speaker, sat opposite to balance the weight.

Turtle had written books about Ireland, and he had told us that his father had told his three sons to sit at the lunch table, and he had called out in Latin *"Primus"* ("the first, the eldest"), *"Secundus"* ("the second and younger") and *"Tertius"* ("the third, the youngest"). Turtle had been crawling on all fours, and one of his older brothers had said, "Not *'Tertius'*, *'Turtle'*." And ever since he had been called 'Turtle'. I later met his father when he came to see his son on the ship, and shook hands with him: a 5th Baron descended from the Butler family that ruled Ireland in Tudor times.

We sped through choppy water to the commercial dock in Galway Bay and clambered off and took off our life-jackets and stuffed them in cotton bags and left them in a large zipped hold-all.

Then we all walked into Galway City. Turtle, who was about 40, said he wanted to visit the Spanish arch first, and I said I had already decided to do that first. So four of us walked round and out of the harbour complex – a man in a high-vis jacket opened a gate for us – and we took a round route.

One of the women walked alongside me and said: "Some of the others on the ship have gone to Clifden. I visited Clifden with my husband before he died two years ago, and he loved it, and I just couldn't go back again. I have dementia and it's made me lose my sense of direction, and I don't want to get lost today."

I said, "It's difficult, memories can be bitter-sweet, sweet because of the happy times and bitter because things have changed. I completely understand your not wanting to go back."

She said, "Yes."

The two women branched off, and Turtle and I walked on to the Spanish arch. The plaque on the wall said it was completed in 1584 as the extension of the medieval wall. It was pre-Spanish Armada, but some while after Columbus's visit to Galway in 1477 (according to the margin of his copy of *Imago Mundi*). It had been looked at by the Galway soldier Gumming, who on 30 January 1649 had beheaded Charles I as a non-English executioner. It had witnessed the bubonic plague of 1649, and had been damaged during the tsunami of 1755.

Turtle then said he wanted to do some research at St Nicholas' Collegiate Church, built in 1320, visited by Columbus and used as stables by Cromwell's troops, where the 13th-century Crusader Adam Bures, a Templar, was buried. Turtle wanted to view the grave.

We walked along narrow streets festooned with flags and festival chains, turning left and right in accordance with what the map on Turtle's phone required, and we found ourselves at the church, which first opened in 1324, dedicated to the fourth-century St Nicholas of Myra who was the inspiration for Santa Claus. It now looked a modern building. It was 10.58 with a church service set to begin at 11am.

"We'd better leave it until after the service," Turtle said, disappointed.

"No," I said, "we'll do it quickly now. Watch me." I went in. The church was packed. Two ladies stood at a table at the back. They greeted us and asked if we had come to attend the service. Turtle said, "Philip here has to go back on his Zodiac to his ship at 11.30. He won't have time."

I said, "We're interested in a grave. A man called Bures."

Turtle gave them details.

A man had joined us. He said, "I don't know him. But I'll find out."

He walked quietly to a bald man who was sitting at the end of a pew by the aisle and whispered in his ear and returned and said, "We don't know where it is. But we have a booklet on it." He went to a cupboard at the back and began searching.

Then there was an announcement that the service would now begin.

I said to Turtle, "I'll slip away now. I hope you find the grave. If there's a leaflet, please get one for me."

"I will," he said, "and thank you for getting them looking."

I left and hurried back through the festooned streets. I recognised a pedestrian crossing we took, and then I went wrong. I was near the sea and after walking down Long Walk found myself on the wrong side of the harbour, a long way from where the Zodiac would come in. I looked around and saw two men in open-necked coloured shirts without jackets parking a car in the only free car-parking space.

I approached them and said to a bald man in a dark-blue shirt, "Sorry to interrupt you, but I'm lost. I'm trying to get to a Zodiac that's there." I showed the place on my map.

"You're from the cruise," the man in the dark-blue shirt said. "I'll drive you there. Get in."

"I don't want to take you out of your way," I said, "and you've just got a parking-space."

"No, it's all right. Jump in."

So I climbed into the front seat and he drove me fast for about three minutes, up and along, and up and further along, and down and round, for well over a mile.

"You've been in Bantry," he said, "and Valentia Island" – he could have said Garinish Island – "and you're going on to –"

I said, "You're very knowledgeable. How do you know all that?"

"I'm the Harbour-master," he said. "I know about your Zodiac."

I was astonished. Out of the thousand people I could have asked, I'd picked the Harbour-master. It seemed a chance meeting, an accident, or was it Providential, had my guiding angel put me in touch with him so I did not miss my Zodiac?

I asked his name. He said, "Brian Sheridan."

Soon I was sitting in the Zodiac, returning to the ship through a choppy sea, and as the Zodiac skimmed and bounced my face was splashed, and my mac beneath my life-jacket and my hood. The Spanish arch, then the church and finally the Harbour-master – had an angel been with me to remind me of seeing the arch in a former life, and the 1324 church, and made sure I did not lose my way by directing me to the Harbour-master?

Aran Knitwear and Cornet Ice-Creams

We landed in Inishmore, the main Aran Island off Ireland, with the sun warm on our cheeks, and got on an antiquated single-decker yellow bus. The fat driver pointed things out in his Irish lilt as we drove along the narrow roads.

He said: "The population is 800. This island is 12 km x 3 km and has 14 villages. There's one policeman, one doctor and one priest. The bank is open one day a week. The language is Gaelic. There was no electricity until 1975, there were kerosene lamps. I had a TV in 1971 run on a battery that was charged by a tractor. The electricity was connected to the mainland in 1995. There are few sheep."

I thought the lack of sheep was strange as the Aran knitwear and wool were in *Vogue* in the 1950s, and Aran sweaters were worn by Picasso, Steve McQueen and Grace Kelly, to name just a few. Perhaps the sheep had supplied so much wool that they had died out.

We drove past tiny stone-walled gardens and a round church, and past one of the five beaches to the Tourist Centre, a low modern building in a cramped square on unmade land surrounded by tiny shops. We looked up at the prehistoric fort with dark limestone walls on three sides and a sheer drop to the rocks below, by the sea. It dated back to 1100BC, and was 300 feet up. Some of the path up was steep with loose stones, and was described as arduous, and we decided against an arduous climb. We headed for the knitwear. The single-storey shop had 'Sale' in the window.

There were Aran sweaters in piles of ten. Many were navy and dark-coloured but I found two that were cream, one large and one medium, for 110 euros for two, 55 euros each. I tried on the large one and an extra-large dark sweater and the assistant said the extra-large was too big on my arms. So I took the large cream sweater and also the medium, which I knew Penny, my PA, would want to take with her to Donegal when she stayed there with her friends. At the other end of the shop Pippa tried on a grey sweater with a hood, a collar and zip that was more like a jacket, and as I settled up for all three I asked about the stitches. The assistant told me that the two cream sweaters had cable, honeycomb and lattice or basket stitches and the one with the hood had cable, diamond, honeycomb and lattice or basket.

I carried the sweaters in two bags out to the ice-cream shop and we had enormous cornets. I had green mint-choc and vanilla-choc scoops, and Pippa had coconut and coffee scoops. I took a long time to eat mine. The ice-creams were very good.

Then we went outside and sat on the coach to be returned to the Zodiac, with our shopping between our feet. I reflected that our brief visit had been a treat: the Aran sweaters would keep us warm in the winter and the ice-creams had cooled us down in the warmth of the summer sun that had reddened my cheeks. And as others from our group staggered to the coach from their arduous climb with tales of youngsters taking selfies above the sheer drop, one backward step from oblivion, I was glad we had had a simple afternoon and had indulged ourselves in a forward-thinking way that would bring warmth and comfort in the winters we still had ahead of us.

Irish Dancers and Singing Birds

At Galway I shared a Zodiac with two elderly ladies. One with a fringe of boyish hair told me she had visited Clifden with her husband before he had died and they were so happy there that she couldn't go back.

Two evenings later at Killybegs there was a surprise after the ship's early-evening briefing. Five slim dancers, all around 20, marched in wearing matching slim black dresses, and were introduced as world champions in Irish dancing from Donegal. With arms down by their sides and looking straight ahead they did elaborate movements with their legs and feet on a metallic sheet pre-laid on the floor, and their shiny black shoes drummed out a patterned clog-like beat that amounted to a communal song. The upper parts of their bodies and arms scarcely moved as their feet nimbly cavorted and rapped out a communal drumbeat.

The next morning, still at Killybegs, I breakfasted at the next table to the ladies I had encountered in Galway city. They sat on their own at a table for six with a white tablecloth and napkins, and I was struck that each looked straight ahead. The lady who had been to Clifden said, "I remember...." I could not hear what she remembered. The other old lady looking straight ahead said, "I used to...." I could not hear what she used to do. I was struck that they were like singing birds. Each had its own song and amid the dawn chorus of breakfasters they were singing their song about their memories, as old people do.

And then I thought how similar they were to the five dancers who, arms by their side and looking straight ahead, were tap-dancing their jigs in their own togetherness and dawn chorus. And I thought: a poet is also a singing bird, in our own way we are all singing birds.

A Security Man and a Swell

As we pulled away from Killybegs the passengers were invited to join the expedition team at the Lido on deck 5. Pippa said she wasn't going, a wise move as there was a two-metre swell as the wind was in the opposite direction to the tide, and the ship was already rolling and the fifty people there were standing, hanging on to chairs and tables. Waiters were circulating with small glasses of Irish whiskey.

I saw our security man standing in the middle. I asked him, "Have you ever been in the SBS, the Special Boat Service?"

"No," he said, taller than me and thickset behind dark glasses, "but I've worked with them on operations. Each operation is assessed and four SBS may be allocated to it, that's the normal range."

"And do they make them retire?"

"They used to. It used to be your eighteenth birthday plus twenty-two years, and retire at forty. But now it's your eighteenth plus thirty-two years, so you retire at fifty."

I asked if he was with us to keep an eye on the real IRA.

"Yes," he said, "that's exactly what I'm doing."

"So you'll be coming to Belfast and Dublin with us?"

"Yes, I will. They should be safe if we keep to the tourist places."

"And Derry?" I asked. "That was where Bloody Sunday happened in 1920, and again in 1972. There were always incidents in Derry when the IRA were active."

"Yes," he said, "but if we keep to the tourist places we should be safe. The young aren't interested, it's not widespread."

"But Sinn Fein are in power in Northern Ireland," I said, "and they want to unite Ireland and are the political wing of the IRA, and after the Protocol it's all awakening again. Do you detect this?"

"Yes," he said. "There's a swell for union, and the Catholic voters will vote for it. I'd think Ireland will be united within twenty years."

"So if Scotland have a referendum and become independent, and Northern Ireland follows, the UK will become a Federation with an English Parliament and four independent nation-states: a Federation of the British Isles."

"That's the way it looks, it's how I see it," he said.

Now the swell had increased and as I supported myself by holding a chair he turned away and that was the end of our conversation.

I looked at the gathering allegedly watching Killybegs recede. Though music was playing, some were holding tiny Irish whiskeys, and elderly women were waving their arms in the air and cavorting and some were singing along to the music, exaggerating the atmosphere of the party that was happening. I crossed to the other side of the ship, took a photo on my phone of a low green bank ending in a rock, and then quietly slipped away.

A Causeway and a Screen

Our coach took us to the Giants' Causeway via Derry. We drove through the Catholic Bogside and lingered at the murals, garish paintings of politicians on walls of houses, and at the Bloody Sunday memorial and Hunger Strikers' Monument, and then on through the Walled City. It had been completed in 1619 and modelled on the French Vitry-le-François that was based on a Roman military camp with two main streets at right angles to each other and four city gates, one at each end of each street.

Then we drove to the Giants' Causeway. We left the coach and walked to the modern National-Trust-built Visitor Experience, found the toilets, were given audio-guides and queued for the public shuttle bus. We sat and looked at the sparkling sea and sunshine and dropped down a long narrow coastal road to the beginning of the stones. We looked at the promontory of closely-packed hexagonal basalt stone columns formed 60 million years ago from a layer of molten basaltic lava. We sat by the sea for a while, and when the shuttle bus returned we returned to the Visitor Experience.

As I got out I had to move away from a little old lady who was walking on a collision course with me. The old lady offered to take Pippa's audio-guide and hand it in for her.

We headed for the toilets again and then I headed towards the café to order coffee. I was slightly ahead of Pippa and negotiated a couple of wide steps without trouble. The little elderly grey-haired, bespectacled lady, who had previously told us she was eighty-seven, was walking beside Pippa. She suddenly lost her footing and fell.

She was lying at the foot of the steps. Hearing a commotion I turned back and Pippa was bending over her telling her not to move (having dislocated a hip herself in the past). The lady nevertheless manoeuvred herself into a sitting position. She tried to get up but couldn't and was in pain.

"I twisted as I fell," she said. "It's my hip." And she sat on.

I did not know her name and there was nothing more I could do except find the expedition leader. I quietly asked Pippa what she wanted.

"Hot chocolate," she said.

So I left her there and walked to the café within the Visitor Experience and queued. Then I saw the expedition leaders Frederic and Rebecca, and told them a lady had fallen.

Eventually Pippa appeared as I was about to order. She said, "I'll have a Rocky Road."

So I had cappuccino and a caramel square, and Pippa had a hot chocolate and Rocky Road.

We sat at a table to drink and eat, and then wandered back towards the stairs. There was now a screen round the old lady, and another member of our group passed and said, "An ambulance has been called." We left to get on our coach to return to our ship. An ambulance was parked at a distance down the road with its back doors wide open and seemingly no one in attendance, possibly because they were attending to the old lady.

On our coach, before we heard that she would be in hospital for several days and would not be returning to the ship, I thought of Derry, where there had been a Bloody Sunday in both 1920 and 1972, and how dangerous it would have been for our coach to go into the Bogside in 1972, fifty years ago. And I thought of the Giants' Causeway and the seemingly harmless causeway with two steps in a Visitor Experience that had consigned the 87-year-old lady to hospital in a fall that might have finished her off.

That was what happened, I thought. Fifty years ago you visited the Catholic nationalistic Bogside and died, and now you go to look at something like a Giants' Causeway and then follow your own causeway and have your own visitor experience and fall over and end up behind a screen, and perhaps die.

Humans keep going until they have some sort of a mishap, and what used to be an IRA bombing or shooting in an untrustworthy place had become a giving-way of your legs as you walked down a causeway of National-Trust steps. But it wasn't a question of trust. When your body let you down and got you in the wrong place, you collapsed and ended up behind a screen. That was how it was these days when you reached eighty-seven, you went out on a sunny day and collapsed and sometimes died.

A Sunken Garden and a Cut Throat

The coach took me from our berth at Belfast past Stormont to Strangford Lough, and from there to Mount Stewart House. It was not open until 11 so I sat in the sunken garden and absorbed the flowers planted by Edith, Lady Londonderry, during and after the Second World War, and the side of the 18th-century Mount Stewart House showing beyond the lawn.

At 11 I was by the front door. I went in wanting to get closer to Robert Stewart, who inherited the family title of Viscount Castlereagh in 1796, and was known as Lord Castlereagh until 1821. Almost immediately I saw his silver penholder, ink-well and sand-holder for the sand he scattered on his letters to dry the ink and then blew off. It had been present at the signing of the Treaty of Vienna in March 1815.

I went on to the dining-room and saw the chairs that were present at the Congress of Vienna and in the drawing-room I found the desk on which the Treaty of Vienna was signed and three chairs: Wellington's, Castlereagh's and Castlereagh's half-brother's. As Foreign Secretary from 1812 to 1822, during the Battle of Waterloo and its aftermath he had appointed the victorious Duke of Wellington to negotiate the exile of Napoleon, and also his half-brother as English Ambassador to Austria, and the brain behind the ninety-nine years of peace from 1815 to 1914 was Castlereagh's.

Castlereagh had been responsible for the 1800 Act of Union which took Ireland into the United Kingdom, but he had crushed an Irish rebellion in the 1790s and was not liked by the Irish. One of the guides said to me, "He took his own life a year after he inherited this house, in 1822. He was depressed, I think it was because of criticism over his involvement in Peterloo."

In fact the Peterloo massacre happened in 1819 without his sanctioning it, it was local law enforcement in Manchester that took the decision to fire on protesters that resulted in between 10 and 20, perhaps 15 dead.

She added, "Criticism by Shelley for example."

Shelley wrote in 'The Masque of Anarchy' in 1819, "I met Murder on the way – /He had a mask like Castlereagh." But his poem was not published until 1832 and Castlereagh did not know of these two lines.

I went upstairs and saw Castlereagh's bedroom. It had a double bed with a red bedspread. I came downstairs and asked the guides in the entrance where Castlereagh killed himself, was it upstairs? They did not know. I went to a new Castlereagh exhibition that was being opened that afternoon in a room at the end of the front terrace, and it did not say either. I went to the gift shop and bought a £5 guide to the house that said he cut his throat, his carotid artery, while still Foreign Secretary, in the house he owned on a farm in Kent, North Cray Farm, near Bexley, now known as Loring Hall.

Castlereagh and his wife were to set off for Greece, he got up and went to his dressing-room and cut his throat with a penknife he had hidden from his wife, who had confiscated his pistols and razors from him in case he harmed himself with one of them on account of his depression. His doctor was called, and he died in his doctor's arms.

In the sunken garden I had seen the house from the outside, but having been in I had a different perspective. Castlereagh had done good things (the Act of Union, the settlement and Treaty after the Battle of Waterloo) but he had also done questionable things (his ruthlessness to the Irish in the 1790s and his defence of the massacre of Peterloo that, despite Shelley's contemptuous words of which he was not aware, he had not ordered).

I was balanced, I was fair-minded and was on Shelley's side but allocated some blame to Castlereagh's defence of the massacre at Peterloo. It was a sensational story, a Foreign Secretary killing himself because of criticism. I was sunk in the politics of 1821–1822 and before, and could understand why Castlereagh cut his throat, but found it wrong and unnecessary. He should have lived in harmony with conflicting points of view, not given up and taken his own life.

Irish Conflict and a Wise Harmony

Our coach stopped at Merrion Square near Kildare Street, and we had forty-five minutes. We set off and within five minutes were in Dublin's national library's standing exhibition on the poet W.B. Yeats.

Pippa sat and rested her hips and knees in a round beehive building within the exhibition room where poems by Yeats were being constantly read and shown on old film on the walls. While she sat I toured the exhibits, some in free-standing glass cases, some in alcoves and some in glass cabinets against walls. There were many manuscripts. While I studied Yeats' 'Innisfree', I heard from the beehive Yeats himself reading 'Innisfree', and recalled visiting the site in 1966. I found myself looking at manuscripts of 'Byzantium' and 'Easter 1916'. I paused over his handwritten line, "All has changed, changed utterly."

I found the manuscript of his epitaph, now on his tombstone in Drumcliffe churchyard, which I had seen in 1966: "Cast a cold eye/ On life and death;/Horse man, pass by." And I winced. He should have checked the last line in his dictionary. It should be "Horseman", one word, not two. That was what it said on the tombstone (no doubt edited by the church).

Then I found a notebook dedicated to the automatic writing of his wife George. There was an astrological chart in his own hand, and there were sentences he had written about the occult. I thought how Yeats had proposed to Maud Gonne twice, and then to her daughter Iseult, and had been turned down each time – Maud Gonne then married John MacBride, who was executed after the Easter 1916 Rising – and had ended with the occult influence of his wife "George" (short for Georgia).

I could have spent the day there, poring over the manuscripts of the poems I knew. I had not found the manuscript of 'The Second Coming', and needed to go round again to see if I had missed his words describing the Second Coming in terms of Satan: "And what rough beast, its hour come round at last,/Slouches towards Bethlehem to be born?"

We had to leave to catch our coach. There was just time for a ten-minute cappuccino at Kilkenny Coffee opposite the coach. We both had a chocolate leaf on our coffee. One final gulp and it was time to go.

I had learned that Yeats had been staying in Gloucestershire when the rising at Easter 1916 took place, and he was frustrated at not getting detailed news. He had mixed views on the uprising, he deplored it and at the same time supported the bravery of the patriots such as Patrick Pearse, and had united his quarrel with himself in his line, "A terrible beauty is born."

Like Yeats I presented two opposites and sought to reconcile them into a wise harmony, and I pronounced him, along with Raleigh, Swift and Tennyson, as one of my main literary forebears.

A Failed Stand and a Final Victory

I took the afternoon shuttle bus – a double-decker, and I was the only passenger – to Dublin's Merrion Square South. A taxi pulled up and two people got out and I got in and was driven to the General Post Office where the Easter 1916 uprising took place, outside which Patrick Pearse read his 'declaration of independence' from the UK, for an independent Ireland. It was a 'Manifesto to the Citizens of Dublin, 25 April 1916' in which "the provisional government" issued a "proclamation of a sovereign independent Irish state" to the "citizens of Dublin".

I had last seen the General Post Office in 1966, fifty years after the uprising, and now I was seeing it in 2022, fifty-six years later. The enormous space before the counters had been filled with display units. Outside I craned my neck looking for the 50 bullet holes still showing in the front of the building, both in the columns and the façade behind them.

The British sent a gunboat up the River Liffey and the uprising was put down within five days. Fifteen of the leaders were arrested and taken to Kilmainham Gaol and executed. (A sixteenth, Roger Casement, was executed in Pentonville Prison, London.)

My Moldovan driver, Igor, took me on to Kilmainham Gaol. I had last been there in 1966: my taxi-driver then was an IRA sympathiser, and he told me he was taking me there without charge as he wanted to show me what the British did to the Irish patriots. He knew someone at the entrance and I was allowed in and was shown the courtyard where the executions happened. The driver made much of the British having shot Connolly in a wheelchair.

I was expecting it to be a functioning gaol as it had been in 1966, but to my astonishment Igor told me it was now a museum. He found it on his phone. I got out and went to an entrance I did not recognise from 1966. At the entrance I was told that the executions happened in the courtyard, the stone-breakers' yard, which I could not see unescorted. I had to be accompanied by a guide, and the earliest slot they had for what I had seen in 1966 was at 4.45pm. This was too late, I would miss the ship's departure from Dublin.

The couple at the entrance told me I might see part of the courtyard from the second floor of the museum. They gave me a free ticket to the museum.

I walked from the new reception-building through a gap in the 1796 prison wall to the newly-built museum and got a lift up to the second floor. I found one rear window that had a view over the wall into the courtyard. I held my phone above my head and took a photograph of the uneven stones. I looked at the 'last words' exhibition that was based on the book by the keeper of the museum who died when the book was in proof, *Last Words*, which the couple at the entrance were both holding. I then returned to the entrance and walked round a tower's curved bulge to the main entrance with railings and an Irish flag.

It came back to me, this was where I had gone in, taken by an IRA driver, in 1966. It was locked behind railings now. I had turned right, stepped into the stone-breakers' yard, and the IRA man had said, "That's where you British shot Connolly in his wheelchair." From the locked gate in the railings I could see an open gate in the right wall, "Connolly's gate" they had called it at the present entrance. That was the gate through which the wheelchair was pushed so he could be shot with sandbags behind him, I was told earlier. I put my phone through the bars and took a picture of the wall behind the open Connolly's gate.

And that was it. I took photos of the prison wall and returned to my driver, who was fending off a woman trying to get into my taxi. He drove me to Merrion Square South, and I paid him by card near where Yeats lived and crossed the road to my Barton double-decker bus. The bus driver said I could find a seat and wait, which I did.

I reflected that the Easter-1916 uprising had resulted in 15 of the 16 executed patriots shot in the stone-breakers' yard in the course of May 1916, while my Uncle Tom (who I never knew) would soon be carrying out spying missions from an RAF plane before he was shot down and killed in 1918. It was a cruel time, with British troops and politicians hardened by the First World War. The uprising for all Ireland had triggered partition on 3 May 1921, and it must have seemed to those executed that they had failed and lost.

But now that Sinn Fein, the political arm of the IRA, was in power in Northern Ireland and would soon be in power in the South, and now that the latest census was about to show that Catholics and Republicans would exceed Protestants and Unionists in Northern Ireland, it seemed clear that Ireland would be united within the next decade or at any rate the next two decades. So the 15 martyrs shot in Kilmainham Gaol had lost in the short term but had partially won by creating Southern Ireland from 1921, and would completely have won within 120 years of their brave stand and sacrifice.

The patriots' stand seemed at the time to have failed, but 106 years later, with the prospect that the UK would decline from a United Kingdom to a Federation of the British Isles, with an English Parliament in Westminster and an independent Scotland, Wales and Northern Ireland, which would be in a union with Southern Ireland, their stand would be seen as having achieved a final victory.

Indignation and Reaching-Out

Our tour of Dublin stopped at St Patrick's Cathedral. We were taken inside by our guide, and knowing what I wanted to see I broke away and found the pulpit where one of my heroes, Jonathan Swift, who was Dean there from 1713 to 1745, had preached every fifth Sunday. His sermons often lasted for several hours.

I studied the table nearby where he distributed the sacrament, and then looked at two death-masks, a sermon on 'Falling asleep in church', and a replica of his skull. I looked at his bust on a wall, and his epitaph, which contained the words "Savage indignation". And I saw his grave in the floor. He had died at 78 and was buried alongside Esther Johnson, "Stella", who had predeceased him aged 46. Swift is said to have gone through a marriage ceremony with Stella, but no evidence for this event has been found.

Then I went to the far end of the Cathedral and looked at the displayed door that had had a panel removed in 1492. When the Butlers had been defeated by the Fitzgeralds they retreated to the Chapter House at St Patrick's Cathedral. Gerald Fitzgerald, the head of the Fitzgeralds, had called through the door that he would give the Butlers safe passage. The Butlers had not trusted him. So Gerald Fitzgerald ordered a panel to be removed from the door and put his arm through as a sign of reconciliation, and the leading Butler shook his hand, giving rise to 'chancing one's arm'. The Butlers *did* receive safe passage, and the door was now in the Cathedral labelled "The Door of Reconciliation".

On my way out I encountered the Cathedral guide, who was a Swift expert. He told me he had sent many of Swift's sermons to be printed as the parchment was fading and was in a fragile condition. He told me, "Swift seems to have had two strokes. The first was in 1740, at the time of Handel's *Messiah*. Handel was often here, practising on the organ, and he and Swift talked, but Swift said he had no recollection of their meeting. The second stroke was just before he died, and he was buried under the Cathedral floor there with 'Stella'."

On the coach I thought of Swift who, as Dean of the Cathedral, was in charge of its day-to-day running; and of Gerald Fitzgerald, who literally reached out to the Butlers during their war. And I thought of Swift's satirical indignation and Fitzgerald's trusting gesture, and realised that between them the two men had excellent qualities: Swift had refused to accept what he believed to be wrong, and had exposed the wrong-doers with biting satire, and Fitzgerald had reunited with those he believed to be wrong, and had brought harmony between them: Swift's indignation and Fitzgerald's reaching-out were what all needed.

An Indian Adviser and Putin

I put the bins out after dark that Thursday evening. It was recycling rubbish. I carried a transparent bag of newspapers and a transparent bag of recycling, and then went back to the house and returned with a black bag, which I put in the bin in the shed, and a green caddy. I put the green bag in the green bin and turned and heard my name called from the dark, "Philip."

It was Raj, our Indian next-door neighbour. He came and shook my hand and said, "I haven't seen you for a long time. You've been away, you're back now."

I said, "Yes, I'm around. How's Aeroflot?"

Until the previous year he was number two in Aeroflot, the Russian airline.

"Oh, I'm still with them. But they've been grounded since June 2021, it's difficult. I'm adviser to the Commonwealth and Foreign Office on aviation, and I've just been asked to be Liz Truss's adviser. I don't know what to do. I'm in the middle, I know Putin. I'm really upset about the invasion of Ukraine, I don't know why he did it. He's killing people. You know about Gazprom? He's killed half a dozen who disagreed with him. I don't want to be a target. If I become an adviser to Truss I'll be a target."

I said, "You'll have to be careful and stay in the middle, face both ways."

"That's what I want to do. I want to suggest at the first meeting that Truss invites Putin to the Queen's funeral, to start peace talks. It can't go on as it is. I dread to think how it will end. It has to be stopped. Johnson provoked Putin. Truss mustn't do that, he could be driven into a corner and use nuclear weapons. But Truss won't make a move towards Putin. If the Queen hadn't died Truss would have been exposed now. She's like a child; Lavrov, the Russian Foreign Secretary, was right. She's not got a plan. Two hundred million, and it's not been borrowed, and it's not to be printed."

I said, "I'll think about your situation, and we'll talk again."

"Good, we must. I can show you some papers. I'm thinking of not being Truss's adviser. I'm fifty and I don't want to be killed by

Putin. I've still got years ahead of me. I need to be in the middle, not Truss's adviser when I know she won't take my advice. Can we please talk again?"

I said we would talk and wished him goodnight and watched him stride to the road in the dark. I had been minding my own business with the bins, and he had told me of his turmoil at being caught between ruthless Putin and a provoking UK. He did not want to follow the Gazprom people to an early grave.

Thumb Wars and Chocolate Cake

It was Simon's birthday on Monday. The family met at the Castle, now a Miller-&-Carter steakhouse, on a Saturday evening. Simon, Kay, Al and Bernard had just got back from watching Arsenal beat Spurs 3–1. We were all shown to a square table by a wall within a large area that had many tables, all full. We sat and ordered. I ordered 'Surf and Turf': steak mignon and lobster (the 'surf') with peppercorn sauce and chips, and we shared a bottle of red wine. Al was going to have one of my two 'turf' steaks.

Simon sat between Al and Minnie; Bernard sat next to Pippa; Al was next to Kay; and I was next to Kay's mother Marjorie.

The previous evening Simon had taken Pippa to the O2 to hear Andrea Bocelli sing, her delayed birthday outing. She recounted for Kay's benefit, prompted by Simon, how they started at Zizzi, just outside the O2, and sat near a couple and exchanged a few words, and then later were looking for a table within the American-Express (Amex) area in the O2. The tables were all taken, but one table had two empty stools. The same couple were sitting at that table, and they waved Simon and Pippa to join them.

There was talk and it turned out that for forty years they had owned a villa in Spain, in San Pedro, very near Simon's two apartments, and that they had eight grandchildren, some of whom were the same age as Al and Minnie. They exchanged phone numbers, and that morning the couple had texted and there was an arrangement to meet them in Spain. I could not help thinking that the manner of their liaising seemed Providential, as though they had been guided towards each other.

The steaks arrived. While we ate I learned that Minnie had fallen over during hockey that afternoon and had hurt her jaw. I heard how Al had received an award as the village's 'Best Under-13 Cricketer' on his return from scout camp. And I heard that Bernard had just started his Masters course and that there were five others, four of whom were international students who did not speak. So he only had one person he could be friendly with, who he knew distantly from the previous year.

I said that the news had reported that Conservative MPs had already sent letters expressing no confidence in the new Prime Minister, Liz Truss, to the 1922 Committee, and that there were a few comments on the national situation, which was dire. Truss had been PM for only 25 days during a period of national mourning, and during that time the Government had spent £160 billion, sterling had dipped to its lowest point since 1985, cheaper mortgages had disappeared from the market and everyone's mortgage was going up hundreds of pounds a month, and the Bank of England had had to make an emergency intervention and spend £55 billion (which the Government would have to repay) to save pension funds. During all this the Conservatives had dropped to their lowest poll rating against Labour since the 1990s, and were according to one poll 19, and another 33, points behind. Tory MPs, City traders and voters all saw economic incompetence and were anxious, and on the evening of the mini-budget the new Chancellor went to an evening with hedge-funders and Tory donors and talked casually about his contempt for the Governor of the Bank of England. The Conservatives looked as if they would be out of power for a generation.

I said, "Grandma and I can't be blamed, we weren't allowed to vote."

Simon said with a straight face, "Grandma can't be trusted to vote as she voted for Brexit."

Kay said, "When I went to Spain, the Spanish border official stamped my passport on two pages, and it's now full so I've got to get another one. That wouldn't have happened if Brexit hadn't happened.

There were no stamps on passports before Brexit." She turned to her mother Marjorie, and said: "That's your fault for voting Brexit."

"I just wanted the UK to have its sovereignty back," she said plaintively, "and I don't approve of our joining a European army."

"You're wrong," Kay said jokingly, but there was a serious point beneath.

I tactfully said to Marjorie, "The trouble is, Brexit hasn't turned out as it was supposed to, because the leaders haven't had a clear idea of what to do. Before Brexit the EU took 44 per cent of our exports, and in 2020 it took 53 per cent and has remained the UK's main trading partner. Things haven't turned out well, and there could be a Third World War. Four pipelines of Nordstream 1 and 2 carrying natural gas from Russia have been blown up, perhaps by the US, and there's talk of possible Russian attacks on our pipelines (including our pipelines from Norway), rigs and cables (including the internet). It's not good, a cable war would cut the UK off and block financial transactions worth $9.2 trillion on the stock market by ending the flow of financial information, and stop the internet."

Minnie had been holding Simon's hand. She had been playing "rock, paper, scissors", a game I played in Japan nearly 60 years ago. I used to say, "*Janken-pon*" ('Beginning with stone'), and present my fist (as a rock), or my flat palm (as paper) or with separated second and third fingers (as scissors). In Japan a clash of opinions between two people was sometimes decided by *Janken-pon*. The two hands thrust out produced one of three results: scissors cut paper (and so won); but were blunted by a rock (and so lost); and paper wrapped a rock (and so won). Could Simon and Minnie have inherited that game from me?

Now Minnie said to Simon, "Shake hands, one-two-three-four, I declare a thumb war. Five-six-seven-eight, winner will get chocolate cake." And *her* thumb and Simon's thumb indulged in a battle as they held hands. She then turned to first Bernard and then Al and repeated her thumb war.

And I thought of the letters going to the 1922 Committee about Truss, and how she was under the thumb of the British electorate who had shown a thumbs-down. And I thought of her thumb war. The UK was in a difficult time with thumb wars going on between

Truss and the Bank of England, other politicians, hedge-funders and Tory donors. "Five-six-seven-eight, winner will get chocolate cake," Minnie chanted.

At that moment a waitress brought in a chocolate caterpillar under a lit candle and laid it in front of Simon, and we all spontaneously sang 'Happy Birthday', stopping the conversation at many surrounding tables, and when we reached "Happy birthday, dear Simon" Simon sang, "Happy birthday, dear me-ee" and blew out the candle in one go.

"Five-six-seven-eight, winner will get chocolate cake." Simon had won the thumb war, and all the other political thumb wars had paled to insignificance in comparison with the moment of our celebration, including moves to force out the new Prime Minister and the possible cable wars in the Atlantic and the North Sea.

A Clot and a Nearly-Lost Leg

We had our annual television servicing. Bill came with a young fellow. They began by replacing the antiquated dish on the roof, which Bill had identified for replacement the previous year.

They carried a ladder round the back and climbed to my balcony and propped the ladder to get on to the roof over my office and access behind the chimney. They dismantled the old dish and replaced it with a brand new one.

Then they went up to the loft and checked the equipment. Then they went round each room that had a television and tested the strength of the signal on a laptop the young fellow carried.

They had finished by lunchtime. I went downstairs to see them out.

"You've kept well?" I asked.

"I had a problem about six months ago," Bill said. "I had my fourth Covid jab and it did something to me. I was in agony in my leg above my knee. I couldn't see a doctor, so I tried ringing the surgery. I stood with difficulty and held a phone near my leg so the doctor could see. The doctor said, 'Stand on a chair.'" Bill laughed. "I could hardly stand but I managed to stand on a chair. He said, 'Come straight in.'

So I went in to see him. As soon as I limped through the door he said, 'I'm calling an ambulance immediately.' He could tell immediately I had a blood clot. I was taken to the hospital and put in a bed and examined. The surgeon said, 'If you hadn't come, you'd have lost your leg.' They gave me a general anaesthetic and cut the clot out of my leg.

"So that's what the Covid jab gave me, a clot about a week later. I'm all right now, but I'm not having another Covid jab."

I did not say, 'Nor am I,' for that would have held the two of them up. They were on their way to the car they had come in.

"See you next year," I said, "and no more clots."

"No," Bill laughed. "Thanks to the doctor I'm still here, and I didn't lose my leg."

But I could see from his face that he had confronted Death and the confrontation had shaken him up. He was sent to people's houses by appointment to test their televisions and make sure they would have a year's straightforward viewing, and facing up to losing a leg had not come into his consideration until then.

A Tumble Down Stairs and Blood

That Monday morning I realised I had not opened the gates for Katie. I got off the phone in my office and walked to the stairs. Pippa had stopped half-way down and was holding on to the handrail on her right. I walked down the stairs holding on to the handrail.

When I reached Pippa I overtook her, hands free, without a handrail to hold on to the other side. She moved to her left, and I swerved to avoid her in mid-step and lost my footing. I missed a stair and fell five stairs. I felt myself diving slowly forward with nothing to hold on to as I stretched out my arms, and I saw the corner of a wall before a low window jutting out and looming as I dived on to the turning platform before the stairs turned. I hit the top of my head a glancing blow as I landed on the turning platform with my head lower than my feet, which were further up the stairs.

I was lying down the stairs, face down, and blood was seeping through my hair and trickling down past my left ear and under my chin. My left ankle hurt. I slowly got myself to my feet, pulling myself up by holding on to the corner post of the handrail. Pippa was standing still, having watched me tumble headlong. I could feel that I had damaged my left ankle, and I wondered if I had strained or slightly torn my calcaneofibular ligament in an ankle sprain.

I limped down the last three stairs beneath the small landing, and turned the key in the cupboard under the stairs to open the gates. Pippa was now in the kitchen giving me a tea towel for the blood coming from under my hair, and asked if she should take me to A&E.

"No," I said, reckoning I did not have a blood clot on my brain, "I shall just carry on." I limped upstairs to the bathroom and washed the blood out of my hair under the shower before my hair became matted. I wrung out the tea towel in the basin and dabbed and cleaned the blood off the side of my face, my neck and under my chin. There was no sign of concussion, and the wound already seemed staunched.

I went back to my office and carried on working normally, and sent an email. I was shaken, and my ankle hurt when I walked on it, and I knew I would not be going to the gym in the afternoon. In due course Dr Erdmann would send me for an MRI, which would confirm that no damage had been done, and there were no signs of a stroke.

'That's how it is,' I reflected ruefully. 'You get up for a normal day's work, realise you've forgotten to open the gates, lose your footing on the stairs and fall and hit your head and die of a head wound. Life ends abruptly when you're not ready for it.'

I vowed that I would finish my work and tidy my papers and live in readiness for Death, who could visit me any time. Was I not already a skeleton-in-waiting?

Laceleaf Spikes and a Dancing Wasp

That Sunday I took Pippa to the Carlyon Bay Hotel for lunch. It was the first time they were taking non-residents since just after lockdown two years previously, when I talked with the grey-top-hatted doorman. Every table had a lily-like laceleaf (*Anthurium andraeanum*) with a pink-to-red spike.

We sat at the sea-end of a row of tables and ordered. We drank sparkling water and munched soft brown seeded bread and butter.

Then we had prawn-and-crab timbale and watched rain creep towards us and darken the smart black-and-white interior so the tiny lights on the broom in large vases on the window-sills could be clearly seen.

Then I had beef and Pippa had pork, and the rain came in and lashed the window-panes. It disturbed a wasp that danced up a window and down, and then danced back up again.

The Asian waitress then brought our chocolate delice with coffee ice-cream, and after that we had coffee. The rain was steady now and the bay outside was misty, and the elderly clientele sitting in pairs at tables in the windows were secondary to the dark clouds that loomed.

I had postprandial coffee and Pippa had Earl Grey tea. We both had a square chocolate in our saucers. There were a couple of flashes of sheet lightning but no thunder, and we sat in the peace of elderly couples bent over their food and Asian waitresses carrying plates to and fro.

The diners were as still and seemingly unaware as the laceleaf spikes, and the artist in me had eyes for every movement. I was like the dancing wasp climbing upwards and after relapsing resuming my climb. I danced up my window on the world and noticed the coming of the rain and the water running down the other side of the windows, but I was separated from the world by glass, like the wasp, and watched with a poet's alertness what the other diners seemed not to notice.

A Plasterer and a Propositioned Wife

Charlie came to paint the hall and breakfast-room walls. From the hall he said to Pippa, who was sitting in her chair in the sitting-room, "Eddie was four last week. I said to him, 'You're going to be four tomorrow.' I explained he was three now, and every year he'll go up one: four, five, six, seven. The next day I said, 'Do you feel four?' He said, 'My heart's telling me I'm still three.' That's quite a statement for a three-year-old."

He unpacked and returned. "My van's being repaired," he said, "so I'm driving a car. I went to work, parked my van in a road, got back into the driver's seat at the end of the day and drove off. I hadn't seen the passenger's door was scratched and dented, and the side wing was crumpled, and the bumper was nearly off. I reckon a heavy lorry, an HGV, reversed into it. I haven't claimed on insurance. They'd write the van off, and I like driving it, and it's still worth a bit, so I've paid a couple of thousand for the work to be done. That was an expensive day going to work."

Pippa asked after his wife. He said, "She's had to look after Eddie for the last week. She doesn't like being at home. She likes to be out there. She's got three jobs. One of the jobs is at Eddie's school. Another one is working with a company. And she helps her friend in the fish-and-chip shop. She's been working with the best man at Harry's wedding. They've been close for a long time but he wants to take it further. She said to me, 'No, I don't want to do that.'"

Charlie narrated it as if it was an ordinary situation, and it was all matter-of-fact and up to her.

He painted the breakfast-room wall which had deep plastering. I had had the central heating on in that room since we came down and it was just about dry. He painted the dry area in the hall and a bit in a wall by the front door. He said at the end, "I'm coming back to do a final coat by the front door and in the breakfast-room next week. There are cracks in the sitting-room wall, look. And the plaster's completely blown there, and it will spread upwards. I'll do that before Christmas if that's all right. And the sill is rotten, look there's a hole in it. I'll do the whole wall next."

"Yes, please," I said.

Pippa asked if he would put up a shelf in a cupboard in the kitchen taken down by plumbers, and I got him to plug a hole where there was a pipe in the main bathroom's skirting-board. Then he left.

As I waved him off I could not forget what he had said about Harry's best man. I thought how different life had become. A husband could now report on someone at work wanting to have an affair with his wife, a married woman with his four-year-old son, and could report her reply as a matter of ordinary conversation, like discovering he had a scratched and dented van. It felt as if we were living in a period of decline, like the decline of the Roman Empire, only in the Western world.

Death in the Evening

As she drove to Porthleven, Pippa talked about her 96-year-old aunt. She told me that Richard had had a hard time coping during his mother Maud's last visit to hospital.

"She didn't want to go back into hospital," she said, thinking aloud. "But she was very incontinent, her water tablets weren't working. Her doctor said she had to go in. He told her that her water tablets had damaged her kidneys, and he got her to sign a DNR ('Do not resuscitate') form, which Richard wasn't pleased about.

"We all knew this but reckoned the water tablets got rid of her water and gave her some quality of life, and that her body would fill with fluid if she stopped them. Richard asked him, 'If she stops them will her body be able to cope?' Her doctor said, 'Oh yes, her heart will be strong enough.' But now she was in hospital because the water tablets had stopped working, another doctor said, 'Her heart won't be strong enough to cope. There's not a lot we can do.' Richard felt he had been misled.

"The hospital did further tests and again found her kidneys were shrivelled, and said they couldn't do anything. Richard and Sue sat with her all that first night. Sandy had a van he'd adapted so they could sleep in the back when they went to places, and that was parked in the hospital outside." (Sandy was their son.) "With my car there were four parked in the hospital car park and we all had permits, the palliative-care staff had organised that for us. Richard took it all badly, he kept having to leave the room, and he rang that Thursday evening as I was coming down and said, 'Are you nearly here?' I said, 'I'm in Truro, I won't be long.' He was waiting for me outside the hospital with my permit.

"We agreed to have a shift system. Maud was conscious that Thursday before she went to sleep, so she knew I was there. Richard and Sue had done twenty-four hours at the hospital. They went home to shower and change their clothes and sleep. I took over, Sandy and Stella and I did shifts." (Stella was their daughter, Sandy's brother.) "She never woke up on the Friday morning. She was unconscious, and her body filled with fluid, her legs and the lower half of her stomach were very swollen, and they wouldn't do anything because she had signed a DNR form.

"I left on the Friday afternoon and went to our house to shower and change, and found Diane there, hoovering, and made her jump. She thought she'd come on the wrong day. I went back and found the four of them together in the room. They were discussing ordering a pizza and eating it in reception. Three of them went downstairs to do this. Stella stayed with me and asked if she could bring a slice of pizza up for me. I said, 'No, you go down and have pizza, I'll stay.'

"I sat with Maud and held her hand and talked to her. The nice nurse had said that the last two things a dying patient has are touch and hearing words. So I kept talking to her and squeezing her hand.

"It was evening. Very soon her breathing changed. I called the nurse and said, 'I think her breathing's become more shallow.' She examined her and said, 'Yes, call the others to come up.' So I texted Sue. Later I rang. They came up but could not get in. The ward's security system had closed the door and the nurses were busy. They were pressing the buzzer and no one came and opened the door. They couldn't get anyone to let them in. Sue texted, 'Can't get in.' So I told the nurse, who went to open the door.

"I stayed with Maud, holding her hand and talking to her. Her breathing got fainter and then it stopped, there was an outbreath and no inbreath, and I knew that she had slipped away, about 8pm. The others then came. I asked the nurse, 'How is she?' The nurse examined her and said, 'She's gone.' I didn't say anything. I knew the others had arrived too late, that she'd gone before they arrived in the room. But no one said anything. The nurse said we could sit with her as long as we liked, so we sat with her and talked about our past memories of events she was involved in."

Pippa fell silent. She drove and I waited, but she did not say any more, perhaps lost in her memories of past events. She had been present at the death of her 96-year-old aunt, and was still coming to terms with her faint breathing and then how her breathing stopped, and how she was then by herself.

Death had tiptoed in and taken her, and she was still processing what had happened. I thought, 'This awaits all of us. Death lurks in the shadows and moves in when our organs begin to fail.' I faced the universe with a quiet acceptance of its inevitable condition.

A Coffin and Petals

We reached Porthleven just after noon. I was in a suit, white shirt, black tie and black overcoat in arctic cold. We sat in Richard's front room with Richard and Sue's mother. Richard was in a white shirt and black tie, and put on a black sweater and then his jacket. Then Sue, Stella and Sandy arrived. Sandy had no black tie, and Sue found him one. He was with his Indian fiancée, Deepa. We all stood and there was awkward chat.

At 12.45 our limousine arrived with a chauffeur in a peaked cap. Pippa and I, Sue and her mother and Richard all got in and at the end of their cul-de-sac we linked up with the hearse. I could see Maud's coffin through the back window. It was made of very light-coloured wood. A Dickensian undertaker with a tall top hat, a stove-pipe hat, walked in front of the hearse, and we followed the coffin in our limousine down into the village to the Methodist chapel. Maud's C of E church was permanently locked up with no vicar, and the Methodist minister had known Maud since his boyhood.

Attendants opened our doors and we got out. Pippa and I followed Richard and Sue, and we walked behind the coffin, which was wheeled by four undertakers, into the chapel. The chapel was decorated for Christmas with life-size wooden effigies in a stable before the altar, and there were Christmas trees on either side. The organ was high above the altar at the front.

The congregation of about 30 were all standing and we stood before our chairs in the front row. On the front of the order of service was a picture of a younger laughing Maud which Kay, Simon's wife, had found on her phone and sent through to Sue.

The service was conducted by a minister who lived a road away from Maud in the old days. Still standing, we sang a hymn ('The Lord's My Shepherd, I'll Not Want'). We then sat for a prayer and a short address on death, and then a résumé of Maud's life which included that Pippa rang her every day between 4 and 5pm for years. There was then a final hymn ('The Day Thou Gavest, Lord, Is Ended'). Then we followed the minister, and the four undertakers wheeling the coffin, past the congregation to the hearse and watched the coffin being loaded back into it.

We rejoined our limousine and proceeded behind the hearse, led by the walking undertaker in a tall stove-pipe hat up through the village to the funeral undertakers, behind which (entered at the side) was a non-denominational cemetery where Maud's husband had been buried in 1973. She had been a widow for 49 years. The limousine drove us at walking pace to her husband's grave, which had been opened and was lined with a green tarpaulin that looked like artificial grass. Another green tarpaulin covered the mound of earth alongside that had been dug out of the grave.

We watched in bitter cold as the coffin was carried to the grave and placed on ropes lying on wooden crossbars that straddled the grave. The crossbars were removed, and as the minister prayed the coffin was lowered. When the minister said, "Dust to dust, ashes to ashes", a lady helping the undertakers threw a handful of sand down onto the coffin. We then queued and each threw a handful of yellow and red petals onto the coffin.

We were then driven out of the cemetery and back to the chapel, where tables with tablecloths had appeared in front of the stable tableau, and some of the congregation were sitting munching pasties or drinking coffee. Some were standing. Pippa was stopped by Maud's neighbour, who said smilingly that Maud waited for her phone call every day between 4 and 5pm. Two 'Age Concern' ladies came and talked to her. Maud had been involved in 'Age Concern' outings.

We got ourselves pasties from the food table, and coffee, and later Pippa asked me to get her saffron bread and butter, a scone with cream and jam and a macaroon, and I brought the same back for myself. We sat near Bill and Daphne, relatives she always visited when we came to Cornwall, and Bill, who used to be in the Navy, and I talked about the Eddystone Lighthouse lights. I could see them from my window, and he could see them from his window at a different angle, and we both agreed they had changed. He said, "They're automated now, controlled by satellite from outer space, it's one – three – two within a ten-second spell." I said I could see seven flashes, the seventh was a strange curved light, like running down a question mark on its back.

We returned to Richard's house in his car. We all sat and there was talk about this and that. At one point Pippa said, "It all went very well, she would have liked it and approved. It's closure."

There was a silence, and thinking of a past colleague at work, whose funeral I had been prevented from attending in 1984 by our hard-line Headmistress, I said, "I used to work with a fellow I lunched with every day, and he died suddenly at home one weekend, leaving a wife and three young children, and I was barred from attending his funeral as I had to front an event at work. Because I couldn't attend his funeral, I had no closure, and for about six months I half-expected to see him in a corridor at work. A funeral helps you to process what's happened so there's closure in that sense. That's right."

We returned home soon afterwards. In the car in the dark I thought of Maud's coffin and of the petals I had tipped out of my right hand onto the coffin below, and I thought of the earth that would now be above the coffin. I knew that at eighty-three my time to face my death was coming. I still had a lot of organising to do before I was ready, and I knew I would get on and finish my work and sort my papers so I could have a neat exit. And I thought that I should find a churchyard where I could lie in peace for the rest of the century and beyond. I was matter-of-fact. This was what would happen, and I should be ahead of it with a practical plan.

Black-Tied Death and Banter

As we were leaving to drive to Exeter we encountered Death – Maisie's husband, Jim – by our car. He was moving the wooden tubs containing shrubs with parking notices on them, wearing his undertaker's funeral clothes (a white shirt, a black tie and dark suit, the dress of Death). Pippa had pulled her car out of our parking area and I had just padlocked the chain where her car had been parked.

"How are you both?" he asked. "Good to see you. The owner of the house beyond ours on the cliff path has told his tenants they have a right of way across our land here, and that they can park where they like. Their tenant has parked in our space. I'm just moving it all back to where it should be. How are you?" He added, seeing our chain was now padlocked, "Are you off?"

Pippa said, "We're going to stay in Exeter for our grandson's graduation."

"Oh, that's good."

Pippa told him her aunt had died. "We had the funeral yesterday," she said. "Strikes did it."

"Oh yes, Strikes," he said, identifying a competitor an hour's drive away.

I said, "A Dickensian man in a stove-pipe hat led the way in front of the hearse."

"Oh, I do that," he said, "but not in a stove-pipe hat. Did he have a stick?"

"To whack people's legs to make them stand back as he walked in front of the hearse?" I asked.

Death laughed.

He said as he shifted another wooden tub with a shrub and a parking notice, "It was good in the old days, everything worked. Now everyone's unhappy, and it's the fault of those who are running the country. They've not run it right. Everyone's going on strike."

"Don't you go on strike," I said. "We need you even if you don't wear a stove-pipe hat."

He laughed and said, "I'm supposed to be retiring in January."

"You've retired once and gone back into it. You'll do the same in January, mark my words."

He laughed again and looked me up and down in his black tie, as if measuring me for a coffin.

"A Happy Christmas to you both," he gushed, "and may everything be good for you in the New Year, even if it's not good for much of the country."

I got in the car and Pippa drove beyond our lawn and saw that the road ahead was blocked. It would also be blocked for Death. The grandson of a neighbour had delivered a child, and taken a pram from the boot. The boot was open.

"It may need you to go and tell him to be off before you sort him out," I said to Jim through the open window. Death laughed.

Then the grandson saw us and waved and closed the boot and reversed.

We waved goodbye to Death and waved our thanks to the grandson.

I thought again of Death. He was jovial and relished walking in front of a hearse with a threatening stick. His joviality allayed anxiety and made those he met believe they were safe. But I knew he was measuring us so he would be able to step in as our undertaker, as he had done for so many local families.

Death posed as a friend and got your confidence with light-heartedness, but was there, waiting to take you under as all good undertakers hope to do, talking in a friendly way but eyeing people up as future clients, no, victims. I bantered back in kind, but I was planning to keep my distance and not be taken under before my time.

A Mortarboard and Open-Mouthed Death

Pippa and I attended Bernard's graduation ceremony the next day, a Friday. We had stayed the night in Exeter's Devon Hotel, and breakfasted at 7 and were driven by taxi to the sloping walk down to the Great Hall, where Simon and Bernard met us. Bernard was in a mortarboard and gown with a curved blue academic hood at the back.

They took us down to the coffee-house, where Angela was sitting. I had a cappuccino there, which Simon bought, and then Bernard went off to join the graduates and be seated at the back of the Great Hall while the rest of us entered the Great Hall at the front and found four chairs at the end of the third row.

There was a roving camera and film of members of the audience on the two screens at the front and on two sloping ceilings. We waited until 10am: music played at the back of the Great Hall. Then a mace-bearer led the key faculty members in. They filled two rows of chairs on the stage. Another mace-bearer of a large mace led in the senior professors, three of whom made speeches of welcome, commending the hard work during the pandemic that had led to these graduates obtaining their degrees.

Then the graduates filed down on one side of the hall, and one of the faculty members called names, following the printed booklet we had found on alternate chairs. The graduates had already received their certificates by post and they all filed past the faculty professor who was fronting the occasion, an elderly woman, with a nod and some waved to their family. One Chinese girl came by with crossed laces up her legs, and another Chinese girl, beaming, nodded so energetically to her supporting family that her mortarboard fell off. She caught it in mid-air before it fell on the floor.

At last it was Bernard's turn. The lady professor did not acknowledge him at first, so he turned to us and beamed under his mortarboard and then she began to applaud after he had passed her, so he turned back to nod at her. He came by as we took pictures and then applauded.

Simon, who had booked a year ago to fly to Amsterdam for an annual get-together with a school friend there, had delayed his flight from City Airport but had to leave. He now ducked and left by arrangement so he could drive to London and catch his flight. He had had dinner with Bernard the previous evening.

The ceremony was all over ten minutes later. Bernard joined us – now without his mortarboard and gown – in the foyer, and we stood and sipped sparkling wine. None of Bernard's five current tutors were there as they had to lecture. Anyway, as postgraduate tutors they had had no input in his graduation, their contact with him was post-graduate.

We were booked to go to the Côte Brasserie by the Cathedral, but there were no taxis available. So Bernard walked to his road and returned half an hour later with his BMW and drove us to a car park. He then walked with Angela to the Côte and the four of us ate tender 6-hour-prepared cheek Bourguignon of beef with French beans on the top floor with a view over the Christmas market and the Cathedral.

I said Bernard had the world at his feet and that he could go into AI and invent a robot that can do all household chores from hoovering to shopping and cooking, and become a billionaire like Elon Musk.

After that we went down to the Christmas market and walked among the stalls. We came to the Cathedral entrance and saw there was free entry. We went in. Pippa and Angela sat in a pew near the entrance and talked quietly, while Bernard and I went in search of all the 12th-century features. We saw the medieval astronomical clock in the north transept and the 14th-century effigies of the Second Earl of Devon and his wife (contemporaries of Chaucer) in the 12th-century south transept. We looked into all the chapels, then headed back to see the Becket boss featuring the murder of Becket above where Pippa and Angela were sitting.

On the way back there were supine statues and effigies of dead bishops and a knight in armour, and then, on our right, there was a statue of an elderly cleric after his death. He was naked with a skeletal chest showing his ribs, and his eyes were closed and his mouth was open. He was open-mouthed Death shown in the last gasp of our lives.

We left the Cathedral and I was sombre as Pippa bought three Scotch eggs from a stall, and some French Brie from another. Bernard was at the start of his life and his mortarboard symbolised his hopes for an energetic, creative and inventive career, and this effigy of open-mouthed Death was where it would all be leading. It put all lives in context, and implied that human achievement was doomed to end in death and that studies leading to a mortarboard were a waste of time.

But no, open-mouthed Death was what awaited all of us at the end of our lives, but humankind went on, and mortarboard success benefited human lives in many ways, including the environment and climate change. Open-mouthed Death would not be ignored, but celebrating the achievements of the mortarboard trumped Death and benefited all humankind.

A Historian and His Last Illness

As I walked to the pharmacy I met Roland Marsh, the local historian, coming towards me with his metallic stick, tall and nearly 87 and pale. I was in my track suit as I was on my way to the gym.

"Hello, Roland," I said as I approached him, "how are you?"

"Not well," he said. "You know I've had cancer – a nine-inch-long thin oval growth that was pressing into my bowel – and have recovered. I've also had a bowel problem. Scar tissue from a past operation has infected my bowel and has blocked its movements. I had that in January, and again in March, and again in May, and again in October. And I was told, 'It can happen again.'"

I looked sympathetic and concerned. "Can't they stop it?"

"It needs a full operation," he said. "I'm prepared to have it, but the doctor said, 'Oh, we can't do it as we don't know how it will affect you.'"

I said, "That means you're in your mid-eighties, and there's a huge waiting-list, and they haven't got the doctors and the nurses, and they're postponing you for a few months or years."

"Yes," he laughed wryly, "you may be right. Otherwise I've been doing a 300-page book on a General who led the army in the War of Independence in the eighteenth century, and was linked to Rolls Park. And still in history, I'm researching Sir William Addison."

"Oh," I said, "I knew him from an early age, since 1945."

"Yes, I know. A mutual historian who saw Addison as the doyen of local historians, with three books on Epping Forest, the last in 1976, had about 20 items connected with Addison, and they came to me in a box, and I gave them to the Epping Forest District Museum. And they've lost the box. They closed during lockdown, and boxes had to be re-stored. Anyway, they're looking for it. I'm going to write a pamphlet on him. I know you met him in a wheelchair in Queen Elizabeth's Hunting-Lodge shortly before he died. You know, in 1945 he wasn't a verderer –"

"But I believe he was then a JP," I said. "He wore a dark suit and white shirt and looked very formal when I first met him in the year his first Epping Forest book came out. He looked as though he was just going to sit on the bench –"

"I can't find a picture of how his bookshop looked in those days."

"I haven't got one I'm afraid."

Then I remembered I had to post a letter and go to the pharmacy and then to the gym. "I must be going," I said.

He nodded and continued walking down Station Road.

I called after him, "Be careful, don't fall, the ambulance men are on strike and you won't be collected."

He nodded and went on walking. Watching him I felt sorry for him. He had been very ill and was trying to get his work done at nearly 87 and it was a struggle for him. He looked frail, and I thought Death was stalking him. He was in his last illness and he would not be alive long.

An Outspoken Girl and an Opinionated Deputy Head

"Did you have a good Christmas?" I asked Penny on her return to work.

"I had the worst Christmas ever," she said. "I spent Friday cooking my turkey, which Rebecca had asked to have as she was too busy to buy one before the large turkeys ran out, and she had to feed Adrian's family on Christmas Day. That was all fine. On Christmas Eve Adrian drove Rebecca and me down to see Andreas and Selena. Selena's three and she fell asleep for an hour or two and I held her while she slept. She's very outspoken for three, and when she woke up, after a couple of minutes, she said in front of her father and the others to me, 'I want you to go now.' No one told her off.

"Christa took her out of the room and we didn't see her after that. Andreas said, 'I'm very sorry, I don't know what to say.' Then Christa came back and said, 'I think it's better if you go.' Rebecca said, 'It's better if we went now.' So we drove home.

"We went to Rebecca's house. Rebecca and Adrian were able to have some of the turkey I had cooked. I was deeply hurt."

I said, "She's three, she may have heard someone say this on TV or heard it from someone at school, and she may have been trying out a new form of words without fully understanding them. I wouldn't take it personally. She may be a young madam who's not been taught social politeness in her nursery school, and this may be remedied when she goes to her next school. There mustn't be a rift over it, you must carry on as if it never happened."

"I've decided I'm going to go away next Christmas," Penny said.

She continued: "The next day, Christmas morning, I went to Rebecca's house to help her get lunch ready. (I had prepped most of it at home for her.) At 12.45 Adrian came and said he had to collect his father, who had had a stroke and had also had cancer. It was a long drive to get him and his wife and he picked up Stacy, Adrian's sister, who is a local Deputy Head and who lives nearby now, so she could drink and not have to drive back home later, and his grandmother.

"They eventually all arrived. Rebecca and I were still in the kitchen, the central heating had been on and I was hot and opened a window. Stacy came into the kitchen and said, 'Oh, it's cold, there's a draught.' I said, 'Cooking's made it hot here, I've opened the window.'

"We served lunch. The talk soon turned to education. Someone mentioned private education, and Stacy the Deputy Head said, 'Oh, that's completely wrong.'

"Rebecca said, 'Parents make sacrifices to get their children forward. My mum and dad sent us to good schools so we could be top of the class.'

"'Oh,' Stacy, a Deputy Head in a local State school, said, 'That's not right. You should have gone to the school you were supposed to go to.'

"'But they wanted us to get on,' Rebecca said. 'They paid for one of the staff to tutor us on Saturday mornings to get us forward.'

"'That's completely wrong, it's a conflict of interest,' Stacy said.

"Rebecca said, 'The staff are allowed to do that in their spare time if they want to.'

"'No, it's wrong. They're with the school, not individual children who attend it.'

"After lunch they sat on the sofa with the television on. The programme was rubbish. They had no conversation while they just sat in silence. There were chocolates and biscuits on the table.

"Stacy said, 'Oh, those are lovely biscuits you've got, where did they come from? I'll ask Adrian to pick me up five packets and deliver them to me.'

"I said, 'You live nearly next door to where you can get them.' I told her the name of the shop. 'But I'd rather Adrian got them,' she said. She was selfish, Adrian had enough to do without getting biscuits from near where she lives and delivering them to her.

"It got to 9.30 and Rebecca was almost asleep on her feet, she was exhausted from working long hours in the NHS. Eventually I said about 10, 'I think we should stop and all go home now, so Rebecca can get some sleep.' Adrian's parents said, 'Oh,' and we all got ourselves together and came away. Adrian had to drive everyone home.

"Adrian was furious. He blamed me for breaking up the Christmas-Day party. Rebecca told me, she said, 'His family demand to see him on Christmas Day and Boxing Day every year, with no alternating or rotating with the other side of the family.'

"The next day, Boxing Day, Stacy had invited everybody to her house, me as well, but she wouldn't have Honey, Rebecca and Adrian's dog. That would mean Honey staying alone and in the dark. I didn't feel well, and after all that had gone on I said to Rebecca that morning on Boxing Day, 'I'm not feeling too good, it may be a good idea if I have Honey and you go to Stacy's.'

"Stacy's house was completely unheated. She said she couldn't afford to turn the heating on, she does have central heating. She complained that Rebecca's house was cold, but she had no heating on at all in hers. They had lunch and it went on and on. Eventually I texted and said, 'Please let me know when you're picking Honey up, I'm tired and need to go to bed.'

"There was no answer to my text. It got really late. In the end they came for Honey around midnight. Adrian didn't say anything, he took Honey and left without a word. Rebecca said, 'They want two full days of Adrian every Christmas, I have to go with it.' She was really tired and was trying to please everybody. She said, 'He's blaming you for everything. He wants an apology. I'm sorry, I have to go with it.' And she followed him home with Honey.

"I had bought myself a turkey while there were still stocks and that was taken from me and given to Adrian's family, and I did the cooking for this. We went to see Selena and she said she wanted me to leave. Adrian's family ate my turkey on Christmas Day, which I had cooked, and blamed me for breaking the party up. Whereas my side of the family was to have no days of Rebecca to ourselves. They didn't pick up Honey until midnight on Boxing Day, so I had her all day and all evening. And the next day Adrian was furious with me for spoiling his two days with his family on my turkey, by cutting short the final day. I really am thinking I'll go away next Christmas, with my friend."

Penny was on the verge of tears and I felt sad for her. She had done nothing wrong but had been the victim of an outspoken granddaughter who had not yet learned social etiquette, and she had been taken advantage of by her in-laws, and her son-in-law, who had assumed that Rebecca had bought and cooked the turkey and had blamed Penny for cutting short Christmas Day. He was irritated that his dog was not being looked after until after midnight by his tired mother-in-law on Boxing Day. Her situation was full of misunderstandings and mistreatments.

I said, "There must be no rift. You must all be speaking to each other in ten years' time. Did you take photos of Selena?" Penny nodded and showed me her pictures on her phone. "Print off and send in the post one of the photos of you holding her while she was asleep, and two pictures of her addressed to her so that receiving a letter in the post is a special gesture to a three-year-old. And as regards Adrian...."

Penny said, "He wants to talk to you. He did not appreciate how much you have done with your life, and that you were taught surveillance. He has applied for a surveillance post in the police. He'd like to come to see you."

"Tell him I'll gladly see him," I said. "Carry on as if nothing has happened, completely normally. I'll talk to him and impress on him the need for stability between Rebecca, you and him."

Suddenly everything looked better, and Penny smiled. "Thank you," she said, "that's a weight off my mind."

After she had gone I thought of the young madam, who would be leaving nursery school for main school soon, and would soon have correct social behaviour towards all members of her family; and of the opinionated socialist Deputy Head who lived near the shop she had asked Adrian to buy from. She was a left-winger with a socialist view of how schools should run and was not afraid to express her slanted opinions.

A Chauffeur and a GP

"Oh," Sam said as he drove me to London for my blood tests, echocardiogram and ECG, "I didn't tell you that I've found my dear friend James a flat. He's lived with me for the last year, he's been unwell. He was a GP but he's retired, he's now 68, and I've looked after him. He had a place in Spain and we all stayed there at different times.

"I had to leave him for a few days before Christmas. I was booked to go to Madeira, my neighbour asked if I'd go with her, then changed her mind and cancelled, so I went on my own. I left him behind as he was unwell. It was a nightmare flight. There were weather problems and they couldn't land in Madeira – we had two unsuccessful landings and circled for another hour – and eventually landed at Porto Santo, a different island, instead. We were stuck in the plane on the tarmac for another four-to-five hours before they decided to fly us to Gran Canaria, which was an hour and twenty minutes away. While we were waiting to leave my phone pinged. It said that we'd be collected the next day at 6.30am for the 11-o'clock flight to Funchal in Madeira, which would land at 1pm. All the other passengers' phones pinged, and there was a collective groan at the early start. At the hotel I couldn't move my feet.

"We had to get up really early the next morning. We were flown to Madeira and arrived at the hotel at 2.30pm. I was so exhausted from it all I lay on the bed in my clothes and fell asleep for five hours. I woke about 9.

"Two days later in Madeira I was ill and had to stay in bed for four days. I went down and helped myself to bits of the breakfast and took it back up to my room. I thought I might have Covid, so I went out and bought a test but I hadn't got it. For four days of my seven I couldn't do anything.

"Anyway, James is getting worse. He's got a chest infection, and I think it might be like what you've had, post-Covid or post-jab. He had a lovely place in Spain. Before the pandemic he worked seven days a week as a GP for 12 hours a day for a fortnight, with just three staff who worked for 12 hours a day. One was the practice manager, James's practice partner's husband. And then he'd have a fortnight off and go to his place in Spain with a view of the ocean, two minutes from a supermarket and a pharmacy, with everything he needed within reach. He played golf and he was on the edge of a golf course.

"Friends of ours wanted him to move near them. We all used to go out and stay near them and meet them every day. They found a place, and he moved – a week before the pandemic. The Spanish lockdown was very strict. Police were in the street enforcing it. You were allowed out once a day to get medicine and once a day to go to the supermarket. The supermarket was now a long way from his home instead of two minutes away, and so was the pharmacy. He was locked up in his room and there was no view of the ocean. Everything was worse. He had a terrible time and his chest infection began then and has got worse.

"He can't work now, he's been living with me. I've been looking after him. But now he's got a place of his own he's got worse, he's really unwell with palpitations, like what you had. I think he had Covid and developed it or had a Covid jab that's given him this, and he hasn't been able to throw it off as you have. And he's 68.

"Now I'm like him. I do some weeks driving many hours a day, and then I want to have time off in Greece. I take after him, intense work with early starts in the morning going on until late in the evening, and then complete relaxation. And he's 68 and unable to throw off his chest infection."

I did not say that I was 83 and had got myself back to normal. I sympathised. I looked at Sam. He had never married, he was about 63, I reckoned, and he had had friends in Spain he stayed with and met every day, just as now he had a place in Greece and out there regularly met up to ten friends from different countries, most of them single, who all had places nearby. I thought of the journeys I had made with him during the last year when he had not said he was looking after a sick GP. I wasn't sure that he had deliberately kept this quiet or had just not got round to telling me when he told me in detail about his plans for his home in Greece.

And I thought how we could rub shoulders with acquaintances we thought we knew well without having much idea of how they spent their time in their private lives.

A Saturday Girl and Leathermen

Arnold, our gardener, left suddenly, without working his notice. He had been cycling and one of the cyclists had told him about a full-time job going with the Council, to start the following week.

He told me, "I've got to find a full-time job bringing in another salary. My wife's been working in a pet shop, as you know. She had a Saturday girl, and found her lying on a mattress on the floor checking through her phone when she should have been painting a wall.

"She said, 'Shouldn't you be getting off your backside and doing what you're supposed to be doing?' That was all.

"The Saturday girl went back home and told her mother that my wife had used bad language – which I know she hadn't, because she never uses bad language – and her mother went to my wife's employer and complained that she had been bullying.

"The employer told my wife, who was aghast that she was being accused of bullying, and said her conduct was being questioned and she couldn't go back to work until it was sorted out.

"The Saturday girl's mother is now doing my wife's job. My wife hasn't been dismissed as she voluntarily stopped working, so on Monday we're going to see a lawyer and see if a case can be brought against the employer. There hasn't been a wrongful dismissal, but there has been lack of support. It's been a terrible time for my wife, she doesn't want to work in that pet shop any more.

"She used to work in a pharmacy, but she needs to refresh her knowledge, so she wants to have time out of work while she does that. She applied to Boots and she was shocked that they weren't insisting on uniforms, and the manager had things wrong with his dress and the way he handled the drugs. So she wasn't going to go there. But that gave her the idea of returning to pharmacy work."

"I am sorry you've got all this to cope with," I said. "None of it's your or your wife's fault. I'm wondering if the mother wanted your wife's job and put her daughter up to be her Saturday girl and whether the whole lying-down while at work was stage-managed to get your wife accused of bullying, so she could take her job."

Arnold's eyes widened. It had not occurred to him that that might be a possibility.

"Thank you for letting me go," he said. "I'll come back and do a 'handing-over', explain everything about the plants and the tools to my successor. And how to maintain the filter."

I later received an email containing his formal resignation on 20 September.

We could not find a suitable replacement for Arnold for a few weeks, and I emailed him towards the end of October.

On the last day of October I had a reply from his wife: "This is Leanne, speaking on behalf of Arnold, he's currently in Eastern Europe working with and I quote 'working with guys with Leathermen' unquote he apologies for his communicate and I've asked Leanne to correspond with you hopefully be back in Early November all the best regards Arnold."

Leanne had clearly forwarded a message from Arnold, and the time at the top of her email reflected the time zone he was in: two hours ahead of ours.

Arnold's friends were all ex-SAS. They had to leave the SAS when they were 41, and they all did things of a survival nature, including running a course in Wales that Arnold helped with. He would drive up on a Friday and return on a Monday. They all had Leathermen. Arnold showed me his Leatherman. It was like an elaborate penknife that had many uses and could deal with all problems. It was a bottle-and-can-opener and a cutter and pliers, and had 21 tools stored in its handles, including knives, screwdrivers, saws, wire-cutters, strippers and crimpers – and it could stab an intruder.

Arnold had told me they had had a discussion as to whether they should all go and do things in Ukraine. I Googled "Ukraine, time now" and I saw it was two hours ahead of our time. I was sure Arnold was in Ukraine, being paid the equivalent of two salaries to do dangerous things with his Leatherman. What had happened to his offer of a job with his local Council?

The next day I had an email from him: "I am back in the UK after a few weeks away. My job at the Council did not work out, it was sold to me as something it definitely was not. I believed I was doing the right thing for my family. I would dearly love to return to you, but could only do so in my current circumstances if there was a possibility of help with travel costs and a higher hourly rate. Would you be open to a discussion? Kindest regards, Arnold."

The next day Arnold emailed Simon that we should disregard this email as it was written in a moment of weakness. He needed to leave.

We appointed a new gardener in mid-November. He used to be a policeman with the Met and was leaving after 28 years with them, having investigated many murders and been in numerous riots. He said he had had enough.

Simon tried to contact Arnold to arrange a handing-over day, but could not get a reply. So I emailed him. Simon also wrote asking if he could arrange a time to 'hand over' to Carl.

Arnold replied on 18 November: "Apologies for the late reply, that's great news. I'm currently working away from home weekdays, but I'll do my utmost to make the appointment for a change-over."

That was the last we heard from him. Both Simon and I emailed but there was no further reply. He was clearly away, back in Ukraine?

I felt sad for Arnold. None of it was his doing. He had been hit with his wife's walk-out from her job, and the solicitor had clearly said there was nothing he could do as regards suing her employer. He had tried to make up her salary, but it involved leaving home with his group of associates who (according to Leanne) all had SAS Leathermen in their pockets. So he had gone from journeying down the A12 to the M25 to reach us to working in Eastern Europe in the same time zone as Ukraine, unable to talk about where he was and what he was doing, and I thought it likely that kind, helpful Arnold had been told by his organisers that he should not come to us so he would not divulge that he was working undercover in Ukraine.

An Ex-Met 'Guardener' and a River

Carl, our new gardener, came to my study's balcony door in January and asked if he could remove a plant that seemed to have taken over the rose beds. He said its roots were entangled with the rose-bushes' roots. I said he should remove it, and we talked about the news. I said police were leaving because the riot control they had to do was putting them at risk.

He said, "When I was in the Met we had to police the eco-protesters. A lot of us were on duty in London, at Oxford Circus, and the protesters were in our face. I remember a well-spoken woman coming up to me and saying, 'I need to go to the toilet.'

"I said, 'Give your name to the officer there and you can go. The toilets are over there.'

"She said, 'How do I know you'll let me back in?'

"If we didn't like the look of someone we very often didn't let them back in, she was right. I repeated, 'Give your name to the officer and then you can go.'

"She said, 'I'm not doing that,' and where she was standing in front of me she hitched up her dress and did what she needed to do from a standing position. A small river began to flow in our direction, and our police line was shoulder to shoulder with policemen standing at attention, and when they saw the river approaching they did an imperceptible shuffle away from it like this." He acted out standing straight and looking in front of him with arms by his side and shuffling imperceptibly to his right. "We all shuffled away from it and when the river reached where we had been standing no policemen got their feet wet."

I laughed. His mimicking of their deadpan avoidance of what the eco-protester had done was very funny.

Carl went on his way to work in the cold on the rose beds. He had left the Met after long nights standing guard outside Buckingham Palace and he had told me he wondered what he was doing, why he wasn't at home. He had left at 51, when after 28 years he qualified for his Met pension of around £22,000, and he was topping up his pension by working for me, getting paid nearly as much as when he was in the police without riots and rivers.

What he had had to put up with at Oxford Circus must have added to his desire to leave. He had done protection in the Met, he was now protecting me. I called him my "guardener", a cross between my guard and gardener. He had settled in to his new work very quickly, and I hoped nothing that happened on my estate would give him cause to leave.

A Mannequin and Unconsciousness

Darren came to finish his first-aid course. Penny, Carl and I sat before him as he unpacked 'Little Anne', a life-size human waist-up torso, a dummy.

He was a fireman in the fire brigade who had often encountered death and the need to save lives, and he emphasised that all parts of the human body regenerate themselves except for the brain, which, if starved of oxygen, can only survive for three minutes. He said that if we encounter one of us lying unconscious, we should assume that the person had stopped breathing and that the three minutes had just begun. We should begin CPR (cardiopulmonary resuscitation). We should cut away clothes in the interests of speed, using scissors in the pack, and place one hand palm down on the middle of the person's chest and place the other hand on top and press down hard. He demonstrated on the mannequin, and carried on demonstrating as he told us what to do next. After every 30 chest compressions, we should give two breaths: hold the person's nose, tilt the head back and blow into the mouth, and watch the chest to see if it rises – twice. If it doesn't, carry on with the CPR. If it does, end the CPR.

He said, "If you're alone with someone unconscious you'll have to break off and dial 999 and open the door for an ambulance and also a gate if necessary. Ideally get someone else to do these things as you're keeping the person alive by your CPR, which elongates their body's oxygen. I realise you're longing to be able to stop, but keep going. If you've got a defibrillator, as you have, then open it like this, put one of the two pads on the right breast – peel off the paper – and the other on the side of the left breast like this. Then stand back and follow the voice, which will tell you to give the person you're with an electric shock – to restart the heart if it's stopped and get oxygen flowing into the brain."

He said, "If you're alone and have a heart attack and are lying down on the floor and are not breathing, then of course you can't give yourself CPR or use a defibrillator. If you're breathing, have a mobile on you and ring 999 and somehow try and open the front door and if necessary a gate. If you're unconscious you'll be found, and if you're not breathing CPR will be done on you."

I pondered. I was 83, and wondered if I should wear a buzzer round my neck to go to a local care home so someone could ring me back or come round themselves – they'd have to have a key – or ring for an ambulance. There was nothing to do when you were on the floor having a heart attack or stroke and couldn't move, except try to reach for the phone in your pocket and try to get help – so long as the ambulance crew and nurses were not on strike that day.

After Darren had gone, having talked and got us to practice on 'Little Anne' for two hours, I sat and faced the stark reality. If I had a heart attack or stroke and lapsed into unconsciousness and was alone, I would not be able to ring. I would remain unconscious and would eventually be found. If I had stopped breathing and had been three minutes without oxygen and had started breathing again, I might be brain-dead.

I sat for some while watching the distant sunset, immersed in the sunset of my life and my inability to prevent my end when it approached, if I was alone that day. I thought, we are all alone. We may be married and have someone who will be back that evening, but at my time of life the end can come at any time, and there may be no going to hospital in an ambulance. I vowed to get on and organise my departure – finish my work and leave everything tidy, so if I were suddenly called aloft I could go in a co-operative spirit.

A Holy Man and Skeletons

During a break from proofreading to rest our eyes from the screen, Penny asked, "Are you going to see your old school friends at this year's Shrove Tuesday dinner?"

"I shan't go this year," I said, sunk in thought. "Derek Minstrel isn't going – his wife's got dementia and is in a home – and last year I was seated near James Pink. He wants to come into the schools and distribute *New Testaments*. He pressed me really hard. He reminds me of Holy Joe in Old Loughton.

"He had *New Testaments* in his bike's saddle-bag. He once stopped me outside the bookshop, having bought enough *New Testaments* to fill his saddle-bag on his building labourer's wages to give away. He worked for W. & C. French and his name was Grey. He was nearly bald with grey hair round his ears. He bent and said to me, when I was about six, 'I'm giving you a *New Testament*. Read it and come to the Lord. And don't play football on a Sunday.'

"He knelt and prayed in the street, in the High Road with traffic whizzing by on either side. I saw him once at the junction of Brook Road and Alderton Hill. He had leaned his bike against a wall and was kneeling in the middle of the road with his arms up and his hands together, praying aloud with eyes closed, talking up to the sky, cycle clips still round his trousers above his ankles, with cars going backwards and forwards on either side. He had told me 'Don't play football on a Sunday,' and I was walking back from church one Sunday morning with my younger brother, who knew this and kicked a stone and said, 'We're playing football on a Sunday.' He was part of Old Loughton. Pink is of the old school, like Grey.

"Another character in Old Loughton was Dafty. He was called Dafty by everyone. He was a road sweeper who pushed a waist-high box on wheels, and he swept up leaves and scooped them up with his spade and tipped them into the top of the box. He was swarthy from the sun and wore a peaked cap and he smiled vacantly at everyone with an open mouth. If a lady was walking in the High Road past him he would interpose himself on her route with his broom and smile vacantly at her. Everyone called him Dafty. Sometimes Mrs. Dafty came by with a pram filled with babies and small children, and she would talk to him briefly.

"Then there was Gladys. She was another Old-Loughton character. She had an open-air greengrocer's opposite St Mary's Church. It had an awning to keep the rain off the vegetables. It was called 'The White

Shop', and she wore a white overall. When I was five or so I was sent up to the High Road with a large wicker basket, and I'd ask for 'Two pounds of potatoes, please'. Gladys had a snub nose and a wrinkled, swarthy face. She wore dark mittens, and with her fingers she would grab large potatoes that had earth and chunks of mud on them, and load them onto her battered gold-coloured brass pan on her scales and tip them into my basket. Then she would wipe her earth-streaked, muddy hands on her white overall, so it had earth-smears all over it. Sometimes she wore a dark beany hat.

"Then there was Freddie Durrant. He was another Old-Loughton character. He was beetle-browed, he had enormously thick black eyebrows, piercing dark eyes and smarmed-back black hair brushed on the sides of his bald head. He looked severe. His shoe shop was where the bookshop is now. He was our neighbour, and towards the end of the war my brother would call through the fence when Durrant was in his garden, 'Dumma, Dumma, Bobbie 'lower.' ('Durrant, Durrant, pick Bobbie a flower.')

"In his shop he had a shoe-fitting fluoroscope or pedoscope, an X-ray machine in a waist-high wooden cabinet, and when my mother was buying me new sandals I would put one of my feet in the opening at the bottom and peer through the black viewing tube and see my foot in a green glow and wiggle my toes. They were skeleton toes in a green sea, I could see all the bones in all my toes. I could see if the sandals were too small for me by assessing the distance between my big toe and the curve of the sandal in the green glow. Durrant would look himself through the second viewing tube and check the new sandals were the right size.

"Fluoroscopes were in many shoe shops in the 1930s and 1940s, but were later banned for exposing shoppers to radiation that could have a lasting impact on their health. But I could remember looking at my toe bones and seeing the feet of my skeleton within their surrounding skin."

I was sunk in thought, back in the year before the end of the war. "That was the first time," I said at last, "I realised I was a living skeleton, seeing my feet in his green X-ray machine. All those people from Old Loughton are now skeletons, and I will soon be one of them, like them."

A Crutch and a Brick Wall

I went to the annual Shrove Tuesday supper to see Derek Minstrel. I wasn't going to go, but the Director of Philanthropy rang me and asked if I'd be going. I said I might not know many there, and asked if Derek Minstrel was going. He said, "Yes, he is." So I emailed Derek and arranged to meet him there.

I knew Derek had had cancer in his throat and had been ill with Covid eighteen months previously. I knew he had spent two weeks in hospital and had been unable to attend last year's Shrove Tuesday supper, and I also knew his wife was now in a care home. I went because I knew he would be there and wanted to catch up.

I registered and took a shiny booklet showing those attending, and saw I was the second oldest in terms of the years Old Boys arrived at the school. Then groups drifted in from chapel, and I saw Minstrel join the queue and was shocked. He had his left arm in a grey metallic crutch and his face looked very lined. He had aged since I last saw him, he looked far older than 84.

I walked over to him and greeted him. He said, "I'm very deaf, you'll have to speak loudly or I can't hear you." He was standing apart from the queue, which was moving, and I guided him back into his place. He stood and said nothing, and I said to the lady who was ticking surnames on a list and who had just registered me, "It's Minstrel."

"That's you?" she asked.

"No," I said, "you've just done me. Him."

Derek did not seem to be hearing what we had been saying. He just stood with his crutch.

His name was ticked and we took glasses of sparkling wine and with difficulty he hobbled a few paces away from the queue on his crutch. We stood.

"Why have you got a crutch?" I asked after I had sipped my wine.

"It's further to coronavirus," he said, and he would not say any more.

"You had it badly, in hospital two weeks."

"Yes," he said, scanning the list of attenders. "Did you know I've got a pacemaker?"

"No," I said. I knew immediately that Covid had caused his heart to beat slowly, at less than 50 beats a minute (bradycardia), and that the pacemaker was there to correct his slow heart. "You're at the opposite end of the spectrum from me. Covid gave you a heart rate of less than 50 and it doubled my heart rate so I have to take a beta-blocker every morning."

I had to speak up so he could hear me. It was as if I was making a public speech.

He said, "I wonder if I had something else in the hospital. Covid and something else?"

He was moving with difficulty, one side of his face looked peculiar. I wondered if he had had a mini-stroke that had not been diagnosed and had made mobility difficult and required a crutch. As a result of Covid he had become deaf, needed a pacemaker, found walking difficult and looked semi-paralysed on his left side. A stroke on the right side of the brain impairs the left side of the body, and he seemed to have difficulty in controlling the crutch with his left hand, and his left leg seemed to be stiff and immobile; and his left ear seemed to be deaf. He could still talk but his words from his left brain seemed slightly slurred, as though he had trouble expressing them. A stroke in his right brain could have been responsible for his deafness and his slow heart rate and his immobility on his left side. And Covid might have caused him to have a stroke.

Vincent Daniel, a multi-millionaire, was there with long hair flowing to his shoulders, looking owl-eyed with slit eyes behind his black-rimmed glasses. He beamed at us. Derek recounted an old story in abrupt sentences, how we had encountered Hitler in Sicily, in Catania. We had stayed in the youth hostel there, sleeping in sleeping-bags in the large foyer as there were no free beds, and Hitler had come and stood near us each dawn and also last thing at night. He only appeared in the foyer late at night or early in the morning, he had not appeared during the day.

I said with assumed sincerity, "I reckon he fled from his bunker to Italy just after Mussolini was hanged upside down, and was hidden in a monastery and later moved to the youth hostel as the warden, who was clearly working in conjunction with him, had a speedboat that could take him across the Aegean to the Turkish coast if he was discovered." There was mirth, and Vincent Daniel beamed.

Derek Minstrel then said he had to sit down, and he was going to find our table and sit at it. He walked slowly with great difficulty. I saw the new Head, a bald, smiley man, and went over and introduced myself. "Welcome," I said. "Have you settled in well?"

We chatted for a short while and then I extricated myself and went in search of table 2. I found Derek Minstrel sitting next to Ronald Panther. I sat round the corner of the table from him, and talked to them and across Derek to Ronald, who told me he lived in Stanford Rivers.

Now everyone came to their tables. A thin bespectacled man came and sat by me and said, "It's Philip Rawley, isn't it? I teach at the school, and I'm recalling Bernard. How is he getting on?"

I turned away from Derek Minstrel and brought him up to date on Bernard's studies.

He said, "I taught him maths, I have a good memory for those I've taught, but not such a good memory for when I taught them."

I said Bernard was doing a Masters now, and he was pleasantly surprised.

Then I recognised the American Director of Philanthropy who had telephoned me. He had said he wanted to chat to me, and I had looked him up on the internet and found he had built a wall of bricks in the school, each brick costing £5,000 (small bricks) or £10,000 (large bricks). On each brick was inscribed the name of the donor. I guessed he wanted to ask me to donate £10,000 for a large brick, and I was keen not to have the chat with him he wanted. He was looking at me, but Bernard's teacher had occupied the place next to me he wanted, so he sat at the far end of the large table, out of speaking range.

We had seafood on a dill pancake, then braised lamb on a pancake roulade, and finally apple cinnamon *tarte tatin* with vanilla ice-cream. I had made my sparkling wine last, and I now had a little red wine Ronald poured me. Derek ate awkwardly, and left much of his meal. He asked for left-overs so he could feed them to his dog, and a waitress brought him a 'doggy bag'.

During the meal I asked Derek about his wife. "She's in a care home on Bell Common."

"How often do you visit?"

"Once or twice a week."

I also said to him, "You should get a private MOT of your health, and ask: 'Could I have had Covid *and* something else – a stroke, for example.' They may be able to give you something so you can get rid of your crutch."

He said, "Good idea. I know a doctor who can do the MOT at my home."

His conversation was answers to questions now, his fluency had gone. And at 9.30, when the speeches had ended, including a speech from the new Head without the hand-held microphone, which wasn't working, Derek said, "I'm going to slip away now."

But he couldn't get up. He stood his crutch upright on the floor and pushed on it, but could not raise his seat from the chair. His crutch fell on the floor with a clatter that turned heads, and I picked it up. Ronald held his left elbow his side, and I held his right elbow my side and pushed upwards and eventually he staggered to his feet, scraping his chair noisily on the floor, and turned slowly and awkwardly. I put his crutch by his left arm, and he crutched through the open door near us to "slip away".

When Derek had gone I thought of his Covid-induced crutch, and looking to the far end of the table I thought of the brick wall the Director of Philanthropy wanted me to contribute to. Derek Minstrel was struggling for mobility with his crutch but was facing a brick wall because his Covid-caused stroke had not been diagnosed, and he was unable to progress from the event that had put him in hospital. I made a note to press him to have an MOT that might confirm he should not be treated for Covid, but for a stroke.

Quince Sauce and a Stained Shirt

We had our anniversary lunch in a restaurant we last visited before lockdown. It was in a converted stable and specialised in fine dining, and was a taste experience. I wore an open-necked white shirt and a blazer, and we sat under a large picture of a stag with seven-branched antlers. Each course was brought and explained and served, sometimes by the owner, who had greeted us warmly: "Hello, haven't seen you for a while."

"When was the last time you were here?" she asked as we sipped champagne and she served chicken, ham and hock.

"Just after you had twins," Pippa said. "Three years ago."

Annabel nodded. She had met a Bermudan and married him. He was the chef, and she was front-of-house. They had spent time in Australia running a restaurant and had been in the UK for several years now.

We had two small courses that were not on the menu, and then brown mushrooms with shallots, and then stone bass. The taste lingered, and we savoured what we had tasted. Then we were served the main course of roasted venison, celeriac and brown quince sauce.

I looked at the quince sauce and thought how quinces, bright yellow fruit, were native to Iran, Turkey, Greece and Crimea, and how quince paste could be made into brown quince sauce. I ate carefully, savouring the tender loin of venison and the venison sausage and thinking of the antlered stag above me. I savoured the caramelised celeriac purée, and dragged bits of the purée through the brown sauce to mop it up and make it edible.

We carried on with a cheese selection, followed by a small pre-dessert, and then a chocolate mousse and mascarpone sorbet. There was a chocolate each, and then a plate arrived saying 'Happy Anniversary' in chocolate with two pastilles on it for us to chew.

I settled up and we left. I lingered near the door and helped Pippa on with her padded jacket.

We went out into the cold, still savouring nine tasty courses on our tongues. It was only when I reached my car in the car park that I looked down and caught sight of the brown stains on my white shirt, where quince sauce had dropped. The front of my shirt had been in full view of the receptionist who gave Pippa her coat.

I was old, I dribbled and drooled and spilt brown sauce down my white shirt when I was in smart casual, I needed a bib, but not to worry.... I was keeping going, that was the main thing. I had got myself to where the quince sauce was.

Then I wondered if some of the venison (deer) was mixed with it. I saw it as a tribute to the taste of the main course, the memory of which – the stag with seven-branched antlers, the venison and quince sauce – was down the front of my shirt for all to see as well as in my stomach and on my satisfied taste buds. Being old meant keeping going, and not worrying if there were understandable accidents now and again.

A King and a Blackbird

Jack's organ composition was being performed at a lunch-time recital in a Cheapside church. Pippa and I were taken to the City by car, and after being driven backwards and forwards in an attempt to get near the church and encountering new 'no entry' signs, we were put out to walk and arrived at the church five minutes before the start. I walked down the nearest of two aisles with arched columns on either side and gated pews seemingly filled with single old men, and Jack, wearing a suit, stood up and greeted us eagerly. As host he had been sitting strategically in the back row near the door.

We walked along the back of the pews and entered a gated pew where Florence was sitting, in the same pew as Jack but in the next aisle and separated from Jack by a low wooden wall, where there were two vacant seats. The organist had played in the proms and had an international reputation, and he began with Buxtehude's phases of the moon and went on to Holst's *Saturn*.

Jack had written a triptych based on the conjunction of Jupiter and Saturn on 21 December 2020, which I had looked for across fields near our home. He saw the conjunction mythologically as ending the astrological Age of Pisces and beginning the Age of Aquarius.

Jack's piece lasted about 20 minutes. It lacked Holst's tunefulness, but had impressive shimmering effects and at the end crashing cadenzas that led to swelling triumphant volume. At the end the organist emerged and bowed, and beckoned Jack down the aisle. Jack strode down, grinning, and they bowed together. Sitting in the back pew, I took a picture of them on my phone, holding it up and taking it quietly as one was not supposed to take pictures in a church.

Jack returned, and the organist then played Holst's *Jupiter*. And then the organist came out for more applause and again beckoned Jack, and the two bowed together. And then we all stood and drifted towards the door.

Pippa and I talked with Florence and then Rex came up, and Jack himself. He chatted to some of the audience and then we walked to a nearby pub, The Counting House, where Jack had booked a room at the back. The pub itself was nearly empty. We walked to our room and were given sparkling wine and offered slices of pork pie. About 20 stood and chatted.

Pippa, Jack's wife and Florence withdrew to a small room on one side that had chairs. It looked like a kind of parlour.

The organist came and greeted me, and then disappeared with his assistant to do technical work on preparing a video. I chatted to Rex, and commiserated with his diagnosis of early Parkinson's disease. His right hand was trembling slightly as he held his glass of sparkling wine, I noticed. I said he would live at least another 15 years. He said, "Would I want to?"

The organist then returned and gave Jack a memory stick saying, "It's all on there," and he then took a sparkling wine Jack offered him. He told me he lived near Ely, and when I said, "Not far from Cambridge" (where I knew he was a Fellow), he confirmed that he was a Fellow at a Cambridge college. He told me he had attended another college, but had opened this college's new organ and they had made him an honorary Fellow, even though he was more in touch with the college where he was an undergraduate.

Eventually I stood with Jack and congratulated him on hosting the small gathering at The Counting House. I chanted, "'The King was in The Counting House, counting out his money.'"

Someone listening said, "The Queen was in the garden, hanging out the clothes.'"

"No," I said, "'The Queen was in the parlour, eating bread and honey. The *maid* was in the garden, hanging out the clothes –'"

Florence interjected, "'And down came a blackbird, and pecked off her nose.'"

"That's right," I said. "The Queen had someone to hang out her clothes." And Jack grinned.

And then I saw Jack as the King, counting out the use he could make of the video. His wife was still in the next room, the parlour, eating and drinking as if there was bread and honey, and the organist had withdrawn to the nearly-empty pub to cope with the video, like hanging out the clothes. But no blackbird had pecked off his nose.

Or was I the blackbird, doing 'not-done' things like taking a photo in church, telling someone diagnosed with Parkinson's disease how long he had to live, and sounding the organist out about the college he was a Fellow of, when he preferred his own Alma Mater?

Then I thought, the blackbird these days doesn't peck off a maid's nose, he observes everything and acts as he pleases and gets to the truth of things and talks to organists truthfully. While a true man of letters talks in disguise, he holds a mirror up to those around him. He also carries on, keeps going in his old age, perseveres with a Latin motto of *Persevera*. The modern blackbird was not cruel and misogynistic towards maids but a harbinger of truth and perseverance.

A Pet Shop and Kyiv

Arnold came, looking more creased and lined during the last seven months. He got out of his car and chatted to Carl, his replacement. When I joined them Carl took a step back and said he would be strimming nearby and would leave us to chat.

Arnold said I was looking well. I told him I had written a reference for his new employer.

"Thank you," he said. "He offered me the job but said it was subject to a reference. He's about five minutes from me, they've got a lot of barns on their field site. They maintain gardens all over, including in London, Arabs' gardens in particular. The Arabs live away and want their gardens maintained even though the house is empty. Their day starts at 4.30am and ends in the early afternoon, so I have to be in at

4.30am. I've already asked to go four days a week so I can sleep late one day.

"I've been helping my friend Declan, one of the ex-SAS men I met on the survival course in Wales. He's had a business storing wheat and grain in Ukraine. It's the bread basket of the world. He said, 'If the Russians come they'll clean it out, and I'll be ruined. I want to move it all to England and store it, and move it back when the war is all over.'

"I made seven trips through Poland and helped him clear the store out completely. It was hard work but he paid well, I got a good lump sum. His store was just outside Kyiv, and employed 250 Ukrainians. I wasn't really aware of the war except at the Polish frontier. There it was like the Second World War, thousands trying to flee to Poland. I had to queue for hours to get across the border, even though I had all the right papers. There were missiles that landed near Poland, they shook me."

Carl approached with his strimmer and I beckoned him to join us and they left together so Arnold could explain how the filter, which he had installed, cleaned the pond.

Later he rang the doorbell, and I invited him to sit in the conservatory for a chat. Pippa joined us. He declined a coffee.

"Carl's generally on top of it," he said, "but the grass is long. I always tried to keep it short so it looked tidy."

I said there had been so much rain he was behind with the grass cutting.

He talked about his mother, who had a leaky heart valve at 96, and was stubborn. "She was so stubborn when the Council offered her equipment she declined. I had to buy it," he said with a laugh.

He talked about his wife. "She got a job at Mercedes Benz in Bishop's Stortford, and loved selling and has been promoted to sell to parts of London. She loves what she's doing. The pet shop she was in has closed. The Saturday girl's mother ran it, and no one came. They used to take three or four thousand over a weekend, but the customers stopped going when Leanne left. I needed to leave you because the meetings with the solicitor were costly. There were three meetings and they mounted up, but then Leanne said, 'I don't want to take any action, I just want to move on.' She's so pleased to be doing what she's doing now, she loves it."

He talked about his sons. One was doing financial speculation online at home during lockdown, and had done sufficiently well to buy a new BMW. The other was doing well in recruitment, placing someone in a job in a London Council and then taking 12 per cent of their salary for some months as his fee.

He then said, "Ever since my accident, the one I told you about, I've gone off cycling. I don't want to cycle any more. We're going to Majorca on Monday. I've left Leanne reading during our past holidays and I've gone cycling, but not this time. I shall sit with her and read a book. I've been selfish. She likes me to be there, even if she's reading. So that's what I'll be doing."

It was time for him to go. I watched him drive off. He had left because he needed to go full-time as his wife had lost her job in the pet shop to the Saturday girl's mother, and he had kept going by taking a job involving visits to Ukraine and now he was still working four days a week but was nearer home than we were. His wife's loss of her job after telling off the Saturday girl and being accused of bullying had caused him to leave us, but there was no bitterness. His life had generally improved, and although he was no longer cycling he was contented with his life. I watched him drive out of our gates with some sadness but a feeling of relief that things had turned out all right.

A Good Samaritan and a Rebuff
(Or: "I Don't Want to be Here")

"James died," said Sam as he drove me to London for my bi-annual medical check. "My friend Alan went to his flat and said there was no answer. He and I got in and James was lying dead on his back. He'd been to the bathroom and had a heart attack. He was 68.

"It's been a nightmare," he said as I commiserated. "He's estranged from his daughter. She's 38. She and his son didn't want anything to do with him because he was shaky. It was the alcohol. James's hands shook and they were embarrassed by it. She didn't want to have anything to do with his death. We phoned an ambulance and they came quickly. The paramedic took one look at him and shook his head and said, 'It happened too long ago.' He turned him over and looked to see if there were any tell-tale signs of violence. Nothing.

"They rang the police. The police didn't come for six hours, so two paramedics had to wait for them with their ambulance, which could have been out doing three calls and visits to hospital with emergencies. We waited with them. They should just have left a junior there.

"The police examined the scene and then locked the door. His funeral's tomorrow. His daughter's relented a bit and taken a suit of his and a shirt from a wardrobe to the undertaker's so he can be dressed in it.

"I got him the flat. It's in our block. I like cooking and my neighbour likes doing laundry, so I cook for everybody and Sue does everybody's laundry. We share. But the first day James went into the flat that I arranged for him, he shut the door. Wouldn't allow me in. That was in January, and it's now May. Since then the only time I've been in his flat was when I found him dead. I used to see him in the pub. It's come to light he said to Alan in the pub, soon after he moved in in January, 'I don't want to be here.'"

"What did he mean by 'here'?" I asked. "'In the flat' or 'alive'?"

"I don't know," Sam said. "I think he meant 'alive'. He was 68 and he had years ahead of him, but his alcohol meant he was shaky – I said to him once, 'I'm not taking you out if you throw your food about' and he laughed – and I think he made up his mind that he wanted to lock himself away and go. And he's had his wish. Look, here's a picture of him on my phone."

He handed me his phone through the gap between the two front seats while driving, and, sitting in the back, I saw an overweight, balding, casually-dressed man laughing with his mouth wide open in what looked like a hotel bar. I handed him back his phone.

Sam was silent as he drove. Then he added, "So I've arranged the funeral. It's where he used to live for many years, I'm hoping some of his old neighbours will attend. It's tomorrow. I'll be there, and I said to his daughter, 'Why don't you just turn up at the back? You don't have to stay on at the end, you can leave at the end of the service.' But she hasn't had a hand in organising the funeral, and because of the estrangement he arranged for me to be his next of kin."

Sam fell silent again. I pondered a bizarre situation. James had been estranged from his family and had made Sam his next of kin, so Sam had organised his funeral, not his family. James had lived with Sam for a year and had then moved into his own flat in the block, which Sam had found, presumably as soon as it became available. He had shut Sam out and said, "I don't want to be here." His hands were shaking because of alcohol after being a hard-working GP. The twists and turns were hard to fathom.

I pondered on Sam's kindness and James shutting him out of his life and not wanting to be alive. Sam had been a Good Samaritan, and James had rebuffed him as he had his family. Inwardly I shook my head.

A Chairman and a Donor

Simon was away, and Pippa and I collected Al from cricket training. We were asked to collect him at 7.45pm, but it was a lovely summery evening and the training had not finished. A semicircle of small boys were taking it in turns to catch high hits from a coach, and both nets had padded, helmeted batsmen who were being bowled at by a queue of bowlers. A coach was sitting on a chair behind the bowlers.

I saw Al in the bowling queue and waved. We talked through the back netting.

"You just missed me batting," he said. "I hit all the balls they bowled at me in all directions."

"Good," I said in an undertone. "Which is your captain?" I asked.

"The one who opens the bowling with you."

At that moment a ball thudded into the coach's chair as he rapidly swung his legs out of the way, and ricocheted into the netting near where I was standing.

"Guess," Al said.

I pointed at the batsman who had hit the ball. He was taller than all the others.

Al nodded. "He's really good. That's why he's in the Essex team."

It was Al's turn to bowl. He was in the queue to bowl in the net next to the captain's. He ran in and bowled, and the ball pitched slightly outside the batsman's leg stump. The batsman hit the ball into the side netting.

I moved away and watched Al bowl two more balls, one straight and one outside the batsman's off stump. Then he moved to the other net and bowled at the captain, who sliced the ball in the air. The coach (still recovering from nearly being hit by the ball that thudded into his chair) said it would have been caught and gave him out, and the captain came out of the nets and bent and took off his pads on the grass. Al looked triumphant.

Then I saw the chairman. He was very white-haired and he was walking towards a new scoreboard. The metal slat blinds rose and revealed a black scoreboard showing yellow scores: batsman 1 with 4 and batsman 2 with 4, and the total 8.

Dusk had begun to fall and the lights on the scoreboard were bright. Then the blinds came down again, and the chairman walked back across the field where catching was happening and spoke to an Indian who was standing a couple of paces from me. He eyed me up while he talked and included me in what he was saying, so I stepped forward.

"You're busy," I said, "things wouldn't happen without your input."

"You're right," the Indian said.

"I was just checking the scoreboard's still working," the chairman said. "Someone has to check."

"We spoke last season," I said. "I'm Al's grandfather. I've come to collect him when he's finished. He greatly appreciated getting a trophy for 'most-improved player' last season. Thank you for doing that."

"We try and encourage them," the chairman said. "I'm glad he was pleased."

"He's very keen," I said.

I said I had first played on the field before us over sixty-six years ago, playing for the local rival club, and the Essex captain Insole (who went on to become the chairman of the Test and

County Cricket Board and England Manager) had told me I was on Essex's watchlist. "You're still a link with Essex, I believe," I said. "If they're good enough they get sent for a trial. If they're not, they don't."

"It's a bit like that," the chairman agreed. "We've got that side under control." And before I could ask if Al was in line for a trial with Essex he said, "Several members of the club who are watching right now have done brilliant things. One's done the car park, one's improved our website online. There's a lady over there who's made fifty thousand from preparing club food. But you know," he added, "I'm worried about the club finances. The energy used to be £300 and it's now £1,200. I know everyone's facing this at this time, it's not just us. I'm seventy-five now, and I worry about the club's money. It's hard. We're closed from October to March but there are still costs. I want to hold events in the pavilion in the winter months to bring some money in."

"Good idea," I said.

"Money's getting tight, and we don't want the club to close. We could do with a donation."

He looked hopefully in my direction. I watched Al bowling and waved to him.

I was now in dangerous territory. If I asked what chance Al had of playing for Essex, I risked being propositioned for a donation. Everyone was at it. I had had a letter only the previous day from my former school showing a wall with bricks and one brick saying: "Rawley family supporting the pupils now and in the future."

I extricated myself and found Pippa in the car park. I chatted for a couple of minutes and then went back to collect Al. The nets were empty. He had gone. I peered at the far end of the car park and saw him walk in from the road. He had been looking for us in the road. He carried a bulging sports bag stuffed with his equipment, which he put in the boot of Pippa's car.

Pippa drove to his house, and I went in with him to check he could find the spaghetti Bolognese his mother had left for him, which just needed heating. He found it immediately. I was struck by how adult he was as he coped with his food. I left him to it, and came away.

So he had done his cricket training and the first match was on Sunday, but he wouldn't be playing as he and his sister were lunching with us. He was of an age when parents had to be full-time drivers, and he would love to have a trial for Essex Under-15s if it could be arranged, but again someone would have to drive him to the ground. And school work had to be done, and his school matches had priority over his club matches. It was difficult. And the chairman and the coaches devoted their lives to the club, they were good club men, and they belonged. They spent their spare moments at the ground, checking the scoreboard, mowing the field and pitch. There was always something to do. And there was always a chance they could find a donor.

I thought of Al's keenness to bowl, and his pride at getting the captain and Essex player out. I thought of the chairman and the Indian as club men. And somehow I had been framed as a possible donor. I had gone to collect Al and was being primed for a donation – and that was what a good club man should do.

Sewn Trousers and a 'Refurb'

When I got back from a medical day in London I got into my car and drove to the High Road to pick up my repaired trousers. The shop was being refitted and as I found my pink ticket saying TRS ('trousers') a fellow said, "I'm the builder. The owner is here but he's gone out, can you come back in a few minutes?"

I had to see if Marks & Spencer stocked some white vinegar to clear some scaling I had to do on a small dehumidifier, so I went there and found they were out of stock for white vinegar. I returned and encountered the owner, a portly Arab, who said, "We're having a 'refurb'. Our stock is next door in the boutique shop and they close at five. So I can't get in and get it. It's 5.10 now. Can you come tomorrow between 10am and 4pm?"

I did not know what to say. I could have said: 'You cleaned the trousers and I wore them and within five minutes discovered there was a tear in the crotch that needed an invisible repair. The tear must have happened while you cleaned them.' But they could have split after I put them on. There was no evidence his shop had caused the tear. I nodded.

I showed up the next day at 10.30am. Four Arab builders were standing around in his shell of a shop, and a huge floor-to-ceiling washing-machine was behind the counter and hid the rest of the shop from the doorway. I now saw a fifth Arab was inside the shop up a ladder. The walls had begun to be lined with grey metallic-looking slats.

The owner, the stout Arab, took my pink ticket and bustled off to the boutique shop next door. He returned with my trousers in a plastic bag, and a newly-sewn seam. It was neatly done, perhaps by the boutique shop. I paid him £15 in cash.

"Is that washing-machine new?" I asked of the huge machine.

"Yes," he said proudly before the five Arabs. "It's German. It's the best. I'm on a mission."

"Well done," I said, looking at the blind-like struts that had been nailed to a stripped wall. I now thought they might be wooden, not metallic. "I hope it goes well. I'm sure your customers will work round you as I have."

I left, pleased that I had mended trousers. Their inside leg measurement was 31 inches, and I had discovered they were no longer made. I had ordered 32-inch trousers to replace them, and when they arrived they turned out to be 31 inches but were not pleated. They no longer made pleated 31-inch trousers, and the new pair were slightly tight. The pleated pair would be more comfortable for office work, so now I had my everyday pair back and usable, and a similar, smarter pair of trousers to wear to events.

I thought of the Arab. He was doing a fundamental 'refurb' at a time of economic crisis, and no doubt the team of Arabs were doing a cut-price job. He was on a mission to take business from other shops, and I wondered if he would now offer a laundry service as well as dry-cleaning.

The main thing from my point of view was that my trousers had been sewn, there was no hint of the gaping split there had been. Yes, I had been inconvenienced by the 'refurb', but the job I had asked to be done had been done, and who knows, there might be a new laundry service I could make use of now and again when the 'refurb' was over.

Stroke: A Wounded Deer and a Healed Heart

My daughter Susan and her late husband had given me a bronze stag and deer for my birthday just over five years previously. They carried them from their car, wrapped up. I stood them near our carp pond, and when Susan visited me we would walk down to where they were grazing near the pond and we would feed the fish. The idea was that I was the stag and she was the deer.

That recent Sunday afternoon I walked down to the pond and found the deer lying on its side with a snapped rear leg. Our gardener must have clipped it when he cut the grass with our tractor the previous Friday. I brought the deer in and stuck its leg back on with superglue.

As I prepared my supper in our kitchen the next evening, on the Monday, there was a phone call from my ex-wife Sibyl about our daughter Susan.

"Something terrible has happened," she said. "Susan has had a stroke. She's in Ipswich Hospital. It's the worst kind of stroke, at the back of the head which does most damage, and she's not speaking or seemingly understanding, just crying. It happened after 10.30 yesterday morning when she had a Sunday delivery. This morning I took round a letter addressed to her that was wrongly delivered through my door, and her front door was open, not closed properly. I looked for her and found her downstairs, lying on the floor. I called an ambulance and went with her to Ipswich Hospital."

I had sat down on a nearby chair to concentrate on the details and adjust to the shock. Susan was now a widow of 60 with no children, and she had sold the house she had lived in with her husband in Essex and was house-sitting two doors down from her mother while waiting to complete on her next house on which she had exchanged contracts. Her mother had a hip operation coming up, and the idea was that Susan would be near her, see her through her operation, and in due course sell the house near her and move elsewhere.

That night I was full of memories from her childhood and over the years. We had always been close, we had talked every week. I was immensely sad but was determined to keep going despite being 84, to see her through and keep her going.

The next morning, a Tuesday, I went to my bank for the last time – the branch was closing as only the elderly were now customers, and the elderly were all now de-banked – and had an early lunch during which Sibyl rang with an update.

She said: "There has been a large area of damage in her brain and she may not survive the next 48 hours. The antibiotics have to work to get rid of a chest infection, and perhaps a heart problem as her heart rate is very low. Her breathing is slow. She is a very sick girl with a torn artery. Her stroke's severe, that's the hospital's category. If she survives she may need care for the rest of her life, in a home or with a carer in her house."

Pippa drove me to Ipswich Hospital. I was apprehensive as to what we would find. Pippa dropped me at a door. Susan was in a ward, and was in a deep sleep, a light coma. She was on a drip and being fed through her nose. There was a cannula in one arm. She stirred, and I sat with her. I found her hand and held it, and talked to her. Her heart rate was on a monitor. It fluctuated between 44 and 50, and the alarm flashed orange for 45 to 49, but red for 44.

Pippa found me, having parked, and I drew her attention to the monitor and lowness of Susan's heart rate. I said, "I'm going to heal her."

I sat beside her and put my right hand on her forehead and said quietly, "Susan, I'm going to heal you." I went into a deep state of relaxation, and almost immediately felt the familiar outside energy flow into the base of my spine and surge up my back to my right shoulder and down through my right arm and my little finger into her head. There were four terrific surges which jolted me as I acted as a conductor for the universal energy. I knew from past healing that the more serious the patient's condition was, the stronger would be the input I channelled. My little right finger was almost white after conducting the energy.

There were never more than four surges when I healed, and I knew the healing had finished. Almost immediately Sibyl came in, leaning on a stick as she walked, with her tall army son, Don, who was dressed casually.

We all sat beside Susan's bed, and I said to her, "Open your eyes if you can hear your mother," and after Sibyl greeted her she opened her eyelids briefly, then closed them again. I went round all of us, asking if she could hear us, and she opened and closed her eyes after each introduction. I held her fingers.

A young doctor came and crouched down beside me. He said quite loudly, "We are observing her, we're not doing anything, her stroke was very severe. The CT scan this morning showed it spread from the right side of her brain to the top of her head. The main stroke was in the stem of the brain. It affected her breathing, her heart and other bodily functions. There's no point in putting her in intensive care. She can't go to rehab as a huge part of her brain is not working. It will probably mean that she will need one-to-one caring if she survives. But that is unlikely. She's not expected to live 48 hours."

He said this loudly, loudly enough for Susan to hear it, and I was shocked. Having seen how she opened her eyes on demand, I said, "Can we talk outside?"

I took him away from the bed and we stood just outside the ward. I said, "She's understanding what I'm saying. I've asked her to open her eyes twenty times, and she does it. We should assume she can hear and understand everything, that she's locked-in and can't speak but can hear and understand."

Chastened, the young doctor followed me back to her bedside and crouched down without saying anything.

I saw that the monitor said her heart rate was now stabilised at 60. I instinctively knew that my healing of her heart had worked. If she only had 48 hours to live, it would not be her heart that would be the cause of her death.

The young doctor left us, and the rest of us all went down the corridor to Costa's and had a cup of tea. We could talk there without Susan hearing. We urged Sibyl to go through with her hip operation despite Susan's inability to help.

Later I looked in on Susan. She was more peaceful and with a better complexion, some red in her cheeks, and she now had a consistently good heart rate that was not fluctuating. The four surges that poured up my back and down my right arm into her head had in a way I did not understand stabilised her heart, and from that moment she had turned a corner, and I knew she would survive.

It was weird, but I had found the bronze deer she gave me lying wounded on the very day she had had her stroke, and after supergluing its leg I had somehow stabilised her heart so she had a chance of surviving, despite her damaged brain. It was as though Providence was alerting me, warning me, that there was a problem with Susan by arranging for me to see the bronze deer lying on its side.

A Father's Day and a Fall
(Or: A Car Guarded by a Fox and a Magpie)

The day before Father's Day Pippa drove Simon, Paul and me to Ipswich Hospital.

Before we set off Pippa gave me Susan's Father's-Day present which Sibyl had given her the previous week: *Shakespeare's Book* on the 400th anniversary of the First Folio, written from a Stratfordian point of view. This could have arrived in the delivery Susan went upstairs to receive when her doorbell rang, and after receiving it wrote a note about being unable to use her left arm.

We arrived in Susan's ward around 2pm. At first Susan looked as if she was still in a coma, but she was more alert, and when I spoke and said, "Susan, Simon's here, open your eyes if you can hear him," and when Simon had greeted her she briefly opened her eyes. She did the same when Paul spoke.

I spoke to her at some length. I told her she was in Ipswich Hospital because she couldn't use her arm last Sunday and had written a note saying she feared she had had a stroke. I told her she was doing well and should keep going. I said she should be arriving at the Premier Inn near us now for Father's Day. I said that I had sorted her booking out. I thanked her for *Shakespeare's Book* and said I would be very interested in what it says.

She understood behind her closed eyes all I was saying about Father's Day and gave a long cry or groan, a frustrated wail indicating she wished she could have arrived there for Father's Day. She was shedding tears and when she opened her eyes they were wet.

I said we would later be visiting her new house. And again she cried from within her coma.

Pippa looped a small bag of crystals over the side of her bed and tied it to hang. It had Susan's name on it, so the stones could send out crystal healing to her during the nights.

We said goodbye several times – the first time elicited a kind of wail saying 'don't go' – and then Pippa drove us all to Sibyl's village in Suffolk, which took us an hour. Sibyl had fallen in her bedroom the previous day and broken her glasses and cut the bridge of her nose. Her son Don was there, a very tall Lieutenant-Colonel in the army but now casually dressed. Sibyl asked him for the key to Susan's house.

We left them and drove four miles to the bungalow on a small newish housing estate in a nearby village. It had a front garden. We let ourselves in and took in the two carpeted bedrooms, bathroom, sitting-room and kitchen. We went out of the back door to the lawned garden and shed at the rear, and then returned to our car.

Back at Sibyl's house Don came out and chatted to Simon and Paul about Susan's maroon mini, which was parked near Sibyl's front door. The plan was that Simon would drive it to our house so it could be parked off the road near the end of our drive.

Pippa and I went into Sibyl's house and she made us cups of tea. I had green tea. We sat round the table and talked, and then Don came in, saying he had given Simon and Paul some tips about the mini and they were sitting in it, getting used to the dashboard.

I asked Don, "Can you get me into the house where Susan had her stroke? I'd like to see where it all happened."

Don and I left through the back door and walked past cramped back gardens to the back door of the house where Susan had been house-sitting. We entered the back basement, stood in the kitchen where Susan worked on the table, and then climbed a flight of narrow, dark stairs to the passage by the front door, which was at street level.

Don said, "This front door was slightly open. She took in her delivery and the parcel was on the floor, there. This is where she felt the stroke coming on and wrote her note, which was found on the floor: 'I think I am having a stroke. I cannot feel my left arm. Sunday,

10.45.' The stroke was in her right brain and affected her left arm. Her phone was charging in the wall, there, see? I don't know why she didn't reach for it and ring her mum. She may have been disorientated by the stroke. She was lying down here, I think, and I think she elbow-crawled back to the stairs there as her elbows have been red. There's a handrail going down on the right, see? She somehow got down the stairs, holding onto the handrail with her right hand, and turned right at the bottom into the front basement room with a small window in the void below the ground. She didn't turn left into the kitchen and garden access where we came in."

We went downstairs and turned right into the basement room.

"The pavement is high up beyond iron railings, see? She seems to have had a fall. She seems to have fallen on her back. Her stroke moved to her brain stem here, and incapacitated her speech. If 10.45 in the note was in the morning, Sibyl found her twenty-four hours later, groaning."

Shocked at being confronted with where it all happened, I said, "Could you lie down in the position where Sibyl found her?"

Don obliged by lying down in front of a sofa with his head alongside a tiled hearth that jutted out in front of a grate.

"Could she have hit her head on the tiles?" I asked.

"The ambulancemen said she didn't," Don said.

"I wonder if she lay on the sofa and fell off onto the carpet."

"There's no evidence that she did. She may have fallen and ended up in this position."

We returned to the kitchen and let ourselves out from where Susan had been house-sitting, and walked back to Sibyl's back door. We joined Pippa and Sibyl, who were still sitting over their tea-cups, and Don summarised what he thought had happened the previous Sunday morning.

Don then said, "I had an army medical. It was found out by an army specialist that Sibyl's stroke was due to a high-cholesterol genetic flaw on her side of the family. She had a stroke in her bathroom in 1999," he said, "and I am on a statin, Atorvastatin 80mg, because of this flaw. Susan was told about it, and had been on Atorvastatin 20mg for three weeks when she had her stroke."

I said, "I had no idea that this genetic flaw existed."

"It explains why I had my stroke in 1999," Sibyl said. "Susan began her statin too late. Her body did not have time to benefit from it."

Sibyl then said, "It's likely that Susan will not survive for long. The first doctor said no one has survived with Susan's level of brain damage."

I said, speaking as a father: "There are different narratives among the doctors. We don't know, and should rule nothing out or in at this stage, and take everything from one day to another until the future becomes clear."

There was a silence. There was a general reluctance to believe that Susan would survive as a quadriplegic with locked-in syndrome, who could not move, swallow or speak. Soon afterwards we left and drove home in convoy, with Simon, accompanied by Paul, driving Susan's mini within our sights.

On the way home I thought of Susan's groaning when Father's Day was mentioned, and I wondered what had led to her fall in the basement the previous Sunday, when she was having her stroke. I did not know that her mini which Simon was driving would be parked off the road near our drive for months and months, and I did not know that it would be guarded by a fox, that would sit in front of it, and a magpie, that would sit on a nearby wall.

It was as if all Nature was aware of the terrible occurrence and was extending its sympathy to the car's immobile human owner. It was as if the event of her stroke and her survival surrounded her car like an aura, and was sensed and acknowledged by passing wildlife.

A Bustling Ward and Peaceful Rehab

Susan had been moved from her bustling ward to a single room next to it. She had had bouts of crying, perhaps because her cerebellum was disconnected from her temporal lobe and her emotions were therefore no longer controlled by her censoring gatekeeper (the Hospital's suggested interpretation). There was now serious talk of moving her to specialist level-1 care in Norwich.

For the third time I was at Ipswich Hospital, after driving through a thunderstorm on a Friday in early August, to meet Norwich level-1 rehab's assessor at his request, and for a third time I was told by the ward clerk when I arrived, "He's not coming, he's ill again."

I stood perplexed, and the physio Audrey came to me and said, "The assessor...." She raised her eyebrows as if to say, 'He's dreadful.'

I said, "It's the third time he's let us down. The trouble is, the first three months after a stroke are supposed to be the best time for the brain to find new pathways and bring the body back, and if he eventually rejects us we could have lost a month in this crucial time and would have to apply elsewhere."

Audrey said, "I agree."

I did not know that she went to her boss, Adrianna, who also agreed – and rang Norwich's level-1 rehab. I did not know that they asked her a few questions and by-passed the assessor. I was with Susan, brushing her hair with a 'scalp brush', when Adrianna came in. She said, with Pippa and me in her room, "Susan, you know we're looking to send you to a specialist unit where you'll receive the best care. I've just been told that a bed has become available on Monday, and you'll be moved there on Monday."

I could not believe what I was hearing. I said, "So she's really going to level-1 care in Norwich?"

"Yes."

"I was told she was twelfth, then ninth, on the list."

"She's gone to first on the list now."

I felt a surge of elation, and had tears in my eyes having got Susan to where I wanted her to be, where she would have the best chance of improving with the specialists in one of the eight level-1 rehab units in the UK. I thanked Adrianna profusely for her efforts, and when she went I said, "That's really good, Susan."

Susan's mother visited her the next day and packed her possessions so they could be placed in the ambulance. Susan moved on Monday.

I visited her the next day. Pippa researched the area and as a surprise drove to the George Hotel, and in the Arlington restaurant we had leek-and-potato soup, prawn sandwiches and cappuccinos.

It was then only a few minutes to Caroline House within Colman Hospital, a low single-storey building with 20 rooms for patients all on ground-floor level. We signed in and were taken to room 6 at the end of the corridor.

Susan was asleep. We quietly sat on chairs in her room, and Susan's consultant came with a nurse and introduced himself as Dr Saatvik. We chatted in the corridor outside. He had worked with Ipswich Hospital's consultant some years ago and said he would contact him as he would be reviewing Susan's medications. He explained they created conditions of quiet so the brain could repair itself in sleep.

Ipswich Hospital had been a bustling place, with nurses and doctors pacing about, coming and going past Susan's open door, but Caroline House was a quieter place where the brain was encouraged to repair itself in sleep.

Pippa and I went and sat in the garden among summery flowers and admired a honeysuckle arch, leaving Saatvik and the nurse to examine Susan. Soon afterwards he beckoned us in. Susan was now awake, quiet and calm, but she then began to be distressed. The speech and language therapist and psychologist arrived, so we returned to the garden and sat among the flowers in the warm sunshine.

They came out and told us we could communicate with Susan by blinks. We then went back and sat with Susan, who was in bed. I talked to her, knowing she understood what I was saying. We told her the family news and talked about why she was there. I looked into her eyes and could see that they were focusing on me and seeing me. She was heavily dosed with medication, and we left her quiet and not tearful.

We returned the following Tuesday. We again stopped at the George for broccoli soup and smoked-salmon sandwiches.

Susan was sitting in her wheelchair and her room was crowded with two nurses and a junior doctor who were doing things, so we went and sat in the garden. A nurse wheeled her out to us and Susan cried, even though her voice was impacting on an elderly man who was pushing his wife in a wheelchair, and spoilt the peace of the garden.

Dr Saatvik came out and took me off to a meeting-room and explained his assessing. He said they would try to match her with an eyegaze machine, a later model of the one that Stephen Hawking used.

When I returned I found Susan was back in her room sitting in her wheelchair. She had just had her blood pressure taken, and it was said she had low blood pressure.

The speech and language therapist came in with the psychologist, and we sat in on an impromptu class. The speech and language therapist, a woman in her early forties, said, "Susan, do you know where you are?" She then gave a very clear explanation that she had had a stroke and after time in Ipswich Hospital had been sent to Caroline House to improve. "And do you know *why* you are here?" She again mentioned Susan's stroke and what they were doing to help her.

Susan listened intently. She did not cry while they gave her information about her predicament.

It was different from Ipswich Hospital, where visiting time brought dozens, perhaps hundreds of visitors into the wards, which were bustling and full of noise. It was like a quiet retreat with a lot of silence, but it was also like a school with timetabled classes. 'Teachers' (therapists) came in and gave one-to-one lessons, and visitors were expected to go and sit in the garden and not interrupt the ongoing repairing care. Thanks to an ill assessor, Susan had somehow arrived early in rehab, and she was now being encouraged by long sleeps within peace and quiet to repair her brain so that once again she could move, swallow and speak. She had left a bustling ward for one of the top eight repairing units' peaceful rehabilitation.

Swapping or Borrowing

My phone rang. "Hello, is that Philip? It's Perry Elmby, we haven't spoken for some time. I've been told by Bill Temple that you've got a tractor you must be wanting to sell as you've had it some while. I've got a newish mower, but there's a problem with the engine, and I'd like to buy yours, swap it for mine. Can I come and see your mower? It's a Massey Ferguson I hear from Bill Temple. I can be with you at 12. I know where you are."

It was true that our tractor was old and would need replacing as all its parts were obsolete.

Taken aback, in the middle of doing things, I said, "You've caught us at a busy time. Come by all means, but I'll have to run it past Simon."

I left a message on Simon's answerphone, and drew his attention to it by email.

He replied, "The cost of a new engine will be a lot. Absolutely not at the present time."

I thought about it and realised he had to replace his engine for several thousand. The 'swap' would be a large payment by me in return for an unwanted dump.

At 12.10 Perry Elmby turned up with his wife in a small white car. They shook my hand at the front door and tried to charm me with smiles and laughter. I cut them short and said, "I've got bad news, I've run it past my son and I'm afraid it's the wrong time to be outlaying for something unbudgeted."

They were crestfallen. Their smiles disappeared.

"But," I said, "you can come and see the mower."

I took them to the back of the house.

"I say," Perry said, pointing to the two fields beyond our lawn, "is all that yours? You must have about five acres."

I called Frankie, our gardener. He heard and appeared, and took Perry down to the mower shed. His wife Pamela engaged me about the history of the untouched countryside in front of us as we walked down to the shed, past the fish-pond.

Perry was saying to Frankie, "This would do us perfectly. I could drive this. My present one" (which he wanted me to have) "is too big." He said to me, "Are you sure you don't want to sell now?"

"Quite sure," I said.

"Can I borrow it?"

The tractor could only be moved on a trailer, and how was he proposing to borrow it? Drive it slowly for three miles to his home, holding up traffic?

"No," I said, "Frankie needs to use it every day to keep the grass cut."

"So we can't have it?"

"No," I said. "Not until we've budgeted for a replacement. It's a difficult time out there, with banks being difficult, and we have a lot of expenditure and we need to budget."

Reluctantly they walked back. I walked with them to their car. They talked about their six grandchildren, whose school fees they paid, and asked questions about the age of our house. They got into the car.

Frankie was walking by. They called to him through their window and gave him a leaflet about a car-boot sale they were holding. Then, with waves, they sped off and waved again as they drove up the drive, and they were gone.

The impression they left was of using me for their own ends. Perry had offered a swap, which turned out to be my paying for his broken engine, and then wanted to borrow my tractor. They wanted Frankie to attend their car-boot sale.

For ever after I would be on my guard against requests to swap or borrow. 'Swapping' meant dumping his expensive repair on us and profiting. 'Borrowing' meant 'my long grass comes before yours'. Self-interest and social ego were behind both.

A Bell-Founder's Funeral and a Bipolar Wife

Pippa came back from Alfred's funeral in Loughborough. I asked her how it went.

She said, "It was held in the Baptist church. I arrived early and sat in the church and Charlotte came in." Charlotte was Alfred's widow. "She's bipolar, and I was concerned. She greeted everyone and seemed up rather than down, as if she'd forgotten she was greeting people who'd come to a funeral. Alfred had to be in a home for more than four years as you know, but there were still a lot of people there, including his twin brother, who's eighty-seven, and his wife and two daughters. They'd turned Catholic and had chains with crosses round their necks.

"The service began at 2.30. It was taken by the Baptist Minister, who knew Alfred, but he stood aside for a Catholic who had known him since his boyhood. He was born in Folkestone and went to the Folkestone parish church. He was a Mason, I think he'd been Master of the Lodge, and there was a Masonic emblem on his coffin, compass and set square. He had vascular dementia, but with his work with the bell foundry there were bell-ringers present. Charlotte wrote a long bit about him in the order-of-service booklet.

"Alfred was brought up to be a High Anglican and he was in a group of bell-founders from the bell foundry, and he volunteered to do lunches for the poor there, he and Charlotte prepared lunches on a Monday. He was a Mason, and at the end twelve Masons from his present and past lodges stepped forward during the committal and sang, like a choral group of singers – a Masonic send-off.

"Charlotte was up and down. One of the tributes ended, 'And Charlotte, he loved you to bits.' She dissolved into tears and was down. But then she was up and smiling at people and nodding at things said and turning round and catching people's eyes and saying, 'That's right.'

"At the end the coffin was taken out to 'The Lord is my shepherd', Psalm 23, and his twin brother, who also has dementia, began singing, and his family joined in. He sang beautifully, and they followed the coffin out and the two girls got into a car and followed it. Charlotte, being as she is, up and down, didn't go with her husband to the cremation, she let him go and be burned on his own. She did the same to Aunt Flora.

"Charlotte stayed in the church talking to people. Everyone waited for her to leave, but she didn't. Some quietly got out, I among them. We all went to have tea. It was beautifully prepared by the Baptist ladies, smoked salmon, carefully-cut square sandwiches, lemon-drizzle cakes beautifully laid out. I sat with his twin brother Martin and his family. He's normal part of the time but during the service he said, 'Whose funeral is this?' He had forgotten it was his twin brother's.

"Charlotte came and spoke to me. She brought Belinda. She had fallen out with Uncle Bob, and I hadn't seen much of her. There was a friar there and he and I talked. I said I'd seen him at their wedding. He said he'd forgotten who was at the wedding. He had rung Charlotte twice in the last couple of weeks and he said to me, 'She's up and down.'

"Charlotte was now very high, laughing and joking, over-calibrated. Up rather than down. She will come down with a big bump. She said to me, 'I've had a spiritual epiphany. I'd like to talk about it with Philip.' I texted Sam and he collected me and drove me home."

I felt sad for Alfred. The bell foundry was his life, and Charlotte had helped him with it. Now she was bipolar she was struggling to cope with the posture expected of her as a recently-bereaved woman, and was behaving inappropriately. Now she was on her own, encouraged by her spiritual epiphany, and had no one to consult except for me, and I was too busy to cope with her as I was struggling for time and unable to attend Alfred's funeral. I was sad at how life isolated people.

Title: 'Bell-founder', "A person who casts large bells in a foundry"
(*Concise Oxford Dictionary*).

A Donkey and Unlocking

Pippa and I arrived at the George Hotel and had potato-and-broccoli soup. Pippa had a salad and I had prawn sandwiches. Then we drove the short distance to the level-1 rehab unit. As we signed into reception's arrival book and logged our car on the hospital's system, someone said, "She's been moved to room 16. The passage on the left."

We found Susan lying in bed. She looked at me as I approached, and slowly started groaning and crying. I thought it might be the pain she was encountering on her left side, and I was told the hospital were coming up with a system of injections to remove her pain.

I sat and talked with her and noticed she was moving her head more and that she could wiggle her right toe. Then a physiotherapist came in, a tall and personable lady who introduced herself. She checked Susan's blood pressure and then asked if she would like to go outside and visit the miniature donkeys. By raising her eyes Susan signalled Yes.

The physiotherapist and an assistant rolled Susan onto her side, placed a black sling beneath her, tied her securely in, and then hoisted her. The arm of the hoist ran along the rail over her bed and lowered her into a wheelchair that was parked near the wall. They straightened her and brushed her hair, and the physiotherapist, Ollie, pushed her out into the garden where a small crowd of about 30 patients in wheelchairs and carers were sitting in the sun and relating to three miniature donkeys. Ollie wheeled Susan to be near the pen that had been erected for the donkeys. Bags of hay hung from its side. I sat on a wall beside Susan's wheelchair.

A donkey was brought to greet her. Its head was the height of Susan's knees in her wheelchair. Its handler discreetly fed it broken bits of ginger-nuts she had in a pocket in her jeans, and the donkey was bribed to put its nose on a pillow where Susan's hand was resting. I moved her hand to touch the nose of the donkey. And then Susan started groaning and crying.

The donkey then chewed Susan's pillow.

Suddenly her mood had changed.

The consultant was watching. He came and shook my hand and said he would like a few words. We went and sat on a seat, and he told me he had started her on new medication which was already improving her groaning, and said he wanted to introduce me to my new key worker, who would be phoning me. He waved to a member of staff, and Geraldine came and found us, an occupational therapist who knew her role.

We stood and chatted, and Geraldine said there would be a review in a fortnight's time. She gave me a date and a time.

Then I looked and saw Ollie pushing Susan's wheelchair, followed by Pippa, back up to her room. I excused myself and set off and returned to her room.

Ollie was saying she had laughed at the donkeys. "She made a deal with me," she said. "If I showed her the donkeys she'd ride on my bike for five minutes and then she can go back and see the donkeys again." She produced a wheel with two pedals.

While Susan sat in her wheelchair, she strapped her feet to the pedals and set the pedals turning. Susan was being cycled and soon it looked as if she was actively cycling rather than keeping up with the electric pedalling.

I said, "She's doing so well I'm sure she can double the speed."

There was mirth and again Susan laughed. Ollie said I wasn't helping her. She said to Susan, "Raise your eyes if you agree." And Susan raised her eyes.

At the end of the five minutes Ollie said, "So she's kept the second part of the deal. Now she can go and have another look at the donkeys." She unstrapped her feet and said to me, "You can take her."

Surprised, good for my years but still 84, I took the two handles and said, "These are the brakes, aren't they?"

"No," Ollie said, "they're the tilts."

"I nearly shot you out of your wheelchair," I said to Susan. And she laughed.

I pushed her out into the garden and back to where she had seen the donkeys earlier, and the same handler saw her and returned with the donkey that had chewed her pillow.

Susan looked intensely at the miniature donkey, whose head was the height of her knees. This donkey was reputed to be excellent in patients' rooms, and picked its way between the pieces of equipment. Susan and the donkey related to each other for a couple of minutes.

"Are you tired?" I asked Susan.

She raised her eyes in a Yes.

"Would you like to go back inside now?"

She raised her eyes in Yes.

So I pushed Susan back up the path and down the corridor to her room, and two occupational therapists came to put her into bed. Pippa and I waited outside in the garden, sitting at a table until we were called.

I had a short monologue with Susan, and told her we were leaving now. She did not groan or cry but looked intently at me. I realised she had not groaned or cried since she saw the donkey at close quarters.

Something had happened. Somehow the pressure of the donkey and its chewing of her pillow had broken into her locked-in syndrome from outside and had made her laugh. She had not groaned throughout her cycling (or being cycled) and her second visit to the donkey with me pushing her, and she had not groaned as we said goodbye. I hoped she was taking possession of her body again. She had moved forward, and I just hoped she had slowly found a new pathway that had allowed her to sit and enjoy her visit to the donkey and derive a meaning from it that had resulted in an unlocking of her body. I hoped the donkey had unlocked her from her locked-in quadriplegic paralysis and inability to speak.

An Ironing Man and Pretend Leaders
(Or: "I'm Not Getting Anywhere")

The ironing man got out of his van and came to the door to collect our ironing. I paid him in advance so he could return it to our porch if I was out, and he said, "That will be £22.50 next time." He had added £3 to the existing price. "I'm not getting anywhere," he said, holding my blue laundry bag over his shoulder. "I don't know what to do. I'm working 13 or 14 hours a day and I'm not getting anywhere."

I told him to keep going.

"I've never known it this bad," he said in his faintly Turkish accent. "When I retire I want to live off an amount. But how can anyone live off £250 a week in this country?"

"When do you want to retire?" I asked.

"Today. I want to buy a house in Turkey and live there four months and then come back and see my grandchildren. They're six, four and one. I always want to see my grandchildren. But I'm just not getting anywhere in this country."

I said, "The leaders aren't very good. Some of them are pretend leaders."

"Yes, that's a good word for them. I admired Cameron, I've always voted Conservative, but he made a mistake in 2015."

"The referendum."

"Yes, that was a big mistake."

"Our trade with the EU was then around 45 per cent, and it hasn't been made up by America – and all the other trade deals we were promised."

"The worst leader was Boris. He was a pretend leader."

"He promised gold," I said. "Vote for me and get gold."

"And the voters believed him, and he's got away with it. He just disappeared. It was the EU, then the pandemic, that hit me, and now the cost-of-living and the price of diesel."

"And the banking crisis in 2009 began it," I said, "and Ukraine hasn't helped."

"I just don't see the point of that war," he said.

"We've given them a lot of weapons but there's been no breakthrough and it's stalemate like the First World War. Look at the grass. No buttercups or daisies or clover. Not for three weeks. Just look as you drive about. I think something happened in Ukraine a month ago, perhaps something nuclear, and it went up into the atmosphere and has been blown over to us and blown down as rain and killed the wild flowers for three weeks. But they're just beginning to come back now."

"That's very interesting, you may be right. I haven't seen any wild flowers recently, it's just grass."

"The grass is still growing but without wild flowers within it."

"Very interesting. I'm sorry to burden you with my problems and my opening up. But I'm not getting anywhere. I'm working hard and not getting anywhere. And the pretend leaders. The Queen was lovely, but the present Queen shouldn't even be Queen, she's a pretend Queen."

I said, "Don't give up. It'll get better next year. Keep going. If necessary you can sell your house and buy a cheaper one and put the difference in the bank. Keep going."

"Thank you," he said, and he got in his van and drove it out of the gates.

I felt sorry for him. He was a hard-working small businessman who ran an ironing business, and the collapse of the country's profitability after Cameron's mistake in allowing a referendum and the consequent cost-of-living crisis had damaged his dream to retire. Things were not good, the country was in decline.

A Fall and a Boot
(Or: A Visit to the Dental Hygienist)

I had an appointment with the hygienist, and had to park above the cricket ground, at the top of the sloping road. I had a walk of several minutes down past the houses, and two bins had been put out on the pavement for the binmen.

I skirted round them and put my left foot on the edge of jagged pavement tarmac and suddenly my left ankle twisted sharply and fell down three inches through weeds into a pothole hidden by greenery between the pavement and the kerb, and, carried by the momentum of my walk downhill, I went flying. In mid-air I dropped my umbrella and bag and put out my arms and landed on the bottom of my hands, the left one in the road beyond the kerb and the right one on the jagged tarmac.

The momentum of my walk had dragged my right knee on the uneven pavement to the kerb and torn and muddied my trousers round my right knee. I saw this as I got myself into a crawling position and managed to stand up.

I was very shaken but seemed to be intact. My hips had not broken. I wiped grit from my hands but could imagine I had grit in my knee. My left ankle hurt moderately. There was no one about, and I resolved to carry on, keep going. So I limped to the dentist's surgery. There was one other patient, a man, in the corner of the waiting-room. I said to the receptionist, "Before anything else happens, could I see someone privately."

A lady in horn rims appeared and without a word led me into the small office off the waiting-room and shut the door.

I said, "I've got an appointment with Dorothy but I've had a fall while getting here. Could someone give me first aid for my right knee?"

The lady said, "I *am* Dorothy."

"Oh yes, you are," I said. "I must be disorientated." I was embarrassed that I had not recognised her in her horn-rimmed glasses I had never seen her wear.

Dorothy cleaned my knee with a sterilised pad and put on a plaster so there would be no more bleeding onto my trousers, and I gingerly climbed the stairs in torn trousers and lay on the tilting flat 'chair', and had my teeth hygienically scoured with water that sprayed my throat as I lay back with my head below my feet until I choked.

I drove home and found Paul there. I asked him to stop a message in my car saying I needed to inflate my tyres, and he found that the tyres could be inflated if I drove. So I drove up to the local roundabout by The Robin Hood and back, time enough for my tyres to inflate and to satisfy the persistent message.

I slept reasonably well that night, but the following night I did not have much sleep. I was in pain, and my ankle was swollen all round. At 2am I took two Nurofen Plus tablets for their ibuprofen content, which was reputed to be anti-inflammatory, and I took two more at 6am.

Simon invited us to look at the end of the work to create a senior school within a local junior school he was involved with, and I climbed the stairs with my father's walking-stick. I got round all right, but it was clear that I was not moving freely, and Pippa said she had a link to a 'minor injuries clinic' a stop along the M25 from where we were.

It took twenty minutes to get there. I was seen immediately and triaged: sent for X-rays. I had my left ankle X-rayed from four angles, and then sat in the waiting-room while Pippa read the papers in her car. Eventually I was seen again.

An Asian nurse studied the X-rays on her screen and said, "You have a broken bone in your ankle. The medial malleolus. No operation, you need to wear an orthopaedic boot."

She left the room and returned with a black boot, took the insole from my left shoe and put it under my left foot. She Velcroed it round my toes and across my shin and placed it within the outside boot, which she strapped through three buckles and Velcroed. I thanked her and returned to Pippa in the car.

I said, "You were right, you and Simon got it right. Thank you."

I was driven home. As I sat in the car I reflected on my fall, on my left ankle-bone which was found to be broken and on the sterilising of my knee. I had got off lightly, I could have broken both hips and ended in hospital. But now I had a boot with a backward tilt so I walked on my heel.

I had gone to Dorothy to make sure my mouth was hygienic, and before I'd got there my right knee and left ankle were unhygienic and needed treatment. I reflected that when you get to 84 it is a real struggle to keep your body hygienic. Judging from the hours I spent on it, it seemed almost a full-time activity.

A Nursery Gardener and a Court Breakdown

I was rung up by the doctor's surgery and asked to have the wound on my knee dressed by a nurse. I parked in the car park and got out and hobbled, leaning on my stick, to fill the meter. A man got out of a van he had just parked and arrived at the meter just ahead of me. He stopped and waved me forward. I said, "No, after you."

He said, "It's Philip."

I said, "Wayne." It was Bill Temple's son. I had not seen him recently. He had a beard now. I said, "It's leaf time, I remember you coming in and blowing a waist-high bank of leaves some years ago. I've broken a bone in my ankle, hence the stick. And I'm on my way to my doctor's, over there."

He smiled and then looked concerned and got his ticket. I followed. Not knowing how long I would have to wait, I put in a £2 coin and took my ticket.

"How's it all going?" I asked, expecting him to tell me about his gardening job.

"I'm in a nightmare time," he said. "My divorce has gone through. I married in 2013 and it was a problem for over eight years. I said nothing to try and sort it out. My wife left me after three years, and we've been to court about the house. She's got thirty-seven per cent, which is not bad since she didn't contribute to it. She's a commercial lawyer who's been earning £200,000 a year, and I'm plodding along as you know and paying for the house and all the bills. It was an unfair decision, and I broke down in court last week. She was questioned for twenty minutes, I was questioned for two-and-a-half days by her barrister. I had to go through everything in my accounts. They claimed there was something wrong in my account. 'Rental' had been put in a wrong column and they claimed I was charging my girlfriend rent and pocketing the money. I'd broken up with her, but she used my office as a base for her work and I let her continue doing it, but the rental had nothing to do with her.

"My wife had an affair at work, and came clean and I forgave her to try and make it work for our children and the family. But she left me after three-and-a-bit years, so the marriage hasn't existed for the last five years, and the strain on me has been immense. I broke down in court and I'm not at work today, I'm getting myself together and trying to work out how I cope with her having thirty-seven per cent of our home and keeping her £200,000 a year, while I pay for our son to go to private school on the small amount I get from gardening."

"I'm really sorry to hear all this," I said, standing with him near the ticket-machine. "What about access to your children?"

"That's in January," he said. "At present it's fifty-fifty, but she wants to restrict me to one weekend every fortnight."

I pulled a sympathetic face and said, "You're doing everything for them and paying school fees and being a good father on your income, and she wants it all, and the lawyers are in with each other. She's one of them, and they've over-cross-examined you."

"You have to laugh," he said. "At the beginning of the court hearing the judge said he had never seen such a messy bundle of papers as the one her lawyers provided. There were papers upside down and some were the wrong way up. The judge suspended the court hearing for two hours so he could sort through and put them in order. They were all lawyers, but handed over a mess. But they questioned her for twenty minutes and me for two-and-a-half days of relentless questioning on minutiae, going line by line through financial statements. I said over 'Rental', 'I can explain it, it's on my phone, can I show you?' I was told, 'No, we don't allow that kind of evidence in court.' So even though what they were saying is wrong, it really got to me. My dad is coming back from Turkey today. I'll see him tonight –"

"Give him my best wishes."

"I will. He hasn't got words for how she's treated me. I have a strong family, and they are a help. But I'm facing a bleak future."

"I've seen it so many times," I said. "One door closes and another one opens, and what seems black now may be the best thing that's ever happened to you in a couple of years' time: a stable family, someone who'll care for your children with you. Keep going, and continue to hope. If you get suicidal thoughts come and see me, and I'll tell you not to do it –"

He smiled and said, "Thank you for saying that."

"Everything we do in life is meant to be, that's how it seems to me. Everything that's happened to me has been helpful in some way. It's as though we're in the hands of Providence which is steering us out of present grim situations into something better. You'll see, in a couple of years' time the way will have opened. Keep going, and hope."

"Thank you for saying that," he said again.

I looked at my watch. "But I must be going, they'll be expecting me. Keep cheerful."

And with that he thanked me and got into his van. I put my ticket in my car window and hobbled to the surgery, where, eventually, a nurse peeled off the old plaster on my wounded knee, soaked my wound in a sterilised cleanser, put on an anti-bacterial strip and then added a new dressing. She said, "There's no infection." She asked me to return in a week's time.

As I walked back to my car I thought of Wayne. He had had a troubled marriage that was over after three years, and it was now nearly eight years after his wife's affair that the court was apportioning the assets, and it was all a shock to him as the apportioning was not based on right and wrong but on power: how a commercial lawyer with £200,000 could manipulate the barristers and judge in awarding her a sum that morally she did not deserve. He had had a breakdown in court, but the court system had broken down before his wife's manipulation.

I felt sorry for Wayne, and was glad that old age had removed me from having to start again with a new home.

Or had it? I thought of my underlying situation with Susan's mother, and the medical staff's fear that their assessment would be taken to court by her, and I hoped that I was now immune from an equivalent injustice.

A Funeral and Shared Fate (Or: 'Dopey' and a Wake)

Patrick Dee died of Parkinson's disease, and his funeral was held at 10.30am at a 13th-century church in the rolling Essex countryside. Paul drove me in his new Kia and parked among the hangars between two farms. We sat for a while and watched a succession of elderly couples dressed in black totter to the narrow railed-in path that led to the church.

We followed, and I opened the door to find the church full. There were just four vacant chairs at the back, and we sat in the back corner of the church. Patrick Dee had been in a class below mine at school, and I had known him well. I looked at the backs of heads and shoulders of the congregation and recognised a couple of now elderly schoolmates.

The service began. The order of service had a large coloured picture of a bespectacled, smiling and younger Patrick standing before daffodils, and inside was a black-and-white picture of him as a young boy with his younger brother, who had had polio and was in a leg-iron at school but I knew would not be present as there had been a fall-out within the family. I turned the pages and found there were nine more coloured pictures. It was a very colourful order of service, but all eleven coloured pictures seemed a bit 'over the top'.

We sang a hymn and there was a long tribute by his son, who spoke, and then read, rapidly without a microphone at the other end of the church. He worked for an oil company.

Patrick's son spoke of how his father was known as 'Dopey' at school and failed Maths at 'O'-level, but became an accountant and worked within a company that did BP's accounts. He had 120 articled clerks, some of whom were present. He had overseen an oil deal in Canada for BP. He had retired at 53 and had become a church warden at this 13th-century church. Nineteen years ago he had been diagnosed with Parkinson's disease.

When he was in mid-flow the church door opened noisily and Derek Minstrel stood leaning on his crutch. He shuffled forward a few steps as heads turned. His hair was uncombed and he was clearly in great discomfort. There were no chairs, but a member of the congregation leapt up and Derek noisily sat on the now-vacant seat. Patrick's son continued, unfazed by the interruption.

When he finished there was a poem, 'Feel no guilt in laughter', a collect, a hymn ('The Lord's my shepherd'), a Bible reading, a sermon (which talked about Patrick's kindness but nothing about his life), the Lord's Prayer, then a final hymn ('Lord of all hopefulness'). Then we went outside for the committal. As I passed Derek Minstrel before the open church door I bent and patted his wrist. He looked up and said, "Good to see you."

Paul and I stood before a semicircle of about 80 of the congregation on the muddy grass in a corner of the churchyard. Behind the semicircle was the Essex countryside disfigured by pylons. There was a groundsheet round the grave and four undertakers in black were holding the coffin by straps. The vicar began his committal, and then the eighty in the semicircle were transfixed. Each seemed to be aware of his or her mortality, there seemed to be a collective feeling in the stillness of 'There but for the grace of God go I'.

Then at a signal from the vicar the four undertakers lowered the coffin, left the ends of the straps by their feet, bowed down into the grave and filed away past us. Patrick's widow and immediate family threw handfuls of earth down onto the coffin and moved away. There were no tears, just an electrifying stillness as all beheld their own fate in the Essex countryside.

There was a 'wake' (according to the invitation) in a 19th-century pub a short drive through the countryside. We parked and entered and made our way up old brick steps to an upstairs room where there were glasses of sparkling wine and some of the elderly were talking. We took our glasses downstairs and while I sat with a couple of my old school's Shrove-Tuesday Old Boys – Patrick had always attended the Shrove-Tuesday dinners without saying very much – Paul brought me a plate of snacks (finger-sandwiches and tiny sausage rolls). Then I went downstairs with Paul in search of Derek Minstrel and his crutch.

I saw him sitting with his lady driver. But I was intercepted and found myself talking to Sheila, who had once worked for me. She asked why I was not at Jimmy Baker's funeral. I was shocked. I said, "Until now I didn't know he had died."

"It was on the 11th of the 11th, 11 November. Didn't his wife invite you?"

"She can't have done. I didn't know about it until just now." But, I said, another member of our staff had died and my invitation arrived two weeks after the funeral because of the slowness of the Royal Mail. "We're all getting old," I said, "we're all elderly, and we're losing people we have been associated with every month."

There was an empty chair in front of where Derek Minstrel was sitting. I sat and chatted to him. He was contorted backwards beside his crutch and spoke up at the ceiling, looking down at me from the bottom of his eyes. He said hearing was a problem, and he could hardly speak, and his hips were a problem. "And I've just had Covid."

Paul was sitting next to him, and I saw him edging away. I instinctively pulled slightly back.

As usual we talked about our visit to Italy, and how he had saved my life when we slept in the Temple of Hera, Zeus's wife, in our sleeping-bags by the altar and I was desperately ill and he walked a long way to buy medication from an all-night-open pharmacy, and how we met Hitler. He was living in a youth-hostel in Catania that was full, and we were allowed to sleep in the foyer on the mosaic floor, and at 6am each morning we woke to see Hitler bending over us, not saying anything. He insisted Hitler faked his suicide in the bunker and had escaped to Mussolini's Italy, still an allied country then.

At the end I said to Paul, "We must be going." I stood and said to Derek, "Shrove Tuesday?"

"Yes," he said, "I'll be there."

"I'll be in touch with you," I said. "I don't want to be attending *your* funeral next, keep well."

From his contorted position he gave a short melancholy laugh.

Outside the pub I thought of the elderly within, still drinking and eating and talking. The leaflet sent out by the family said the 'wake' would be an opportunity to reminisce, share stories and honour Patrick's memory, but I had not heard one word said about Patrick in the pub, the conversation was all about our connections with the Old Boys.

The whole morning had been about each member of the elderly congregation's facing up to his or her impending death. It was present throughout the funeral service, and very evident at the committal, and the 'wake' had enabled all to process their own fate. The funeral we had attended had, for all of us, including me, been a dress rehearsal for our funeral – *my* funeral. We were losing people each month, I couldn't keep up with the number dying, and all had watched the committal with fascination as 'there but for the grace of God' went each one of us.

The elderly had attended a funeral and looked out for Old Boys, but each of us had been shown our own fate, and our recognition of the Old Boys was in fact a facing up to our own funeral which was out there waiting to happen one day soon, and a fate we all shared.

A Locker Key and Dementia

Dr Erdmann was convinced I should be tested for prostate cancer as three years had passed since my last test. He sent me to his urology consultant, a youngish vigorous man in a suit who asked me to do an input (food) and output (urine) chart for two whole days at home, and then have a urine test, ultrasound and MRI at King Edward VII Hospital. I had to arrive with a full bladder. Sam collected me after an early lunch and drove me to London, and from time to time I sipped from a bottle of water.

A thin man in a tall stove-pipe hat and tails opened my car door outside the hospital. He had a grey lined face, and he looked like Death. I went into reception and a smart man told me I should go across the road to their other building. I was escorted across the road by an assistant, and I passed Death and thought I had escaped him.

I had my urine test (mid-flow in a small specimen container) and was told I still had to have a full bladder for my ultrasound. I was told to go downstairs to the lower-ground floor, where another receptionist gave me forms to complete in the waiting-room, including the forms for my MRI. I sat with half a dozen others and sipped more water.

One of the forms asked me when I last had a scan. I had had one about a week earlier, but I could not work out when. I was asked when I had last had an MRI. My mind was blank, and I guessed three or four years previously. I was also asked if I had ever had arrhythmia. I had, after Covid, but I could not remember which year that was and I could not recall the name for what I had had or the name of the specialist who had diagnosed me. It was only hours later that I recalled I had had perimyocarditis: fluid in the sac round (peri) the heart and an accelerated, more-than-double heart rate caused by an infection of my heart muscle (myo). And an hour later still that I remembered the name of my consultant who had sorted out the problem with a tiny tablet I had to take each morning.

I was shown through to the ultrasound room and lay back on a narrow couch and pulled up my shirt. A thin semi-elderly woman came in with a very authoritative manner and did my ultrasound rapidly. She applied gel to my body between my two hips and pressed the ultrasound probe (or traducer) hard above my bladder, kidneys, liver and prostate, and eventually said, "I'm happy with that." I then had to go down the corridor and wee into a loo with a hole in the bottom, beneath which was a measuring jug, and I returned for her to check that I had an empty bladder, which I had.

I returned to the receptionist, who asked me to go back to the waiting-room for my MRI. "You won't have eaten anything for the four hours before, will you?" she asked. No one had said I had to fast for four hours, but luckily my early lunch had ended exactly four hours before I was due to go in.

I was called and had to go down another floor in the lift to the basement. There I had to change in a small room, take off my clothes and shoes so I was in my underwear and socks, put on a gown that tied at the back and then carry my clothes and possessions, my watch and my hearing-aids to a metal locker at the end of a short corridor. I had to lock the locker and keep the key, then go to the loo one final time, which I did. I had to have my MRI with an empty bladder. There was a small jutting-out shelf and I put my locker key, which was attached to a wooden wedge on a keyring, on it.

As I came out of the loo I was accosted and taken straight to the MRI room. Two operators asked me to sit in front of the tunnel and then lie back with my head on a pillow while a cannula was fitted into my left arm, and I was then shunted inside the tunnel. I closed my eyes, and earphones reduced the sound of the ensuing clanking and knocking.

After twenty-five minutes I was asked if I was all right. I replied yes. A voice said, "The dye is going in now. You'll feel it in your left arm."

Then I remembered my key. I could not remember giving it to the MRI operators, so I added, "Have you got the key to my locker? If not, I might have left it in the loo."

There was silence. The dye went into my arm, there was more clanking and knocking, and then silence. The voice said, "You're done."

I was slid out of the tunnel. "Did you hear my message about the key?" I asked.

"Yes. We've got it."

"*Was* it in the loo?"

"Yes."

I sat up and waited while they checked their MRI. I thought how I could not recall when I had my last scan and my last MRI and what Covid had done to my heart or the name of the consultant who sorted the problem out, and I had forgotten my key. Anyone could have taken it from the loo and opened my locker and stolen my wallet. I must have early dementia.

I was being tested for cancer, but really should I not be being tested for dementia? I ruefully thought, 'I am eighty-four and falling apart despite my attempts to keep going by going to the gym once a week.' My memory was going, I had failing powers. I could still write and choose words carefully, but my memory, which had always been good, was suffering temporary malfunctions. I wondered if I had had a TIA, a transient ischaemic attack, a mini-stroke. But no, I concluded sadly, not wanting to declare this to Dr Erdmann and trigger more investigations, it was more likely that I had early dementia and could expect my sharp mind, which had often imposed an ordered pattern on seemingly random and unrelated chaotic events, to undergo shut-downs like the shut-down I had experienced in the waiting-room until the lapse involving the key immediately before I had my MRI.

I was old and for much of the time still brimming, but I was entering my twilight and a concerning twilight in the lapses in my memory. I might not have escaped Death in his stove-pipe hat after all.

A Delayed Discharge and New Spectacles (Or: Providence Supportive)

Pippa drove me to Norwich for the three-monthly review of my daughter Susan's progress on 15 December. Susan had been told she must leave by the end of January, and we arrived early in the car park and had rolls containing smoked salmon for lunch and sipped coffee from our thermoses. We went in early so I could go to their loo, and then Sibyl and Don, Susan's half-brother, arrived, Sibyl walking awkwardly with a stick having recently had a hip replacement and now in pain from her other hip. Don had managed to get away from his Army commitments.

Susan was wheeled in a wheelchair. As she came through a normally-locked door she saw Don and began to cry. It looked as if she did not want to see him, but she may have thought he would not attend and the emotion of surprise may have come out as crying in her locked-in syndrome, wordless, quadriplegic state.

The nurse parked the wheelchair and disappeared. A member of staff came up, and said to Susan, "Are you Mandy?"

"No," I said, "she's Susan."

The member of staff consulted her clipboard. "Have you an intolerance of tomatoes?"

"No," I said. "You've got the wrong person." She stared at her clipboard.

"Sometimes Susan goes under the name of Mandy," I said, "when she's trying to escape." And Susan's crying turned to laughter.

The member of staff apologised and left us, and we chatted. Then a nearby door opened, and we were invited to go into a room where there were tables, each with a chair, round the walls for a senior nurse, an occupational therapist, a physiotherapist, a speech and language therapist, a psychologist, and the consultant. There were chairs on either side of the central aisle, and Sibyl and I sat on them. Pippa squashed past me and sat on a chair behind me, and Don sat on a chair at the far end of the room. Susan was wheeled in her wheelchair and parked next to me.

The consultant asked us all to introduce ourselves. Then began a report on Susan's medical condition. The consultant covered her eleven medications and reported that her doses were coming down but in a way that made sure she would have no seizures. The senior nurse repeated that Susan would need two nurses, and said that her health was progressing.

Something she said made Susan cry, and I held her hand and urged her to stop crying so we could all hear the progress she had been making.

The occupational therapist spoke of the work she had been doing with Susan and the machine that the communication-aid company based at Addenbrooke's Hospital had in mind for Susan to use when they returned to complete their assessment.

The physiotherapist spoke at length of the MOTOmed bicycle Susan had used in the gym and of the standing machine I had seen, and how the aim was that Susan should reach ten minutes' standing from her present record of six minutes despite her low blood pressure.

The speech and language therapist spoke about the drive to improve her swallowing, and her progress on the e-tran board.

The psychologist said that Susan's inner experiences now conformed to their outer expression, and Susan promptly cried, silencing the progress of her report.

After all this the occupational therapist said, "Susan has made good progress and is still improving, and we have recommended she should stay until the end of March. Susan will decide and she has until after Christmas to make up her mind."

There was a silence.

I said, "So to put it in other words, she's been making good progress but is still improving, and needs more level-1 work, and instead of the upheaval of her going elsewhere she can stay here and finish her level-1 course with you."

"Exactly," said the consultant. "She knows us and we know her. If she went elsewhere, the staff would have to get to know her. It's better for Susan to work with therapists she knows and achieve the rehab goals they've set her."

"I would think that's excellent," I said, "thank you very much. And Ipswich is still possibly her next place?"

"Yes. Her consultant at Ipswich Hospital is still her stroke consultant, and if she moves to the nursing home in Ipswich he will visit her. But it may take two or three weeks of waiting to get there while a bed becomes available."

"It will be level-2?" I asked.

"Yes."

Everything had worked out perfectly.

The meeting ended. A nurse came in and wheeled Susan into the foyer, and we talked. The receptionist called, "Two packages have arrived for her."

I said, "One of them may be her new spectacles."

The receptionist looked. "Yes," she said, "these are her new spectacles."

They had asked me to book an optician, and most opticians would not go to a hospital-based patient unless they were permanently based in hospital. I had visited and seen the optician through as the rehab unit was short-staffed, and the optician had confirmed that Susan's stroke had had an impact on her vision, and her previous spectacles should not be used for the next six months till her vision returned to how it used to be.

"Excellent," I said. Susan had been wheeled through the normally-locked door into her corridor. "I'll take them to her, to her room." And I did.

I tried the spectacles on Susan's nose, making sure they went over her ears, and I held up the e-tran board. "Is that an improvement?" She eyes-upped in a Yes.

"Excellent," I said.

The speech and language therapist came by with the occupational therapist. I told them and they said they would contact Addenbrooke's Hospital and get the communication-aid specialist back.

Everything had come together. Discharge had been kicked three months down the road, everything would continue. The communication-aid specialist had requested that Susan should have new spectacles, I had made that happen and the spectacles had arrived. It would take longer than until the end of January for their work to have effects, for their benefit to be felt, and so they had extended the discharge date by a further two months. They were all caring professionals who were doing their best for Susan.

I was elated as Sibyl and Don arrived to see Susan, and I, knowing that only two were allowed in her room, squeezed Susan's hand as she sat in her wheelchair and said goodbye, and that I would return on Tuesday, the day before the solicitor visited her to take her instructions so she could give us Powers of Attorney to speak for her on property and finance, and health and welfare.

I walked down the corridor sensing that the Angels were with me. Everything had turned out well, Providence seemed supportive. After six months of a nightmare I was now awake and looking ahead. It was as if the new spectacles had given me a new way of seeing the wonderful order in the universe's management and maintenance of the status quo.

A Snowman and a Wail

Pippa drove me to Norwich in her car through rain and we sat in the car park of the level-1 rehab unit and I ate my sandwiches and sipped coffee from a thermos. Then I got out and Pippa drove to a garden centre.

I was slightly early and was asked to wait in the lounge until visiting time. I felt awkward as the lounge had three patients in wheelchairs and their nursing staff. I walked beyond them and sat on a settee facing the large TV, which was off.

Susan's door was shut, a notice said, 'Quiet Time'. I opened her door and peered at her. She was lying back watching her wall-mounted TV that was above head height. She saw and half-smiled. She was very relaxed, and I wondered if she was on a new medication.

I turned her TV off and sat with her and talked. She was not really participating, and her alarm was going off. A nurse came and turned it off. I reminded Susan that a solicitor was coming the next day to get her instructions for Powers of Attorney, and went through some of the questions she might be asked. She listened with minimum interaction.

Then two nurses came and said they needed to change her. So I took my chair and sat in the corridor outside her room. Pippa arrived, and when the nurses left we both went in to Susan's room. She was higher up on her pillow but more remote, with a slight frown, and slipping down on one side.

Pippa had brought a bag with her Christmas present. I unpacked her card and opened it for her. It showed Father Christmas reading a long wish list in front of a Christmas tree – and I had written inside that the wish list included my wish that she would continue her improvement in the New Year. I had wondered whether to give her a card of a snowman with a carrot for a nose, but the snowman would melt and vanish, and I thought it would be inappropriate to give her a card on the transience and imminent melting-away of her life.

I opened the present Pippa had wrapped: a light navy dress that could be worn when she was too hot, with flowers on it. It was easy to put on, it had magnetic catches at the back. Pippa had got her two neck decorations that were on magnets, and could be popped on and unpopped off without difficulty. Susan lay back and showed little reaction. I hung her present in her wardrobe.

I talked to her while Pippa rearranged her cards from her friends with my help, and put up her new birthday and Christmas cards. "You'll be able to look at these from your wheelchair," Pippa said.

Susan eye-gazed a stand-up picture of her and me, taken five years earlier, which I had given her on her birthday. Her husband (not in the picture) was next to her, and she was made up and laughing. I nodded and innocently said, "That was when you came to my birthday five years ago. We'll be thinking of you over Christmas, so many will be thinking of you then."

Then she began crying, and we could not stop her. I put lip salve on her lips and put cream on both sides of her fingers and hands, and brushed her hair, all activities that normally stopped her crying, but the crying got worse. It went on and on and turned (after a deep breath) into a long wail of despair. It was as if she had begun saying she would miss us all at Christmas and it had turned into 'I don't want to be here in rehab this Christmas' and 'I don't want to be locked-in and quadriplegic', and had become, 'I don't want to live like this, I'd be happier dead.'

Pippa was aghast at the rawness of the wail. I was shaken by it, and squeezed her fingers, standing over her. Then Libby came in and, having heard the commotion, said briskly, "Hello, Susan, we've arranged a physio session for you, would you like that?" When Susan eyes-upped in a yes Libby said, "We'll be back in a couple of minutes. You can say goodbye to your dad and Pippa now." And she went.

Susan still cried but the depth of the wail had gone now, and when Libby returned with another physiotherapist she said to me aside, "We could see you were in difficulty, this has got her out of it."

I said, "Bye" and squeezed Susan's hand and left as quickly as I could as the crying began again (saying: 'Don't go'). I listened outside the door and could hear Libby talking, and soon Susan was laughing.

Back in Pippa's car I reflected. The intensity of her despair had shaken me. It seemed that six months after her stroke she was crying with a depth I had not encountered before, and that her willing participation in the exercises which the staff arranged for her was co-existing with a howl of wretchedness she could do nothing about.

Virtual Reality and the Christmas Spirit

Simon had us for his annual Boxing-Day family lunch. We began with champagne in the sitting-room before the tree and went through to the kitchen when lunch was served. We had lamb, beef, turkey and gammon and many vegetables and sauces, and soon our plates were heaped. Our bantering grandchildren dominated the conversation, we grandparents conversed safely with our children.

Simon had played Santa at 2.30am and had left stockings in Al's and Minnie's rooms. Al had discovered his stocking at 5.30am and had woken Minnie, and Simon had been woken by the excited squeals as they opened their first presents. He was short of sleep, but as we saw when we returned to the sitting-room for a lull before Christmas pudding he had catered for everyone's wishes.

He handed out many wrapped presents which were piled on the floor before the ceiling-high tree covered with tiny coloured electric lights. I opened what he gave me and found myself looking at a portrait of myself in a red military tunic, white trousers and knee-high black boots (Wellington's uniform) and a Lord's scarlet robe with an ermine cape (sleeveless cloak), holding a short ceremonial sceptre.

He encouraged me to open the next present and I found that I now owned a small piece of land near Coniston in the Lake District, with a grid number, that entitled me to change my name to Lord Philip Rawley if I wanted to. It was like a deed-poll change from my title Mr and if I implemented it I would be Lord Philip Rawley from now on, but not for passports, driving licences or bank cards. Simon saw it as a piece of fun.

Al, who was six foot three inches and still only 14, had put on a virtual-reality helmet he had been given and was holding a cricket-bat handle that looked like a truncheon. He was playing cricket shots. He stopped and said to me, "I've got 30. You can have a go now if you like." He handed me the truncheon.

I put the helmet on. It contained a headset, and I found I was on a realistic pitch that could have been at Lord's or the Oval, with a capacity crowd and eleven players dressed in white crowding my bat: a silly mid-off and silly mid-on who were aggressively near, and three slips. In my virtual reality I was holding a full-length realistic cricket bat and not a truncheon, and I touched a sign 'new over' with it, and a fast left-arm bowler ran in behind an umpire and I glimpsed the ball was a Yorker and slammed down my bat on the pitch (i.e. my 'truncheon' in mid-air) and the ball shot past me. My wicket was intact so I was not out. Each ball during the rest of the over was too fast for me, at 84, to hit. The last ball uprooted my middle stump and all the fielders rushed at me and through me to congratulate the bowler.

Kay came in and said the virtual-reality helmet could be linked to the wall-mounted television, and all in the room were now able to see what I, in the middle of the aggressive fielders, was experiencing. When I hit the ball, they saw an arrow indicate where the ball went. They saw my middle stump uprooted again. Two of the players rushed at me and stared at me aggressively, their scowling faces in my face, and the rest of the team rushed to the bowler and stood in a circle with their arms round each other's shoulders. I was relieved to undo my helmet and hand the 'truncheon' to Al, and take stock of what I had seen of the crowd and the players from the detachment of my settee as I watched the gigantic wall-mounted television.

I sat on the settee and rested. I looked up at the screen on the wall. Al was batting with his helmet on and hit a six. I could see he was playing his shots before the bowler had released the ball, so the ball did not flash past his bat.

I thought of Al in his virtual-reality world, smashing each ball for a boundary. I had contributed some misses, which kept alive the frightening speed of the fast bowler. And I looked again at the picture of my head superimposed on a Lord wearing an ermine cape, holding a small short ceremonial sceptre. I had dignity, but it was a virtual-reality picture to give a taste of what it was like to be ennobled, just as Al's helmet gave him a taste of what it was like to be a county or Test cricketer. In both the cricket and the Lord wearing an ermine cape the 'I' had been relegated into a background, so a replacement 'I' could be in a county or Test match and in the military regalia and ermine cape that could precede a seat in the House of Lords.

And all this was possible because of the Christmas spirit which Simon had brought to bear on us, using modern technology. He had chosen Christmas presents that took the young and the elderly out of their everyday context and placed them in a different context – a competitive Test match and a Lord dressed for the House of Lords. I marvelled at the way AI (artificial intelligence) had got the fielders acting with the spirit of a cricket team and had superimposed my face on a Lord's to act in the spirit of the House of Lords, and we had received these examples of AI while we prepared to go back to the kitchen and have Christmas pudding with brandy butter and brandy sauce to keep us in the Christmas spirit.

And in a sense this Christmas spirit was a virtual reality that was far removed from three wise men leaving a town in Iran and crossing the red-sanded Iraqi desert to Bethlehem, following Sirius, the brightest star in the night sky which on 24 December aligns with the three brightest stars in Orion's belt (called "the three kings", and later "the three wise men"). The legendary journey of the three wise men was in itself a virtual reality for the northern hemisphere's winter solstice's disappearance of the sun for the longest and darkest night of the year and rebirth three days later, as reflected in the Persian Zoroastrian feast of Yalda (a word meaning 'birth'), that was celebrated with an evergreen tree (the ice on top of which resembled a star) and marked the eve of the 40-day-long winter season that ushered in spring and the rebirth of the sun; and passed into Mithraic rituals and in the 4th century morphed into our Christmas festival. The whole of the belief system which was the context for our festive season and Christmas spirit was a virtual reality.

A Six-Hitter and a Sacred Sight-Screen

Al was batting at school when his new coach served for him. He hit three sixes in an over, and the new coach, a recent Essex opening batsman, immediately spoke of him as "the six-hitter". When he met Al later, he said, "Here comes the six-hitter," and that was how he always referred to him.

Al was only 14, and in the school holidays he played for Loughton's Under-15 team.

My father took me to watch Loughton play on Saturday afternoons at the end of the war, and, sitting near the sight-screen near the road, on one occasion I had more than 40 gnat bites. In due course, on Saturdays I sometimes walked to the cricket ground on my own and sat on a wooden bench the other side of the ground, near Charles Albert George "Jack" Russell (erroneously written during his playing career as Albert Charles Russell), who first played cricket for Essex in 1908 and scored 1,000 runs in the 1913, 1914 and 1915 seasons. In 1923 he was the leading run-scorer, and scored more than Jack Hobbs. He looked very old in the 1940s, very lined though only around 60, and he signed my autograph album as A.C. Russell. He died in 1961.

Sometimes I sat next to Russell, and asked him what it was like playing for Essex before the First World War. He told me about the grounds he played on, how players he knew were killed. Each time I sat with him to hear his tales I was near the wooden white sight-screen. It was sacred, it seemed to have survived the First and Second World Wars, and was still intact.

Recently Bernard sent me a video via email of Al batting at the road end. He danced down the pitch and whacked the ball high back over the bowler's head. The ball crashed into the top right corner of the sight-screen, and broke a small chunk off. The video showed it fall. Al had also seen the bit fall, and after his innings he went and picked the piece of wood up and took it home as a souvenir.

The sight-screen had been undamaged for more than a century, and "the six-hitter" had broken it. It was sacred to Jack Russell's 1908 generation and to my generation when I, Al's Grandpa, played for the MCC against Loughton here in 1955. More than 67 years later, Al had broken it.

Next time I saw him I said, "You need to get yourself a trial with Essex in the coming year. Get your new coach, who recently played for Essex, to recommend you. Show him the bit of the Loughton sight-screen you, 'the six-hitter', broke and get him to report what happened. And do it quickly. I'm 84, and I want to sit in the pavilion near the aisle so when you go out to bat I can pat you on your arm or your back and wish you luck in your first game for Essex."

Al smiled, 6ft 3 although only 14 and heading for 6ft 6 or even 6ft 8. To build up his height he would sometimes have his school lunch, slip out to the Carvery and have a second lunch, and then return and have a second school lunch. He specialised in having a lot of potatoes and several Yorkshire puddings (five, on one occasion) to build up his fast-bowling strength – and his hitting strength so he could open the bowling and bat as a regular no.3 and six-hitter.

I did not know that Al would tour Holland with his school Under-15 team, and that he would have a bet with one of the team that if either of them got out first ball the first-baller would suffer the indignity of wearing the other's favourite football club's shirt at his school's next 'non-uniform' day. I did not know that they would play the Netherlands' Under-17 national eleven, who would be a man short, and that Al would volunteer to play for them and open the bowling, or that the player he had made the bet with would open the batting for his school's side. I did not know that Al would clean bowl him first ball – and cause him to wear Al's Arsenal-team shirt at school instead of his own Tottenham-team shirt, at the 'non-uniform' day, which he hated doing. Nor did I know that Al would captain his school's Under-15 team, and in 10 overs would take six wickets for 12 runs during his opponents' total of 227, and would then win the match by hitting three fours in the last over which took him to a score of 85 not out, and be named Man of the Match.

Having broken the sight-screen, the six-hitter was now breaking records, and it could only be a matter of time before he would have a trial for the Essex county team.

A Liquefied Eye and a Plastered Dressing (Or: A One-Eyed Cyclops and a Victim)

Dr Erdmann referred me to Professor Gallinger for my cataracts. I did not think they needed removing, but after his examination I noticed that my vision in both eyes was getting blurred. Suddenly I had difficulties in reading the straplines beneath the TV news. I was fast-tracked, had my biomeasuring just before Christmas and was to have my two cataracts lasered on the first two working Mondays in January. I had to arrive at Moorfields Hospital by 7.30am.

On the first Monday I got up at 4.45 and was driven to the hospital by 6.40. At reception I was told, "The Hospital doesn't open until 7.30am." A mixture of NHS and private patients were sitting on chairs round the walls and in front of the windows, and I was told to join them until I was called.

The call was communicated. One of the receptionists stood up, a man, and announced, "All NHS patients follow the orange line on the floor to the left and go to the first floor. All private patients follow the red and blue lines on the floor to the left and go to the fourth floor." Twelve of us squashed into the private patients' lift, and two then said they needed to get out on the first floor, as they were in the wrong lift.

Ten of us queued at reception on the fourth floor. An African lady tried to find our names on four pages of handwritten notes on each patient. When she found one of our names she ticked the name and asked the bearer of that name to sit down. Eventually a nurse came and read out three names and took the three sitting patients away. Another nurse came and said, "Everyone else, follow me."

I was led down two or three corridors to the private rooms. I was put in room 17. It had a bed, a television, a table and a comfortable chair, which I sat in. I unpacked a newspaper and read it.

Eventually several nurses came, one after another, to take my blood pressure and temperature, finalise paperwork and put me in a gown, tying the strings at the back. Then Professor Gallinger came in, wearing green scrubs and a green surgical cap, and asked me to sign two consent forms. He said I was first that day and he would see me shortly. He put a cross above my left eye with a skin-marking pen.

A nurse led me through several corridors to his room, about 8.55. While I was approaching, another nurse rang Pippa and asked if I was coming today as they were waiting for me.

Soon I lay on a padded trolley and had drops put in my left eye and was then asked to look at a red light and keep still for 20 seconds while a green light appeared. I was then escorted by a nurse on a long walk to the anaesthetist's room, and had my eye frozen with more drops. My nose and surrounding cheek and forehead all felt numb. I was then asked to lie on a padded trolley and was wheeled through to the theatre.

After a delay, I had a bag put over my head. There was an opening to access my left eye. Professor Gallinger said my left eye could not move or see now. I was blind in my left eye as a result of the anaesthetic. He asked me to be still for 20 minutes.

I remained still. I could see nothing as my face was covered and I could not see through the hole. I could hear instructions, requests Professor Gallinger made to his female Portuguese assistant. I felt liquid trickle down my left cheek. It seemed like water, as if I was shedding tears. I knew the laser would liquefy my cataract and my lens, but I could not see any laser, and did not know that had happened yet. I heard Professor Gallinger ask for my new lens. More liquid trickled down my cheek. He then put a padded dressing over my eye, and fastened it with two long strips of plaster. Later he said, "We're done."

I thanked him and the Portuguese assistant and unsteadily climbed off the padded trolley and sat in a wheelchair. I was then wheelchaired down several corridors, biffing a wall and the edge of a door-frame on the way. I was careful to keep my fingers clear of hazards.

I was wheeled to Recovery, a long room in which I was the only patient. A Filipino sat and asked me questions to assess whether I was disorientated.

I was then wheelchaired back to my room. I was brought the lunch they had insisted I ordered: tomato soup, egg mayonnaise sandwiches, ice-cream, cappuccino and two biscuits. It was a strategy to keep me occupied for an hour while they observed my progress.

Eventually a junior doctor brought in my medication: two bottles of drops, one of which had to be kept in a fridge, so I could have drops four times daily for four weeks, and a transparent eye-patch to be taped to my forehead and cheek to cover my eye at night for a week.

Now at last I could go.

I was one-eyed and found walking down the corridor to the lift difficult. I could not see to my left and hugged the wall on my right, and managed to get downstairs and to the entrance where I had come in. Then I rang my driver, and he collected me outside in his car.

I still could not feel a thing. My left eye's cataract had been liquefied and some of the liquid, perhaps mixed with water, had trickled down my cheek. Professor Gallinger had concealed my wound with a plastered dressing.

I felt like the one-eyed Cyclops in blind Homer's *Odyssey*, Polyphemus, who had groped his sheep in Serifos in the Western Cyclades when blinded, only I was not going to imprison the people I passed. I felt conspicuous, and a bit of a monster. But no, I was a mariner, who had been imprisoned in Professor Gallinger's cave and, a victim, had clung to the underbelly of his sheep and had escaped. I had escaped from the Cyclops' cave and now had to recover. But I had to go back to the Cyclops' cave next week to lose my other eye to this eye-devouring giant.

But in reality I was full of awe and admiration for this giant of an ophthalmologist who had pioneered and carried out the first laser treatment for cataracts in the UK in 1989, and who was a legend within the medical profession for having been such an innovating pioneer.

A Heart Pain and a Repaired Eye

I was to return to Moorfields Eye Hospital a week later to have the cataract removed from my other eye.

I went to sleep at 9.45pm the previous evening to be up at 4.45am the next day. At 3.15 I woke with pain in the region of my heart. It was quite considerable, and I lay and breathed calmly, but each out-breath hurt. I checked my Fitbit. My heart rate was under 70 beats per minute. I thought: 'It's not certain that I am having a heart attack, it could be heartburn or reflux, or even indigestion. Covid is returning, and I want to get today's procedure done before operations are cancelled.'

I got up and, to walk about, went to the loo. Then I sat on the side of my bed and breathed in and out, as if meditating. There was still pain, and it was cold outside, sub-zero, so I lay back in bed and turned off the light and breathed by inhaling through my nostrils to a count of four, holding my breath for a count of seven, then exhaling through my mouth to a count of eight. The pain continued.

Eventually I got up at 4.15am and busied myself to get ready. I shaved, dressed, took eye drops, went downstairs and took my tablets, and poured milk on my cereal (both prepared overnight). All the bustling to and fro eased the pressure on my heart.

I was collected at 6.15am. My driver had picked up my newspapers on the way in. I was in Moorfields by 7am. I sat until the announcement that we could all go up in the lifts, and I went to the fourth floor and the receptionist found my name. I sat near the door and was called to go to my room early. The nurse said I was second, not first as last week.

In room 18 I had four lots of drops, put a gown over my clothes that tied at the back and removed a hearing-aid, and put it, my watch and my Fitbit into a pocket. I put my bag in the locker beside my coat, locked it and pocketed my key. I was taken to the room where (after a wait as no.2) I looked at red and then green lights up a tube and had my right eye sealed by something gauze-like so I could only see outlines of people. I was eventually taken to the foyer of the theatre, and was given a local anaesthetic of drops and felt the sting of the anaesthetic on the surface of my eye for more than a dozen seconds.

The anaesthetist told me that after Claude Monet had surgery for his cataracts in 1923, his paintings of water lilies in his garden became a blaze of red and gold. His series of 250 oil paintings of water lilies, done over many years, shows (towards their end) how cataracts affected his work by reducing its colour.

After that there was no pain. My heart pain had gone with the local anaesthetic, and I was wheeled into the theatre and, my right eye numb and unable to move or see, lay back under the cover that lay over all my face and upper body except for a hole round my right eye, which I could not see through as that eye was now blind.

The operation went well. There was a bright white light, and the laser flushed out the cataract – I could feel it and my lens pour down my right cheek – and the new lens was fitted. I had a pad and eye shield placed over my right eye and plaster from my forehead down to the bottom of my right cheek.

At last Professor Gallinger said I should sit up and swing my legs over the side of the trolley and sit in the wheelchair parked next to it. As I swung my legs the pain returned in my heart, and I thought how lucky I had been that it had not hurt during the operation, when I had to lie still.

I was wheeled down the corridor to Recovery. I thought of Susan in her wheelchair at the mercy of the nurse, therapist or orderly who wheeled her to and from the gym. From Recovery I was collected by a nurse and wheeled back to my room.

My heart still hurt, but as I again tucked into the welcome hot tomato soup, prawn sandwiches (this time) and ice-cream washed down with cappuccino, I thought I had done right to keep going and not get side-tracked into ringing for an ambulance to have my heart checked, which would have ruled out the procedure involving my cataract. Eventually I had my blood pressure checked (119/77 as opposed to the ideal of 120/80) and my temperature taken (37C), and received my medication, and I was discharged. I rang my driver, and set off for the lift with my bag. The lift came up from below, and Professor Gallinger got out, scrubbed up.

"Oh," he said, "you're going."

I thought he might be about to stop me.

"Thank you for all you did today," I said. "I'll see you on Thursday week."

The doors closed and I descended. I had escaped. It was a military operation. I had had an operation under local anaesthetic with a possible heart attack going on and I had survived. I felt elated as the lift doors opened and I found the way out and stood in the biting cold for my driver to drive up and take me away. I had kept my painful heart a secret, and my eye had been repaired without anyone knowing.

An Algorithm and Extra-Crisp Bacon

Our grandson Bernard came, with a trimmed beard, combed-back hair and horn-rimmed glasses, looking very much a City-worker. He had started as an intern to be a trader in a French bank near Liverpool Street station.

He said, "There are 400 on the open-plan floor. My desk has six screens and is coveted."

He showed me pictures of his desk and the large room on his phone.

"I'm near Martin," he continued, "who's head of a team of 15. I'm being looked after by Ahmed, a second-year intern. He told me he picked my application out as other Masters graduates with excellent qualifications had fluffed their interviews.

"Banks want to buy bonds. Some will buy a lot, a billion pounds' worth. Others just five million. The biggest get the most attention, about 30 per cent. The smallest don't. But my boss Martin has vision. He's devised an algorithm that will work independently of the teams and cope with the 70 per cent we can't respond to. He took me to lunch on Friday with Ahmed, the new Chinese intern and a French intern. I want to work with him when I've finished my year's internship and help set up this new algorithm.

"I get in at 6, half an hour before everyone else, and that's already been noted. We can't leave our desks for more than five minutes except for lunchtime, and it takes about five minutes to walk to the coffee urns. The drinks are all free. On Friday you can take your credit card and come back with breakfast, only on a Friday. Next week I can get away about 5, this last week not until about 6.

"On Wednesday about 15 interns from different teams went out at lunchtime to the bar next door just to meet each other. The lunch with Martin on Friday took two hours, and when the conversation flagged and Martin put his head forward, Ahmed did circular movements with one hand meaning 'Keep talking'. I did, but the Chinese girl hardly said anything. She's very clever but very shy. The French intern didn't say much, I did the talking. Ahmed's Turkish Cypriot. He spent a year in Paris. They don't like it in France, they all have to speak French. There's a French team sitting near me, they speak in French all the time.

"Martin has a boss. He's Australian, he's very belittling. He asked me to get him breakfast and he said, 'I like my bacon extra-crisp.' We have to message on the screen, and he said to me, 'Your messages will go into my junk mail. I won't read them.' He said to me, 'I've no idea what you do. You work under me but I don't know what you do.' He was very slighting, but if he doesn't know what his team are doing he's not a very good manager. That's what we think. But he did compliment me on his bacon. He said that was how he liked extra-crisp. He's Martin's boss and is looked on with awe.

"Martin's team made 16 million pounds last year," Bernard concluded. "They made 8 of the 16 million in two weeks. I'm looking forward to being a trader, keeping up to date with the markets and buying bonds for banks at good rates. I can't wait to be doing that."

Bernard clearly loved what he was doing. He reckoned he had fallen on his feet, and he could see a way forward as he worked through being an intern earning more than many are earning at the end of their careers. He really liked his boss who had a vision of what his algorithm could do, and he contrasted him with *his* boss who insisted on extra-crisp bacon. Bernard was now in effect an observer-helper within a team of 15, and he longed for the time when he could join and be a trader in his own right and bring in millions more for the bank that employed him.

And if he was lucky he might find himself overseeing the algorithm that would deal with 70 per cent of the banks that wanted bonds. He did not then know that two weeks later he would be told to his delight that he had been picked to concentrate on getting the algorithm up and running, and that he would not be doing some of the intern work so he would have time to establish the algorithm. He was prepared to supply his boss's boss with extra-crisp bacon so he could have access to the new algorithm that would dramatically increase what the team made and propel him up the bank's tree so one day interns' messages would go into *his* junk mail.

A Wheelchair and a 'No'
(Or: Snowdrops and a Crocus of Early Spring)

I ate my sandwiches in the Norwich car park, got out and waved Pippa off to go shopping, and entered Susan's rehab unit shortly before 2pm.

In the corridor I encountered the "key worker", and I showed her the floss sticks she had requested to go with the battery-operated toothbrush I had brought previously. She picked up a chair and carried it into Susan's room for me to sit on. Susan was in her wheelchair with a nurse bending over her, and when she saw me her eyes widened and her face filled with pleasure and delight.

I showed Susan the floss sticks and put them in her drawer. When the nurse and the key worker had left I asked her if she was more comfortable now in her wheelchair, and she eyes-upped a Yes. She eye-gazed coloured letters on her e-tran board, "The head rest sore."

I said, "The head-rest made your neck sore?"

She nodded and e-tranned, "Sorted."

I nodded in approval.

I told her that Paul would be coming with his nearly-one-year-old daughter (her niece) and his dog in two days' time, and that Simon was coming with us in a week's time. She was pleased. I told her that at last, after four months of letters, the Council had agreed to exempt her from Council tax – a good result. They had wanted evidence of permanent care, and I was reluctant to ask her consultant for this as it would have to be with her listening, and I did not want to plunge her into despair at hearing she would need lifelong permanent care in a home. The Council had reviewed her case and had decided it was unique and they would exempt her until further notice, as I had requested.

The speech and language therapist came in. She was on the timetable to have a session, but said she did not want to interrupt my visit, she wanted to chat to both of us. She talked about the BISSkiT (Biofeedback in Strength and Skill Training) swallowing programme, and the goal (on the wall) of five swallows. She agreed the swallowing muscles were the same as the speaking muscles, but said the muscles were used in different ways for swallowing and speaking. But improvement in swallowing would improve speaking.

I said, "She's so nearly speaking. She mouths the words. If I were a lip-reader I could almost work out what she's saying from the movement in her mouth."

She agreed.

After the therapist went Susan e-tranned me by gazing on her letter board: "The nurse has just tested me for diabetes." I said it was probably a routine blood test they have to do from time to time, and Susan agreed. In the course of spelling out the letters that made the words, she said "R" aloud.

I said, "The letter 'R'?" She eyes-upped a Yes.

And on one occasion she said, "No."

I said, "You've just said 'No'," and she nodded, pleased. I said, "You're doing so well, you're in month 8 and powers are coming back." She eyes-upped Yes and moved her fingers and her elbow. When I pressed her, she indicated she had signed her Powers of Attorney the previous week unaided, with no help to her elbow.

Then a young therapist came in and said, "Guess what, ta-rra, I'm back, you've got me again. I've just been told by your speech and language therapist I'm going to do sound and speed with you, we might chant nursery rhymes to get you to speak." She said, "I'm writing a new session on her timetable on the wall." And she wrote herself in for a session on Thursday morning.

463

I said, "Susan has just said 'No'." And Susan nodded.

When we were alone again I talked to Susan about her house. I said we were all worried as she was not ready for risky living yet. I said, "You need your medications, and someone shouldn't be buying them at a pharmacy, which may not have had a delivery and may not stock them. It's better to be in the care centre near your mum, they'll have your medications. And agencies are losing staff, and what happens if one of the staff doesn't turn up? At a care centre staff will always be there, there's no risk of your being left alone. If they say they want to discharge you into a risky set-up, can you say you want to consult your family before you agree?"

Susan eyes-upped a Yes.

I said, "Your house is a possibility in the future. It needs plastering and painting, and adapting for a hoist and a wheelchair, and perhaps some of this will require planning permission, which will take time. It's not going to be ready to move into when they discharge you from here next month. Do you see that?"

Susan eyes-upped a Yes.

I told her how on the day she had had her stroke I found the deer she gave me lying on the grass with a snapped leg, and how I had repaired it. (I did not know that I would see out of my window early next morning a stag and three deer grazing in the meadow at the bottom of our lawn, a hint that everything would be all right between me and my three children, including her, from now on.) I also told her how in the course of my first visit to her in Ipswich Hospital I had healed her with four great surges.

I did some more healing. I sat and put the little finger of my right hand on her forehead. There was activity as energy entered my back and passed down my right arm through my finger into her forehead, but there were no massive surges as on that first day. She did not need surges now, just a faint flow of healing energy.

Then I showed her printed-off pictures I had brought of her car being guarded by a magpie and a fox, and she roared with laughter at the thought of Nature co-operating in looking after her.

Then Pippa arrived. I summarised what had happened and what had been said, and Pippa said her mum wanted to order some trousers. "Do you mind what kind?" Susan shook her head. "Size 14?" Susan looked horrified, and it was clear she wanted size 12. When I suggested size 11 she laughed, as I had suggested a non-existent size: women's clothes have only even numbers.

A nurse came in and fed clear liquid into her PEG, and then asked if I would like to wheel her into the garden. It was a mild day, 12C in February, but it was nearly 4pm and dusk was not far off.

I said, "For five minutes, yes."

I put another blanket over her upper front and wheeled her for the first time this year out down the slope and round and then between the waist-high raised flower-beds and stopped at a group of snowdrops and held them in my fingers and said, "See, they have three white petals, and three shorter green ones beneath." And I stopped at a solitary crocus and held its brilliant orangey yellow in my fingers. We stopped to look at ivy and honeysuckle leaves. The fresh air did her good, and she loved it. I heard her chuckling as I avoided hazards and steered her back up the slope into her room.

Back inside I lip-salved her lips, brushed her hair and rubbed cream into her fingers and hands. I wiped saliva which had dribbled from the side of her mouth to her neck. Then I pressed the buzzer, and when the nurse came I said Susan would like to get back into bed. (I had put a typed notice on her chest, "Please put me back into bed.") Another nurse arrived to help.

We slipped away. There had been no crying or groaning at all for nearly two-and-a-half hours, the first time a visit had been crying-free.

In the car I reflected that things were improving. She had stopped crying. She was now happy to sit in her wheelchair, the problems of preferring to stay in her bed had been resolved, and following our journey round the garden she would be more likely to agree to sit in the wheelchair for our visits in the hope that this would happen again. And she was nearly speaking, she had said "No". She had seen the first signs of spring. Just as the snowdrops and crocus had pushed through the recently frosty ground, so her silent words were pushing through the frozen muscles of her paralysed throat. Her swallowing and her speaking were like the snowdrops and crocus of early spring.

In the car I felt very positive and forward-looking, and now longed to hear where, following her impending discharge, her next place would be.

A Normal Routine and Chaos

Paul came with us to Norwich, and brought his dog, a cross between a Jack Russell and a Bichon Frisé, and his nearly-one-year-old daughter Alice. Susan had held her when she visited me for my birthday three weeks before her stroke. Alice was then nearly three months old, and was recovering from an operation.

She had been born with PDA, *patent ductus arteriosus*, a foetal blood vessel that normally closes after birth. The *ductus arteriosus* had not closed and had leaked oxygenated blood from her left heart, causing it to flow back through her aorta to her lungs. Half her heart was working extra hard to pump her blood round her limbs, half her heart had been doing the work of the other half of her heart and she had a bulge on one side of her heart. She had a heart murmur and breathing was a struggle. She was reluctant to be bottle-fed while this was being discovered, and she failed to gain weight at a normal rate, and her weight was behind what a normal child's weight should be.

Paul had taken her to the Royal London Hospital, and it so happened that a specialist from Great Ormond Street Hospital (GOSH) was present and had a look, and luckily identified the problem. GOSH had her in before she reached three months, and threaded a tube from her groin up inside her and closed what had remained open, so her heart problem was solved. Paul had taken her in at 7am, the procedure took nearly three hours, and at 1pm she had an echocardiogram to check that everything had gone well. Everything was fine when Susan last held her and the return to normal weight was just beginning.

That had now happened, and a few days short of her first birthday she was normal, she had progressed to eating solids and had started at her local nursery three days a week.

It had been a wet journey and the rain eased as we ate our sandwiches in the car park. Then Paul took his dog, leaving Alice asleep in the car in the care of Pippa, and he and I and the dog entered Susan's room soon after 2pm. She was in her wheelchair with two nurses bending over her, and when she saw Paul, the dog and then me, her eyes widened in delight.

I stooped and kissed her forehead and said, "You're winning," trying to be encouraging, and she cried as if to say, 'I'm not, my recovery is frustratingly slow.'

Paul put his dog on the two pillows over her knees in the wheelchair. Susan's mood calmed. The dog sat very quietly for half an hour as if it knew what was wrong with Susan, and sympathised. It displayed the sensitive behaviour in front of a sick patient shown by therapeutic dogs. On two occasions the dog shifted and touched the buzzer near Susan's hand, and twice nurses had to come and turn the alarm off. Susan laughed.

Paul then took the dog back to the car and I monologued to Susan. I put lip salve on her lips and tried healing her forehead. No surge came through, suggesting she did not need major healing, even in her throat.

Then Pippa appeared, saying Paul was changing Alice. Pippa read from her phone a message from her mother about trousers she was ordering for her.

Pippa left to look after the dog, and soon Paul arrived with Alice. Paul took her coat off and sat her on the pillows looking at Susan – she quickly made eye contact with Susan and watched her eyes – and Susan had a face-to-face look at a fellow human who could not speak but had said simple words. I said, "Alice, it's Auntie Susan." Now it was as if Susan was looking at herself in a mirror, herself in a few weeks' time, able to do a little more. Alice had more movement and freedom than Susan had.

Very soon Alice was lying quietly on her back on the pillows, cradled by Susan's right arm for another half-hour. It was as if Alice had the same therapeutic sense as the dog and instinctively knew what was wrong with Susan and consequently kept very still and calm. Alice also set the buzzer off twice, and nurses looked in to stop the alarm, and again Susan laughed at the chaos.

I rang Pippa and she came with the dog. We all sat with Susan, and Paul got the dog lying on her left side and Alice on her right side, so she cradled both. I reminded Susan that there was a picture of her holding Alice seven days after her operation, taken on my birthday, and she was holding Alice and also fondling the dog. And Susan briefly cried as if to say, 'I wish I could go back to that time and do that now.'

Then Paul turned Alice and sat her looking at Susan on one of the pillows, and Alice blew raspberries through bubbling lips, which made Susan laugh. Susan e-tranned, knowing that Alice's birthday was only ten days away: "I will sort Alice's birthday when I can." And she promptly cried as if to say, 'I wish I could do it now, I hate being unable to send birthday presents.'

It was time to be going. Paul got me to hold Alice while he lifted the dog to the floor and put him on the lead. Then he lifted Alice and put her coat back on. I busied myself putting cream on Susan's hands and tried to turn the TV back on for her. Then Susan started crying. She did not want us to leave.

Two nurses were waiting in the corridor outside to hoist her from her wheelchair back into bed. One said to me, "We'll cope with the TV and make sure it's on for her."

I said to Susan, "See you next Tuesday with Simon, bye." Susan tried to mouth 'Bye' but nothing came out, and that made her cry more.

We left. At the end of the corridor we encountered the speech and language therapist. I said I wanted to ask her something, and she took me to an empty room so we had some privacy.

I said, "Sibyl is worried that the neurological care centre at Ipswich has been taken over. The team have to decide whether she will still need level-1 care next month or if she can go down to level 2. If it's level 2, can you confirm that everything at the care centre in Ipswich will go on just the same? I've been online and they'll still do level 2 in 6 beds and residential care in 26 beds, and your referral process won't change – is that right? Have I understood correctly? It will all go on just the same?"

"Oh, yes," she said. "Nothing will have changed. It will have the same staff and programme, and we'll approach them in the same way as before."

Relieved, having heard what I wanted to hear, I rejoined the others in the foyer. And Pippa was soon driving us back.

It had been a good day. Susan's normal routine had been replaced by a chaotic relay of ins and outs, the buzzer going off, and the hospital's limit of two visitors becoming three with a child and a dog as well. Susan had reconstructed the photo of her taken nine months previously on my last birthday.

There had been a lot of laughter and delight, and a lot of tears. Susan had been torn by different emotions, but she understood everything, and Paul was surprised at how much of the old Susan had come back. She was very interested to hear the family news, it made her feel included even though she was sad she could not be part of it, part of marking birthdays as she had always been able to do.

Her normal routine was a timetabled day with therapists and nurses, and a lot of peace and quiet. The chaotic toing and froing had brought back the outer world and all she had been missing. The chaos had invaded her locked-in syndrome and had made her feel less locked-in. The chaos had brought the outer world home to her, and I hoped it would give her an added incentive to recover her lost powers.

A Madonna and a Fire-Ball

Penny returned from her visit to Amsterdam, where she had booked to spend two nights in a hotel with her daughter and son-in-law to celebrate her 65th birthday near her childhood.

"I had a really good time in Amsterdam, even though it rained much of the time," she said. "The first day, Wednesday, I visited where I used to live and the building where I went to school. My father left Holland for Singapore before the war and had a hotel there, and fled with his wife and three children from the invading Japanese with nothing and came to Amsterdam. The hotel we were staying in was where he worked as a chef. I asked if they had records, archives, from that time, but the hotel has changed hands several times since then and they hadn't. My grandfather was a sculptor, and he worked on the Central Station in Amsterdam. We saw his sculptures on the front of the Central Station when we arrived and when we left.

"The second day, Thursday, we had lunch with my sister Greta, who's now 82, in a restaurant. Her daughter was there, it was lovely. On our wall when I was a child was a carving by my grandfather of a Madonna. The face of the Madonna is my mother's. My mother died when I was seven, and my father when I was 15, and I had to live alone and get myself off to school in those days. The Madonna went to my sister Greta, who gave it to her daughter, who didn't like it, and in the restaurant Greta gave it to me. I was so pleased to have it. I've brought it home. It's a sculpture of my mother.

"We set off for home on Friday on a Eurostar train and everything went well until we reached Rotterdam that evening. We were held on the train for two hours. Then we were told the train would terminate there. It was said that a migrant had climbed onto the roof of a Eurostar train in Paris's Gare du Nord station and had stood up and put his hands on the electric cable above him, and his body burst into flames, he had become a fire-ball and there was little left to identify.

"We were told to find a hotel. Eurostar cancelled our tickets from Rotterdam to London without telling us. It was very stressful. There were 600 seeking a hotel and the hotels were all pretty full. Adrian got on his phone and managed to book into the Marriott Hotel near the station, and we tried to rebook tickets to London. We found a really early train to Brussels on Saturday morning, and an onward train to London that afternoon. We booked it for £1,000 with no help or guidance from Eurostar. There were 50 schoolchildren on the train, how could their teachers find them a hotel and book them to come home? There was no help from Eurostar.

"We only had three hours' sleep that night. We had to go through customs and British Border Force three times because of stupid Brexit: first in Amsterdam, then in Rotterdam, then in Brussels. The tickets were all electronic, on our phones. At Brussels Rebecca pleaded to be put on an earlier train back to London as – I didn't know it until then – they had a surprise for me that evening. Through Eurostar managers she managed it.

"I found out that my son Andreas and his wife were to meet us in London as a surprise, have dinner and then have front-row seats for *The King and I*. The cast includes an actress I like from *Call the Midwife*. It all happened, it was amazing. Andreas's wife ordered a bottle of champagne, and we all drank champagne. It was a wonderful evening.

"But now I have to get a refund from Eurostar. The wait of two hours meant we should be refunded for our journey to Rotterdam. Eurostar cancelled our tickets to London. There was our hotel booking at the Marriott. Eurostar left us stranded with no help, and we now have to get our money back.

"But it was so lovely to be back where I spent my childhood, and to have the Madonna. I wonder about the migrant. Didn't he know that electric cables above the train must not be touched, and turn you into a fire-ball if you touch them?"

I had listened with sympathy and admiration for how they all coped, and carried through their plans. On the migrant I too had questions. Many migrants were economic migrants from Africa and the Middle East who were not escaping wars but looking to improve their income from black-market jobs. Had this one come from a desert and had he never learned about electric cables? Was it ignorance of the modern world that led to his death? He had wanted to travel from Paris to London, perhaps on the top of a Eurostar train.

Word had got round that the UK was a soft touch: "It's good, you land there and apply for asylum and they put you in a 5-star hotel for two years, with free meals and a white tablecloth, waited on hand and foot." Was he one of the economic migrants who had been lured by the stories of royal treatment while his claim was processed, and by the prospect that on the black market he would be able to earn four-fifths of the going rate that the English received?

He hadn't thought about the consequences of his selfish attempt to be a stowaway, and he may have been ignorant of the Western life from which he sought to benefit. Was he unaware of the hazards, had he done no research into the situation into which he was putting himself? Was it ignorance of the Western way of life and use of electric cables that killed him? It was said he had been running away from the police before he climbed onto the train.

I was haunted by Penny's present of her grandfather's carving of her mother. It was so appropriate that it had finally come to Penny, and Greta (who, Penny said, bled easily under her skin as I do) had done right by presenting the carving to her. And I was also haunted by the migrant who had apparently been running away from the police, having embarked on a project where he was out of his depth, and had consequently been turned into a fire-ball. I could only shake my head at his ill-considered decision.

A Golden Pilgrimage and a Honeycomb

For our Golden Wedding on a Thursday towards the end of February, Pippa got Simon to book us in at The Savoy, and Simon obliged by maximising our experience there. He told me he had paid for everything, including breakfast, except for our other meals, and we had been upgraded to a junior suite because of our anniversary and would have their butler service for suites.

I was getting old, and packing was more of a struggle. I had completely forgotten that our suitcases had built-in locks and would not need padlocks, as Pippa reminded me, and I wondered if I had early dementia.

Our driver drove us to the grand Strand entrance around 11.15am. The receptionist in the lobby immediately wished us a happy anniversary and as our room was not ready gave us a complimentary voucher to have coffee in a sitting area, which we did. Our cases would be delivered to our room, we kept our hand luggage with us.

Pippa had not been well. She had bronchitis and a chest, throat and ear infection, and was on antibiotics. This was her first foray out into society, and she felt under the weather.

I savoured the atmosphere. Peter, Count of Savoy, had built the Savoy Palace on the site in 1246, having been granted the land between the Strand and the River Thames by Henry III. It was the greatest house in England, and Chaucer began *The Canterbury Tales* in Middle English in 1387 while in residence there with its owner John of Gaunt, a younger son of Edward III who had inherited the lands of the Dukes of Lancaster. Chaucer's long poem begins in

April, when the weather turns warmer after winter and people begin to go on pilgrimages. The Savoy Palace was destroyed during rioting in Wat Tyler's Peasants' Revolt of 1381. The rioters blamed John of Gaunt for introducing the poll tax. I imagined Chaucer sitting where I was sitting in John of Gaunt's palace amid thoughts of a pilgrimage to Canterbury.

By 12 noon we had gone up shallow stairs to the American Bar. The current Savoy was built by Richard D'Oyly Carte from profits from his Gilbert-and-Sullivan opera productions, and opened in 1889. It attracted the artistic world in the 1890s. Oscar Wilde lived in it, and it became notorious during his trial. I knew the American Bar had often been visited by T.S. Eliot, Ezra Pound, Scott Fitzgerald and Ernest Hemingway, and again as we sat before a window and drank King's Cobbler cocktails and munched Cornish lobster, chilli chews and olives, I savoured the atmosphere from a hundred years ago, recalling how I had met Hemingway and Pound as a young man.

We went back to reception and a new receptionist, a young girl, confirmed that our room was now ready. She made a call and gave me a card to hold over the door-opener. She said, "It's your Golden Wedding." (Impressively, all the staff seemed to know.) She said, "I'm getting married in September, have you any tips for a long and happy marriage?"

I said, "Have separate interests, and keep talking."

She smiled and thanked me profusely, and said she would remember what I had said.

Then a butler appeared. After congratulating us on our Golden Wedding he told me he had been at The Savoy for seven years, and he would take us up to our room. He was Greek, from Athens, and he walked us to a lift and took us up to the fourth floor and to our room, room 426.

The fourth-floor suite had a sitting-room with a head-high white-and-gold balloon weighted to the floor, saying '50 Happy Years'; and a bathroom off; and a bedroom with a wardrobe area and another bathroom off.

The two rooms overlooked the River Thames from Waterloo Bridge on our left down to a distant bend, and from Charing Cross Bridge on our right up to and beyond the Houses of Parliament. There was a large book on Claude Monet, and I immediately found a picture of his showing Waterloo Bridge, one of the hundred pictures of London he painted while he stayed at The Savoy between 1899 and 1901. I established he had occupied room 618.

The butler showed us a button on a phone on the sitting-room desk, and said we could have breakfast brought to our room if we ordered it that evening over the phone. Our luggage arrived, and he left us to unpack.

Just before 2pm we took the lift down a floor to the Spa, where Simon had booked us in for two-hour signature treatments. I changed into a dressing-gown and slippers in a changing-room, and then had a working over: aromatherapy oil and a back scrub that nourished my skin, and then a massage that melted the oily moisture into my skin, and a facial. It soon had me so relaxed that I was on the fringe of sleep. Pippa told me afterwards that she felt the same. I came out very drowsy and after changing we went back to our room to look at the river. By arrangement, a butler had already brought tea, and I sat and drank green tea overlooking the river and light rain.

We then exchanged cards. Pippa's card showed 50 gold hearts as balloons anchored in the 0 of 50 years. In my card I thanked her for having joined me in a journey that had built up a fund that had led to a good life for ourselves, our children and grandchildren, and for having provided a good daily routine and food for our family.

We then exchanged presents. Pippa gave me a high-quality American gold tie-pin, and another she had bought as a substitute as it seemed that the main one would not arrive in time. I gave her gold earrings and a gold bracelet. Then I ordered our breakfast over the butler phone and changed for dinner.

We had a tasting supper in Restaurant 1890 (now a Gordon Ramsay restaurant). We had a window table overlooking The Savoy's entrance and turning-circle, and Savoy Theatre (where early Gilbert-and-Sullivan operettas were performed), where theatre-goers were queueing in the rain to get in. They were waiting to see *Plaza Suite*, a play showing what happened in The Plaza Hotel, New York. We had just left our suite in The Savoy Hotel, London.

I was wearing a pale gold shirt and a gold tie, and the gold American tie-pin Pippa had given me. Pippa wore a black dress with white trees on it, and she wore the gold earrings and bracelet I had given her, and a brooch of a large finely-carved bee.

I said, "It's a bee."

She said, "It's a Gucci antique bee."

Pippa had always been very attentive to what our lives needed, and had gone out like a bee gathering nectar to turn it into honey in our hive. She had always been a busy bee, going from flower to flower to advance our family.

The restaurant staff all knew we were celebrating our Golden Wedding, and we were told the menu was a surprise. Each of the eleven mini-courses – that included lobster, crab, sardines, chicken, cheesecake, quince and spiced ice-cream – was explained, and at the end we were given a printed-out menu of what we had had with a card wishing us a Happy Anniversary, signed by the half-dozen waiters and waitresses who had served us.

After our dinner we returned to our room, and Pippa asked to sit in the dark so she could look at the river. She changed into her dressing-gown and sat in the window. A full moon was now high in the sky. The lights on the water our side of Waterloo Bridge were flecked as in Monet's 1899–1901 paintings. Monet painted nearly 100 paintings of the River Thames, 41 of which were of Waterloo Bridge and another series of the Houses of Parliament. The lights on the far bank of the Thames were red (indicating dangerously high buildings to low-flying helicopters), blue and purple (the gigantic wheel known as the London Eye). It was all spellbinding.

I changed into my dressing-gown and in the darkened room, looking at the clear full moon, I reflected on our Golden Anniversary. But I also thought again of Chaucer beginning *The Canterbury Tales* in the vicinity of where I was sitting, and thinking of what it meant to be a pilgrim. Earlier in my life I had been journeying towards a Reality which I had found, and had returned with a deeper knowledge of Truth in all its forms. We had both followed our own interests, and in my case I had been on a pilgrimage. For me, I was celebrating as a Golden Pilgrim like one of Chaucer's pilgrims, and celebrating the daily routine Pippa had established for the family as a busy antique bee in the sense that she had followed the antique way of doing things for a family, gathering nectar for family honey. She was younger than me and whereas I was ancient she had a commendably antique way of doing things. She was a mature antique, an antique bee.

We had a long sleep and woke to a sunny morning with blue sky the next day, a Friday. I got up first and, having showered, on a whim, ran a shallow bath in an old-style white tub with curved sides. I got in all right by holding on to the handles. I lay in the warm water and relaxed, and then sat up to get out. But at first I could not haul myself up gripping the handles. With difficulty I grasped the curved open side of the bath with both hands and heaved myself slowly up and out, aware of my advancing years.

As I patted myself dry I was astonished to see there were about 20 spots lying in the water. The back scrub must have dislodged some of my seborrhoeic spots and small warts, and their debris, lodged in my oily skin, had come off in the bath's water. My skin was healthier than it had been for a long while.

Breakfast was delivered to our door at 9am. A formally-suited new butler (one of the 25 who looked after the 73 suites) wheeled in a laid and laden oval table on wheels. We chatted about Monet and his perspective on Waterloo Bridge, and we made an arrangement that he would take me to Monet's room 618 after breakfast.

For breakfast I had cereal, a cooked breakfast with poached eggs, toast, honey and coffee. I then finished packing and went downstairs to settle for the meals that were not included in what Simon had paid. An invoice had been tucked under our door just before the butler arrived. I paid at reception, and was met by the butler who had brought breakfast, Atilla.

He took me up in a lift and walked with me to room 618. There was a huge reception room with an abandoned pair of steps near the door, and a bedroom off it. It was in the dead centre of The Savoy, and was farther from Waterloo Bridge than we were, and nearer Charing Cross Bridge (and the Houses of Parliament). Brilliant sunshine poured through the modernised windows and made me screw up my eyes.

I talked with Atilla. A workman came and adjusted the steps and politely said, "I hope you've enjoyed your stay."

Back in our room, I did a final search to check that we had packed everything, and was ready when at 11.15 another butler collected our suitcases and wheeled them off on his trolley. We went downstairs, Pippa holding the balloon saying "50 Happy Years", and she and I waited outside the lobby alongside our cases. Four doormen, two in black top hats, greeted us and hoped we had had a pleasant stay and a Happy Anniversary.

In our car, Pippa, holding the balloon saying "50 Happy Years", told our driver that she had texted Simon the previous day that she was going to live in The Savoy from now on. Simon had texted back, "Your card will be declined."

I smiled at the vast expense of Pippa's proposal, which, if it had not been humorous, would have been delusional. I had picked up the first of several cuttings I had taken from the previous day's newspapers to read more carefully. It spoke of lazy, defenceless, near-bankrupt Britain living beyond its means, and detached from reality. It said Britain was a second-order global power looking back to a bygone age. It claimed the British wanted free public services paid from borrowing while all enjoyed low tax despite there being no growth. It said the country's prospects were dire, and national delusions had to be punctured.

Pippa was sitting in the back of the car with the balloon saying "50 Happy Years". I reflected that we had lived through 50 years of national decline and were under no illusions following the passing of a bygone age. I had set out on a pilgrimage to Truth in all its forms as Chaucer had in *The Canterbury Tales*, and to give myself the time to do it I had created a fund that would protect our family from what had always seemed dire times. I had teamed up with an excellent provider of a smooth-running household that had allowed me time at my desk. She had collected nectar during the long outer decline and had contributed to our golden honeycomb. Things had turned out well. I had pursued my quest and recorded my pilgrimage through social events to the Reality, the Golden Truth of the One I had found, and had been sustained by a stable home. In that sense, everything seemed Golden; despite my time of decline, I was living in a Golden Age.

I reflected in my advanced old age that our Golden Anniversary had quietly celebrated the long alliance and union between a now-ancient pilgrim whose Golden pilgrimage mirrored Truth and a now-antique nectar-gathering honey-bee who had lived together in a honeycomb of Golden calm.

Title 'Pilgrimage', "life viewed as a journey"
   (*Concise Oxford Dictionary*).

A Demudding and a Turned Corner

That Tuesday morning ten minutes before I was leaving for Norwich, Frankie, our gardener, came to my balcony door in a T-shirt, shorts and trainers. He said, "The mower's stuck in mud at the bottom of the field."

Then I realised his arms, legs and feet, and parts of his face, were covered in thick mud. The mower's wheels had spun while he tried to give it a push to get it out of the mud, and had spattered mud all over him.

I said, "I'm just about to leave. The best I can do is hose you so you can go home and get a hot shower and change of clothes."

He said he would go home and then come back with a tarpaulin to cover the mower until the field dried out.

So I clambered down the spiral staircase, took him to the hose on the side of the annexe and squirted cold water on each limb in turn and demudded him enough to enable him to get into his car. Then I returned up the spiral staircase to collect what I was taking and leave.

On the way to Norwich I reflected on recent events. The February Tuesday after our stay in The Savoy I found Susan sitting in her wheelchair with Geraldine outside the front sliding doors, holding an anniversary card with 50 hearts like balloons, which she had signed "Susan xxx" in legible handwriting. Then with her right fingers she steered her wheelchair along the corridor. Geraldine, slim and very much in control, guided her through the door to her room and she then, sitting in the wheelchair, demonstrated the Possum (Freeway) the environmental-control team had left for her.

She pressed on a large button and switched a lamp on and then off, then turned her wall-mounted TV on, went down four channels to Radio 2 and turned it on, and adjusted the volume. Then she turned it off so we could speak. Geraldine had already said that the consultant would be discussing her discharge the following Monday with her. She said we would be kept informed.

The next Tuesday, the first Tuesday in March, I found Susan in her wheelchair in her room. I asked her what the consultant had said, and by eyegazing one of four groups of alphabetical letters on her e-tran board and then a colour, I could spell out letter by letter that she had been asked to stay until the end of May. I was delighted, as she was in a time of great progress and this extension would carry her forward during the next two months. I took her out into the garden to look at the early spring flowers.

The following Tuesday Pippa and I took in four blouses Pippa had found for her in a Seasalt sale. Before we hung them in her wardrobe she told me via e-tran that a doctor had let slip that her discharge date was 20 May. It was later confirmed in an update Geraldine emailed. It transpired that Susan had swallowed five teaspoonfuls, and was actually saying a few words now and then.

Now we arrived at her level-1 hospital at 1.45pm. Pippa, who was driving, slowed to let a wheelchair across the hospital road, and in it was Susan wearing her old glasses, being pushed by Geraldine. With the car still moving very slowly, I opened my passenger door and called to her, "Hello, Susan and Geraldine."

Geraldine turned the wheelchair and Susan saw us and looked delighted. Geraldine called, "We've just been round the block outside the gates, looking at the houses."

Pippa found a parking space and said she was going to a garden centre and would join me later. I walked to the foyer, and Susan was sitting in her wheelchair. I signed in and went to the loo, and then joined them in Susan's room. Geraldine showed me that the environmental-control team had rewired the Possum to include calling a nurse, and said she would be applying in mid-April to the care home in Ipswich we had chosen so she could be taken by 20 May.

Geraldine said, "I did some of my training there, I know them. Ipswich Town football club train there in mid-week. It's got 100 acres, and Susan will be able to drive her powered wheelchair near them."

I said, "You'll need a whistle to referee their practice game."

Susan and Geraldine both laughed.

Geraldine said that Susan had asked to wear her old glasses, and she asked Susan if she could take them off. Susan nodded. Geraldine left, and I talked to Susan.

I asked her if she still had black blocks in the left corners of each eye, and she shook her head. I asked, "Can you see all of me, not just part of me? All of me?" She eyes-upped yes. "Even looking sideways?" She eyes-upped yes. Her sight had come back, as the optician who visited her before Christmas said it would.

Then I realised she was wearing one of the Seasalt blouses. It looked very good with small yellow and blue flowers on white. I said, "Is it the crinkle blouse?"

She nodded. The blouse did not look crinkly at all, it suited her.

I told her Pippa had a problem with driving for too long because of her arthritic hands, and Susan indicated she wanted to write by wiggling her right hand rather than eyegaze the e-tran board, so I put a biro in her hand and paper on the small tray her button was on. And she wrote, "To make it easier for Pippa's driving, come every other week."

I could just about read it. I was touched.

"No, we'll still come every week," I said. "We want to see you safely in the new place. But what a nice thought. The old Susan's back, thinking of others before herself, being considerate." And I brushed her hair, applied lip salve and creamed her hands.

Then Pippa arrived. She told Susan she had bought some pinks at the garden centre, and she said she was researching a phone with large buttons that could be operated like her Possum and would allow her to WhatsApp her friends and family. She said, "I don't know what phone you'd need here and in the new place. 2G, 4G or 5G?"

Both of us saw Susan mouth and faintly say, "4G."

Then I put a blanket over her front for warmth and pushed her in her wheelchair out into the garden while Pippa tidied her drawers-on-wheels, sitting on the side of her bed. I wheeled Susan to some orange tulips and we looked at narcissi. We listened to a blackbird. Pippa came out and joined us. She confirmed that Susan could hear the blackbird's song. Pippa later told me, "She liked being in the garden with you."

We sat on chairs in a deserted sitting-area. I sensed Susan was getting cold and asked if she'd like to go in, and she eyes-upped a yes.

I wheeled her back into her room, and soon after Pippa went, saying she would be in the foyer. Susan mouthed 'Bye' and waved the fingers in her right hand.

I asked Susan to turn her TV on and select her Radio 2, which she did, and adjust the volume. Then I asked her to call the nurse to get her out of her wheelchair and into her bed, and she did. The alarm went off within her room and in the corridor, but no one came, so I said I had to rejoin Pippa and would see her next Tuesday. She laughed 'Bye' and waved the fingers on her right hand.

Back in the foyer I found Pippa talking to Geraldine, who stopped and had a word with me. I said I had left Susan in her wheelchair, could she arrange for a nurse to put her back into bed, and she said she would. She said Susan would be holding a drumstick in her fingers and would be beating a drum in their next music session.

I signed out and went to the loo. Pippa was heading outside and the consultant came by, Dr Saatvik. "Nice to see you," he said, 'can't stop as I'm dealing with an emergency, but nice to see you."

I wondered if he was responding to Susan's call bell, as the alarm was still going off in the corridor.

In the car Pippa said, "I had a long chat with Geraldine. She said, 'Susan's a completely different person. She's up for everything, including going out into the community, she does whatever we ask and she's making progress. She's turned a corner, and the staff are all thrilled.'"

I nodded and said, "She looks more normal, she looks more natural. Her eyes are moving, her head's moving all the time. I reckon for a while she was under Sibyl's and Don's influence, that if she has capacity she can decline to do what she's asked to do of a strenuous nature, and have undemanding passive palliative care and an easier time. I reckon she's listened to me and is discovering that doing everything is bringing her powers back."

Pippa said, "But Geraldine also said that there can't be any more extensions. This is the last one. She really is going to be discharged in May."

Then I thought of Frankie. It was as if Susan's stroke had got her stuck in mud like the mower, and had had her arms and legs, all four limbs, spattered in mud. She had gone through a time of not wanting to struggle with 'stuckness', exert herself with physios in the gym, but now she was up for everything. Somehow the team of therapists and my morale-boosting had hosed her down and demudded her, and she was already escaping being locked-in with her heroic letter-by-letter eyegazing communication and circumventing her quadriplegia with the Possum device and her powered wheelchair with the fingers on her right hand, and writing sentences as an alternative to eyegaze. I had no doubt that having been stuck in mud for a while her limbs would once again be on the move, and she would possibly visit shops while out in the community – she had expressed a wish to go to Marks & Spencer – and reconnect herself to the social life out there.

I did not then know that exactly four weeks later, a week after referring her to the care home in Ipswich, Dr Saatvik would come in while I was visiting Susan and talk about her ability to raise her right arm when it fell downwards from the arm of her wheelchair, and about the movement in the fingers of her right hand, and that he would say to her: "You are a different person from the one who arrived. If you go back to Ipswich your consultant will be the same one you had in Ipswich Hospital. He won't recognise you. You came to us locked-in and now you're no longer locked-in, and your hand movements mean you can be regarded as level 2, and we can recommend you to a level-2 rehab unit."

I did not know that during April Susan would be visited by the lead therapist of a care home and offered a level-2 room, subject to the approval of the ICB (Integrated Care Board), and that this approval would be given. I did not know Susan would be promised there would be baking every Thursday and that she would visit a farm with hens and ducks. Nor did I know that the staff would nickname her 'The

Queen' as she would wave to them silently with her fingers when they entered her room.

Nor did I know that Susan would be asked to move upstairs into permanent care at the end of her twelve weeks of level-2 downstairs, and would have continuous health care, and that her goals and therapies would continue beyond the end of her level-2 care.

Her stroke had brought her life to a complete standstill and confined her to lying in a bed or sitting in a wheelchair and not moving. But now she had been hosed with urging and manipulating and morale-strengthening and had recovered her energy and had had her limbs demudded, and was set to make a heroic return that could not have been predicted nine months earlier, immediately after her stroke when she was given only forty-eight hours to live. She had made a stunning recovery, she had turned a corner and established a new direction she would pursue in the coming months and years.

A Bracelet and Bone People
(Or: A Dark Age and a Nuthatch)

Having diagnosed my post-Covid perimyocarditis, Dr Lennon put me on a small daily dose of bisoprolol. I was still on this, and he checked me every six months: blood tests, 12-lead ECG, echocardiogram, and a 24-hour Holter ECG monitor.

In January the tests showed that my blood pressure was up, he said when I saw him. It was borderline-elevated at 142/67mmHg, which alerted him to other things. He studied my past blood tests and remarked that the previous May my troponin was mildly raised.

He said, "This would normally suggest you have had a heart attack, but it may be down to your perimyocarditis. I'm aware you've been under significant stress and pressure coping with your daughter. I'd like you to have regular blood-pressure tests in the coming year."

I sensed that Death was not far away, and that he was shielding me from him.

He stood up from his desk and came round to where I sat in a chair and showed me a black Fitbit-like strap round his wrist.

"Look," he said, "this is completely new. It's an Aktiia bracelet. I've had this for 20 days now. I had my blood pressure taken with a cuff when it arrived, and have to repeat that every four weeks. I wear this bracelet. It automatically takes my blood pressure every half-hour or so by sending out a green light into my wrist, and it sends the reading to my phone. You see," he said, producing his phone, "my 28 measurements today are all here." I saw two graphs showing circles connected by lines zigzagging up and down. "The beauty is I can share it all with my doctor from my phone.

"I'd like you to buy one like this, get it sent from Switzerland, and wear it round your wrist all the time. You have to keep the bracelet charged, and take your blood pressure in your arm once a month with the cuff, but otherwise you can go about your life without thinking about it. You could begin a blood-pressure diary and record the main readings so you can see at a glance if your blood pressure is up. And you can send your readings for the year in one sharing to me next January. Could you order an Aktiia bracelet and cuff and begin this?"

I sensed that he thought my regular journeys to Norwich were stressing me and might result in a heart attack, and that he was trying to manage the possibility. "Yes," I said. "I'll do my best to get this up and running."

And that was what I did. On 26 January the bracelet and cuff arrived and I began. I had survived pericarditis (fluid in the sac round my heart) and myocarditis (infection of my heart muscle which could have been life-threatening), and now I had to survive increased troponin, which might still be due to a heart attack I had already had without knowing it, and the stress of visiting Susan and guiding her recovery required regular travelling, continuous involvement and dealing with the therapists' requests while setting a positive example to Susan.

I had to stay alive for Susan, to help her out of locked-in quadriplegia, and I had a feeling that Death might come for me at any time in view of my advanced years, and take me with a heart attack. I had a feeling that I was once again among the bone people: not far off from becoming a heap of bones.

Now, quietly at home in the evening, I looked back over the seven decades of my working life. I had been full of discovery in Japan, and had found my way through meditation and a centre-shift to the wisdom of the East, an inner calm that saw beyond all opposites and reflected the harmony within the universe. I had been through a turbulent time full of emotions, and had settled into a stable life that had kept me independent from the world of work and had given me time to process and set down my experiences, and reflect on them and learn from them. And now although I had grown old I had kept going – *Persevera* could have been my motto – and had not given in. I was more frail than I had been, but I still went to my gym every week and forced myself to do 15 minutes of strenuous walking at 5.5 km per hour and a gradient of 6.5 (an incline of 6.5 per cent); do 10 minutes cycling, do five minutes treadling; pull two lots of weights; and keep my back flexible by lying back and sitting up on a large ball. Each day I set myself targets and fulfilled them.

I had to complete my life's work and prepare to leave behind an orderly place. I had many arrangements still to make, I was not ready to go at 84. I would not be ready for at least another two years.

On my television screen were images of Death: rubble in Ukraine, and homeless wounded people; rubble in Gaza and homeless wounded people camping in tents; rubble in the Yemen, rubble in Syria and rubble in Iraq following US attacks. Death was everywhere, walking in a black hood with a scythe, turning people into bones. So all knew they were bone people, waiting to be removed in a heap of bones. Future attacks on Europe? Never, said Putin, who had said never regarding Ukraine. A Third World War? I saw bone people in groups on screen, wanting to know their future, sensing a new Dark Age amid all the decay.

I sat among the bone people and knew I would soon be one of them, but until then I would keep going, be positive, look for a way of hope in all situations, send out a message that a new Dark Age can be avoided, and that there can be a new World Order and an escape from the World War I experienced as a boy, whose senselessness left an indelible mark on my soul.

The next morning my nuthatch came to my bird feeder outside my study window. I sat three feet away and watched its streamlined lemon-yellow underbelly feed on seed and then upside-down on nuts. Then it flew off, with no idea that we were facing a Dark Age. I thought, 'That's what I am doing, keeping myself going. It may be terrible out there, but I must carry on as if there is no catastrophic Dark Age ahead.' I was in a deeper rhythm of Nature, living off the largesse of the universe, feeding on what the universe had made available, reflecting the universe in my river-like soul that still had a current and was still brimming despite my twilit years, and assuming that (with the help of my bracelet) I could keep going and complete my life's task regardless of a looming Dark Age.

INDEXES

DATES OF STORIES

Dates of stories in *The Still Brimming Twilit River*
in chronological order

Date

Part One
The Still Brimming Twilit River

The Still Brimming Twilit River	3, 10 June 2016
A Cliff Path and Dark Winter Evenings	4 June 2016
Cricket and Champagne	27 June 2016
A Doctor and his Godmother	9 July 2016
A Burnt Croissant and a Wrong-Way-Round Cap	24 July 2016
A Rape and a Dying Mother's Love	7 August 2016
A Cut Wire and a Whippersnapper Bully	17 August 2016
A Walled Garden on the Cliff	22 August 2016
Rock Pipits and iPads	22, 23 August 2016
A Drone and a Child	23 August 2016
Wasting Muscles and White Dust	5 September 2016
A Salon and Just Looking	30 September 2016
A Chaplain, a Funeral and God	2 October 2016
A Car-Park Attendant and Interference	3 October 2016
Barley Risotto	3 October 2016 (Written in the Stansted departure lounge.)
Three Negotiations and Pleased Faces	25 October 2016
A Pinged Cable and a Dark Hole	27 October 2016
Portraits and Harps (Or: A Napkin and a Bath)	7, 8 January 2017
A Baby in the Bookshop	5 February 2017
A Furred-Up Heart and Wobbly Stress	3, 4 February 2017
Screams and a Tool-Box (Or: A Carer and a Painful Knee)	21 February 2017

A Fallen Snowman and a Ghost	15, 16 December 2017
A Rod and Seasons	15, 16 December 2017
A Deer and Hospitals	15, 16 December 2017
A Sale and Providence	15, 16 December 2017
Good Manners and a Bull	15, 16 December 2017
Drama Queens and Pink Pheasant	9, 13 January 2018
A Mince Pie and Vacant Eyes	9, 14 January 2018
A Broken Christian	9, 14 January 2018
A Cleaner and a Prefab	16, 20 January 2018
A Surgeon and a Red-Stained Shirt (Or: A White Shirt like a Pure Soul)	14, 15 February 2018
A Locked Memory and a Reconfigured Bar	9, 11 April 2018
Smiling Sun and Si Si	9, 11 April 2018
Orange Trees and a Tossing Catamaran	9, 11 April 2018
A Barbary Ape and a Full English	9, 12 April 2018
Leaping Towards the Sun (Or: Yachts and McLarens)	10, 12 April 2018
Ladies by the Pool	10, 12 April 2018
A Tearful Sun and a Mohican Skull	10, 12 April 2018
Swollen Legs and a Fractured Shoulder	28 April, 28 May 2018
A Laundry Bag and an Enlarged Heart	30 April 2018
Mountbatten and a Magpie	29, 30 May 2018
A Coffin Trunk and a Dressing-Room Honours Board	29, 30 May 2018
A Great Star and a Green Band	29, 30 May 2018
A Hole in the Carpet and a Stately Garden	29, 30 May 2018
A New Wife and a Septic Tank	29, 30 May 2018
A Lurch and a Wall	14, 20 June 2018
A Shower and a Threat	14, 20 June 2018
A Mask and a Quiche	14, 20 June 2018
A Tudor Hall and a Woman Priest	15, 20 June 2018
A Car Park and Marathons	20 June 2018
A Scraped Knee and Tattered Hands	20 June 2018

A Slipper and a Clout	20 June 2018
Tests and Cappuccinos	20 June 2018
Lunching Ladies and Solitary Work	20 June 2018
A French Court and a Retreating World	5, 21 August 2018
A Mystery Play and Death	16 September 2018
A Canon and Everlasting Life	17 September 2018
A Crypt and Hot Coals	17 September 2018
Vikings and a Skeleton	17 September 2018
A New Garden and a Dead Baby	9 November 2018
An Angel among Belsen People	15 January 2019
A Fall and a Nursing Home	11 February 2019
A Legless Man and a Child with a Moustache	17 May 2019
A Monk and a Right Hand	22 May, 16 December 2019
A Tiller and a North Wind	11 June, 15 December 2019
Lugworms and Snakes	20 July 2019
Death at My Door	4 August 2019
A Toiling Mower and a Dancing Wasp	11 August 2019
A White Face and Pasties	11, 12 August 2019
Rain and Ten Thousand Steps	16 August 2019
An RSM and a Blocked Drain	21 October 2019
A Baited Trap and Two Mice	3 November 2019
A Purple-Nailed Man and Clattering	3 December 2019
A Schoolboy and Death	16 December 2019
A Donkey and Precipices (Or: A Cave-Dweller and a Monastery)	2 March 2020; 29 July 2021
A Fairy Shirt and a Cleaning Boss	30 June 2020
A Fluffy Cloud and Swallow Harbingers	30 June 2020
An Open Bonnet and Trickling Oil	30 June 2020
Red Kites High Above the Virus	12 August 2020
Isolations and Masks	22 August 2020
A Rapid Death and a Stoical Wife	15 February 2024
A Humanist Funeral and a Self-Controlled Widow	15 February 2024

Part Two
A Death-Mask and the Bone People

Indignation and Reaching-Out	13 August 2022
An Indian Adviser and Putin	15 September 2022
Thumb Wars and Chocolate Cake	1 October 2022
Chest Pain and Pericarditis (Or: Fluid on the Heart Sac)	9 October 2022
A Fall and a Puzzle Ring	10 October 2022
Covid Inflammation and Double Heartbeats	10 October 2022
A Clot and a Nearly-Lost Leg	14 October 2022
A Tumble Down Stairs and Blood	16 October 2022
Laceleaf Spikes and a Dancing Wasp	23 October 2022
A Plasterer and a Propositioned Wife	26 October 2022
Death in the Evening	14 December 2022
A Coffin and Petals	14 December 2022
Black-Tied Death and Banter	15 December 2022
A Mortarboard and Open-Mouthed Death	16 December 2022
A Historian and His Last Illness	21, 29 December 2022
An Outspoken Girl and an Opinionated Deputy Head	28 December 2022
A Chauffeur and a GP	12 January 2023
A Saturday Girl and Leathermen	18 January 2023
An Ex-Met 'Guardener' and a River	20 January, 4 February 2023
A Mannequin and Unconsciousness	22 January, 4 February 2023
A Holy Man and Skeletons	3 February 2023
A Crutch and a Brick Wall	25 February 2023
Quince Sauce and a Stained Shirt	25 February 2023
A King and a Blackbird	30 March 2023
A Pet Shop and Kyiv	12 April 2023
A Good Samaritan and a Rebuff (Or: "I Don't Want to be Here")	3, 5 May 2023
A Chairman and a Donor	4, 5 May 2023
Sewn Trousers and a 'Refurb'	4, 5 May 2023
Swapping or Borrowing	7 August 2023

A Bell-Founder's Funeral and a Bipolar Wife	14 August 2023
A Donkey and Unlocking	23 August 2023; 28 January, 4 February 2024
An Ironing Man and Pretend Leaders (Or: "I'm Not Getting Anywhere")	11 September 2023; 5 February 2024
A Fall and a Boot (Or: A Visit to the Dental Hygienist)	16 October 2023; 5 February 2024
A Nursery Gardener and a Court Breakdown	16 October 2023; 5 February 2024
A Funeral and Shared Fate (Or: 'Dopey' and a Wake)	8, 9 December 2023
A Locker Key and Dementia	9, 10 December 2023
A Delayed Discharge and New Spectacles (Or: Providence Supportive)	17, 23 December 2023
A Snowman and a Wail	23 December 2023
Virtual Reality and the Christmas Spirit	27, 29 December 2023
A Six-Hitter and a Sacred Sight-Screen	7 January, 6 February 2024
A Liquefied Eye and a Plastered Dressing (Or: A One-Eyed Cyclops and a Victim)	8 January, 6 February 2024
A Heart Pain and a Repaired Eye	15 January, 7 February 2024
An Algorithm and Extra-Crisp Bacon	21 January, 9 February 2024
Stroke: A Wounded Deer and a Healed Heart	29, 30 January, 4, 5 February 2024
A Bustling Ward and Peaceful Rehab	2, 9 February 2024
A Father's Day and a Fall (Or: A Car Guarded by a Fox and a Magpie)	3, 5 February 2024
A Wheelchair and a 'No' (Or: Snowdrops and a Crocus of Early Spring)	6, 7 February 2024
A Normal Routine and Chaos	8, 9 February 2024
A Bracelet and Bone People (Or: A Dark Age and a Nuthatch)	9, 10, 26 February 2024
A Madonna and a Fire-Ball	13 February 2024
A Golden Pilgrimage and a Honeycomb	23, 24 February 2024
A Demudding and a Turned Corner	20, 21 March 2024

INDEX OF TITLES

(Stories in alphabetical order, part titles in italics.)

B

C

LIBERALIS
B O O K S

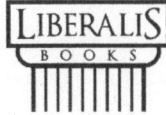

Liberalis is a Latin word which evokes ideas of freedom, liberality, generosity of spirit, dignity, honour, books, the liberal arts education tradition and the work of the Greek grammarian and storyteller Antoninus Liberalis. We seek to combine all these inter-linked aspects in the books we publish.

We bring classical ways of thinking and learning in touch with traditional storytelling and the latest thinking in terms of educational research and pedagogy in an approach that combines the best of the old with the best of the new.

As classical education publishers, our books are designed to appeal to readers across the globe who are interested in expanding their minds in the quest of knowledge. We cater for primary, secondary and higher education markets, homeschoolers, parents and members of the general public who have a love of ongoing learning.

If you have a proposal that you think would be of interest to Liberalis, submit your inquiry in the first instance via the website: www.liberalisbooks.com.